Raymond Chandler was born in Chicago in 1888. He came to England at an early age and studied at Dulwich College, completing his education in France and Germany.

In addition to his service with a Canadian infantry regiment in the First World War, he worked in many trades and professions – teacher, book reviewer, poet, paragraph writer, essayist, student pilot, accountant, oil executive and 'pulp' writer.

For the last forty years of his life he lived in the United States, largely in the Southern California region which provided the background for his classic series of Philip Marlowe crime novels. Raymond Chandler died in 1959.

Also by Raymond Chandler in Picador

The Chandler Collection
Volume 2

The High Window
The Long Good-bye
Playback

The Chandler Collection
Volume 3

Pearls Are a Nuisance
Smart-Alec Kill
Killer in the Rain

The Chandler Collection

Volume 1

The Big Sleep

—☆—

The Lady in the Lake

—☆—

The Little Sister

published by Pan Books

The Big Sleep first published in Great Britain 1939
by Hamish Hamilton Ltd
First Pan Books edition published 1979
© Helga Greene 1959
The Lady in the Lake first published in Great Britain 1944 by
Hamish Hamilton Ltd
First Pan Books edition published 1979
© Helga Greene 1959
The Little Sister first published in Great Britain 1949 by
Hamish Hamilton Ltd
First Pan Books edition published 1979
© Raymond Chandler 1949
This collected Picador edition published 1983 by Pan Books Ltd,
Cavaye Place, London SW10 9PG
9 8 7
ISBN 0 330 028152 6
Printed and bound in Great Britain by
Cox & Wyman Ltd, Reading

Contents

The Big Sleep

1

It was about eleven o'clock in the morning, mid-October, with the sun not shining and a look of hard wet rain in the clearness of the foothills. I was wearing my powder-blue suit, with dark blue shirt, tie and display handkerchief, black brogues, black wool socks with dark blue clocks on them. I was neat, clean, shaved and sober, and I didn't care who knew it. I was everything the well-dressed private detective ought to be. I was calling on four million dollars.

The main hallway of the Sternwood place was two storeys high. Over the entrance doors, which would have let in a troop of Indian elephants, there was a broad stained-glass panel showing a knight in dark armour rescuing a lady who was tied to a tree and didn't have any clothes on but some very long and convenient hair. The knight had pushed the vizor of his helmet back to be sociable, and he was fiddling with the knots on the ropes that tied the lady to the tree and not getting anywhere. I stood there and thought that if I lived in the house, I would sooner or later have to climb up there and help h'm. He didn't seem to be really trying.

There were french doors at the back of the hall, beyond them a wide sweep of emerald grass to a white garage, in front of which a slim dark young chauffeur in shiny black leggings was dusting a maroon Packard convertible. Beyond the garage were some decorative trees trimmed as carefully as poodle dogs. Beyond them a large greenhouse with a domed roof. Then more trees and beyond everything the solid, uneven, uncomfortable line of the foothills.

On the east side of the hall a free staircase, tile-paved, rose to a gallery with a wrought-iron railing and another piece of stained-glass romance. Large hard chairs with rounded red plush seats were backed into the vacant spaces of the wall around about. They didn't look as if anybody ever sat in them. In the middle of the west wall there was a big empty fireplace with a brass screen in four hinged panels, and over the fireplace a marble mantel with cupids at the corners. Above the mantel there was a large oil portrait, and above the portrait two bullet-torn or moth-eaten cavalry pennants crossed in a glass frame. The portrait was a stiffly posed job of an officer in full regimentals of about the time of the Mexican War. The officer had a neat black imperial, black moustachios, hot hard coal-black eyes, and the general look of a man it would pay to get along with. I thought this might be General Sternwood's grandfather. It could hardly be the General himself, even though I had heard he was pretty far gone in years to have a couple of daughters still in the dangerous twenties.

I was still staring at the hot black eyes when a door opened far back under the stairs. It wasn't the butler coming back. It was a girl.

She was twenty or so, small and delicately put together, but she looked durable. She wore pale blue slacks and they looked well on her. She walked as if she were floating. Her hair was a fine tawny wave cut much shorter than the current fashion of pageboy tresses curled in at the bottom. Her eyes were slate-grey, and had almost no expression when they looked at me. She came over near me and smiled with her mouth and she had little sharp predatory teeth, as white as fresh orange pith and as shiny as porcelain. They glistened between her thin, too taut lips. Her face lacked colour and didn't look too healthy.

'Tall, aren't you?' she said.

'I didn't mean to be.'

Her eyes rounded. She was puzzled. She was thinking. I could see, even on that short acquaintance, that thinking was always going to be a bother to her.

'Handsome too,' she said. 'And I bet you know it.'

I grunted.

'What's your name?'

'Reilly,' I said. 'Doghouse Reilly.'

'That's a funny name.' She bit her lip and turned her head a little and looked at me along her eyes. Then she lowered her lashes until they almost cuddled her cheeks and slowly raised them again, like a theatre curtain. I was to get to know that trick. That was supposed to make me roll over on my back with all four paws in the air.

'Are you a prizefighter?' she asked, when I didn't.

'Not exactly, I'm a sleuth.'

'A – a—' She tossed her head angrily, and the rich colour of it glistened in the rather dim light of the big hall. 'You're making fun of me.'

'Uh-uh.'

'What?'

'Get on with you,' I said. 'You heard me.'

'You didn't say anything. You're just a big tease.' She put a thumb up and bit it. It was a curiously shaped thumb, thin and narrow like an extra finger, with no curve in the first joint. She bit it and sucked it slowly, turning it around in her mouth like a baby with a comforter.

'You're awfully tall,' she said. Then she giggled with secret merriment. Then she turned her body slowly and lithely, without lifting her feet. Her hands dropped limp at her sides. She tilted herself towards me on her toes. She fell straight back into my arms. I had to catch her or let her crack her head on the tessellated floor. I caught her under her arms and she went rubber-legged on me instantly. I had to hold her close to hold her up. When her head was against my chest she screwed it around and giggled at me.

'You're cute,' she giggled. 'I'm cute too.'

I didn't say anything. So the butler chose that convenient moment to come back through the french doors and see me holding her.

It didn't seem to bother him. He was a tall, thin, silver man, sixty or close to it or a little past it. He had blue eyes as remote as eyes could be. His skin was smooth and bright and he moved like a man with very sound muscles. He walked slowly across the floor towards us and the girl jerked away from me. She flashed across the room to the foot of the stairs and went up them like a deer. She was gone before I could draw a long breath and let it out.

The butler said tonelessly: 'The General will see you now, Mr Marlowe.'

I pushed my lower jaw up off my chest and nodded at him. 'Who was that?'

'Miss Carmen Sternwood, sir.'

'You ought to wean her. She looks old enough.'

He looked at me with grave politeness and repeated what he had said.

2

We went out at the french doors and along a smooth red-flagged path that skirted the far side of the lawn from the garage. The boyish-looking chauffeur had a big black and chromium sedan out now and was dusting that. The path took us along to the side of the greenhouse and the butler opened a door for me and stood aside. It opened into a sort of vestibule that was about as warm as a slow oven. He came in after me, shut the outer door, opened an inner door and we went through that. Then it was really hot. The air was thick, wet, steamy and larded with the cloying smell of tropical orchids in bloom. The glass walls and roof were heavily misted and big drops of moisture splashed down on the plants. The light had an unreal greenish colour, like light filtered through an aquarium tank. The plants filled the place, a forest of them, with nasty meaty leaves and stalks like the newly washed fingers of dead men. They smelled as overpowering as boiling alcohol under a blanket.

The butler did his best to get me through without being smacked in the face by the sodden leaves, and after a while we came to a clearing in the middle of the jungle, under the domed roof. Here, in a space of hexagonal flags, an old red Turkish rug was laid down and on the rug was a wheel chair, and in the wheelchair an old and obviously dying man watched us come with black eyes from which all fire had died long ago, but which still had the coal-black directness of the eyes in the portrait that hung above the mantel in the hall. The rest of his face was a leaden mask, with the bloodless lips and the sharp nose and the sunken temples and the outward-turning earlobes of approaching dissolution. His long narrow body was wrapped – in that heat – in a travelling rug and a faded red bathrobe. His thin clawlike hands were folded loosely on the rug, purple-nailed. A few locks of dry white hair clung to his scalp, like wild flowers fighting for life on a bare rock.

The butler stood in front of him and said: 'This is Mr Marlowe, General.'

The old man didn't speak or move, or even nod. He just looked at me lifelessly. The butler pushed a damp wicker chair against the backs of my legs and I sat down. He took my hat with a deft scoop.

Then the old man dragged his voice up from the bottom of a well and said: 'Brandy, Norris. How do you like your brandy, sir?'

'Any way at all,' I said.

The butler went away among the abominable plants. The General spoke again, slowly, using his strength as carefully as an out-of-work showgirl uses her last good pair of stockings.

'I used to like mine with champagne. The champagne as cold as Valley Forge and about a third of a glass of brandy beneath it. You may take your coat off, sir. It's too hot in here for a man with blood in his veins.'

I stood up and peeled off my coat and got a handkerchief out and mopped my face and neck and the backs of my wrists. St Louis in August had nothing on that place. I sat down again and felt automatically for a cigarette and then stopped. The old man caught the gesture and smiled faintly.

'You may smoke, sir. I like the smell of tobacco.'

I lit the cigarette and blew a lungful at him and he sniffed at it like a terrier at a rathole. The faint smile pulled at the shadowed corners of his mouth.

'A nice state of affairs when a man has to indulge his vices by proxy,' he said dryly. 'You are looking at a very dull survival of a rather gaudy life, a cripple paralysed in both legs and with only half of his lower belly. There's very little that I can eat and my sleep is so close to waking that it is hardly worth the name. I seem to exist largely on heat, like a newborn spider, and the orchids are an excuse for the heat. Do you like orchids?'

'Not particularly,' I said.

The General half closed his eyes. 'They are nasty things. Their flesh is too much like the flesh of men. And their perfume has the rotten sweetness of a prostitute.'

I stared at him with my mouth open. The soft wet heat was like a pall around us. The old man nodded, as if his neck was afraid of the weight of his head. Then the butler came pushing back through the jungle with a tea-wagon, mixed me a brandy and soda, swathed the copper ice bucket with a damp napkin, and went away softly among the orchids. A door opened and shut behind the jungle.

I sipped the drink. The old man licked his lips watching me, over and over again, drawing one lip slowly across the other with a funereal absorption, like an undertaker dry-washing his hands.

'Tell me about yourself, Mr Marlowe. I suppose I have a right to ask?'

'Sure, but there's very little to tell. I'm thirty-three years old, went to college once and can still speak English if there's any demand for it. There isn't much in my trade. I worked for Mr Wilde, the District Attorney, as an investigator once. His chief investigator, a man named Bernie Ohls, called me and told me you wanted to see me. I'm unmarried because I don't like police-men's wives.'

'And a little bit of a cynic,' the old man smiled. 'You didn't like working for Wilde?'

'I was fired. For insubordination. I test very high on insubor-dination, General.'

'I always did myself, sir. I'm glad to hear it. What do you know about my family?'

'I'm told you are a widower and have two young daughters, both pretty and both wild. One of them has been married three times, the last time to an ex-bootlegger, who went in the trade by the name of Rusty Regan. That's all I heard, General.'

'Did any of it strike you as peculiar?'

'The Rusty Regan part, maybe. But I always got along with bootleggers myself.'

He smiled his faint economical smile. 'It seems I do too. I'm very fond of Rusty. A big curly-headed Irishman from Clonmel, with sad eyes and a smile as wide as Wilshire Boulevard. The first time I saw him I thought he might be what you are probably thinking he was, an adventurer who happened to get himself wrapped up in some velvet.'

'You must have liked him,' I said. 'You learned to talk the language.'

He put his thin bloodless hands under the edge of the rug. I put my cigarette stub out and finished my drink.

'He was the breath of life to me – while he lasted. He spent hours with me, sweating like a pig, drinking brandy by the quart and telling me stories of the Irish revolution. He had been an officer in the IRA. He wasn't even legally in the United States. It was a ridiculous marriage, of course, and it probably didn't last a month, as a marriage. I'm telling you the family secrets, Mr Marlowe.'

'They're still secrets,' I said. 'What happened to him?'

The old man looked at me woodenly. 'He went away, a month ago. Abruptly, without a word to anyone. Without saying goodbye to me. That hurt a little, but he had been raised in a rough school. I'll hear from him one of these days. Meantime I am being blackmailed again.'

I said: 'Again?'

He brought his hands from under the rug with a brown envelope in them. 'I should have been very sorry for anybody who tried to blackmail me while Rusty was around. A few months before he came – that is to say about nine or ten months ago – I paid a man named Joe Brody five thousand dollars to let my younger daughter Carmen alone.'

'Ah,' I said.

He moved his thin white eyebrows. 'That means what?'

'Nothing,' I said.

He went on staring at me, half frowning. Then he said: 'Take this envelope and examine it. And help yourself to the brandy.'

I took the envelope off his knees and sat down with it again. I wiped off the palms of my hands and turned it around. It was addressed to General Guy Sternwood, 3765 Alta Brea Crescent, West Hollywood, California. The address was in ink, in the slanted printing engineers use. The envelope was slit. I opened it up and took out a brown card and three slips of stiff paper. The card was of thin brown linen, printed in gold: 'Mr Arthur Gwynn Geiger.' No address. Very small in the lower left-hand corner: 'Rare Books and De Luxe Editions.' I turned the card over. More of the slanted printing on the back. 'Dear Sir: In spite of the legal uncollectability of the enclosed, which frankly represent gambling debts, I assume you might wish them honoured. Respectfully, A. G. Geiger.'

I looked at the slips of stiffish white paper. They were promissory notes filled out in ink, dated on several dates early in the month before, September. 'On Demand I promise to pay to Arthur Gwynn Geiger or Order the sum of One Thousand Dollars ($1000.00) without interest. Value Received. Carmen Sternwood.'

The written part was in a sprawling moronic handwriting with a lot of fat curlicues and circles for dots. I mixed myself another drink and sipped it and put the exhibit aside.

'Your conclusions?' the General asked.

'I haven't any yet. Who is this Arthur Gwynn Geiger?'

'I haven't the faintest idea.'

'What does Carmen say?'

'I haven't asked her. I don't intend to. If I did, she would suck her thumb and look coy.'

I said: 'I met her in the hall. She did that to me. Then she tried to sit in my lap.'

Nothing changed in his expression. His clasped hands rested peacefully on the edge of the rug, and the heat, which made me feel like a New England boiled dinner, didn't seem to make him even warm.

'Do I have to be polite?' I asked. 'Or can I just be natural?'

'I haven't noticed that you suffer from many inhibitions, Mr Marlowe.'

'Do the two girls run around together?'

'I think not. I think they go their separate and slightly divergent roads to perdition. Vivian is spoiled, exacting, smart and quite ruthless. Carmen is a child who likes to pull wings off flies. Neither of them has any more moral sense than a cat. Neither have I. No Sternwood ever had. Proceed.'

'They're well educated, I suppose. They know what they're doing.'

'Vivian went to good schools of the snob type and to college. Carmen went to half a dozen schools of greater and greater liberality, and ended up where she started. I presume they both had, and still have, all the usual vices. If I sound a little sinister as a parent, Mr Marlowe, it is because my hold on life is too slight to include any Victorian hypocrisy.' He leaned his head back and closed his eyes, then opened them again suddenly. 'I need not add that a man who indulges in parenthood for the first time at the age of fifty-four deserves all he gets.'

I sipped my drink and nodded. The pulse in his lean grey throat throbbed visibly and yet so slowly that it was hardly a pulse at all. An old man two-thirds dead and still determined to believe he could take it.

'Your conclusions?' he asked suddenly.

'I'd pay him.'

'Why?'

'It's a question of a little money against a lot of annoyance. There has to be something behind it. But nobody's going to break your heart, if it hasn't been done already. And it would take an awful lot of chisellers an awful lot of time to rob you of enough so that you'd even notice it.'

'I have pride, sir,' he said coldly.

'Somebody's counting on that. It's the easiest way to fool them. That or the police. Geiger can collect on these notes, unless you can show fraud. Instead of that he makes you a present of them and admits they are gambling debts, which gives you a defence, even if he had kept the notes. If he's a crook, he knows his onions, and if he's an honest man doing a little loan business on the side, he ought to have his money. Who was this Joe Brody you paid the five thousand dollars to?'

'Some kind of gambler. I hardly recall. Norris would know. My butler.'

'Your daughters have money in their own right, General?'

'Vivian has, but not a great deal. Carmen is still a minor under her mother's will. I give them both generous allowances.'

I said: 'I can take this Geiger off your back, General, if that's what you want. Whoever he is and whatever he has. It may cost you a little money, besides what you pay me. And of course it won't get you anything. Sugaring them never does. You're already listed on their book of nice names.'

'I see.' He shrugged his wide sharp shoulders in the faded red bathrobe. 'A moment ago you said pay him. Now you say it won't get me anything.'

'I mean it might be cheaper and easier to stand for a certain amount of squeeze. That's all.'

'I'm afraid I'm rather an impatient man, Mr Marlowe. What are your charges?'

'I get twenty-five a day and expenses – when I'm lucky.'

'I see. It seems reasonable enough for removing morbid growths from people's backs. Quite a delicate operation. You realize that, I hope. You'll make your operation as little of a shock to the patient as possible? There might be several of them, Mr Marlowe.'

I finished my second drink and wiped my lips and my face. The heat didn't get any less hot with the brandy in me. The General blinked at me and plucked at the edge of his rug.

'Can I make a deal with this guy, if I think he's within hooting distance of being on the level?'

'Yes. The matter is now in your hands. I never do things by halves.'

'I'll take him out,' I said. 'He'll think a bridge fell on him.'

'I'm sure you will. And now I must excuse myself. I am tired.' He reached out and touched the bell on the arm of his chair.

The cord was plugged into a black cable that wound along the side of the deep dark green boxes in which the orchids grew and festered. He closed his eyes, opened them again in a brief bright stare, and settled back among his cushions. The lids dropped again and he didn't pay any more attention to me.

I stood up and lifted my coat off the back of the damp wicker chair and went off with it among the orchids, opened the two doors and stood outside in the brisk October air getting myself some oxygen. The chauffeur over by the garage had gone away. The butler came along the red path with smooth light steps and his back as straight as an ironing board. I shrugged into my coat and watched him come.

He stopped about two feet from me and said gravely: 'Mrs Regan would like to see you before you leave, sir. And in the matter of money the General has instructed me to give you a cheque for whatever seems desirable.'

'Instructed you how?'

He looked puzzled, then he smiled. 'Ah, I see, sir. You are, of course, a detective. By the way he rang his bell.'

'You write his cheques?'

'I have that privilege.'

'That ought to save you from a pauper's grave. No money now, thanks. What does Mrs Regan want to see me about?'

His blue eyes gave me a smooth level look. 'She has a misconception of the purpose of your visit, sir.'

'Who told her anything about my visit?'

'Her windows command the greenhouse. She saw us go in. I was obliged to tell her who you were.'

'I don't like that,' I said.

His blue eyes frosted. 'Are you attempting to tell me my duties, sir?'

'No. But I'm having a lot of fun trying to guess what they are.'

We stared at each other for a moment. He gave me a blue glare and turned away.

3

This room was too big, the ceiling was too high, the doors were too tall, and the white carpet that went from wall to wall looked like a fresh fall of snow at Lake Arrowhead. There were full-length mirrors and crystal doodads all over the place. The ivory furniture had chromium on it, and the enormous ivory drapes lay tumbled on the white carpet a yard from the windows. The white made the ivory look dirty and the ivory made the white look bled out. The windows stared towards the darkening foothills. It was going to rain soon. There was pressure in the air already.

I sat down on the edge of a deep soft chair and looked at Mrs Regan. She was worth a stare. She was trouble. She was stretched out on a modernistic chaise-longue with her slippers off, so I stared at her legs in the sheerest silk stockings. They seemed to be arranged to stare at. They were visible to the knee and one of them well beyond. The knees were dimpled, not bony and sharp. The calves were beautiful, the ankles long and slim and with enough melodic line for a tone poem. She was tall and rangy and strong-looking. Her head was against an ivory satin cushion. Her hair was black and wiry and parted in the middle and she had the hot black eyes of the portrait in the hall. She had a good mouth and a good chin. There was a sulky droop to her lips and the lower lip was full.

She had a drink. She took a swallow from it and gave me a cool level stare over the rim of the glass.

'So you're a private detective,' she said. 'I didn't know they really existed, except in books. Or else they were greasy little men snooping around hotels.'

There was nothing in that for me, so I let it drift with the current. She put her glass down on the flat arm of the chaise-longue and flashed an emerald and touched her hair. She said slowly: 'How did you like Dad?'

'I liked him,' I said.

'He liked Rusty. I suppose you know who Rusty is?'

'Uh-huh.'

'Rusty was earthy and vulgar at times, but he was very real. And he was a lot of fun for Dad. Rusty shouldn't have gone off like that. Dad feels very badly about it, although he won't say so. Or did he?'

'He said something about it.'

'You're not much of a gusher, are you, Mr Marlowe? But he wants to find him, doesn't he?'

I stared at her politely through a pause. 'Yes and no,' I said.

'That's hardly an answer. Do you think you can find him?'

'I didn't say I was going to try. Why not try the Missing Persons Bureau? They have the organization. It's not a one-man job.'

'Oh, Dad wouldn't hear of the police being brought into it.' She looked at me smoothly across her glass again, emptied it, and rang a bell. A maid came into the room by a side door. She was a middle-aged woman with a long yellow gentle face, a long nose, no chin, large wet eyes. She looked like a nice old horse that had been turned out to pasture after long service. Mrs Regan waved the empty glass at her and she mixed another drink and handed it to her and left the room, without a word, without a glance in my direction.

When the door shut Mrs Regan said: 'Well, how will you go about it then?'

'How and when did he skip out?'

'Didn't Dad tell you?'

I grinned at her with my head on one side. She flushed. Her hot black eyes looked mad. 'I don't see what there is to be cagey about,' she snapped. 'And I don't like your manners.'

'I'm not crazy about yours,' I said. 'I didn't ask to see you. You sent for me. I don't mind your ritzing me or drinking your lunch out of a Scotch bottle. I don't mind your showing me your legs. They're very swell legs and it's a pleasure to make their acquaintance. I don't mind if you don't like my manners. They're pretty bad. I grieve over them during the long winter evenings. But don't waste your time trying to cross-examine me.'

She slammed her glass down so hard that it slopped over on an ivory cushion. She swung her legs to the floor and stood up with her eyes sparkling fire and her nostrils wide. Her mouth was open and her bright teeth glared at me. Her knuckles were white.

'People don't talk like that to me,' she said thickly.

I sat there and grinned at her. Very slowly she closed her mouth and looked down at the spilled liquor. She sat down on the edge of the chaise-longue and cupped her chin in one hand.

'My God, you big dark handsome brute! I ought to throw a Buick at you.'

I snicked a match on my thumbnail and for once it lit. I puffed smoke into the air and waited.

'I loathe masterful men,' she said. 'I simply loathe them.'

'Just what is it you're afraid of, Mrs Regan?'

Her eyes whitened. Then they darkened until they seemed to be all pupil. Her nostrils looked pinched.

'That wasn't what he wanted with you at all,' she said in a strained voice that still had shreds of anger clinging to it. 'About Rusty. Was it?'

'Better ask him.'

She flared up again. 'Get out! Damn you, get out!'

I stood up. 'Sit down!' she snapped. I sat down. I flicked a finger at my palm and waited.

'Please,' she said. 'Please. You could find Rusty – if Dad wanted you to.'

That didn't work either. I nodded and asked: 'When did he go?'

'One afternoon a month back. He just drove away in his car without saying a word. They found the car in a private garage somewhere.'

'They?'

She got cunning. Her whole body seemed to go lax. Then she smiled at me winningly. 'He didn't tell you then.' Her voice was almost gleeful, as if she had outsmarted me. Maybe she had.

'He told me about Mr Regan, yes. That's not what he wanted

to see me about. Is that what you've been trying to get me to say?'

'I'm sure I don't care what you say.'

I stood up again. 'Then I'll be running along.' She didn't speak. I went over to the tall white door I had come in at. When I looked back she had her lip between her teeth and was worrying it like a puppy at the fringe of a rug.

I went out, down the tile staircase to the hall, and the butler drifted out of somewhere with my hat in his hand. I put it on while he opened the door for me.

'You made a mistake,' I said. 'Mrs Regan didn't want to see me.'

He inclined his silver head and said politely: 'I'm sorry, sir. I make many mistakes.' He closed the door against my back.

I stood on the step breathing my cigarette smoke and looking down a succession of terraces with flowerbeds and trimmed trees to the high iron fence with gilt spears that hemmed in the estate. A winding driveway dropped down between retaining walls to the open iron gates. Beyond the fence the hill sloped for several miles. On this lower level, faint and far off I could just barely see some of the old wooden derricks of the oilfield from which the Sternwoods had made their money. Most of the field was public park now, cleaned up and donated to the city by General Sternwood. But a little of it was still producing in groups of wells pumping five or six barrels a day. The Sternwoods, having moved up the hill, could no longer smell the stale sump water or the oil, but they could still look out of their front windows and see what had made them rich. If they wanted to. I don't suppose they would want to.

I walked down a brick path from terrace to terrace, followed along inside the fence and so out of the gates to where I had left my car under a pepper tree on the street. Thunder was crackling in the foothills now and the sky above them was purple-black. It was going to rain hard. The air had the damp foretaste of rain. I put the top up on my convertible before I started down-town.

She had lovely legs. I would say that for her. They were a

couple of pretty smooth citizens, she and her father. He was probably just trying me out; the job he had given me was a lawyer's job. Even if Mr Arthur Gwynn Geiger, *Rare Books and De Luxe Editions,* turned out to be a blackmailer, it was still a lawyer's job. Unless there was a lot more to it than met the eye. At a casual glance I thought I might have a lot of fun finding out.

I drove down to the Hollywood public library and did a little superficial research in a stuffy volume called *Famous First Editions.* Half an hour of it made me need my lunch.

4

A. G. Geiger's place was a store frontage on the north side of the boulevard near Las Palmas. The entrance door was set far back in the middle and there was a copper trim on the windows, which were backed with Chinese screens, so I couldn't see into the store. There was a lot of oriental junk in the windows. I didn't know whether it was any good, not being a collector of antiques, except unpaid bills. The entrance door was plate glass, but I couldn't see much through that either, because the store was very dim. A building entrance adjoined it on one side and on the other was a glittering credit jewellery establishment. The jeweller stood in his entrance, teetering on his heels and looking bored, a tall handsome white-haired Jew in lean dark clothes, with about nine carats of diamond on his right hand. A faint knowing smile curved his lips when I turned into Geiger's store. I let the door close softly behind me and walked on a thick blue rug that paved the floor from wall to wall. There were blue leather easy chairs with smoke stands beside them. A few sets of tooled leather bindings were set out on narrow polished tables, between book ends. There were more tooled bindings in glass cases on the walls. Nice-looking merchandise, the kind a rich promoter would buy by the yard and have somebody paste his book-plate in. At the back there was a grained wood partition with a door in the middle of it, shut. In the corner made by the partition and one wall a woman sat behind a small desk with a carved wooden lantern on it.

She got up slowly and swayed towards me in a tight black dress that didn't reflect any light. She had long thighs and she walked with a certain something I hadn't often seen in book-stores. She was an ash blonde with greenish eyes, beaded lashes, hair waved smoothly back from ears in which large jet buttons glittered. Her fingernails were silvered. In spite of her get-up she looked as if she would have a hall bedroom accent.

She approached me with enough sex appeal to stampede a businessmen's lunch and tilted her head to finger a stray, but not very stray, tendril of softly glowing hair. Her smile was tentative, but could be persuaded to be nice.

'Was it something?' she inquired.

I had my horn-rimmed sun-glasses on. I put my voice high and let a bird twitter in it. 'Would you happen to have a *Ben Hur* 1860?'

She didn't say 'Huh?' but she wanted to. She smiled bleakly. 'A first edition?'

'Third,' I said. 'The one with the erratum on page 116.'

'I'm afraid not – at the moment.'

'How about a *Chevalier Audubon* 1840 – the full set, of course?'

'Er – not at the moment,' she said harshly. Her smile was now hanging by its teeth and eyebrows and wondering what it would hit when it dropped.

'You *do* sell books?' I said in my polite falsetto.

She looked me over. No smile now. Eyes medium to hard. Pose very straight and stiff. She waved silver fingernails at the glassed-in shelves. 'What do they look like – grapefruit?' she inquired tartly.

'Oh, that sort of thing hardly interests me, you know.

Probably has duplicate sets of steel engravings, tuppence coloured and a penny plain. The usual vulgarity. No. I'm sorry. No.'

'I see.' She tried to jack the smile back up on her face. She was as sore as an alderman with the mumps. 'Perhaps Mr Geiger – but he's not in at the moment.' Her eyes studied me carefully. She knew as much about rare books as I knew about handling a flea circus.

'He might be in later?'

'I'm afraid not until late.'

'Too bad,' I said. 'Ah, too bad. I'll sit down and smoke a cigarette in one of these charming chairs. I have rather a blank afternoon. Nothing to think about but my trigonometry lesson.'

'Yes,' she said. 'Ye-es, of course.'

I stretched out in one and lit a cigarette with the round nickel lighter on the smoking stand. She still stood, holding her lower lip with her teeth, her eyes vaguely troubled. She nodded at last, turned slowly and walked back to her little desk in the corner. From behind the lamp she stared at me. I crossed my ankles and yawned. Her silver nails went out to the cradle phone on the desk, didn't touch it, dropped and began to tap on the desk.

Silence for about five minutes. The door opened and a tall hungry-looking bird with a cane and a big nose came in neatly, shut the door behind him against the pressure of the door closer, marched over to the corner and placed a wrapped parcel on the desk. He took a pin-seal wallet with gold corners from his pocket and showed the blonde something. She pressed a button on the desk. The tall bird went to the door in the panelled partition and opened it barely enough to slip through.

I finished my cigarette and lit another. The minutes dragged by. Horns tooted and grunted on the boulevard. A big red interurban car grumbled past. A traffic light gonged. The blonde leaned on her elbow and cupped a hand over her eyes and stared at me behind it. The partition door opened and the tall bird with the cane slid out. He had another wrapped parcel, the shape of a large book. He went over to the desk and paid money. He left as he had come, walking on the balls of his feet, breathing with his mouth open, giving me a sharp side glance as he passed.

I got to my feet, tipped my hat to the blonde and went out after him. He walked west, swinging his cane in a small tight arc just above his right shoe. He was easy to follow. His coat was cut from a rather loud piece of horse robe with shoulders so wide that his neck stuck up out of it like a celery stalk and his head wobbled on it as he walked. We went a block and a half. At the Highland Avenue traffic signal I pulled up beside him and let him see me. He gave me a casual, then a suddenly sharpened side glance, and quickly turned away. We crossed Highland with the green light and made another block. He stretched his long legs and had twenty yards on me at the corner. He turned right. A hundred feet up the hill he stopped and hooked his cane over his arm and fumbled a leather cigarette case out of an inner pocket. He put a cigarette in his mouth, dropped his match, looked back when he picked it up, saw me watching him from the corner, and straightened up as if somebody had booted him from behind. He almost raised dust going up the block, walking with long gawky strides and jabbing his cane into the pavement. He turned left again. He had at least half a block on me when I reached the place where he had turned. He had me wheezing. This was a narrow tree-lined street with a retaining wall on one side and three bungalow courts on the other.

He was gone. I loafed along the block peering this way and that. At the second bungalow court I saw something. It was called 'The La Baba', a quiet dim place with a double row of tree-shaded bungalows. The central walk was lined with Italian cypresses trimmed short and chunky, something the shape of the oil jars in Ali Baba and the Forty Thieves. Behind the third jar a loud-patterned sleeve edge moved.

I leaned against a pepper tree in the parkway and waited. The thunder in the foothills was rumbling again. The glare of lightning was reflected on piled-up black clouds off to the south. A few tentative raindrops splashed down on the pavement and

27

made spots as large as nickels. The air was as still as the air in General Sternwood's orchid house.

The sleeve behind the tree showed again, then a big nose and one eye and some sandy hair without a hat on it. The eye stared at me. It disappeared. Its mate reappeared like a woodpecker on the other side of the tree. Five minutes went by. It got him. His type are half nerves. I heard a match strike and then whistling started. Then a dim shadow slipped along the grass to the next tree. Then he was out on the walk coming straight towards me, swinging the cane and whistling. A sour whistle with jitters in it. I stared vaguely up at the dark sky. He passed within ten feet of me and didn't give me a glance. He was safe now. He had ditched it.

I watched him out of sight and went up the central walk of 'The La Baba' and parted the branches of the third cypress. I drew out a wrapped book and put it under my arm and went away from there. Nobody yelled at me.

5

Back on the boulevard I went into a drugstore phone booth and looked up Mr Arthur Gwynn Geiger's residence. He lived on Laverne Terrace, a hillside street off Laurel Canyon Boulevard. I dropped my nickel and dialled his number just for fun. Nobody answered. I turned to the classified section and noted a couple of bookstores within blocks of where I was.

The first I came to was on the north side, a large lower floor devoted to stationery and office supplies, a mass of books on the mezzanine. It didn't look the right place. I crossed the street and walked two blocks east to the other one. This was more like it, a narrow cluttered little shop stacked with books from floor to ceiling and four or five browsers taking their time putting thumb marks on the new jackets. Nobody paid any attention to them. I shoved on back into the store, passed through a partition and found a small dark woman reading a law book at a desk.

I flipped my wallet open on her desk and let her look at the buzzer pinned to the flap. She looked at it, took her glasses off and leaned back in her chair. I put the wallet away. She had the fine-drawn face of an intelligent Jewess. She stared at me and said nothing.

I said: 'Would you do me a favour, a very small favour?'

'I don't know. What is it?' She had a smoothly husky voice.

'You know Geiger's store across the street, two blocks west?'

'I think I may have passed it.'

'It's a bookstore,' I said. 'Not your kind of bookstore. You know darn well.'

She curled her lip slightly and said nothing. 'You know Geiger by sight?' I asked.

'I'm sorry. I don't know Mr Geiger.'

'Then you couldn't tell me what he looks like?'

Her lip curled some more. 'Why should I?'

'No reason at all. If you don't want to, I can't make you.'

She looked out through the partition door and leaned back again. 'That was a sheriff's star, wasn't it?'

'Honorary deputy. Doesn't mean a thing. It's worth a dime cigar.'

'I see.' She reached for a pack of cigarettes and shook one loose and reached for it with her lips. I held a match for her. She thanked me, leaned back again and regarded me through smoke. She said carefully:

'You wish to know what he looks like and you don't want to interview him?'

'He's not there,' I said.

'I presume he will be. After all, it's his store.'

'I don't want to interview him just yet,' I said.

She looked out through the open doorway again. I said: 'Know anything about rare books?'

'You could try me.'

'Would you have a *Ben Hur,* 1860, third edition, the one with the duplicated line on page 116?'

She pushed her yellow law book to one side and reached a fat volume up on the desk, leafed it through, found her page, and studied it. 'Nobody would,' she said without looking up. 'There isn't one.'

'Right.'

'What in the world are you driving at?'

'The girl in Geiger's store didn't know that.'

She looked up. 'I see. You interest me. Rather vaguely.'

'I'm a private dick on a case. Perhaps I ask too much. It didn't seem much to me somehow.'

She blew a soft grey smoke ring and poked her finger through. It came to pieces in frail wisps. She spoke smoothly, indifferently. 'In his early forties, I should judge. Medium height, fattish. Would weigh about a hundred and sixty pounds. Fat face, Charlie Chan moustache, thick soft neck. Soft all over. Well dressed, goes without a hat, affects a knowledge of antiques and hasn't any. Oh yes. His left eye is glass.'

'You'd make a good cop,' I said.

She put the reference book back on an open shelf at the end of her desk, and opened the law book in front of her again. 'I hope not,' she said. She put her glasses on.

I thanked her and left. The rain had started. I ran for it, with the wrapped book under my arm. My car was on a side street pointing at the boulevard almost opposite Geiger's store. I was well sprinkled before I got there. I tumbled into the car and ran both windows up and wiped my parcel off with my handkerchief. Then I opened it up.

I knew about what it would be, of course. A heavy book, well bound, handsomely printed in handset type on fine paper. Larded with full-page arty photographs. Photos and letterpress were alike of an indescribable filth. The book was not new. Dates were stamped on the front endpaper, in and out dates. A rent book. A lending library of elaborate smut.

I rewrapped the book and locked it up behind the seat. A racket like that, out in the open on the boulevard seemed to

mean plenty of protection. I sat there and poisoned myself with
cigarette smoke and listened to the rain and thought about it.

6

Rain filled the gutters and splashed knee-high off the pavement.
Big cops in slickers that shone like gun barrels had a lot of fun
carrying giggling girls across the bad places. The rain drummed
hard on the roof of the car and the burbank top began to leak.
A pool of water formed on the floorboards for me to keep my
feet in. It was too early in the fall for that kind of rain. I
struggled into a trench coat and made a dash for the nearest
drugstore and bought myself a pint of whisky. Back in the
car I used enough of it to keep warm and interested. I was long
overparked, but the cops were too busy carrying girls and
blowing whistles to bother about that.

In spite of the rain, or perhaps even because of it, there was
business done at Geiger's. Very nice cars stopped in front and
very nice-looking people went in and out with wrapped parcels.
They were not all men.

He showed about four o'clock. A cream-coloured coupé
stopped in front of the store and I caught a glimpse of the fat
face and the Charlie Chan moustache as he dodged out of it
and into the store. He was hatless and wore a belted green
leather raincoat. I couldn't see his glass eye at that distance. A
tall and very good-looking kid in a jerkin came out of the store
and rode the coupé around the corner and came back walking,
his glistening black hair plastered with rain.

Another hour went by. It got dark and the rain-clouded lights
of the stores were soaked up by the black street. Street-car
bells jangled crossly. At around five-fifteen the tall boy in the
jerkin came out of Geiger's with an umbrella and went after
the cream-coloured coupé. When he had it in front Geiger

31

came out and the tall boy held the umbrella over Geiger's bare head. He folded it, shook it off and handed it into the car. He dashed back into the store. I started my motor.

The coupé went west on the boulevard, which forced me to make a left turn and a lot of enemies, including a motorman who stuck his head out into the rain to bawl me out. I was two blocks behind the coupé before I got in the groove. I hoped Geiger was on his way home. I caught sight of him two or three times and then made him turning north into Laurel Canyon Drive. Half-way up the grade he turned left and took a curving ribbon of wet concrete which was called Laverne Terrace. It was a narrow street with a high bank on one side and a scattering of cabin-like houses built down the slope on the other side, so that their roofs were not very much above road level. Their front windows were masked by hedges and shrubs. Sodden trees dripped all over the landscape.

Geiger had his lights on and I hadn't. I speeded up and passed him on a curve, picked a number off a house as I went by and turned at the end of the block. He had already stopped. His car lights were tilted at the garage of a small house with a square box hedge so arranged that it masked the front door completely. I watched him come out of the garage with his umbrella up and go in through the hedge. He didn't act as if he expected anybody to be tailing him. Light went on in the house. I drifted down to the next house above it, which seemed empty but had no signs out. I parked, aired out the convertible, had a drink from my bottle, and sat. I didn't know what I was waiting for, but something told me to wait. Another army of sluggish minutes dragged by.

Two cars came up the hill and went over the crest. It seemed to be a very quiet street. At a little after six more bright lights bobbed through the driving rain. It was pitch black by then. A car dragged to a stop in front of Geiger's house. The filaments of its lights glowed dimly and died. The door opened and a woman got out. A small slim woman in a vagabond hat and a transparent raincoat. She went in through the box maze. A bell rang faintly, light through the rain, a closing door, silence.

I reached a flash out of my car pocket and went down-grade and looked at the car. It was a Packard convertible, maroon or dark brown. The left window was down. I felt for the licence holder and poked light at it. The registration read: Carmen Sternwood, 3765 Alta Brea Crescent, West Hollywood. I went back to my car again and sat and sat. The top dripped on my knees and my stomach burned from the whisky. No more cars came up the hill. No lights went on in the house before which I was parked. It seemed like a nice neighbourhood to have bad habits in.

At seven-twenty a single flash of hard white light shot out of Geiger's house like a wave of summer lightning. As the darkness folded back on it and ate it up a thin tinkling scream echoed out and lost itself among the drain-drenched trees. I was out of the car and on my way before the echoes died.

There was no fear in the scream. It had a sound of half-pleasurable shock, an accent of drunkenness, an overtone of pure idiocy. It was a nasty sound. It made me think of men in white and barred windows and hard narrow cots with leather wrist and ankle straps fastened to them. The Geiger hide-away was perfectly silent again when I hit the gap in the hedge and dodged around the angle that masked the front door. There was an iron ring in a lion's mouth for a knocker. I reached for it, I had hold of it. At that exact instant, as if somebody had been waiting for the cue, three shots boomed in the house. There was a sound that might have been a long harsh sigh. Then a soft messy thump. And then rapid footsteps in the house – going away.

The door fronted on a narrow run, like a foot-bridge over a gully, that filled the gap between the house wall and the edge of the bank. There was no porch, no solid ground, no way to get around to the back. The back entrance was at the top of a flight of wooden steps that rose from the alley-like street below. I knew this because I heard a clatter of feet on the steps, going down. Then I heard the sudden roar of a starting car. It faded swiftly into the distance. I thought the sound was echoed by another car, but I wasn't sure. The house in front of me was as silent as a vault. There wasn't any hurry. What was in there was in there.

I straddled the fence at the side of the runway and leaned far out to the draped but unscreened french window and tried to look in at the crack where the drapes came together. I saw lamplight on a wall and one end of a bookcase. I got back on the runway and took all of it and some of the hedge and gave the front door the heavy shoulder. This was foolish. About the only part of a California house you can't put your foot through is the front door. All it did was hurt my shoulder and make me mad. I climbed over the railing again and kicked the french window in, used my hat for a glove and pulled out most of the lower small pane of glass. I could now reach in and draw a bolt that fastened the window to the sill. The rest was easy. There was no top bolt. The catch gave. I climbed in and pulled the drapes off my face.

Neither of the two people in the room paid any attention to the way I came in, although only one of them was dead.

7

It was a wide room, the whole width of the house. It had a low beamed ceiling and brown plaster walls decked out with strips of Chinese embroidery and Chinese and Japanese prints in grained wood frames. There were low bookshelves, there was a thick pinkish Chinese rug in which a gopher could have spent a week without showing his nose above the nap. There were floor cushions, bits of odd silk tossed around, as if whoever lived there had to have a piece he could reach out and thumb. There was a broad low divan of old rose tapestry. It had a wad of clothes on it, including lilac-coloured silk underwear. There was a big carved lamp on a pedestal, two other standing lamps with jade-green shades and long tassels. There was a black desk with carved gargoyles at the corners and behind it a yellow satin cushion on a polished black chair with carved arms and back. The room contained an odd assortment of odours, of which the most emphatic at the moment seemed to be the pungent aftermath of cordite and the sickish aroma of ether.

On a sort of low dais at one end of the room there was a high-backed teakwood chair in which Miss Carmen Sternwood was sitting on a fringed orange shawl. She was sitting very straight, with her hands on the arms of the chair, her knees close together, her body stiffly erect in the pose of an Egyptian goddess, her chin level, her small bright teeth shining between her parted lips. Her eyes were wide open. The dark slate colour of the iris had devoured the pupil. They were mad eyes. She seemed to be unconscious, but she didn't have the pose of unconsciousness. She looked as if, in her mind, she was doing something very important and making a fine job of it. Out of her mouth came a tinny chuckling noise which didn't change her expression or even move her lips.

She was wearing a pair of long jade ear-rings. They were nice ear-rings and had probably cost a couple of hundred dollars. She wasn't wearing anything else.

She had a beautiful body, small, lithe, compact, firm, rounded. Her skin in the lamplight had the shimmering lustre of a pearl. Her legs didn't quite have the raffish grace of Mrs Regan's legs, but they were very nice. I looked her over without either embarrassment or ruttishness. As a naked girl she was not there in that room at all. She was just a dope. To me she was always just a dope.

I stopped looking at her and looked at Geiger. He was on his back on the floor, beyond the fringe of the Chinese rug, in front of a thing that looked like a totem pole. It had a profile like an eagle and its wide round eye was a camera lens. The lens was aimed at the naked girl in the chair. There was a blackened flash bulb clipped to the side of the totem pole. Geiger was wearing Chinese slippers with thick felt soles, and his legs were in black satin pyjamas and the upper part of him wore a Chinese embroidered coat, the front of which was mostly blood. His glass eye shone brightly up at me and was by far the most lifelike thing about him. At a glance none of the three shots I heard had missed. He was very dead.

The flash bulb was the sheet lightning I had seen. The crazy scream was the doped and naked girl's reaction to it. The three shots had been somebody else's idea of how the proceedings might be given a new twist. The idea of the lad who had gone down the back steps and slammed into a car and raced away. I could see merit in his point of view.

A couple of fragile gold-veined glasses rested on a red lacquer tray on the end of the black desk, beside a pot-bellied flagon of brown liquid. I took the stopper out and sniffed at it. It smelled of ether and something else, possibly laudanum. I had never tried the mixture but it seemed to go pretty well with the Geiger ménage.

I listened to the rain hitting the roof and the north windows. Beyond was no other sound, no cars, no siren, just the rain beating. I went over to the divan and peeled off my trench coat and pawed through the girl's clothes. There was a pale green rough wool dress of the pull-on type, with half sleeves, I thought I might be able to handle it. I decided to pass up her under-clothes, not from feelings of delicacy, but because I couldn't see myself putting her pants on and snapping her brassière. I took the dress over to the teak chair on the dais. Miss Stern-wood smelled of ether also, at a distance of several feet. The tinny chuckling noise was still coming from her and a little froth oozed down her chin. I slapped her face. She blinked and stopped chuckling. I slapped her again.

'Come on,' I said brightly. 'Let's be nice. Let's get dressed.'

She peered at me, her slaty eyes as empty as holes in a mask. 'Gugugoterell,' she said.

I slapped her around a little more. She didn't mind the slaps. They didn't bring her out of it. I set to work with the dress. She didn't mind that either. She let me hold her arms up and she spread her fingers out wide, as if that was cute. I got her hands through the sleeves, pulled the dress down over her back and got her stockings and shoes on her.

'Let's take a little walk,' I said. 'Let's take a nice little walk.'

We took a little walk. Part of the time her ear-rings banged against my chest and part of the time we did the splits in unison, like adagio dancers. We walked over to Geiger's body and back. I had her look at him. She thought he was cute. She giggled and tried to tell me so, but she just bubbled. I walked her over to the divan and spread her out on it. She hiccuped twice, giggled a little and went to sleep. I stuffed her belongings into my pockets and went over behind the totem pole thing. The camera was there all right, set inside it, but there was no plateholder in the camera. I looked around on the floor, thinking he might have got it out before he was shot. No plateholder. I didn't like this development.

I went into a hall at the back of the room and investigated the house. There was a bathroom on the right and a locked door, a kitchen at the back. The kitchen window had been jimmied. The screen was gone and the place where the hook had pulled out showed on the sill. The back door was unlocked. I left it unlocked and looked into a bedroom on the left side of the hall. It was neat, fussy, womanish. The bed had a flounced cover. There was perfume on the triple-mirrored dressing table, beside a handkerchief, some loose money, a man's brushes, a keyholder. A man's clothes were in the closet and a man's slippers under the flounced edge of the bed cover. Mr Geiger's room. I took the keyholder back to the living-room and went through the desk. There was a locked steel box in the deep drawer. I used one of the keys on it. There was nothing in it but a blue leather book with an index and a lot of writing in code, in the same slanting printing that had written to General Sternwood. I put the notebook in my pocket, wiped the steel box where I had touched it, locked the desk up, pocketed the keys, turned the gas logs off in the fireplace, wrapped myself in my coat and tried to rouse Miss Sternwood. It couldn't be done. I crammed her vagabond hat on her head and swathed her in her coat and carried her out to her car. I went back and put all the lights out and shut the front door, dug her keys out of her bag and started the Packard. We went off down the hill without lights. It was less than ten minutes' drive to Alta Brea Crescent. Carmen spent them snoring and breathing ether in my face. I couldn't keep her head off my shoulder. It was all I could do to keep it out of my lap.

8

There was a dim light behind narrow leaded panes in the side door of the Sternwood mansion. I stopped the Packard under the porte-cochère and emptied my pockets out on the seat. The girl snored in the corner, her hat tilted rakishly over her nose, her hands hanging limp in the folds of the raincoat. I got out and rang the bell. Steps came slowly, as if from a long dreary distance. The door opened and the straight, silvery butler looked out at me. The light from the hall made a halo of his hair.

He said: 'Good evening, sir,' politely and looked past me at the Packard. His eyes came back to look at my eyes.

'Is Mrs Regan in?'

'No, sir.'

'The General is asleep, I hope?'

'Yes. The evening is his best time for sleeping.'

'How about Mrs Regan's maid?'

'Mathilda? She's here, sir.'

'Better get her down here. The job needs the woman's touch. Take a look in the car and you'll see why.'

He took a look in the car. He came back. 'I see,' he said. 'I'll get Mathilda.'

'Mathilda will do right by her,' I said.

'We all try to do right by her,' he said.

'I guess you'll have had practice,' I said.

He let that one go. 'Well, good night,' I said. 'I'm leaving it in your hands.'

'Very good, sir. May I call you a cab?'

'Positively not,' I said. 'As a matter of fact I'm not here. You're just seeing things.'

He smiled then. He gave me a duck of his head and I turned and walked down the driveway and out of the gates.

Ten blocks of that, winding down curved rain-swept streets, under the steady drip of trees, past lighted windows in big houses in ghostly enormous grounds, vague clusters of eaves and gables and lighted windows high on the hillside, remote and inaccessible, like witch houses in a forest. I came out at a service station glaring with wasted light, where a bored attendant in a white cap and a dark blue windbreaker sat hunched on a stool, inside the steamed glass, reading a paper. I started in, then kept going. I was as wet as I could get already. And on a night like that you can grow a beard waiting for a taxi. And taxi drivers remember.

I made it back to Geiger's house in something over half an hour of nimble walking. There was nobody there, no car on the street except my own car in front of the next house. It looked as dismal as a lost dog. I dug my bottle of rye out of it and poured half of what was left down my throat and got inside to light a cigarette. I smoked half of it, threw it away, got out again and went down to Geiger's. I unlocked the door and stepped into the still warm darkness and stood there, dripping quietly on the floor and listening to the rain. I groped to a lamp and lit it.

The first thing I noticed was that a couple of strips of embroidered silk were gone from the wall. I hadn't counted them, but the spaces of brown plaster stood out naked and obvious. I went a little farther and put another lamp on. I looked at the totem pole. At its foot, beyond the margin of the Chinese rug, on the bare floor another rug had been spread. It hadn't been there before. Geiger's body had. Geiger's body was gone.

That froze me. I pulled my lips against my teeth and leered

at the glass eye in the totem pole. I went through the house again. Everything was exactly as it had been. Geiger wasn't in his flounced bed or under it or in his closet. He wasn't in the kitchen or the bathroom. That left the locked door on the right of the hall. One of Geiger's keys fitted the lock. The room inside was interesting, but Geiger wasn't in it. It was interesting because it was so different from Geiger's room. It was a hard bare masculine bedroom with a polished wood floor, a couple of small throw rugs in Indian design, two straight chairs, a bureau in dark grained wood with a man's toilet set and two black candles in foot-high brass candlesticks. The bed was narrow and looked hard and had a maroon batik cover. The room felt cold. I locked it up again, wiped the knob off with my handkerchief, and went back to the totem pole. I knelt down and squinted along the nap of the rug to the front door. I thought I could see two parallel grooves pointing that way, as though heels had dragged. Whoever had done it had meant business. Dead men are heavier than broken hearts.

It wasn't the law. They would have been there still, just about getting warmed up with their pieces of string and chalk and their cameras and dusting powders and their nickel cigars. They would have been very much there. It wasn't the killer. He had left too fast. He must have seen the girl. He couldn't be sure she was too batty to see him. He would be on his way to distant places. I couldn't guess the answer, but it was all right with me if somebody wanted Geiger missing instead of just murdered. It gave me a chance to find out if I could tell it leaving Carmen Sternwood out. I locked up again, choked my car to life and rode off home to a shower, dry clothes and a late dinner. After that I sat around in the apartment and drank too much hot toddy trying to crack the code in Geiger's blue indexed notebook. All I could be sure of was that it was a list of names and addresses, probably of the customers. There were over four hundred of them. That made it a nice racket, not to mention any blackmail angles, and there were probably plenty of those. Any name on the list might be a prospect as the killer. I didn't envy the police their job when it was handed to them,

I went to bed full of whisky and frustration and dreamed about a man in a bloody Chinese coat who chased a naked girl with long jade ear-rings while I ran after them and tried to take a photograph with an empty camera.

9

The next morning was bright, clear and sunny. I woke up with a motorman's glove in my mouth, drank two cups of coffee and went through the morning papers. I didn't find any reference to Mr Arthur Gwynn Geiger in either of them. I was shaking the wrinkles out of my damp suit when the phone rang. It was Bernie Ohls, the DA's chief investigator, who had given me the lead to General Sternwood.

'Well, how's the boy?' he began. He sounded like a man who had slept well and didn't owe too much money.

'I've got a hangover,' I said.

'Tsk, tsk.' He laughed absently and then his voice became a shade too casual, a cagey cop voice. 'Seen General Sternwood yet?'

'Uh-huh.'

'Done anything for him?'

'Too much rain,' I answered, if that was an answer.

'They seem to be a family things happen to. A big Buick belonging to one of them is washing about in the surf off Lido fish pier.'

I held the telephone tight enough to crack it. I also held my breath.

'Yeah,' Ohls said cheerfully. 'A nice new Buick sedan all messed up with sand and sea water . . . Oh, I almost forgot. There's a guy inside it.'

I let my breath out so slowly that it hung on my lip. 'Regan?' I asked.

'Huh? Who? Oh, you mean the ex-legger the eldest girl picked up and went and married. I never saw him. What would he be doing down there?'

'Quit stalling. What would anybody be doing down there?'

'I don't know, pal. I'm dropping down to look see. Want to go along?'

'Yes.'

'Snap it up,' he said. 'I'll be in my hutch.'

Shaved, dressed and lightly breakfasted, I was at the Hall of Justice in less than an hour. I rode up to the seventh floor and went along to the group of small offices used by the DA's men. Ohls's was no larger than the others, but he had it to himself. There was nothing on his desk but a blotter, a cheap pen set, his hat and one of his feet. He was a medium-sized blondish man with stiff white eyebrows, calm eyes and well-kept teeth. He looked like anybody you would pass on the street. I happened to know he had killed nine men – three of them when he was covered, or somebody thought he was.

He stood up and pocketed a flat tin of toy cigars called Entractes, jiggled the one in his mouth up and down and looked at me carefully along his nose, with his head thrown back.

'It's not Regan,' he said. 'I checked. Regan's a big guy, as tall as you and a shade heavier. This is a young kid.'

I didn't say anything.

'What made Regan skip out?' Ohls asked. 'You interested in that?'

'I don't think so,' I said.

'When a guy out of the liquor traffic marries into a rich family and then waves good-bye to a pretty dame and a couple million legitimate bucks – that's enough to make even me think. I guess you thought that was a secret.'

'Uh-huh.'

'Okay, keep buttoned, kid. No hard feelings.' He came around the desk tapping his pockets and reaching for his hat.

'I'm not looking for Regan,' I said.

He fixed the lock on his door and we went to the official parking lot and got into a small blue sedan. We drove out

Sunset, using the siren once in a while to beat a signal. It was a crisp morning, with just enough snap in the air to make life seem simple and sweet, if you didn't have too much on your mind. I had.

It was thirty miles to Lido on the coast highway, the first ten of them through traffic. Ohls made the run in three-quarters of an hour. At the end of that time we skidded to a stop in front of a faded stucco arch and I took my feet out of the floorboards and we got out. A long pier railed with white two-by-fours stretched seaward from the arch. A knot of people leaned out at the far end and a motor-cycle officer stood under the arch keeping another group of people from going out on the pier. Cars were parked on both sides of the highway, the usual ghouls, of both sexes. Ohls showed the motor-cycle officer his badge and we went out on the pier, into a loud fish smell which one night's hard rain hadn't even dented.

'There she is – on the power barge,' Ohls said, pointing with one of his toy cigars.

A low black barge with a wheelhouse like a tug's was crouched against the pilings at the end of the pier. Something that glistened in the morning sunlight was on its deck, with hoist chains still around it, a large black and chromium car. The arm of the hoist had been swung back into position and lowered to deck level. Men stood around the car. We went down slippery steps to the deck.

Ohls said hello to a deputy in green khaki and a man in plain clothes. The barge crew of three men leaned against the front of the wheelhouse and chewed tobacco. One of them was rubbing at his wet hair with a dirty bathtowel. That would be the man who had gone down into the water to put the chains on.

We looked the car over. The front bumper was bent, one headlight smashed, the other bent up but the glass still unbroken. The radiator shell had a big dent in it, and the paint and nickel were scratched up all over the car. The upholstery was sodden and black. None of the tyres seemed to be damaged.

The driver was still draped around the steering post with his head at an unnatural angle to his shoulders. He was a slim

43

dark-haired kid who had been good-looking not so long ago. Now his face was bluish white and his eyes were a faint dull gleam under the lowered lids and his open mouth had sand in it. On the left side of his forehead there was a dull bruise that stood out against the whiteness of the skin.

Ohls backed away, made a noise in his throat and put a match to his little cigar. 'What's the story?'

The uniformed man pointed up at the rubbernecks on the end of the pier. One of them was fingering a place where the white two-by-fours had been broken through in a wide space. The splintered wood showed yellow and clean, like fresh-cut pine.

'Went through there. Must have hit pretty hard. The rain stopped early down here, around 9 p.m. The broken wood's dry inside. That puts it after the rain stopped. She fell in plenty of water not to be banged up worse, not more than half tide or she'd have drifted farther, and not more than half tide going out or she'd have crowded the piles. That makes it around ten last night. Maybe nine-thirty, not earlier. She shows under the water when the boys come down to fish this morning, so we get the barge to hoist her out and we find the dead guy.'

The plain-clothes man scuffed at the deck with the toe of his shoe. Ohls looked sideways along his eyes at me, and twitched his little cigar like a cigarette.

'Drunk?' he asked, of nobody in particular.

The man who had been towelling his head went over to the rail and cleared his throat in a loud hawk that made everybody look at him. 'Got some sand,' he said, and spat. 'Not as much as the boy friend got – but some.'

The uniformed man said: 'Could have been drunk. Showing off all alone in the rain. Drunks will do anything.'

'Drunk, hell,' the plain-clothes man said. 'The hand throttle's set half-way down and the guy's been sapped on the side of the head. Ask me and I'll call it murder.'

Ohls looked at the man with the towel. 'What do you think, buddy?'

The man with the towel looked flattered. He grinned. 'I say

suicide, Mac. None of my business, but you ask me, I say suicide. First off the guy ploughed an awful straight furrow down that pier. You can read his tread marks all the way nearly. That puts it after the rain like the Sheriff said. Then he hit the pier hard and clean or he don't go through and land right side up. More likely turned over a couple of times. So he had plenty of speed and hit the rail square. That's more than half-throttle. He could have done that with his hand falling and he could have hurt his head falling too.'

Ohls said: 'You got eyes, buddy. Frisked him?' he asked the deputy. The deputy looked at me, then at the crew against the wheelhouse. 'Okay, save that,' Ohls said.

A small man with glasses and a tired face and a black bag came down the steps from the pier. He picked out a fairly clean spot on the deck and put the bag down. Then he took his hat off and rubbed the back of his neck and stared out to sea, as if he didn't know where he was or what he had come for.

Ohls said: 'There's your customer, Doc. Dived off the pier last night. Around nine to ten. That's all we know.'

The small man looked in at the dead man morosely. He fingered the head, peered at the bruise on the temple, moved the head around with both hands, felt the man's ribs. He lifted a lax dead hand and stared at the finger-nails. He let it fall and watched it fall. He stepped back and opened his bag and took out a printed pad of DOA forms and began to write over a carbon.

'Broken neck's the apparent cause of death,' he said, writing. 'Which means there won't be much water in him. Which means he's due to start getting stiff pretty quick now he's out in the air. Better get him out of the car before he does. You won't like doing it after.'

Ohls nodded. 'How long dead, Doc?'

'I wouldn't know.'

Ohls looked at him sharply and took the little cigar out of his mouth and looked at that sharply. 'Pleased to know you, Doc. A coroner's man that can't guess within five minutes has me beat.'

The little man grinned sourly and put his pad in his bag and clipped his pencil back on his waistcoat. 'If he ate dinner last night, I'll tell you – if I know what time he ate it. But not within five minutes.'

'How would he get that bruise – falling?'

The little man looked at the bruise again. 'I don't think so. That blow came from something covered. And it had already bled subcutaneously while he was alive.'

'Blackjack, huh?'

'Very likely.'

The little ME's man nodded, picked his bag off the deck and went back up the steps to the pier. An ambulance was backing into position outside the stucco arch. Ohls looked at me and said: 'Let's go. Hardly worth the ride, was it?'

We went back along the pier and got into Ohls's sedan again. He wrestled it around on the highway and drove back towards town along a three-lane highway washed clean by the rain, past low rolling hills of yellow-white sand terraced with pink moss. Seaward a few gulls wheeled and scooped over something in the surf and far out a white yacht looked as if it was hanging in the sky.

Ohls cocked his chin at me and said: 'Know him?'

'Sure. The Sternwood chauffeur. I saw him dusting that very car out there yesterday.'

'I don't want to crowd you, Marlowe. Just tell me, did the job have anything to do with him?'

'No. I don't even know his name.'

'Owen Taylor. How do I know? Funny about that. About a year or so back we had him in the cooler on a Mann Act rap. It seems he run Sternwood's hotcha daughter, the young one, off to Yuma. The sister ran after them and brought them back and had Owen heaved into the icebox. Then next day she comes down to the DA and gets him to beg the kid off with the US 'cutor. She says the kid meant to marry her sister and wanted to, only the sister can't see it. All *she* wanted was to kick a few high ones off the bar and have herself a party. So we let the kid go and then darned if they don't have him come back to work. And a little later we get the routine report on his prints from Washington, and he's got a prior back in Indiana, attempted hold-up six years ago. He got off with a six months in the county jail, the very one Dillinger bust out of. We hand that to the Sternwoods and they keep him on just the same. What do you think of that?'

'They seem to be a screwy family,' I said. 'Do they know about last night?'

'No. I gotta go up against them now.'

'Leave the old man out of it, if you can.'

'Why?'

'He has enough troubles and he's sick.'

'You mean Regan?'

I scowled. 'I don't know anything about Regan, I told you. I'm not looking for Regan. Regan hasn't bothered anybody that I know of.'

Ohls said: 'Oh,' and stared thoughtfully out to sea and the sedan nearly went off the road. For the rest of the drive back to town he hardly spoke. He dropped me off in Hollywood near the Chinese Theatre and turned back west to Alta Brea Crescent. I ate lunch at a counter and looked at an afternoon paper and couldn't find anything about Geiger in it.

After lunch I walked east on the boulevard to have another look at Geiger's store.

10

The lean black-eyed credit jeweller was standing in his entrance in the same position as the afternoon before. He gave me the same knowing look as I turned in. The store looked just the same. The same lamp glowed on the small desk in the corner and the same ash blonde in the same black suede-like dress got up from behind it and came towards me with the same tentative smile on her face.

'Was it—?' she said and stopped. Her silver nails twitched at her side. There was an overtone of strain in her smile. It wasn't a smile at all. It was a grimace. She just thought it was a smile.

'Back again,' I said airily, and waved a cigarette. 'Mr Geiger in today?'

'I'm afraid—I'm afraid not. No – I'm afraid not. Let me see – you wanted—?'

I took my dark glasses off and tapped them delicately on the inside of my left wrist. If you can weigh a hundred and ninety pounds and look like a fairy, I was doing my best.

'That was just a stall about those first editions,' I whispered. 'I have to be careful. I've got something he'll want. Something's he's wanted for a long time.'

The silver finger-nails touched the blonde hair over one small jet-buttoned ear. 'Oh, a salesman,' she said. 'Well – you might come in tomorrow. I think he'll be here tomorrow.'

'Drop the veil,' I said. 'I'm in the business too.'

Her eyes narrowed until they were a faint greenish glitter, like a forest pool far back in the shadow of trees. Her fingers clawed at her palm. She stared at me and chopped off a breath.

'Is he sick? I could go up to the house,' I said impatiently. 'I haven't got for ever.'

'You—a—you—a—' her throat jammed. I thought she was going to fall on her nose. Her whole body shivered and her face fell apart like a bride's pie crust. She put it together again slowly, as if lifting a great weight, by sheer will power. The smile came back, with a couple of corners badly bent.

'No,' she said. 'No. He's out of town. That – wouldn't be any use. Can't you – come in – tomorrow?'

I had my mouth open to say something when the partition door opened a foot. The tall dark handsome boy in the jerkin looked out, pale-faced and tight-lipped, saw me, shut the door quickly again, but not before I had seen on the floor behind him a lot of wooden boxes lined with newspapers and packed loosely with books. A man in very new overalls was fussing with them. Some of Geiger's stock was being moved out.

When the door shut I put my dark glasses on again and touched my hat. 'Tomorrow, then. I'd like to give you a card, but you know how it is.'

'Ye-es. I know how it is.' She shivered a little more and made a faint sucking noise between her bright lips. I went out of the store and west on the boulevard to the corner and north on the street to the alley which ran behind the stores. A small black truck with wire sides and no lettering on it was backed up to Geiger's place. The man in the very new overalls was just heaving a box up on the tailboard. I went back to the boulevard and along the block next to Geiger's and found a taxi standing at a fireplug. A fresh-faced kid was reading a horror magazine behind the wheel. I leaned in and showed him a dollar: 'Tail job?'

He looked me over. 'Cop?'

'Private.'

He grinned. 'My meat, Jack.' He tucked the magazine over his rear view mirror and I got into the cab. We went around the block and pulled up across from Geiger's alley, beside another fireplug.

There were about a dozen boxes on the truck when the man in overalls closed the screened doors and hooked the tailboard up and got in behind the wheel.

'Take him,' I told my driver.

The man in overalls gunned his motor, shot a glance up and down the alley and ran away fast in the other direction. He turned left out of the alley. We did the same. I caught a glimpse of the truck turning east on Franklin and I told my driver to close in a little. He didn't or couldn't do it. I saw the truck two blocks away when we got to Franklin. We had it in sight to Vine and across Vine and all the way to Western. We saw it twice after Western. There was a lot of traffic and the fresh-faced kid tailed from too far back. I was telling him about that without mincing words when the truck, now far ahead, turned north again. The street at which it turned was called Brittany

Place. When we got to Brittany Place the truck had vanished.

The fresh-faced kid made comforting sounds at me through the panel and we went up the hill at four miles an hour looking for the truck behind bushes. Two blocks up, Brittany Place swung to the east and met Randall Place in a tongue of land on which there was a white apartment house with its front on Randall Place and its basement garage opening on Brittany. We were going past that and the fresh-faced kid was telling me the truck couldn't be far away when I looked through the arched entrance of the garage and saw it back in the dimness with its rear doors open again.

We went around to the front of the apartment house and I got out. There was nobody in the lobby, no switchboard. A wooden desk was pushed back against the wall beside a panel of gilt mailboxes. I looked the names over. A man named Joseph Brody had Apartment 405. A man named Joe Brody had received five thousand dollars from General Sternwood to stop playing with Carmen and find some other little girl to play with. It could be the same Joe Brody. I felt like giving odds on it.

I went around an elbow of wall to the foot of tiled stairs and the shaft of the automatic elevator. The top of the elevator was level with the floor. There was a door beside the shaft lettered 'Garage'. I opened it and went down narrow steps to the basement. The automatic elevator was propped open and the man in new overalls was grunting hard as he stacked heavy boxes in it. I stood beside him and lit a cigarette and watched him. He didn't like my watching him.

After a while I said: 'Watch the weight, bud. She's only tested for half a ton. Where's the stuff going?'

'Brody, four-o-five,' he said. 'Manager?'

'Yeah. Looks like a nice lot of loot.'

He glared at me with pale white-rimmed eyes. 'Books,' he snarled. 'A hundred pounds a box, easy, and me with a seventy-five pound back.'

'Well, watch the weight,' I said.

He got into the elevator with six boxes and shut the doors. I went back up the steps to the lobby and out to the street and the cab took me down-town again to my office building. I gave the fresh-faced kid too much money and he gave me a dog-eared business card which for once I didn't drop into the majolica jar of sand beside the elevator bank.

I had a room and a half on the seventh floor at the back. The half-room was an office split in two to make reception-rooms. Mine had my name on it and nothing else, and that only on the reception-room. I always left this unlocked, in case I had a client, and the client cared to sit down and wait.

I had a client.

11

She wore brownish speckled tweeds, a mannish shirt and tie, hand-carved walking shoes. Her stockings were just as sheer as the day before, but she wasn't showing as much of her legs. Her black hair was glossy under a brown Robin Hood hat that might have cost fifty dollars and looked as if you could have made it with one hand out of a desk blotter.

'Well, you *do* get up,' she said, wrinkling her nose at the faded red settee, the two odd semi-easy chairs, the net curtains that needed laundering and the boy's size library table with the venerable magazines on it to give the place a professional touch. 'I was beginning to think perhaps you worked in bed, like Marcel Proust.'

'Who's he?' I put a cigarette in my mouth and stared at her. She looked a little pale and strained, but she looked like a girl who could function under a strain.

'A French writer, a connoisseur in degenerates. You wouldn't know him.'

'Tut, tut,' I said. 'Come into my boudoir.'

She stood up and said: 'We didn't get along very well yesterday. Perhaps I was rude.'

'We were both rude,' I said. I unlocked the communicating door and held it for her. We went into the rest of my suite, which contained a rust-red carpet, not very young, five green filing cases, three of them full of California climate, an advertising calendar showing the Quints rolling around on a sky-blue floor, in pink dresses, with seal-brown hair and sharp black eyes as large as mammoth prunes. There were three near-walnut chairs, the usual desk with the usual blotter, pen set, ashtray and telephone, and the usual squeaky swivel chair behind it.

'You don't put on much of a front,' she said, sitting down at the customer's side of the desk.

I went over to the mail slot and picked up six envelopes, two letters and four pieces of advertising matter. I hung my hat on the telephone and sat down.

'Neither do the Pinkertons,' I said. 'You can't make much money at this trade, if you're honest. If you have a front, you're making money – or expect to.'

'Oh – are you honest?' she asked and opened her bag. She picked a cigarette out of a French enamel case, lit it with a pocket lighter, dropped case and lighter back into the bag and left the bag open.

'Painfully.'

'How did you ever get into this slimy kind of business then?'

'How did you come to marry a bootlegger?'

'My God, let's not start quarrelling again. I've been trying to get you on the phone all morning. Here and at your apartment.'

'About Owen?'

Her face tightened sharply. Her voice was soft. 'Poor Owen,' she said. 'So you know about that.'

'A DA's man took me down to Lido. He thought I might know something about it. But he knew much more than I did. He knew Owen wanted to marry your sister – once.'

She puffed silently at her cigarette and considered me with steady black eyes. 'Perhaps it wouldn't have been a bad idea,' she said quietly. 'He was in love with her. We don't find much of that in our circle.'

'He had a police record.'

She shrugged. She said negligently: 'He didn't know the right people. That's all a police record means in this rotten crime-ridden country.'

'I wouldn't go that far.'

She peeled her right glove off and bit her index finger at the first joint, looking at me with steady eyes. 'I didn't come to see you about Owen. Do you feel that you can tell me what my father wanted to see you about?'

'Not without his permission.'

'Was it about Carmen?'

'I can't even say that.' I finished filling a pipe and put a match to it. She watched the smoke for a moment. Then her hand went into her open bag and came out with a thick white envelope. She tossed it across the desk.

'You'd better look at it anyway,' she said.

I picked it up. The address was typewritten to Mrs Vivian Regan, 3765 Alta Brea Crescent, West Hollywood. Delivery had been by messenger service and the office stamp showed 8.35 a.m. as the time out. I opened the envelope and drew out the shiny 4¼ by 3¼ photo that was all there was inside.

It was Carmen sitting in Geiger's high-backed teakwood chair on the dais, in her ear-rings and her birthday suit. Her eyes looked even a little crazier than as I remembered them. The back of the photo was blank. I put it back in the envelope.

'How much do they want?' I asked.

'Five thousand – for the negative and the rest of the prints. The deal has to be closed tonight or they give the stuff to some scandal sheet.'

'The demand came how?'

'A woman telephoned me, about half an hour after this thing was delivered.'

'There's nothing in the scandal sheet angle. Juries convict without leaving the box on that stuff nowadays. What else is there?'

'Does there have to be something else?'

'Yes.'

She stared at me, a little puzzled. 'There is. The woman said there was a police jam connected with it and I'd better lay it on the line fast, or I'd be talking to my little sister through a wire screen.'

'Better,' I said. 'What kind of jam?'

'I don't know.'

'Where is Carmen now?'

'She's at home. She was sick last night. She's still in bed, I think.'

'Did she go out last night?'

'No. I was out, but the servants say she wasn't. I was down at Las Olindas, playing roulette at Eddie Mars's Cypress Club. I lost my shirt.'

'So you like roulette. You would.'

She crossed her legs and lit another cigarette. 'Yes. I like roulette. All the Sternwoods like losing games, like roulette and marrying men that walk out on them and riding steeplechases at fifty-eight years old and being rolled on by a jumper and crippled for life. The Sternwoods have money. All it has bought them is a rain cheque.'

'What was Owen doing last night with your car?'

'Nobody knows. He took it without permission. We always let him take a car on his night off, but last night wasn't his night off.' She made a wry mouth. 'Do you think—?'

'He knew about the nude photo? How would I be able to say? I don't rule him out. Can you get five thousand in cash right away?'

'Not unless I tell Dad – or borrow it. I could probably borrow it from Eddie Mars. He ought to be generous with me, heaven knows.'

'Better try that. You may need it in a hurry.'

She leaned back and hung an arm over the back of the chair. 'How about telling the police?'

'It's a good idea. But you won't do it.'

'Won't I?'

'No. You have to protect your father and your sister. You don't know what the police might turn up. It might be something they couldn't sit on. Though they usually try in blackmail cases.'

'Can you do anything?'

'I think I can. But I can't tell you why or how.'

'I like you,' she said suddenly. 'You believe in miracles. Would you have a drink in the office?'

I unlocked my deep drawer and got out my office bottle and two pony glasses. I filled them and we drank. She snapped her bag shut and pushed her chair back.

'I'll get the five grand,' she said. 'I've been a good customer of Eddie Mars. There's another reason why he should be nice to me, which you may not know.' She gave me one of those smiles the lips have forgotten before they reach the eyes. 'Eddie's blonde wife is the lady Rusty ran away with.'

I didn't say anything. She stared tightly at me and added: 'That doesn't interest you?'

'It ought to make it easier to find him – if I was looking for him. You don't think he's in this mess, do you?'

She pushed her empty glass at me. 'Give me another drink. You're the hardest guy to get anything out of. You don't even move your ears.'

I filled the little glass. 'You've got all you wanted out of me – a pretty good idea I'm not looking for your husband.'

She put the drink down very quickly. It made her gasp – or gave her an opportunity to gasp. She let a breath out slowly.

'Rusty was no crook. If he had been, it wouldn't have been for nickels. He carried fifteen thousand dollars, in bills. He called it his mad money. He had it when I married him and he had it when he left me. No – Rusty's not in on any cheap blackmail racket.'

She reached for the envelope and stood up. 'I'll keep in touch with you,' I said. 'If you want to leave me a message, the phone girl at my apartment house will take care of it.'

We walked over to the door. Tapping the white envelope against her knuckles, she said: 'You still feel you can't tell me what Dad—'

'I'd have to see him first.'

She took the photo out and stood looking at it, just inside the door. 'She has a beautiful little body, hasn't she?'

'Uh-huh.'

She leaned a little towards me. 'You ought to see mine,' she said gravely.

'Can it be arranged?'

She laughed suddenly and sharply and went half-way through the door, then turned her head to say coolly: 'You're as cold-blooded a beast as I ever met, Marlowe. Or can I call you Phil?'

'Sure.'

'You can call me Vivian.'

'Thanks, Mrs Regan.'

'Oh, go to hell, Marlowe.' She went on out and didn't look back.

I let the door shut and stood with my hand on it, staring at the hand. My face felt a little hot. I went back to the desk and put the whisky away and rinsed out the two pony glasses and put them away.

I took my hat off the phone and called the DA's office and asked for Bernie Ohls.

He was back in his cubby hole. 'Well, I let the old man alone,' he said. 'The butler said he or one of the girls would tell him. This Owen Taylor lived over the garage and I went through his stuff. Parents at Dubuque, Iowa. I wired the Chief of Police there to find out what they want done. The Sternwood family will pay for it.'

'Suicide?' I asked.

'No can tell. He didn't leave any notes. He had no leave to take the car. Everybody was home last night but Mrs Regan. She was down at Las Olindas with a playboy named Larry Cobb. I checked on that. I know a lad on one of the tables.'

'You ought to stop some of that flash gambling,' I said.

'With the syndicate we got in this county? Be your age, Marlowe. That sap mark on the boy's head bothers me. Sure you can't help me on this?'

I liked his putting it that way. It let me say no without actually lying. We said good-bye and I left the office, bought all three afternoon papers and rode a taxi down to the Hall of Justice to get my car out of the lot. There was nothing in any of the papers about Geiger. I took another look at his blue note-book, but the code was just as stubborn as it had been the night before.

12

The trees on the upper side of Laverne Terrace had fresh green leaves after the rain. In the cool afternoon sunlight I could see the steep drop of the hill and the flight of steps down which the killer had run after his three shots in the darkness. Two small houses fronted on the street below. They might or might not have heard the shots.

There was no activity in front of Geiger's house or anywhere along the block. The box hedge looked green and peaceful and the shingles on the roof were still damp. I drove past slowly, gnawing at an idea. I hadn't looked in the garage the night before. Once Geiger's body slipped away I hadn't really wanted to find it. It would force my hand. But dragging him to the garage, to his own car and driving that off into one of the hundred odd lonely canyons around Los Angeles would be a good way to dispose of him for days or even weeks. That supposed two things: a key to his car and two in the party. It would narrow the sector of search quite a lot, especially as I had had his personal keys in my pocket when it happened.

I didn't get a chance to look at the garage. The doors were shut and padlocked and something moved behind the hedge as I drew level. A woman in a green and white check coat and a small button of a hat on soft blonde hair stepped out of the maze and stood looking wild-eyed at my car, as if she hadn't heard it come up the hill. Then she turned swiftly and dodged back out of sight. It was Carmen Sternwood, of course.

I went on up the street and parked and walked back. In the daylight it seemed an exposed and dangerous thing to do. I went in through the hedge. She stood there straight and silent against the locked front door. One hand went slowly up to her teeth and her teeth bit at her funny thumb. There were purple smears under her eyes and her face was gnawed white by nerves.

She half smiled at me. She said: 'Hello,' in a thin, brittle voice. 'Wha—what—?' That tailed off and she went back to the thumb.

'Remember me?' I said. 'Doghouse Reilly, the man that grew too tall. Remember?'

She nodded and a quick jerky smile played across her face.

'Let's go in,' I said. 'I've got a key. Swell, huh?'

'Wha—wha—?'

I pushed her to one side and put the key in the door and opened it and pushed her in through it. I shut the door again and stood there sniffing. The place was horrible by daylight. The Chinese junk on the walls, the rug, the fussy lamps, the teakwood stuff, the sticky riot of colours, the totem pole, the flagon of ether and laudanum – all this in the daytime had a stealthy nastiness, like a fag party.

The girl and I stood looking at each other. She tried to keep a cute little smile on her face but her face was too tired to be bothered. It kept going blank on her. The smile would wash off like water off sand and her pale skin had a harsh granular texture under the stunned and stupid blankness of her eyes. A whitish tongue licked at the corners of her mouth. A pretty, spoilt and not very bright little girl who had gone very, very wrong, and nobody was doing anything about it. To hell with the rich. They made me sick. I rolled a cigarette in my fingers and pushed some books out of the way and sat on the end of the black desk. I lit my cigarette, puffed a plume of smoke and watched the thumb and tooth act for a while in silence. Carmen stood in front of me, like a bad girl in the principal's office.

'What are you doing here?' I asked her finally.

She picked at the cloth of her coat and didn't answer.

'How much do you remember of last night?'

She answered that – with a foxy glitter rising at the back of her eyes. 'Remember what? I was sick last night. I was home.' Her voice was a cautious throaty sound that just reached my ears.

'Like hell you were.'

Her eyes flickered up and down very swiftly.

'Before you went home,' I said. 'Before I took you home. Here. In that chair' – I pointed to it – 'on that orange shawl. You remember all right.'

A slow flush crept up her throat. That was something. She could blush. A glint of white showed under the clogged grey irises. She chewed hard on her thumb.

'You – were the one?' she whispered.

'Me. How much of it stays with you?'

She said vaguely: 'Are you the police?'

'No. I'm a friend of your father's.'

'You're not the police?'

'No.'

She let out a thin sigh. 'Wha—what do you want?'

'Who killed him?'

Her shoulders jerked, but nothing more moved in her face. 'Who else – knows?'

'About Geiger? I don't know. Not the police, or they'd be camping here. Maybe Joe Brody.'

It was a stab in the dark but it got her. 'Joe Brody! Him!'

Then we were both silent. I dragged at my cigarette and she ate her thumb.

'Don't get clever, for God's sake,' I urged her. 'This is a spot for a little old-fashioned simplicity. Did Brody kill him?'

'Kill who?'

'Oh, Christ,' I said.

She looked hurt. Her chin came down an inch. 'Yes,' she said solemnly. 'Joe did it.'

'Why?'

'I don't know.' She shook her head, persuading herself that she didn't know.

'Seen much of him lately?'

Her hands went down and made small white knots. 'Just once or twice. I hate him.'

'Then you know where he lives.'

'Yes.'

'And you don't like him anymore?'

'I hate him!'

'Then you'd like him for the spot.'

A little blank again. I was going too fast for her. It was hard not to. 'Are you willing to tell the police it was Joe Brody?' I probed.

Sudden panic flamed all over her face. 'If I can kill the nude photo angle, of course,' I added soothingly.

She giggled. That gave me a nasty feeling. If she had screeched or wept or even nosedived to the floor in a dead faint, that would have been all right. She just giggled. It was suddenly a lot of fun. She had had her photo taken as Isis and somebody had swiped it and somebody had bumped Geiger off in front of her and she was drunker than a Legion convention, and it was suddenly a lot of nice clean fun. So she giggled. Very cute. The giggles got louder and ran around the corners of the room like rats behind the wainscoting. She started to go hysterical. I slid off the desk and stepped up close to her and gave her a smack on the side of the face.

'Just like last night,' I said. 'We're a scream together. Reilly and Sternwood, two stooges in search of a comedian.'

The giggles stopped dead, but she didn't mind the slap any more than last night. Probably all her boy friends got around to slapping her sooner or later. I could understand how they might. I sat down on the end of the black desk again.

'Your name isn't Reilly,' she said seriously. 'It's Philip Marlowe. You're a private detective. Viv told me. She showed me your card.' She smoothed the cheek I had slapped. She smiled at me, as if I was nice to be with.

'Well, you do remember,' I said. 'And you came back to look for that photo and you couldn't get into the house. Didn't you?'

Her chin ducked down and up. She worked the smile. I was

60

having the eye put on me. I was being brought into camp. I was going to yell 'Yippee!' in a minute and ask her to go to Yuma.

'The photo's gone,' I said. 'I looked last night, before I took you home. Probably Brody took it with him. You're not kidding me about Brody?'

She shook her head earnestly.

'It's a pushover,' I said. 'You don't have to give it another thought. Don't tell a soul you were here, last night or today. Not even Vivian. Just forget you were here. Leave it to Reilly.'

'Your name isn't—' she began, and then stopped and shook her head vigorously in agreement with what I had said or with what she had just thought of. Her eyes became narrow and almost black and as shallow as enamel on a cafeteria tray. She had had an idea. 'I have to go home now,' she said, as if we had been having a cup of tea.

'Sure.'

I didn't move. She gave me another cute glance and went on towards the front door. She had her hand on the knob when we both heard a car coming. She looked at me with questions in her eyes. I shrugged. The car stopped, right in front of the house. Terror twisted her face. There were steps and the bell rang. Carmen stared back at me over her shoulder, her hand clutching the door knob, almost drooling with fear. The bell kept on ringing. Then the ringing stopped. A key tickled at the door and Carmen jumped away from it and stood frozen. The door swung open. A man stepped through it briskly and stopped dead, staring at us quietly, with complete composure.

13

He was a grey man, all grey, except for his polished black shoes and two scarlet diamonds in his grey satin tie that looked like the diamonds on roulette layouts. His shirt was grey and his double-breasted soft, beautifully cut flannel. Seeing Carmen he took a grey hat off and his hair underneath it was grey and as fine as if it had been sifted through gauze. His thick grey eyebrows had that indefinably sporty look. He had a long chin, a nose with a hook to it, thoughtful grey eyes that had a slanted look because the fold of skin over his upper lid came down over the corner of the lid itself.

He stood there politely, one hand touching the door at his back, the other holding the grey hat and flapping it gently against his thigh. He looked hard, not the hardness of the tough guy. More like the hardness of a well-weathered horseman. But he was no horseman. He was Eddie Mars.

He pushed the door shut behind him and put that hand in the lap-seamed pocket of his coat and left the thumb outside to glisten in the rather dim light of the room. He smiled at Carmen. He had a nice easy smile. She licked her lips and stared at him. The fear went out of her face. She smiled back.

'Excuse the casual entrance,' he said. 'The bell didn't seem to rouse anybody. Is Mr Geiger around?'

I said: 'No. We don't know just where he is. We found the door a little open. We stepped inside.'

He nodded and touched his long chin with the brim of his hat. 'You're friends of his, of course?'

'Just business acquaintances. We dropped by for a book.'

'A book, eh?' He said that quickly and brightly and, I thought, a little slyly, as if he knew all about Geiger's books. Then he looked at Carmen again and shrugged.

I moved towards the door. 'We'll trot along now,' I said. I took hold of her arm. She was staring at Eddie Mars. She liked him.

'Any message – if Geiger comes back?' Eddie Mars asked gently.

'We won't bother you.'

'That's too bad,' he said, with too much meaning. His grey eyes twinkled and then hardened as I went past him to open the door. He added in a casual tone: 'The girl can dust. I'd like to talk to you a little, soldier.'

I let go of her arm. I gave him a blank stare. 'Kidder, eh?' he said nicely. 'Don't waste it. I've got two boys outside in a car that always do just what I want them to.'

Carmen made a sound at my side and bolted through the door. Her steps faded rapidly downhill. I hadn't seen her car, so she must have left it down below. I started to say: 'What the hell—!'

'Oh, skip it,' Eddie Mars sighed. 'There's something wrong around here. I'm going to find out what it is. If you want to pick lead out of your belly, get in my way.'

'Well, well,' I said, 'a tough guy.'

'Only when necessary, soldier.' He wasn't looking at me any more. He was walking around the room, frowning, not paying any attention to me. I looked out above the broken pane of the front window. The top of a car showed over the hedge. Its motor idled.

Eddie Mars found the purple flagon and the two gold-veined glasses on the desk. He sniffed at one of the glasses, then at the flagon. A disgusted smile wrinkled his lips. 'The lousy pimp,' he said tonelessly.

He looked at a couple of books, grunted, went on around the desk and stood in front of the little totem pole with the camera eye. He studied it, dropped his glance to the floor in front of it. He moved the small rug with his foot, then bent swiftly, his body tense. He went down on the floor with one grey knee. The desk hid him from me partly. There was a sharp exclamation and he came up again. His arm flashed under his coat and a black Luger appeared in his hand. He held it in long brown fingers, not pointing it at me, not pointing it at anything.

'Blood,' he said. 'Blood on the floor there, under the rug. Quite a lot of blood.'

'Is that so?' I said, looking interested.

He slid into the chair behind the desk and hooked the mulberry-coloured phone towards him and shifted the Luger to his left hand. He frowned sharply at the telephone, bringing his thick grey eyebrows close together and making a hard crease in the weathered skin at the top of his hooked nose. 'I think we'll have some law,' he said.

I went over and kicked at the rug that lay where Geiger had lain. 'It's old blood,' I said. 'Dried blood.'

'Just the same we'll have some law.'

'Why not?' I said.

His eyes went narrow. The veneer had flaked off him, leaving a well-dressed hard boy with a Luger. He didn't like my agreeing with him.

'Just who the hell are you, soldier?'

'Marlowe is the name. I'm a sleuth.'

'Never heard of you. Who's the girl?'

'Client. Geiger was trying to throw a loop on her with some blackmail. We came to talk it over. He wasn't here. The door being open we walked in to wait. Or did I tell you that?'

'Convenient,' he said. 'The door being open. When you didn't have a key.'

'Yes. How come *you* had a key?'

'Is that any of your business, soldier?'

'I could make it my business.'

He smiled tightly and pushed his hat back on his grey hair. 'And I could make your business my business.'

'You wouldn't like it. The pay's too small.'

'All right bright eyes. I own this house. Geiger is my tenant. Now what do you think of that?'

'You know such lovely people.'

'I take them as they come. They come all kinds.' He glanced down at the Luger, shrugged and tucked it back under his arm. 'Got any good ideas, soldier?'

'Lots of them. Somebody gunned Geiger. Somebody got gunned by Geiger, who ran away. Or it was two other fellows. Or Geiger was running from a cult and made blood sacrifices in front of that totem pole. Or he had chicken for dinner and liked to kill his chickens in the front parlour.'

The grey man scowled at me.

'I give up,' I said. 'Better call your friends downtown.'

'I don't get it,' he said. 'I don't get your game here.'

'Go ahead, call the buttons. You'll get a big reaction from it.'

He thought that over without moving. His lips went back against his teeth. 'I don't get that, either,' he said tightly.

'Maybe it just isn't your day. I know you, Mr Mars. The Cypress Club at Las Olindas. Flash gambling for flash people. The local law in your pocket and a well-greased line into LA. In other words, protection. Geiger was in a racket that needed that too. Perhaps you spared him a little now and then, seeing he's your tenant.'

His mouth became a hard white grimace. 'Geiger was in what racket?'

'The smut book racket.'

He stared at me for a long level minute. 'Somebody got to him,' he said softly. 'You know something about it. He didn't show at the store today. They don't know where he is. He didn't answer the phone here. I came up to see about it. I find blood on the floor, under a rug. And you and a girl here.'

'A little weak,' I said. 'But maybe you can sell the story to a willing buyer. You missed a little something, though. Somebody moved his books out of the store today – the nice books he rented out.'

He snapped his fingers sharply and said: 'I should have thought of that, soldier. You seem to get around. How do you figure it?'

'I think Geiger was rubbed. I think that is his blood. And the books being moved out gives a motive for hiding the body for a while. Somebody is taking over the racket and wants a little time to organize.'

'They can't get away with it,' Eddie Mars said grimly.

'Who says so? You and a couple of gunmen in your car outside? This is a big town now, Eddie. Some very tough people have checked in here lately. The penalty of growth.'

'You talk too damned much,' Eddie Mars said. He bared his teeth and whistled twice sharply. A car door slammed outside and running steps came through the hedge. Mars flicked the Luger out again and pointed it at my chest. 'Open the door.'

The knob rattled and a voice called out. I didn't move. The

muzzle of the Luger looked like the mouth of the Second Street tunnel, but I didn't move. Not being bullet proof is an idea I had had to get used to.

'Open it yourself, Eddie. Who the hell are you to give me orders? Be nice and I might help you out.'

He came to his feet rigidly and moved around the end of the desk and over to the door. He opened it without taking his eyes off me. Two men tumbled into the room, reaching busily under their arms. One was an obvious pug, a good-looking pale-faced boy with a bad nose and one ear like a club steak. The other man was slim, blond, deadpan, with close-set eyes and no colour in them.

Eddie Mars said: 'See if this bird is wearing any iron.'

The blond flicked a short-barrelled gun out and stood pointing it at me. The pug sidled over flat-footed and felt my pockets with care. I turned around for him like a bored beauty modelling an evening gown.

'No gun,' he said in a burry voice.

'Find out who he is.'

The pug slipped a hand into my breast pocket and drew out my wallet. He flipped it open and studied the contents. 'Name's Philip Marlowe, Eddie. Lives at the Hobart Arms on Franklin. Private licence, deputy's badge and all. A shamus.' He slipped the wallet back in my pocket, slapped my face lightly and turned away.

'Beat it,' Eddie Mars said.

The two gunmen went out again and closed the door. There was the sound of them getting back into the car. They started its motor and kept it idling once more.

'All right. Talk,' Eddie Mars said. The peaks of his eyebrows made sharp angles against his forehead.

'I'm not ready to give out. Killing Geiger to grab his racket would be a dumb trick and I'm not sure it happened that way, assuming he has been killed. But I'm sure that whoever got the books knows what's what, and I'm sure that the blonde lady at his store is scared batty about something or other. And I have a guess who got the books.'

'Who?'

'That's the part I'm not ready to give out. I've got a client, you know.'

He wrinkled his nose. 'That—' he chopped it off quickly.

'I expected you would know the girl,' I said.

'Who got the books, soldier?'

'Not ready to talk, Eddie. Why should I?'

He put the Luger down on the desk and slapped it with his open palm. 'This,' he said. 'And I might make it worth your while.'

'That's the spirit. Leave the gun out of it. I can always hear the sound of money. How much are you clinking at me?'

'For doing what?'

'What did you want done?'

He slammed the desk hard. 'Listen, soldier. I ask you a question and you ask me another. We're not getting anywhere. I want to know where Geiger is, for my own personal reasons. I didn't like his racket and I didn't protect him. I happen to own this house. I'm not so crazy about that right now. I can believe that whatever you know about all this is under glass, or there would be a flock of johns squeaking sole leather around this dump. You haven't got anything to sell. My guess is you need a little protection yourself. So cough up.'

It was a good guess, but I wasn't going to let him know it. I lit a cigarette and blew the match out and flicked it at the glass eye of the totem pole. 'You're right,' I said. 'If anything has happened to Geiger, I'll have to give what I have to the law. Which puts it in the public domain and doesn't leave me anything to sell. So with your permission I'll just drift.'

His face whitened under the tan. He looked mean, fast and tough enough for a moment. He made a movement to lift the gun. I added casually: 'By the way, how is Mrs Mars these days?'

I thought for a moment I had kidded him a little too far. His hand jerked at the gun, shaking. His face was stretched out by hard muscles. 'Beat it,' he said quite softly. 'I don't give a damn where you go or what you do when you get there. Only take a word of advice, soldier. Leave me out of your plans or you'll wish your name was Murphy and you lived in Limerick.'

'Well, that's not so far from Clonmel, I said. 'I hear you had a pal came from there.'

He leaned down on the desk, frozen-eyed, unmoving. I went over to the door and opened it and looked back at him. His eyes had followed me, but his lean grey body had not moved. There was hate in his eyes. I went out and through the hedge and up the hill to my car and got into it. I turned it around and drove up over the crest. Nobody shot at me. After a few blocks I turned off, cut the motor and sat for a few moments. Nobody followed me either. I drove back into Hollywood.

14

It was ten minutes to five when I parked near the lobby entrance of the apartment house on Randall Place. A few windows were lit and radios were bleating at the dusk. I rode the automatic elevator up to the fourth floor and went along a wide hall carpeted in green and panelled in ivory. A cool breeze blew down the hall from the open screened door to the fire escape.

There was a small ivory pushbutton beside the door marked '405'. I pushed it and waited what seemed a long time. Then the door opened noiselessly about a foot. There was a steady, furtive air in the way it opened. The man was long-legged, long-waisted, high-shouldered, and he had dark brown eyes in a brown expressionless face that had learned to control its expressions long ago. Hair like steel wool grew far back on his head and gave him a great deal of domed brown forehead that might at a careless glance have seemed a dwelling-place for brains. His sombre eyes probed at me impersonally. His long thin brown fingers held the edge of the door. He said nothing.

I said: 'Geiger?'

Nothing in the man's face changed that I could see. He brought a cigarette from behind the door and tucked it between his lips and drew a little smoke from it. The smoke came towards me in a lazy, contemptuous puff and behind it words in a cool unhurried voice that had no more inflection than the voice of a faro dealer.

'You said what?'

'Geiger. Arthur Gwynn Geiger. The guy that has the books.'

The man considered that without any haste. He glanced down at the tip of his cigarette. His other hand, the one that had been holding the door, dropped out of sight. His shoulder had a look as though his hidden hand might be making motions.

'Don't know anybody by that name,' he said. 'Does he live around here?'

I smiled. He didn't like the smile. His eyes got nasty. I said: 'You're Joe Brody?'

The brown face hardened. 'So what? Got a grift, brother – or just amusing yourself?'

'So you're Joe Brody,' I said. 'And you don't know anybody named Geiger. That's very funny.'

'Yeah? You got a funny sense of humour, maybe. Take it away and play on it somewhere else.'

I leaned against the door and gave him a dreamy smile. 'You got the books, Joe. I got the sucker list. We ought to talk things over.'

He didn't shift his eyes from my face. There was a faint sound in the room behind him, as though a metal curtain ring clicked lightly on a metal rod. He glanced sideways into the room. He opened the door wider.

'Why not – if you think you've got something?' he said coolly. He stood aside from the door. I went past him into the room.

It was a cheerful room with good furniture and not too much of it. French windows in the end wall opened on a stone porch and looked across the dusk at the foothills. Near the windows a closed door in the west wall and near the entrance door another door in the same wall. This last had a plush curtain drawn across it on a thin brass rod below the lintel.

That left the east wall, in which there were no doors. There was a davenport backed against the middle of it, so I sat down on the davenport. Brody shut the door and walked crab-fashion to a tall oak desk studded with square nails. A cedarwood box with gilt hinges lay on the lower leaf of the desk. He carried the box to an easy chair midway between the other two doors and sat down. I dropped my hat on the davenport and waited.

'Well, I'm listening,' Brody said. He opened the cigar box and dropped his cigarette stub into a dish at his side. He put a long thin cigar in his mouth. 'Cigar?' He tossed one at me through the air.

I reached for it. Brody took a gun out of the cigar box and pointed it at my nose. I looked at the gun. It was a black Police .38. I had no argument against it at the moment.

'Neat, huh?' Brody said. 'Just kind of stand up a minute. Come forward just about two yards. You might grab a little air while you're doing that.' His voice was the elaborately casual voice of the tough guy in pictures. Pictures have made them all like that.

'Tsk, tsk,' I said, not moving at all. 'Such a lot of guns around town and so few brains. You're the second guy I've met within hours who seems to think a gat in the hand means a world by the tail. Put it down and don't be silly, Joe.'

His eyebrows came together and he pushed his chin at me. His eyes were mean.

'The other guy's name is Eddie Mars,' I said. 'Ever hear of him?'

'No.' Brody kept the gun pointed at me.

'If he ever gets wise to where you were last night in the rain, he'll wipe you off the way a cheque raiser wipes a cheque.'

'What would I be to Eddie Mars?' Brody asked coldly. But he lowered the gun to his knee.

'Not even a memory,' I said.

We stared at each other. I didn't look at the pointed black slipper that showed under the plush curtain on the doorway to my left.

Brody said quietly: 'Don't get me wrong. I'm not a tough

70

guy – just careful. I don't know hell's first whisper about you. You might be a lifetaker for all I know.'

'You're not careful enough,' I said. 'That play with Geiger's books was terrible.'

He drew a long slow breath and let it out silently. Then he leaned back and crossed his long legs and held the Colt on his knee.

'Don't kid yourself I won't use this heat, if I have to,' he said. 'What's your story?'

'Have your friend with the pointed slippers come on in. She gets tired of holding her breath.'

Brody called out without moving his eyes off my stomach. 'Come on in, Agnes.'

The curtain swung aside and the green-eyed, thigh-swinging ash blonde from Geiger's store joined us in the room. She looked at me with a kind of mangled hatred. Her nostrils were pinched and her eyes had darkened a couple of shades. She looked very unhappy.

'I knew damn well you were trouble,' she snapped at me. 'I told Joe to watch his step.'

'It's not his step, it's the back of his lap he ought to watch,' I said.

'I suppose that's funny,' the blonde said.

'It has been,' I said. 'But it probably isn't any more.'

'Save the gags,' Brody advised me. 'Joe's watchin' his step plenty. Put some lights on so I can see to pop this guy, if it works out that way.'

The blonde snicked on a light in a big square standing lamp. She sank down into a chair beside the lamp and sat stiffly, as if her girdle was too tight. I put my cigar in my mouth and bit the end off. Brody's Colt took a close interest in me while I got matches out and lit the cigar. I tasted the smoke and said:

'The sucker list I spoke of is in code. I haven't cracked it yet, but there are about five hundred names. You got twelve boxes of books that I know of. You should have at least five hundred books. There'll be a bunch more out on loan, but say five hundred is the full crop, just to be cautious. If it's a good active list and you could run it even fifty per cent down the line, that would be one hundred and twenty-five thousand rentals. Your girl friend knows all about that. I'm only guessing. Put the average rental as low as you like, but it won't be less than a dollar, That merchandise costs money. At a dollar a rental you take one hundred and twenty-five grand and you still have your capital. I mean, you still have Geiger's capital. That's enough to spot a guy for.'

The blonde said: 'You're crazy, you goddamn egg-headed—!'

Brody put his teeth sideways at her and snarled: 'Pipe down, for Chrissake. Pipe down!'

She subsided into an outraged mixture of slow anguish and bottled fury. Her silvery nails scraped on her knees.

'It's no racket for bums,' I told Brody almost affectionately. 'It takes a smooth worker like you, Joe. You've got to get confidence and keep it. People who spend their money for second-hand sex jags are as nervous as dowagers who can't find the rest room. Personally I think the blackmail angles are a big mistake. I'm for shedding all that and sticking to legitimate sales and rentals.'

Brody's dark brown stare moved up and down my face. His Colt went on hungering for my vital organs. 'You're a funny guy,' he said tonelessly. 'Who has this lovely racket?'

'*You* have,' I said. 'Almost.'

The blonde choked and clawed her ear. Brody didn't say anything. He just looked at me.

'What?' the blonde called. 'You sit there and try to tell us Mr Geiger ran that kind of business right down to the main drag? You're nuts!'

I leered at her politely. 'Sure I do. Everybody knows the racket exists. Hollywood's made to order for it. If a thing like that has to exist, then right out on the street is where all practical coppers want it to exist. For the same reason they favour red light districts. They know where to flush the game when they want to.'

'My God,' the blonde said. 'You let this cheesehead sit there

72

and insult me, Joe? You with a gun in your hand and him holding nothing but a cigar and his thumb?'

'I like it,' Brody said. 'The guy's got good ideas. Shut your trap and keep it shut, or I'll slap it shut for you with this.' He flicked the gun around in an increasingly negligent manner.

The blonde gasped and turned her face to the wall. Brody looked at me and said cunningly: '*How* have I got that lovely racket?'

'You shot Geiger to get it. Last night in the rain. It was dandy shooting weather. The trouble is he wasn't alone when you whiffed him. Either you didn't notice that, which seems unlikely, or you got the wind up and lammed. But you had nerve enough to take the plate out of his camera and you had nerve enough to come back later on and hide his corpse, so you could tidy up on the books before the law knew it had a murder to investigate.'

'Yah,' Brody said contemptuously. The Colt wobbled on his knee. His brown face was as hard as a piece of carved wood. 'You take chances mister. It's kind of goddamned lucky for you I *didn't* bop Geiger.'

'You can step off for it just the same,' I told him cheerfully. 'You're made to order for the rap.'

Brody's voice went rough. 'Think you got me framed for it?'

'Positive.'

'How come?'

'There's somebody who'll tell it that way. I told you there was a witness. Don't go simple on me, Joe.'

He exploded then. 'That goddamned little hot pants!' he shouted. 'She would, goddamn her! She would – just that!'

I leaned back and grinned at him. 'Swell. I thought you had those nude photos of her.'

He didn't say anything. The blonde didn't say anything. I let them chew on it. Brody's face cleared slowly, with a sort of greyish relief. He put his Colt down on the end table beside his chair but kept his right hand close to it. He knocked ash from his cigar on the carpet and stared at me with eyes that were a tight shine between narrowed lids.

'I guess you think I'm dumb,' Brody said.

'Just average, for a grifter. Get the pictures.'

'What pictures?'

I shook my head. 'Wrong play, Joe. Innocence gets you nowhere. You were either there last night, or you got the nude photo from somebody that was there. You know *she* was there, because you had your girl friend threaten Mrs Regan with a police rap. The only ways you could know enough to do that would be by seeing what happened or by holding the photo and knowing where and when it was taken. Cough up and be sensible.'

'I'd have to have a little dough,' Brody said. He turned his head a little at the green-eyed blonde. Not now green-eyed and only superficially a blonde. She was as limp as a fresh-killed rabbit.

'No dough,' I said.

He scowled bitterly. 'How'd you get to me?'

I flicked my wallet out and let him look at my buzzer. 'I was working on Geiger – for a client. I was outside last night, in the rain. I heard the shots. I crashed in. I didn't see the killer. I saw everything else.'

'And kept your lip buttoned,' Brody sneered.

I put my wallet away. 'Yes,' I admitted. 'Up till now. Do I get the photos or not?'

'About these books,' Brody said. 'I don't get that.'

'I tailed them here from Geiger's store. I have a witness.'

'That punk kid?'

'What punk kid?'

He scowled again. 'The kid that works at the store. He skipped out after the truck left. Agnes don't even know where he flops.'

'That helps,' I said, grinning at him. 'That angle worried me a little. Either of you ever been in Geiger's house – before last night?'

'Not even last night,' Brody said sharply. 'So she says I gunned him, eh?'

'With the photos in hand I might be able to convince her she was wrong. There was a little drinking being done.'

Brody sighed. 'She hates my guts. I bounced her out. I got paid, sure, but I'd have had to do it anyway. She's too screwy for a simple guy like me.' He cleared his throat. 'How about a little dough? I'm down to nickels. Agnes and me gotta move on.'

'Not from my client.'

'Listen—'

'Get the pictures, Brody.'

'Oh, hell,' he said. 'You win.' He stood up and slipped the Colt into his side pocket. His left hand went up inside his coat. He was holding it there, his face twisted with disgust, when the door buzzer rang and kept on ringing.

15

He didn't like that. His lower lip went in under his teeth, and his eyebrows drew down sharply at the corners. His whole face became sharp and foxy and mean.

The buzzer kept up its song. I didn't like it either. If the visitors should happen to be Eddie Mars and his boys, I might get chilled off just for being there. If it was the police, I was caught with nothing to give them but a smile and a promise. And if it was some of Brody's friends – supposing he had any – they might turn out to be tougher than he was.

The blonde didn't like it. She stood up in a surge and chipped at the air with one hand. Nerve tension made her face old and ugly.

Watching me, Brody jerked a small drawer in the desk and picked a bone-handled automatic out of it. He held it at the blonde. She slid over to him and took it, shaking.

'Sit down next to him,' Brody said. 'Hold it on him low down, away from the door. If he gets funny use your own judgement. We ain't licked yet, baby.'

'Oh, Joe,' the blonde wailed. She came over and sat next to me on the davenport and pointed the gun at my leg artery. I didn't like the jerky look in her eyes.

The door buzzer stopped humming and a quick impatient rapping on the wood followed it. Brody put his hand in his pocket, on his gun, and walked over to the door and opened it with his left hand. Carmen Sternwood pushed him back into the room by putting a little revolver against his lean brown lips.

Brody backed away from her with his mouth working and an expression of panic on his face. Carmen shut the door behind her and looked neither at me nor Agnes. She stalked Brody carefully, her tongue sticking out a little between her teeth. Brody took both hands out of his pockets and gestured placatingly at her. His eyebrows designed themselves into an odd assortment of curves and angles. Agnes turned the gun away from me and swung it at Carmen. I shot my hand out and closed my fingers down hard over her hand and jammed my thumb on the safety catch. It was already on. I kept it on. There was a short silent tussle, to which neither Brody nor Carmen paid any attention whatever. I had the gun. Agnes breathed deeply and shivered the whole length of her body. Carmen's face had a bony scraped look and her breath hissed. Her voice said without tone:

'I want my pictures, Joe.'

Brody swallowed and tried to grin. 'Sure kid, sure.' He said it in a small flat voice that was as much like the voice he had used to me as a scooter is like a ten-ton truck.

Carmen said: 'You shot Arthur Geiger. I saw you. I want my pictures.' Brody turned green.

'Hey, wait a minute, Carmen,' I called.

Blonde Agnes came to life with a rush. She ducked her head and sank her teeth in my right hand. I made more noises and shook her off.

'Listen, kid,' Brody said. 'Listen a minute—'

The blonde spat at me and threw herself on my leg and tried to bite that. I cracked her on the head with the gun, not very hard, and tried to stand up. She rolled down my legs and wrapped her arms around them. I fell back on the davenport. The blonde was strong with the madness of love or fear, or a mixture of both, or maybe she was just strong.

Brody grabbed for the little revolver that was so close to his face. He missed. The gun made a sharp rapping noise that was not very loud. The bullet broke glass in a folded-back french window. Brody groaned horribly and fell down on the floor and jerked Carmen's feet from under her. She landed in a heap and the little revolver went skidding off into a corner. Brody jumped up on his knees and reached for his pocket.

I hit Agnes on the head with less delicacy than before, kicked her off my feet, and stood up. Brody flicked his eyes at me. I showed him the automatic. He stopped trying to get his hand into his pocket.

'Christ!' he whined. 'Don't let her kill me!'

I began to laugh. I laughed like an idiot, without control. Blonde Agnes was sitting up on the floor with her hands flat on the carpet and her mouth wide open and a wick of metallic blonde hair down over her right eye. Carmen was crawling on her hands and knees, still hissing. The metal of her little revolver glistened against the baseboard over in the corner. She crawled towards it relentlessly.

I waved my share of the guns at Brody and said: 'Stay put. You're all right.'

I stepped past the crawling girl and picked the gun up. She looked at me and began to giggle. I put her gun in my pocket and patted her on the back. 'Get up, angel. You look like a Pekinese.'

I went over to Brody and put the automatic against his midriff and reached his Colt out of his side pocket. I now had all the guns that had been exposed to view. I stuffed them into my pockets and held my hand out to him.

'Give.'

He nodded, licking his lips, his eyes still scared. He took a fat envelope out of his breast pocket and gave it to me. There was a developed plate in the envelope and five glossy prints.

'Sure these are all?'

He nodded again. I put the envelope in my own breast pocket and turned away. Agnes was back on the davenport, straightening her hair. Her eyes ate Carmen with a green distillation of hate. Carmen was up on her feet too, coming towards me with her hand out, still giggling and hissing. There was a little froth at the corners of her mouth. Her small white teeth glinted close to her lips.

'Can I have them now?' she asked me with a coy smile.

'I'll take care of them for you. Go on home.'

'Home?'

I went to the door and looked out. The cool night breeze was blowing peacefully down the hall. No excited neighbours hung out of doorways. A small gun had gone off and broken a pane of glass, but noises like that don't mean much any more. I held the door open and jerked my head at Carmen. She came towards me, smiling uncertainly.

'Go on home and wait for me,' I said soothingly.

She put her thumb up. Then she nodded and slipped past me into the hall. She touched my cheek with her fingers as she went by. 'You'll take care of Carmen, won't you?' she said.

'Check.'

'You're cute.'

'What you see is nothing,' I said. 'I've got a Bali dancing girl tattooed on my right thigh.'

Her eyes rounded. She said: 'Naughty,' and wagged a finger at me. Then she whispered: 'Can I have my gun?'

'Not now. Later. I'll bring it to you.'

She grabbed me suddenly around the neck and kissed me on the mouth. 'I like you,' she said. 'Carmen likes you a lot.' She ran off down the hall as gay as a thrush, waved at me from the stairs and ran down the stairs out of my sight.

I went back into Brody's apartment.

16

I went over to the folded-back french window and looked at the small broken pane in the upper part of it. The bullet from Carmen's gun had smashed the glass like a blow. It had not made a hole. There was a small hole in the plaster which a keen eye would find quickly enough. I pulled the drapes over the broken pane and took Carmen's gun out of my pocket. It was a Banker's Special, .22 calibre, hollow point cartridges. It had a pearl grip, and a small round silver plate set into the butt was engraved: 'Carmen from Owen.' She made saps of all of them.

I put the gun back in my pocket and sat down close to Brody and stared into his bleak brown eyes. A minute passed. The blonde adjusted her face by the aid of a pocket mirror. Brody fumbled around with a cigarette and jerked: 'Satisfied?'

'So far. Why did you put the bite on Mrs Regan instead of the old man?'

'Tapped the old man once. About six, seven months ago. I figure maybe he gets sore enough to call in some law.'

'What made you think Mrs Regan wouldn't tell him about it?'

He considered that with some care, smoking his cigarette and keeping his eyes on my face. Finally he said: 'How well you know her?'

'I've met her twice. You must know her a lot better to chance on that squeeze with the photo.'

'She skates around plenty. I figure maybe she has a couple of soft spots she don't want the old man to know about. I figure she can raise five grand easy.'

'A little weak,' I said. 'But pass it. You're broke, eh?'

'I been shaking two nickels together for a month, trying to get them to mate.'

'What do you do for a living?'

'Insurance. I got a desk room in Puss Walgreen's office, Fulwider Building, Western and Santa Monica.'

'When you open up, you open up. The books here in your apartment?'

He snapped his teeth and waved a brown hand. Confidence was oozing back into his manner. 'Hell, no. In storage.'

'You had a man bring them here and then you had a storage outfit come and take them away again right afterwards?'

'Sure. I don't want them moved direct from Geiger's place, do I?'

'You're smart,' I said admiringly. 'Anything incriminating in the joint right now?'

He looked worried again. He shook his head sharply.

'That's fine,' I told him. I looked across at Agnes. She had finished fixing her face and was staring at the wall, blank-eyed, hardly listening. Her face had the drowsiness which strain and shock induce, after their first incidence.

Brody flicked his eyes warily. 'Well?'

'How'd you come by the photo?'

He scowled. 'Listen, you got what you came after, got it plenty cheap. You done a nice neat job. Now go peddle it to your top man. I'm clean. I don't know nothing about any photo, do I, Agnes?'

The blonde opened her eyes and looked at him with vague but uncomplimentary speculation. 'A half smart guy,' she said with a tired sniff. 'That's all I ever draw. Never once a guy that's smart all the way around the course. Never once.'

I grinned at her. 'Did I hurt your head much?'

'You and every other man I ever met.'

I looked back at Brody. He was pinching his cigarette between his fingers, with a sort of twitch. His hand seemed to be shaking a little. His brown poker face was still smooth.

'We've got to agree on a story,' I said. 'For instance, Carmen wasn't here. That's very important. She wasn't here. That was a vision you saw.'

'Huh!' Brody sneered. 'If you say so, pal, and if—' he put his hand out palm up and cupped the fingers and rolled the thumb gently against the index and middle fingers.

I nodded. 'We'll see. There might be a small contribution.

You won't count it in grands, though. Now where did you get the picture?'

'A guy slipped it to me.'

'Uh-huh. A guy you just passed in the street. You wouldn't know him again. You never saw him before.'

Brody yawned. 'It dropped out of his pocket,' he said.

'Uh-huh. Got an alibi for last night, poker pan?'

'Sure. I was right here. Agnes was with me. Okay, Agnes?'

'I'm beginning to feel sorry for you again,' I said.

His eyes flicked wide and his mouth hung loose, the cigarette balanced on his lower lip.

'You think you're smart and you're so goddamned dumb,' I told him. 'Even if you don't dance off up in Quentin, you have such a bleak long lonely time ahead of you.'

His cigarette jerked and dropped ash on his waistcoat.

'Thinking about how smart you are,' I said.

'Take the air,' he growled suddenly. 'Dust. I got enough chinning with you. Beat it.'

'Okay.' I stood up and went over to the tall oak desk and took his two guns out of my pockets, laid them side by side on the blotters so that the barrels were exactly parallel. I reached my hat off the floor beside the davenport and started for the door.

Brody called: 'Hey!'

I turned and waited. His cigarette was jiggling like a doll on a coiled spring. 'Everything's smooth, ain't it?' he asked.

'Why, sure. This is a free country. You don't have to stay out of jail, if you don't want to. That is, if you're a citizen. Are you a citizen?'

He just stared at me, jiggling the cigarette. The blonde Agnes turned her head slowly and stared at me along the same level. Their glances contained almost the exact same blend of foxiness, doubt and frustrated anger. Agnes reached her silvery nails up abruptly and yanked a hair out of her head and broke it between her fingers, with a bitter jerk.

Brody said tightly: 'You're not going to any cops, brother. Not if it's the Sternwoods you're working for. I've got too much stuff on that family. You got your pictures and you got your hush. Go and peddle your papers.'

'Make your mind up,' I said. 'You told me to dust. I was on my way out, you hollered at me and I stopped, and now I'm on my way out again. Is that what you want?'

'You ain't got anything on me,' Brody said.

'Just a couple of murders. Small change in your circle.'

He didn't jump more than an inch, but it looked like a foot. The white cornea showed all around the tobacco coloured iris of his eyes. The brown skin of his face took on a greenish tinge in the lamplight.

Blonde Agnes let out a low animal wail and buried her head in a cushion on the end of the davenport. I stood there and admired the long line of her thighs.

Brody moistened his lips slowly and said: 'Sit down, pal. Maybe I have a little more for you. What's that crack about two murders mean?'

I leaned against the door. 'Where were you last night about seven-thirty, Joe?'

His mouth dropped sulkily and he stared down at the floor. 'I was watching a guy, a guy who had a nice racket I figured he needed a partner in. Geiger. I was watching him now and then to see had he any tough connections. I figure he has friends or he don't work the racket as open as he does. But they don't go to his house. Only dames.'

'You didn't watch hard enough,' I said. 'Go on.'

'I'm there last night on the street below Geiger's house. It's raining hard and I'm buttoned up in my coupé and I don't see anything. There's a car in front of Geiger's and another car a little way up the hill. That's why I stay down below. There's a big Buick parked down where I am and after a while I go over and take a gander into it. It's registered to Vivian Regan. Nothing happens, so I scram. That's all.'

He waved his cigarette. His eyes crawled up and down my face.

'Could be,' I said. 'Know where that Buick is now?'

'Why would I?'

'In the Sheriff's garage. It was lifted out of twelve feet of water off Lido fish pier this morning. There was a dead man in it. He had been sapped and the car pointed out to the pier and the hand throttle pulled down.'

Brody was breathing hard. One of his feet tapped restlessly. 'Jesus, guy, you can't pin that one on me,' he said thickly.

'Why not? This Buick was down back of Geiger's according to you. Well, Mrs Regan didn't have it out. Her chauffeur, a lad named Owen Taylor, had it out. He went over to Geiger's place to have words with him, because Owen Taylor was sweet on Carmen, and he didn't like the kind of games Geiger was playing with her. He let himself in the back way with a jimmy and a gun and he caught Geiger taking a photo of Carmen without any clothes on. So his gun went off, as guns will, and Geiger fell down dead and Owen ran away, but not without the photo negative Geiger had just taken. So you ran after him and took the photo from him. How else would you have got hold of it?'

Brody licked his lips. 'Yeah,' he said. 'But don't make me knock him off. Sure, I heard the shots and saw this killer come slamming down the back steps into the Buick and off. I took out after him. He hit the bottom of the canyon and went west on Sunset. Beyond Beverly Hills he skidded off the road and had to stop and I came up and played copper. He had a gun but his nerve was bad and I sapped him down. So I went through his clothes and found out who he was and I lifted the plate-holder, just out of curiosity. I was wondering what it was all about and getting my neck wet when he came out of it all of a sudden and knocked me off the car. He was out of sight when I picked myself up. That's the last I saw of him.'

'How did you know it was Geiger he shot?' I asked gruffly.

Brody shrugged. 'I figure it was, but I can be wrong. When I had the plate developed and saw what was on it, I was pretty damn sure. And when Geiger didn't come down to the store this morning and didn't answer his phone I was plenty sure. So I figure it's a good time to move his books out and make a quick touch on the Sternwoods for travel money and blow for a while.'

I nodded. 'That seem reasonable. Maybe you didn't murder anybody at that. Where did you hide Geiger's body?'

He lifted his eyebrows. Then he grinned. 'Nix, nix. Skip it. You think I'd go back there and handle him, not knowing when a couple carloads of law would come tearing around the corner? Nix.'

'Somebody hid the body,' I said.

Brody shrugged. The grin stayed on his face. He didn't believe me. While he was still not believing me the door buzzer started to ring again. Brody stood up sharply, hard-eyed. He glanced over at his guns on the desk.

'So she's back again,' he growled.

'If she is, she doesn't have her gun,' I comforted him. 'Don't you have any other friends?'

'Just about one,' he growled. 'I got enough of this puss-in-the-corner game.' He marched to the desk and took the Colt. He held it down at his side and went to the door. He put his left hand to the knob and twisted it and opened the door a foot and leaned into the opening, holding the gun tight against his thigh.

A voice said: 'Brody?'

Brody said something I didn't hear. The two quick reports were muffled. The gun must have been pressed tight against Brody's body. He tilted forward against the door and the weight of his body pushed it shut with a bang. He slid down the wood. His feet pushed the carpet away behind him. His left hand dropped off the knob and the arm slapped the floor with a thud. His head was wedged against the door. He didn't move. The Colt clung to his right hand.

I jumped across the room and rolled him enough to get the door open and crowd through. A woman peered out of a door almost opposite. Her face was full of fright and she pointed along the hall with a claw-like hand.

I raced down the hall and heard thumping feet going down the tile steps and went down after the sound. At the lobby level the front door was closing itself quietly and running feet slapped the pavement outside. I made the door before it was shut, clawed it open again and charged out.

A tall hatless figure in a leather jerkin was running diagonally across the street between the parked cars. The figure turned and flame spurted from it. Two heavy hammers hit the stucco wall beside me. The figure ran on, dodged between two cars, vanished.

A man came up beside me and asked: 'What happened?'

'Shooting going on,' I said.

'Jesus!' He scuttled into the apartment house.

I walked quickly down the pavement to my car and got in and started it. I pulled out from the kerb and drove down the hill, not fast. No other car started up on the other side of the street. I thought I heard steps, but I wasn't sure about that. I rode down the hill a block and a half, turned at the intersection and started to back up. The sound of a muted whistling came to me faintly along the pavement. Then steps. I double parked and slid out between two cars and went down low. I took Carmen's little revolver out of my pocket.

The sound of the steps grew louder, and the whistling went on cheerfully. In a moment the jerkin showed. I stepped out between the two cars and said: 'Got a match, buddy?'

The boy spun towards me and his right hand darted up to go inside the jerkin. His eyes were a wet shine in the glow of the round electroliers. Moist dark eyes shaped like almonds, and a pallid handsome face with wavy black hair growing low on the forehead in two points. A very handsome boy indeed, the boy from Geiger's store.

He stood there looking at me silently, his right hand on the edge of the jerkin, but not inside it yet. I held the little revolver down at my side.

'You must have thought a lot of that queen,' I said.

'Go — yourself,' the boy said softly, motionless between the parked cars and the five-foot retaining wall on the inside of the pavement.

A siren wailed distantly coming up the long hill. The boy's head jerked towards the sound. I stepped in close and put my gun into his jerkin.

'Me or the cops?' I asked him.

His head rolled a little sideways as if I had slapped his face. 'Who are you?' he said.

'Friend of Geiger's.'

'Get away from me, you son of a bitch.'

'This is a small gun, kid. I'll give it you through the navel and it will take three months to get you well enough to walk. But you'll get well. So you can walk to the nice new gas chamber up in Quentin.'

He said: 'Go — yourself.' His hand moved inside the jerkin. I pressed harder on his stomach. He let out a long soft sigh, took his hand away from the jerkin and let it fall limp at his side. His wide shoulders sagged. 'What you want?' he whispered.

I reached inside the jerkin and plucked out the automatic. 'Get into my car, kid.'

He stepped past me and I crowded him from behind. He got into the car.

'Under the wheel, kid. You drive.'

He slid under the wheel and I got into the car beside him. I said: 'Let the prowl car pass up the hill. They'll think we moved over when we heard the siren. Then turn her downhill and we'll go home.'

I put Carmen's gun away and leaned the automatic against the boy's ribs. I looked back through the window. The whine of the siren was very loud now. Two red lights swelled in the middle of the street. They grew larger and blended into one and the car rushed by in a wild flurry of sound.

'Let's go,' I said.

The boy swung the car and started off down the hill.

'Let's go home,' I said. 'To Laverne Terrace.'

His smooth lips twitched. He swung the car west on Franklin. 'You're a simple-minded lad. What's your name?'

'Carol Lundgren,' he said lifelessly.

'You shot the wrong guy, Carol. Joe Brody didn't kill your queen.'

He spoke three words to me and kept on driving.

17

A moon half gone from the full glowed through a ring of mist among the high branches of the eucalyptus trees on Laverne Terrace. A radio sounded loudly from a house low down the hill. The boy swung the car over to the box hedge in front of Geiger's house, killed the motor and sat looking straight before him with both hands on the wheel. No light showed through Geiger's hedge.

I said 'Anybody home, son?'

'You ought to know.'

'How would I know?'

'Go — yourself.'

'That's how people get false teeth.'

He showed me his in a tight grin. Then he kicked the door open and got out. I scuttled out after him. He stood with his fists on his hips, looking silently at the house above the top of the hedge.

'All right,' I said. 'You have a key. Let's go in.'

'Who said I had a key?'

'Don't kid me, son. The fag gave you one. You've got a nice clean manly little room in there. He shooed you out and locked it up when he had lady visitors. He was like Caesar, a husband to women and a wife to men. Think I can't figure people like him and you out?'

I still held his automatic more or less pointed at him, but he swung on me just the same. It caught me flush on the chin. I backstepped fast enough to keep from falling, but I took plenty of the punch. It was meant to be a hard one, but a pansy has no iron in his bones, whatever he looks like.

I threw the gun down at the kid's feet and said: 'Maybe you need this.'

He stooped for it like a flash. There was nothing slow about his movements. I sank a fist in the side of his neck. He toppled over sideways, clawing for the gun and not reaching it. I picked it up again and threw it in the car. The boy came up on all fours, leering with his eyes too wide open. He coughed and shook his head.

'You don't want to fight,' I told him. 'You're giving away too much weight.'

He wanted to fight. He shot at me like a plane from a catapult, reaching for my knees in a diving tackle. I sidestepped and reached for his neck and took it into chancery. He scraped the dirt hard and got his feet under him enough to use his hands on me where it hurt. I twisted him around and heaved him a little higher. I took hold of my right wrist with my left hand and turned my right hipbone into him and for a moment it was a balance of weights. We seemed to hang there in the misty moonlight, two grotesque creatures whose feet scraped on the road and whose breath panted with effort.

I had my right forearm against his windpipe now and all the strength of both arms in it. His feet began a frenetic shuffle and he wasn't panting any more. He was ironbound. His left foot sprawled off to one side and the knee went slack. I held on half a minute longer. He sagged on my arm, an enormous weight I could hardly hold up. Then I let go. He sprawled at my feet, out cold. I went to the car and got a pair of handcuffs out of the glove compartment and twisted his wrists behind him and snapped them on. I lifted him by the armpits and managed to drag him in behind the hedge, out of sight from the street. I went back to the car and moved it a hundred feet up the hill and locked it.

He was still out when I got back. I unlocked the door, dragged him into the house, shut the door. He was beginning to gasp now. I switched a lamp on. His eyes fluttered open and focused on me slowly.

I bent down, keeping out of the way of his knees and said: 'Keep quiet or you'll get the same and more of it. Just lie quiet and hold your breath. Hold it until you can't hold it any longer and then tell yourself that you have to breathe, that you're black in the face, that your eyeballs are popping out, and that you're going to breathe right now, but that you're sitting strapped in the chair in the clean little gas chamber up in San Quentin and when you take that breath you're fighting with all your soul not to take it, it won't be air you'll get, it will be cyanide fumes. And that's what they call humane execution in our state now.'

'Go — yourself,' he said with a soft stricken sigh.

'You're going to cop a plea, brother, don't ever think you're not. And you're going to say just what we want you to say and nothing we don't want you to say.'

'Go — yourself.'

'Say that again and I'll put a pillow under your head.'

His mouth twitched. I left him lying on the floor with his wrists shackled behind him and his cheek pressed into the rug and an animal brightness in his visible eye. I put on another lamp and stepped into the hallway at the back of the living-room. Geiger's bedroom didn't seem to have been touched. I opened the door, not locked now, of the bedroom across the hall from it. There was a dim flickering light in the room and a smell of sandalwood. Two cones of incense ash stood side by side on a small brass tray on the bureau. The light came from the two tall black candles in the foot-high candlesticks. They were standing on straight-backed chairs, one on either side of the bed.

Geiger lay on the bed. The two missing strips of Chinese tapestry made a St Andrew's Cross over the middle of his body, hiding the blood-smeared front of his Chinese coat. Below the cross his black-pyjama'd legs lay stiff and straight. His feet were in the slippers with thick white felt shoes. Above the cross his arms were crossed at the wrists and his hands lay flat against his shoulders, palms down, fingers close together and stretched out evenly. His mouth was closed and his Charlie Chan moustache was as unreal as a toupee. His broad nose was pinched and white. His eyes were almost closed, but not entirely. The faint glitter of his glass eye caught the light and winked at me.

I didn't touch him. I didn't go very near him. He would be as cold as ice and as stiff as a board.

The black candles guttered in the draught from the open door.

Drops of black wax crawled down their sides. The air of the room was poisonous and unreal. I went out and shut the door again and went back to the living-room. The boy hadn't moved. I stood still, listening for sirens. It was all a question of how soon Agnes talked and what she said. If she talked about Geiger, the police would be there any minute. But she might not talk for hours. She might even have got away.

I looked down at the boy. 'Want to sit up, son?'

He closed his eyes and pretended to go to sleep. I went over to the desk and scooped up the mulberry-coloured phone and dialled Bernie Ohls's office. He had left to go home at six o'clock. I dialled the number of his home. He was there.

'This is Marlowe,' I said. 'Did your boys find a revolver on Owen Taylor this morning?'

I could hear him clearing his throat and then I could hear him trying to keep the surprise out of his voice. 'That would come under the heading of police business,' he said.

'If they did, it had three empty shells in it.'

'How the hell did you know that?' Ohls asked quietly.

'Come over to 7244 Laverne Terrace, off Laurel Canyon Boulevard. I'll show you where the slugs went.'

'Just like that, huh?'

'Just like that.'

Ohls said: 'Look out the window and you'll see me coming round the corner. I thought you acted a little cagey on that one.'

'Cagey is no word for it,' I said.

18

Ohls stood looking down at the boy. The boy sat on the couch leaning sideways against the wall. Ohls looked at him silently, his pale eyebrows bristling and stiff and round like the little vegetable brushes the Fuller Brush man gives away.

He asked the boy: 'Do you admit shooting Brody?'

The boy said his favourite three words in a muffled voice.

Ohls sighed and looked at me. I said: 'He doesn't have to admit that. I have his gun.'

Ohls said: 'I wish to Christ I had a dollar for every time I've had that said to me. What's funny about it?'

'It's not meant to be funny,' I said.

'Well, that's something,' Ohls said. He turned away. 'I've called Wilde. We'll go over and see him and take this punk. He can ride with me and you can follow on behind in case he tries to kick me in the face.'

'How do you like what's in the bedroom?'

'I like it fine,' Ohls said. 'I'm kind of glad that Taylor kid went off the pier. I'd hate to have to help send him to the death-house for rubbing that skunk.'

I went back into the small bedroom and blew out the black candles and let them smoke. When I got back to the living-room Ohls had the boy up on his feet. The boy stood glaring at him with sharp black eyes in a face as hard and white as cold mutton fat.

'Let's go,' Ohls said and took him by the arms as if he didn't like touching him. I put the lamps out and followed them out of the house. We got into our cars and I followed Ohls's twin tail-lights down the long curving hill. I hoped this would be my last trip to Laverne Terrace.

Taggart Wilde, the District Attorney, lived at the corner of Fourth and Lafayette Park, in a white frame house the size of a carbarn, with red sandstone porte-cochère built on to one side and a couple of acres of soft rolling lawn in front. It was one of those solid old-fashioned houses which it used to be the thing to move bodily to new locations as the city grew westward. Wilde came of an old Los Angeles family and had probably been born in the house when it was on West Adams or Figueroa or St James Park.

There were two cars in the driveway already, a big private sedan and a police car with a uniformed chauffeur who leaned smoking against his rear fender and admired the moon. Ohls went over and spoke to him and the chauffeur looked in at the boy in Ohls's car.

We went up to the house and rang the bell. A slick-haired blond man opened the door and led us down the hall and through a huge sunken living-room on the far side of it. He knocked at a door and stepped inside, then held the door wide and we went into a panelled study with an open french door at the end and a view of dark garden and mysterious trees. A smell of wet earth and flowers came in at the window. There were large dim oils on the walls, easy chairs, books, a smell of good cigar smoke which blended with the smell of wet earth and flowers.

Taggart Wilde sat behind a desk, a middle-aged plump man with clear blue eyes that managed to have a friendly expression without really having any expression at all. He had a cup of black coffee in front of him and he held a dappled thin cigar between the neat careful fingers of his left hand. Another man sat at the corner of the desk in a blue leather chair, a cold-eyed hatchet-faced man, as lean as a rake and as hard as the manager of a loan office. His neat well-kept face looked as if it had been shaved within the hour. He wore a well-pressed brown suit and there was a black pearl in his tie. He had the long nervous fingers of a man with a quick brain. He looked ready for a fight.

Ohls pulled a chair up and sat down and said: 'Evening, Cronjager. Meet Phil Marlowe, a private eye who's in a jam.' Ohls grinned.

Cronjager looked at me without nodding. He looked me over as if he was looking at a photograph. Then he nodded his chin about an inch. Wilde said: 'Sit down, Marlowe. I'll try to handle Captain Cronjager, but you know how it is. This is a big city now.'

I sat down and lit a cigarette. Ohls looked at Cronjager and asked: 'What did you get on the Randall Place killing?'

The hatchet-faced man pulled one of his fingers until the knuckle cracked. He spoke without looking up. 'A stiff, two slugs in him. Two guns that hadn't been fired. Down on the street we got a blonde trying to start a car that didn't belong to her. Hers was right next to it, the same model. She acted rattled so the boys brought her in and she spilled. She was in there when this guy Brody got it. Claims she didn't see the killer.'

'That all?' Ohls asked.

Cronjager raised his eyebrows a little. 'Only happened about an hour ago. What did you expect – moving pictures of the killing?'

'Maybe a description of the killer,' Ohls said.

'A tall guy in a leather jerkin – if you call that a description.'

'He's outside in my heap,' Ohls said. 'Handcuffed. Marlowe put the arm on him for you. Here's his gun.' Ohls took the boy's automatic out of his pocket and laid it on a corner of Wilde's desk. Cronjager looked at the gun but didn't reach for it.

Wilde chuckled. He was leaning back and puffing his dappled cigar without letting go of it. He bent forward to sip from his coffee cup. He took a silk handkerchief from the breast pocket of the dinner-jacket he was wearing and touched his lips with it and tucked it away again.

'There's a couple more deaths involved,' Ohls said, pinching the soft flesh at the end of his chin.

Cronjager stiffened visibly. His surly eyes became points of steely light.

Ohls said: 'You heard about a car being lifted out of the Pacific Ocean off Lido pier this morning with a dead guy in it?'

Cronjager said: 'No,' and kept on looking nasty.

'The dead guy in the car was chauffeur to a rich family,' Ohls said. 'The family was being blackmailed on account of one of the daughters. Mr Wilde recommended Marlowe to the family, through me. Marlowe played it kind of close to the waistcoat.'

'I love private dicks that play murders close to the waistcoat,' Cronjager said. 'You don't have to be so goddamned coy about it.'

'Yeah,' Ohls said. 'I don't have to be so goddamned coy about it. It's not so goddamned often I get a chance to be coy with a city copper. I spend most of my time telling them where to put their feet so they won't break an ankle.'

Cronjager whitened around the corners of his sharp nose. His breath made a soft hissing sound in the quiet room. He said very quietly: 'You haven't had to tell any of *my* men where to put their feet, smart guy.'

'We'll see about that,' Ohls said. 'This chauffeur I spoke of that's drowned off Lido shot a guy last night in your territory. A guy named Geiger who ran a dirty book racket in a store on Hollywood Boulevard. Geiger was living with the punk I got outside in my car. I mean living with him, if you get the idea.'

Cronjager was staring at him levelly now. 'That sounds like it might grow up to be a dirty story,' he said.

'It's my experience most police stories are,' Ohls growled and turned to me, his eyebrows bristling. 'You're on the air, Marlowe. Give it to him.'

I gave it to him.

I left out two things, not knowing just why, at the moment, I left out one of them. I left out Carmen's visit to Brody's apartment and Eddie Mars's visit to Geiger's in the afternoon. I told the rest of it just as it happened.

Cronjager never took his eyes off my face and no expression of any kind crossed his as I talked. At the end of it he was perfectly silent for a long minute. Wilde was silent, sipping his coffee, puffing gently at his dappled cigar. Ohls stared at one of his thumbs.

Cronjager leaned slowly back in his chair and crossed one ankle over his knee and rubbed the ankle-bone with his thin nervous hand. His lean face wore a harsh frown. He said with deadly politeness:

'So all you did was not report a murder that happened last night and then spend today foxing around so that this kid of Geiger's could commit a second murder this evening.'

'That's all,' I said. 'I was in a pretty tough spot. I guess I did wrong, but I wanted to protect my client and I hadn't any reason to think the boy would go gunning for Brody.'

'That kind of thinking is police business, Marlowe. If Geiger's death had been reported last night, the books could never have been moved from the store to Brody's apartment. The kid wouldn't have been led to Brody and wouldn't have killed him. Say Brody was living on borrowed time. His kind usually are. But a life is a life.'

'Right,' I said. 'Tell that to your coppers next time they shoot down some scared petty larceny crook running away up an alley with a stolen spare.'

Wilde put both his hands down on his desk with a solid smack. 'That's enough of that,' he snapped. 'What makes you so sure, Marlowe, that this Taylor boy shot Geiger? Even if the gun that killed Geiger was found on Taylor's body or in the car, it doesn't absolutely follow that he was the killer. The gun might have been planted – say by Brody, the actual killer.'

'It's physically possible,' I said, 'but morally impossible. It assumes too much coincidence and too much that's out of character for Brody and his girl, and out of character for what he was trying to do. I talked to Brody for a long time. He was a crook, but not a killer type. He had two guns, but he wasn't wearing either of them. He was trying to find a way to cut in on Geiger's racket, which naturally he knew all about from the girl. He says he was watching Geiger off and on to see if he had any tough backers. I believe him. To suppose he killed Geiger in order to get his books, then scrammed with the nude photo Geiger had just taken of Carmen Sternwood, then planted the gun on Owen Taylor and pushed Taylor into the ocean off Lido, is to suppose a hell a lot too much. Taylor had the motive, jealous rage, and the opportunity to kill Geiger. He was out in one of the family cars without permission. He killed Geiger right in front of the girl, which Brody would never have done, even if he had been a killer. I can't see anybody with a purely commercial interest in Geiger doing that. But Taylor would have done it. The nude photo business was just what would have made him do it.'

Wilde chuckled and looked along his eyes at Cronjager. Cronjager cleared his throat with a snort. Wilde asked: 'What's this business about hiding the body? I don't see the point of that.'

I said: 'The kid hasn't told us, but he must have done it. Brody wouldn't have gone into the house after Geiger was shot. The boy must have got home when I was away taking Carmen to her house. He was afraid of the police, of course, being what he is, and he probably thought it a good idea to have the body hidden until he had removed his effects from the house. He dragged it out of the front door, judging by the marks on the rug, and very likely put it in the garage. Then he packed up whatever belongings he had there and took them away. And later on, sometime in the night and before the body stiffened, he had a revulsion of feeling and thought he hadn't treated his dead friend very nicely. So he went back and laid him out on the bed. That's all guessing of course.'

Wilde nodded. 'Then this morning he goes down to the store as if nothing had happened and keeps his eyes open. And when Brody moved the books out he found out where they were going and assumed that whoever got them had killed Geiger just for that purpose. He may even have known more about Brody and the girl than they suspected. What do you think, Ohls?'

Ohls said: 'We'll find out – but that doesn't help Cronjager's troubles. What's eating him is all this happened last night and he's only just been rung in on it.'

Cronjager said sourly: 'I think I can find some way to deal with that angle too.' He looked at me sharply and immediately looked away again.

Wilde waved his cigar and said: 'Let's see the exhibits, Marlowe.'

I emptied my pockets and put the catch on his desk: the three notes and Geiger's card to General Sternwood, Carmen's photos, and the blue note-book with the code list of names and addresses. I had already given Geiger's keys to Ohls.

Wilde looked at what I gave him, puffing gently at his cigar. Ohls lit one of his own toy cigars and blew smoke peacefully at the ceiling. Cronjager leaned on the desk and looked at what I had given Wilde.

Wilde tapped the three notes signed by Carmen and said: 'I

guess these were just a come-on. If General Sternwood paid them, it would be through fear or something worse. Then Geiger would have tightened the screws. Do you know what he was afraid of?' He was looking at me.

I shook my head.

'Have you told your story complete in all relevant details?'

'I left out a couple of personal matters. I intend to keep on leaving them out, Mr Wilde.'

Cronjager said: 'Hah!' and snorted with deep feeling.

'Why?' Wilde asked quietly.

'Because my client is entitled to that protection, short of anything but a Grand Jury. I have a licence to operate as a private detective. I suppose that word "private" has some meaning. The Hollywood Division has two murders on its hands, both solved. They have both killers. They have the motive, the instrument in each case. The blackmail angle has got to be suppressed, as far as the names of the parties are concerned.'

'Why?' Wilde asked again.

'That's okay,' Cronjager said dryly. 'We're glad to stooge for a shamus of his standing.'

I said: 'I'll show you.' I got up and went back out of the house to my car and got the book from Geiger's store out of it. The uniformed police driver was standing beside Ohls's car. The boy was inside it, leaning back sideways in the corner.

'Has he said anything?' I asked.

'He made a suggestion,' the copper said and spat. 'I'm letting it ride.'

I went back into the house, put the book on Wilde's desk and opened up the wrappings. Cronjager was using a telephone on the end of the desk. He hung up and sat down as I came in.

Wilde looked through the book, wooden-faced, closed it and pushed it towards Cronjager. Cronjager opened it, looked at a page or two, shut it quickly. A couple of red spots the size of half-dollars showed on his cheek-bones.

I said: 'Look at the stamped dates at the front end-paper.'

Cronjager opened the book again and looked at them. 'Well?'

'If necessary,' I said, 'I'll testify under oath that that book came from Geiger's store. The blonde, Agnes, will admit what kind of business the store did. It's obvious to anybody with eyes that that store is just a front for something. But the Hollywood police allowed it to operate, for their own reasons. I dare say the Grand Jury would like to know what those reasons are.'

Wilde grinned. He said: 'Grand Juries do ask those embarrassing questions sometimes – in a rather vain effort to find out just why cities are run as they are run.'

Cronjager stood up suddenly and put his hat on. 'I'm one against three here,' he snapped. 'I'm a homicide man. If this Geiger was running indecent literature, that's no skin off my nose. But I'm ready to admit it won't help my division any to have it washed over in the papers. What do you birds want?'

Wilde looked at Ohls. Ohls said calmly: 'I want to turn a prisoner over to you. Let's go.'

He stood up. Cronjager looked at him fiercely and stalked out of the room. Ohls went after him. The door closed again. Wilde tapped on his desk and stared at me with his clear blue eyes.

'You ought to understand how any copper would feel about a cover-up like this,' he said. 'You'll have to make statements of all of it – at least for the files. I think it may be possible to keep the two killings separate and to keep General Sternwood's name out of both of them. Do you know why I'm not tearing your ear off?'

'No. I expected to get both ears torn off.'

'What are you getting for it all?'

'Twenty-five dollars a day and expenses.'

'That would make fifty dollars and a little gasolene so far.'

'About that.'

He put his head on one side and rubbed the back of his left little finger along the lower edge of his chin.

'And for that amount of money you're willing to get yourself in Dutch with half the law enforcement of this country?'

'I don't like it,' I said. 'But what the hell am I to do? I'm on a case. I'm selling what I have to sell to make a living. What little guts and intelligence the Lord gave me and a willingness to get pushed around in order to protect a client. It's against my principles to tell as much as I've told tonight, without consulting with the General. As for the cover-up, I've been in police business myself, as you know. They come a dime a dozen in any big city. Cops get very large and emphatic when an outsider tries to hide anything, but they do the same things themselves every other day, to oblige their friends or anybody with a little pull. And I'm not through. I'm still on the case. I'd do the same thing again, if I had to.'

'Providing Cronjager doesn't get your licence,' Wilde grinned. 'You said you held back a couple of personal matters. Of what import?'

'I'm still on the case,' I said, and stared straight back into his eyes.

Wilde smiled at me. He had the frank daring smile of an Irishman. 'Let me tell you something, son. My father was a close friend of old Sternwood. I've done all my office permits – and maybe a good deal more – to save the old man from grief. But in the long run it can't be done. Those girls of his are bound certain to hook up with something that can't be hushed, especially that little blonde brat. They ought not to be running around loose. I blame the old man for that. I guess he doesn't realize what the world is today. And there's another thing I might mention while we're talking man to man and I don't have to growl at you. I'll bet a dollar to a Canadian dime that the General's afraid his son-in-law, the ex-bootlegger, is mixed up in this somewhere, and what he really hoped you would find out is that he isn't. What do you think of that?'

'Regan didn't sound like a blackmailer, what I heard of him. He had a soft spot where he was and he walked out on it.'

Wilde snorted. 'The softness of that spot neither you nor I could judge. If he was a certain sort of man, it would not have been so very soft. Did the General tell you he was looking for Regan?'

'He told me he wished he knew where he was and that he

was all right. He liked Regan and was hurt the way he bounced off without telling the old man good-bye.'

Wilde leaned back and frowned. 'I see,' he said in a changed voice. His hand moved the stuff on his desk around, laid Geiger's blue note-book to one side and pushed the other exhibits towards me. 'You may as well take these,' he said. 'I've no further use for them.'

19

It was close to eleven when I put my car away and walked around to the front of the Hobart Arms. The plate-glass door was put on the lock at ten, so I had to get my keys out. Inside, in the square barren lobby, a man put a green evening paper down beside a potted palm and flicked a cigarette butt into the tub the palm grew in. He stood up and waved his hat at me and said: 'The boss wants to talk to you. You sure keep your friends waiting, pal.'

I stood still and looked at his flattened nose and club steak ear.

'What about?'

'What do you care? Just keep your nose clean and everything will be jake.' His hands hovered near the upper buttonhole of his open coat.

'I smell of policemen,' I said. 'I'm too tired to talk, too tired to eat, too tired to think. But if you think I'm not too tired to take orders from Eddie Mars – try getting your gat before I shoot your good ear off.'

'Nuts. You ain't got no gun.' He stared at me levelly. His dark wiry brows closed in together and his mouth made a downward curve.

'That was then,' I told him. 'I'm not always naked.'

He waved his left hand. 'Okay. You win. I wasn't told to blast anybody. You'll hear from him.'

'Too late will be too soon,' I said, and turned slowly as he passed me on his way to the door. He opened it and went out without looking back. I grinned at my own foolishness, went along to the elevator and upstairs to the apartment. I took Carmen's little gun out of my pocket and laughed at it. Then I cleaned it thoroughly, oiled it, wrapped it in a piece of canton flannel and locked it up. I made myself a drink and was drinking it when the phone rang. I sat down beside the table on which it stood.

'So you're tough tonight,' Eddie Mars's voice said.

'Big, fast, tough and full of prickles. What can I do for you?'

'Cops over there – you know where. You keep me out of it?'

'Why should I?'

'I'm nice to be nice to, soldier. I'm not nice not to be nice to.'

'Listen hard and you'll hear my teeth chattering.'

He laughed dryly. 'Did you – or did you?'

'I did. I'm damned if I know why. I guess it was just complicated enough without you.'

'Thanks, soldier. Who gunned him?'

'Read it in the paper tomorrow – maybe.'

'I want to know now.'

'Do you get everything you want?'

'No. Is that an answer, soldier?'

'Somebody you never heard of gunned him. Let it go at that.'

'If that's on the level, some day I may be able to do you a favour.'

'Hang up and let me go to bed.'

He laughed again. 'You're looking for Rusty Regan, aren't you?'

'A lot of people seem to think I am, but I'm not.'

'If you were, I could give you an idea. Drop in and see me down at the beach. Any time. Glad to see you.'

'Maybe.'

'Be seeing you then.' The phone clicked and I sat holding it with a savage patience. Then I dialled the Sternwoods' number and heard it ring four or five times and then the butler's suave voice saying: 'General Sternwood's residence.'

'This is Marlowe. Remember me? I met you about a hundred years ago – or was it yesterday?'

'Yes, Mr Marlowe. I remember, of course.'

'Is Mrs Regan home?'

'Yes, I believe so. Would you—'

I cut in on him with a sudden change of mind. 'No. You give her the message. Tell her I have the pictures, all of them, and that everything is all right.'

'Yes . . . yes . . .' The voice seemed to shake a little. 'You have the pictures – all of them – and everything is all right . . . Yes, sir. I may say – thank you very much, sir.'

The phone rang back in five minutes. I had finished my drink and it made me feel as if I could eat the dinner I had forgotten all about; I went out leaving the telephone ringing. It was ringing when I came back. It rang at intervals until half-past twelve. At that time I put my lights out and opened the windows up and muffled the phone bell with a piece of paper and went to bed. I had a bellyful of the Sternwood family.

I read all three of the morning papers over my eggs and bacon the next morning. Their accounts of the affair came as close to the truth as newspaper stories usually come – as close as Mars is to Saturn. None of the three connected Owen Taylor, driver of the Lido Pier Suicide Car, with the Laurel Canyon Exotic Bungalow Slaying. None of them mentioned the Sternwoods, Bernie Ohls or me. Owen Taylor was 'chauffeur to a wealthy family'. Captain Cronjager of the Hollywood Division got all the credit for solving the two slayings in his district, which were supposed to arise out of a dispute over the proceeds from a wire service maintained by one Geiger in the back of the bookstore on Hollywood Boulevard. Brody had shot Geiger and Carol Lundgren had shot Brody in revenge. Police were holding Carol Lundgren in custody. He had confessed. He had a bad record – probably in high school. Police were also holding one Agnes Lozelle, Geiger's secretary, as a material witness.

It was a nice write-up. It gave the impression that Geiger had been killed the night before, that Brody had been killed about an hour later, and that Captain Cronjager had solved both murders while lighting a cigarette. The suicide of Taylor made Page One of Section II. There was a photo of the sedan on the deck of the power lighter, with the licence plate blacked out, and something covered with a cloth lying on the deck beside the running board. Owen Taylor had been despondent and in poor health. His family lived in Dubuque, and his body would be shipped there. There would be no inquest.

20

Captain Gregory of the Missing Persons Bureau laid my card down on his wide flat desk and arranged it so that its edges exactly paralleled the edges of the desk. He studied it with his head on one side, grunted, swung around in his swivel chair and looked out of his window at the barred top floor of the Hall of Justice half a block away. He was a burly man with tired eyes and the slow deliberate movements of a night watchman. His voice was toneless, flat and uninterested.

'Private dick, eh?' he said, not looking at me at all, but looking out of his window. Smoke wisped from the blackened bowl of a briar that hung on his eye tooth. 'What can I do for you?'

'I'm working for General Guy Sternwood, 3765 Alta Brea Crescent, West Hollywood.'

Captain Gregory blew a little smoke from the corner of his mouth without removing the pipe. 'On what?'

'Not exactly on what you're working on, but I'm interested. I thought you could help me.'

'Help you on what?'

'General Sternwood's a rich man,' I said. 'He's an old friend of the DA's father. If he wants to hire a full-time boy to run errands for him, that's no reflection on the police. It's just a luxury he is able to afford himself.'

'What makes you think I'm doing anything for him?'

I didn't answer that. He swung round slowly and heavily in his swivel chair and put his large feet flat on the bare linoleum that covered his floor. His office had the musty smell of years of routine. He stared at me bleakly.

'I don't want to waste your time, Captain,' I said and pushed my chair back – about four inches.

He didn't move. He kept on staring at me out of his washed-out tired eyes. 'You know the DA?'

'I've met him. I worked for him once. I know Bertie Ohls, his chief investigator, pretty well.'

Captain Gregory reached for a phone and mumbled into it: 'Get me Ohls at the DA's office.'

He sat holding the phone down on its cradle. Moments passed. Smoke drifted from his pipe. His eyes were heavy and motionless like his hand. The bell tinkled and he reached for my card with his left hand. 'Ohls? . . . Al Gregory at head-quarters. A guy named Philip Marlowe is in my office. His card says he's a private investigator. He wants information from me . . . Yeah? What does he look like? . . . Okay, thanks.'

He dropped the phone and took his pipe out of his mouth and tamped the tobacco with the brass cap of a heavy pencil. He did it carefully and solemnly, as if that was as important as anything he would have to do that day. He leaned back and stared at me some more.

'What do you want?'

'An idea of what progress you're making, if any.'

He thought that over, 'Regan?' he asked finally.

'Sure.'

'Know him?'

'I never saw him. I hear he's a good-looking Irishman in his late thirties, that he was once in the liquor racket, that he married General Sternwood's older daughter and that they didn't click. I'm told he disappeared about a month back.'

'Sternwood oughta think himself lucky instead of hiring private talent to beat around in the tall grass.'

'The General took a big fancy to him. Such things happen. The old man is crippled and lonely. Regan used to sit around with him and keep him company.'

'What you think you can do that we can't do?'

'Nothing at all, in so far as finding Regan goes. But there's a rather mysterious blackmail angle. I want to make sure Regan isn't involved. Knowing where he is or isn't might help.'

'Brother, I'd like to help you, but I don't know where he is. He pulled down the curtain and that's that.'

'Pretty hard to do against your organization, isn't it, Captain?'

'Yeah – but it can be done – for a while.' He touched a bell button on the side of his desk. A middle-aged woman put her head in at a side door. 'Get me the file on Terence Regan, Abba.'

The door closed. Captain Gregory and I looked at each other in some more heavy silence. The door opened again and the woman put a tabbed green file on his desk. Captain Gregory nodded her out, put a pair of heavy horn-rimmed glasses on his veined nose and turned the papers in the file over slowly. I rolled a cigarette around in my fingers.

'He blew the 16th of September,' he said. 'The only thing important about that is it was the chauffeur's day off and nobody saw Regan take his car out. It was late afternoon, though. We found the car four days later in a garage belonging to a ritzy bungalow court place near the Sunset Towers. A garage man reported it to the stolen car detail, said it didn't belong there. The place is called the Casa de Oro. There's an angle to that I'll tell you about in a minute. We couldn't find out anything about who put the car in there. We print the car but don't find any prints that are on the file anywhere. The car in the garage don't jibe with foul play, although there's a reason to suspect foul play. It jibes with something else I'll tell you about in a minute.'

I said: 'That jibes with Eddie Mars's wife being on the missing list.'

He looked annoyed. 'Yeah. We investigate the tenants and find she's living there. Left about the time Regan did, within two days anyway. A guy who sounds a bit like Regan had been seen with her, but we don't get a positive identification. It's goddamned funny in this police racket how an old woman can look out of a window and see a guy running and pick him out of a line-up six months later, but we can show hotel help a clear photo and they just can't be sure.'

'That's one of the qualifications for good hotel help,' I said.

'Yeah. Eddie Mars and his wife didn't live together, but they were friendly, Eddie says. Here's some of the possibilities. First off Regan carried fifteen grand, packed it in his clothes all the time. Real money, they tell me. Not just a top card and a bunch of hay. That's a lot of jack but this Regan might be the boy to have it around so he could take it out and look at it when somebody was looking at him. Then again maybe he wouldn't give a damn. His wife says he never made a nickel off old man Sternwood except room and board and a Packard 120 his wife gave him. Tie that for an ex-legger in the rich gravy.'

'It beats me,' I said.

'Well, here we are with a guy who ducks out and has fifteen grand in his pants and folks know it. Well, that's money. I might duck out myself, if I had fifteen grand, and me with two kids in high school. So the first thought is somebody rolls him for it and rolls him too hard, so they have to take him out in the desert and plant him among the cactuses. But I don't like that too well. Regan carried a gat and had plenty of experience using it, and not just in a greasy-faced liquor mob. I understand he commanded a whole brigade in the Irish troubles back in 1922 or whenever it was. A guy like that wouldn't be white meat to a heister. Then, his car being in that garage makes whoever rolled him know he was sweet on Eddie Mars's wife, which he was, I guess, but it ain't something every poolroom bum would know.'

'Got a photo?' I asked.

'Him, not her. That's funny too. There's a lot of funny angles to this case. Here.' He pushed a shiny print across the desk and I looked at an Irish face that was more sad than merry and more reserved than brash. Not the face of a tough guy and not the face of a man who could be pushed around much by anybody. Straight dark brows with strong bone under them. A forehead wide rather than high, a mat of dark clustering hair, a thin short nose, a wide mouth. A chin that had strong lines but was small for the mouth. A face that looked a little taut, the face of a man who would move fast and play for keeps. I passed the print back. I would know that face, if I saw it.

Captain Gregory knocked his pipe out and refilled it and tamped the tobacco down with his thumb. He lit it, blew smoke and began to talk again.

'Well, there could be people who would know he was sweet on Eddie Mars's frau. Besides Eddie himself. For a wonder *he* knew it. But he don't seem to give a damn. We check him pretty thoroughly around that time. Of course Eddie wouldn't have knocked him off out of jealousy. The set-up would point to him too obvious.'

'It depends how smart he is,' I said. 'He might try the double bluff.'

Captain Gregory shook his head. 'If he's smart enough to get by in his racket, he's too smart for that. I get your idea. He pulls the dumb play because he thinks we wouldn't expect him to pull the dumb play. From a police angle that's wrong. Because he'd have us in his hair so much it would interfere with his business. *You* might think a dumb play would be smart. I might think so. The rank and file wouldn't. They'd make his life miserable. I've ruled it out. If I'm wrong, you can prove it on me and I'll eat my chair cushion. Till then I'm leaving Eddie in the clear. Jealousy is a bad motive for his type. Top-flight racketeers have business brains. They learn to do things that are good policy and let their personal feelings take care of themselves. I'm leaving that out.'

'What are you leaving in?'

'The dame and Regan himself. Nobody else. She was a blonde then, but she won't be now. We don't find her car, so they probably left in it. They had a long start on us – fourteen days.

Except for that car of Regan's I don't figure we'd have got the case at all. Of course I'm used to them that way, especially in good-class families. And of course everything I've done has had to be under the hat.'

He leaned back and thumped the arms of his chair with the heels of his large heavy hands.

'I don't see nothing to do but wait,' he said. 'We've got readers out, but it's too soon to look for results. Regan had fifteen grand we know of. The girl had some, maybe a lot in rocks. But they'll run out of dough some day. Regan will cash a cheque, drop a marker, write a letter. They're in a strange town and they've got new names, but they've got the same old appetites. They got to get back in the fiscal system.'

'What did the girl do before she married Eddie Mars?'

'Torcher.'

'Can't you get any old professional photos?'

'No. Eddie must have had some, but he won't loosen up. He wants her let alone. I can't make him. He's got friends in town, or he wouldn't be what he is.' He grunted. 'Any of this doing you any good?'

I said: 'You'll never find either of them. The Pacific Ocean is too close.'

'What I said about my chair cushion still goes. We'll find him. It may take time. It could take a year or two.'

'General Sternwood may not live that long,' I said.

'We've done all we could, brother. If he wants to put out a reward and spend some money, we might get results. The city don't give me the kind of money it takes.' His large eyes peered at me and his scratchy eyebrows moved. 'You serious about thinking Eddie put them both down?'

I laughed. 'No. I was just kidding. I think what you think, Captain. That Regan ran away with a woman who meant more to him than a rich wife he didn't get along with. Besides, she isn't rich yet.'

'You met her, I suppose?'

'Yes. She'd make a jazzy week-end, but she'd be wearing for a steady diet.'

He grunted and I thanked him for his time and information and left. A grey Plymouth sedan tailed me away from the City Hall. I gave it a chance to catch up with me on a quiet street. It refused the offer, so I shook it off and went about my business.

21

I didn't go near to the Sternwood family. I went back to the office and sat in my swivel chair and tried to catch up on my foot-dangling. There was a gusty wind blowing in at the windows and the soot from the oil burners of the hotel next door was down-draughted into the room and rolling across the top of the desk like tumbleweed drifting across a vacant lot. I was thinking about going out to lunch and that life was pretty flat and that it would probably be just as flat if I took a drink and that taking a drink all alone at that time of day wouldn't be any fun anyway. I was thinking this when Norris called up. In his carefully polite manner he said that General Sternwood was not feeling very well and that certain items in the newspaper had been read to him and he assumed that my investigation was now completed.

'Yes, as regards Geiger,' I said. 'I didn't shoot him, you know.'

'The General didn't suppose you did, Mr Marlowe.'

'Does the General know anything about those photographs Mrs Regan was worrying about?'

'No, sir. Decidedly not.'

'Did you know what the General gave me?'

'Yes, sir. Three notes and a card, I believe.'

'Right. I'll return them. As to the photos I think I'd better just destroy them.'

'Very good, sir. Mrs Regan tried to reach you a number of times last night—'

'I was out getting drunk,' I said.

'Yes. Very necessary, sir, I'm sure. The General has instructed me to send you a cheque for five hundred dollars. Will that be satisfactory?'

'More than generous,' I said.

'And I presume we may now consider the incident closed?'

'Oh, sure. Tight as a vault with a busted time lock.'

'Thank you, sir. I am sure we all appreciate it. When the General is feeling a little better – possibly tomorrow – he would like to thank you in person.'

'Fine,' I said. 'I'll come out and drink some more of his brandy, maybe with champagne.'

'I shall see that some is properly iced,' the old boy said, almost with a smirk in his voice.

That was that. We said good-bye and hung up. The coffee shop smell from next door came in at the windows with the soot but failed to make me hungry. So I got out my office bottle and took the drink and let my self-respect ride its own race.

I counted it up on my fingers. Rusty Regan had run away from a lot of money and a handsome wife to go wandering with a vague blonde who was more or less married to a racketeer named Eddie Mars. He had gone suddenly without good-byes and there might be any number of reasons for that. The General had been too proud, or, at the first interview he gave me, too careful, to tell me the Missing Persons Bureau had the matter in hand. The Missing Persons people were dead on their feet on it and evidently didn't think it worth bothering over. Regan had done what he had done and that was his business. I agreed with Captain Gregory that Eddie Mars would have been very unlikely to involve himself in a double murder just because another man had gone to town with the blonde he was not even living with. It might have annoyed him, but business is business, and you have to hold your teeth clamped around Hollywood to keep from chewing on stray blondes. If there had been a lot of money involved, that would be different. But fifteen grand wouldn't be a lot of money to Eddie Mars. He was no two-bit chiseller like Brody.

Geiger was dead and Carmen would have to find some other shady character to drink exotic blends of hooch with. I didn't suppose she would have any trouble. All she would have to do would be to stand on the corner for five minutes and look coy. I hoped that the next grifter who dropped the hook on her would play her a little more smoothly, a little more for the long haul rather than the quick touch.

Mrs Regan knew Eddie Mars well enough to borrow money from him. That was natural, if she played roulette and was a good loser. Any gambling house owner would lend a good client money in a pinch. Apart from this they had an added bond of interest in Regan. He was her husband and he had gone off with Eddie Mars's wife.

Carol Lundgren, the boy killer with the limited vocabulary, was out of circulation for a long, long time, even if they didn't strap him in a chair over a bucket of acid. They wouldn't, because he would take a plea and save the county money. They all do when they don't have the price of a big lawyer. Agnes Lozelle was in custody as a material witness. They wouldn't need her for that, if Carol took a plea, and if he pleaded guilty on arraignment, they would turn her loose. They wouldn't want to open up any angles on Geiger's business, apart from which they had nothing on her.

That left me. I had concealed a murder and suppressed evidence for twenty-four hours, but I was still at large and had a five-hundred-dollar cheque coming. The smart thing for me to do was to take another drink and forget the whole mess.

That being the obviously smart thing to do, I called Eddie Mars and told him I was coming down to Las Olindas that evening to talk to him. That was how smart I was.

I got down there about nine, under a hard high October moon that lost itself in the top layers of a beach fog. The Cypress Club was at the far end of the town, a rambling frame mansion that had once been the summer residence of a rich man named De Cazens, and later had been a hotel. It was now a big dark outwardly shabby place in a thick grove of wind-twisted Monterey cypresses, which gave it its name. It had enormous scrolled porches, turrets all over the place, stained-glass trims around the big windows, big empty stables at the back, a general air of nostalgic decay. Eddie Mars had left the outside much as he had found it, instead of making it over to look like an MGM set. I left my car on a street with sputtering arc lights and walked into the grounds along a damp gravel path to the main entrance. A doorman in a double-breasted guards coat let me into a huge dim silent lobby from which a white oak staircase curved majestically up to the darkness of an upper floor. I checked my hat and coat and waited, listening to music and confused voices behind heavy double doors. They seemed a long way off, and not quite of the same world as the building itself. Then the slim pasty-faced blond man who had been with Eddie Mars and the peg at Geiger's place came through a door under the staircase, smiled at me bleakly and took me back with him along a carpeted hall to the boss's office.

This was a square room with a deep old bay window and a stone fireplace in which a fire of juniper logs burned lazily. It was wainscoted in walnut and had a frieze of faded damask above the panelling. The ceiling was high and remote. There was a smell of cold sea.

Eddie Mars's dark sheenless desk didn't belong in the room, but neither did anything made after 1900. His carpet had a Florida suntan. There was a bartop radio in the corner and a Sèvres china tea set on a copper tray beside a samovar. I wondered who that was for. There was a door in the corner that had a time lock on it.

Eddie Mars grinned at me sociably and shook hands and moved his chin at the vault. 'I'm a pushover for a heist mob here except for that thing,' he said cheerfully. 'The local johns drop in every morning and watch me open it. I have an arrangement with them.'

'You hinted you had something for me,' I said. 'What is it?'

'What's your hurry? Have a drink and sit down.'

'No hurry at all. You and I haven't anything to talk about but business.'

'You'll have the drink and like it,' he said. He mixed a couple and put mine down beside a red leather chair and stood cross-legged against the desk himself, one hand in the side pocket of his midnight-blue dinner jacket, the thumb outside and the nail glistening. In dinner clothes he looked a little harder than in grey flannel, but he still looked like a horseman. We drank and nodded at each other.

'Ever been here before?' he asked

'During prohibition. I don't get any kick out of gambling.'

'Not with money,' he smiled. 'You ought to look in tonight. One of your friends is outside betting the wheels. I hear she's doing pretty well. Vivian Regan.'

I sipped my drink and took one of his monogrammed cigarettes.

'I kind of liked the way you handled that yesterday,' he said. 'You made me sore at the time but I could see afterwards how right you were. You and I ought to get along. How much do I owe you?'

'For doing what?'

'Still careful, eh? I have my pipe line into headquarters, or I wouldn't be here. I get them the way they happen, not the way you read them in the papers.' He showed me his large white teeth.

'How much have you got?' I asked.

'You're not talking money?'

'Information was the way I understood it.'

'Information about what?'

'You have a short memory. Regan.'

'Oh, that.' He waved his glistening nails in the quiet light from one of those bronze lamps that shoot a beam at the ceiling. 'I hear you got the information already. I felt I owed you a fee. I'm used to paying for nice treatment.'

'I didn't drive down here to make a touch. I get paid for what I do. Not much by your standards, but I make out. One customer at a time is a good rule. You didn't bump Regan off, did you?'

'No. Did you think I did?'

'I wouldn't put it past you.'

He laughed. 'You're kidding.'

I laughed. 'Sure, I'm kidding. I never saw Regan, but I saw his photo. You haven't got men for the work. And while we're on that subject don't send me any more gun punks with orders. I might get hysterical and blow one down.'

He looked through his glass at the fire, set it down on the end of the desk and wiped his lips with a sheer lawn handkerchief.

'You talk a good game,' he said. 'But I dare say you can break a hundred and ten. You're not really interested in Regan, are you?'

'No, not professionally. I haven't been asked to be. But I know somebody who would like to know where he is.'

'She doesn't give a damn,' he said.

'I mean her father.'

He wiped his lips again and looked at the handkerchief almost as if he expected to find blood on it. He drew his thick grey eyebrows close together and fingered the side of his weatherbeaten nose.

'Geiger was trying to blackmail the General,' I said. 'The General wouldn't say so, but I figure he was at least half scared Regan might be behind it.'

Eddie Mars laughed. 'Uh-huh. Geiger worked that one on everybody. It was strictly his own idea. He'd get notes from people that looked legal – were legal, I dare say, except that he wouldn't have dared sue on them. He'd present notes, with a nice flourish, leaving himself empty-handed. If he drew an ace, he had a prospect that scared and he went to work. If he didn't draw an ace, he just dropped the whole thing.'

'Clever guy,' I said. 'He dropped it all right. Dropped it and fell on it. How come *you* know all this?'

He shrugged impatiently. 'I wish to Christ I didn't know half the stuff that's brought to me. Knowing other people's business is the worst investment a man can make in my circle. Then if it was just Geiger you were after, you're washed up on that angle.'

'Washed up and paid off.'

'I'm sorry about that. I wish old Sternwood would hire himself a soldier like you on a straight salary, to keep those girls of his home at least a few nights a week.'

'Why?'

His mouth looked sulky. 'They're plain trouble. Take the dark one. She's a pain in the neck around here. If she loses, she plunges and I end up with a fistful of paper which nobody will discount at any price. She has no money of her own except an allowance and what's in the old man's will is a secret. If she wins, she takes my money home with her.'

'You get it back the next night,' I said.

'I get some of it back. But over a period of time I'm loser.'

He looked earnestly at me, as if that was important to me. I wondered why he thought it necessary to tell me at all. I yawned and finished my drink.

'I'm going out and look the joint over,' I said.

'Yes, do.' He pointed to a door near the vault door. 'That leads to a door behind the tables.'

'I'd rather go in the way the suckers enter.'

'Okay. As you please. We're friends, aren't we, soldier?'

'Sure.' I stood up and we shook hands.

'Maybe I can do you a real favour some day,' he said. 'You got it all from Gregory this time.'

'So you own a piece of him too.'

'Oh not that bad. We're just friends.'

I stared at him for a moment, then went over to the door I had come in at. I looked back at him when I had it open.

'You don't have anybody tailing me around in a grey Plymouth sedan, do you?'

His eyes widened sharply. He looked jarred. 'Hell, no. Why should I?'

'I couldn't imagine,' I said, and went on out. I thought his surprise looked genuine enough to be believed. I thought he even looked a little worried. I couldn't think of any reason for that.

22

It was about ten-thirty when the little yellow-sashed Mexican orchestra got tired of playing a low-voiced prettied-up rumba that nobody was dancing to. The gourd player rubbed his finger tips together as if they were sore and got a cigarette into his mouth almost with the same movement. The other four, with a timed simultaneous stoop, reached under their chairs for glasses from which they sipped, smacking their lips and flashing their eyes. Tequila, their manner said. It was probably mineral water. The pretence was as wasted as the music. Nobody was looking at them.

The room had been a ballroom once and Eddie Mars had changed it only as much as his business compelled him. No chromium glitter, no indirect lighting from behind angular cornices, no fused glass pictures, or chairs in violent leather and polished metal tubing, none of the pseudo-modernistic circus of the typical Hollywood night trap. The light was from heavy crystal chandeliers and the rose-damask panels of the wall were still the same rose damask, a little faded by time and darkened by dust, that had been matched long ago against the parquetry floor, of which only a small glass-smooth space in front of the little Mexican orchestra showed bare. The rest was covered by a heavy old-rose carpeting that must have cost plenty. The parquetry was made of a dozen kinds of hardwood, from Burma teak through half a dozen shades of oak and ruddy wood that looked like mahogany, and fading out to the hard pale wild lilac of the California hills, all laid in elaborate patterns, with the accuracy of a transit.

It was still a beautiful room and now there was roulette in it instead of measured, old-fashioned dancing. There were three tables close to the far wall. A low bronze railing joined them and made a fence around the croupiers. All three tables were working, but the crowd was at the middle one. I could see

Vivian Regan's black head close to it, from across the room where I was leaning against the bar and turning a small glass of bacardi around on the mahogany.

The bartender leaned beside me watching the cluster of well-dressed people at the middle table. 'She's pickin' 'em tonight, right on the nose,' he said. 'That tall blackheaded frail.'

'Who is she?'

'I wouldn't know her name. She comes here a lot though.'

'The hell you wouldn't know her name.'

'I just work here, mister,' he said without any animosity. 'She's all alone too. The guy was with her passed out. They took him out to his car.'

'I'll take her home,' I said.

'The hell you will. Well, I wish you luck anyways. Should I gentle up that bacardi or do you like it the way it is?'

'I like it the way it is as well as I like it at all,' I said.

'Me, I'd just as leave drink croup medicine,' he said.

The crowd parted and two men in evening clothes pushed their way out and I saw the back of her neck and her bare shoulders in the opening. She wore a low-cut dress of dull green velvet. It looked too dressy for the occasion. The crowd closed and hid all but her black head. The two men came across the room and leaned against the bar and asked for Scotch and soda. One of them was flushed and excited. He was mopping his face with a black-bordered handkerchief. The double satin stripes down the side of his trousers were wide enough for tyre tracks.

'Boy, I never saw such a run,' he said in a jittery voice. 'Eight wins and two stand-offs in a row on that red. That's roulette, boy, that's roulette.'

'It gives me the itch,' the other one said. 'She's betting a grand at a crack. She can't lose.' They put their beaks in their drinks, gurgled swiftly and went back.

'So wise the little men are,' the barkeeper said. 'A grand a crack, huh. I saw an old horseface in Havana once—'

The noise swelled over at the middle table and a chiselled foreign voice rose above it saying: 'If you will just be patient

117

a moment, madam. The table cannot cover your bet. Mr Mars will be here in a moment.'

I left my bacardi and padded across the carpet. The little orchestra started to play a tango, rather loud. No one was dancing or intending to dance. I moved through a scattering of people in dinner clothes and full evening dress and sports clothes and business suits to the end table at the left. It had gone dead. Two croupiers stood behind it with their heads together and their eyes sideways. One moved a rake back and forth aimlessly over the empty layout. They were both staring at Vivian Regan.

Her long lashes twitched and her face looked unnaturally white. She was at the middle table, exactly opposite the wheel. There was a disordered pile of money and chips in front of her. It looked like a lot of money. She spoke to the croupier with a cool, insolent, ill-tempered drawl.

'What kind of a cheap outfit is this, I'd like to know. Get busy and spin that wheel, highpockets. I want one more play and I'm playing table stakes. You take it away fast enough, I've noticed, but when it comes to dishing it out you start to whine.'

The croupier smiled a cold polite smile that had looked at thousands of boors and millions of fools. His tall dark disinterested manner was flawless. He said gravely: 'The table cannot cover your bet, madam. You have over sixteen thousand dollars there.'

'It's your money,' the girl jeered. 'Don't you want it back?'

A man beside her tried to tell her something. She turned swiftly and spat something at him and he faded back into the crowd red-faced. A door opened in the panelling at the far end of the enclosed place made by the bronze railing. Eddie Mars came through the door with a set indifferent smile on his face, his hands thrust into the pockets of his dinner jacket, both thumb-nails glistening outside. He seemed to like that pose. He strolled behind the croupiers and stopped at the corner of the middle table. He spoke with lazy calm, less politely than the croupier.

'Something the matter, Mrs Regan?'

She turned her face to him with a sort of lunge. I saw the curve of her cheek stiffen, as if with an almost unbearable inner tautness. She didn't answer him.

Eddie Mars said gravely: 'If you're not playing any more, you must let me send someone home with you.'

The girl flushed. Her cheekbones stood out white in her face. Then she laughed off-key. She said bitterly:

'One more play, Eddie. Everything I have on the red. I like red. It's the colour of blood.'

Eddie Mars smiled faintly, then nodded and reached into his inner breast pocket. He drew out a large pinseal wallet with gold corners and tossed it carelessly along the table to the croupier. 'Cover the bet in even thousands,' he said, 'if no one objects to this turn of the wheel being just for the lady.'

No one objected. Vivian Regan leaned down and pushed all her winnings savagely with both hands on to the large red diamond on the layout.

The croupier leaned over the table without haste. He counted and stacked her money and chips, placed all but a few chips and bills in a neat pile and pushed the rest back off the layout with his rake. He opened Eddie Mars's wallet and drew out two flat packets of thousand-dollar bills. He broke one, counted six bills out, added them to the unbroken packet, put the four loose bills in the wallet and laid it aside as carelessly as if it had been a packet of matches. Eddie Mars didn't touch the wallet. Nobody moved except the croupier. He spun the wheel left-handed and sent the ivory ball skittering along the upper edge with a casual flirt of his wrist. Then he drew his hands back and folded his arms.

Vivian's lips parted slowly until her teeth caught the light and glittered like knives. The ball drifted lazily down the slope of the wheel and bounced on the chromium ridges above the numbers. After a long time and then very suddenly motion left it with a dry click. The wheel slowed, carrying the ball around with it. The croupier didn't unfold his arms until the wheel had entirely ceased to revolve.

'The red wins,' he said formally, without interest. The little ivory ball lay in Red 25, the third number from the Double Zero. Vivian Regan put her head back and laughed triumphantly.

The croupier lifted his rake and slowly pushed the stack of thousand-dollar bills across the layout, added them to the stake, pushed everything slowly out of the field of play.

Eddie Mars smiled, put his wallet back in his pocket, turned on his heel and left the room through the door in the panelling.

A dozen people let their breath out at the same time and broke for the bar. I broke with them and got to the far end of the room before Vivian had gathered up her winnings and turned away from the table. I went out into the large quiet lobby, got my hat and coat from the check girl, dropped a quarter in her tray and went out on the porch. The doorman loomed up beside me and said: 'Can I get your car for you, sir?'

I said: 'I'm just going for a walk.'

The scrollwork along the edge of the porch roof was wet with the fog. The fog dripped from the Monterey cypresses that shadowed off into nothing towards the cliff above the ocean. You could see a scant dozen feet in any direction. I went down the porch steps and drifted off through the trees, following an indistinct path until I could hear the wash of the surf licking at the fog, low down at the bottom of the cliff. There wasn't a gleam of light anywhere. I could see a dozen trees clearly at one time, another dozen dimly, then nothing at all but the fog. I circled to the left and drifted back towards the gravel path that went around to the stables where they parked the cars. When I could make out the outlines of the house I stopped. A little in front of me I had heard a man cough.

My steps hadn't made any sound on the soft moist turf. The man coughed again, then stifled the cough with a handkerchief or a sleeve. While he was still doing that I moved forward closer to him. I made him out, a vague shadow close to the path. Something made me step behind a tree and crouch down. The man turned his head. His face should have been a white blur when he did that. It wasn't. It remained dark. There was a mask over it.

I waited, behind the tree.

23

Light steps, the steps of a woman, came along the invisible pathway and the man in front of me moved forward and seemed to lean against the fog. I couldn't see the woman, then I could see her indistinctly. The arrogant carriage of her head seemed familiar. The man stepped out very quickly. The two figures blended in the fog, seemed to be part of the fog. There was dead silence for a moment. The man said:

'This is a gun, lady. Gentle now. Sound carries in the fog. Just hand me the bag.'

The girl didn't make a sound. I moved forward a step. Quite suddenly I could see the foggy fuzz on the man's hat brim. The girl stood motionless. Then her breathing began to make a rasping sound, like a small file on soft wood.

'Yell,' the man said, 'and I'll cut you in half.'

She didn't yell. She didn't move. There was a movement from him, and a dry chuckle. 'It better be in here,' he said. A catch clicked and a fumbling sound came to me. The man turned towards my tree. When he had taken three or four steps he chuckled again. The chuckle was something out of my own memories. I reached a pipe out of my pocket and held it like a gun.

I called out softly: 'Hi, Lanny.'

The man stopped dead and started to bring his hand up. I said: 'No. I told you never to do that, Lanny. You're covered.'

Nothing moved. The girl back on the path didn't move. I didn't move. Lanny didn't move.

'Put the bag down between your feet, kid,' I told him. 'Slow and easy.'

He bent down. I jumped out and reached him still bent over. He straightened up against me breathing hard. His hands were empty.

'Tell me I can't get away with it,' I said. I leaned against him and took the gun out of his overcoat pocket. 'Somebody's always giving me guns,' I told him. 'I'm weighted down with them till I walk all crooked. Beat it.'

Our breaths met and mingled, our eyes were like the eyes of two tomcats on a wall. I stepped back.

'On your way, Lanny. No hard feelings. You keep it quiet and I keep it quiet. Okay?'

'Okay,' he said thickly.

The fog swallowed him. The faint sound of his steps and then nothing. I picked the bag up and felt in it and went towards the path. She still stood there motionless, a grey fur coat held tight around her throat with an ungloved hand on which a ring made a faint glitter. She wore no hat. Her dark parted hair was part of the darkness of the night. Her eyes too.

'Nice work, Marlowe. Are you my bodyguard now?' Her voice had a harsh note.

'Looks that way. Here's the bag.'

She took it. I said: 'Have you a car with you?'

She laughed. 'I came with a man. What are you doing here?'

'Eddie Mars wanted to see me.'

'I didn't know you knew him. Why?'

'I don't mind telling you. He thought I was looking for somebody he thought had run away with his wife.'

'Were you?'

'No.'

'Then what did you come for?'

'To find out why he thought I was looking for somebody he thought had run away with his wife.'

'Did you find out?'

'No.'

'You leak information like a radio announcer,' she said. 'I suppose it's none of my business – even if the man was my husband. I thought you weren't interested in that.'

'People keep throwing it at me.'

She clicked her teeth in annoyance. The incident of the masked man with the gun seemed to have made no impression on her at all. 'Well, take me to the garage,' she said. 'I have to look in at my escort.'

We walked along the path and around a corner of the building and there was light ahead, then around another corner and came to a bright enclosed stable yard lit with two floodlights. It was still paved with brick and still sloped down to a grating in the middle. Cars glistened and a man in a brown smock got up off a stool and came forward.

'Is my boy friend still blotto?' Vivian asked him carelessly.

'I'm afraid he is, miss. I put a rug over him and run the windows up. He's okay, I guess. Just kind of resting.'

We went over to a big Cadillac and the man in the smock pulled the rear door open. On the wide back seat, loosely arranged, covered to the chin with a plaid robe, a man lay snoring with his mouth open. He seemed to be a big blond man who would hold a lot of liquor.

'Meet Mr Larry Cobb,' Vivian said. 'Mister Cobb – Mister Marlowe.'

I grunted.

'Mr Cobb was my escort,' she said. 'Such a nice escort, Mr Cobb. So attentive. You should see him sober. *I* should see him sober. Somebody should see him sober. I mean, just for the record. So it could become a part of history, that brief flashing moment, soon buried in time, but never forgotten – when Larry Cobb was sober.'

'Yeah,' I said.

'I've even thought of marrying him,' she went on in a high strained voice, as if the shock of the stick-up was just beginning to get to her. 'At odd times when nothing pleasant would come into my mind. We all have those spells. Lots of money, you know. A yacht, a place on Long Island, a place at Newport, a place at Bermuda, places dotted here and there all over the world probably – just a good Scotch bottle apart. And to Mr Cobb a bottle of Scotch is not very far.'

'Yeah,' I said. 'Does he have a driver to take him home?'

'Don't say "yeah". It's common.' She looked at me with arched eyebrows. The man in the smock was chewing his lower lip hard. 'Oh, undoubtedly a whole platoon of drivers. They probably do squads right in front of the garage every morning, buttons shining, harness gleaming, white gloves immaculate – a sort of West Point elegance about them.'

'Well, where the hell is this driver?' I asked.

'He drove hisself tonight,' the man in the smock said, almost apologetically. 'I could call his home and have somebody come down for him.'

Vivian turned around and smiled at him as if he had just presented her with a diamond tiara. 'That would be lovely,' she said. 'Would you do that? I really wouldn't want Mr Cobb to die like that – with his mouth open. Someone might think he had died of thirst.'

The man in the smock said: 'Not if they sniffed him, miss.'

She opened her bag and grabbed a handful of paper money and pushed it at him. 'You'll take care of him, I'm sure.'

'Jeeze,' the man said, pop-eyed. 'I sure will, miss.'

'Regan is the name,' she said sweetly. 'Mrs Regan. You'll probably see me again. Haven't been here long, have you?'

'No'm.' His hands were doing frantic things with the fistful of money he was holding.

'You'll get to love it here,' she said. She took hold of my arm. 'Let's ride in your car, Marlowe.'

'It's outside on the street.'

'Quite all right with me, Marlowe. I love a nice walk in the fog. You meet such interesting people.'

'Oh nuts,' I said.

She held on to my arm and began to shake. She held me hard all the way to the car. She had stopped shaking by the time we reached it. I drove down a curving lane of trees on the blind side of the house. The lane opened on De Cazens Boulevard, the main drag of Las Olindas. We passed under the ancient sputtering arc lights and after a while there was a town, buildings, dead-looking stores, a service station with a light over a night bell, and at last a drugstore that was still open.

'You better have a drink,' I said.

She moved her chin, a point of paleness in the corner of the seat. I turned diagonally into the kerb and parked. 'A little black coffee and a smattering of rye would go well,' I said.

'I could get as drunk as two sailors and love it.'

I held the door for her and she got out close to me, brushing my cheek with her hair. We went into the drugstore. I bought a pint of rye at the liquor counter and carried it over to the stools and set it down on the cracked marble counter.

'Two coffees,' I said. 'Black, strong and made this year.'

'You can't drink liquor in here,' the clerk said. He had a washed-out blue smock, was thin on top as to hair, had fairly honest eyes and his chin would never hit a wall before he saw it.

Vivian Regan reached into her bag for a packet of cigarettes and shook a couple loose just like a man. She held them towards me.

'It's against the law to drink liquor in here,' the clerk said.

I lit the cigarettes and didn't pay any attention to him. He drew two cups of coffee from a tarnished nickel urn and set them in front of us. He looked at the bottle of rye, muttered under his breath and said wearily: 'Okay I'll watch the street while you pour it.'

He went and stood at the display window with his back to us and his ears hanging out.

'My heart's in my mouth doing this,' I said, and unscrewed the top of the whisky bottle and loaded the coffee. 'The law enforcement in this town is terrific. All through prohibition Eddie Mars's place was a night club and they had two uniformed men in the lobby every night – to see that the guests didn't bring their own liquor instead of buying it from the house.'

The clerk turned suddenly and walked back behind the counter and went in behind the little glass window of the prescription room.

We sipped our loaded coffee. I looked at Vivian's face in the mirror back of the coffee urn. It was taut, pale, beautiful and wild. Her lips were red and harsh.

'You have wicked eyes,' I said. 'What's Eddie Mars got on you?'

She looked at me in the mirror. 'I took plenty away from him tonight at roulette – starting with five grand I borrowed from him yesterday and didn't have to use.'

125

'That might make him sore. You think he sent that loogan after you?'

'What's a loogan?'

'A guy with a gun.'

'Are you a loogan?'

'Sure,' I laughed. 'But strictly speaking a loogan is on the wrong side of the fence.'

'I often wonder if there is a wrong side.'

'We're losing the subject. What has Eddie Mars got on you?'

'You mean a hold on me of some sort?'

'Yes.'

Her lip curled. 'Wittier, please, Marlowe. Much wittier.'

'How's the General? I don't pretend to be witty.'

'None too well. He didn't get up today. You could at least stop questioning me.'

'I remember a time when I thought the same about you. How much does the General know?'

'He probably knows everything.'

'Norris would tell him?'

'No. Wilde, the District Attorney, was out to see him. Did you burn those pictures?'

'Sure. You worry about your little sister, don't you – from time to time.'

'I think she's all I do worry about. I worry about Dad in a way, to keep things from him.'

'He hasn't many illusions,' I said, 'but I suppose he still has pride.'

'We're his blood. That's the hell of it.' She stared at me in the mirror with deep, distant eyes. 'I don't want him to die despising his own blood. It was always wild blood, but it wasn't always rotten blood.'

'Is it now?'

'I guess you think so.'

'Not yours. You're just playing the part.'

She looked down. I sipped some more coffee and lit another cigarette for us. 'So you shoot people,' she said quietly. 'You're a killer.'

'Me? How?'

'The papers and the police fixed it up nicely. But I don't believe everything I read.'

'Oh, you think I accounted for Geiger – or Brody – or both of them.'

She didn't say anything. 'I didn't have to,' I said. 'I might have, I suppose, and got away with it. Neither of them would have hesitated to throw lead at me.'

'That makes you just a killer at heart, like all cops.'

'Oh, nuts.'

'One of those dark deadly quiet men who have no more feelings than a butcher has for slaughtered meat. I knew it the first time I saw you.'

'You've got enough shady friends to know different.'

'They're all soft compared to you.'

'Thanks lady. You're no English muffin yourself.'

'Let's get out of this rotten little town.'

I paid the check, put the bottle of rye in my pocket, and we left. The clerk still didn't like me.

We drove away from Las Olindas through a series of little dank beach towns with shack-like houses built down on the sand close to the rumble of the surf and larger houses built back on the slopes behind. A yellow window shone here and there, but most of the houses were dark. A smell of kelp came in off the water and lay on the fog. The tyres sang on the moist concrete of the boulevard. The world was a wet emptiness.

We were close to Del Rey before she spoke to me for the first time since we left the drugstore. Her voice had a muffled sound, as if something was throbbing deep under it.

'Drive down by the Del Rey beach club. I want to look at the water. It's the next street on the left.'

There was a winking yellow light at the intersection. I turned the car and slid down a slope with a high bluff on one side, interurban tracks to the right, a low straggle of lights far off beyond the tracks, and then very far off a glitter of pier lights and a haze in the sky over a city. That way the fog was almost gone. The road crossed the tracks where they turned to run under the bluff, then reached a paved strip of waterfront high-way that bordered an open and uncluttered beach. Cars were parked along the pavement, facing out to sea, dark. The lights of the beach club were a few hundred yards away.

I braked against the kerb and switched the headlights off and sat with my hands on the wheel. Under the thinning fog the surf curled and creamed, almost without sound, like a thought trying to form itself on the edge of consciousness.

'Move closer,' she said almost thickly.

I moved out from under the wheel into the middle of the seat. She turned her body a little away from me as if to peer out of the window. Then she let herself fall backwards, without a sound, into my arms. Her head almost struck the wheel. Her eyes were closed, her face was dim. Then I saw that her eyes opened and flickered, the shine of them visible even in the darkness.

'Hold me close, you beast,' she said.

I put my arms around her loosely at first. Her hair had a harsh feeling against my face. I tightened my arms and lifted her up. I brought her face slowly up to my face. Her eyelids were flickering rapidly, like moth wings.

I kissed her tightly and quickly. Then a long slow clinging kiss. Her lips opened under mine. Her body began to shake in my arms.

'Killer,' she said softly, her breath going into my mouth.

I strained her against me until the shivering of her body was almost shaking mine. I kept on kissing her. After a long time she pulled her head away enough to say: 'Where do you live?'

'Hobart Arms. Franklin near Kenmore.'

'I've never seen it.'

'Want to?'

'Yes.'

'What has Eddie Mars got on you?'

Her body stiffened in my arms and her breath made a harsh sound. Her head pulled back until her eyes, wide open, ringed with white, were staring at me.

'So that's the way it is,' she said in a soft dull voice.

'That's the way it is. Kissing is nice, but your father didn't hire me to sleep with you.'

'You son of a bitch,' she said calmly, without moving.

I laughed in her face. 'Don't think I'm an icicle,' I said. 'I'm not blind or without senses. I have warm blood like the next guy. You're easy to take – too damned easy. What has Eddie Mars got on you?'

'If you say that again, I'll scream.'

'Go ahead and scream.'

She jerked away and pulled herself upright, far back in the corner of the car.

'Men have been shot for little things like that, Marlowe.'

'Men have been shot for practically nothing. The first time we met I told you I was a detective. Get it through your lovely head. I work at it, lady. I don't play at it.'

She fumbled in her bag and got a handkerchief out and bit on it, her head turned away from me. The tearing sound of the handkerchief came to me. She tore it, with her teeth, slowly, time after time.

'What makes you think he has anything on me?' she whispered, her voice muffled by the handkerchief.

'He lets you win a lot of money and sends a gunpoke around to take it back for him. You're not more than mildly surprised. You didn't even thank me for saving it for you. I think the whole thing was just some kind of an act. If I wanted to flatter myself, I'd say it was at least partly for my benefit.'

'You think he can win or lose as he pleases.'

'Sure. On even money bets, four times out of five.'

'Do I have to tell you I loathe your guts, Mister Detective?'

'You don't owe me anything. I'm paid off.'

She tossed the shredded hankerchief out of the car window. 'You have a lovely way with women.'

'I liked kissing you.'

'You kept your head beautifully. That's so flattering. Should I congratulate you, or my father?'

'I liked kissing you.'

Her voice became an icy drawl. 'Take me away from here,

if you will be so kind. I'm quite sure I'd like to go home.'

'You won't be a sister to me?'

'If I had a razor, I'd cut your throat – just to see what ran out of it.'

'Caterpillar blood,' I said.

I started the car and turned it and drove back across the interurban tracks to the highway and so on into town and up to West Hollywood. She didn't speak to me. She hardly moved all the way back. I drove through the gates and up the sunken drive-way to the porte-cochère of the big house. She jerked the car door open and was out of it before it had quite stopped. She didn't speak even then. I watched her back as she stood against the door after ringing the bell. The door opened and Norris looked out. She pushed past him quickly and was gone. The door banged shut and I was sitting there looking at it.

I turned back down the driveway and home.

24

The apartment house lobby was empty this time. No gunman waiting under the potted palm to give me orders. I took the automatic elevator up to my floor and walked along the hall-way to the tune of a muted radio behind a door. I needed a drink and was in a hurry to get one. I didn't switch the light on inside the door. I made straight for the kitchenette and brought up short in three or four feet. Something was wrong. Something on the air, a scent. The shades were down at the windows and the street light leaking in at the sides made a dim light in the room. I stood still and listened. The scent on the air was a perfume, a heavy, cloying perfume.

There was no sound, no sound at all. Then my eyes adjusted themselves more to the darkness and I saw there something across the floor in front of me that shouldn't have been there. I backed, reached the wall switch with my thumb and flicked the light on.

The bed was down. Something in it giggled. A blonde head was pressed into my pillow. Two bare arms curved up and the hands belonging to them were clasped on top of the blonde head. Carmen Sternwood lay on her back, in my bed, giggling at me. The tawny wave of her hair was spread out on the pillow as if by a careful and artificial hand. Her slaty eyes peered at me and had the effect, as usual, of peering from behind a barrel. She smiled. Her small sharp teeth glinted.

'Cute, aren't I?' she said.

I said harshly: 'Cute as a Filipino on Saturday night.'

I went over to a floor lamp and pulled the switch, went back to put off the ceiling light, and went across the room again to the chessboard on a card table under the lamp. There was a problem laid out on the board, a six-mover. I couldn't solve it, like a lot of my problems. I reached down and moved a knight, then pulled my hat and coat off and threw them somewhere. All this time the soft giggling went on from the bed, that sound made me think of rats behind a wainscoting in an old house.

'I bet you can't even guess how I got in.'

I dug a cigarette out and looked at her with bleak eyes. 'I bet I can. You came through the keyhole, just like Peter Pan.'

'Who's he?'

'Oh, a fellow I used to know around the poolroom.'

She giggled. 'You're cute, aren't you?' she said.

I began to say: 'About that thumb—' but she was ahead of me. I didn't have to remind her. She took her right hand from behind her head and started sucking the thumb and eyeing me with very round and naughty eyes.

'I'm all undressed,' she said, after I had smoked and stared at her for a minute.

'By God,' I said, 'it was right at the back of my mind. I was groping for it. I almost had it, when you spoke. In another minute I'd have said "I bet you're all undressed". I always

131

wear my rubbers in bed myself, in case I wake up with a bad conscience and have to sneak away from it.'

'You're cute.' She rolled her head a little, kittenishly. Then she took her left hand from under her head and took hold of the covers, paused dramatically, and swept them aside. She was undressed all right. She lay there on the bed in the lamplight, as naked and glistening as a pearl. The Sternwood girls were giving me both barrels that night.

I pulled a shred of tobacco off the edge of my lower lip.

'That's nice,' I said. 'But I've already seen it all. Remember? I'm the guy that keeps finding you without any clothes on.'

She giggled some more and covered herself up again. 'Well, how *did* you get in?' I asked her.

'The manager let me in. I showed him your card. I'd stolen it from Vivian. I told him you told me to come here and wait for you. I was – I was mysterious.' She glowed with delight.

'Neat,' I said. 'Managers are like that. Now I know how you got in tell me how you're going to go out.'

She giggled. 'Not going – not for a long time . . . I like it here. You're cute.'

'Listen,' I pointed my cigarette at her. 'Don't make me dress you again. I'm tired. I appreciate all you're offering me. It's just more than I could possibly take. Doghouse Reilly never let a pal down that way. I'm your friend. I won't let you down – in spite of yourself. You and I have to keep on being friends, and this isn't the way to do it. Now will you dress like a nice little girl?'

She shook her head from side to side.

'Listen,' I ploughed on, 'you don't really care anything about me. You're just showing how naughty you can be. But you don't have to show me. I knew it already. I'm the guy that found—'

'Put the light out,' she giggled.

I threw my cigarette on the floor and stamped on it. I took a handkerchief out and wiped the palms of my hands. I tried it once more.

'It isn't on account of the neighbours,' I told her. 'They don't really care a lot. There's a lot of stray broads in any apartment house and one more won't make the building rock. It's a question of professional pride. You know – professional pride. I'm working for your father. He's a sick man, very frail, very helpless. He sort of trusts me not to pull any stunts. Won't you please get dressed, Carmen?'

'Your name isn't Doghouse Reilly,' she said. 'It's Philip Marlowe. You can't fool me.'

I looked down at the chessboard. The move with the knight was wrong. I put it back where I had moved it from. Knights had no meaning in this game. It wasn't a game for knights.

I looked at her again. She lay still now, her face pale against the pillow, her eyes large and dark and empty as rain barrels in a drought. One of her small five-fingered thumbless hands picked at the cover restlessly. There was a vague glimmer of doubt starting to get born in her somewhere. She didn't know about it yet. It's so hard for women – even nice women – to realize that their bodies are not irresistible.

I said: 'I'm going out in the kitchen and mix a drink. Want one?'

'Uh-huh.' Dark silent mystified eyes stared at me solemnly, the doubt growing larger in them, creeping into them noiselessly, like a cat in long grass stalking a young blackbird.

'If you're dressed when I get back, you'll get the drink. Okay?'

Her teeth parted and a faint hissing noise came out of her mouth. She didn't answer me. I went to the kitchenette and got out some Scotch and fizzwater and mixed a couple of highballs. I didn't have anything really exciting to drink, like nitroglycerine or distilled tiger's breath. She hadn't moved when I got back with the glasses. The hissing had stopped. Her eyes were dead again. Her lips started to smile at me. Then she sat up suddenly and threw all the covers off her body and reached.

'Gimme.'

'When you're dressed. Not *until* you're dressed.'

I put the two glasses down on the card table and sat down myself and lit another cigarette. 'Go ahead. I won't watch you.'

I looked away. Then I was aware of the hissing noise very

sudden and sharp. It startled me into looking at her again. She sat there naked, propped on her hands, her mouth open a little, her face like scraped bone. The hissing noise came tearing out of her mouth as if she had nothing to do with it. There was something behind her eyes, blank as they were, that I had never seen in a woman's eyes.

Then her lips moved very slowly and carefully, as if they were artificial lips and had to be manipulated with springs.

She called me a filthy name.

I didn't mind that. I didn't mind what she called me, what anybody called me. But this was the room I had to live in. It was all I had in the way of a home. In it was everything that was mine, that had any association for me, any past, anything that took the place of a family. Not much; a few books, pictures, radio, chessmen, old letters, stuff like that. Nothing. Such as they were they had all my memories.

I couldn't stand her in that room any longer. What she called me only reminded me of that.

I said carefully: 'I'll give you three minutes to get dressed and out of here. If you're not out by then, I'll throw you out – by force. Just the way you are, naked. And I'll throw your clothes after you into the hall. Now – get started.'

Her teeth chattered and the hissing noise was sharp and animal. She swung her feet to the floor and reached for her clothes on a chair beside the bed. She dressed. I watched her. She dressed with stiff awkward fingers – for a woman – but quickly at that. She was dressed in a little over two minutes. I timed it.

She stood there beside the bed, holding a green bag tight against a fur-trimmed coat. She wore a rakish green hat crooked on her head. She stood there for a moment and hissed at me, her face still like scraped bone, her eyes still empty and yet full of some jungle emotion. Then she walked quickly to the door and opened it and went out, without speaking, without looking back. I heard the elevator lurch into motion and move in the shaft.

I walked to the windows and pulled the shades up and opened

134

the windows wide. The night air came drifting in with a kind of stale sweetness that still remembered automobile exhausts and the streets of the city. I reached for my drink and drank it slowly. The apartment house door closed itself down below me. Steps tinkled on the quiet pavement. A car started up not far away. It rushed off into the night with a rough clashing of gears. I went back to the bed and looked down at it. The imprint of her head was still in the pillow, of her small corrupt body still on the sheets.

I put my empty glass down and tore the bed to pieces savagely.

25

It was raining again the next morning, a slanting grey rain like a swung curtain of crystal beads. I got up feeling sluggish and tired and stood looking out of the windows, with a dark harsh taste of Sternwoods still in my mouth. I was as empty of life as a scarecrow's pockets. I went out to the kitchenette and drank two cups of black coffee. You can have a hangover from other things than alcohol. I had one from women. Women made me sick.

I shaved and showered and dressed and got my raincoat out and went downstairs and looked out of the front door. Across the street, a hundred feet up, a grey Plymouth sedan was parked. It was the same one that had tried to trail me around the day before, the same one that I had asked Eddie Mars about. There might be a cop in it, if a cop had that much time on his hands and wanted to waste it following me around. Or it might be a smoothie in the detective business trying to get a noseful of somebody'e else's case in order to chisel a way into it. Or it might be the Bishop of Bermuda disapproving of my night life.

I went out back and got my convertible from the garage and

drove it around front past the grey Plymouth. There was a small man in it, alone. He started up after me. He worked better in the rain. He stayed close enough so that I couldn't make a short block and leave that before he entered it, and he stayed back far enough so that other cars were between us most of the time. I drove down to the boulevard and parked in the lot next to my building and came out of there with my raincoat collar up and my hat brim low and the raindrops tapping icily at my face in between. The Plymouth was across the way at a fireplug. I walked down to the intersection and crossed with the green light and walked back, close to the edge of the pavement and the parked cars. The Plymouth hadn't moved. Nobody got out of it. I reached it and jerked open the door on the kerb side.

A small bright-eyed man was pressed back into the corner behind the wheel. I stood and looked in at him, the rain thumping my back. His eyes blinked behind the swirling smoke of a cigarette. His hands tapped restlessly on the thin wheel.

I said: 'Can't you make your mind up?'

He swallowed and the cigarette bobbed between his lips. 'I don't think I know you,' he said, in a tight little voice.

'Marlowe's the name. The guy you've been trying to follow around for a couple of days.'

'I ain't following anybody, doc.'

'This jalopy is. Maybe you can't control it. Have it your own way. I'm now going to eat breakfast in the coffee shop across the street, orange juice, bacon and eggs, toast, honey, three or four cups of coffee and a toothpick. I am then going up to my office, which is on the seventh floor of the building right opposite you. If you have anything that's worrying you beyond endurance, drop up and chew it over. I'll only be oiling my machine-gun.'

I left him blinking and walked away. Twenty minutes later I was airing the scrubwoman's Soirée d'Amour out of my office and opening up a thick rough envelope addressed in a fine old-fashioned pointed handwriting. The envelope contained a brief formal note and a large mauve cheque for five hundred dollars, payable to Philip Marlowe and signed, Guy de Brisay Stern-wood, by Vincent Norris. That made it a nice morning. I was making out a bank slip when the buzzer told me somebody had entered my two by four reception room. It was the little man from the Plymouth.

'Fine,' I said. 'Come in and shed your coat.'

He slid past me carefully as I held the door, as carefully as though he feared I might plant a kick in his minute buttocks. We sat down and faced each other across the desk. He was a very small man, not more than five feet three and would hardly weigh as much as a butcher's thumb. He had tight brilliant eyes that wanted to look hard, and looked as hard as oysters on the half-shell. He wore a double-breasted dark grey suit that was too wide in the shoulders and had too much lapel. Over this, open, an Irish tweed coat with some badly worn spots. A lot of foulard tie bulged out and was rain-spotted above his crossed lapels.

'Maybe you know me,' he said. 'I'm Harry Jones.'

I said I didn't know him. I pushed a flat tin of cigarettes at him. His small neat fingers speared one like a trout taking the fly. He lit it with the desk lighter and waved his hand.

'I been around,' he said. 'Know the boys and such. Used to do a little liquor-running down for Hueneme Point. A tough racket, brother. Riding the scout car with a gun in your lap and a wad on your hip that would choke a coal chute. Plenty of times we paid off four sets of law before we hit Beverly Hills. A tough racket.'

'Terrible,' I said.

He leaned back and blew smoke at the ceiling from the small tight corner of his small tight mouth.

'Maybe you don't believe me,' he said.

'Maybe I don't,' I said. 'And maybe I do. And then again maybe I haven't bothered to make my mind up. Just what is the build-up supposed to do to me?'

'Nothing,' he said tartly.

'You've been following me around for a couple of days,' I said. 'Like a fellow trying to pick up a girl and lacking the last inch of nerve. Maybe you're selling insurance. Maybe you knew a fellow called Joe Brody. That's a lot of maybes, but I have a lot on hand in my business.'

His eyes bulged and his lower lip almost fell in his lap. 'Christ, how'd you know that?' he said.

'I'm psychic. Shake your business up and pour it. I haven't got all day.'

The brightness of his eyes almost disappeared between the suddenly narrowed lids. There was silence. The rain pounded down on the flat tarred roof over the Mansion House lobby below my windows. His eyes opened a little, shined again, and his voice was full of thought.

'I was trying to get a line on you, sure,' he said. 'I've got something to sell – cheap, for a couple of C notes. How'd you tie me to Joe?'

I opened a letter and read it. It offered me a six months' correspondence course in fingerprinting at a special professional discount. I dropped it into the waste basket and looked at the little man again. 'Don't mind me. I was just guessing. You're not a cop. You don't belong to Eddie Mars's outfit. I asked him last night. I couldn't think of anybody else but Joe Brody's friends who would be that much interested in me.'

'Jesus,' he said and licked his lower lip. His face turned white as paper when I mentioned Eddie Mars. His mouth drooped open and his cigarette hung to the corner of it by some magic, as if it had grown there. 'Aw, you're kidding me,' he said at last, with the sort of smile the operating-room sees.

'All right. I'm kidding you.' I opened another letter. This one wanted to send me a daily newsletter from Washington, all inside stuff, straight from the cook-house. 'I suppose Agnes is loose,' I added.

'Yeah. She sent me. You interested?'

'Well – she's a blonde.'

'Nuts. You made a crack when you were up there that night – the night Joe got squibbed off. Something about Brody must have known something good about the Sternwoods or he wouldn't have taken the chance on that picture he sent them.'

'Uh-huh. So he had? What was it?'

'That's what the two hundred bucks pays for.'

I dropped some more fan mail into the basket and lit myself a fresh cigarette.

'We gotta get out of town,' he said. 'Agnes is a nice girl. You can't hold that stuff on her. It's not so easy for a dame to get by these days.'

'She's too big for you,' I said. 'She'll roll on you and smother you.'

'That's kind of a dirty crack, brother,' he said with something that was near enough to dignity to make me stare at him.

I said: 'You're right. I've been meeting the wrong kind of people lately. Let's cut out the gabble and get down to cases. What have you got for the money?'

'Would you pay it?'

'If it does what?'

'If it helps you find Rusty Regan.'

'I'm not looking for Rusty Regan.'

'Says you. Want to hear it or not?'

'Go ahead and chirp. I'll pay for anything I use. Two C notes buys a lot of information in my circle.'

'Eddie Mars had Regan bumped off,' he said calmly, and leaned back as if he had just been made a vice-president.

I waved a hand in the direction of the door. 'I wouldn't even argue with you,' I said. 'I wouldn't waste the oxygen. On your way, small size.'

He leaned across the desk, white lines at the corners of his mouth. He snubbed his cigarette out carefully, over and over again, without looking at it. From behind a communicating door came the sound of a typewriter clacking monotonously to the bell, to the shift, line after line.

'I'm not kidding,' he said.

'Beat it. Don't bother me. I have work to do.'

'No you don't,' he said sharply. 'I ain't that easy. I came here to speak my piece and I'm speaking it. I knew Rusty myself. Not well, well enough to say "How's a boy?" and he answered me or he wouldn't, according to how he felt. A nice guy though.

I always like him. He was sweet on a singer named Mona Grant. Then she changed her name to Mars. Rusty got sore and married a rich dame that hung around the joints like she couldn't sleep well at home. You know all about her, tall, dark, enough looks for a Derby winner, but the type would put a lot of pressure on a guy. High-strung Rusty wouldn't get along with her. But Jesus, he'd get along with her old man's dough, wouldn't he? That's what you think. This Regan was a cockeyed sort of buzzard. He had long-range eyes. He was looking over into the next valley all the time. He wasn't scarcely around where he was. I don't think he gave a damn about dough. And coming from me, brother, that's a compliment.'

The little man wasn't so dumb after all. A three for a quarter grifter wouldn't even think such thoughts, much less know how to express them.

I said: 'So he ran away.'

'He started to run away, maybe. With this girl Mona. She wasn't living with Eddie Mars, didn't like his rackets. Especially the side lines, like blackmail, bent cars, hideouts for hot boys from the east, and so on. The talk was Regan told Eddie one night, right out in the open, that if he ever messed Mona up in any criminal rap, he'd be around to see him.'

'Most of this is on the record, Harry,' I said. 'You can't expect money for that.'

'I'm coming to what isn't. So Regan blew. I used to see him every afternoon in Vardi's drinking Irish whiskey and staring at the wall. He don't talk much any more. He'd give me a bet now and then, which was what I was there for, to pick up bets for Puss Walgreen.'

'I thought he was in the insurance business.'

'That's what it says on the door. I guess he'd sell you insurance at that, if you tramped on him. Well, about the middle of September I don't see Regan any more. I don't notice it right away. You know how it is. A guy's there and you see him and then he ain't there and you don't see him until something makes you think of it. What makes me think about it is I hear a guy say laughing that Eddie Mars's woman lammed out with Rusty

Regan and Mars is acting like he was best man, instead of being sore. So I tell Joe Brody and Joe was smart.'

'Like hell he was,' I said.

'Not copper smart, but still smart. He's out for the dough. He gets to figuring could he get a line somehow on the two lovebirds he could maybe collect twice – once from Eddie Mars and once from Regan's wife. Joe knew the family a little.'

'Five grand worth,' I said. 'He nicked them for that a while back.'

'Yeah?' Harry Jones looked mildly surprised. 'Agnes ought to have told me that. There's a frail for you. Always holding out. Well, Joe and me watch the papers and we don't see anything, so we know old Sternwood has a blanket on it. Then one day I see Lash Canino in Vardi's. Know him?'

I shook my head.

'There's a boy that is tough like some guys think they are tough. He does a job for Eddie Mars when Mars needs him – trouble shooting. He'd bump a guy off between drinks. When Mars don't need him he don't go near him. And he don't stay in LA. Well it might be something and it might not. Maybe they got a line on Regan and Mars has just been sitting back with a smile on his puss, waiting for the chance. Then again it might be something else entirely. Anyway I tell Joe and Joe gets on Canino's tail. He can tail. Me, I'm no good at it. I'm giving that one away. No charge. And Joe tails Canino out to the Sternwood place and Canino parks outside the estate and a car comes up beside him with a girl in it. They talk for a while and Joe thinks the girl passes something over, like maybe dough. The girl beats it. It's Regan's wife. Okay, she knows Canino and Canino knows Mars. So Joe figures Canino knows something about Regan and is trying to squeeze a little on the side for himself. Canino blows and Joe loses him. End of Act One.'

'What does this Canino look like?'

'Short, heavy set, brown hair, brown eyes, and always wears brown clothes and a brown hat. Even wears a brown suede raincoat. Drives a brown coupé. Everything brown for Mr Canino.'

'Let's have Act Two,' I said.

'Without some dough, that's all.'

'I don't see two hundred bucks in it. Mrs Regan married an ex-bootlegger out of the joints. She'd know other people of his sort. She knows Eddie Mars well. If she thought anything had happened to Regan, Eddie would be the very man she'd go to, and Canino might be the man Eddie would pick to handle the assignment. Is that all you have?'

'Would you give the two hundred to know where Eddie's wife is?' the little man asked calmly.

He had all my attention now. I almost cracked the arms of my chair leaning on them.

'Even if she was alone?' Harry Jones added in a soft, rather sinister tone. 'Even if she never run away with Regan at all, and was being kept now about forty miles from LA in a hideout – so the law would keep on thinking she had dusted with him? Would you pay two hundred bucks for that, shamus?'

I licked my lips. They tasted dry and salty. 'I think I would,' I said. 'Where?'

'Agnes found her,' he said grimly. 'Just by a lucky break. Saw her out riding and managed to tail her home. Agnes will tell you where that is – when she's holding the money in her hand.'

I made a hard face at him. 'You could tell the coppers for nothing, Harry. They have some good wreckers down at Central these days. If they killed you trying, they still have Agnes.'

'Let 'em try,' he said. 'I ain't so brittle.'

'Agnes must have something I didn't notice.'

'She's a grifter, shamus. I'm a grifter. We're all grifters. So we sell each other out for a nickel. Okay. See can you make me.' He reached for another of my cigarettes, placed it neatly between his lips and lit it with a match the way I do myself, missing twice on his thumb-nail and then using his foot. He puffed evenly and stared at me level-eyed, a funny little hard guy I could have thrown from home plate to second base. A small man in a big man's world. There was something I liked about him.

'I haven't pulled anything in here,' he said steadily. 'I come in talking two Cs. That's still the price. I come because I thought I'd get a take it or leave it, one right gee to another. Now you're waving cops at me. You oughta be ashamed of yourself.'

I said: 'You'll get the two hundred – for that information. I have to get the money myself first.'

He stood up and nodded and pulled his worn little Irish tweed coat tight around his chest. 'That's okay. After dark is better anyway. It's a leery job – buckin' guys like Eddie Mars. But a guy has to eat. The book's been pretty dull lately. I think the big boys have told Puss Walgreen to move on. Suppose you come over there to the office, Fulwider Building, Western and Santa Monica, four-twenty-eight at the back. You bring the money, I'll take you to Agnes.'

'Can't you tell me yourself? I've seen Agnes.'

'I promised her,' he said simply. He buttoned his overcoat, cocked his hat jauntily, nodded again and strolled to the door. He went out. His steps died along the hall.

I went down to the bank and deposited my five-hundred-dollar cheque and drew out two hundred in currency. I went upstairs again and sat in my chair thinking about Harry Jones and his story. It seemed a little too pat. It had the austere simplicity of fiction rather than the tangled woof of fact. Captain Gregory ought to have been able to find Mona Mars, if she was that close to his beat. Supposing, that is, he had tried.

I thought about it most of the day. Nobody came into the office. Nobody called me on the phone. It kept on raining.

26

At seven the rain had stopped for a breathing spell, but the gutters were still flooded. On Santa Monica the water was level with the pavement and a thin film of it washed over the top of the kerbing. A traffic cop in shining black rubber from boots to cap sloshed through the flood on his way from the shelter of a sodden awning. My rubber heels slithered on the pavement as I turned into the narrow lobby of the Fulwider Building. A single drop light burned far back, beyond an open, once gilt elevator. There was a tarnished and well-missed spittoon on a gnawed rubber mat. A case of false teeth hung on the mustard-coloured wall like a fuse box in a screen porch. I shook the rain off my hat and looked at the building directory beside the case of teeth. Numbers with names and numbers without names. Plenty of vacancies or plenty of tenants who wished to remain anonymous. Painless dentists, shyster detective agencies, small sick businesses that had crawled there to die, mail order schools that would teach you how to become a railway clerk or a radio technician or a screen writer – if the postal inspectors didn't catch up with them first. A nasty building. A building in which the smell of stale cigar butts would be the cleanest odour.

An old man dozed in the elevator, on a ramshackle stool, with a burst-out cushion under him. His mouth was open, his veined temples glistened in the weak light. He wore a blue uniform coat that fitted him the way a stall fits a horse. Under that grey trousers with frayed cuffs, white cotton socks and black kid shoes, one of which was slit across the bunion. On the stool he slept miserably, waiting for a customer. I went past him softly, the clandestine air of the building prompting me, found the fire door and pulled it open. The fire stairs hadn't been swept in a month. Bums had slept on them, eaten on them, left crusts and fragments of greasy newspaper, matches, a gutted imitation-leather pocket-book. In a shadowy angle against the scribbled wall a pouched ring of pale rubber had fallen and had not been disturbed. A very nice building.

I came out at the fourth floor sniffing for air. The hallway had the same dirty spittoon and frayed mat, the same mustard walls, the same memories of low tide. I went down the line and turned a corner. The name: 'L. D. Walgreen – Insurance', showed on a dark pebbled glass door, on a second dark door, on a third behind which there was a light. One of the dark doors said: 'Entrance'.

A glass transom was open above the lighted door. Through it the sharp birdlike voice of Harry Jones spoke, saying:

'Canino? . . . Yeah, I've seen you around somewhere. Sure.'

I froze. The other voice spoke. It had a heavy purr, like a small dynamo behind a brick wall. It said: 'I thought you would.' There was a vaguely sinister note in that voice.

A chair scraped on linoleum, steps sounded, the transom above me squeaked shut. A shadow melted from behind the pebbled glass.

I went back to the first of the three doors marked with the name Walgreen. I tried it cautiously. It was locked. It moved in a loose frame, an old door fitted many years past, made of half-seasoned wood and shrunken now. I reached my wallet out and slipped the thick hard window of celluloid from over my driver's licence. A burglar's tool the law had forgotten to proscribe. I put my gloves on, leaned softly and lovingly against the door and pushed the knob hard away from the frame. I pushed the celluloid plate into the wide crack and felt for the slope of the spring lock. There was a dry click, like a small icicle breaking. I hung there motionless, like a lazy fish in the water. Nothing happened inside. I turned the knob and pushed the door back into darkness. I shut it behind me as carefully as I had opened it.

The lighted oblong of an uncurtained window faced me, cut by the angle of a desk. On the desk a hooded typewriter took form, then the metal knob of a communicating door. This was unlocked. I passed into the second of the three offices. Rain rattled suddenly against the closed window. Under its noise

I crossed the room. A tight fan of light spread from an inch opening of the door into the lighted office. Everything very convenient. I walked like a cat on a mantel and reached the hinged side of the door, put an eye to the crack and saw nothing but light against the angle of the wood.

The purring voice was now saying quite pleasantly: 'Sure, a guy could sit on his fanny and crab what another guy done if he knows what it's all about. So you go to see this peeper. Well, that was your mistake. Eddie don't like it. The peeper told Eddie some guy in a grey Plymouth was tailing him. Eddie naturally wants to know who and why, see.'

Harry Jones laughed lightly. 'What makes it his business?'

'That don't get you no place.'

'You know why I went to the peeper. I already told you. Account of Joe Brody's girl. She has to blow and she's shatting on her uppers. She figures the peeper can get her some dough. I don't have any.'

The purring voice said gently: 'Dough for what? Peepers don't give that stuff out to punks.'

'He could raise it. He knows rich people.' Harry Jones laughed, a brave little laugh.

'Don't fuss with me, little man.' The purring voice had an edge, like sand in the bearings.

'Okay, okay. You know the dope on Brody's bump-off. That screwy kid done it all right, but the night it happened this Marlowe was right there in the room.'

'That's known, little man. He told it to the law.'

'Yeah – here's what isn't. Brody was trying to peddle a nudist photo of the young Sternwood girl. Marlowe got wise to him. While they were arguing about it the young Sternwood girl dropped around herself – with a gat. She took a shot at Brody. She lets one fly and breaks a window. Only the peeper didn't tell the coppers about that. And Agnes didn't neither. She figures it's railway fare for her not to.'

'This ain't got anything to do with Eddie?'

'Show me how.'

'Where's this Agnes at?'

'Nothing doing.'

'You'll tell me, little man. Here, or in the back room where the boys pitch dimes against the wall.'

'She's my girl now, Canino. I don't put my girl in the middle for anybody.'

A silence followed. I listened to the rain lashing the windows. The smell of cigarette smoke came through the crack of the door. I wanted to cough. I bit hard on a handkerchief.

The purring voice said, still gentle: 'From what I hear this blonde broad was just a shill for Geiger. I'll talk it over with Eddie. How much you tap the peeper for?'

'Two centuries.'

'Get it?'

Harry Jones laughed again. 'I'm seeing him tomorrow. I have hopes.'

'Where's Agnes?'

'Listen—'

'Where's Agnes?'

Silence.

'Look at it, little man.'

I didn't move. I wasn't wearing a gun. I didn't have to see through the crack of the door to know that a gun was what the purring voice was inviting Harry Jones to look at. But I didn't think Mr Canino would do anything with his gun beyond showing it. I waited.

'I'm looking at it,' Harry Jones said, his voice squeezed tight as if it could hardly get past his teeth. 'And I don't see anything I didn't see before. Go ahead and blast and see what it gets you.'

'A Chicago overcoat is what it would get *you*, little man.'

Silence.

'Where's Agnes?'

Harry Jones sighed. 'Okay,' he said wearily. 'She's in an apartment house at 28 Court Street, up on Bunker Hill. Apartment 301. I guess I'm yellow all right. Why should I front for that twist?'

'No reason. You got good sense. You and me'll go out and talk to her. All I want is to find out is she dummying up on you, kid. If it's the way you say it is, everything is jakeloo. You can put the bite on the peeper and be on your way. No hard feelings?'

'No,' Harry Jones said. 'No hard feelings, Canino.'

'Fine. Let's dip the bill. Got a glass?' The purring voice was now as false as an usherette's eyelashes and as slippery as a watermelon seed. A drawer was pulled open. Something jarred on wood. A chair squeaked. A scuffing sound on the floor. 'This is bond stuff,' the purring voice said.

There was a gurgling sound. 'Moths in your ermine, as the ladies say.'

Harry Jones said softly: 'Success.'

I heard a short sharp cough. Then a violent retching. There was a small thud on the floor, as if a thick glass had fallen. My fingers curled against my raincoat.

The purring voice said gently: 'You ain't sick from just one drink, are you pal?'

Harry Jones didn't answer. There was laboured breathing for a short moment. Then thick silence folded down. Then a chair scraped.

'So long, little man,' said Mr Canino.

Steps, a click, the wedge of light died at my feet, a door opened and closed quietly. The steps faded, leisurely and assured.

I stirred around the edge of the door and pulled it wide and looked into the blackness relieved by the dim shine of a window. The corner of a desk glittered faintly. A hunched shape took form in a chair behind it. In the close air there was a heavy clogged smell, almost a perfume. I went across to the corridor door and listened. I heard the distant clang of the elevator.

I found the light switch and light glowed in a dusty glass bowl hanging from the ceiling by three brass chains. Harry Jones looked at me across the desk, his eyes wide open, his face frozen in a tight spasm, the skin bluish. His small dark head was tilted to one side. He sat upright against the back of the chair.

A tramcar bell clanged at an almost infinite distance and the sound came buffeted by innumerable walls. A brown half-pint of whisky stood on the desk with the cap off. Harry Jones's glass glinted against a castor of the desk. The second glass was gone.

I breathed shallowly, from the top of my lungs, and bent above the bottle. Behind the charred smell of the bourbon another odour lurked, faintly, the odour of bitter almonds. Harry Jones dying had vomited on his coat. That made it cyanide.

I walked around him carefully, and lifted a phone book from a hook on the wooden frame of the window. I let it fall again, reached the telephone as far as it would go from the little dead man. I dialled information. The voice answered.

'Can you give me the phone number of Apartment 301, 28 Court Street?'

'One moment, please.' The voice came to me borne on the smell of bitter almonds. A silence. 'The number is Wentworth 2528. It is listed under Glendower Apartments.'

I thanked the voice and dialled the number. The bell rang three times, then the line opened. A radio blared along the wire and was muted. A burly male voice said: 'Hello.'

'Is Agnes there?'

'No Agnes here, buddy. What number you want?'

'Wentworth two-five-two-eight.'

'Right number, wrong gal. Ain't that a shame?' The voice cackled.

I hung up and reached for the phone book again and looked up the Wentworth Apartments. I dialled the manager's number. I had a blurred vision of Mr Canino driving fast through rain to another appointment with death.

'Glendower Apartments. Mr Schiff speaking.'

'This is Wallis, Police Identification Bureau. Is there a girl named Agnes Lozelle registered in your place?'

'Who did you say you were?'

I told him again.

'If you give me your number, I'll—'

'Cut the comedy,' I said sharply, 'I'm in a hurry. Is there or isn't there?'

149

'No. There isn't.' The voice was as stiff as a breadstick.

'Is there a tall blonde with green eyes registered in the flop?'

'Say, this isn't any flop—'

'Oh, can it, *can it*!' I rapped at him in a police voice. 'You want me to send the vice squad over there and shake the joint down? I know all about Bunker Hill apartment houses, mister. Especially the ones that have phone numbers listed for each apartment.'

'Hey, take it easy, officer. I'll co-operate. There's a couple of blondes here, sure. Where isn't there? I hadn't noticed their eyes much. Would yours be alone?'

'Alone with a little chap about five feet three, a hundred and ten, sharp black eyes, wears double-breasted dark grey suit and Irish tweed overcoat, grey hat. My information is Apartment 301, but all I get there is the big razzoo.'

'Oh, she ain't there. There's a couple of car salesmen living in three-o-one.'

'Thanks, I'll drop around.'

'Make it quiet, won't you? Come to my place, direct?'

'Much obliged, Mr Schiff.' I hung up.

I wiped sweat off my face. I walked to the far corner of the office and stood with my face to the wall, patted it with a hand. I turned around slowly and looked across at little Harry Jones grimacing in his chair.

'Well, you fooled him, Harry,' I said out loud, in a voice that sounded queer to me. 'You lied to him and you drank your cyanide, like a little gentleman. You died like a poisoned rat, Harry, but you're no rat to me.'

I had to search him. It was a nasty job. His pockets yielded nothing about Agnes, nothing that I wanted at all. I didn't think they would, but I had to be sure. Mr Canino might be back. Mr Canino would be the kind of self-confident gentleman who would not mind returning to the scene of his crime.

I put the light out and started to open the door. The phone bell rang jarringly down on the baseboard. I listened to it, my jaw muscles drawn into a knot, aching. Then I shut the door and put the light on again and went across to it.

'Yeah?'

A woman's voice. Her voice. 'Is Harry around?'

'Not for a minute, Agnes.'

She waited a while on that. Then she said slowly: 'Who's talking?'

'Marlowe, the guy that's trouble to you.'

'Where is he?' sharply.

'I came over to give him two hundred bucks in return for certain information. The offer holds. I have the money. Where are you?'

'Didn't he tell you?'

'No.'

'Perhaps you'd better ask him. Where is he?'

'I can't ask him. Do you know a man named Canino?'

Her gasp came as clearly as though she had been beside me.

'Do you want the two C's or not?' I asked.

'I – I want it pretty bad, mister.'

'All right then. Tell me where to bring it.'

'I – I—' Her voice trailed off and came back with a panic rush. 'Where's Harry?'

'Got scared and blew. Meet me somewhere – anywhere at all – I have the money.'

'I don't believe you – about Harry. It's a trap.'

'Oh, stuff. I could have had Harry hauled in long ago. There isn't anything to make a trap for. Canino got a line on Harry somehow and he blew. I want quiet, you want quiet, Harry wants quiet.' Harry already had it. Nobody could take it away from him. 'You don't think I'd stooge for Eddie Mars, do you angel?'

'No-o, I guess not. Not that. I'll meet you in half an hour. Beside Bullocks Wilshire, the east entrance to the parking lot.'

'Right,' I said.

I dropped the phone in its cradle. The wave of almond odour flooded me again, and the sour smell of vomit. The little dead man sat silent in his chair, beyond fear, beyond change.

I left the office. Nothing moved in the dingy corridor. No pebbled glass door had light behind it. I went down the fire stairs to the second floor and from there looked down at the lighted roof of the elevator cage. I pressed the button. Slowly the car lurched into motion. I ran down the stairs again. The car was above me when I walked out of the building.

It was raining hard again. I walked into it with the heavy drops slapping my face. When one of them touched my tongue I knew that my mouth was open and the ache at the side of my jaws told me it was open wide and strained back, mimicking the rictus of death carved upon the face of Harry Jones.

27

'Give me the money.'

The motor of the grey Plymouth throbbed under her voice and the rain pounded above it. The violet light at the top of Bullocks green-tinged tower was far above us, serene and withdrawn from the dark, dripping city. Her black-gloved hand reached out and I put the bills in it. She bent over to count them under the dim light of the dash. A bag clicked open, clicked shut. She let a spent breath die on her lips. She leaned towards me.

'I'm leaving, copper. I'm on my way. This is a get-away stake and God how I need it. What happened to Harry?'

'I told you he ran away. Canino got wise to him somehow. Forget Harry. I've paid and I want my information.'

'You'll get it. Joe and I were riding Foothill Boulevard Sunday before last. It was late and the lights coming up and the usual mess of cars. We passed a brown coupé and I saw the girl who was driving it. There was a man beside her, a dark short man. The girl was blonde. I'd seen her before. She was Eddie Mars's wife. The guy was Canino. You wouldn't forget either of them, if you ever saw them. Joe trailed the coupé from in front. He was good at that. Canino, the watch-dog, was taking her out for air. A mile or so east of Realito a road turns towards the foothills. That's orange country to the south but to the north it's as bare as hell's back yard and smack up against the hills there's a cyanide plant where they make the stuff for fumigation. Just off the highway there's a small garage and paint-shop run by a gee named Art Huck. Hot car drop, likely. There's a frame house beyond this, and beyond the house nothing but the foothills and the bare stone outcrop and the cyanide plant a couple of miles on. That's the place where she's holed up. They turned off on this road and Joe swung around and went back and we saw the car turn off the road where the frame house was. We sat there half an hour looking through the cars going by. Nobody came back out. When it was quite dark Joe sneaked up there and took a look. He said there were lights in the house and a radio was going and just the one car out in front of the coupé. So we beat it.

She stopped talking and I listened to the swish of tyres on Wilshire. I said: 'They might have shifted quarters since then but that's what you have to sell – that's what you have to sell. Sure you knew her?'

'If you ever see her, you won't make a mistake the second time. Good-bye, copper, and wish me luck. I got a raw deal.'

'Like hell you did,' I said, and walked away across the street to my own car.

The Grey Plymouth moved forward, gathered speed, and darted around the corner on to Sunset Place. The sound of its motor died, and with it blonde Agnes wiped herself off the slate for good, so far as I was concerned. Three men dead, Geiger, Brody and Harry Jones, and the woman went riding off in the rain with my two hundred in her bag and not a mark on her. I kicked my starter and drove on down-town to eat. I ate a good dinner. Forty miles in the rain is a hike, and I hoped to make it a round trip.

I drove north across the river, on into Pasadena, through Pasadena and almost at once I was in orange groves. The tumbling rain was solid white spray in the headlights. The windshield wiper could hardly keep the glass clear enough to see through. But not even the drenched darkness could hide the flawless lines of the orange trees wheeling away like endless spokes into the night.

Cars passed with a tearing hiss and a wave of dirty spray. The highway jerked through a little town that was all packing houses and sheds, and railway sidings nuzzling them. The groves thinned out and dropped away to the south and the road climbed and it was cold and to the north the black foothills crouched closer and sent a bitter wind whipping down their flanks. Then faintly out of the dark two yellow vapour lights showed high up in the air and a neon sign between them said 'Welcome to Realito'.

Frame houses were spaced far back from a wide main street, then a sudden knot of stores, the lights of a drugstore behind fogged glass, the fly-cluster of cars in front of the movie theatre, a dark bank on a corner with a clock sticking out over the pavement and a group of people standing in the rain looking at its windows, as if they were some kind of a show. I went on. Empty fields closed in again.

Fate stage-managed the whole thing. Beyond Realito, just about a mile beyond, the highway took a curve and the rain fooled me and I went too close to the shoulder. My right front tyre let go with an angry hiss. Before I could stop the right rear went with it. I jammed the car to a stop, half on the pavement, half on the shoulder, got out and flashed a spotlight around. I had two flats and one spare. The flat butt of a heavy galvanized tack stared at me from the front tyre. The edge of the pavement was littered with them. They had been swept off, but not far enough off.

I snapped the flash off and stood there breathing rain and looking up a side road at a yellow light. It seemed to come from a skylight. The skylight could belong to a garage, the garage could be run by a man named Art Huck, and there could be a frame house next door to it. I tucked my chin down in my collar and started towards it, then went back to unstrap the licence holder from the steering post and put it in my pocket. I leaned lower under the wheel. Behind a weighted flap, directly under my right leg as I sat in the car, there was a hidden compartment. There were two guns in it. One belonged to Eddie Mars's boy Lanny and one belonged to me. I took Lanny's. It would have had more practice than mine. I stuck it nose down in an inside pocket and started up the side road.

The garage was a hundred yards from the highway. It showed the highway a blank side wall. I played the flash on it quickly. 'Art Huck—Motor Repairs and Painting.' I chuckled, then Harry Jones's face rose up in front of me, and I stopped chuckling. The garage doors were shut, but there was an edge of light under them and a thread of light where the halves met. I went on past. The frame house was there, light in two front windows, shades down. It was set well back from the road, behind a thin clump of trees. A car stood on the gravel drive in front. It was dark, indistinct, but it would be a brown coupé and it would belong to Mr Canino. It squatted there peacefully in front of the narrow wooden porch.

He would let her take it out for a spin once in a while and sit beside her, probably with a gun handy. The girl Rusty Regan ought to have married, that Eddie Mars couldn't keep, the girl that hadn't run away with Regan. Nice Mr Canino.

I trudged back to the garage and banged on the wooden door with the butt of my flash. There was a hung instant of silence, as heavy as thunder. The light inside went out. I stood there grinning and licking the rain off my lip. I clicked the spot on the middle of the doors. I grinned at the circle of white. I was where I wanted to be.

A voice spoke through the door, a surly voice: 'Wha'd'ya want?'

'Open up. I've got two flats back on the highway and only one spare. I need help.'

'Sorry, mister. We're closed up. Realito's a mile west. Better try there.'

I didn't like that. I kicked the door hard. I kept on kicking it. Another voice made itself heard, a purring voice, like a small dynamo behind a wall. I liked this voice. It said: 'A wise guy, huh? Open up, Art.'

A bolt squealed and half of the door bent inward. My flash

155

burned briefly on a gaunt face. Then something that glittered swept down and knocked the flash out of my hand. A gun had peaked at me. I dropped low where the flash burned on the wet ground and picked it up.

The surly voice said: 'Kill that spot, bo. Folks get hurt that way.'

I snapped the flash off and straightened. Light went on inside the garage, outlined a tall man in overalls. He backed away from the open door and kept a gun levelled at me.

'Step inside and shut the door, stranger. We'll see what we can do.'

I stepped inside, and shut the door behind my back. I looked at the gaunt man, but not at the other man who was shadowy over by a workbench, silent. The breath of the garage was sweet and sinister with the smell of hot pyroxylin paint.

'Ain't you got no sense?' the gaunt man chided me. 'A bank job was pulled at Realito this noon.'

'Pardon,' I said, remembering the people staring at the bank in the rain. 'I didn't pull it. I'm a stranger here.'

'Well, there was,' he said morosely. 'Some say it was a couple of punk kids and they got 'em cornered back here in the hills.'

'It's a nice night for hiding,' I said. 'I suppose they threw tacks out. I got some of them. I thought you just needed the business.'

'You didn't ever get socked in the kisser, did you?' the gaunt man asked me briefly.

'Not by anybody your weight.'

The purring voice from over in the shadows said: 'Cut out the heavy menace, Art. This guy's in a jam. You run a garage, don't you?'

'Thanks,' I said, and didn't look at him even then.

'Okay, okay,' the man in the overalls grumbled. He tucked his gun through a flap in his clothes and bit a knuckle, staring at me moodily over it. The smell of the pyroxylin paint was as sickening as ether. Over in the corner, under a drop light, there was a big new-looking sedan with a paint gun lying on its fender.

156

I looked at the man by the workbench now. He was short and thick-bodied with strong shoulders. He had a cool face and cool dark eyes. He wore a belted brown suède raincoat that was heavily spotted with rain. His brown hat was tilted rakishly. He leaned his back against the workbench and looked me over without haste, without interest, as if he was looking at a slab of cold meat. Perhaps he thought of people that way.

He moved his dark eyes up and down slowly and then glanced at his finger-nails one by one, holding them up against the light and studying them with care, as Hollywood has taught it should be done. He spoke around a cigarette.

'Got two flats, huh? That's tough. They swept them tacks, I thought.'

'I skidded a little on the curve.'

'Stranger in town you said?'

'Travelling through. On the way to L.A. How far is it?'

'Forty miles. Seems longer this weather. Where from, stranger?'

'Santa Rosa.'

'Come the long way, eh? Tahoe and Lone Pine?'

'Not Tahoe. Reno and Carson City.'

'Still the long way.' A fleeting smile curved his lips.

'Any law against it?' I asked him.

'Huh? No, sure not. Guess you think we're nosey. Just on account of that heist back there. Take a jack and get his flats, Art.'

'I'm busy,' the gaunt man growled. 'I've got work to do. I got this spray job. And it's raining, you might have noticed.'

The man in brown said pleasantly: 'Too damp for a good spray job, Art. Get moving.'

I said: 'They're front and rear on the right side. You could use the spare for one spot, if you're busy.'

'Take two jacks, Art,' the brown man said.

'Now listen—' Art began to bluster.

The brown man moved his eyes, looked at Art with a soft quiet-eyed stare, lowered them again almost shyly. He didn't speak. Art rocked as if a gust of wind had hit him. He stamped over to the corner and put a rubber coat over his overalls, a sou'wester on his head. He grabbed a socket wrench and a hand jack and wheeled a dolly jack over to the doors.

He went out silently, leaving the door yawning. The rain blustered in. The man in brown strolled over and shut it and strolled back to the workbench and put his hips exactly where they had been before. I could have taken him then. We were alone. He didn't know who I was. He looked at me lightly and threw his cigarette on the cement floor and stamped on it without looking down.

'I bet you could use a drink,' he said. 'Wet the inside and even up.' He reached a bottle from the workbench behind him and set it on the edge and set two glasses beside it. He poured a stiff jolt into each and held one out.

Walking like a dummy I went over and took it. The memory of the rain was still cold on my face. The smell of hot paint drugged the close air of the garage.

'That Art,' the brown man said. 'He's like all mechanics. Always got his face in a job he ought to have done last week. Business trip?'

I sniffed my drink delicately. It had the right smell. I watched him drink some of his before I swallowed mine. I rolled it around on my tongue. There was no cyanide in it. I emptied the little glass and put it down beside him and moved away.

'Partly,' I said. I walked over to the half-painted sedan with the big metal paint gun lying along its fender. The rain hit the flat roof hard. Art was out in it, cursing.

The brown man looked at the big car. 'Just a panel job, to start with,' he said casually, his purring voice still softer from the drink. 'But the guy had dough and his driver needed a few bucks. You know the racket.'

I said: 'There's only one that's older.' My lips felt dry. I didn't want to talk. I lit a cigarette. I wanted my tyres fixed. The minutes passed on tiptoe. The brown man and I were two strangers chance-met, looking at each other across a little dead man named Harry Jones. Only the brown man didn't know that yet.

Feet crunched outside and the door was pushed open. The light hit pencils of rain and made silver wires of them. Art trundled two muddy flats in sullenly, kicked the door shut, let one of the flats fall over on its side. He looked at me savagely.

'You sure pick spots for a jack to stand on,' he snarled.

The brown man laughed and took a rolled cylinder of nickels out of his pocket and tossed it up and down on the palm of his hand.

'Don't crab so much,' he said dryly. 'Fix those flats.'

'I'm fixin' them, ain't I?'

'Well, don't make a song about it.'

'Yah!' Art peeled his rubber coat and sou'wester off and threw them away from him. He heaved one tyre up on a spreader and tore the rim loose viciously. He had the tube out and cold-patched in nothing flat. Still scowling, he strode over to the wall beside me and grabbed an air hose, put enough air into the tube to give it body and let the nozzle off the air hose smack against the whitewashed wall.

I stood watching the roll of wrapped coins dance in Canino's hand. The moment of crouched intensity had left me. I turned my head and watched the gaunt mechanic beside me toss the air-stiffened tube up and catch it with his hands wide, one in each side of the tube. He looked it over sourly, glanced at a big galvanized tub of dirty water in the corner and grunted.

The teamwork must have been very nice. I saw no signal, no glance of meaning, no gesture that might have a special import. The gaunt man had the stiffened tube high in the air, staring at it. He half turned his body, took one long quick step, and slammed it down over my head and shoulders, a perfect ringer.

He jumped behind me and leaned hard on the rubber. His weight dragged on my chest, pinned my upper arms tight to my sides. I could move my hands, but I couldn't reach the gun in my pocket.

The brown man came almost dancing towards me across the floor. His hand tightened over the roll of nickels. He came up to me without sound, without expression. I bent forward and tried to heave Art off his feet.

The fist with the weighted tube inside it went through my spread hands like a stone through a cloud of dust. I had the stunned moment of shock when the lights danced and the visible world went out of focus but was still there. He hit me again. There was no sensation in my head. The bright glare got brighter. There was nothing but hard aching white light. Then there was darkness in which something red wriggled like a germ under a microscope. Then there was nothing bright or wriggling, just darkness and emptiness and a rushing wind and a falling as of great trees.

28

It seemed there was a woman and she was sitting near a lamp, which was where she belonged, in a good light. Another light shone hard on my face, so I closed my eyes again and tried to look at her through the lashes. She was so platinumed that her hair shone like a silver fruit bowl. She wore a green knitted dress with a broad white collar turned over it. There was a sharp-angled glossy bag at her feet. She was smoking and a glass of amber fluid was tall and pale at her elbow.

I moved my head a little, carefully. It hurt, but not more than I expected. I was trussed like a turkey ready for the oven. Hand-cuffs held my wrists behind me and a rope went from them to my ankles and then over the end of the brown davenport on which I was sprawled. I moved enough to make sure it was tied down.

I stopped these furtive movements and opened my eyes again and said: 'Hello.'

The woman withdrew her gaze from some distant mountain peak. Her small firm chin turned slowly. Her eyes were the blue of mountain lakes. Overhead the rain still pounded, with a remote sound, as if it was somebody else's rain.

'How do you feel?' It was a smooth silvery voice that matched her hair. It had a tiny tinkle in it, like bells in a doll's house. I thought that was silly as soon as I thought of it.

'Great,' I said. 'Somebody built a filling station on my jaw.'

'What did you expect, Mr Marlowe – orchids?'

'Just a plain pine box,' I said. 'Don't bother with bronze or silver handles. And don't scatter my ashes over the blue Pacific. I like the worms better. Did you know that worms are of both sexes and that any worm can love any other worm?'

'You're a little light-headed,' she said, with a grave stare.

'Would you mind moving this light?'

She got up and went behind the davenport. The light went off. The dimness was a benison.

'I don't think you're so dangerous,' she said. She was tall rather than short, but no bean-pole. She was slim, but not a dried crust. She went back to her chair.

'So you know my name.'

'You slept well. They had plenty of time to go through your pockets. They did everything but embalm you. So you're a detective.'

'Is that all they have on me?'

She was silent. Smoke floated dimly from the cigarette. She moved it in the air. Her hand was small and had shape, not the usual bony garden tool you see on women nowadays.

'What time is it?' I asked.

She looked sideways at her wrist, beyond the spiral of smoke, at the edge of the grave lustre of the lamplight. 'Ten-seventeen. You have a date?'

'I wouldn't be surprised. Is this the house next to Art Huck's garage?'

'Yes.'

'What are the boys doing – digging a grave?'

'They had to go somewhere.'

'You mean they left you here alone?'

Her head turned slowly again. She smiled. 'You don't look dangerous.'

'I thought they were keeping you a prisoner.'

It didn't seem to startle her. It even slightly amused her. 'What made you think that?'

'I know who you are.'

Her very blue eyes flashed so sharply that I could almost see the sweep of their glance, like the sweep of a sword. Her mouth tightened. But her voice didn't change.

'Then I'm afraid you're in a bad spot. And I hate killing.'

'And you Eddie Mars's wife? Shame on you.'

She didn't like that. She glared at me. I grinned. 'Unless you can unlock these bracelets, which I'd advise you not to do, you might spare me a little of that drink you're neglecting.'

She brought the glass over. Bubbles rose in it like false hopes. She bent over me. Her breath was as delicate as the eyes of a fawn. I gulped from the glass. She took it away from my mouth and watched some of the liquid run down my neck.

She bent over me again. Blood began to move around in me, like a prospective tenant looking over a house.

'Your face looks like a collision mat,' she said.

'Make the most of it. It won't last long even this good.'

She swung her head sharply and listened. For an instant her face was pale. The sounds were only the rain drifting against the walls. She went back across the room and stood with her side to me, bent forward a little, looking down at the floor.

'Why did you come here and stick your neck out?' she asked quietly. 'Eddie wasn't doing you any harm. You know perfectly well that if I hadn't hit out there, the police would have been certain Eddie murdered Rusty Regan.'

'He did,' I said.

She didn't move, didn't change position an inch. Her breath made a harsh quick sound. I looked around the room. Two doors, both in the same wall, one half open. A carpet of red and tan squares, blue curtains at the windows, a wallpaper with bright green pine trees on it. The furniture looked as if it had come from one of those places that advertise on bus benches. Gay, but full of resistance.

She said softly: 'Eddie didn't do anything to him. I haven't seen Rusty in months. Eddie's not that sort of man.'

'You left his bed and board. You were living alone. People at the place where you lived identified Regan's photo.'

'That's a lie,' she said coldly.

I tried to remember whether Captain Gregory had said that or not. My head was too fuzzy. I couldn't be sure.

'And it's none of your business,' she added.

'The whole thing is my business. I'm hired to find out.'

'Eddie's not that sort of man.'

'Oh, you like racketeers.'

'As long as people will gamble there will be places for them to gamble.'

'That's just protective thinking. Once outside the law you're all the way outside. You think he's just a gambler. I think he's a pornographer, a blackmailer, a hot car broker, a killer by remote control, and a suborner of crooked cops. He's whatever looks good to him, whatever has the cabbage pinned to it. Don't try to sell me on any high-souled racketeers. They don't come in that pattern.'

'He's not a killer.' She frowned.

'Not personally. He has Canino. Canino killed a man tonight, a harmless little guy who was trying to help somebody out. I almost saw him killed.'

She laughed wearily.

'All right,' I growled. 'Don't believe it. If Eddie is such a nice guy, I'd like to get to talk to him without Canino around. You know what Canino will do – beat my teeth out and then kick me in the stomach for mumbling.'

She put her head back and stood there thoughtful and withdrawn, thinking something out.

'I thought platinum hair was out of style,' I went on, just to keep sound alive in the room, just to keep from listening.

'It's a wig, silly. While mine grows out.' She reached up and yanked it off. Her own hair was clipped short all over, like a boy's. She put the wig back on.

'Who did that to you?'

She looked surprised. 'I had it done. Why?'

'Yes. Why?'

'Why, to show Eddie I was willing to do what he wanted me to do – hide out. That he didn't need to have me guarded. I wouldn't let him down. I love him.'

'Good grief,' I groaned. 'And you have me right here in the room with you.'

She turned a hand over and stared at it. Then abruptly she walked out of the room. She came back with a kitchen knife. She bent and sawed at my rope.

'Canino has the key to the handcuffs,' she said. 'I can't do anything about those.'

She stepped back, breathing rapidly. She had cut the rope at every knot.

'You're a kick,' she said. 'Kidding with every breath – the spot you're in.'

'I thought Eddie wasn't a killer.'

She turned away quickly and went back to her chair by the lamp and sat down and put her face in her hands. I swung my feet to the floor and stood up. I tottered around, stiff-legged. The nerve on the left side of my face was jumping in all its branches. I took a step. I could still walk. I could run, if I had to.

'I guess you mean me to go,' I said.

She nodded without lifting her head.

'You'd better go with me – if you want to keep on living.'

'Don't waste time. He'll be back any minute.'

'Light a cigarette for me.'

I stood beside her, touching her knees. She came to her feet with a sudden lurch. Our eyes were only inches apart.

'Hello, Silver-Wig,' I said softly.

She stepped back, around the chair, and swept a package of cigarettes up off the table. She jabbed one loose and pushed it roughly into my mouth. Her hand was shaking. She snapped a small green leather lighter and held it to the cigarette. I drew in the smoke, staring into her lake-blue eyes. While she was still close to me I said:

'A little bird named Harry Jones led me to you. A little bird that used to hop in and out of cocktail bars picking up horse bets for crumbs. Picking up information too. This little bird picked up an idea about Canino. One way and another he and his friends found out where you were. He came to me to sell the information because he knew – how he knew is a long story – that I was working for General Sternwood. I got his information, but Canino got the little bird. He's a dead little bird now, with his feathers ruffled and his neck limp and a pearl of blood on his beak. Canino killed him. But Eddie Mars wouldn't do that, would he, Silver-Wig? He never killed anybody. He just hires it done.'

'Get out,' she said harshly. 'Get out of here quick.'

Her hand clutched in midair on the green lighter. The fingers strained. The knuckles were as white as snow.

'But Canino doesn't know I know that,' I said. 'About the little bird. All he knows is I'm nosing around.'

Then she laughed. It was almost a racking laugh. It shook her as the wind shakes a tree. I thought there was puzzlement in it, not exactly surprise, but as if a new idea had been added to something already known and it didn't fit. Then I thought that was too much to get out of a laugh.

'It's very funny,' she said breathlessly. 'Very funny, because you see – I still love him. Women—' She began to laugh again.

I listened hard, my head throbbing. 'Let's go,' I said. 'Fast.'

She took two steps back and her face set hard. 'Get out, you! Get out! You can walk to Realito. You can make it – and you can keep your mouth shut – for an hour or two at least. You owe me that much.'

'Let's go,' I said. 'Got a gun, Silver-Wig?'

'You know I'm not going. You know that. Please, please get out of here quickly.'

I stepped up close to her, almost pressing against her. 'You're going to stay here after turning me loose? Wait for that killer to come back so you can say sorry? A man who kills like swatting a fly. Not much. You're going with me, Silver-Wig.'

'No.'

'Suppose,' I said, 'your handsome husband *did* kill Regan? Or suppose Canino did, without Eddie's knowing it. Just suppose. How long will *you* last, after turning me loose?'

'I'm not afraid of Canino. I'm still his boss's wife.'

'Eddie's a handful of mush,' I snarled. 'Canino would take him with a teaspoon. He'll take him the way the cat took the canary. A handful of mush. The only time a girl like you goes for a wrong gee is when he's a handful of mush.'

'Get out!' she almost spat at me.

'Okay.' I turned away from her and moved out through the half-open door into a dark hallway. Then she rushed after me and pushed past to the front door and opened it. She peered out into the wet blackness and listened. She motioned me forward.

'Goodbye,' she said under her breath. 'Good luck in everything but one thing. Eddie didn't kill Rusty Regan. You'll find him alive and well somewhere, when he wants to be found.'

I leaned against her and pressed her against the wall with my body. I pushed my mouth against her face. I talked to her that way.

'There's no hurry. All this was arranged in advance, rehearsed to the last detail, timed to the split second. Just like a radio programme. No hurry at all. Kiss me, Silver-Wig.'

Her face under my mouth was like ice. She put her hands up and took hold of my head and kissed me hard on the lips. Her lips were like ice, too.

I went out through the door and closed it behind me, without sound, and the rain blew in under the porch, not as cold as her lips.

29

The garage next door was dark. I crossed the gravel drive and a patch of sodden lawn. The road ran with small rivulets of water. It gurgled down a ditch on the far side. I had no hat. That must have fallen in the garage. Canino hadn't bothered to give it back to me. He hadn't thought I would need it any more. I imagined him driving back jauntily through the rain, alone, having left the gaunt and sulky Art and the probably stolen sedan in a safe place. She loved Eddie Mars and she was hiding to protect him. So he would find her there when he came back, calm beside the light and the untasted drink, and me tied up on the davenport. He would carry her stuff out to the car and go through the house carefully to make sure nothing incriminating was left. He would tell her to go out and wait. She wouldn't hear a shot. A blackjack is just as effective at short range. He would tell her he had left me tied up and I would get loose after a while. He would think she was that dumb. Nice Mr Canino.

The raincoat was open in front and I couldn't button it, being handcuffed. The skirts flapped against my legs like the wings of a large and tired bird. I came to the highway. Cars went by in a wide swirl of water illuminated by headlights. The tearing noise of their tyres died swiftly. I found my convertible where I had left it, both tyres fixed and mounted, so it could be driven away, if necessary. They thought of everything. I got into it and leaned down sideways under the wheel and fumbled aside the flap of leather that covered the pocket. I got the other gun, stuffed it up under my coat and started back. The world was small, shut in, black. A private world for Canino and me.

Half-way there the headlights nearly caught me. They turned swiftly off the highway and I slid down the bank into the wet ditch and flopped there breathing water. The car hummed by without slowing. I lifted my head, heard the rasp of its tyres as it left the road and took the gravel of the driveway. The motor died, the lights died, a door slammed. I didn't hear the house door shut, but a fringe of light trickled through the clump of trees, as though a shade had been moved aside from a window, or the light had been put on in the hall.

I came back to the soggy grass plot and sloshed across it. The car was between me and the house, the gun was down at my side, pulled as far around as I could get it, without pulling my left arm out by the roots. The car was dark, empty, warm.

Water gurgled pleasantly in the radiator. I peered in at the door. The keys hung on the dash. Canino was very sure of himself. I went around the car and walked carefully across the gravel to the window and listened. I couldn't hear any voices, any sound but the swift bong-bong of the raindrops hitting the metal elbows at the bottom of the rain gutters.

I kept on listening. No loud voices, everything quiet and refined. He would be purring at her and she would be telling him she had let me go and I promised to let them get away. He wouldn't believe me, as I wouldn't believe him. So he wouldn't be in there long. He would be on his way and take her with him. All I had to do was wait for him to come out.

I couldn't do it. I shifted the gun to my left hand and leaned down to scoop up a handful of gravel. I tossed it against the screen of the window. It was a feeble effort. Very little of it reached the glass above the screen, but the loose rattle of that little was like a dam bursting.

I ran back to the car and got on the running board behind it. The house had already gone dark. That was all. I dropped quietly on the running board and waited. No soap. Canino was too cagey.

I straightened up and got into the car backwards, fumbled around for the ignition key and turned it. I reached with my foot, but the starter button had to be on the dash. I found it at last, pulled it and the starter ground. The warm motor caught at once. It purred softly, contentedly. I got out of the car again and crouched down by the rear wheels.

I was shivering now but I knew Canino wouldn't like that last effect. He needed that car badly. A darkened window slid down inch by inch, only some shifting of light on the glass showing it moved. Flame spouted from it abruptly, the blended roar of three swift shots. Glass starred in the coupé. I yelled with agony. The yell went off into a wailing groan. The groan became a wet gurgle, choked with blood. I let the gurgle die sickeningly, on a choked gasp. It was nice work. I liked it. Canino liked it very much. I heard him laugh. It was a large booming laugh, not at all like the purr of his speaking voice.

Then silence for a little while, except for the rain and the quietly throbbing motor of the car. Then the house door crawled open, a deeper blackness in the black night. A figure showed in it cautiously, something white around the neck. It was her collar. She came out on the porch stiffly, a wooden woman. I caught the pale shine of her silver wig. Canino came crouched methodically behind her. It was so deadly it was almost funny.

She came down the steps. Now I could see the white stiffness of her face. She started towards the car. A bulwark of defence for Canino, in case I could still spit in his eye. Her voice spoke through the lisp of the rain, saying slowly, without any tone: 'I can't see a thing, Lash. The windows are misted.'

He grunted something and the girl's body jerked hard, as though he had jammed a gun into her back. She came on again and drew near the lightless car. I could see him behind her now, his hat, a side of his face, the bulk of his shoulder. The girl stopped rigid and screamed. A beautiful thin tearing scream that rocked me like a left hook.

'I can see him!' she screamed. 'Through the window. Behind the wheel, Lash!'

He fell for it like a bucket of lead. He knocked her roughly to one side and jumped forward, throwing his hand up. Three more spurts of flame cut the darkness. More glass scarred. One bullet went on through and smacked into a tree on my side. A ricochet whined off into the distance. But the motor went quietly on.

He was low down, crouched against the gloom, his face a greyness without form that seemed to come back slowly after the glare of the shots. If it was a revolver he had, it might be empty. It might not. He had fired six times, but he might have reloaded inside the house. I hoped he had. I didn't want him with an empty gun. But it might be an automatic.

I said: 'Finished?'

He whirled at me. Perhaps it would have been nice to allow him another shot or two, just like a gentleman of the old school. But his gun was still up and I couldn't wait any longer. Not long enough to be a gentleman of the old school. I shot him four times, the Colt straining against my ribs. The gun jumped out of his hand as if it had been kicked. He reached both hands for his stomach. I could hear them smack hard against his body. He fell like that, straight forward, holding himself together with his broad hands. He fell face down in the wet gravel. And after that there wasn't a sound from him.

Silver-Wig didn't make a sound either. She stood rigid, with the rain swirling at her. I walked around Canino and kicked his gun, without any purpose. Then I walked after it and bent over sideways and picked it up. That put me close beside her. She spoke moodily, as if she was talking to herself.

'I – I was afraid you'd come back.'

I said: 'We had a date. I told you it was all arranged.' I began to laugh like a loon.

Then she was bending down over him, touching him. And after a little while she stood up with a small key on a thin chain.

She said bitterly: 'Did you have to kill him?'

I stopped laughing as suddenly as I had started. She went behind me and unlocked the handcuffs.

'Yes,' she said softly. 'I suppose you did.'

30

This was another day and the sun was shining again.

Captain Gregory of the Missing Persons Bureau looked heavily out of his office window at the barred upper floor of the Hall of Justice, white and clean after the rain. Then he turned ponderously in his swivel chair and tamped his pipe with a heat-scarred thumb and stared at me bleakly.

'So you got yourself in another jam.'

'Oh, you heard about it.'

'Brother, I sit here all day on my fanny and I don't look as if I had a brain in my head. But you'd be surprised what I hear. Shooting this Canino was all right, I guess, but I don't figure the homicide boys pinned any medals on you.'

'There's been a lot of killing going on around me,' I said. 'I haven't been getting my share of it.'

He smiled patiently. 'Who told you this girl out there was Eddie Mars's wife?'

I told him. He listened carefully and yawned. He tapped his gold-studded mouth with a palm like a tray. 'I guess you figure I ought to have found her.'

'That's a fair deduction.'

'Maybe I knew,' he said. 'Maybe I thought if Eddie and his woman wanted to play a little game like that, it would be smart – or as smart as I ever get – to let them think they were getting away with it. And then again maybe you think I was letting Eddie get away with it for more personal reasons.' He held his big hand out and revolved the thumb against the index and second fingers.

'No,' I said. 'I didn't really think that. Not even when Eddie seemed to know all about our talk here the other day.'

He raised his eyebrows as if raising them was an effort, a trick he was out of practice on. It furrowed his whole forehead and when it smoothed out it was full of white lines that turned reddish as I watched them.

'I'm a copper,' he said. 'Just a plain ordinary copper. Reasonably honest. As honest as you could expect a man to be in a world where it's out of style. That's mainly why I asked you to come in this morning. I'd like you to believe that. Being a copper I'd like to see the law win. I'd like to see the flashy well-dressed mugs like Eddie Mars spoiling their manicures in the rock quarry at Folsom, alongside of the poor little slum-bred hard guys that got knocked over on their first caper and never had a break since. That's what I'd like. You and me both lived too long to think I'm likely to see it happen. Not in this town, not in any town half this size, in any part of this wide, green and beautiful USA. We just don't run our country that way.'

I didn't say anything. He blew smoke with a backward jerk of his head, looked at the mouthpiece of his pipe and went on:

'But that don't mean I think Eddie Mars bumped off Regan or had any reason to or would have done it if he had. I just figured maybe he knows something about it, and maybe sooner or later something will sneak out into the open. Hiding his wife out at Realito was childish, but it's the kind of childishness a smart monkey thinks is smart. I had him in here last night, after the DA got through with him. He admitted the whole thing. He said he knew Canino was a reliable protection guy and that's what he had him for. He didn't know anything about his hobbies or want to. He didn't know Harry Jones. He didn't know Joe Brody. He did know Geiger, of course, but claims he didn't know about his racket. I guess you heard all that.'

'Yes.'

'You played it smart down there at Realito, brother. Not trying to cover up. We keep a file on unidentified bullets nowadays. Some day you might use that gun again. Then you'd be over a barrel.'

'I played it smart,' I said, and leered at him.

He knocked his pipe out and stared down at it broodingly. 'What happened to the girl?' he asked, not looking up.

'I don't know. They didn't hold her. We made statements, three sets of them, for Wilde, for the Sheriff's office, for the Homicide Bureau. They turned her loose. I haven't seen her since. I don't expect to.'

'Kind of a nice girl, they say. Wouldn't be one to play dirty games.'

'Kind of a nice girl,' I said.

Captain Gregory sighed and rumpled his mousy hair. 'There's just one more thing,' he said almost gently. 'You look like a nice guy, but you play too rough. If you really want to help the Sternwood family – leave 'em alone.'

'I think you're right, Captain.'

'How you feel?'

'Swell,' I said. 'I was standing on various pieces of carpet most of the night, being balled out. Before that I got soaked to the skin and beaten up. I'm in perfect condition.'

'What the hell did you expect, brother?'

'Nothing else.' I stood up and grinned at him and started for the door. When I had almost reached it he cleared his throat suddenly and said in a harsh voice: 'I'm wasting my breath, huh? You still think you can find Regan.'

I turned round and looked him straight in the eyes. 'No, I don't think I can find Regan. I'm not even going to try. Does that suit you?'

He nodded slowly. Then he shrugged. 'I don't know what the hell I even said that for. Good luck, Marlowe. Drop around any time.'

'Thanks, Captain.'

I went down out of the City Hall and got my car from the parking lot and drove home to the Hobart Arms. I lay down on the bed with my coat off and stared at the ceiling and listened to the traffic sounds on the street outside and watched the sun move slowly across a corner of the ceiling, I tried to go to sleep, but sleep didn't come. I got up and took a drink, although it was the wrong time of day, and lay down again. I still couldn't go to sleep. My brain ticked like a clock. I sat up on the side of the bed and stuffed a pipe and said out loud:

'That old buzzard knows something.'

The pipe tasted as bitter as lye. I put it aside and lay down again. My mind drifted through waves of false memory, in which I seemed to do the same thing over and over again, go to the same places, meet the same people, say the same words to them, over and over again, and yet each time it seemed real, like something actually happening, and for the first time. I was driving hard along the highway through the rain, with Silver-Wig in the corner of the car, saying nothing, so that by the time we reached Los Angeles we seemed to be utter strangers again. I was getting out at an all-night drugstore and phoning Bernie Ohls that I had killed a man at Realito and was on my way over to Wilde's house with Eddie Mars's wife, who had seen me do it. I was pushing the car along the silent, rain-polished streets to Lafayette Park and up under the porte-cochère of Wilde's big frame house and the porch light was already on, Ohls having telephoned ahead that I was coming. I was in Wilde's study and he was behind his desk in a flowered dressing-gown and a tight hard face and a dappled cigar moved in his fingers and up to the bitter smile on his lips. Ohls was there and a slim grey scholarly man from the Sheriff's office who looked and talked more like a professor of economics than a cop. I was telling the story and they were listening quietly and Silver-Wig sat in a shadow with her hands folded in her lap, looking at nobody. There was a lot of telephoning. There were two men from the Homicide Bureau who looked at me as if I was some kind of strange beast escaped from a travelling circus. I was driving again, with one of them beside me, to the Fulwider Building. We were there in the room where Harry Jones was still in the chair behind the desk, the twisted stiffness of his dead face and the sour-sweet smell in the room. There was a medical examiner, very young and husky, with red bristles on his neck. There was a fingerprint man fussing around and I was telling him not to forget the latch of the transom. (He found Canino's thumb print on it, the only print the brown man had left to back up my story.)

I was back again at Wilde's house, signing a typewritten statement his secretary had run off in another room. Then the door opened and Eddie Mars came in and an abrupt smile flashed to his face when he saw Silver-Wig, and he said: 'Hello, sugar,' and she didn't look at him or answer him. Eddie Mars fresh and cheerful, in a dark business suit, with a fringed white scarf hanging outside his tweed overcoat. Then they were gone, everybody was gone out of the room but myself and Wilde, and Wilde was saying in a cold, angry voice: 'This is the last time, Marlowe. The next fast one you pull I'll throw you to the lions, no matter whose heart it breaks.'

It was like that, over and over again, lying on the bed and watching the patch of sunlight slide down the corner of the wall. Then the phone rang, and it was Norris, the Sternwood butler, with his usual untouchable voice.

'Mr Marlowe? I telephoned your office without success, so I took the liberty of trying to reach you at home.'

'I was out most of the night,' I said. 'I haven't been down.'

'Yes, sir. The General would like to see you this morning, Mr Marlowe, if it's convenient.'

'Half an hour or so,' I said. 'How is he?'

'He's in bed, sir, but not doing badly.'

'Wait till he sees me,' I said, and hung up.

I shaved, changed clothes and started for the door. Then I went back and got Carmen's little pearl-handed revolver and dropped it into my pocket. The sunlight was so bright that it danced. I got to the Sternwood place in twenty minutes and drove up under the arch at the side door. It was eleven-fifteen. The birds in the ornamental trees were crazy with song after the rain, the terraced lawns were as green as the Irish flag, and the whole estate looked as though it had been made about ten minutes before. I rang the bell. It was five days since I had rung it for the first time. It felt like a year.

A maid opened the door and led me along a side hall to the main hallway and left me there, saying Mr Norris would be down in a moment. The main hallway looked just the same. The portrait over the mantel had the same hot black eyes and the knight in the stained-glass window still wasn't getting anywhere untying the naked damsel from the tree.

In a few minutes Norris appeared, and he hadn't changed either. His acid-blue eyes were as remote as ever, his greyish-pink skin looked healthy and rested, and he moved as if he was twenty years younger than he really was. I was the one who felt the weight of the years.

We went up the tiled staircase and turned the opposite way from Vivian's room. With each step the house seemed to grow larger and more silent. We reached a massive old door that looked as if it had come out of a church. Norris opened it softly and looked in. Then he stood aside and I went past him across what seemed to be about a quarter of a mile of carpet to a huge canopied bed like the one Henry the Eighth died in.

General Sternwood was propped up on pillows. His bloodless hands were clasped on top of the sheet. They looked grey against it. His black eyes were still full of fight and the rest of his face still looked like the face of a corpse.

'Sit down, Mr Marlowe.' His voice sounded weary and a little stiff.

I pulled a chair close to him and sat down. All the windows were shut tight. The room was sunless at that hour. Awnings cut off what glare there might be from the sky. The air had the faint sweetish smell of old age.

He stared at me silently for a long minute. He moved a hand, as if to prove to himself that he could still move it, then folded it back over the other. He said lifelessly:

'I didn't ask you to look for my son-in-law, Mr Marlowe.'

'You wanted me to, though.'

'I didn't ask you to. You assume a great deal. I usually ask for what I want.'

I didn't say anything.

'You have been paid,' he went on coldly. 'The money is of no consequence one way or the other. I merely feel that you have, no doubt unintentionally, betrayed a trust.'

He closed his eyes on that. I said: 'Is that all you wanted to see me about?'

He opened his eyes again, very slowly, as though the lids were made of lead. 'I suppose you are angry at that remark,' he said.

I shook my head. 'You have an advantage over me, General. It's an advantage I wouldn't want to take away from you, not a hair of it. It's not much, considering what you have to put up with. You can say anything you like to me and I wouldn't think of getting angry. I'd like to offer you your money back. It may mean nothing to you. It might mean something to me.'

'What does it mean to you?'

'It means I have refused payment for an unsatisfactory job. That's all.'

'Do you do many unsatisfactory jobs?'

'A few. Everyone does.'

'Why did you go to see Captain Gregory?'

I leaned back and hung an arm over the back of the chair. I studied his face. It told me nothing. I didn't know the answer to his question – no satisfactory answer.

I said: 'I was convinced you put those Geiger notes up to me chiefly as a test, and that you were a little afraid Regan might somehow be involved in an attempt to blackmail you. I didn't know anything about Regan then. It wasn't until I talked to Captain Gregory that I realized Regan wasn't that sort of guy in all probability.'

'That is scarcely answering my question.'

I nodded. 'No. That is scarcely answering your question. I guess I just don't like to admit that I played a hunch. The morning I was here, after I left you in the orchid house, Mrs Regan sent out for me. She seemed to assume I was hired to look for her husband and she didn't seem to like it. She let drop however that "they" had found his car in a certain garage. The "they" could only be the police. Consequently the police must know something about it. If they did, the Missing Persons Bureau would be the department that would have the case. I didn't know whether you had reported it, of course, or somebody else, or whether they had found the car through somebody reporting it abandoned in a garage. But I know cops, and I knew that if they got that much, they would get a little more – especially as your driver happened to have a police record. I didn't know how much more they would get. That started me thinking about the Missing Persons Bureau. What convinced me was something in Mr Wilde's manner the night we had the conference over at his house about Geiger and so on. We were alone for a minute and he asked me whether you had told me you were looking for Regan. I said you had told me you wished you knew where he was and that he was all right. Wilde pulled his lip in and looked funny. I knew just as plainly as though he had said it that by "looking for Regan" he meant using the machinery of the law to look for him. Even then I tried to go up against Captain Gregory in such a way that I wouldn't tell him anything he didn't know already.'

'And you allowed Captain Gregory to think I had employed you to find Rusty?'

'Yeah. I guess I did – when I was sure he had the case.'

He closed his eyes. They twitched a little. He spoke with them closed. 'And do you consider that ethical?'

'Yes,' I said. 'I do.'

The eyes opened again. The piercing blackness of them was startling coming suddenly out of that dead face. 'Perhaps I don't understand,' he said.

'Maybe you don't. The head of a Missing Persons Bureau isn't a talker. He wouldn't be in that office if he was. This one is a very smart cagey guy who tries, with a lot of success at first, to give the impression he's a middle-aged hack fed up with his job. The game I play is not spillikins. There's always a large element of bluff connected with it. Whatever I might say to a cop, he would be apt to discount it. And to *that* cop it wouldn't make much difference what I said. When you hire a boy in my line of work it isn't like hiring a window-washer and showing him eight windows and saying: "Wash those and you're through." *You* don't know what I have to go through or over or under to do your job for you. I do it in my way. I do my best to protect you and I may break a few rules, but I break them in your favour. The client comes first, unless he's crooked. Even then all I do is hand the job back to him and keep my mouth shut. After all you didn't tell me *not* to go to Captain Gregory.'

'That would have been rather difficult,' he said with a faint smile.

'Well, what have I done wrong? Your man Norris seemed to think when Geiger was eliminated the case was over. I don't see it that way. Geiger's method of approach puzzled me and still does. I'm not Sherlock Holmes or Philo Vance. I don't expect to go over ground the police have covered and pick up a broken pen point and build a case from it. If you think there is anybody in the detective business making a living doing that sort of thing, you don't know much about cops. It's not things like that they overlook if they overlook anything. I'm not saying they often overlook anything when they're really allowed to work. But if they do, it's apt to be something looser and vaguer, like a man of Geiger's type sending you his evidence of debt and asking you to pay like a gentleman – Geiger, a man in a shady racket, in a vulnerable position, protected by a racketeer and having at least some negative protection from some of the police. Why did he do that? Because he wanted to find out if there was anything putting pressure on you. If there was, you would pay him. If not, you would ignore him and wait for his next move. But there was something putting a pressure on you, Regan. You were afraid he was not what he had appeared to be, that he had stayed around and been nice to you just long enough to find out how to play games with your bank account.'

He started to say something but I interrupted him. 'Even at that it wasn't your money you cared about. It wasn't even your daughters. You've more or less written them off. It's that you're still too proud to be played for a sucker – and you really liked Regan.'

There was a silence. Then the General said quietly: 'You talk too damn much, Marlowe. Am I to understand you are still trying to solve that puzzle?'

'No. I've quit. I've been warned off. The boys think I play too rough. That's why I thought I should give you back your money – because it isn't a completed job by my standards.'

He smiled. 'Quit, nothing,' he said. 'I'll pay you another thousand dollars to find Rusty. He doesn't have to come back. I don't even have to know where he is. A man has a right to live his own life. I don't blame him for walking out on my daughter, nor even for going so abruptly. It was probably a sudden impulse. I want to know that he is all right wherever he is. I want to know it from him directly, and if he should happen to need money, I should want him to have that also. Am I clear?'

I said: 'Yes, General.'

He rested a little while, lax on the bed, his eyes closed and dark-lidded, his mouth tight and bloodless. He was used up.

He was pretty nearly licked. He opened his eyes again and tried to grin at me.

'I guess I'm a sentimental old goat,' he said. 'And no soldier at all. I took a fancy to that boy. He seemed pretty clean to me. I must be a little too vain about my judgement of character. Find him for me, Marlowe. Just find him.'

'I'll try,' I said. 'You'd better rest now. I've talked your arm off.'

I got up quickly and walked across the wide floor and out. He had his eyes shut again before I opened the door. His hands lay limp on the sheet. He looked a lot more like a dead man than most dead men look. I shut the door quietly and went back along the upper hall and down the stairs.

31

The butler appeared with my hat. I put it on and said: 'What do you think of him?'

'He's not as weak as he looks, sir.'

'If he was, he'd be ready for burial. What did this Regan fellow have that bored into him so?'

The butler looked at me levelly and yet with a queer lack of expression. 'Youth, sir,' he said. 'And the soldier's eye.'

'Like yours,' I said.

'If I may say so, sir, not unlike yours.'

'Thanks. How are the ladies this morning?'

He shrugged politely.

'Just what I thought,' I said, and he opened the door for me.

I stood outside on the step and looked down the vistas of grassed terraces and trimmed trees and flowerbeds to the tall metal railing at the bottom of the gardens. I saw Carmen about half-way down, sitting on a stone bench, with her head between her hands, looking forlorn and alone.

I went down the red brick steps that led from terrace to terrace. I was quite close before she heard me. She jumped up and whirled like a cat. She wore the light blue slacks she had worn the first time I saw her. Her blonde hair was the same loose tawny wave. Her face was white. Red spots flared in her cheeks as she looked at me. Her eyes were slaty.

'Bored?' I said.

She smiled slowly, rather shyly, then nodded quickly. Then she whispered: 'You're not mad at me?'

'I thought you were mad at me.'

She put her thumb up and giggled. 'I'm not.' When she giggled I didn't like her any more. I looked around. A target hung on a tree about thirty feet away, with some darts sticking to it. There were three or four more on the stone bench where she had been sitting.

'For people with money you and your sister don't seem to have much fun,' I said.

She looked at me under her long lashes. This was the look that was supposed to make me roll over on my back. I said: 'You like throwing those darts?'

'Uh-huh.'

'That reminds me of something.' I looked back towards the house. By moving about three feet I made a tree hide me from it. I took her little pearl-handled gun out of my pocket. 'I brought you back your artillery. I cleaned it and loaded it up. Take my tip – don't shoot it at people, unless you get to be a better shot. Remember?'

Her face went paler and her thin thumb dropped. She looked at me, then at the gun I was holding. There was fascination in her eyes. 'Yes,' she said and nodded. Then suddenly: 'Teach me to shoot.'

'Huh?'

'Teach me how to shoot. I'd like that.'

'Here? It's against the law.'

She came close to me and took the gun out of my hand,

cuddled her hand around the butt. Then she tucked it quickly inside her slacks, almost with a furtive movement, and looked around.

'I know where,' she said in a secret voice. 'Down by some of the old wells.' She pointed off down the hill. 'Teach me?'

I looked into her slaty blue eyes. I might as well have looked at a couple of bottle-tops. 'All right. Give me back the gun until I see if the place looks all right.'

She smiled and made a mouth, then handed it back with a secret naughty air, as if she was giving me a key to her room. We walked up the steps and round to my car. The gardens seemed deserted. The sunshine was as empty as a headwaiter's smile. We got into the car and I drove down the sunken drive-way and out through the gates.

'Where's Vivian?' I asked.

'Not up yet.' She giggled.

I drove on down the hill through the quiet opulent streets with their faces washed by the rain, bore east to La Brea, then south. We reached the place she meant in about ten minutes.

'In there.' She leaned out of the window and pointed.

It was a narrow dirt road, not much more than a track, like the entrance to some foothill ranch. A wide five-barred gate was folded back against a stump and looked as if it hadn't been shut in years. The road was fringed with tall eucalyptus trees and deeply rutted. Trucks had used it. It was empty and sunny now, but not yet dusty. The rain had been too hard and too recent. I followed the ruts along and the noise of city traffic grew curiously and quickly faint, as if this were not in the city at all, but far away in a daydream land. Then the oil-stained, motionless walking-beam of a squat wooden derrick stuck up over a branch. I could see the rusty old steel cable that connected this walking-beam with half a dozen others. The beams didn't move, probably hadn't moved for a year. The wells were no longer pumping. There was a pile of rusted pipe, a loading platform that sagged at one end, half a dozen empty oil drums lying in a ragged pile. There was the stagnant, oil-scummed water of an old slump iridescent in the sunlight.

'Are they going to make a park of all this?' I asked.

She dipped her chin down and gleamed at me.

'It's about time. The smell of that sump would poison a herd of goats. This the place you had in mind?'

'Uh-huh. Like it?'

'It's beautiful.' I pulled up beside the loading platform. We got out. I listened. The hum of the traffic was a distant web of sound, like the buzzing of bees. The place was as lonely as a churchyard. Even after the rain the tall eucalyptus trees still looked dusty. They always look dusty. A branch broken off by the wind had fallen over the edge of the sump and the flat leathery leaves dangled in the water.

I walked around the sump and looked into the pump-house. There was some junk in it, nothing that looked like recent activity. Outside a big wooden bull wheel was tilted against the wall. It looked like a good place all right.

I went back to the car. The girl stood beside it preening her hair and holding it out in the sun.

'Gimme,' she said, and held her hand out.

I took the gun and put it in her palm. I bent down and picked up a rusty can.

'Take it easy now,' I said. 'It's loaded in all five. I'll go over and set this can in that square opening in the middle of that big wooden wheel. See?' I pointed. She ducked her head, delighted. 'That's about thirty feet. Don't start shooting until I get back beside you. Okay?'

'Okay,' she giggled.

I went back around the sump and set the can up in the middle of the bull wheel. It made a swell target. If she missed the can, which she was certain to do, she would probably hit the wheel. That would stop a small slug completely. However, she wasn't going to hit even that.

I went back towards her around the sump. When I was about ten feet from her, at the edge of the sump, she showed me all her sharp little teeth and brought the gun up and started to hiss.

I stopped dead, the sump water stagnant and stinking at my back.

'Stand there, you son of a bitch,' she said.

The gun pointed at my chest. Her hand seemed to be quite steady. The hissing sound grew louder and her face had the scraped bone look. Aged, deteriorated, become animal, and not a nice animal.

I laughed at her. I started to walk towards her. I saw her small finger tighten on the trigger and grow white at the tip. I was about six feet away from her when she started to shoot.

The sound of the gun made a sharp slap, without body, a brittle crack in the sunlight. I didn't see any smoke. I stopped again and grinned at her.

She fired twice more, very quickly. I don't think any of the shots would have missed. There were five in the little gun. She had fired four. I rushed her.

I didn't want the last one in my face, so I swerved to one side. She gave it to me quite carefully, not worried at all. I think I felt the hot breath of the powder blast a little.

I straightened up. 'My, but you're cute,' I said.

Her hand holding the empty gun began to shake violently. The gun fell out of it. Her mouth began to shake. Her whole face went to pieces. Then her head screwed up towards her left ear and froth showed on her lips. Her breath made a whining sound. She swayed.

I caught her as she fell. She was already unconscious. I pried her teeth open with both hands and stuffed a wadded handkerchief in between them. It took all my strength to do it. I lifted her up and got her into the car, then went back for the gun and dropped it into my pocket. I climbed in under the wheel, backed the car and drove back the way we had come along the rutted road, out of the gateway, back up the hill and so home.

Carmen lay crumpled in the corner of the car, without motion. I was half-way up the drive to the house before she stirred. Then her eyes suddenly opened wide and wild. She sat up.

'What happened?' she gasped.

'Nothing. Why?'

'Oh, yes it did,' she giggled. 'I wet myself.'

'They always do,' I said.

She looked at me with a sudden sick speculation and began to moan.

32

The gentle-eyed, horse-faced maid let me into the long grey and white upstairs sitting-room with the ivory drapes tumbled extravagantly on the floor and the white carpet from wall to wall. A screen star's boudoir, a place of charm and seduction, artificial as a wooden leg. It was empty at the moment. The door closed behind me with the unnatural softness of a hospital door. A breakfast table on wheels stood by the chaise-longue. Its silver glittered. There were cigarette ashes in the coffee cup. I sat down and waited.

It seemed a long time before the door opened again and Vivian came in. She was in oyster-white lounging pyjamas trimmed with white fur, cut as flowingly as a summer sea frothing on the beach of some small exclusive island.

She went past me in long smooth strides and sat down on the edge of the chaise-longue. There was a cigarette in her lips, at the corner of her mouth. Her nails today were copper red from quick to tip, without half-moons.

'So you're just a brute after all,' she said quietly, staring at me. 'An utter callous brute. You killed a man last night. Never mind how I heard it. I heard it. And now you have to come out here and frighten my kid sister into a fit.'

I didn't say a word. She began to fidget. She moved over to a slipper chair and put her head back against a white cushion that lay along the back of the chair against the wall. She blew pale grey smoke upwards and watched it float towards the ceiling and come apart in wisps that were for a little while distinguishable from the air and then melted and were nothing. Then very slowly she lowered her eyes and gave me a cool hard glance.

'I don't understand you,' she said. 'I'm thankful as hell one of us kept his head the night before last. It's bad enough to have a bootlegger in my past. Why don't you for Christ's sake say something?'

'How is she?'

'Oh, she's all right, I suppose. Fast asleep. She always goes to sleep. What did you do to her?'

'Not a thing. I came out of the house after seeing your father and she was out in front. She had been throwing darts at a target on a tree. I went down to speak to her because I had something that belonged to her. A little revolver Owen Taylor gave her once. She took it over to Brody's place the other evening, the evening he was killed. I had to take it away from her there. I didn't mention it, so perhaps you didn't know it.'

The black Sternwood eyes got large and empty. It was her turn not to say anything.

'She was pleased to get her little gun back and she wanted me to teach her how to shoot and she wanted to show me the old oil wells down the hill where your family made some of its money. So we went down there and the place was pretty creepy, all rusted metal and old wood and silent wells and greasy scummy sumps. Maybe that upset her. I guess you've been there yourself. It was kind of eerie.'

'Yes – it is.' It was a small breathless voice now.

'So we went in there and I stuck a can up in a bull wheel for her to pop at. She threw a wingding. Looked like a mild epileptic fit to me.'

'Yes.' The same minute voice. 'She has them once in a while. Is that all you wanted to see me about?'

'I guess you still wouldn't tell me what Eddie Mars has on you?'

'Nothing at all. And I'm getting a little tired of that question,' she said coldly.

'Do you know a man named Canino?'

She drew her fine black brows together in thought. 'Vaguely. I seem to remember the name.'

'Eddie Mars's trigger man. A tough hombre, they said. I guess he was. Without a little help from a lady I'd be where he is – in the morgue.'

'The ladies seem to—' She stopped dead and whitened. 'I can't joke about it,' she said simply.

'I'm not joking, and if I seem to talk in circles, it just seems that way. It all ties together – everything. Geiger and his cute little blackmail tricks, Brody and his pictures, Eddie Mars and his roulette tables, Canino and the girl Rusty Regan didn't run away with. It all ties together.'

'I'm afraid I don't know what you're talking about.'

'Suppose you did – it would be something like this. Geiger got his hooks into your sister, which isn't very difficult, and got some notes from her and tried to blackmail your father with them, in a nice way. Eddie Mars was behind Geiger, protecting him and using him for a cat's paw. Your father sent for me instead of paying up, which showed he wasn't scared about anything. Eddie Mars wanted to know that. He had something on you and he wanted to know if he had it on the General too. If he had, he could collect a lot of money in a hurry. If not, he would have to wait until you got your share of the family fortune, and in the meantime be satisfied with whatever spare cash he could take away from you across the roulette table. Geiger was killed by Owen Taylor, who was in love with your silly little sister and didn't like the kind of games Geiger played with her. That didn't mean anything to Eddie. He was playing a deeper game than Geiger knew anything about, or than Brody knew anything about or anybody except you and Eddie and a tough guy named Canino. Your husband disappeared and Eddie, knowing everybody knew there had been bad blood between him and Regan hid his wife out at Realito and put Canino to guard her, so that it would look as if she had run away with Regan. He even got Regan's car into the garage of the place where Mona Mars had been living. But that sounds a little silly taken merely as an attempt to divert suspicion that Eddie had killed your husband or had him killed. It isn't so silly, really. He had another motive. He was playing for a million or so. He knew where Regan had gone and why and he didn't want the police to have to find out. He wanted them to have an explanation of the disappearance that would keep them satisfied. Am I boring you?'

'You tire me,' she said in a dead, exhausted voice. 'God, how you tire me!'

'I'm sorry. I'm not just fooling around trying to be clever. Your father offered me a thousand dollars this morning to find Regan. That's a lot of money to me, but I can't do it.'

Her mouth jumped open. Her breath was suddenly strained and harsh. 'Give me a cigarette,' she said thickly. 'Why?' The pulse in her throat had begun to throb.

I gave her a cigarette and lit a match and held it for her. She drew in a lungful of smoke and let it out raggedly and then the cigarette seemed to be forgotten between her fingers. She never drew on it again.

'Well, the Missing Persons Bureau can't find him,' I said. 'It's not so easy. What they can't do it's not likely that I can do.'

'Oh.' There was a shade of relief in her voice.

'That's one reason. The Missing Persons people think he just disappeared on purpose, pulled down the curtain, as they call it. They don't think Eddie Mars did away with him.'

'Who said anybody did away with him?'

'We're coming to it,' I said.

For a brief instant her face seemed to come to pieces, to become merely a set of features without form or control. Her mouth looked like the prelude to a scream. But only for an instant. The Sternwood blood had to be good for something more than her black eyes and her recklessness.

I stood up and took the smoking cigarette from between her fingers and killed it in an ashtray. Then I took Carmen's little gun out of my pocket and laid it carefully, with exaggerated care, on her white satin knee. I balanced it there, and stepped back with my head on one side like a window-dresser getting the effect of a new twist of a scarf around a dummy's neck.

I sat down again. She didn't move. Her eyes came down millimetre by millimetre and looked at the gun.

'It's harmless,' I said. 'All five chambers empty. She fired them all. She fired them all at me.'

The pulse jumped wildly in her throat. Her voice tried to say something and couldn't. She swallowed.

'From a distance of five or six feet,' I said. 'Cute little thing, isn't she? Too bad I had loaded the gun with blanks.' I grinned nastily. 'I had a hunch about what she would do – if she got the chance.'

She brought her voice back from a long way off. 'You're a horrible man,' she said. 'Horrible.'

'Yeah. You're her big sister. What are you going to do about it?'

'You can't prove a word of it.'

'Can't prove what?'

'That she fired at you. You said you were down there around the wells with her alone. You can't prove a word of what you say.'

'Oh that,' I said. 'I wasn't thinking of trying. I was thinking of another time – when the shells in the little gun had bullets in them.'

Her eyes were pools of darkness, much emptier than darkness.

'I was thinking of the day Regan disappeared,' I said. 'Late in the afternoon. When he took her down to those old wells to teach her to shoot and put up a can somewhere and told her to pop at it and stood near her while she shot. And she didn't shoot at the can. She turned the gun and shot him, just the way she tried to shoot me today, and for the same reason.'

She moved a little and the gun slid off her knee and fell to the floor. It was one of the loudest sounds I ever heard. Her eyes were riveted on my face. Her voice was a stretched whisper of agony. 'Carmen . . . Merciful God, Carmen! . . . Why?'

'Do I really have to tell you why she shot at me?'

'Yes.' Her eyes were still terrible. 'I'm – I'm afraid you do.'

'Night before last when I got home she was in my apartment. She'd kidded the manager into letting her in to wait for me. She was in my bed – naked. I threw her out on her ear. I guess maybe Regan did the same thing to her some time. But you can't do that to Carmen.'

She drew her lips back and made a half-hearted attempt to lick them. It made her, for a brief instant, look like a frightened child. The lines of her cheeks sharpened and her hand went up slowly like an artificial hand worked by wires and its fingers closed slowly and stiffly around the white fur at her collar. They drew the fur tight against her throat. After that she just sat staring.

'Money,' she croaked. 'I suppose you want money.'

'How much money?' I tried not to sneer.

'Fifteen thousand dollars?'

I nodded. 'That would be about right. That would be the established fee. That was what he had in his pockets when she shot him. That would be what Mr Canino got for disposing of the body when you went to Eddie Mars for help. But that would be small change to what Eddie expects to collect one of these days, wouldn't it?'

'You son of a bitch!' she said.

'Uh-huh. I'm a very smart guy. I haven't a feeling or a scruple in the world. All I have the itch for is money. I am so money greedy that for twenty-five bucks a day and expenses, mostly gasolene and whisky, I do my thinking myself, what there is of it; I risk my whole future, the hatred of the cops and of Eddie Mars and his pals, I dodge bullets and eat saps, and say thank you very much, if you have any more trouble, I hope you'll think of me, I'll just leave one of my cards in case anything comes up. I do all this for twenty-five bucks a day – and maybe just a little to protect what little pride a broken and sick old man has left in his blood, in the thought that his blood is not poison, and that although his two little girls are a trifle wild, as many nice girls are these days, they are not perverts or killers. And that makes me a son of a bitch. All right I don't care anything about that. I've been called that by people of all sizes and shapes, including your little sister. She called me worse than that for not getting into bed with her. I got five hundred dollars from your father, which I didn't ask for, but he can afford to give it to me. I can get another thousand for finding Mr Rusty Regan, if I could find him. Now you offer me fifteen grand. That makes me a big shot. With fifteen grand I could own a home and a new car and four suits of clothes. I might even take a vacation without worrying about losing a case. That's fine. What are you offering it to me for? Can I go on being a son of a bitch, or do I have to become a gentleman, like that lush that passed out in his car the other night?'

She was as silent as a stone woman.

'All right,' I went on heavily. 'Will you take her away? Somewhere far off from here where they can handle her type, where they will keep guns and knives and fancy drinks away from her? Hell, she might even get herself cured, you know. It's been done.'

She got up and walked slowly to the windows. The drapes lay in heavy ivory folds beside her feet. She stood among the folds and looked out towards the quiet darkish foothills. She stood motionless, almost blending into the drapes. Her hands hung loose at her sides. Utterly motionless hands. She turned and came back along the room and walked past me blindly. When she was behind me she caught her breath sharply and spoke.

'He's in the sump,' she said. 'A horrible decayed thing. I did it. I did just what you said. I went to Eddie Mars. She came home and told me about it, just like a child. She's not normal. I knew the police would get it all out of her. In a little while she would even brag about it. And if dad knew, he would call them instantly and tell them the whole story. And some time in that night he would die. It's not his dying – it's what he would be thinking just before he died. Rusty wasn't a bad fellow. I didn't love him. He was all right, I guess. He just didn't mean anything to me, one way or another, alive or dead, compared with keeping it from dad.'

'So you let her run around loose,' I said, 'getting into other jams.'

'I was playing for time. Just for time. I played the wrong way, of course. I thought she might even forget it herself. I've heard they do forget what happens in those fits. Maybe she has forgotten it. I knew Eddie Mars would bleed me white, but I didn't care. I had to have help and I could only get it from somebody like him . . . There have been times when I hardly believed it all myself. And other times when I had to get drunk quickly – whatever time of day it was. Awfully damn quickly.'

'You'll take her away,' I said. 'And do that awfully damn quickly.'

She still had her back to me. She said softly now: 'What about you?'

'Nothing about me. I'm leaving. I'll give you three days. If you're gone by then – okay. If you're not, out it comes. And don't think I don't mean that.'

She turned suddenly. 'I don't know what to say to you. I don't know how to begin.'

'Yeah. Get her out of here and see that she's watched every minute. Promise?'

'I promise. Eddie—'

'Forget Eddie. I'll go see him after I get some rest. I'll handle Eddie.'

'He'll try to kill you.'

'Yeah,' I said. 'His best boy couldn't. I'll take a chance on the others. Does Norris know?'

'He'll never tell.'

'I thought he knew.'

I went quickly away from her down the room and out and down the tiled staircase to the front hall. I didn't see anybody when I left. I found my hat alone this time. Outside the bright gardens had a haunted look, as though small wild eyes were watching me from behind the bushes, as though the sunshine itself had a mysterious something in its light. I got into my car and drove off down the hill.

What did it matter where you lay once you were dead? In a dirty sump or in a marble tower on top of a high hill? You were dead, you were sleeping the big sleep, you were not bothered by things like that. Oil and water were the same as wind and air to you. You just slept the big sleep, not caring about the nastiness of how you died or where you fell. Me, I was part of the nastiness now. Far more a part of it than Rusty Regan was. But the old man didn't have to be. He could lie quiet in his canopied bed, with his bloodless hands folded on the sheet, waiting. His heart was a brief, uncertain murmur. His thoughts were as grey as ashes. And in a little while he too, like Rusty Regan would be sleeping the big sleep.

On the way downtown I stopped at a bar and had a couple of double Scotches. They didn't do me any good. All they did was make me think of Silver-Wig and I never saw her again.

The Lady in the Lake

1

The Treloar Building was, and is, on Oliver Street, near Sixth, on the west side. The sidewalk in front of it had been built of black and white rubber blocks. They were taking them up now to give to the government, and a hatless pale man with a face like a building superintendent was watching the work and looking as if it was breaking his heart.

I went past him through an arcade of speciality shops into a vast black and gold lobby. The Gillerlain Company was on the seventh floor, in front, behind swinging double plate glass doors bound in platinum. Their reception room had Chinese rugs, dull silver walls, angular but elaborate furniture, sharp shiny bits of abstract sculpture on pedestals and a tall display in a triangular showcase in the corner. On tiers and steps and islands and promontories of shining mirror-glass it seemed to contain every fancy bottle and box that has ever been designed. There were creams and powders and soaps and toilet waters for every season and every occasion. There were perfumes in tall thin bottles that looked as if a breath would blow them over and perfumes in little pastel phials tied with ducky satin bows, like little girls at a dancing class. The cream of the crop seemed to be something very small and simple in a squat amber bottle. It was in the middle at eye height, had a lot of space to itself, and was labelled *Gillerlain Regal, The Champagne of Perfumes.* It was definitely the stuff to get. One drop of that in the hollow of your throat and the matched pink pearls started falling on you like summer rain.

A neat little blonde sat off in a far corner at a small PBX, behind a railing and well out of harm's way. At a flat desk in line with the doors was a tall, lean, light-haired lovely whose name, according to the tilted embossed plaque on her desk, was Miss Adrienne Fromsett.

She wore a steel-grey business suit and under the jacket a dark blue shirt and a man's tie of lighter shade. The edges of the folded handkerchief in the breast pocket looked sharp enough to slice bread. She wore a linked bracelet and no other jewellery. Her light hair was parted and fell in loose but not unstudied waves. She had smooth ivory skin and rather severe eyebrows and large dark eyes that looked as if they might warm up at the right time and in the right place.

I put my plain card, the one without the tommy gun in the corner, on her desk and asked to see Mr Derace Kingsley.

She looked at the card and said: 'Have you an appointment?'

'No appointment.'

'It is very difficult to see Mr Kingsley without an appointment.'

That wasn't anything I could argue about.

'What is the nature of your business, Mr Marlowe?'

'Personal.'

'I see. Does Mr Kingsley know you, Mr Marlowe?'

'I don't think so. He may have heard of my name. You might say I'm from Lieutenant M'Gee.'

'And does Mr Kingsley know Lieutenant M'Gee?'

She put my card beside a pile of freshly typed letterheads. She leaned back and put one arm on the desk and tapped lightly with a small gold pencil.

I grinned at her. The little blonde at the PBX cocked a shell-like ear and smiled a small fluffy smile. She looked playful and eager, but not quite sure of herself, a new kitten in a house where they don't care much about kittens.

'I'm hoping he does,' I said. 'But maybe the best way to find out is to ask him.'

She initialled three letters rapidly, to keep from throwing her pen set at me. She spoke again without looking up.

'Mr Kingsley is in conference. I'll send your card in when I have an opportunity.'

I thanked her and went and sat in a chromium and leather chair that was a lot more comfortable than it looked. Time passed and silence descended on the scene. Nobody came in or went out. Miss Fromsett's elegant hand moved over her papers and the muted peep of the kitten at the PBX was audible at moments, and the little click of the plugs going in and out.

I lit a cigarette and dragged a smoking stand beside the chair. The minutes went by on tiptoe, with their fingers to their lips. I looked the place over. You can't tell anything about an outfit like that. They might be making millions, and they might have the sheriff in the back room, with his chair tilted against the safe.

Half an hour and three or four cigarettes later a door opened behind Miss Fromsett's desk and two men came out backwards

198

laughing. A third man held the door for them and helped them laugh. They all shook hands heartily and the two men went across the office and out. The third man dropped the grin off his face and looked as if he had never grinned in his life. He was a tall bird in a grey suit and he didn't want any nonsense.

'Any calls?' he asked in a sharp bossy voice.

Miss Fromsett said softly: 'A Mr Marlowe to see you. From Lieutenant M'Gee. His business is personal.'

'Never heard of him,' the tall man barked. He took my card, didn't even glance at me, and went back into his office. His door closed on the pneumatic closer and made a sound like 'phooey'. Miss Fromsett gave me a sweet sad smile and I gave it back to her in the form of an obscene leer. I ate another cigarette and more time staggered by. I was getting to be very fond of the Gillerlain Company.

Ten minutes later the same door opened again and the big shot came out with his hat on and sneered that he was going to get a hair-cut. He started off across the Chinese rug in a swinging athletic stride, made about half the distance to the door and then did a sharp cutback and came over to where I was sitting.

'You want to see me?' he barked.

He was about six feet two and not much of it soft. His eyes were stone grey with flecks of cold light in them. He filled a large size in smooth grey flannel with a narrow chalk stripe, and filled it elegantly. His manner said he was very tough to get along with.

I stood up. 'If you're Mr Derace Kingsley.'

'Who the hell did you think I was?'

I let him have that trick and gave him my other card, the one with the business on it. He clamped it in his paw and scowled down at it.

'Who's M'Gee?' he snapped.

'He's just a fellow I know.'

'I'm fascinated,' he said, glancing back at Miss Fromsett. She liked it. She liked it very much. 'Anything else you would care to let drop about him?'

'Well, they call him Violets M'Gee,' I said. 'On account of he chews little throat pastilles that smell of violets. He's a big man with soft silvery hair and a cute little mouth made to kiss babies with. When last seen he was wearing a neat blue suit, wide-toed brown shoes, grey homburg hat, and was smoking opium in a short briar pipe.'

'I don't like your manner,' Kingsley said in a voice you could have cracked a brazil nut on.

'That's all right,' I said. 'I'm not selling it.'

He reared back as if I had hung a week-old mackerel under his nose. After a moment he turned his back on me and said over his shoulder:

'I'll give you exactly three minutes. God knows why.'

He burned the carpet back past Miss Fromsett's desk to his door, yanked it open and let it swing to in my face. Miss Fromsett liked that too, but I thought there was a little sly laughter behind her eyes now.

2

The private office was everything a private office should be. It was long and dim and quiet and air-conditioned and its windows were shut and its grey venetian blinds half-closed to keep out the July glare. Grey drapes matched the grey carpeting. There was a large black and silver safe in the corner and a low row of low filing cases that exactly matched it. On the wall there was a huge tinted photograph of an elderly party with a chiselled beak and whiskers and a wing collar. The Adam's apple that edged through his wing collar looked harder than most people's chins. The plate underneath the photograph read: *Mr Matthew Gillerlain, 1860–1934.*

Derace Kingsley marched briskly behind about eight hundred dollars' worth of executive desk and planted his backside in a tall leather chair. He reached himself a panatela out of a copper and mahogany box and trimmed it and lit it with a fat copper desk lighter. He took his time about it. It didn't matter about my time. When he had finished this, he leaned back and blew a little smoke and said:

'I'm a business man. I don't fool around. You're a licensed detective your card says. Show me something to prove it.'

I got my wallet out and handed him things to prove it. He looked at them and threw them back across the desk. The celluloid holder with the photostat of my licence in it fell to the floor. He didn't bother to apologize.

'I don't know M'Gee,' he said. 'I know Sheriff Petersen. I asked for the name of a reliable man to do a good job. I suppose you are the man.'

'M'Gee is in the Hollywood sub-station of the sheriff's office,' I said. 'You can check on that.'

'Not necessary. I guess you might do, but don't get flip with me. And remember when I hire a man he's my man. He does exactly what I tell him and he keeps his mouth shut. Or he goes out fast. Is that clear? I hope I'm not too tough for you.'

'Why not leave that an open question?' I said.

He frowned. He said sharply: 'What do you charge?'

'Twenty-five a day and expenses. Eight cents a mile for my car.'

'Absurd,' he said. 'Far too much. Fifteen a day flat. That's plenty. I'll pay the mileage, within reason, the way things are now. But no joyriding.'

I blew a little grey cloud of cigarette smoke and fanned it with my hand. I said nothing. He seemed a little surprised that I said nothing.

He leaned over the desk and pointed with his cigar. 'I haven't hired you yet,' he said, 'but if I do, the job is absolutely confidential. No talking it over with your cop friend. Is that understood?'

'Just what do you want done, Mr Kingsley?'

'What do you care? You do all kinds of detective work, don't you?'

'Not all kinds. Only the fairly honest kinds.'

He stared at me level-eyed, his jaw tight. His grey eyes had an opaque look.

'For one thing I don't do divorce business,' I said. 'And I get a hundred down as a retainer – from strangers.'

'Well, well,' he said, in a voice suddenly soft. 'Well, well.'

'And as for your being too tough for me,' I said, 'most of the clients start out either by weeping down my shirt or bawling me out to show who's boss. But usually they end up very reasonable – if they're still alive.'

'Well, well,' he said again, in the same soft voice, and went on staring at me. 'Do you lose very many of them?' he asked.

'Not if they treat me right,' I said.

'Have a cigar,' he said.

I took a cigar and put it in my pocket.

'I want you to find my wife,' he said. 'She's been missing for a month.'

'Okay,' I said. 'I'll find your wife.'

He patted his desk with both hands. He stared at me solidly. 'I think you will at that,' he said. Then he grinned. 'I haven't been called down like that in four years,' he said.

I didn't say anything.

'Damn it all,' he said, 'I liked it. I liked it fine.' He ran a hand through his thick dark hair. 'She's been gone a whole month,' he said. 'From a cabin we have in the mountains. Near Puma Point. Do you know Puma Point?'

I said I knew Puma Point.

'Our place is three miles from the village,' he said, 'partly over a private road. It's on a private lake. Little Fawn Lake. There's a dam three of us put up to improve the property. I own the tract with two other men. It's quite large, but undeveloped and won't be developed now for some time, of course. My friends have cabins, I have a cabin and a man named Bill Chess lives with his wife in another cabin rent-free and looks after the place. He's a disabled veteran with a pension. That's all there is up there. My wife went up in the middle of May, came down twice for week-ends, was due down the twelfth of June for a party and never showed up. I haven't seen her since.'

'What have you done about it?' I asked.

'Nothing. Not a thing. I haven't even been up there.' He waited, wanting me to ask why.

I said: 'Why?'

He pushed his chair back to get a locked drawer open. He took out a folded paper and passed it over. I unfolded it and saw it was a Postal Telegraph form. The wire had been filed at El Paso on June 14th, at 9.19 a.m. It was addressed to Derace Kingsley, 965 Carson Drive, Beverly Hills, and read:

'AM CROSSING TO GET MEXICAN DIVORCE STOP WILL MARRY CHRIS STOP GOOD LUCK AND GOOD-BYE CRYSTAL.'

I put this down on my side of the desk and he was handing me a large and very clear snapshot on glazed paper which showed a man and a woman sitting on the sand under a beach umbrella. The man wore trunks and the woman what looked like a very daring white sharkskin bathing suit. She was a slim blonde, young and shapely and smiling. The man was a hefty dark handsome lad with fine shoulders and legs, sleek dark hair and white teeth. Six feet of a standard type of home-wrecker. Arms to hold you close and all his brains in his face. He was holding a pair of dark glasses in his hand and smiling at the camera with a practised and easy smile.

'That's Crystal,' Kingsley said, 'and that's Chris Lavery. She can have him and he can have her and to hell with them both.'

I put the photo down on the telegram. 'All right, what's the catch?' I asked him.

'There's no telephone up there,' he said, and there was nothing important about the affair she was coming down for. So I got the wire before I gave much thought to it. The wire surprised me only mildly. Crystal and I have been washed up for years. She lives her life and I live mine. She has her own money and plenty of it. About twenty thousand a year from a family holding corporation that owns valuable oil leases in Texas. She plays around and I knew Lavery was one of her playmates. I might have been a little surprised that she would actually marry him, because the man is nothing but a professional chaser. But the picture looked all right so far, you understand?'

'And then?'

'Nothing for two weeks. Then the Prescott Hotel in San Bernadino got in touch with me and said a Packard Clipper registered to Crystal Grace Kingsley at my address was unclaimed in their garage and what about it. I told them to keep it and I sent them a cheque. There was nothing much in that either. I figured she was still out of the state and that if they had gone in a car at all, they had gone in Lavery's car. The day before yesterday, however, I met Lavery in front of the Athletic Club down on the corner here. He said he didn't know where Crystal was.'

Kingsley gave me a quick look and reached a bottle and two tinted glasses up on the desk. He poured a couple of drinks and pushed one over. He held his against the light and said slowly:

'Lavery said he hadn't gone away with her, hadn't seen her in two months, hadn't had any communication with her of any kind.'

I said: 'You believed him?'

He nodded, frowning, and drank his drink and pushed the glass to one side. I tasted mine. It was Scotch. Not very good Scotch.

'If believed him—' Kingsley said, 'and I was probably wrong to do it – it wasn't because he's a fellow you have to believe. Far from it. It's because he's a no-good son of a bitch who thinks it is smart to lay his friends' wives and brag about it. I feel he would have been tickled pink to stick it into me and break it off that he had got my wife to run away with him and leave me flat. I know these tomcats and I know this one too well. He rode a route for us for a while and he was in trouble all the time. He couldn't keep his hands off the office help. And apart from all that there was this wire from El Paso and I told him about it and why would he think it worth while to lie about it?'

'She might have tossed him out on his can,' I said. 'That would have hurt him in his deep place – his Casanova complex.'

Kingsley brightened up a little, but not very much. He shook his head. 'I still more than half-way believe him,' he said. 'You'll have to prove me wrong. That's part of why I wanted you. But there's another and very worrying angle. I have a good job here, but a job is all it is, I can't stand scandal. I'd be out of here in a hurry if my wife got mixed up with the police.'

'Police?'

'Among her other activities,' Kingsley said grimly, 'my wife occasionally finds time to lift things in department stores. I think it's just a sort of delusion of grandeur she gets when she has been hitting the bottle too hard, but it happens, and we have had some pretty nasty scenes in managers' offices. So far I've been able to keep them from filing charges, but if something like that happened in a strange city where nobody knew her' – he lifted his hands and let them fall with a smack on the desk – 'well, it might be a prison matter, mightn't it?'

'Has she ever been fingerprinted?'

'She has never been arrested,' he said.

'That's not what I mean. Sometimes in large department stores they make it a condition of dropping shoplifting charges that you give them your prints. It scares the amateurs and builds up a file of kleptomaniacs in their protective association. When the prints come in a certain number of times they call time on you.'

'Nothing like that has happened to my knowledge,' he said.

'Well, I think we might almost throw the shoplifting angle out of this for the time being,' I said. 'If she got arrested, she would get searched. Even if the cops let her use a Jane Doe name on the police blotter, they would be likely to get in touch with you. Also she would start yelling for help when she found herself in a jam.' I tapped the blue-and-white telegraph form. 'And this is a month old. If what you are thinking about happened around that time, the case would have been settled by now. If it was a first offence she would get off with a scolding and a suspended sentence.'

He poured himself another drink to help him with his worrying. 'You're making me feel better,' he said.

'There are too many other things that could have happened,' I said. 'That she did go away with Lavery and they split up. That she went away with some other man and the wire is a gag That she went away alone or with a woman. That she drank herself over the edge and is holed up in some private sanitorium taking a cure. That she got into some jam we have no idea of. That she met with foul play.'

'Good God, don't say that,' Kingsley exclaimed.

'Why not? You've got to consider it. I get a very vague idea of Mrs Kingsley — that she is young, pretty, reckless and wild. That she drinks and does dangerous things when she drinks. That she is a sucker for the men and might take up with a stranger who might turn out to be a crook. Does that fit?'

He nodded. 'Every word of it.'

'How much money would she have with her?'

'She liked to carry enough. She has her own bank and her own bank account. She could have any amount of money.'

'Any children?'

'No children.'

'Do you have the management of her affairs?'

He shook his head. 'She hasn't any — except depositing cheques and drawing out money and spending it. She never invests a nickel. And her money certainly never does me any good, if that's what you are thinking.' He paused and then said: 'Don't think I haven't tried. I'm human and it's not fun to watch twenty thousand a year go down the drain and nothing to show for it but hangovers and boy friends of the class of Chris Lavery.'

'How are you with her bank? Could you get a detail of the cheques she has drawn for the past couple of months?'

'They wouldn't tell me. I tried to get some information of the sort once, when I had an idea she was being blackmailed. All I got was ice.'

'We can get it,' I said, 'and we may have to. It will mean going to the Missing Persons Bureau. You wouldn't like that?'

'If I had liked that, I wouldn't have called you,' he said.

I nodded, gathered my exhibits together and put them away in my pockets. 'There are more angles to this than I can even see now,' I said, 'but I'll start by talking to Lavery and then taking a run up to Little Fawn Lake and asking questions there. I'll need Lavery's address and a note to your man in charge at the mountain place.'

He got a letterhead out of his desk and wrote and passed it over. I read: 'Dear Bill: This will introduce Mr Philip Marlowe who wishes to look over the property. Please show him my cabin and assist him in every way. Yrs. Derace Kingsley.'

I folded this up and put it in the envelope he had addressed while I was reading it. 'How about the other cabins up there?' I asked.

'Nobody up this year so far. One man's in government service in Washington and the other is at Fort Leavenworth. Their wives are with them.'

'Now Lavery's address,' I said.

He looked at a point well above the top of my head. 'In Bay City. I could find the house but I forgot the address. Miss Fromsett can give it to you, I think. She needn't know why you want it. She probably will. And you want a hundred dollars, you said.'

'That's right,' I said. 'That's just something I said when you were tramping on me.'

He grinned. I stood up and hesitated by the desk looking at him. After a moment I said: 'You're not holding anything back, are you – anything important?'

He looked at his thumb. 'No. I'm not holding anything back. I'm worried and I want to know where she is. I'm damn worried. If you get anything at all, call me any time, day or night.'

I said I would do that, and we shook hands and I went back down the long cool office and out to where Miss Fromsett sat elegantly at her desk.

'Mr Kingsley thinks you can give me Chris Lavery's address,' I told her and watched her face.

She reached very slowly for a brown leather address book and turned the leaves. Her voice was tight and cold when she spoke.

'The address we have is 623 Altair Street, in Bay City. Telephone Bay City 12523. Mr Lavery has not been with us for more than a year. He may have moved.'

I thanked her and went on to the door. From there I glanced back at her. She was sitting very still, with her hands clasped on her desk, staring into space. A couple of red spots burned in her cheeks. Her eyes were remote and bitter.

I got the impression that Mr Chris Lavery was not a pleasant thought to her.

3

Altair Street lay on the edge of the V forming the inner end of a deep canyon. To the north was the cool blue sweep of the bay out to the point about Malibu. To the south the beach town of Bay City was spread out on a bluff above the coast highway.

It was a short street, not more than three or four blocks, and ended in a tall iron fence enclosing a large estate. Beyond the gilded spikes of the fence I could see trees and shrubs and a glimpse of lawn and part of a curving driveway, but the house was out of sight. On the inland side of Altair Street the houses were well kept and fairly large, but the few scattered bungalows on the edge of the canyon were nothing much. In the short half-block ended by the iron fence were only two houses on opposite sides of the street and almost directly across from each other. The smaller was number 623.

I drove past it, turned the car in the paved half-circle at the end of the street and came back to park in front of the lot next to Lavery's place. His house was built downwards, one of those clinging vine effects, with the front door a little below street level, the patio on the roof, the bedrooms in the basement, and a garage like the corner pocket on a pool table. A crimson bougainvillea was rustling against the front wall and the flat stones of the front walk were edged with Korean moss. The door was narrow, grilled and topped by a lancet arch. Below the grill there was an iron knocker. I hammered on it.

Nothing happened. I pushed the bell at the side of the door and heard it ring inside not very far off and waited and nothing happened. I worked on the knocker again. Still nothing. I went back up the walk and along to the garage and lifted the door far enough to see the car with white side-walled tyres was inside. I went back to the front door.

A neat black Cadillac coupé came out of the garage across the way, backed, turned and came along past Lavery's house, slowed, and a thin man in dark glasses looked at me sharply, as if I hadn't any business to be there. I gave him my steely glare and he went on his way.

I went down Lavery's walk again and did some more hammering on his knocker. This time I got results. The judas window opened and I was looking at a handsome bright-eyed number through the bars of the grill.

'You make a hell of a lot of noise,' a voice said.

'Mr Lavery?'

He said he was Mr Lavery and what about it. I poked a card through the grill. A large brown hand took the card. The bright brown eyes came back and the voice said: 'So sorry. Not needing any detectives today please.'

'I'm working for Derace Kingsley.'

'The hell with both of you,' he said, and banged the judas window.

I leaned on the bell beside the door and got a cigarette out with my free hand and had just struck the match on the woodwork beside the door when it was yanked open and a big guy in bathing trunks, beach sandals and a white terrycloth bathing robe started to come out at me.

I took my thumb off the bell and grinned at him. 'What's the matter?' I asked him. 'Scared?'

'Ring that bell again,' he said, 'and I'll throw you clear across the street.'

'Don't be childish,' I told him. 'You know perfectly well I'm going to talk to you and you're going to talk to me.'

I got the blue-and-white telegram out of my pocket and held it in front of his bright brown eyes. He read it morosely, chewed his lip and growled:

'Oh, for Chrissake, come on in then.'

He held the door wide and I went in past him, into a dim pleasant room with an apricot Chinese rug that looked expensive, deep-sided chairs, a number of white drum lamps, a big Capehart in the corner, a long and very wide davenport in pale tan mohair shot with dark brown, and a fireplace with a copper screen and an overmantel in white wood. A fire was laid behind the screen and partly masked by a large spray of manzanita bloom. The bloom was turning yellow in places but was still pretty. There was a bottle of Vat 69 and glasses on a tray and a copper ice-bucket on a low round burl walnut table with a glass top. The room went clear to the back of the house and ended in a flat arch through which showed three narrow windows and the top few feet of the white iron railings of the staircase going down.

Lavery swung the door shut and sat on the davenport. 'He grabbed a cigarette out of a hammered silver box and lit it and looked at me irritably. I sat down opposite him and looked him over. He had everything in the way of good looks the snap shot had indicated. He had a terrific torso and magnificent thighs. His eyes were chestnut brown and the whites of them sightly grey-white. His hair was rather long and curled a little over his temples. His brown skin showed no signs of dissipation. He was a nice piece of beef, but to me that was all he was. I could understand that women would think he was something to yell for.

'Why not tell us where she is?' I said. 'We'll find out eventually anyway, and if you tell us now we won't be bothering you.'

'It would take more than a private dick to bother me,' he said.

'No it wouldn't. A private dick can bother anybody. He's persistent and used to snubs. He's paid for his time and he would just as soon use it to bother you as any other way.'

'Look,' he said, leaning forward and pointing his cigarette at me. 'I know what that wire says, but it's the bunk. I didn't go to El Paso with Crystal Kingsley. I haven't seen her in a long time – long before the date of that wire. I haven't had any contact with her. I told Kingsley that.'

'He didn't have to believe you.'

'Why would I lie to him?' He looked surprised.

'Why wouldn't you?'

'Look,' he said earnestly, 'it might seem so to you, but you don't know her. Kingsley has no strings on her. If he doesn't like the way she behaves he has a remedy. These proprietary husbands make me sick.'

'If you didn't go to El Paso with her,' I said, 'why did she send this telegram?'

'I haven't the faintest idea.'

'You can do better than that,' I said. I pointed to the spray of manzanita on the fireplace. 'You pick that up at Little Fawn Lake?'

'The hills around here are full of manzanita,' he said contemptuously.

'It doesn't bloom like that down here.'

He laughed. 'I was up there the third week in May. If you have to know. I suppose you can find out. That's the last time I saw her.'

'You didn't have any idea of marrying her?'

He blew smoke and said through it: 'I've thought of it, yes. She has money. Money is always useful. But it would be too tough a way to make it.'

I nodded, but didn't say anything. He looked at the manzanita spray in the fireplace and leaned back to blow smoke in the air and show me the strong brown line of his throat. After a moment, when I still didn't say anything, he began to get restless. He glanced down at the card I had given him and said:

'So you hire yourself out to dig up dirt? Doing well at it?'

'Nothing to brag about. A dollar herè, a dollar there.'

'And all of them pretty slimy,' he said.

'Look, Mr Lavery, we don't have to get into a fight. Kingsley thinks you know where his wife is, but won't tell him. Either out of meanness or motives of delicacy.'

'Which way would he like it?' the handsome brown-faced man sneered.

'He doesn't care, as long as he gets the information. He doesn't care a great deal what you and she do together or where you go or whether she divorces him or not. He just wants to feel sure that everything is all right and that she isn't in trouble of any kind.'

Lavery looked interested. 'Trouble? What kind of trouble?' He licked the word around on his brown lips, tasting it.

'Maybe you won't know the kind of trouble he is thinking of.'

'Tell me,' he pleaded sarcastically. 'I'd just love to hear about some kind of trouble I didn't know about.'

'You're doing fine,' I told him. 'No time to talk business, but always time for a wisecrack. If you think we might try to get a hook into you because you crossed a state line with her, forget it.'

'Go climb up your thumb, wise guy. You'd have to prove I paid the freight, or it wouldn't mean anything.'

'This wire has to mean something,' I said stubbornly. It seemed to me that I had said it before, several times.

'It's probably just a gag. She's full of little tricks like that. All of them silly, and some of them vicious.'

'I don't see any point in this one.'

He flicked cigarette ash carelessly at the glass-top table. He gave me a quick up from under look and immediately looked away.

'I stood her up,' he said slowly. 'It might be her idea of a way to get back at me. I was supposed to run up there one week-end. I didn't go. I was – sick of her.'

I said: 'Uh-huh,' and gave him a long steady stare. 'I don't like that so well. I'd like it better if you did go to El Paso with her and had a fight and split up. Could you tell it that way?'

He flushed solidly behind the sunburn.

'God damn it,' he said, 'I told you I didn't go anywhere with her. Not anywhere. Can't you remember that?'

'I'll remember it when I believe it.'

He leaned over to snub out his cigarette. He stood up with an easy movement, not hurried at all, pulled the belt of his robe tight, and moved out to the end of the davenport.

'All right,' he said in a clear tight voice. 'Out you go. Take the air. 'I've had enough of your third-degree tripe. You're wasting my time and your own – if it's worth anything.'

I stood up and grinned at him. 'Not a lot, but for what it's worth I'm being paid for it. It couldn't be, for instance, that you ran into a little unpleasantness in some departmental store – say at the stocking or jewellery counter.'

He looked at me carefully, drawing his eyebrows down at the corners and making his mouth small.

'I don't get it,' he said, but there was thought behind his voice.

'That's all I wanted to know,' I said. 'And thanks for listening. By the way, what line of business are you in – since you left Kingsley?'

'What the hell business is it of yours?'

'None. But of course I can always find out,' I said, and moved a little way towards the door, not very far.

'At the moment I'm not doing anything,' he said coldly. 'I expect a commission in the navy almost any day.'

'You ought to do well at that,' I said.

'Yeah. So long, snooper. And don't bother to come back. I won't be at home.'

I went over to the door and pulled it open. It stuck on the lower sill, from the beach moisture. When I had it open, I looked back at him. He was standing there narrow-eyed, full of muted thunder.

'I may have to come back,' I said. 'But it won't be just to swop gags. It will be because I find something out that needs talking over.'

'So you still think I'm lying,' he said savagely.

'I think you have something on your mind. I've looked at too many faces not to know. It may not be any of my business. If it is, you're likely to have to throw me out again.'

'A pleasure,' he said. 'And next time bring somebody to drive you home. In case you land on your fanny and knock your brains out.'

Then without any rhyme or reason that I could see, he spat on the rug in front of his feet.

It jarred me. It was like watching the veneer peel off and leave a tough kid in an alley. Or like hearing an apparently re-fined woman start expressing herself in four-letter words.

'So long, beautiful hunk,' I said, and left him standing there. I closed the door, had to jerk it to get it shut, and went up the path to the street. I stood on the sidewalk looking at the house across the way.

4

It was a wide shallow house with rose stucco walls faded out to a pleasant pastel shade and trimmed with dull green at the window frames. The roof was of green tiles, round rough ones. There was a deeply inset front door framed in a mosaic of multi-coloured pieces of tiling and a small flower garden in front, behind a low stucco wall topped by an iron railing, which the beach moisture had begun to corrode. Outside the wall to the left was the three-car garage, with a door opening inside the yard and a concrete path going from there to a side door of the house.

Set into the gate post was a bronze tablet which read: 'Albert S. Almore, MD.'

While I was standing there staring across the street, the black Cadillac I had already seen came purring around the corner and then down the block. It slowed and started to sweep outwards to get turning space to get into the garage, decided my car was in the way of that, and went on to the end of the road and turned in the widened-out space in front of the ornamental iron railing. It came back slowly and went into the empty third of the garage across the way.

The thin man in sun-glasses went along the sidewalk to the house, carrying a double-handled doctor's bag. Halfway along he slowed down to stare across at me. I went along towards my car. At the house he used a key and as he opened the door he looked across at me again.

I got into the Chrysler and sat there smoking and trying to make up my mind whether it was worth while hiring somebody to pull a tail on Lavery. I decided it wasn't, not the way things looked so far.

Curtains moved at a lower window close to the side door Dr Almore had gone in at. A thin hand held them aside and I caught the glint of light on glasses. They were held aside for quite some time, before they fell together again.

I looked along the street at Lavery's house. From this angle I could see that his service porch gave on a flight of painted wooden steps to a sloping concrete walk and a flight of concrete steps ending in the paved alley below.

I looked across at Dr Almore's house again, wondering idly if he knew Lavery and how well. He probably knew him, since theirs were the only two houses in the block. But being a doctor, he wouldn't tell me anything about him. As I looked, the curtains which had been lifted apart were now completely drawn aside.

The middle segment of the triple window they had masked had no screen. Behind it, Dr Almore stood staring across my way, with a sharp frown on his thin face. I shook cigarette ash out of the window and he turned abruptly and sat down at a desk. His double-handled bag was on the desk in front of him. He sat rigidly, drumming on the desk beside the bag. His hand reached for the telephone, touched it and came away again. He lit a cigarette and shook the match violently, then strode to the window and stared out at me some more.

This was interesting, if at all, only because he was a doctor. Doctors, as a rule, are the least curious of men. While they are still interns they hear enough secrets to last them a lifetime. Dr Almore seemed interested in me. More than interested, bothered.

I reached down to turn the ignition key, then Lavery's front door opened and I took my hand away and leaned back again. Lavery came briskly up the walk of his house, shot a glance down the street and turned to go into his garage. He was dressed as I had seen him. He had a rough towel and a steamer rug over his arm. I heard the garage door lift up, then the car door open and shut, then the grind and cough of a starting car. It backed up the steep incline to the street, white steamy exhaust pouring from its rear end. It was a cute little blue convertible, with the top folded down and Lavery's sleek dark head just rising above it. He was now wearing a natty pair of sun-goggles with very wide white sidebows. The convertible swooped off down the block and danced around the corner.

There was nothing in that for me. Mr Christopher Lavery was bound for the edge of the broad Pacific, to lie in the sun and let the girls see what they didn't necessarily have to go on missing.

I gave my attention back to Dr Almore. He was on the telephone now, not talking, holding it to his ear, smoking and waiting. Then he leaned forward as you do when the voice comes back, listened, hung up and wrote something on a pad in front of him. Then a heavy book with yellow sides appeared on his desk and he opened it just about in the middle. While he was doing this he gave one quick look out of the window, straight at the Chrysler.

He found his place in the book, leaned down over it and quick puffs of smoke appeared in the air over the pages. He wrote something else, put the book away, and grabbed for the telephone again. He dialled, waited, began to speak quickly, pushing his head down and making gestures in the air with his cigarette.

He finished his call and hung up. He leaned back and sat there brooding, staring down at his desk, but not forgetting to look out of the window every half-minute. He was waiting, and I waited with him, for no reason at all. Doctors make many phone calls, talk to many people. Doctors look out of their front windows, doctors frown, doctors show nervousness, doctors have things on their mind and show the strain. Doctors are just people, born to sorrow, fighting the long grim fight like the rest of us.

But there was something about the way this one behaved that intrigued me. I looked at my watch, decided it was time to get something to eat, lit another cigarette and didn't move.

It took about five minutes. Then a green sedan whisked around the corner and bore down the block. It coasted to a stop in front of Dr Almore's house and its tall buggy-whip aerial quivered. A man with dusty blond hair got out and went up to Dr Almore's front door. He rang the bell and leaned down to strike a match on the step. His head came around and he stared across the street exactly at where I was sitting.

The door opened and he went into the house. An invisible hand gathered the curtains at Dr Almore's study window and blanked the room. I sat there and stared at the sun-darkened lining of the curtains. More time trickled by.

The front door opened again and the big man loafed casually down the steps and through the gate. He snapped his cigarette end off into the distance and rumpled his hair. He shrugged once, pinched the end of his chin, and walked diagonally across the street. His steps in the quiet were leisurely and distinct. Dr Almore's curtains moved apart again behind him. Dr Almore stood in his window and watched.

A large freckled hand appeared on the sill of the car door at my elbow. A large face, deeply lined, hung above it. The man had eyes of metallic blue. He looked at me solidly and spoke in a deep harsh voice.

'Waiting for somebody?' he asked.

'I don't know,' I said. 'Am I?'

'I'll ask the questions.'

'Well, I'll be damned,' I said. 'So that's the answer to the pantomime.'

'What pantomime?' He gave me a hard level unfriendly stare from his very blue eyes.

I pointed across the street with my cigarette. 'Nervous Nellie and the telephone. Calling the cops, after first getting my name from the Auto Club, probably, then looking it up in the city directory. What goes on?'

'Let me see your driver's licence.'

I gave him back his stare. 'You fellows ever flash a buzzer – or is acting tough all the identification you need?

'If I have to get tough, fellow, you'll know it.'

I leaned down and turned my ignition key and pressed the starter. The motor caught and idled down.

'Cut that motor,' he said savagely, and put his foot on the running-board.

I cut the motor again and leaned back and looked at him.

215

'God damn it,' he said, 'do you want me to drag you out of there and bounce you on the pavement?'

I got my wallet out and handed it to him. He drew the celluloid pocket out and looked at my driver's licence, then turned the pocket over and looked at the photostat of my other licence on the back. He rammed it contemptuously back into the wallet and handed me the wallet. I put it away. His hand dipped and came up with a blue-and-gold police badge.

'Degarmo, detective-lieutenant,' he said in his heavy brutal voice.

'Pleased to meet you, Lieutenant.'

'Skip it. Now tell why you're down here casing Almore's place.'

'I'm not casing Almore's place, as you put it, Lieutenant. I never heard of Dr Almore and I don't know of any reason why I should want to case his house.'

He turned his head to spit. I was meeting the spitting boys today.

'What's your grift then? We don't like peepers down here. We don't have one in town.'

'Is that so?'

'Yeah, that's so. So come on, talk it up. Unless you want to ride down to the clubhouse and sweat it out under the bright lights.'

I didn't answer him.

'Her folks hire you?' he asked suddenly.

I shook my head.

'The last boy that tried it ended up on the road gang, sweetheart.'

'I bet it's good,' I said, 'If only I could guess. Tried what?'

'Tried to put the bite on him,' he said thinly.

'Too bad I don't know how,' I said. 'He looks like an easy man to bite.'

'That line of talk don't buy you anything,' he said.

'All right,' I said. 'Let's put it this way. I don't know Dr Almore, never heard of him, and I'm not interested in him. I'm down here visiting a friend and looking at the view. If I'm doing anything else, it doesn't happen to be any of your business. If you don't like that, the best thing to do is to take it down to headquarters and see the day captain.'

He moved a foot heavily on the running-board and looked doubtful. 'Straight goods?' he asked slowly.

'Straight goods.'

'Aw hell, the guy's screwy,' he said suddenly and looked back over his shoulder at the house. 'He ought to see a doctor.' He laughed without any amusement in the laugh. He took his foot off my running board and rumpled his wiry hair.

'Go on – beat it,' he said. 'Stay off our reservation, and you won't make any enemies.'

I pressed the starter again. When the motor was idling gently I said: 'How's Al Norgaard these days?'

He stared at me, 'You knew Al?'

'Yeah. He and I worked on a case down here a couple of years ago – when Wax was chief of police.'

'Al's in the military police. Wish I was,' he said bitterly. He started to walk away and then swung sharply on his heel. 'Go on, beat it before I change my mind,' he snapped.

He walked heavily across the street and through Dr Almore's front gate again.

I let the clutch in and drove away. On the way back to the city, I listened to my thoughts. They moved fitfully in and out, like Dr Almore's thin nervous hands pulling at the edges of his curtains.

Back in Los Angeles I ate lunch and went up to my office in the Cahuenga Building to see what mail there was. I called Kingsley from there.

'I saw Lavery,' I told him. 'He told me just enough dirt to sound frank. I tried to needle him a little, but nothing came of it. I still like the idea that they quarrelled and split up and that he hopes to fix it up with her yet.'

'Then he must know where she is,' Kingsley said.

'He might, but it doesn't follow. By the way a rather curious thing happened to me on Lavery's street. There are only two houses. The other belongs to a Dr Almore.' I told him briefly about the rather curious thing.

He was silent for a moment at the end and then he said: 'Is this Dr Albert Almore?'

'Yes.'

'He was Crystal's doctor for a time. He came to the house several times when she was – well, when she had been over-drinking. I thought him a little too quick with a hypodermic needle. His wife – let me see, there was something about his wife. Oh yes, she committed suicide.'

I said: 'When?'

'I don't remember. Quite a long time now. I never knew them socially. What are you going to do now?'

I told him I was going up to Puma Lake, although it was a little late in the day to start.

He said I would have plenty of time and that they had an hour more of daylight in the mountains.

I said that was fine and we hung up.

5

San Bernadino baked and shimmered in the afternoon heat. The air was hot enough to blister my tongue I drove through it gasping, stopped long enough to buy a pint of liquor in case I fainted before I got to the mountains, and started up the long grade to Crestline. In fifteen miles the road climbed five thousand feet, but even then it was far from cool. Thirty miles of mountain driving brought me to the tall pines and a place called Bubbling Springs. It had a clapboard store and a gas pump, but it felt like paradise. From there on it was cool all the way.

The Puma Lake dam had an armed sentry at each end and one in the middle. The first one I came to had me close all the windows of the car before crossing over the dam. About a hundred yards from the dam a rope with cork floats barred the pleasure boats from coming any closer. Beyond these details the war did not seem to have done anything much to Puma Lake.

Canoes paddled about on the blue water and rowing-boats with outboard motors put-putted and speedboats showing off like fresh kids made wide swathes of foam and turned on a dime and girls in them shrieked and dragged their hands in the water. Jounced around in the wake of the speedboats people who had paid two dollars for a fishing licence were trying to get a dime of it back in tired-tasting fish.

The road skimmed along a high granite outcrop and dropped to meadows of coarse grass in which grew what was left of the wild irises and white and purple lupin and bugle flowers and columbine and pennyroyal and desert paint brush. Tall yellow pines probed at the clear blue sky The road dropped again to lake level and the landscape began to be full of girls in gaudy slacks and snoods and peasant handkerchiefs and rat rolls and fat-soled sandals and fat white thighs. People on bicycles wobbled cautiously over the highway and now and then an anxious-looking bird thumped past on a power-scooter.

A mile from the village the highway was joined by another lesser road which curved back into the mountains. A rough wooden sign under the highway sign said: *Little Fawn Lake* 1¾ *miles*. I took it. Scattered cabins were perched along the slopes for the first mile and then nothing. Presently another very narrow road debouched from this one and another rough wood sign said: *Little Fawn Lake. Private Road. No Trespassing.*

I turned the Chrysler into this and crawled carefully around huge bare granite rocks and past a little waterfall and through a maze of black oak-trees and ironwood and manzanita and silence. A blue jay squawked on a branch and a squirrel scolded at me and beat one paw angrily on the pine cone it was holding. A scarlet-topped woodpecker stopped probing in the bark long enough to look at me with one beady eye and then dodge behind the tree trunk to look at me with the other one. I came to a five-barred gate and another sign.

Beyond the gate the road wound for a couple of hundred yards through trees and then suddenly below me was a small oval lake deep in trees and rocks and wild grass, like a drop of dew caught in a curled leaf. At the near end of it was a rough concrete dam with a rope hand-rail across the top and an old millwheel at the side. Near that stood a small cabin of native pine with the bark on it.

Across the lake the long way by the road and the short way by the top of the dam a large redwood cabin overhung the water, and farther along, each well separated from the others. were two other cabins. All three were shut up and quiet, with drawn curtains. The big one had orange-yellow venetian blinds and a twelve-paned window facing on the lake.

At the far end of the lake from the dam was what looked like a small pier and pavilion. A warped wooden sign on it was painted in large white letters: *Camp Kilkare*. I couldn't see any sense in that in these surroundings, so I got out of the car and started down towards the nearest cabin. Somewhere behind it an axe thudded.

I pounded on the cabin door. The axe stopped. A man's voice yelled from somewhere. I sat down on a rock and lit a cigarette. Steps came around the corner of the cabin, uneven steps. A man with a harsh face and a swarthy skin came into view carrying a double-bitted axe.

He was heavily built and not very tall and he limped as he walked, giving his right leg a little kick out with each step and swinging the foot in a shallow arc. He had a dark unshaven chin and steady blue eyes and grizzled hair that curled over his ears and needed cutting badly. He wore blue denim pants and a blue shirt open on a brown muscular neck. A cigarette hung from the corner of his mouth. He spoke in a tight tough city voice.

'Yeah?'

'Mr Bill Chess?'

'That's me.'

I stood up and got Kingsley's note of introduction out of my pocket and handed it to him. He squinted at the note, then clumped into the cabin and came back with glasses perched on his nose. He read the note carefully and then again. He put it in his shirt pocket, buttoned the flap of the pocket and put his hand out.

'Pleased to meet you, Mr Marlowe.'

We shook hands. He had a hand like a wood rasp.

'You want to see Kingsley's cabin, huh? Glad to show you. He ain't selling for Chrissake?' He eyed me steadily and jerked a thumb across the lake.

'He might,' I said. 'Everything's for sale in California.'

'Ain't that the truth? That's his – the redwood job. Lined with knotty pine, composition roof, stone foundations and porches, full bath and shower, venetian blinds all around, big fireplace, oil-stove in the big bedroom – and brother, you need it in the spring and autumn – Pilgrim combination gas and wood range, everything first class. Cost about eight thousand and that's money for a mountain cabin. And private reservoir in the hills for water.'

'How about electric light and telephone?' I asked, just to be friendly.

'Electric light, sure. No phone. You couldn't get one now. If you could, it would cost plenty to string the lines out here.'

He looked at me with steady blue eyes and I looked at him. In spite of his weathered appearance he looked like a drinker.

He had the thickened and glossy skin, the too noticeable veins, the bright glitter in the eyes.

I said: 'Anybody living there now?'

'Nope. Mrs Kingsley was here a few weeks back. She went down the hill. Back any day, I guess. Didn't he say?'

I looked surprised. 'Why? Does she go with the cabin?'

He scowled and then put his head back and burst out laughing. The roar of laughter was like a tractor backfiring. It blasted the woodland silence to shreds.

'Jesus, if that ain't a kick in the pants!' he gasped. 'Does she go with the—' He put out another bellow and then his mouth shut tight as a trap.

'Yeah, it's a swell cabin,' he said, eyeing me carefully.

'The beds comfortable?' I asked.

He leaned forward and smiled. 'Maybe you'd like a face full of knuckles,' he said.

I stared at him with my mouth open. 'That one went by me too fast,' I said, 'I never laid an eye on it.'

'How would I know if the beds are comfortable?' he snarled, bending down a little so that he could reach me with a hard right, if it worked out that way.

'I don't know why you wouldn't know,' I said. 'I won't press the point. I can find out for myself.'

'Yah,' he said bitterly, 'think I can't smell a dick when I meet one? I played hit and run with them in every state in the Union. Nuts to you pal. And nuts to Kingsley. So he hires himself a dick to come up here and see am I wearing his pyjamas, huh? Listen, Jack, I might have a stiff leg and all, but the women I could get—'

I put a hand out, hoping he wouldn't pull it off and throw it in the lake.

'You're slipping your clutch,' I told him. 'I didn't come up here to inquire into your love life. I never saw Mrs Kingsley. I never saw Mr Kingsley until this morning. What the hell's the matter with you?'

He dropped his eyes and rubbed the back of his hand viciously across his mouth, as if he wanted to hurt himself. Then he held the hand in front of his eyes and squeezed it into a hard fist and opened it again and stared at the fingers. They were shaking a little.

'Sorry, Mr Marlowe,' he said slowly. 'I was out on the roof last night and I've got a hangover like seven Swedes. I've been up here alone for a month and it's got me talking to myself. A thing happened to me.'

'Anything a drink would help?'

His eyes focused sharply on me and glinted. 'You got one?'

I pulled the pint of rye out of my pocket and held it so that he could see the green label over the cap.

'I don't deserve it,' he said. 'God damn it, I don't. Wait till I get a couple of glasses or would you come into the cabin?'

'I like it out here. I'm enjoying the view.'

He swung his stiff leg and went into his cabin and came back carrying a couple of small cheese glasses. He sat down on the rock beside me smelling of dried perspiration.

I tore the metal cap off the bottle and poured him a stiff drink and a light one for myself. We touched glasses and drank. He rolled the liquor on his tongue and a bleak smile put a little sunshine into his face.

'Man, that's from the right bottle,' he said. 'I wonder what made me sound off like that. I guess a guy gets the blues up here all alone. No company, no real friends, no wife.' He paused and added with a sideways look. 'Especially no wife.'

I kept my eyes on the blue water of the tiny lake. Under an over-hanging rock a fish surfaced in a lance of light and a circle of widening ripples. A light breeze moved the tops of the pines with a noise like a gentle surf.

'She left me,' he said slowly. 'She left me a month ago. Friday the 12th of June. A day I'll remember.'

I stiffened, but not too much to pour whisky into his empty glass. Friday the 12th of June was the day Mrs Crystal Kingsley was supposed to have come into town for a party.

'But you don't want to hear about that,' he said. And in his faded blue eyes was the deep yearning to talk about it, as plain as anything could possibly be.

'It's none of my business,' I said. 'But if it would make you feel any better—'

He nodded sharply. 'Two guys will meet on a park bench,' he said, 'and start talking about God. Did you ever notice that? Guys that wouldn't talk about God to their best friend.'

'I know that,' I said.

He drank and looked across the lake. 'She was one swell kid,' he said softly. 'A little sharp in the tongue sometimes, but one swell kid. It was love at first sight with me and Muriel. I met her in a joint in Riverside, a year and three months ago. Not the kind of joint where a guy would expect to meet a girl like Muriel, but that's how it happened. We got married. I loved her. I knew I was well off. And I was too much of a skunk to play ball with her.'

I moved a little to show him I was still there, but I didn't say anything for fear of breaking the spell. I sat with my drink untouched in my hand. I liked to drink, but not when people are using me for a diary.

He went on sadly: 'But you know how it is with marriage – any marriage. After a while a guy like me, a common no-good guy like me, he wants to feel a leg. Some other leg. Maybe it's lousy, but that's the way it is.'

He looked at me and I said I had heard the idea expressed.

He tossed his second drink off. I passed him the bottle. A blue jay went up a pine-tree hopping from branch to branch without moving his wings or even pausing to balance.

'Yeah,' Bill Chess said. 'All these hillbillies are half-crazy and I'm getting that way too. Here I am sitting pretty, no rent to pay, a good pension cheque every month, half my bonus money in war bonds. I'm married to as neat a little blonde as ever you clapped an eye on and all the time I'm nuts and I don't know it. I go for *that*.' He pointed hard at the redwood cabin across the lake. It was turning the colour of ox blood in the late afternoon light. 'Right in the front yard,' he said, 'right under the windows, and a showy little tart that means no more to me than a blade of grass. Jesus, what a sap a guy can be.'

He drank his third drink and steadied the bottle on a rock. He fished a cigarette out of his shirt, fired a match on his thumbnail and puffed rapidly. I breathed with my mouth open, as silent as a burglar behind a curtain.

'Hell,' he said at last, 'you'd think if I had to jump off the dock I'd go a little ways from home and pick me a change in types at least. But little roundheels over there ain't even that. She's a blonde like Muriel, same size and weight, same type, almost the same colour eyes. But, brother, how different from then on in. Pretty, sure, but no prettier to anybody and not half. so pretty to me. Well, I'm over there burning trash that morning and minding my own business, as much as I ever mind it. And she comes to the back door of the cabin in peekaboo pyjamas so thin you can see the pink of her nipples against the cloth. And she says in her lazy, no-good voice: 'Have a drink, Bill. Don't work so hard on such a beautiful morning.' And me, I like a drink too well and I go to the kitchen door and take it. And then I take another and then I take another and then I'm in the house. And the closer I get to her the more bedroom her eyes are.'

He paused and swept me with a hard level look.

'You asked me if the beds over there were comfortable and I got sore. You didn't mean a thing. It was just too full of remembering. Yeah – the bed I was in was comfortable.'

He stopped talking and I let his words hang in the air. They fell slowly and then after them was silence. He leaned to pick the bottle off the rock and stare at it. He seemed to fight with it in his mind. The whisky won the fight, as it always does. He took a long savage drink out of the bottle and then screwed the cap on tightly. as if that meant something. He picked up a stone and flicked it into the water.

'I came back across the dam,' he said slowly, in a voice already thick with alcohol. 'I'm as smooth as a new piston head. I'm getting away with something. Us boys can be so wrong about those little things, can't we? I'm not getting away with anything at all. Not anything at all. I listen to Muriel telling me and she don't even raise her voice. But she tells me things about myself I didn't even imagine. Oh yeah, I'm getting away with it lovely.'

'So she left you,' I said, when he fell silent.

'That night. I wasn't even here. I felt too mean to stay even half-sober. I hopped into my Ford and went over to the north side of the lake and holed up with a couple of no-goods like myself and got good and stinking. Not that it did me any good. Along about 4 a.m. I got back home and Muriel had gone, packed up and gone, nothing left but a note on the bureau and some cold cream on the pillow.'

He pulled a dog-eared piece of paper out of a shabby old wallet and passed it over. It was written in pencil on blue-lined paper from a note-book. It read:

'I'm sorry, Bill, but I'd rather be dead than live with you any longer. Muriel.'

I handed it back. 'What about over there?' I asked, pointing across the lake with a glance.

Bill Chess picked up a flat stone and tried to skip it across the water, but it refused to skip.

'Nothing over there,' he said. 'She packed up and went down the same night. I didn't see her again, I don't want to see her

224

again. I haven't heard a word from Muriel in the whole month, not a single word. I don't have any idea at all where she's at. With some other guy; maybe. I hope he treats her better than I did.'

He stood up and took the keys out of his pocket and shook them. 'So if you want to go across and look at Kingsley's cabin, there isn't a thing to stop you. And thanks for listening to the soap opera. And thanks for the liquor. Here.' He picked the bottle up and handed me what was left of the pint.

6

We went down the slope to the bank of the lake and the narrow top of the dam. Bill Chess swung his stiff leg in front of me, holding on to the rope hand-rail set in iron stanchions. At one point water washed over the concrete in a lazy swirl.

'I'll let some out through the wheel in the morning,' he said over his shoulder. 'That's all the darn thing is good for. Some movie outfit put it up three years ago. They made a picture up here. That little pier down at the other end is some more of their work. Most of what they built is torn down and hauled away, but Kingsley had them leave the pier and the millwheel. Kind of gives the place a touch of colour.'

I followed him up a flight of heavy wooden steps to the porch of the Kingsley cabin. He unlocked the door and we went into hushed warmth. The closed-up room was almost hot. The light filtering through the slatted blinds made narrow bars across the floor. The living-room was long and cheerful and had Indian rugs, padded mountain furniture with metal-strapped joints, chintz curtains, a plain hardwood floor, plenty of lamps and a little built-in bar with round stools in one corner. The room was neat and clean and had no look of having been left at short notice.

We went into the bedrooms. Two of them had twin beds and one a large double bed with a cream-coloured spread having a design in plum-coloured wool stitched over it. This was the master bedroom, Bill Chess said. On a dresser of varnished wood there were toilet articles and accessories in jade green enamel and stainless steel, and an assortment of cosmetic oddments. A couple of cold cream jars had the wavy gold brand of the Gillerlain Company on them. One whole side of the room consisted of closets with sliding doors. I slid one open and peeked inside. It seemed to be full of women's clothes of the sort they wear at resorts. Bill Chess watched me sourly while I pawed them over. I slid the door shut and pulled open a deep shoe drawer underneath. It contained at least half a dozen pairs of new-looking shoes. I heaved the drawer shut and straightened up.

Bill Chess was planted squarely in front of me, with his chin pushed out and his hard hands in knots on his hips.

'So what did you want to look at the lady's clothes for?' he asked in an angry voice.

'Reasons,' I said. 'For instance Mrs Kingsley didn't go home when she left here. Her husband hasn't seen her since. He does not know where she is.'

He dropped his fists and twisted them slowly at his sides. 'Dick it is,' he snarled. 'The first guess is always right. I had myself about talked out of it. Boy, did I open up to you. Nellie with her hair in her lap. Boy, am I a smart little egg!'

'I can respect a confidence as well as the next fellow,' I said and walked around him into the kitchen.

There was a big green-and-white combination range, a sink of lacquered yellow pine, an automatic water-heater in the service porch, and opening off the other side of the kitchen a cheerful breakfast-room with many windows and an expensive plastic breakfast set. The shelves were gay with coloured dishes and glasses and a set of pewter serving-dishes.

Everything was in apple-pie order. There were no dirty cups or plates on the drain-board, no smeared glasses or empty liquor bottles hanging around. There were no ants and no flies. Whatever loose living Mrs Derace Kingsley indulged in she managed without leaving the usual Greenwich Village slop behind her.

I went back to the living-room and out on the front porch again and waited for Bill Chess to lock up. When he had done that and turned to me with his scowl well in place I said:

'I didn't ask you to take your heart out and squeeze it for me, but I didn't try to stop you either. Kingsley doesn't have to know his wife made a pass at you, unless there's a lot more behind all this than I can see now.'

'The hell with you,' he said, and the scowl stayed right where it was.

'All right, the hell with me. Would there be any chance your wife and Kingsley's wife went away together?'

'I don't get it,' he said.

'After you went to drown your troubles they could have had a fight and made up and cried down each other's necks. Then Mrs Kingsley might have taken your wife down the hill. She had to have something to ride in, didn't she?'

It sounded silly, but he took it seriously enough.

'Nope. Muriel didn't cry down anybody's neck. They left the weeps out of Muriel. And if she did want to cry on a shoulder, she wouldn't have picked little roundheels. And as for transportation she has a Ford of her own. She couldn't drive mine easily on account of the way the controls are switched over for my stiff leg.'

'It was just a passing thought,' I said.

'If any more like it pass you, let them go right on,' he said.

'For a guy that takes his long wavy hair down in front of complete strangers you're pretty damn touchy,' I said.

He took a step towards me. 'Want to make something of it?'

'Look, pal,' I said. 'I'm working hard to think you are a fundamentally good egg. Help me out a little can't you?'

He breathed hard for a moment and then dropped his hands and spread them helplessly.

'Boy, can I brighten up anybody's afternoon,' he sighed. 'Want to walk back around the lake?'

'Sure, if your leg will stand it.'

'Stood it plenty of times before.'

We started off side by side, as friendly as puppies again. It would probably last all of fifty yards. The roadway, barely wide enough to pass a car, hung above the level of the lake and dodged between high rocks. About half-way to the far end another smaller cabin was built on a rock foundation. The third was well beyond the end of the lake, on a patch of almost level ground. Both were closed up and had that long-empty look.

Bill Chess said after a minute or two: 'That straight good little roundheels lammed off?'

'So it seems.'

'You are a real dick or just a shamus?'

'Just a shamus.'

'She go with some guy?'

'I should think it likely.'

'Sure she did. It's a cinch. Kingsley ought to be able to guess that. She had plenty of friends.'

'Up here?'

He didn't answer me.

'Was one of them named Lavery?'

'I wouldn't know,' he said.

'There's no secret about this one,' I said. 'She sent a wire from El Paso saying she and Lavery were going to Mexico.' I dug the wire out of my pocket and held it out. He fumbled his glasses loose from his shirt and stopped to read it. He handed the paper back and put his glasses away again and stared out over the blue water.

'That's a little confidence for you to hold against some of what you gave me,' I said.

'Lavery was up here once,' he said slowly.

'He admits he saw her a couple of months ago, probably up here. He claims he hasn't seen her since. We don't know whether to believe him. There's no reason why we should and no reason why we shouldn't.'

'She isn't with him now, then?'

'He says not.'

'I wouldn't think she would fuss with little details like getting married,' he said soberly. 'A Florida honeymoon would be more in her line.'

'But you can't give me any positive information? You didn't see her go or hear anything that sounded authentic?'

'Nope,' he said. 'And if I did, I doubt if I would tell. I'm dirty, but not that kind of dirty.'

'Well, thanks for trying,' I said.

'I don't owe you any favours,' he said. 'The hell with you and every other goddamn snooper.'

We had come to the end of the lake now. I left him standing there and walked out on the little pier. I leaned on the wooden railing at the end of it and saw what had looked like a band pavilion was nothing but two pieces of propped up wall meeting at a flat angle towards the dam. About two feet deep of overhanging roof was stuck on the wall, like a coping. Bill Chess came up behind me and leaned on the railing at my side.

'Not that I don't thank you for the liquor,' he said.

'Yeah. Any fish in the lake?'

'Some smart old bastards of trout. No fresh stock. I don't go for fish much myself. I don't bother with them. Sorry I got tough again.'

I grinned and leaned on the railing and stared down into the deep still water. It was green when you looked down into it. There was a swirl of movement down there and a swift greenish form moved in the water.

'There's Granpa,' Bill Chess said. 'Look at the size of that old bastard. He ought to be ashamed of himself getting so fat.'

Down below the water there was what looked like an underwater flooring. I couldn't see the sense of that. I asked him.

'Used to be a boat landing before the damn was raised. That lifted the water level so far the old landing was six feet under.'

A flat-bottomed boat dangled in a frayed rope tied to a post of the pier. It lay in the water almost without motion, but not quite. The air was peaceful and calm and sunny and held a quiet you don't get in cities. I could have stayed there for hours doing nothing but forgetting all about Derace Kingsley and his wife and her boy friends.

There was a hard movement at my side and Bill Chess said, 'Look there!' in a voice that growled like mountain thunder.

His hard fingers dug into the flesh of my arm until I started to get mad. He was bending far out over the railing, staring down like a loon, his face as white as the weather tan would let it get. I looked down with him into the water at the edge of the submerged staging.

Languidly at the edge of this green and sunken shelf of wood something waved out from the darkness, hesitated, waved back again out of sight under the flooring.

The something had looked far too much like a human arm.

Bill Chess straightened his body rigidly. He turned without a sound and clumped back along the pier. He bent to a loose pile of stones and heaved. His panting breath reached me. He got a big one free and lifted it breast high and started back out on the pier with it. It must have weighed a hundred pounds. His neck muscles stood out like ropes under canvas under his taut brown skin. His teeth were clamped tight and his breath hissed between them.

He reached the end of the pier and steadied himself and lifted the rock high. He held it a moment poised, his eyes staring down now, measuring. His mouth made a vague distressful sound and his body lurched forward hard against the quivering rail and the heavy stone smashed down into the water.

The splash it made went over both of us. The rock fell straight and true and struck on the edge of the submerged planking, almost exactly where we had seen the thing wave in and out.

For a moment the water was a confused boiling, then the ripples widened off into the distance, coming smaller and smaller with a trace of froth at the middle, and there was a dim sound as of wood breaking under water, a sound that seemed to come to us a long time after it should have been audible. An ancient rotted plank popped suddenly through the surface, stuck out a full foot of its jagged end, and fell back with a flat slap and floated off.

The depths cleared again. Something moved in them that was not a board. It rose slowly, with an infinitely careless languor, a long dark twisted something that rolled lazily in the water as it rose. It broke surface casually, lightly without haste. I saw wool, sodden and black, a leather jerkin blacker than ink, a pair of slacks. I saw shoes and something that bulged nastily between the shoes and the cuffs of the slacks. I saw a wave of dark blond hair straighten out in the water and hold still for a brief instant as if with a calculated effect, and then swirl into a tangle again.

The thing rolled over once more and an arm flapped up barely above the skin of the water and the arm ended in a bloated hand that was the hand of a freak. Then the face come. A swollen pulpy grey-white mass without features, without eyes, without mouth. A blotch of grey dough, a nightmare with human hair on it.

A heavy necklace of green stone showed on what had been a neck, half-embedded, large rough green stones with something that glittered joining them together.

Bill Chess held the hand-rail and his knuckles were polished bones.

'Muriel!' his voice said croakily. 'Sweet Christ, it's Muriel!'

His voice seemed to come to me from a long way off, over a hill, through a thick silent growth of trees.

7

Behind the window of the board shack one end of a counter was piled with dusty folders. The glass upper half of the door was lettered in flaked black paint. *Chief of Police. Fire Chief. Town Constable. Chamber of Commerce.* In the lower corner a USO card and a Red Cross emblem were fastened to the glass.

I went in. There was a pot-bellied stove in the corner and a roll-top desk in the other corner behind the counter. There was a large blue print map of the district on the wall and beside that a board with four hooks on it, one of which supported a frayed and much mended mackinaw. On the counter beside the dusty folders lay the usual sprung pen, exhausted blotter and smeared bottle of gummy ink. The end wall beside the desk was covered with telephone numbers written in hard-bitten figures that would last as long as the wood and looked as if they had been written by a child.

A man sat at the desk in a wooden arm-chair whose legs were anchored to flat boards, fore and aft, like skis. A spittoon big enough to coil a hose in was leaning against the man's right leg. He had a sweat-stained Stetson on the back of his head and his large hairless hands were clasped comfortably over his stomach, above the waistband of a pair of khaki pants that had been scrubbed thin years ago. His shirt matched the pants except that it was even more faded. It was buttoned tight to the man's thick neck and undecorated by a tie. His hair was mousy brown except at the temples, where it was the colour of old snow. He sat more on his left hip than his right, because there was a hip holster down inside his right hip pocket, and a half foot of forty-five gun reared and bored into his solid back. The star on his left breast had a bent point.

He had large ears and friendly eyes and his jaws munched slowly and he looked as dangerous as a squirrel and much less nervous. I liked everything about him. I leaned on the counter and looked at him and he looked at me and nodded and loosed half a pint of tobacco juice down his right leg into the spittoon. It made a nasty sound of something falling into water.

I lit a cigarette and looked round for an ash-tray.

'Try the floor, son,' the large friendly man said.

'Are you Sheriff Patton?'

'Constable and deputy sheriff. What law we got to have around here I'm it. Come election anyways. There's a couple of good boys running against me this time and I might get whupped. Job pays eighty a month, cabin, firewood and electricity. That ain't hay in these little old mountains.'

'Nobody's going to whip you,' I said. 'You're going to get a lot of publicity.'

'That so?' he asked indifferently and ruined the spittoon again.

'That is, if your jurisdiction extends over to Little Fawn Lake.'

'Kingsley's place. Sure. Something bothering over there, son?'

'There's a dead woman in the lake.'

That shook him to the core. He unclasped his hands and scratched one ear. He got to his feet by grasping the arms of his chair and deftly kicking it back from under him. Standing up, he was a big man and hard. The fat was just cheerfulness.

'Anybody I know?' he inquired uneasily.

'Muriel Chess. I guess you know her. Bill Chess's wife.'

'Yep, I know Bill Chess.' His voice hardened a little.

'Looks like suicide. She left a note which sounded as if she was just going away. But it could be a suicide note just as well. She's not nice to look at. Been in the water a long time, about a month judging by the circumstances.'

He scratched his other ear. 'What circumstances would that be?' His eyes were searching my face now, slowly and calmly, but searching. He didn't seem in any hurry to blow his whistle.

'They had a fight a month ago. Bill went over to the north shore of the lake and was gone some hours. When he got home she was gone. He never saw her again.'

'I see. Who are you, son?'

'My name is Marlowe. I'm up from LA to look at the property. I had a note from Kingsley to Bill Chess. He took me around the lake and went out on that little pier the movie people built. We were leaning on the rail and looking down into the water and something that looked like an arm waved out under the submerged flooring, the old boat landing. Bill dropped a heavy rock in and the body popped up.'

Patton looked at me without moving a muscle.

'Look, sheriff, hadn't we better run over there? The man's half-crazy with shock and he's there all alone.'

'How much liquor has he got?'

'Very little when I left. I had a pint but we drank most of it talking.'

He moved over to the roll-top desk and unlocked a drawer. He brought up three or four bottles and held them against the light.

'This baby's near full,' he said, patting one of them. 'Mount Vernon. That ought to hold him. County don't allow me no money for emergency liquor, so I just have to seize a little here and there. Don't use it myself. Never could understand folks letting theirselves get gummed up with it.'

He put the bottle on his left hip and locked the desk up and lifted the flap in the counter. He fixed a card against the inside of the glass door panel. I looked at the card as we went out. It read: *Back in Twenty Minutes – Maybe.*

'I'll run down and get Doc Hollis,' he said. 'Be right back and pick you up. That your car?'

'Yes.'

'You can follow along then, as I come back by.'

He got into a car which had a siren on it, two red spotlights, two fog lights, a red and white fire plate, a new air-raid horn on top, three axes, two heavy coils of rope and a fire-extinguisher in the back seat, extra petrol and oil and water cans in a frame on the running-board, an extra spare tyre roped to the one on the rack, the stuffing coming out of the upholstery in dingy wads, and half an inch of dust over what was left of the paint.

Behind the right-hand lower corner of the windshield there was a white card printed in block capitals. It read:

'VOTERS, ATTENTION! KEEP JIM PATTON CONSTABLE. HE IS TOO OLD TO GO TO WORK.'

He turned the car and went off down the street in a swirl of white dust.

8

He stopped in front of a white frame building across the road from the stage depot. He went into the white building and presently came out with a man who got into the back seat with the axes and the rope. The official car came back up the street and I fell in behind it. We sifted along the main stem through the slacks and shorts and French sailor jerseys and knotted bandannas and knobby knees and scarlet lips. Beyond the village we went up a dusty hill and stopped at a cabin. Patton touched the siren gently and a man in faded blue overalls opened the cabin door.

'Get in, Andy. Business.'

The man in blue overalls nodded morosely and ducked back into the cabin. He came back out wearing an oyster-grey lion-hunter's hat and got in under the wheel of Patton's car while Patton slid over. He was about thirty, dark, lithe, and had the slightly dirty and slightly underfed look of the native.

We drove out to Little Fawn Lake with me eating enough dust to make a batch of mudpies. At the five-barred gate Patton got out and let us through and we went on down to the lake. Patton got out again and went to the edge of the water and looked along towards the little pier. Bill Chess was sitting naked on the floor of the pier with his head in his hands. There was something stretched out on the wet planks beside him.

'We can ride a ways more,' Patton said.

The two cars went on to the end of the lake and all four of us trooped down to the pier behind Bill Chess's back. The doctor stopped to cough rackingly into a handkerchief and then look thoughtfully at the handkerchief. He was an angular bug-eyed man with a sad sick face.

The thing that had been a woman lay face down on the boards with a rope under the arms. Bill Chess's clothes lay to one side. His stiff leg, flat and scarred at the knee, was stretched out in front of him, the other leg bent up and his forehead resting against it. He didn't move or look up as we came down behind him.

Patton took the pint bottle of Mount Vernon off his hip and unscrewed the top and handed it.

234

'Drink hearty, Bill.'

There was a horrible, sickening smell in the air. Bill Chess didn't seem to notice it, nor Patton nor the doctor. The man called Andy got a dusty brown blanket out of the car and threw it over the body. Then without a word he went and vomited under a pine-tree.

Bill Chess drank a long drink and sat holding the bottle against his bare bent knee. He began to talk in a stiff wooden voice, not looking at anybody, not talking to anybody in particular. He told about the quarrel and what happened after it, but not why it had happened. He didn't mention Mrs Kingsley even in the most casual way. He said that after I left him he had got a rope and stripped and gone down into the water and got the thing out. He had dragged it ashore and then got it up on his back and carried it out on the pier. He didn't know why. He had gone back into the water again then. He didn't have to tell us why.

Patton put a cut of tobacco into his mouth and chewed on it silently, his calm eyes full of nothing. Then he shut his teeth tight and leaned down to pull the blanket off the body. He turned the body over carefully, as if it might come to pieces. The late afternoon sun winked on the necklace of large green stones that were partially embedded in the swollen neck. They were roughly carved and lustreless, like soapstone or false jade. A gilt chain with an eagle clasp set with small brilliants joined the ends. Patton straightened his broad back and blew his nose on a tan handkerchief.

'What you say, Doc?'

'About what?' the bug-eyed man snarled.

'Cause and time of death.'

'Don't be a damn fool, Jim Patton.'

'Can't tell nothing, huh?'

'By looking at that? Good God!'

Patton sighed. 'Looks drowned all right,' he admitted. 'But you can't always tell. There's been cases where a victim would be knifed or poisoned or something, and they would soak him in the water to make things look different.'

'You get many like that up here?' the doctor inquired nastily.

'Only honest to God murder I ever had up here,' Patton said, watching Bill Chess out of the corner of his eye, 'was old Dad Meacham over on the north shore. He had a shack in Sheedy Canyon, did a little panning in summer on an old placer claim he had back in the valley near Belltop. Folks didn't see him around for a while in late fall, then come a heavy snow and his roof caved in to one side. So we was over there trying to prop her up a bit, figuring Dad had gone down the hill for the winter without telling anybody, the way them old prospectors do things. Well by gum, old Dad never went down the hill at all. There he was in bed with most of a kindling axe in the back of his head. We never did find out who done it. Somebody figured he had a little bag of gold hid away from the summer's panning.'

He looked thoughtfully at Andy. The man in the lion-hunter's hat was feeling a tooth in his mouth. He said:

"Course we know who done it. Guy Pope done it. Only Guy was dead nine days of pneumonia before we found Dad Meacham.'

'Eleven days,' Patton said.

'Nine,' the man in the lion-tamer's hat said.

'Was all of six years ago, Andy. Have it your own way, son. How you figure Guy Pope done it?'

'We found about three ounces of small nuggets in Guy's cabin along with some dust. Never was anything bigger'n sand on Guy's claim. Dad had nuggets all of a pennyweight, plenty of times.'

'Well, that's the way it goes,' Patton said, and smiled at me in a vague manner. 'Fellow always forgets something, don't he? No matter how careful he is.'

'Cop stuff,' Bill Chess said disgustedly and put his pants on and sat down again to put on his shoes and shirt. When he had them on he stood up and reached down for the bottle and took a good drink and laid the bottle carefully on the planks. He thrust his hairy wrists out towards Patton.

'That's the way you guys feel about it, put the cuffs on and get it over,' he said in a savage voice.

Patton ignored him and went over to the railing and looked down. 'Funny place for a body to be,' he said. 'No current here to mention, but what there is would be towards the dam.'

Bill Chess lowered his wrists and said quietly: 'She did it herself, you darn fool. Muriel was a fine swimmer. She dived down in and swum under the boards there and just breathed water in. Had to. No other way.'

'I wouldn't quite say that, Bill,' Patton answered him mildly. His eyes were as blank as new plates.

Andy shook his head. Patton looked at him with a sly grin.
'Crabbin' again, Andy?'

'Was nine days, I tell you. I just counted back,' the man in
the lion-tamer's hat said morosely.

The doctor threw his arms up and walked away, with one
hand to his head. He coughed into his handkerchief again
and again looked into the handkerchief with passionate attention.

Patton winked at me and spat over the railing. 'Let's get on
to this one, Andy.'

'You ever try to drag a body six feet under water?'

'Nope, can't say I ever did, Andy. Any reason it couldn't be
done with a rope?'

Andy shrugged. 'If a rope was used, it will show on the
corpse. If you got to give yourself away like that, why bother
to cover up at all?'

'Question of time,' Patton said. 'Fellow has his arrangements
to make.'

Bill Chess snarled at them and reached down for the whisky.
Looking at their solemn mountain faces I couldn't tell what
they were really thinking.

Patton said absently: 'Something was said about a note.'

Bill Chess rummaged in his wallet and drew the folded piece
of ruled paper loose. Patton took it and read it slowly.

'Don't seem to have any date,' he observed.

Bill Chess shook his head sombrely. 'No. She left a month
ago. June 12th.'

'Left you once before, didn't she?'

'Yeah.' Bill Chess stared at him fixedly. 'I got drunk and
stayed with a chippy. Just before the first snow last December.
She was gone a week and came back all prettied up. Said she
just had to get away for a while and had been staying with a
girl she used to work with in LA.'

'What was the name of this party?' Patton asked.

'Never told me and I never asked her. What Muriel did was
all silk with me.'

'Sure. Note left that time, Bill?' Patton asked smoothly.

'No.'

'No.'

'This note here looks middling old,' Patton said, holding it up.

'I carried it a month,' Bill Chess growled. 'Who told you she
left me before?'

'I forget,' Patton said. 'You know how it is in a place like this. Not much folks don't notice. Except maybe in summer time where there's a lot of strangers about.'

Nobody said anything for a while and then Patton said absently: 'June 12th you say she left? Or you thought she left. Did you say the folks across the lake were up here then?'

Bill Chess looked at me and his face darkened again. 'Ask this snoopy guy – if he didn't already spill his guts to you.'

Patton didn't look at me at all. He looked at the line of mountains far beyond the lake. He said gently: 'Mr Marlowe here didn't tell me anything at all, Bill, except how the body come up out of the water and who it was. And that Muriel went away, as you thought, and left a note you showed him. I don't guess there's anything wrong in that, is there?'

There was another silence and Bill Chess stared down at the blanket-covered corpse a few feet away from his. He clenched his hands and a thick tear ran down his cheek.

'Mrs Kingsley was here,' he said. 'She went down the hill that same day. Nobody was in the other cabins. Perrys and Farquars ain't been up at all this year.'

Patton nodded and was silent. A kind of charged emptiness hung in the air, as if something that had not been said was plain to all of them and didn't need saying.

Then Bill Chess said wildly: 'Take me in, you sons of bitches! Sure I did it! I drowned her. She was my girl and I loved her. I'm a heel, always was a heel, always will be a heel, but just the same I loved her. Maybe you guys wouldn't understand that. Just don't bother to try. Take me in, damn you!'

Nobody said anything at all.

Bill Chess looked down at his hard brown fist. He swung it up viciously and hit himself in the face with all his strength.

'You rotten son of a bitch,' he breathed in a harsh whisper.

His nose began to bleed slowly. He stood and the blood ran down his lip, down the side of his mouth, to the point of his chin. A drop fell sluggishly to his shirt.

Patton said quietly: 'Got to take you down the hill for questioning, Bill. You know that. We ain't accusing you of anything, but the folks down there have got to talk to you.'

Bill Chess said heavily: 'Can I change my clothes?'

'Sure. You go with him, Andy. And see what you can find to kind of wrap up what he got here.'

They went off along the path at the edge of the lake. The

doctor cleared his throat and looked out over the water and sighed.

'You'll want to send the corpse down in my ambulance, Jim, won't you?'

Patton shook his head. 'Nope. This is a poor county, Doc. I figure the lady can ride cheaper than what you get for that ambulance.'

The doctor walked away from him angrily, saying over his shoulder: 'Let me know if you want me to pay for the funeral.'

'That ain't no way to talk,' Patton sighed.

9

The Indian Head Hotel was a brown building on a corner across from the new dance hall. I parked in front of it and used its rest room to wash my face and hands and comb the pine needles out of my hair, before I went into the dining-drinking parlour that adjoined the lobby. The whole place was full to overflowing with males in leisure jackets and liquor breaths and females in high-pitched laughs, ox-blood fingernails and dirty knuckles. The manager of the joint, a low budget tough guy in shirt sleeves and a mangled cigar, was prowling the room with watchful eyes. At the cash desk a pale-haired man was fighting to get the war news on a small radio that was as full of static as the mashed potatoes were full of water. In the deep back corner of the room, a hillbilly orchestra of five pieces, dressed in ill-fitting white jackets and purple shirts, was trying to make itself heard above the brawl at the bar and smiling glassily into the fog of cigarette smoke and the blur of alcoholic voices. At Puma Point summer, that lovely season, was in full swing.

I gobbled what they called the regular dinner, drank a brandy to sit on its chest and hold it down, and went out on to the main street. It was still broad daylight but some of the neon signs had been turned on, and the evening reeled with the cheerful din of motor horns, children screaming, bowls rattling, skeeballs clunking, .22s snapping merrily in shooting-galleries, juke boxes playing like crazy, and behind all this out on the lake the hard barking roar of the speedboats going nowhere at all and acting as though they were racing with death.

In my Chrysler a thin, serious-looking, brown-haired girl in dark slacks was sitting smoking a cigarette and talking to a dude ranch cowboy who sat on my running-board. I walked around the car and got into it. The cowboy strolled away hitching his jeans up. The girl didn't move.

'I'm Birdie Keppel,' she said cheerfully, 'I'm the beautician here daytimes and evenings I work on the *Puma Point Banner*. Excuse me sitting in your car.'

'That's all right,' I said. 'You want to just sit or you want me to drive you somewhere?'

'You can drive down the road a piece where it's quieter, Mr Marlowe. If you're obliging enough to talk to me.'

'Pretty good grapevine you've got up here,' I said and started the car.

I drove down past the post office to a corner where a blue-and-white arrow marked *Telephone* pointed down a narrow road towards the lake. I turned down that, drove down past the telephone office, which was a log cabin with a tiny railed lawn in front of it, passed another small cabin and pulled up in front of a huge oak-tree that flung its branches all the way across the road and a good fifty feet beyond it.

'This do, Miss Keppel?'

'Mrs. But just call me Birdie. Everybody does. This is fine. Pleased to meet you, Mr Marlowe. I see you come from Hollywood, that sinful city.'

She put a firm brown hand out and I shook it. Clamping bobbie pins into fat blondes had given her a grip like a pair of iceman's tongs.

'I was talking to Doc Hollis,' she said, 'about poor Muriel Chess. I thought you could give me some details. I understand you found the body.'

'Bill Chess found it really. I was just with him. You talk to Jim Patton?'

'Not yet. He went down the hill. Anyway I don't think Jim would tell me much.'

'He's up for re-election,' I said. 'And you're a newspaper woman.'

'Jim's no politician, Mr Marlowe, and I could hardly call myself a newspaper woman. This little paper we get out up here is a pretty amateurish proposition.'

'Well, what do you want to know?' I offered her a cigarette and lit it for her.

'You might just tell me the story.'

'I came up here with a letter from Derace Kingsley to look at his property. Bill Chess showed me around, got talking to me, told me his wife had moved out on him and showed me the note she left. I had a bottle along and he punished it. He was feeling pretty blue. The liquor loosened him up, but he was lonely and aching to talk anyway. That's how it happened. I didn't know him. Coming back around the end of the lake we went out on the pier and Bill spotted an arm waving out from under the planking down in the water. It turned out to belong to what was left of Muriel Chess. I guess that's all.'

'I understand from Doc Hollis she had been in the water a long time. Pretty badly decomposed and all that.'

'Yes. Probably the whole month he thought she had been gone. There's no reason to think otherwise. The note's a suicide note.'

'Any doubts about that, Mr Marlowe?'

I looked at her sideways. Thoughtful dark eyes looked out at me under fluffed-out brown hair. The dusk had begun to fall now, very slowly. It was no more than a slight change in the quality of the light.

'I guess the police always have doubts in these cases,' I said.

'How about you?'

'My opinion doesn't go for anything.'

'But for what it's worth?'

'I only met Bill Chess this afternoon,' I said. 'He struck me as a quick-tempered lad and from his own accounts he's no saint. But he seems to have been in love with his wife. And I can't see him hanging around for a month knowing she was rotting down in the water under that pier. Coming out of his cabin in the sunlight and looking along that soft blue water and seeing in his mind what was under it and what was happening to it. And knowing he put it there.'

'No more can I,' Birdie Keppel said softly. 'No more could anybody. And yet we know in our minds that such things have happened and will happen again. Are you in the real-estate business, Mr Marlowe?'

'No.'

'What line of business are you in, if I may ask?'

'I'd rather not say.'

'That's almost as good as saying,' she said. 'Besides Doc Hollis heard you tell Jim Patton your full name. And we have an LA city directory in our office. I haven't mentioned it to anyone.'

'That's nice of you,' I said.

'And what's more, I won't,' she said. 'If you don't want me to.'

'What does it cost me?'

'Nothing,' she said. 'Nothing at all. I don't claim to be a very good newspaper man. And we wouldn't print anything that would embarrass Jim Patton. Jim's the salt of the earth. But it does open up, doesn't it?'

'Don't draw any wrong conclusions,' I said. 'I had no interest in Bill Chess whatever.'

'No interest in Muriel Chess?'

'Why should I have any interest in Muriel Chess?'

She snuffed her cigarette out carefully into the ash-tray under the dashboard. 'Have it your own way,' she said. 'But here's a little item you might like to think about, if you don't know it already. There was a Los Angeles copper named De Soto up here about six weeks back, a big roughneck with damn poor manners. We didn't like him and we didn't open up to him much. I mean the three of us in the *Banner* office didn't. He had a photograph with him and he was looking for a woman called Mildred Haviland, he said. On police business. It was an ordinary photograph, an enlarged snapshot, not a police photo. He said he had information the woman was staying up here. The photo looked a good deal like Muriel Chess. The hair seemed to be reddish and in a very different style than she has worn it here, and the eyebrows were all plucked to narrow arches, and that changes a woman a good deal. But it did look a good deal like Bill Chess's wife.'

I drummed on the door of the car and after a moment I said: 'What did you tell him?'

'We didn't tell him anything. First off, we couldn't be sure. Second, we didn't like his manner. Third, even if we had been sure and had liked his manner, we likely would not have sicked him on to her. Why would we? Everybody's done something to be sorry for. Take me. I was married once – to a professor of classical languages at Redlands University.' She laughed lightly.

'You might have got yourself a story,' I said.

'Sure. But up here we're just people.'

'Did this man De Soto see Jim Patton?'

'Sure, he must have. Jim didn't mention it.'

'Did he show you his badge?'

She thought and then shook her head. 'I don't recall that he did. We just took him for granted, from what he said. He certainly acted like a tough city cop.'

'To me that's a little against his being one. Did anyone tell Muriel about this guy?'

She hesitated, looking quietly out through the windshield for a long moment before she turned her head and nodded,

'I did. Wasn't any of my damn business, was it?'

'What did she say?'

'She didn't say anything. She gave a funny little embarrassed laugh, as if I had been making a bad joke. Then she walked away. But I did get the impression that there was a queer look in her eyes, just for an instant. You still not interested in Muriel Chess, Mr Marlowe?'

'Why should I be? I never heard of her until I came up here this afternoon. Honest. And I never heard of anybody called Mildred Haviland either. Drive you back to town?'

'Oh no, thanks. I'll walk. It's only a few steps. Much obliged to you. I kind of hope Bill doesn't get into a jam. Especially a nasty jam like this.'

She got out of the car and hung on one foot, then tossed her head and laughed. 'They say I'm a pretty good beauty operator,' she said. 'I hope I am. As an interviewer I'm terrible. Good night.'

I said good night and she walked off into the evening. I sat there watching her until she reached the main street and turned out of sight. Then I got out of the Chrysler and went over towards the telephone company's little rustic building.

10

A tame doe deer with a leather dog collar on wandered across the road in front of me. I patted her rough hairy neck and went into the telephone office. A small girl in slacks sat at a small desk working on the books. She got me the rate to Beverly Hills and the change for the coin box. The booth was outside, against the front wall of the building.

'I hope you like it up here,' she said. 'It's very quiet, very restful.'

I shut myself into the booth. For ninety cents I could talk to Derace Kingsley for five minutes. He was at home and the call came through quickly, but the connection was full of mountain static.

'Find anything up there?' he asked me in a three-highball voice. He sounded tough and confident again.

'I've found too much,' I said. 'And not at all what we want. Are you alone?'

'What does that matter?'

'It doesn't matter to me. But I know what I'm going to say. You don't.'

'Well, get on with it, whatever it is,' he said.

'I had a long talk with Bill Chess. He was lonely. His wife had left him – a month ago. They had a fight and he went out and got drunk and when he came back she was gone. She left a note saying she would rather be dead than live with him any more.'

'I guess Bill drinks too much,' Kingsley's voice said from very far off.

'When he got back, both the women had gone. He has no idea where Mrs Kingsley went. Lavery was up here in May, but not since. Lavery admitted that much himself. Lavery could, of course, have come up again while Bill was out getting drunk, but there wouldn't be a lot of point to that and there would be two cars to drive down the hill. And I thought that possibly Mrs K. and Muriel Chess might have gone away together, only Muriel also had a car of her own. But that idea, little as it was worth, has been thrown out by another development, Muriel Chess didn't go away at all. She went down into your little private lake. She came back up today. I was there.'

'Good God!' Kingsley sounded properly horrified. 'You mean she drowned herself?'

'Perhaps. The note she left could be a suicide note. It would read as well that way as the other. The body was stuck down under that old submerged landing below the pier. Bill was the one who spotted an arm moving down there while we were standing on the pier looking down into the water. He got her out. They've arrested him. The poor guy's pretty badly broken up.'

'Good God!' Kingsley said again. 'I should think he would be. Does it look as if he –' He paused as the operator came in on the line and demanded another forty-five cents. I put in two quarters and the little line cleared.

'Look as if he what?'

Suddenly very clear, Kingsley's voice said: 'Look as if he murdered her?'

I said: 'Very much. Jim Patton, the constable up here, doesn't like the note not being dated. It seems she left him once before over some woman. Patton of course suspects Bill might have saved up an old note. Anyhow they've taken Bill down to San Bernadino for questioning and they've taken the body down to be post-mortemed.'

'And what do you think?' he asked slowly.

'Well, Bill found the body himself. He didn't have to take me around by that pier. She might have stayed down in the water very much longer, or for ever. The note could be old because Bill had carried it in his wallet and handled it from time to time, brooding over it. It could just as easily be undated this time as another time. I'd say notes like that are undated more often than not. The people who write them are apt to be in a hurry and not concerned with dates.'

'The body must be pretty far gone. What can they find out now?'

'I don't know how well equipped they are. They can find out if she died by drowning. I guess. And whether there are any marks of violence that wouldn't be erased by water and decomposition. They could tell if she had been shot or stabbed. If the hyoid bone in the throat was broken, they could assume she was throttled. The main thing for us is that I'll have to tell why I came up here. I'll have to testify at an inquest.'

'That's bad,' Kingsley growled. 'Very bad. What do you plan to do now?'

'On my way home I'll stop at the Prescott Hotel and see if I can pick up anything there. Were your wife and Muriel Chess friendly?'

'I guess so. Crystal's easy enough to get along with most of the time. I hardly knew Muriel Chess.'

'Did you ever know anybody named Mildred Haviland?'

'What?'

I repeated the name.

'No,' he said. 'Is there any reason why I should?'

'Every question I ask you ask another right back,' I said. 'No, there isn't any reason why you should know Mildred Haviland. Especially if you hardly knew Muriel Chess. I'll call you in the morning.'

'Do that,' he said, and hesitated. 'I'm sorry you had to work into such a mess,' he added and then hesitated again and said good night and hung up.

The bell rang again immediately and the long-distance operator told me sharply I had put in five cents too much money. I said the sort of thing I would be likely to put into an opening like that. She didn't like it.

I stepped out of the booth and gathered some air into my lungs. The tame doe with the leather collar was standing in the gap in the fence at the end of the walk. I tried to push her out of the way, but she just leaned against me and wouldn't push. So I stepped over the fence and went back to the Chrysler and drove back to the village.

There was a hanging light in Patton's headquarters but the shack was empty and his 'Back in Twenty Minutes' sign was still against the inside of the glass part of the door. I kept on going down to the boat landing and beyond to the edge of a deserted swimming-beach. A few put-puts and speedboats were still fooling around on the silky water. Across the lake tiny yellow lights began to show in toy cabins perched on miniature slopes. A single bright star glowed low in the north-east above the ridge of mountains. A robin sat on the spike top of a hundred-foot pine and waited for it to be dark enough for him to sing his good night song.

In a little while it was dark enough and he sang and went away into the invisible depths of sky. I snapped my cigarette into the motionless water a few feet away and climbed back into the car and started back in the direction of Little Fawn Lake.

11

The gate across the private road was padlocked. I put the Chrysler between two pine-trees and climbed the gate and pussy-footed along the side of the road until the glimmer of the little lake bloomed suddenly at my feet. Bill Chess's cabin was dark. The three cabins on the other side were abrupt shadows against the pale granite outcrop. Water gleamed white where it trickled across the top of the dam, and fell almost soundlessly along the sloping outer face to the brook below. I listened and heard no other sound at all.

The front door of the Chess cabin was locked. I padded along to the back and found a brute of a padlock hanging at that. I went along the walls feeling window screens. They were all fastened. One window higher up was screenless, a small double cottage window half-way down the north wall. This was locked too. I stood still and did some more listening. There was no breeze and the trees were as quiet as their shadows.

I tried a knife blade between the two halves of the small window. No soap. The catch refused to budge. I leaned against the wall and thought and then suddenly I picked up a large stone and smacked it against the place where the two frames met in the middle. The catch pulled out of dry wood with a tearing noise. The window swung back into darkness. I heaved up on the sill and wangled a cramped leg over and edged through the opening. I rolled and let myself down into the room. I turned, grunting a little from the exertion at that altitude, and listened again.

A blazing flash beam hit me square in the eyes.

A very calm voice said: 'I'd rest right there, son. You must be all tuckered out.'

The flash pinned me against the wall like a squashed fly. Then a light switch clicked and a table lamp glowed. The flash went out. Jim Patton was sitting in an old brown Morris chair beside the table. A fringed brown scarf hung over the end of the table and touched his thick knee. He wore the same clothes he had worn that afternoon, with the addition of a leather jerkin which must have been new once, say about the time of Grover Cleveland's first term. His hands were empty except for the flash. His eyes were empty. His jaws moved in gentle rhythm.

'What's on your mind, son – besides breaking and entering?'

I poked a chair out and straddled it and leaned my arms on the back and looked around the cabin.

'I had an idea,' I said. 'It looked pretty good for a while, but I guess I can learn to forget it.'

The cabin was larger than it had seemed from the outside. The part I was in was the living-room. It contained a few articles of modest furniture, a rag rug on the pineboard floor, a round table against the end wall and two chairs set against it. Through an open door the corner of a big black cookstove showed.

Patton nodded and his eyes studied me without rancour. 'I heard a car coming,' he said. 'I knew it had to be coming here. You walk right nice though. I didn't hear you walk worth a darn. I've been a mite curious about you, son.'

I said nothing.

'I hope you don't mind me callin' you "son",' he said. 'I hadn't ought to be so familiar, but I got myself into the habit and I can't seem to shake it. Anybody that don't have a long white beard and arthritis is "son" to me.'

I said he could call me anything that came to mind. I wasn't sensitive.

He grinned. 'There's a mess of detectives in the LA phone book,' he said. 'But only one of them is called Marlowe.'

'What made you look?'

'I guess you might call it lowdown curiosity. Added to which Bill Chess told me you was some sort of dick. You didn't bother to tell me yourself.'

'I'd have got around to it,' I said. 'I'm sorry it bothered you.'

'It didn't bother me none. I don't bother at all easy. You got any identification with you?'

I got my wallet out and showed him this and that.

'Well, you got a good build on you for the work,' he said satisfied. 'And your face don't tell a lot of stories. I guess you was aiming to search the cabin.'

'Yeah.'

'I already pawed around considerable myself. Just got back and come straight here. That is, I stopped by my shack a minute and then come. I don't figure I could let you search the place, though.' He scratched his ear. 'That is, dum if I know whether I could or not. You telling who hired you?'

'Derace Kingsley. To trace his wife. She skipped out on him a month ago. She started from here. So I started from here. She's supposed to have gone away with a man. The man denies it. I thought maybe something up here might give me a lead.'

'And did anything?'

'No. She's traced pretty definitely as far as San Bernadino and then El Paso. There the trail ends. But I've only just started.'

Patton stood up and unlocked the cabin door. The spicy smell of the pines surged in. He spat outdoors and sat down again and rumpled the mousy brown hair under his Stetson. His head with the hat off had the indecent look of heads that are seldom without hats.

'You didn't have no interest in Bill Chess at all?'

'None whatever.'

'I guess you fellows do a lot of divorce business,' he said. 'Kind of smelly work, to my notion.'

I let that ride.

'Kingsley wouldn't have asked help from the police to find his wife, would he?'

'Hardly,' I said. 'He knows her too well.'

'None of what you've been saying don't hardly explain your wanting to search Bill's cabin,' he said judiciously.

'I'm just a great guy to poke around.'

'Hell,' he said, 'you can do better than that.'

'Say I am interested in Bill Chess then. But only because he's in trouble and rather a pathetic case – in spite of being a good deal of a heel. If he murdered his wife, there's something here to point that way. If he didn't, there's something to point that way too.'

He held his head sideways, like a watchful bird. 'As for instance what kind of thing?'

'Clothes, personal jewellery, toilet articles, whatever a woman takes with her when she goes away, not intending to come back.'

He leaned back slowly. 'But she didn't go away, son.'

'Then the stuff should be still here. But if it was still there, Bill would have noticed she hadn't taken it. He would know she hadn't gone away.'

'By gum, I don't like it either way,' he said.

'But if he murdered her,' I said, 'then he would have to get rid of the things she ought to have taken with her, if she had gone away.'

'And how do you figure he would do that, son?' The yellow lamplight made bronze of one side of his face.

'I understand she had a Ford car of her own. Except for that I'd expect him to burn what he could burn and bury what he could not burn out in the woods. Sinking it in the lake might be dangerous. But he couldn't burn or bury her car. Could he drive it?'

Patton looked surprised. 'Sure. He can't bend his right leg at the knee, so he couldn't use the footbrake very handy. But he could get by with the handbrake. All that's different on Bill's own Ford is the brake pedal is set over on the left side of the post, close to the clutch, so he can shove them both down with one foot.'

I shook ash from my cigarette into a small blue jar that had once contained a pound of orange honey, according to the small gilt label on it.

'Getting rid of the car would be his big problem,' I said. 'Wherever he took it he would have to get back, and he would rather not be seen coming back. And if he simply abandoned it on a street, say, down in San Bernadino, it would be found and identified very quickly. He wouldn't want that either. The best stunt would be to unload it on a hot car dealer, but he probably doesn't know one. So the chances are he hid it in the woods within walking distance of here. And walking distance for him would not be very far.'

'For a fellow that claims not to be interested, you're doing some pretty close figuring on all this,' Patton said dryly. 'So now you've got the car hid in the woods. What then?'

'He has to consider the possibility of its being found. The woods are lonely, but rangers and woodcutters get around in them from time to time. If the car is found, it would be better for Muriel's stuff to be found in it. That would give him a couple of outs – neither one very brilliant but both at least possible. One, that she was murdered by some unknown party who fixed things to implicate Bill when and if the murder was discovered. Two, that Muriel did actually commit suicide, but fixed things so that he would be blamed. A revenge suicide.'

Patton thought all this over with calm and care. He went to the door to unload again. He sat down and rumpled his hair again. He looked at me with solid scepticism.

'The first one's possible like you say,' he admitted. 'But only just, and I don't have anybody in mind for the job. There's that little matter of the note to be got over.'

I shook my head, 'Say Billy already had the note from another time. Say she went away, as he thought, without leaving a note. After a month had gone by without any word from her he might be just worried and uncertain enough to show the note, feeling it might be some protection to him in case anything had happened to her. He didn't say any of this, but he could have had it in his mind.'

Patton shook his head. He didn't like it. Neither did I. He said slowly: 'As to your other notion, it's just plain crazy. Killing yourself and fixing things so as somebody else would get accused of murdering you don't fit in with my simple ideas of human nature at all.'

'Then your ideas of human nature are too simple,' I said. 'Because it has been done, and when it has been done, it has nearly always been done by a woman.'

'Nope,' he said, 'I'm a man fifty-seven years old and I've seen a lot of crazy people, but I don't go for that worth a peanut shell. What I like is that she did plan to go away and did write the note, but he caught her before she got clear and saw red and finished her off. Then he would have to do all them things we been talking about.'

'I never met her,' I said. 'So I wouldn't have any idea what she would be likely to do. Bill said he met her in a place in Riverside something over a year ago. She may have had a long and complicated history before that. What kind of girl was she?'

'A mighty cute little blonde when she fixed herself up. She kind of let herself go with Bill. A quiet girl, with a face that kept its secrets. Bill says she had a temper, but I never seen any of it. I seen plenty of nasty tempers in him.'

'And did you think she looked like the photo of somebody called Mildred Haviland?'

His jaws stopped munching and his mouth became almost primly tight. Very slowly he started chewing again.

'By gum,' he said, 'I'll be mighty careful to look under the bed before I crawl in tonight. To make sure you ain't there. Where did you get that information?'

'A nice little girl called Birdie Keppel told me. She was interviewing me in the course of her spare-time newspaper job. She happened to mention that an LA cop named De Soto was showing the photo around.'

Patton smacked his thick knee and hunched his shoulders forward.

'I done wrong there,' he said soberly, 'I made one of my mistakes. This big bruiser showed his picture to darn near everybody in town before he showed it to me. That made me kind of sore. It looked some like Muriel, but not enough to be sure by any manner of means. I asked him what she was wanted for. He said it was police business. I said I was in that way of business myself, in an ignorant countrified kind of way. He said his instructions were to locate the lady and that was all he knew. Maybe he did wrong to take me up short like that. So I guess I done wrong to tell him I didn't know anybody that looked like his little picture.'

The big calm man smiled vaguely at the corner of the ceiling, then brought his eyes down and looked at me steadily.

'I'll thank you to respect this confidence, Mr Marlowe. You done right nicely in your figuring too. You ever happen to go over to Coon Lake?'

'Never heard of it.'

'Back about a mile,' he said pointing over his shoulder with a thumb, 'there's a little narrow wood road turns over west. You can just drive in and miss the trees. It climbs about five hundred feet in another mile and comes out by Coon Lake. Pretty little place. Folks go up there to picnic once in a while, but not often. It's hard on tyres. There's two three small shallow lakes full of reeds. There's snow up there even now in the shady places. There's a bunch of old hand-hewn log cabins that's been falling down ever since I recall, and there's a big broken-down frame building that Montclair University used to use for a summer camp maybe ten years back. They ain't used it in a very long time. This building sits back from the lakes in heavy timber. Round at the back of it there's a warehouse with an old rusty boiler and along of that there's a big woodshed with a sliding door hung on rollers. It was built for a garage but they kept their wood in it and they locked it up out of season. Wood's one of the few things people will steal up here, but folks who might steal it off a pile wouldn't break a lock to get it. I guess you know what I found in that woodshed.'

'I thought you went down to San Bernadino.'

'Changed my mind. Didn't seem right to let Bill ride down there with his wife's body in the back of the car. So I sent it down in Doc's ambulance and I sent Andy down with Bill. I figured I kind of ought to look around a little more before I put things up to the sheriff and the coroner.'

'Muriel's car was in the woodshed?'

'Yep. And two unlocked suitcases in the car. Packed with clothes and packed kind of hasty, I thought. Women's clothes. The point is, son, no stranger would have known about that place.'

I agreed with him. He put his hand in the slanting side pocket of his jerkin and brought out a small twist of tissue paper. He opened it up on his palm and held the hand out flat.

'Take a look at this.'

I went over and looked. What lay on the tissue was a thin gold chain with a tiny lock hardly larger than a link of the chain. The gold had been snipped through, leaving the lock intact. The chain seemed to be about seven inches long. There was white powder sticking to both chain and paper.

'Where would you guess I found that?' Patton asked.

I picked the chain up and tried to fit the cut ends together. They didn't fit. I made no comment on that, but moistened a finger and touched the powder and tasted it.

'In a can or box of confectioner's sugar,' I said. 'The chain is an anklet. Some women never take them off, like wedding rings. Whoever took this one off didn't have the key.'

'What do you make of it?'

'Nothing much,' I said. 'There wouldn't be any point in Bill cutting it off Muriel's ankle and leaving that green necklace on her neck. There wouldn't be any point in Muriel cutting it off herself – assuming she had lost the key – and hiding it to be found. A search thorough enough to find it wouldn't be made unless her body was found first. If Bill cut it off, he would have thrown it into the lake. But if Muriel wanted to keep it and yet hide it from Bill, there's some sense in the place where it was hidden.'

Patton looked puzzled this time. 'Why is that?'

'Because it's a woman's hiding-place. Confectioner's sugar is used to make cake icing. A man would never look there. Pretty clever of you to find it, sheriff.'

He grinned a little sheepishly. 'Hell, I knocked the box over and some of the sugar spilled,' he said. 'Without that I don't guess I ever would have found it.' He rolled the paper up again and slipped it back into his pocket. He stood up with an air of finality.

'You staying up here or going back to town, Mr Marlowe?'

'Back to town. Until you want me for the inquest. I suppose you will.'

'That's up to the coroner, of course. If you'll kind of shut that window you bust in, I'll put this lamp out and lock up.'

I did what he said and he snapped his flash on and put out the lamp. We went out and he felt the cabin door to make sure the lock had caught. He closed the screen softly and stood looking across the moonlit lake.

'I don't figure Bill meant to kill her,' he said sadly. 'He could choke a girl to death without meaning to at all. He has mighty strong hands. Once done he has to use what brains God gave him to cover up what he done. I feel real bad about it, but that don't alter the facts and the probabilities. It's simple and natural and the simple and natural things usually turn out to be right.'

I said: 'I should think he would have run away. I don't see how he could stand it to stay here.'

Patton spat into the black velvet shadow of a manzanita bush. He said slowly: 'He had a government pension and he would have to run away from that too. And most men can stand what they've got to stand, when it steps up and looks them straight in the eye. Like they're doing all over the world right now. Well, good night to you. I'm going to walk down to that little pier again and stand there awhile in the moonlight and feel bad. A night like this, and we got to think about murders.'

He moved quietly off into the shadows and became one of them himself. I stood there until he was out of sight and then went back to the locked gate and climbed over it. I got into the car and drove back down the road looking for a place to hide.

12

Three hundred yards from the gate a narrow track, sifted over with brown oak leaves from last autumn, curved around a granite boulder and disappeared. I followed it around and bumped along the stones of the outcrop for fifty or sixty feet, then swung the car around a tree and set it pointing back the way it had come. I cut the lights and switched off the motor and sat there waiting.

Half an hour passed. Without tobacco it seemed a long time. Then far off I heard a car motor start up and grow louder and the white beam of headlights passed below me on the road. The sound faded into the distance and a faint dry tang of dust hung in the air for a while after it was gone.

I got out of my car and walked back to the gate and to the Chess cabin. A hard push opened the sprung window this time. I climbed in again and let myself down to the floor and poked the flash I had brought across the room to the table lamp. I switched the lamp on and listened a moment, heard nothing and went out to the kitchen. I switched on a hanging bulb over the sink.

The wood-box beside the stove was neatly piled with split wood. There were no dirty dishes in the sink, no foul-smelling pots on the stove. Bill Chess, lonely or not, kept his house in good order. A door opened from the kitchen into the bedroom, and from that very narrow door led into a tiny bathroom which had evidently been built on to a cabin fairly recently. The clean celotex lining showed that. The bathroom told me nothing.

The bedroom contained a double bed, a pinewood dresser with a round mirror on the wall above it, a bureau, two straight chairs and a tin waste basket. There were two oval rag rugs on the floor, one on each side of the bed. On the walls Bill Chess had tacked up a set of war maps from the National Geographic. There was a silly-looking red-and-white flounce on the dressing table.

I poked around in the drawers. An imitation leather trinket box with an assortment of gaudy costume jewellery had not been taken away. There was the usual stuff women use on their faces and fingernails and eyebrows, and it seemed to me that there was too much of it. But that was just guessing. The bureau contained both man's and woman's clothes, not a great deal of either. Bill Chess had a very noisy check shirt with starched matching collar, among other things. Underneath a sheet of blue tissue paper in one corner I found something I didn't like. A seemingly brand-new peach-coloured silk slip trimmed with lace. Silk slips were not being left behind that year, not by any woman in her senses.

This looked bad for Bill Chess. I wondered what Patton had thought of it.

I went back to the kitchen and prowled the open shelves above and beside the sink. They were thick with cans and jars of household staples. The confectioner's sugar was in a square brown box with a torn corner. Patton had made an attempt to clean up what he had spilled. Near the sugar were salt, borax, baking-soda, cornstarch, brown sugar and so on. Something might be hidden in any of them.

Something that had been clipped from a chain anklet whose cut ends did not fit together.

I shut my eyes and poked a finger out at random and it came to rest on the baking-soda. I got a newspaper from the back of the woodbox and spread it out and dumped the soda out of the box. I stirred it around with a spoon. There seemed to be an indecent lot of baking-soda, but that was all there was. I funnelled it back into the box and tried the borax. Nothing but borax. Third time lucky. I tried the cornstarch. It made too much fine dust, and there was nothing but cornstarch.

The sound of distant steps froze me to the ankles. I reached up and yanked the light out and dodged back into the living-room and reached for the lamp switch. Much too late to be of any use, of course. The steps sounded again, soft and cautious. The hackles rose on my neck.

I waited in the dark, with the flash in my left hand. A deadly long two minutes crept by. I spent some of the time breathing, but not all.

It wouldn't be Patton. He would walk up to the door and open it and tell me off. The careful quiet steps seemed to move this way and that, a movement, a long pause, another movement, another long pause. I sneaked across to the door and twisted the knob silently. I yanked the door wide and stabbed out with the flash.

It made golden lamps of a pair of eyes. There was a leaping movement and a quick thudding of hoofs back among the trees. It was only an inquisitive deer.

I closed the door again and followed my flashlight beam back into the kitchen. The small round glow rested squarely on the box of confectioner's sugar.

I put the light on again, lifted the box down and emptied it on the newspaper.

Patton hadn't gone deep enough. Having found one thing by accident he had assumed that was all there was. He hadn't seemed to notice that there ought to be something else.

Another twist of white tissue showed in the fine white powdered sugar. I shook it clean and unwound it. It contained a tiny gold heart, no larger than a woman's little fingernail.

I spooned the sugar back into the box and put the box back on the shelf and crumpled the piece of newspaper into the stove. I went back to the living-room and turned the table lamp on. Under that brighter light the tiny engraving on the back of the gold heart could just be read without a magnifying glass.

It was in script. It read: 'Al to Mildred. June 28th, 1938. With all my love.'

Al to Mildred. Al somebody to Mildred Haviland. Mildred Haviland was Muriel Chess. Muriel Chess was dead – two weeks after a cop named De Soto had been looking for her.

I stood there, holding it, wondering what it had to do with me. Wondering, and not having the faintest glimmer of an idea.

I wrapped it up again and left the cabin and drove back to the village.

Patton was in his office telephoning when I got around there. The door was locked. I had to wait while he talked. After a while he hung up and came to unlock the door.

I walked in past him and put the twist of tissue paper on his counter and opened it up.

'You didn't go deep enough into the powdered sugar,' I said.

He looked at the little gold heart, looked at me, went around behind the counter and got a cheap magnifying glass off his desk. He studied the back of the heart. He put the glass down and frowned at me.

'Might have known if you wanted to search that cabin, you was going to do it,' he said gruffly. 'I ain't going to have trouble with you, am I, son.'

'You ought to have noticed that the cut ends of the chain didn't fit,' I told him.

He looked at me sadly. 'Son, I don't have your eyes.' He pushed the little heart around with his square blunt finger. He stared at me and said nothing.

I said: 'If you were thinking that anklet meant something Bill could have been jealous about, so was I – provided he ever saw it. But strictly on the cuff I'm willing to bet he never did see it and that he never heard of Mildred Haviland.'

Patton said slowly: 'Looks like maybe I owe this De Soto party an apology, don't it?'

'If you ever see him,' I said.

He gave me another long empty stare and I gave it right back to him. 'Don't tell me, son,' he said. 'Let me guess all for myself that you got a brand-new idea about it.'

'Yeah. Bill didn't murder his wife.'

'No?'

'No. She was murdered by somebody out of her past. Somebody who had lost track of her and then found it again and found her married to another man and didn't like it. Somebody who knew the country up here – as hundreds of people do who don't live here – and knew a good place to hide the car and the clothes. Somebody who hated and could dissimulate. Who persuaded her to go away with him and when everything was ready and the note was written, took her around the throat and gave her what he thought was coming to her and put her in the lake and went his way. Like it?'

'Well,' he said judiciously, 'it does make things kind of complicated, don't you think? But there ain't anything impossible about it. Not one bit impossible.'

'When you get tired of it, let me know. I'll have something else,' I said.

'I'll just be doggone sure you will,' he said, and for the first time since I had met him he laughed.

I said good night again and went out, leaving him there moving his mind around with the ponderous energy of a homesteader digging up a stump.

13

At somewhere around eleven I got down to the bottom of the grade and parked in one of the diagonal slots at the side of the Prescott Hotel in San Bernadino. I pulled an overnight bag out of the boot and had taken three steps with it when a bellhop in braided pants and a white shirt and black bow tie yanked it out of my hand.

The clerk on duty was an egg-headed man with no interest in me or in anything else. He wore parts of a white linen suit and he yawned as he handed me the desk pen and looked off into the distance as if remembering his childhood.

The hop and I rode a four by four elevator to the second floor and walked a couple of blocks around corners. As we walked it got hotter and hotter. The hop unlocked a door into a boy's size room with one window on an air-shaft. The air conditioner inlet up in the corner of the ceiling was about the size of a woman's handkerchief. The bit of ribbon tied to it fluttered weakly, just to show that something was moving.

The hop was tall and thin and yellow and not young and as cool as a slice of chicken in aspic. He moved his gum around in his face, put my bag on a chair, looked up at the grating and then stood looking at me. He had eyes the colour of a drink of water.

'Maybe I ought to have asked for one of the dollar rooms,' I said. 'This one seems a mite close-fitting.'

'I reckon you're lucky to get one at all. This town's fair bulgin' at the seams.'

'Bring us up some ginger ale and glasses and ice,' I said.

'Us?'

'That is, if you happen to be a drinking man.'

'I reckon I might take a chance this late.'

He went out. I took off my coat, tie, shirt and undershirt and walked around in the warm draught from the open door. The draught smelled of hot iron. I went into the bathroom sideways – it was that kind of bathroom – and doused myself with tepid cold water. I was breathing a little more freely when the tall languid hop returned with a tray. He shut the door and I brought out a bottle of rye. He mixed a couple of drinks and we made the usual insincere smiles over them and drank. The perspiration started from the back of my neck down my spine and was half-way to my socks before I put the glass down. But I felt better all the same. I sat on the bed and looked at the hop.

'How long can you stay?'

'Doin' what?'

'Remembering.'

'I ain't a damn bit of use at it,' he said.

'I have money to spend,' I said, 'in my own peculiar way.' I got my wallet unstuck from the lower part of my back and spread tired-looking dollar bills along the bed.

'I beg yore pardon,' the hop said, 'I reckon you might be a dick.'

'Don't be silly,' I said. 'You never saw a dick playing solitaire with his own money. You might call me an investigator.'

'I'm interested,' he said. 'The likker makes my mind work.'

I gave him a dollar bill. 'Try that on your mind. And can I call you Big Tex from Houston?'

'Amarillo,' he said. 'Not that it matters. And how do you like my Texas drawl? It makes me sick, but I find people go for it.'

'Stay with it,' I said. 'It never lost anybody a dollar yet.'

He grinned and tucked the folded dollar neatly into the watch pocket of his pants.

'What were you doing on Friday, June 12th?' I asked him. 'Late afternoon or evening. It was a Friday.'

He sipped his drink and thought, shaking the ice around gently and drinking past his gum. 'I was right here, six to twelve shift,' he said.

'A woman, slim, pretty blonde, checked in here and stayed until time for the night train to El Paso. I think she must have taken that because she was in El Paso Sunday morning. She came here driving a Packard Clipper registered to Crystal Grace Kingsley, 965 Carson Drive, Beverly Hills. She may have registered as that, or under some other name, and she may not have registered at all. Her car is still in the hotel garage. I'd like to talk to the boys that checked her in and out. That wins another dollar – just thinking about it.'

I separated another dollar from my exhibit and it went into his pocket with a sound like caterpillars fighting.

'Can do,' he said calmly.

He put his glass down and left the room, closing the door. I finished my drink and made another. I went into the bathroom and used some more warm water on my torso. While I was doing this the telephone on the wall tinkled and I wedged myself into the minute space between the bathroom door and the bed to answer it.

The Texas voice said: 'That was Sonny. He was inducted last week. Another boy called Les checked her out. He's here.'

'Okay. Shoot him up, will you?'

I was playing with my second drink and thinking about the third when a knock came and I opened the door to a small, green-eyed rat with a tight, girlish mouth.

He came in almost dancing and stood looking at me with a faint sneer.

'Drink?'

'Sure,' he said coldly. He poured himself a large one, and added a whisper of ginger ale, put the mixture down in one long swallow, tucked a cigarette between his smooth little lips and snapped a match alight while it was coming up from his pocket. He blew smoke and went on staring at me. The corner of his eye caught the money on the bed without looking directly at it. Over the pocket of his shirt, instead of a number, the word *Captain* was stitched.

'You Les?' I asked him.

'No.' He paused. 'We don't like dicks here,' he added. 'We don't have one of our own and we don't care to bother with dicks that are working for other people.'

'Thanks,' I said. 'That will be all.'

'Huh?' The small mouth twisted unpleasantly,

'Beat it,' I said.

'I thought you wanted to see me,' he sneered,

'You're the bell captain?'

'Check.'

'I wanted to buy you a drink. I wanted to give you a buck. Here.' I held it out to him. 'Thanks for coming up.'

He took the dollar and pocketed it, without a word of thanks. He hung there, smoke trailing from his nose, his eyes tight and mean.

'What I say here goes,' he said.

'It goes as far as you can push it,' I said. 'And that couldn't be very far. You had your drink and you had your graft. Now you can scram out.'

He turned with a swift tight shrug and slipped out of the room noiselessly.

Four minutes passed, then another knock, very light. The tall boy came in grinning. I walked away from him and sat on the bed again.

'You didn't take to Les, I reckon?'

'Not a great deal. Is he satisfied?'

'I reckon so. You know what captains are. They have to have their cut. Maybe you better call me Les, Mr Marlowe.'

'So you checked her out.'

'No, that was all a stall. She never checked in at the desk. But I remember the Packard. She gave me a dollar to put it away for her and to look after her stuff until train time. She ate dinner here. A dollar gets you remembered in this town. And there's been talk about the car bein' left so long.'

'What was she like to look at?'

'She wore a black and white outfit, mostly white, and a panama hat with a black and white band. She was a neat blonde lady like you said. Later on she took a hack to the station. I put her bags into it for her. They had initials on them but I'm sorry I can't remember the initials.'

'I'm glad you can't,' I said. 'It would be too good. Have a drink. How old would she be?'

He rinsed the other glass and mixed a civilized drink for himself.

'It's mighty hard to tell a woman's age these days,' he said. 'I reckon she was about thirty, or a little more or a little less.'

I dug in my coat for the snapshot of Crystal and Lavery on the beach and handed it to him.

He looked at it steadily and held it away from his eyes, then close.

'You won't have to swear to it in court,' I said.

He nodded. 'I wouldn't want to. These small blondes are so much of a pattern that a change of clothes or light or make-up makes them all alike or all different.' He hesitated, staring at the snapshot.

'What's worrying you?' I asked.

'I'm thinking about the gent in this snap. He enter into it at all?'

'Go on with that,' I said.

'I think this fellow spoke to her in the lobby, and had dinner with her. A tall good-lookin' jasper, built like a fast light-heavy. He went in the hack with her too.'

'Quite sure about that?'

He looked at the money on the bed.

'Okay, how much does it cost?' I asked wearily.

He stiffened, laid the snapshot down and drew the two folded bills from his pocket and tossed them on the bed.

'I thank you for the drink,' he said, 'and to hell with you.' He started for the door.

'Oh sit down and don't be so touchy,' I growled.

He sat down and looked at me stiff-eyed.

'And don't be so damn southern,' I said. 'I've been knee-deep

262

in hotel hops for a lot of years. If I've met one who wouldn't pull a gag, that's fine. But you can't expect me to expect to meet one that wouldn't pull a gag.'

He grinned slowly and nodded quickly. He picked the snapshot up again and looked at me over it.

'This gent takes a solid photo,' he said. 'Much more so than the lady. But there was another little item that made me remember him. I got the impression the lady didn't quite like him walking up to her so openly in the lobby.'

I thought that over and decided it didn't mean anything much. He might have been late or have missed some earlier appointment. I said:

'There's a reason for that. Did you notice what jewellery the lady was wearing? Rings, ear-pendants, anything that looked conspicious or valuable?'

He hadn't noticed, he said.

'Was her hair long or short, straight or waved or curly, natural blonde or bleached?'

He laughed. 'Hell, you can't tell that last point, Mr Marlowe. Even when it's natural they want it lighter. As to the rest, my recollection is it was rather long, like they're wearing it now and turned in a little at the bottom and rather straight. But I could be wrong.' He looked at the snapshot again. 'She has it bound back here. You can't tell a thing.'

'That's right,' I said. 'And the only reason I asked you was to make sure that you didn't over-observe. The guy that sees too much detail is just as unreliable a witness as the guy that doesn't see any. He's nearly always making half of it up. You check just about right, considering the circumstances. Thanks very much.'

I gave him back his two dollars and a five to keep them company. He thanked me, finished his drink and left softly. I finished mine and washed off again and decided I would rather drive home than sleep in that hole. I put my shirt and coat on again and went downstairs with my bag.

The redheaded rat of a captain was the only hop in the lobby. I carried my bag over to the desk and he didn't move to take it off my hands. The eggheaded clerk separated me from two dollars without even looking at me.

'Two bucks to spend the night in this manhole,' I said, 'when for free I could have a nice airy ashcan.'

The clerk yawned, got a delayed reaction and said brightly:

'It gets quite cool here about three in the morning. From then on until eight, or even nine, it's quite pleasant.'

I wiped the back of my neck and staggered out to the car. Even the seat of the car was hot at midnight.

I got home about two-forty-five and Hollywood was an icebox. Even Pasadena had felt cool.

14

I dreamed I was far down in the depths of icy green water with a corpse under my arm. The corpse had long blonde hair that kept floating around in front of my face. An enormous fish with bulging eyes and a bloated body and scales shining with putrescence swam around leering like an elderly roué. Just as I was about to burst from lack of the air, the corpse came alive under my arm and got away from me and then I was fighting with the fish and the corpse was rolling over and over in the water, spinning its long hair.

I woke up with a mouth full of sheet and both hands hooked on the head-frame of the bed and pulling hard. The muscles ached when I let go and lowered them. I got up and walked the room and lit a cigarette, feeling the carpet with bare toes. When I had finished the cigarette, I went back to bed.

It was nine o'clock when I woke up again. The sun was on my face. The room was hot. I showered and shaved and partly dressed and made the morning toast and eggs and coffee in the dinette. While I was finishing up there was a knock at the apartment door.

I went to open it with my mouth full of toast. It was a lean serious-looking man in a severe grey suit.

'Lloyd Greer, lieutenant, Central Detective Bureau,' he said, and walked into the room.

He put out a dry hand and I shook it. He sat down on the edge of a chair, the way they do, and turned his hat in his hands and looked at me with the quiet stare they have.

'We got a call from San Bernadino about that business up at

Puma Lake. Drowned woman. Seems you were on hand when the body was discovered.'

I nodded and said: 'Have some coffee?'

'No thanks. I had breakfast two hours ago.'

I got my coffee and sat down across the room from him.

'They asked us to look you up,' he said. 'Give them a line on you.'

'Sure.'

'So we did that. Seems like you have a clean bill of health so far as we are concerned. Kind of coincidence a man in your line would be around when the body was found.'

'I'm like that,' I said. 'Lucky.'

'So I just thought I'd drop around and say howdy.'

'That's fine. Glad to know you, Lieutenant.'

'Kind of coincidence,' he said again, nodding. 'You up there on business, so to speak?'

'If I was,' I said, 'my business had nothing to do with the girl who was drowned, so far as I know.'

'But you couldn't be sure?'

'Until you've finished with a case, you can't ever be quite sure what its ramifications are, can you?'

'That's right.' He circled his hat brim through his fingers again, like a bashful cowboy. There was nothing bashful about his eyes. 'I'd like to feel sure that if these ramifications you speak of happened to take in this drowned woman's affairs, you would put us wise.'

'I hope you can rely on that,' I said.

He bulged his lower lip with his tongue. 'We'd like a little more than a hope. At the present time you don't care to say?'

'At the present time I don't know anything that Patton doesn't know.'

'Who's he?'

'The constable up at Puma Point.'

The lean serious man smiled tolerantly. He cracked a knuckle and after a pause said: 'The San Berdoo DA will likely want to talk to you – before the inquest. But that won't be very soon. Right now they're trying to get a set of prints. We lent them a technical man.'

'That will be tough. The body's pretty far gone.'

'It's done all the time,' he said. 'They worked out the system back in New York where they're all the time pulling in floaters. They cut patches of skin off the fingers and harden them in a

265

tanning solution and make stamps. It works well enough as a rule.'

'You think this woman had a record of some kind?'

'Why we always take prints of a corpse,' he said. 'You ought to know that.'

I said: 'I didn't know the lady. If you thought I did and that was why I was up there, there's nothing in it.'

'But you wouldn't care to say just why you *were* up there,' he persisted.

'So you think I'm lying to you,' I said.

He spun his hat on a bony forefinger. 'You got me wrong, Mr Marlowe. We don't think anything at all. What we do is investigate and find out. This stuff is just routine. You ought to know that. You been around long enough.' He stood up and put his hat on.'You might let me know if you have to leave town. I'd be obliged.'

I said I would and went to the door with him. He went out with a duck of his head and a sad half-smile. I watched him drift languidly down the hall and punch the elevator button.

I went back out to the dinette to see if there was any more coffee. There was about two-thirds of a cup. I added cream and sugar and carried my cup over to the telephone. I dialled Police Headquarters downtown and asked for the Detective Bureau and then for Lieutenant Floyd Greer.

The voice said: 'Lieutenant Greer is not in the office. Anybody else do?'

'De Soto in?'

'Who?'

I repeated the name.

'What's his rank and department?'

'Plain clothes something or other.'

'Hold the line.'

I waited. The blurring male voice came back after a while and said: 'What's the gag? We don't have a De Soto on the roster. Who's this talking?'

I hung up, finished my coffee and dialled the number of Derace Kingsley's office. The smooth and cool Miss Fromsett said he had just come in and put me through without a murmur.

'Well,' he said, loud and forceful at the beginning of a fresh day, 'what did you find out at the hotel?'

'She was there all right. And Lavery met her there. The hop who gave me the dope brought Lavery into it himself, without

266

any prompting from me. He had dinner with her and went with her in a cab to the railroad station.'

'Well, I ought to have known he was lying,' Kingsley said slowly. 'I got the impresson he was surprised when I told him about the telegram from El Paso. I was just letting my impressions get too sharp. Anything else?'

'Not there. I had a cop calling on me this morning, giving me the usual looking over and warning me not to leave town without letting him know. Trying to find out why I went to Puma Point. I didn't tell him as he wasn't even aware of Jim Patton's existence, it's evident that Patton didn't tell anybody.'.

'Jim would do his best to be decent about it,' Kingsley said. 'Why were you asking me last night about some name – Mildred something or other?'

I told him, making it brief. I told him about Muriel Chess's car and clothes being found and where.

'That looks bad for Bill,' he said. 'I know Coon Lake myself, but it would never have occurred to me to use that old wood shed – or even that there was an old woodshed. It not only looks bad, it looks pre-meditated.'

'I disagree with that. Assuming he knew the country well enough it wouldn't take him any time to search his mind for a likely hiding-place. He was very restricted as to distance.'

'Maybe. What do you plan to do now?' he asked.

'Go up against Lavery again, of course.'

He agreed that that was the thing to do. He added: 'This other, tragic as it is, is really no business of ours, is it?'

'Not unless your wife knew something about it.'

His voice sounded sharply, saying: 'Look here, Marlowe, I think I can understand your detective instinct to tie everything that happens into one compact knot, but don't let it run away with you. Life isn't like that at all – not life as I have known it. Better leave the affairs of the Chess family to the police and keep your brains working on the Kingsley family.'

'Okay,' I said.

'I don't mean to be domineering,' he said.

I laughed heartily, said good-bye, and hung up. I finished dressing and went down to the basement for the Chrysler. I started for Bay City again.

15

I drove past the intersection of Altair Street to where the cross street continued to the edge of the canyon and ended in a semicircular parking place with a sidewalk and a white wooden guard fence around it. I sat there in the car a little while, thinking, looking out to sea and admiring the blue-grey fall of the foothills towards the ocean. I was trying to make up my mind whether to try handling Lavery with a feather or go on using the back of my hand and the edge of my tongue I decided I could lose nothing by the soft approach. If that didn't produce for me – and I didn't think it would – nature could take its course and we could bust up the furniture.

The paved alley that ran along half-way down the hill below the houses on the outer edge was empty. Below that, on the next hillside street, a couple of kids were throwing a boomerang up the slope and chasing it with the usual amount of elbowing and mutual insult. Farther down still a house was enclosed in trees and a red brick wall. There was a glimpse of washing on the line in the backyard and two pigeons strutted along the slope of the roof bobbing their heads. A blue and tan bus trundled along the street in front of the brick house and stopped, and a very old man got off with slow care and settled himself firmly on the ground and tapped with a heavy cane before he started to crawl back up the slope.

The air was clearer than yesterday. The morning was full of peace. I left the car where it was and walked along Altair Street to No. 623.

The venetian blinds were down across the front windows and the place had a sleepy look. I stepped down over the Korean moss and punched the bell and saw that the door was not quite shut. It had dropped in its frame, as most of our doors do, and the spring bolt hung a little on the lower edge of the lock plate. I remembered that it had wanted to stick the day before, when I was leaving.

I gave the door a little push and it moved inward with a light click. The room beyond was dim, but there was some light from west windows. Nobody answered my ring. I didn't ring again. I pushed the door a little wider and stepped inside.

The room had a hushed warm smell, the smell of late morning in a house not yet opened up. The bottle of Vat 69 on the table by the davenport was almost empty and another full bottle waited beside it. The copper ice bucket had a little water in the bottom. Two glasses had been used, and half a siphon of carbonated water.

I fixed the door about as I had found it and stood there and listened. If Lavery was away I thought I would take a chance and frisk the joint. I didn't have anything much on him, but it was probably enough to keep him from calling the cops.

In the silence time passed. It passed in the dry whirr of the electric clock on the mantel, in the far-off toot of an auto horn on Aster Drive, in the hornet drone of a plane over the foothills across the canyon, in the sudden lurch and growl of the electric refrigerator in the kitchen.

I went farther into the room and stood peering around and listening and hearing nothing except those fixed sounds belonging to the house and having nothing to do with the humans in it. I started along the rug towards the archway at the back.

A hand in a glove appeared on the slope of the white metal railing, at the edge of the archway, where the stairs went down. It appeared and stopped.

It moved and a woman's hat showed, then her head. The woman came quietly up the stairs. She came all the way up, turned through the arch and still didn't seem to see me. She was a slender woman of uncertain age, with untidy brown hair, a scarlet mess of a mouth, too much rouge on her cheekbones, shadowed eyes. She wore a blue tweed suit that looked like the dickens with a purple hat that was doing its best to hang on to the side of her head.

She saw me and didn't stop or change expression in the slightest degree. She came slowly on into the room, holding her right hand away from her body. Her left hand wore the brown glove I had seen on the railing. The right-hand glove that matched it was wrapped around the butt of a small automatic.

She stopped then and her body arched back and a quick distressful sound came out of her mouth. Then she giggled, a high nervous giggle. She pointed the gun at me, and came steadily on.

I kept on looking at the gun and not screaming.

The woman came close. When she was close enough to be confidential she pointed the gun at my stomach and said:

'All I wanted was my rent. The place seems well taken care of. Nothing broken. He has always been a good tidy careful tenant. I just didn't want him to get too far behind in the rent.'

A fellow with a kind of strained and unhappy voice said politely: 'How far behind is he?'

'Three months,' she said. 'Two hundred and forty dollars. Eighty dollars is very reasonable for a place as well furnished as this. I've had a little trouble collecting before, but it always came out very well. He promised me a cheque this morning. Over the telephone. I mean he promised to give it to me this morning.'

'Over the telephone,' I said. 'This morning.'

I shuffled around a bit in an inconspicuous sort of way. The idea was to get close enough to make a side swipe at the gun. knock it outwards and then jump in fast before she could bring it back in line. I've never had a lot of luck with the technique, but you have to try it once in a while. This looked like the time to try it.

I made about six inches, but not nearly enough for a first down. I said: 'And you're the owner?' I didn't look at the gun directly. I had a faint, a very faint hope that she didn't know she was pointing it at me.

'Why, certainly. I'm Mrs Fallbrook. Who did you think I was?'

'Well, I thought you might be the owner,' I said. 'You talking about the rent and all. But I didn't know your name.' Another eight inches. Nice smooth work. It would be a shame to have it wasted.

'And who are you, if I may inquire?'

'I just came about the car payment,' I said. 'The door was open just a teensy weensy bit and I kind of shoved in. I don't know why.'

I made a face like a man from the finance company coming about the car payment. Kind of tough, but ready to break into a sunny smile.

'You mean Mr Lavery is behind in his car payments?' she asked, looking worried.

'A little. Not a great deal,' I said soothingly.

I was all set now. I had the reach and I ought to have the speed. All it needed was a clean sharp sweep inside the gun and outward. I started to take my left foot out of the rug.

'You know,' she said, 'it's funny about this gun. I found it on

270

the stairs. Nasty oily things, aren't they? And the stair carpet is a very nice grey chenille. Quite expensive.'

And she handed me the gun.

My hand went out for it, as stiff as an eggshell, almost as brittle. I took the gun. She sniffed with distaste at the glove which had been wrapped around the butt. She went on talking in exactly the same tone of cockeyed reasonableness. My knees cracked, relaxing.

'Well of course it's much easier for you,' she said. 'About the car, I mean. You can just take it away, if you have to. But taking a house with nice furniture in it isn't so easy. It takes time and money to evict a tenant. There is apt to be bitterness and things get damaged, sometimes on purpose. The rug on this floor cost over two hundred dollars, second-hand. It's only a jute rug, but it has a lovely colouring, don't you think? You'd never know it was only jute, second-hand. But that's silly too because they're always second-hand after you've used them. And I walked over here too, to save my tyres for the government. I could have taken a bus part way, but the darn things never come along except going in the wrong direction.'

I hardly heard what she said. It was like surf breaking beyond a point, out of sight. The gun had my interest.

I broke the magazine out. It was empty. I turned the gun and looked into the breech. That was empty too. I sniffed the muzzle. It reeked.

I dropped the gun into my pocket. A six-shot .25-calibre automatic. Emptied out. Shot empty, and not too long ago. But not in the last half-hour either.

'Has it been fired?' Mrs Fallbrook inquired pleasantly. 'I certainly hope not.'

'Any reason why it should have been fired?' I asked her. The voice was steady, but the brain was still bouncing.

'Well, it was lying on the stairs,' she said. 'After all, people do fire them.'

'How true that is,' I said. 'But Mr Lavery probably had a hole in his pocket. He isn't home, is he?'

'Oh no.' She shook her head and looked disappointed. 'And I don't think it's very nice of him. He promised me the cheque and I walked over—'

'When was it you phoned him?' I asked.

'Why, yesterday evening.' She frowned, not liking so many questions.

271

'He must have been called away,' I said.

She stared at a spot between my big brown eyes.

'Look, Mrs Fallbrook,' I said. 'Let's not kid around any more, Mrs Fallbrook. Not that I don't love it. And not that I like to say this. But you didn't shoot him, did you – on account of he owed you three months' rent?'

She sat down very slowly on the edge of a chair and worked the tip of her tongue along the scarlet slash of her mouth.

'Why, what a perfectly horrid suggestion,' she said angrily. 'I don't think you are nice at all. Didn't you say the gun had not been fired?'

'All guns have been fired sometime. All guns have been loaded sometime. This one is not loaded now.'

'Well, then—' she made an impatient gesture and sniffed at her oily glove.

'Okay, my idea was wrong. Just a gag anyway. Mr Lavery was out and you went through the house. Being the owner, you have a key. Is that correct?'

'I didn't mean to be interfering,' she said, biting a finger. 'Perhaps I ought not to have done it. But I have a right to see how things are kept.'

'Well, you looked. And you're sure he's not here?'

'I didn't look under the beds or in the icebox,' she said coldly. 'I called out from the top of the stairs when he didn't answer my ring. Then I went down to the lower hall and called out again. I even peeped into the bedroom.' She lowered her eyes as if bashfully and twisted a hand on her knee.

'Well, that's that,' I said.

She nodded briefly. 'Yes, that's that. And what did you say your name was?'

'Vance,' I said. 'Philo Vance.'

'And what company are you employed with, Mr Vance?'

'I'm out of work right now,' I said. 'Until the police commissioner gets in a jam again.'

She looked startled. 'But you said you came about a car payment.'

'That's just part-time work,' I said. 'A fill-in job.'

She rose to her feet and looked at me steadily. Her voice was cold saying: 'Then in that case I think you had better leave now.'

I said: 'I thought I might take a look around first, if you don't mind. There might be something you missed.'

'I don't think that is necessary,' she said. 'This is my house. I'll thank you to leave now, Mr Vance.'

I said: 'And if I don't leave, you'll get somebody who will. Take a chair again, Mrs Fallbrook. I'll just glance through. This gun, you know, is kind of queer.'

'But I told you I found it lying on the stairs,' she said angrily. 'I don't know anything else about it. I don't know anything about guns at all. I – I never shot one in my life.' She opened a large blue bag and pulled a handkerchief out of it and sniffed.

'That's your story,' I said. 'I don't have to get stuck with it.'

She put her left hand to me with a pathetic gesture, like the erring wife in *East Lynne*.

'Oh, I shouldn't have come in! she cried. 'It was horrid of me. I know it was. Mr Lavery will be furious.'

'What you shouldn't have done,' I said, 'was let me find out the gun was empty. Up to then you were holding everything in the deck.'

She stamped her foot. That was all the scene lacked. That made it perfect.

'Why, you perfectly loathsome man,' she squawked. 'Don't you dare touch me! Don't you take a single step towards me! I won't stay in this house another minute with you. How *dare* you be so insulting—'

She caught her voice and snapped it in mid-air like a rubber band. Then she put her head down, purple hat and all, and ran for the door. As she passed me she put a hand out as if to stiff-arm me but she wasn't near enough and I didn't move. She jerked the door wide and charged out through it and up the walk to the street. The door came slowly shut and I heard her rapid steps above the sound of its closing.

I ran a finger nail along my teeth and punched the point of my jaw with a knuckle, listening. I didn't hear anything anywhere to listen to. A six-shot automatic, fired empty.

'Something,' I said out loud, 'is all wrong with this scene.'

The house seemed now to be abnormally still. I went along the apricot rug and through the archway to the head of the stairs. I stood there for another moment and listened again.

I shrugged and went quietly down the stairs.

16

The lower hall had a door at each end and two in the middle side by side. One of these was a linen closet and the other was locked. I went along to the end and looked in at a spare bedroom with drawn blinds and no sign of being used. I went back to the other end of the hall and stepped into a second bedroom with a wide bed, a café-au-lait rug, angular furniture in light wood, a box mirror over the dressing-table and a long fluorescent lamp over the mirror. In the corner a crystal greyhound stood on a mirror-top table and beside him a crystal box with cigarettes in it.

Face powder was spilled around on the dressing-table There was a smear of dark lipstick on a towel hanging over the waste basket. On the bed were pillows side by side, with depressions in them that could have been made by heads. A woman's handkerchief peeped from under one pillow. A pair of sheer black pyjamas lay across the foot of the bed. A rather too emphatic trace of chypre hung in the air.

I wondered what Mrs Fallbrook had thought of all this.

I turned around and looked at myself in the long mirror of a closet door. The door was painted white and had a crystal knob. I turned the knob in my handkerchief and looked inside. The cedar-lined closet was fairly full of man's clothes. There was a nice friendly smell of tweed. The closet was not entirely full of man's clothes.

There was also a woman's black and white tailored suit, mostly white, black and white shoes under it, a panama with a black and white rolled band on a shelf above it. There were other woman's clothes, but I didn't examine them.

I shut the closet door and went out of the bedroom, holding my handkerchief ready for more doorknobs.

The door next to the linen closet, the locked door, had to be the bathroom. I shook it, but it went on being locked. I bent down and saw there was a short, slit-shaped opening in the middle of the knob. I knew then that the door was fastened by pushing a button in the middle of the knob inside, and that the slit-like opening was was for a metal key without wards that would spring the lock open in case somebody fainted in the bathroom, or the kids locked themselves in and got sassy.

The key for this ought to be kept on the top shelf of the linen closet but it wasn't. I tried my knife blade, but that was too thin. I went back to the bedroom and got a flat nail file off the dresser. That worked. I opened the bathroom door.

A man's sand-coloured pyjamas were tossed over a painted hamper. A pair of heelless green slippers lay on the floor. There was a safety razor on the edge of the washbowl and a tube of cream with the cap off. The bathroom window was shut, and there was a pungent smell in the air that was not quite like any other smell.

Three empty shells lay bright and coppery on the nile green tiles of the bathroom floor, and there was a nice clean hole in the frosted pane of the window. To the left and a little above the window were two scarred places in the plaster where the white showed behind the paint and where something, such as a bullet, had gone in.

The shower curtain was green and white oiled silk and it hung on shiny chromium rings and it was drawn across the shower opening. I slid it aside, the rings making a thin scraping noise, which for some reason sounded indecently loud.

I felt my neck creak a little as I bent down. He was there all right – there wasn't anywhere else for him to be. He was huddled in the corner under the two shining faucets, and water dripped slowly on his chest from the chromium showerhead.

His knees were drawn up but slack. The two holes in his naked chest were dark blue and both of them were close enough to his heart to have killed him. The blood seemed to have been washed away.

His eyes had a curiously bright and expectant look, as if he smelled the coffee and would be coming right out.

Nice efficient work. You have just finished shaving and stripped for the shower and you are leaning in against the shower curtain and adjusting the temperature of the water. The door opens behind you and somebody comes in. The somebody appears to have been a woman. She has a gun. You look at the gun and she shoots it.

She misses with three shots. It seems impossible, at such short range, but there it is. Maybe it happens all the time. I've been around so little.

You haven't anywhere to go. You could lunge at her and take a chance if you were that kind of fellow, and if you were braced for it. But leaning in over the shower faucets, holding the curtains closed, you are off balance. Also you are apt to be some-what petrified with panic, if you are at all like other people.

That is where you go. You go into it as far as you can, but a shower stall is a small place and the tiled wall stops you. You are backed up against the last wall there is now. You are all out of space, and you are all out of living. And then there are two more shots, possibly three, and you slide down the wall, and your eyes are not even frightened any more now. They are just the empty eyes of the dead.

She reaches in and turns the shower off. She sets the locks of the bathroom door. On her way out of the house she throws the empty gun on the stair carpet. She should worry. It is probably your gun.

Is that right? It had better be right.

I bent and pulled at his arm. Ice couldn't have been any colder or any stiffer. I went out of the bathroom, leaving it unlocked. No need to lock it now. It only makes work for the cops.

I went into the bedroom and pulled the handkerchief out from under the pillow. It was a minute piece of linen rag with a scalloped edge embroidered in red. Two small initials were stitched in the corner, in red. *AF*.

'Adrienne Fromsett,' I said. I laughed. It was a rather ghoulish laugh.

I shook the handkerchief to get some of the chypre out of it and folded it up in a tissue and put it in a pocket. I went back upstairs to the living-room and poked around in the desk against the wall. The desk contained no interesting letters, phone numbers or provocative match folders. Or if it did, I didn't find them.

I looked at the phone. It was on a small table against the wall beside the fireplace. It had a long cord so that Mr Lavery could be lying on his back on the davenport, a cigarette between his smooth brown lips, a tall cool one at the table at his side, and plenty of time for a nice cosy conversation with a lady friend. An easy, languid, flirtatious, kidding, not too subtle and not too blunt conversation, of the sort he would be apt to enjoy.

All that wasted too. I went away from the telephone to the door and set the lock so I could come in again and shut the door tight, pulling it hard over the sill until the lock clicked. I went up the walk and stood in the sunlight looking across the street at Dr Almore's house.

Nobody yelled or ran out of the door. Nobody blew a police

whistle. Everything was quiet and sunny and calm. No cause for excitement whatever. It's only Marlowe, finding another body. He does it rather well by now. Murder-a-day Marlowe, they call him. They have the meat wagon following him around to follow up on the business he finds.

A nice enough fellow, in an ingenious sort of way.

I walked back to the intersection and got into my car and started it and backed it and drove away from there.

17

The bellhop at the Athletic Club was back in three minutes with a nod for me to come with him. We rode up to the fourth floor and went around a corner and he showed me a half-open door.

'Around to the left, sir. As quietly as you can. A few of the members are sleeping.'

I went into the club library. It contained books behind glass doors and magazines on a long central table and a lighted portrait of the club's founder. But its real business seemed to be sleeping. Outward-jutting bookcases cut the room into a number of small alcoves and in the alcoves were high-backed leather chairs of an incredible size and softness. In a number of the chairs old boys were snoozing peacefully, their faces violet with high blood pressure, thin racking snores coming out of their pinched noses.

I climbed over a few feet and stole around to the left. Derace Kingsley was in the very last alcove in the far end of the room. He had two chairs arranged side by side, facing into the corner. His big dark head just showed over the top of one of them. I slipped into the empty one and gave him a quick nod.

'Keep your voice down,' he said. 'This room is for after-luncheon naps. Now what is it? When I employed you it was to save me trouble, not to add trouble to what I already had. You made me break an important engagement.'

'I know,' I said, and put my face close to his. He smelled of highballs, in a nice way. 'She shot him.'

His eyebrows jumped and his face got that stony look. His teeth clamped tight. He breathed softly and twisted a large hand on his kneecap.

'Go on,' he said, in a voice the size of a marble.

I looked back over the top of my chair. The nearest old geezer was sound asleep and blowing the dusty fuzz in his nostrils back and forth as he breathed.

'No answer at Lavery's place,' I said. 'Door slightly open. But I noticed yesterday it sticks on the sill. Pushed it open. Room dark, two glasses with drinks having been in them. House very still. In a moment a slim dark woman calling herself Mrs Fallbrook, landlady, came up the stairs with her glove wrapped around a gun. Said she had come to collect her three months' back rent. Used her key to get in. Inference is she took the chance to snoop around and look the house over. Took the gun from her and found it had been fired recently, but didn't tell her so. She said Lavery was not home. Got rid of her by making her mad and she departed in high dudgeon. She may call the police, but it's much more likely she will just go out and hunt butterflies and forget the whole thing – except the rent.'

I paused. Kingsley's head was turned towards me and his jaw muscles bulged with the way his teeth were clamped. His eyes looked sick.

'I went downstairs. Signs of a woman having spent the night. Pyjamas, face powder, perfume, and so on. Bathroom locked, but got it open. Three empty shells on the floor, two shots in the wall, one in the window. Lavery in the shower stall, naked and dead.'

'My God!' Kingsley whispered. 'Do you mean to say he had a woman with him last night and she shot him this morning in the bathroom?'

'Just what did you think I was trying to say?' I asked.

'Keep your voice down,' he groaned. 'It's a shock, naturally. Why in the bathroom?'

'Keep your own voice down,' I said. 'Why not in the bathroom? Could you think of a place where a man would be more completely off guard?'

He said: 'You don't know that a woman shot him. I mean, you're not sure, are you?'

'No,' I said. 'That's true. It might have been somebody who

used a small gun and emptied it carelessly to look like a woman's work. The bathroom is downhill, facing outwards on space and I don't think shots down there would be easily heard by anyone not in the house. The woman who spent the night might have left – or there need not have been any woman at all. The appearances could have been faked. *You* might have shot him.'

'What would I want to shoot him for?' he almost bleated, squeezing both kneecaps hard. 'I'm a civilized man.'

That didn't seem to be worth an argument either. I said: 'Does your wife own a gun?'

He turned a drawn miserable face to me and said hollowly: 'Good God, man, you can't really think that!'

'Well, does she?'

He got the words out in small gritty pieces. 'Yes – she does. A small automatic.'

'You buy it locally?'

'I – I didn't buy it at all. I took it away from a drunk at a party in San Francisco a couple of years ago. He was waving it around, with an idea that that was very funny. I never gave it back to him.' He pinched his jaw hard until his knuckles whitened. 'He probably doesn't even remember how or when he lost it. He was that kind of a drunk.'

'This is working out almost too neatly,' I said. 'Could you recognize this gun?'

He thought hard, pushing his jaw out and half-closing his eyes. I looked back over the chairs again. One of the elderly snoozers had waked himself up with a snort that almost blew him out of his chair. He coughed, scratched his nose with a thin dried-up hand, and fumbled a gold watch out of his vest. He peered at it bleakly, put it away, and went to sleep again.

I reached into my pocket and put the gun in Kingsley's hand. He stared down at it miserably.

'I don't know,' he said slowly. 'It's like it, but I can't tell.'

'There's a serial number on the side,' I said.

'Nobody remembers the serial numbers of guns.'

'I was hoping you wouldn't,' I said. 'It would have worried me very much.'

His hand closed around the gun and he put it down beside him in the chair.

'The dirty rat,' he said softly. 'I suppose he ditched her.'

'I don't get it,' I said. 'The motive was inadequate for you, on account of you're a civilized man. But it was adequate for her.'

'It's not the same motive,' he snapped. 'And women are more impetuous than men.'

'Like cats are more impetuous than dogs.'

'How?'

'Some women are more impetuous than some men. That's all that means. We'll have to have a better motive, if you want your wife to have done it.'

He turned his head enough to give me a level stare in which there was no amusement. White crescents were bitten into the corners of his mouth.

'This doesn't seem to me a very good spot for the light touch,' he said. 'We can't let the police have this gun. Crystal had a permit and the gun was registered. So they will know the number, even if I don't. We can't let them have it.'

'But Mrs Fallbrook knows I had the gun.'

He shook his head stubbornly. 'We'll have to chance that. Yes, I know you're taking a risk. I intend to make it worth your while. It the set-up were possible for suicide, I'd say put the gun back. But the way you tell it, it isn't.'

'No. He'd have to have missed himself with the first three shots. But I can't cover up a murder, even for a ten-dollar bonus. The gun will have to go back.'

'I was thinking of more money than that,' he said quietly. 'I was thinking of five hundred dollars.'

'Just what did you expect to buy with it?'

He leaned close to me. His eyes were serious and bleak, but not hard. 'Is there anything in Lavery's place, apart from the gun, that might indicate Crystal has been there lately?

'A black and white dress and a hat like the bellhop in Bernadino described on her. There may be a dozen things I don't know about. There almost certainly will be finger-prints. You say she was never printed, but that doesn't mean they won't get her prints to check. Her bedroom at home will be full of them. So will the cabin at Little Fawn Lake. And her car.'

'We ought to get the car –' he started to say. I stopped him.

'No use. Too many other places. What kind of perfume does she use?'

He looked blank for an instant. 'Oh – Gillerlain Regal, the

Champagne of Perfumes,' he said woodenly. 'A Chanel number once in a while.'

'What's this stuff of yours like?'

'A kind of chypre. Sandalwood chypre.'

'The bedroom reeks with it,' I said. 'It smelled like cheap stuff to me. But I'm no judge.'

'Cheap?' he said, stung to the quick. 'My God, cheap? We get thirty dollars an ounce for it.'

'Well, this stuff smelled more like three dollars a gallon.'

He put his hands down hard on his knees and shook his head.

'I'm talking about money,' he said. 'Five hundred dollars. A cheque for it right now.'

I let the remark fall to the ground, eddying like a soiled feather. One of the old boys behind us stumbled to his feet and groped his way wearily out of the room.

Kingsley said gravely: 'I hired you to protect me from scandal and of course to protect my wife, if she needed it. Through no fault of yours the chance to avoid scandal is pretty well shot. It's a question of my wife's neck now. I don't believe she shot Lavery. I have no reason for that belief. None at all. I just feel the conviction. She may even have been there last night, this gun may even be her gun. It doesn't prove she killed him. She would be as careless with the gun as with anything else. Anybody could have got hold of it.'

'The cops down there won't work very hard to believe that,' I said. 'If the one I met is a fair specimen, they'll just pick the first head they see and start swinging with their blackjacks. And hers will certainly be the first head they see when they look the situation over.'

He ground the heels of his hands together. His misery had a theatrical flavour, as real misery so often has.

'I'll go along with you up to a point,' I said. 'The set-up down there is almost too good, at first sight. She leaves clothes there she has been seen wearing and which can probably be traced. She leaves the gun on the stairs. It's hard to think she would be as dumb as that.'

'You give me a little heart,' Kingsley said wearily.

'But none of that means anything,' I said. 'Because we are looking at it from the angle of calculation, and people who commit crimes of passion or hatred, just commit them and walk out. Everything I have heard indicates that she is a reckless foolish woman. There's no sign of planning in any of the scene down there. There's every sign of a complete lack of planning. But even if there wasn't a thing down there to point to your wife, the cops would tie her up to Lavery. They will investigate his background, his friends, his women. Her name is bound to crop up somewhere along the line, and when it does, the fact that she has been out of sight for a month will make them sit up and rub their horny palms with glee. And of course they'll trace the gun, and if it's her gun—'

His hand dived for the gun in the chair beside him.

'Nope,' I said. 'They'll have to have the gun. Marlowe may be a very smart guy and very fond of you personally but he can't risk the suppression of such vital evidence as the gun that killed a man. Whatever I do has to be on the basis that your wife is an obvious suspect, but that the obviousness can be wrong.'

He groaned, and put his big hand out with the gun in it. I took it and put it away. Then I took it out again and said: 'Lend me your handkerchief. I don't want to use mine. I might be searched.'

He handed me a stiff white handkerchief and I wiped the gun carefully all over and dropped it into my pocket. I handed him back the handkerchief.

'My prints are all right,' I said. 'But I don't want yours on it. Here's the only thing I can do. Go back down there and replace the gun and call the law. Ride it out with them and let the chips fall where they have to. The story will have to come out. What I was doing down there and why. At the worst they'll find her and prove she killed him. At the best they'll find her a lot quicker than I can and let me use my energies proving that she didn't kill him, which means, in effect, proving that someone else did. Are you game for that?'

He nodded slowly. He said: 'Yes – and the five hundred stands. For showing Crystal didn't kill him.'

'I don't expect to earn it,' I said. 'You may as well understand that now. How well did Miss Fromsett know Lavery? Out of the office hours?'

His face tightened up like a charleyhorse. His fists went into hard lumps on his thighs. He said nothing.

'She looked kind of queer when I asked her for his address yesterday morning,' I said.

He let a breath out slowly.

'Like a bad taste in the mouth,' I said. 'Like a romance that fouled out. Am I too blunt?'

His nostrils quivered a little and his breath made noise in them for a moment. Then he relaxed and said quietly:

'She – knew him rather well – at one time. She's a girl who would do about what she pleased in that way. Lavery was, I guess, a fascinating bird – to women.'

'I'll have to talk to her,' I said.

'Why?' he asked shortly. Red patches showed in his cheeks.

'Never mind why. It's my business to ask all sorts of questions of all sorts of people.'

'Talk to her then,' he said tightly. 'As a matter of fact she knew the Almores. She knew Almore's wife, the one who killed herself. Lavery knew her too. Could that have any possible connection with this business?'

'I don't know. You're in love with her, aren't you?'

'I'd marry her tomorrow if I could,' he said stiffly.

I nodded and stood up. I looked back along the room. It was almost empty now. At the far end a couple of elderly relics were still blowing bubbles. The rest of the soft chair boys had staggered back to whatever it was they did when they were conscious.

'There's just one thing,' I said, looking down at Kingsley. 'Cops get very hostile when there is a delay in calling them after a murder. There's been delay this time and there will be more. I'd like to go down there as if it was the first visit today. I think I can make it that way, if I leave the Fallbrook woman out.'

'Fallbrook?' He hardly knew what I was talking about. 'Who the hell – oh yes, I remember.'

'Well, don't remember. 'I'm almost certain they'll never hear a peep from her. She's not the kind to have anything to do with the police of her own free will.'

'I understand,' he said.

'Be sure you handle it right then. Questions will be asked you *before* you are told Lavery is dead, before I'm allowed to get in touch with you – so far as they know. Don't fall into any traps. If you do, I won't be able to find anything out. I'll be in the clink.'

'You could call me from the house down there – before you call the police,' he said reasonably.

'I know. But the fact that I don't will be in my favour. And they'll check the phone calls one of the first things they do. And if I call you from anywhere else, I might just as well admit that I came up here to see you.'

'I understand,' he said again. 'You can trust me to handle it.'

We shook hands and I left him standing there.

18

The Athletic Club was on a corner across the street and half a block down from the Treloar Building. I crossed and walked north to the entrance. They had finished laying rose-coloured concrete where the rubber sidewalk had been. It was fenced around, leaving a narrow gangway in and out of the building. The space was clotted with office help going in from lunch.

The Gillerlain Company's reception room looked even emptier than the day before. The same fluffy little blonde was tucked in behind the PBX in the corner. She gave me a quick smile and I gave her the gunman's salute, a stiff forefinger pointing at her, the three lower fingers tucked back under it, and the thumb wiggling up and down like a western gun-fighter fanning his hammer. She laughed heartily, without making a sound. This was more fun than she had had in a week.

I pointed to Miss Fromsett's empty desk and the little blonde nodded and pushed a plug in and spoke. A door opened and Miss Fromsett swayed elegantly out to her desk and sat down and gave me her cool expectant eyes.

'Yes, Mr Marlowe? Mr Kingsley is not in, I'm afraid.'

'I just came from him. Where do we talk?'

'Talk?'

'I have something to show you.'

'Oh, yes?' She looked me over thoughtfully. A lot of guys had probably tried to show her things, including etchings. At another time I wouldn't have been above taking a flutter at it myself.

'Business,' I said. 'Mr Kingsley's business.'

She stood up and opened the gate in the railing. 'We may as well go into his office then.'

We went in. She held the door for me. As I passed her I sniffed. Sandalwood. I said:

'Gillerlain Regal, the Champagne of Perfumes?'

She smiled faintly, holding the door. 'On my salary?'

'I didn't say anything about your salary. You don't look like a girl who has to buy her own perfume.'

'Yes, that's what it is,' she said. 'And if you want to know, I detest wearing perfume in the office. He makes me.'

We went down the long dim office and she took a chair at the end of the desk. I sat where I had sat the day before. We looked at each other. She was wearing tan today, with a ruffled jabot at her throat. She looked a little warmer, but still no prairie fire.

I offered her one of Kingsley's cigarettes. She took it, took a light from his lighter, and leaned back.

'We needn't waste time being cagey,' I said. 'You know by now who I am and what I am doing. If you didn't know yesterday morning, it's only because he loves to play big shot.'

She looked down at the hand that lay on her knee, then lifted her eyes and smiled almost shyly.

'He's a great guy,' she said. 'In spite of the heavy executive act he likes to put on. He's the only guy that gets fooled by it after all. And if you only knew what he has stood from that little tramp—' She waved her cigarette. 'Well, perhaps I'd better leave that out. What was it you wanted to see me about?'

'Kingsley said you knew the Almores.'

'I knew Mrs Almore. That is, I met her a couple of times.'

'Where?'

'At a friend's house. Why?'

'At Lavery's house?'

'You're not going to be insolent, are you, Mr Marlowe?'

'I don't know what your definition of that would be. I'm going to talk business as if it was business, not international diplomacy.'

'Very well.' She nodded slightly. 'At Chris Lavery's house, yes. I used to go there – once in a while. He had cocktail parties.'

'Then Lavery knew the Almores – or Mrs Almore.'

She flushed very slightly. 'Yes. Quite well.'

'And a lot of other women – quite well, too. I don't doubt that. Did Mrs Kingsley know her too?'

'Yes, better than I did. They called each other by their first names. Mrs Almore is dead, you know. She committed suicide, about a year and a half ago.'

'Any doubt about that?'

She raised her eyebrows, but the expression looked artificial to me, as if it just went with the question I asked, as a matter of form.

She said: 'Have you any particular reason for asking that question in that particular way? I mean, has it anything to do with – with what you are doing?'

'I didn't think so. I still don't know that it has. But yesterday Dr Almore called a cop just because I looked at his house. After he had found out from my car licence who I was. The cop got pretty tough with me, just for being there. He didn't know what I was doing and I didn't tell him I had been calling on Lavery. But Dr Almore must have known that. He had seen me in front of Lavery's house. Now why would he think it necessary to call a cop? And why would the cop think it smart to say that the last fellow who tried to put the bite on Almore ended up on the road gang? And why would the cop ask me if her folks – meaning Mrs Almore's folks, I suppose – had hired me? If you can answer any of those questions, I might know whether it's any of my business.'

She thought about it for a moment, giving me one quick glance while she was thinking, and then looking away again.

'I only met Mrs Almore twice,' she said slowly. 'But I think I can answer your questions – all of them. The last time I met her was at Lavery's place, as I said, and there were quite a lot of people there. There was a lot of drinking and loud talk. The women were not with their husbands and the men were not with their wives, if any. There was a man there named Brownwell who was very tight. He's in the navy now, I heard. He was ribbing Mrs Almore about her husband's practice. The idea seemed to be that he was one of those doctors who run around all night with a case of loaded hypodermic needles, keeping the local fast set from having pink elephants for breakfast. Florence Almore said she didn't care how her husband got his money, as long as he got plenty of it and she had the spending of it. She was tight too and not a very nice person sober, I should imagine. One of the slinky glittering females who laugh too much and sprawl all over their chairs, showing a great deal of leg. A very light blonde with a high colour and indecently large baby-blue eyes. Well, Brownwell told her not to worry, it would always be a good racket. In and out of the patient's house in fifteen minutes and anywhere from ten to fifty bucks a trip. But one thing bothered him, he said, however a doctor would get hold of so much dope without underworld contacts. He asked Mrs Almore if they had many nice gangsters to dinner at their house. She threw a glass of liquor in his face.'

I grinned, but Miss Fromsett didn't. She crushed her cigarette out in Kingsley's big copper and glass tray and looked at me soberly.

'Fair enough,' I said. 'Who wouldn't, unless he had a large hard fist to throw?'

'Yes. A few weeks later, Florence Almore was found dead in the garage late at night. The door of the garage was shut and the car motor was running.' She stopped and moistened her lips slightly. 'It was Chris Lavery who found her. Coming home at God knows what o'clock in the morning. She was lying on the concrete floor in pyjamas, with her head under a blanket which was also over the exhaust pipe of the car. Dr Almore was out. There was nothing about the affair in the papers, except that she had died suddenly. It was well hushed up.'

She lifted her clasped hands a little and then let them fall slowly into her lap again. I said:

'Was something wrong with it, then?'

'People thought so, but they always do. Some time later I heard what purported to be the lowdown. I met this man Brownwell on Vine Street and he asked me to have a drink with him. I didn't like him, but I had half an hour to kill. We sat at the back of Levy's bar and he asked me if I remembered the babe who threw the drink in his face. I said I did. The conversation then went something very like this. I remember it very well.

'Brownwell said: "Our pal Chris Lavery is sitting pretty, if he ever runs out of girl friends he can touch for dough."

'I said: "I don't understand."

'He said: "Hell, maybe you don't want to. The night the Almore woman died she was over at Lou Condy's place losing her shirt at roulette. She got into a tantrum and said the wheels were crooked and made a scene. Condy practically had to drag her into his office. He got hold of Dr Almore through the Physicians' Exchange and after a while the doc came over. He shot her with one of his busy little needles. Then he went away, leaving Condy to get her home. It seems he had a very urgent case. So Condy took her home and the doc's office nurse showed up, having been called by the doc, and Condy carried her upstairs and the nurse put her to bed. Condy went back to his chips. So she had to be carried to bed and yet the same night she got up and walked down to the family garage and finished herself off with monoxide. What do you think of that?" Brown-well was asking me.

'I said: "I don't know anything about it. How do you?"

'He said: "I know a reporter on the rag they call a newspaper down there. There was no inquest and no autopsy. If any tests were made, nothing was told about them. They don't have a regular coroner down there. The undertakers take turns at being acting coroner a week at a time. They're pretty well subservient to the political gang naturally. It's easy to fix a thing like that in a small town, if anybody with any pull wants it fixed. And Condy had plenty at that time. He didn't want the publicity of an investigation and neither did the doctor." '

Miss Fromsett stopped talking and waited for me to say something. When I didn't, she went on: 'I suppose you know what all this meant to Brownwell.'

'Sure. Almore finished her off and then he and Condy between them bought a fix. It has been done in cleaner little cities than Bay City ever tried to be. But that isn't all the story, is it?'

'No. It seems Mrs Almore's parents hired a private detective. He was a man who ran a night watchman service down there and he was actually the second man on the scene that night, after Chris. Lavery said he must have had something in the way of information but he never got a chance to use it. They arrested him for drunk driving and he got a jail sentence.'

I said: 'Is that all?'

She nodded. 'And if you think I remember it too well, it's part of my job to remember conversations.'

'What I was thinking was that it doesn't have to add up to very much. I don't see where it has to touch Lavery, even if he was the one who found her. Your gossipy friend Brownwell seems to think what happened gave somebody a chance to blackmail the doctor. But there would have to be some evidence, especially when you're trying to put the bite on a man who has already cleared himself with the law.'

Miss Fromsett said: 'I think so too. And I'd like to think blackmail was one of the nasty little tricks Chris Lavery didn't quite run to. I think that's all I can tell you, Mr Marlowe. And I ought to be outside.'

She started to get up. I said: 'It's not quite all. I have something to show you.'

I got the little perfumed rag that had been under Lavery's pillow out of my pocket and leaned over to drop it on the desk in front of her.

19

She looked at the handkerchief, looked at me picked up a pencil and pushed the little piece of linen around with the eraser end.

'What's on it?' she asked. 'Flyspray?'

'Some kind of sandalwood, I thought.'

'A cheap synthetic. Repulsive is a mild word for it. And why did you want me to look at this handkerchief, Mr Marlowe?' She leaned back again and stared at me with level cool eyes.

'I found it in Chris Lavery's house, under the pillow on his bed. It has initials on it.'

She unfolded the handkerchief without touching it by using the rubber tip of the pencil. Her face got a little grim and taut.

'It has two letters embroidered on it,' she said in a cold angry voice. 'They happen to be the same letters as my initials. Is that what you mean?'

'Right,' I said. 'He probably knows half a dozen women with the same initials.'

'So you're going to be nasty after all,' she said quietly.

'Is it your handkerchief – or isn't it?'

She hesitated. She reached out to the desk and very quietly got herself another cigarette and lit it with a match. She shook the match slowly, watching the small flame creep along the wood.

'Yes, it's mine,' she said, 'I must have dropped it there. It's a long time ago. And I assure you I didn't put it under a pillow on his bed. Is that what you wanted to know?'

I didn't say anything, and she added: 'He must have lent it to some woman who – who would like this kind of perfume.'

'I get a mental picture of the woman,' I said. 'And she doesn't quite go with Lavery.'

Her upper lip curled a little. It was a long upper lip. I like long upper lips.

'I think,' she said, 'you ought to do a little more work on your mental picture of Chris Lavery. Any touch of refinement you may have noticed is purely coincidental.'

'That's not a nice thing to say about a dead man,' I said.

For a moment she just sat there and looked at me as if I hadn't said anything and she was waiting for me to say something. Then a slow shudder started at her throat and passed over her whole body. Her hands clenched and the cigarette bent into a crook. She looked down at it and threw it into the ashtray with a quick jerk of her arm.

'He was shot in his shower,' I said. 'And it looks as if it was done by some woman who spent the night there. He had just been shaving. The woman left a gun on the stairs and this handkerchief on the bed.'

She moved very slightly in her chair. He eyes were perfectly empty now. Her face was as cold as a carving.

'And did you expect me to be able to give you information about that?' she asked me bitterly.

'Look, Miss Fromsett, I'd like to be smooth and distant and subtle about all this too. I'd like to play this sort of game just once the way somebody like you would like it to be played. But nobody will let me – not the clients, nor the cops, nor the people I play against. However hard I try to be nice I always end up with my nose in the dirt and my thumb feeling for somebody's eye.'

She nodded as if she had only just barely heard me. 'When was he shot?' she asked, and then shuddered slightly again.

'This morning, I suppose. Not long after he got up. I said he had just shaved and was going to take a shower.'

'That,' she said, 'would probably have been quite late. I've been here since eight-thirty.'

'I didn't think you shot him.'

'Awfully kind of you,' she said. 'But it is my handkerchief, isn't it? Although not my perfume. But I don't suppose policemen are very sensitive to quality in perfume – or in anything else.'

'No – and that goes for private detectives too,' I said. 'Are you enjoying this a lot?'

'God,' she said, and put the back of her hand hard against her mouth.

'He was shot at five or six times,' I said. 'And missed all but twice. He was cornered in the shower-stall. It was a pretty grim scene, I should think. There was a lot of hate on one side of it. Or a pretty cold-blooded mind.'

'He was quite easy to hate,' she said emptily. 'And poisonously easy to love. Women – even decent women – make such ghastly mistakes about men.'

'All you're telling me is that you once thought you loved him, but not any more, and that you didn't shoot him.'

'Yes.' Her voice was light and dry now, like the perfume she didn't like to wear at the office. 'I'm sure you'll respect the confidence.' She laughed shortly and bitterly. 'Dead,' she said. 'The poor, egotistical, cheap, nasty, handsome, treacherous guy. Dead and cold and done with. No, Mr Marlowe, I didn't shoot him.'

I waited, letting her work it out of her. After a moment she said quietly: 'Does Mr Kingsley know?'

I nodded.

'And the police, of course.'

'Not yet. At least not from me. I found him. The house door wasn't quite shut. I went in. I found him.'

She picked the pencil up and poked at the handkerchief again. 'Does Mr Kingsley know about this scented rag?'

'Nobody knows about that, except you and me, and whoever put it there.'

'Nice of you,' she said dryly. 'And nice of you to think what you thought.'

'You have a certain quality of aloofness and dignity that I like,' I said. 'But don't run it into the ground. What would you expect me to think? Do I pull the hankie out from under the pillow and sniff it and hold it out and say, "Well, well, Miss Adrienne Fromsett's initials and all. Miss Fromsett must have known Lavery, perhaps very intimately. Let's say, just for the book, as intimately as my nasty little mind can conceive. And that would be pretty damn intimately. But this is cheap synthetic sandalwood and Miss Fromsett wouldn't use cheap scent. And this was under Lavery's pillow and Miss Fromsett just never keeps her hankies under a man's pillow. Therefore this has absolutely nothing to do with Miss Fromsett. It's just an optical delusion."'

'Oh, shut up,' she said.

I grinned.

'What kind of girl do you think I am?' she snapped.

'I came in too late to tell you.'

She flushed, but delicately and all over her face this time. Then, 'Have you any idea who did it?'

'Ideas, but that's all they are. I'm afraid the police are going to find it simple. Some of Mrs Kingsley's clothes are hanging in Lavery's closet. And when they know the whole story – including what happened at Little Fawn Lake yesterday – I'm afraid they'll just reach for the handcuffs. They have to find her first. But that won't be so hard for them.'

'Crystal Kingsley,' she said emptily. 'So he couldn't be spared even that.'

I said: 'It doesn't have to be. It could be an entirely different motivation, something we know nothing about. It could have been somebody like Dr Almore.'

She looked up quickly, then shook her head. 'It could be,' I insisted. 'We don't know anything against it. He was pretty nervous yesterday, for a man who has nothing to be afraid of. But, of course, it isn't only the guilty who are afraid.'

I stood up and tapped on the edge of the desk looking down at her. She had a lovely neck. She pointed to the handkerchief.

'What about that?' she asked dully.

'If it was mine, I'd wash that cheap stuff out of it.'

'It has to mean something doesn't it? It might mean a lot.'

I laughed. 'I don't think it means anything at all. Women are always leaving their handkerchiefs around. A fellow like Lavery would collect them and keep them in a drawer with a sandalwood sachet. Somebody would find the stock and take one out to use. Or he would lend them, enjoying the reaction to the other girl's initials. I'd say he was that kind of a heel. Goodbye, Miss Fromsett, and thanks for talking to me.'

I started to go, then I stopped and asked her: 'Did you hear the name of the reporter down there who gave Brownwell all his information?'

She shook her head.

'Or the name of Mrs Almore's parents?'

'Not that either. But I could probably find that out for you. I'd be glad to try.'

'How?'

'Those things are usually printed in death notices, aren't they? There is pretty sure to have been a death notice in the Los Angeles papers.'

'That would be very nice of you,' I said. I ran a finger along the edge of the desk and looked at her sideways. Pale ivory skin, dark and lovely eyes, and hair as dark as hair can be and eyes as dark as night can be.

I walked back down the room and out. The little blonde at the PBX looked at me expectantly, her small red lips parted, waiting for more fun.

I didn't have any more. I went out.

20

No police cars stood in front of Lavery's house, nobody hung around on the sidewalk, and when I pushed the front door open there was no smell of cigar or cigarette smoke inside. The sun had gone away from the windows and a fly buzzed softly over one of the liquor glasses. I went down to the end and hung over the railing that led downstairs. Nothing moved in Mr Lavery's house. Nothing made sound except very faintly down below in the bathroom the quiet trickle of water dripping on a dead man's shoulder.

I went to the telephone and looked up the number of the police department in the directory. I dialled and while I was waiting for an answer, I took the little automatic out of my pocket and laid it on the table beside the telephone.

When the male voice said: 'Bay City police – Smoot talking,' I said: 'There's been a shoooting at 623 Altair Street. Man named Lavery lives there. He's dead.'

'Six-two-three Altair. Who are you?'

'The name is Marlowe.'

'You there in the house?'

'Right.'

'Don't touch anything at all.'

I hung up, sat down on the davenport and waited.

Not very long. A siren whined far off, growing louder with great surges of sound. Tyres screamed at a corner, and the siren wail died to a metallic growl, then to silence, and the tyres screamed again in front of the house. The Bay City Police conserving rubber. Steps hit the sidewalk and I went over to the front door and opened it.

Two uniformed cops barged into the room. They were the usual large size and they had the usual weathered faces and suspicious eyes. One of them had a carnation tucked under his cap, behind his right ear. The other one was older, a little grey and grim. They stood and looked at me warily, then the older one said briefly:

'All right, where is it?'

'Downstairs in the bathroom, behind the shower curtain.'

'You stay here with him, Eddie.'

He went rapidly along the room and disappeared. The other one looked at me steadily and said out of the corner of his mouth:

'Don't make any false moves, buddy.'

I sat down on the davenport again. The cop ranged the room with his eyes. There were sounds below stairs, feet walking. The cop with me suddenly spotted the gun lying on the telephone table. He charged at it violently, like a downfield blocker.

'This is the death gun?' he almost shouted.

'I should imagine so. It's been fired.'

'Ha!' He leaned over the gun, baring his teeth at me, and put his hand to his holster. His fingers tickled the flap off the stud and he grasped the butt of the black revolver.

'You should what?' he barked.

'I should imagine so.'

'That's very good,' he sneered. 'That's very good indeed.'

'It's not that good,' I said.

He reeled back a little. His eyes were being careful of me. 'What you shoot him for?' he growled.

'I've wondered and wondered.'

'Oh, a wisenheimer.'

'Let's just sit down and wait for the homicide boys,' I said. 'I'm reserving my defence.'

'Dont give me none of that,' he said.

'I'm not giving you any of anything. If I had shot him, I wouldn't be here. I wouldn't have called up. You wouldn't have found the gun. Don't work so hard on the case. You won't be on it more than ten minutes.'

His eyes looked hurt. He took his cap off and the carnation dropped to the floor. He bent and picked it up and twirled it between his fingers, then dropped it behind the fire screen.

'Better not do that,' I told him. 'They might think it's a clue and waste a lot of time on it.'

'Aw hell.' He bent over the screen and retrieved the carnation and put it in his pocket. 'You know all the answers, don't you, buddy?'

The other cop came back up the stairs, looking grave. He stood in the middle of the floor and looked at his wrist watch and made a note in a note-book and then looked out of the front windows, holding the venetian blinds to one side to do it.

The one who had stayed with me said: 'Can I look now?'

'Let it lie, Eddie. Nothing in it for us. You call the coroner?'

'I thought Homicide would do that.'

'Yeah, that's right. Captain Webber will be on it and he likes to do everything himself.' He looked at me and said: 'You're a man named Marlowe?'

I said I was a man named Marlowe.

'He's a wise guy, knows all the answers' Eddie said.

The older one looked at me absently, looked at Eddie absently, spotted the gun lying on the telephone table and looked at that not at all absently.

'Yeah, that's the death gun,' Eddie said. 'I ain't touched it.'

The other nodded. 'The boys are not so fast today. What's your line, mister? Friend of his?' He made a thumb towards the floor.

'Saw him yesterday for the first time. I'm a private operative from LA.'

'Oh.' He looked at me very sharply. The other cop looked at me with deep suspicion.

'Cripes, that means everything will be all balled up,' he said.

That was the first sensible remark he had made. I grinned at him affectionately.

The older cop looked out of the front window again. 'That's the Almore place across the street, Eddie,' he said.

Eddie went and looked with him. 'Sure is,' he said. 'You can read the plate. Say, this guy downstairs might be the guy—'

'Shut up,' the other one said and dropped the venetian blind. They both turned around and stared at me woodenly.

A car came down the block and stopped and a door slammed and more steps came down the walk. The older of the prowl car boys opened the door to two men in plain clothes, one of whom I already knew.

21

The one who came first was a small man for a cop, middle-aged, thin-faced, with a permanently tired expression. His nose was sharp and bent a little to one side, as if somebody had given it the elbow one time when it was into something. His blue porkpie hat was set very square on his head and chalk-white hair showed under it. He wore a dull brown suit and his hands were in the side pockets of the jacket, with the thumbs outside the seam.

The man behind him was Degarmo, the big cop with the dusty blond hair and the metallic blue eyes and the savage, lined face who had not liked my being in front of Dr Almore's house.

The two uniformed men looked at the small man and touched their caps.

'The body's in the basement, Captain Webber. Been shot twice after a couple of misses, looks like. Dead quite some time. This party's name is Marlowe. He's a private eye from Los Angeles. I didn't question him beyond that.'

'Quite right,' Webber said sharply. He had a suspicious voice. He passed a suspicious eye over my face and nodded briefly. 'I'm Captain Webber,' he said: 'This is Lieutenant Degarmo. We'll look at the body first.'

He went along the room. Degarmo looked at me as if he had never seen me before and followed him. They went downstairs, the older of the two prowl men with him. The cop called Eddie and I stared each other down for a while.

I said: 'This is right across the street from Dr Almore's place, isn't it?'

All the expression went out of his face. There hadn't been much to go. 'Yeah. So what?'

'So nothing,' I said.

He was silent. The voices came up from below, blurred and indistinct. The cop cocked his ear and said in a more friendly tone: 'You remember that one?'

'A little.'

He laughed. 'They killed that one pretty,' he said. 'They wrapped it up and hid it in back of the shelf. The top shelf in the bathroom closet. The one you can't reach without standing on a chair.'

'So they did,' I said. 'I wonder why.'

The cop looked at me sternly. 'There was good reasons, pal. Don't think there wasn't. You know this Lavery well?'

'Not well.'

'On to him for something?'

'Working on him a little,' I said. 'You knew him?'

The cop called Eddie shook his head. 'Nope, I just remembered it was a guy from this house found Almore's wife in the garage that night.'

'Lavery may not have been here then,' I said.

'How long's he been here?'

'I don't know,' I said.

'Would be about a year and a half,' the cop said, musingly. 'The LA papers give it any play?'

'Paragraph on the Home Counties page,' I said, just to be moving my mouth.

He scratched his ear and listened. Steps were coming back up the stairs. The cop's face went blank and he moved away from me and straightened up.

Captain Webber hurried over to the telephone and dialled the number and spoke, then he held the phone away from his ear and looked back over his shoulder.

'Who's deputy coroner this week, Al?'

'Ed Garland,' the big Lieutenant said woodenly.

'Call Ed Garland,' Webber said into the phone. 'Have him come over right away. And tell the flash squad to step on it.'

He put the phone down and barked sharply: 'Who handled this gun?'

'I said: 'I did.'

He came over and teetered on his heels in front of me and pushed his small sharp chin up at me. He held the gun delicately on a handkerchief in his hand.

'Don't you know enough not to handle a weapon found at the scene of a crime?'

'Certainly,' I said. 'But when I handled it I didn't know there had been a crime. I didn't know the gun had been fired. It was lying on the stairs and I thought it had been dropped.'

'A likely story,' Webber said bitterly. 'You get a lot of that sort of thing in your business?'

'A lot of what sort of thing?'

He kept his hard stare on me and didn't answer.

I said: 'How would it be for me to tell you my story as it happened?'

He bridled at me like a cockerel. 'Suppose you answer my questions exactly as I choose to put them.'

I didn't say anything to that. Webber swivelled sharply and said to the two uniformed men: 'You boys can get back to your car and check in with the dispatcher.'

They saluted and went out, closing the door softly until it stuck, then getting as mad at it as anybody else. Webber listened until their car went away. Then he put the bleak and callous eye on me once more.

'Let me see your identification.'

I handed him my wallet and he rooted in it. Degarmo sat in a chair and crossed his legs and stared up blankly at the ceiling. He got a match out of his pocket and chewed the end of it. Webber gave me back my wallet. I put it away.

'People in your line make a lot of trouble,' he said.

'Not necessarily,' I said.

He raised his voice. It had been sharp enough before. 'I said they make a lot of trouble, and a lot of trouble is what I meant. But get this straight. You're not going to make any in Bay City.'

I didn't answer him. He jabbed a forefinger at me.

'You're from the big town,' he said. 'You think you're tough and you think you're wise. Don't worry. We can handle you. We're a small place, but we're very compact. We don't have any political tug-of-war down here. We work on the straight line and we work fast. Don't worry about us, mister.'

'I'm not worrying,' I said. 'I don't have anything to worry about. I'm just trying to make a nice clean dollar.'

'And don't give me any of the flip talk,' Webber said. 'I don't like it.'

Degarmo brought his eyes down from the ceiling and curled a forefinger to stare at the nail. He spoke in a heavy bored voice.

'Look, chief, the fellow downstairs is called Lavery. He's dead. I knew him a little. He was a chaser.'

'What of it?' Webber snapped, not looking away from me.

'The whole set-up indicates a dame,' Degarmo said. 'You know what these private eyes work at. Divorce stuff. Suppose we'd let him tie into it, instead of just trying to scare him dumb.'

'If I'm scaring him,' Webber said, 'I'd like to know it. I don't see any signs of it.'

He walked over to the front window and yanked the venetian blind up. Light poured into the room almost dazzlingly, after the long dimness. He came back bouncing on his heels and poked a thin hard finger at me and said:

'Talk.'

I said: 'I'm working for a Los Angeles business man who can't take a lot of publicity. That's why he hired me. A month ago his wife ran off and later a telegram came which indicated she had gone with Lavery. But my client met Lavery in town a couple of days ago and he denied it. The client believed him enough to get worried. It seems the lady is pretty reckless. She might have taken up with some bad company and got into a jam. I came down to see Lavery and he denied to me that he had gone with her. I half believed him but later I got reasonable proof that he had been with her in a San Bernadino hotel the night she was believed to have left the mountain cabin where she had been staying. With that in my pocket I came down to tackle Lavery again. No answer to the bell, the door was slightly open. I came inside, looked around, found the gun and searched the house. I found him. Just the way he is now.'

'You had no right to search the house,' Webber said coldly.

'Of course not,' I agreed. 'But I wouldn't be likely to pass up the chance either.'

'The name of this man you're working for?'

'Kingsley.' I gave him the Beverly Hills address. 'He manages a cosmetic company in the Treloar Building on Olive. The Gillerlain Company.'

Webber looked at Degarmo. Degarmo wrote lazily on an envelope. Webber looked back at me and said: 'What else?'

'I went up to this mountain cabin where the lady had been staying. It's a place called Little Fawn Lake, near Puma Point, forty-six miles into the mountains from San Bernadino.'

I looked at Degarmo. He was writing slowly. His hand stopped a moment and seemed to hang in the air stiffly, then it dropped to the envelope and wrote again. I went on:

'About a month ago the wife of the caretaker at Kingsley's place up there had a fight with him and left, as, everybody thought. Yesterday she was found drowned in the lake.'

Webber almost closed his eyes and rocked on his heels. Almost softly he asked: 'Why are you telling me this? Are you implying a connection?'

'There's a connection in time. Lavery had been up there. I don't know of any other connection, but I thought I'd better mention it.'

Degarmo was sitting very still, looking at the floor in front of him. His face was tight and he looked even more savage than usual. Webber said:

'This woman that was drowned? Suicide?'

'Suicide or murder. She left a good-bye note. But her husband has been arrested on suspicion. The name is Chess. Bill and Muriel Chess, his wife.'

'I don't want part of that,' Webber said sharply. 'Let's confine ourselves to what went on here.'

'Nothing went on here,' I said, looking at Degarmo. 'I've been down here twice. The first time I talked to Lavery and didn't get anywhere. The second time I didn't talk to him and didn't get anywhere.'

Webber said slowly: 'I'm going to ask you a question and I want an honest answer. You won't want to give it, but now will be as good a time as later. You know I'll get it eventually. The question is this. You have looked through the house and I imagine pretty thoroughly. Have you seen anything that suggests to you that this Kingsley woman has been here?'

'That's not a fair question,' I said. 'It calls for a conclusion of the witness.'

'I want an answer to it,' he said grimly. 'This isn't a court of law.'

'The answer is yes,' I said. 'There are women's clothes hanging in a closet downstairs that have been described to me as being worn by Mrs Kingsley at San Bernadino the night she met Lavery there. The description was not exact though. A black and white suit, mostly white, and a panama hat with a rolled black and white band.'

Degarmo snapped a finger against the envelope he was holding. 'You must be a great guy for a client to have working for him,' he said. 'That puts the woman right in this house where a murder has been committed and she is the woman he's supposed to have gone away with. I don't think we'll have to look far for the killer, chief.'

Webber was staring at me fixedly, with little or no expression on his face but a kind of tight watchfulness. He nodded absently to what Degarmo had said.

'I said: 'I'm assuming you fellows are not a pack of damn fools. The clothes are tailored and easy to trace. I've saved you an hour by telling you, perhaps even no more than a phone call.'

'Anything else?' Webber asked quietly.

Before I could answer, a car stopped outside the house, and then another. Webber skipped over to open the door. Three men came in, a short curly-haired man and a large ox-like man, both carrying heavy black leather cases. Behind them a tall thin man in a dark grey suit and black tie. He had very bright eyes and a poker face.

Webber pointed a finger at the curly-haired man and said: 'Downstairs in the bathroom, Busoni. I want a lot of prints from all over the house, particularly any that seem to be made by a woman. It will be a long job.'

'I do all the work,' Busoni grunted. He and the ox-like man went along the room and down the stairs.

We have a corpse for you, Garland,' Webber said to the third man. 'Let's go down and look at him. You've ordered the wagon?'

The bright-eyed man nodded briefly and he and Webber went downstairs after the other two.

Degarmo put the envelope and pencil away. He stared at me woodenly.

I said: 'Am I supposed to talk about our conversation yesterday – or is that a private transaction?'

'Talk about it all you like,' he said. 'It's our job to protect the citizen.'

'You talk about it,' I said. 'I'd like to know more about the Almore case.'

He flushed slowly and his eyes got mean. 'You said you didn't know Almore.'

'I didn't yesterday, or know anything about him. Since then I've learned that Lavery knew Mrs Almore, that she committed suicide, that Lavery found her dead, and that Lavery has at least been suspected of blackmailing him – or of being in a position to blackmail him.. Also both your prowl-car boys seeemed interested in the fact that Almore's house was across the street from here. And one of them remarked that the case had been killed pretty, or words to that effect.'

Degarmo said in a slow deadly tone: 'I'll have the badge off the son of a bitch. All they do is flap their mouths. Goddamn empty-headed bastards.'

'Then there's nothing in it,' I said.

He looked at his cigarette. 'Nothing in what?'

Nothing in the idea that Almore murdered his wife, and had enough pull to get it fixed.'

Degarmo came to his feet and walked over to lean down at me. 'Say that again,' he said softly.

'I said it again.

He hit me across the face with his open hand. It jerked my head around hard. My face felt hot and large.

'Say it again,' he said softly.

I said it again. His hands swept and knocked my head to one side again.

'Say it again.'

'Nope. Third time lucky. You might miss.' I put a hand up and rubbed my cheek.

He stood leaning down his lips drawing back over his teeth, a hard animal glare in his very blue eyes.

'Any time you talk like that to a cop,' he said, 'you know what you got coming. Try it on again and it won't be the flat of a hand I'll use on you.'

I bit hard on my lips and rubbed my cheek.

'Poke your nose into our business and you'll wake up in an alley with the cats looking at you,' he said.

I didn't say anything. He went and sat down again, breathing hard. I stopped rubbing my face and held my hand out and worked the fingers slowly, to get the hard clench out of them.

'I'll remember that,' I said. 'Both ways.'

22

It was early evening when I got back to Hollywood and up to the office. The building had emptied out and the corridors were silent. Doors were open and the cleaning women were inside with their vacuum cleaners and their dry mops and dusters.

I unlocked the door to mine and picked up an envelope that lay in front of the mail slot and dropped it on the desk without looking at it. I ran the windows up and leaned out, looking at the early neon lights glowing, smelling the warm, foody air that drifted up from the alley ventilator of the coffee shop next door.

I peeled off my coat and tie and sat down at the desk and got the office bottle out of the deep drawer and bought myself a drink. It didn't do any good. I had another, with the same result.

By now Webber would have seen Kingsley. There would be a general alarm for his wife, already or very soon. The thing looked cut and dried to them. A nasty affair between two rather nasty people, too much loving, too much drinking, too much proximity ending in a savage hatred and a murderous impulse and death.

I thought this was all a little too simple.

I reached for the envelope and tore it open. It had no stamp. It read: 'Mr Marlowe: Florence Amore's parents are a Mr and Mrs Eustace Grayson, at present residing at the Rossmore Arms, 640 South Oxford Avenue. I checked this by calling the listed phone number. YRS. ADRIENNE FROMSETT.'

An elegant handwriting, like the elegant hand that wrote it. I pushed it to one side and had another drink. I began to feel a little less savage. I pushed things around on the desk. My hands felt thick and hot and awkward. I ran a finger across the corner of the desk and looked at the streak made by the wiping off of the dust. I looked at the dust on my finger and wiped that off. I looked at my watch. I looked at the wall. I looked at nothing.

I put the liquor bottle away and went over to the washbowl to rinse the glass out. When I had done that I washed my hands and bathed my face in cold water and looked at it. The flush was gone from the left cheek, but it looked a little swollen. Not very much, but enough to make me tighten up again. I brushed my hair and looked at the grey in it. There was getting

to be plenty of grey in it. The face under the hair had a sick
look. I didn't like the face at all.

I went back to the desk and read Miss Fromsett's note again.
I smoothed it out on the glass and sniffed it and smoothed it
out some more and folded it and put it in my coat pocket.

I sat very still and listened to the evening grow quiet outside
the open windows. And very slowly I grew quiet with it.

23

The Mossmore Arms was a gloomy pile of dark red brick built
around a huge forecourt. It had a plush-lined lobby containing
silence, tubbed plants, a bored canary in a cage as big as a doghouse, a smell of old carpet dust and the cloying fragrance of
gardenias long ago.

The Graysons were on the fifth floor in front, in the north
wing. They were sitting together in a room which seemed to be
deliberately twenty years out of date. It had fat overstuffed
furniture and brass doorknobs, shaped like eggs, a huge wall
mirror in a gilt frame, a marble-topped table in the window and
dark red plush side drapes by the windows. It smelled of tobacco
smoke and behind that the air was telling me they had lamb
chops and broccoli for dinner.

Grayson's wife was a plump woman who might once have
had big baby-blue eyes. They were faded out now and dimmed
by glasses and slightly protuberant. She had kinky white hair.
She sat darning socks with her thick ankles crossed, her feet
just reaching the floor, and a big wicker sewing basket in her
lap.

Grayson was a long, stooped, yellow-faced man with his high
shoulders, bristly eyebrows and almost no chin. The upper part
of his face meant business. The lower part was just saying
good-bye. He wore bifocals and he had been gnawing fretfully
at the evening paper. I had looked him up in the city directory.
He was a CPA and looked it every inch. He even had ink on his

fingers and there were four pencils in the pocket of his open vest.

He read my card carefully for the seventh time and looked me up and down and said slowly:

'What is it you want to see us about, Mr Marlowe?'

'I'm interested in a man named Lavery. He lives across the street from Dr Almore. Your daughter was the wife of Dr Almore. Lavery is the man who found your daughter the night she – died.'

They both pointed like bird dogs when I deliberately hesitated on the last word. Grayson looked at his wife and she shook her head.

'We don't care to talk about that,' Grayson said promptly. 'It is much too painful to us.'

I waited a moment and looked gloomy with them. Then I said: 'I don't blame you. I don't want to make you. I'd like to get in touch with the man you hired to look into it, though.'

They looked at each other again. Mrs Grayson didn't shake her head this time.

Grayson asked: 'Why?'

'I'd better tell you a little of my story.' I told them what I had been hired to do, not mentioning Kingsley by name. I told them the incident with Degarmo outside Almore's house the day before. They pointed again on that.

Grayson said sharply: 'Am I to understand that you were unknown to Dr Almore, had not approached him in any way, and that he nevertheless called a police officer because you were outside his house?'

I said: 'That's right. Had been outside for at least an hour though. That is, my car had.'

'That's very queer,' Grayson said.

'I'd say that was one very nervous man,' I said. 'And Degarmo asked me if her folks – meaning your daughter's folks – had hired me. Looks as if he didn't feel safe yet, wouldn't you say?'

'Safe about what?' He didn't look at me saying this. He relit his pipe, slowly, then tamped the tobacco down with the end of a big metal pencil and lit it again.

I shrugged and didn't answer. He looked at me quickly and looked away. Mrs Grayson didn't look at me, but her nostrils quivered.

'How did he know who you were?' Grayson asked suddenly.

'Made a note of the car licence, called the Auto Club, looked up the name in the directory. At least that's what I'd have done and I saw him through his window making some of the motions.'

'So he has the police working for him,' Grayson said.

'Not necessarily. If they made a mistake that time, they wouldn't want it found out now.'

'Mistake!' He laughed almost shrilly.

'Okay,' I said. 'The subject is painful but a little fresh air won't hurt it. You've always thought he murdered her, haven't you? That's why you hired this dick – detective.'

Mrs Grayson looked up with quick eyes and ducked her head down and rolled up another pair of mended socks.

Grayson said nothing.

I said: 'Was there any evidence, or was it just that you didn't like him?'

'There was evidence,' Grayson said bitterly, and with a sudden clearness of voice, as if he had decided to talk about it after all. 'There must have been. We were told there was. But we never got it. The police took care of that.'

'I heard they had this fellow arrested and sent up for drunk driving.'

'You heard right.'

'But he never told you what he had to go on?'

'No.'

'I don't like that,' I said. 'That sounds a little as if this fellow hadn't made up his mind whether to use his information for your benefit or keep it and put a squeeze on the doctor.'

Grayson looked at his wife again. She said quietly: 'Mr Talley didn't impress me that way. He was a quiet unassuming little man. But you can't always judge, I know.'

I said: 'So Talley was his name. That was one of the things I hoped you would tell me.'

'And what were the others?' Grayson asked.

'How can I find Talley – and what it was that laid the groundwork of suspicion in your minds. It must have been there, or you wouldn't have hired Talley without a better showing from him that *he* had grounds.'

Grayson smiled very thinly and primly. He reached for his little chin and rubbed it with one long yellow finger.

Mrs Grayson said 'Dope.'

'She means that literally,' Grayson said at once, as if the single word had been a green light. 'Almore was, and no doubt is, a dope doctor. Our daughter made that clear to us. In his hearing too. He didn't like it.'

'Just what do you mean by a dope doctor, Mr Grayson?'

'I mean a doctor whose practice is largely with people who are living on the raw edge of nervous collapse, from drink and dissipation. People who have to be given sedatives and narcotics all the time. The stage comes when an ethical physician refuses to treat them any more, outside a sanatorium. But not the Dr Almores. *They* will keep on as long as the money comes in, as long as the patient remains alive and reasonably sane, even if he or she becomes a hopeless addict in the process. A lucrative practice,' he said primly, 'and I imagine a dangerous one to the doctor.'

'No doubt of that,' I said. 'But there's a lot of money in it. Did you know a man named Condy?'

'No. We know who he was. Florence suspected he was a source of Almore's narcotic supply.'

I said: 'Could be. He probably wouldn't want to write himself too many prescriptions. Did you know Lavery?'

'We never saw him. We knew who he was.'

'Ever occur to you that Lavery might have been blackmailing Almore?'

It was a new idea to him. He ran his hand over the top of his head and brought it down over his face and dropped it to his bony knee. He shook his head.

'No. Why should it?'

'He was first to the body,' I said. 'Whatever looked wrong to Talley must have been equally visible to Lavery.'

'Is Lavery that kind of a man?'

'I don't know. He has no visible means of support, no job. He gets around a lot, especially with women.'

'It's an idea,' Grayson said. 'And those things can be handled very discreetly.' He smiled wryly. 'I have come across traces of them in my work. Unsecured loans, long outstanding. Investments on the face of them worthless made by men who would not be likely to make worthless investments. Bad debts that should obviously be charged off and have not been, for fear of inviting scrutiny from the income-tax people. Oh yes, those things can easily be arranged.'

I looked at Mrs Grayson. Her hands had never stopped working. She had a dozen pairs of darned socks finished. Grayson's long bony feet would be hard on socks.

'What's happened to Talley? Was he framed?'

'I don't think there's any doubt about it. His wife was very bitter. She said he had been given a doped drink in a bar and he had been drinking with a policeman. She said a police car was waiting across the street for him to start driving and that he was picked up at once. Also that he was given only the most perfunctory examination at the jail.'

'That doesn't mean too much. That's what he told her after he was arrested. He'd tell her something like that automatically.'

'Well I hate to think the police are not honest,' Grayson said. 'But these things are done, and everybody knows it.'

I said: 'If they made an honest mistake about your daughter's death, they would hate to have Talley show them up. It might mean several lost jobs. If they thought what he was really after was blackmail, they wouldn't be too fussy about how they took care of him. Where is Talley now? What it all boils down to is that if there was any solid clue, he either had it or was on the track of it and he knew what he was looking for.'

Grayson said: 'We don't know where he is. He got six months, but that expired long ago.'

'How about his wife?'

He looked at his own wife. She said briefly: '1618½ Westmore Street, Bay City. Eustace and I sent her a little money. She was badly off.'

I made a note of the address and leaned back in my chair and said: 'Somebody shot Lavery this morning in his bathroom.'

Mrs Grayson's pudgy hands became still on the edges of the basket. Grayson sat with his mouth open, holding his pipe in front of it. He made a noise of clearing his throat softly, as if in the presence of the dead. Nothing ever moved slower than his old black pipe going back between his teeth.

'Of course it would be too much to expect,' he said and let it hang in the air and blew a little pale smoke at it, and then added, 'that Dr Almore had any connection with that.'

'I'd like to think he had,' I said. 'He certainly lives at a handy distance. The police think my client's wife shot him. They have a good case too, when they find her. But if Almore had anything to do with it, it must surely arise out of your daughter's death. That's why I'm trying to find out something about that.'

Grayson said: 'A man who has done one murder wouldn't have more than twenty-five per cent hesitation in doing another.' He spoke as if he had given the matter considerable study.

I said: 'Yeah, maybe. What was supposed to be the motive for the first one?'

'Florence was wild,' he said sadly. 'A wild and difficult girl. She was wasteful and extravagant, always picking up new and rather doubtful friends, talking too much and too loudly, and generally acting the fool. A wife like that can be very dangerous to a man like Albert S. Almore. But I don't believe that was the prime motive, was it, Lettie?'

He looked at his wife, but she didn't look at him. She jabbed a darning needle into a round ball of wool and said nothing.

Grayson sighed and went on: 'We had reason to believe he was carrying on with his office nurse and that Florence had threatened him with a public scandal. He couldn't have anything like that, could he? One kind of scandal might too easily lead to another.'

I said: 'How did he do the murder?'

'With morphine, of course. He always had it, he always used it. He was an expert in the use of it. Then when she was in a deep coma he would have placed her in the garage and started the car motor. There was no autopsy, you know. But if there had been, it was known that she had been given a hypodermic injection that night.'

I nodded and he leaned back satisfied and ran his hand over his head and down his face and let it fall slowly to his bony knee. He seemed to have given a lot of study to this angle too.

I looked at them. A couple of elderly people sitting there quietly, poisoning their minds with hate, a year and a half after it had happened. They would like it if Almore had shot Lavery. They would love it. It would warm them clear down to their ankles.

After a pause I said: 'You're believing a lot of this because you want to. It's always possible that she committed suicide, and that the cover-up was partly to protect Condy's gambling club and partly to prevent Almore having to be questioned at a public hearing.'

'Rubbish,' Grayson said sharply. 'He murdered her all right. She was in bed, asleep.'

'You don't know that. She might have been taking dope herself. She might have established a tolerance for it. The effect wouldn't last long in that case. She might have got up in the middle of the night and looked at herself in the glass and seen devils pointing at her. These things happen.'

'I think you have taken up enough of our time,' Grayson said.

I stood up. I thanked them both and made a yard towards the door and said: 'You didn't do anything more about it after Talley was arrested?'

'Saw an assistant district attorney named Leach,' Grayson grunted. 'Got exactly nowhere. He saw nothing to justify his office in interfering. Wasn't even interested in the narcotic angle. But Condy's place was closed up about a month later. That might have come out of it somehow.'

'That was probably the Bay City cops throwing a little smoke. You'd find Condy somewhere else, if you knew where to look. With all his original equipment intact.'

I started for the door again and Grayson hoisted himself out of his chair and dragged across the room after me. There was a flush on his yellow face.

'I didn't mean to be rude,' he said. 'I guess Lettie and I oughtn't to brood about this business the way we do.'

'I think you've both been very patient,' I said. 'Was there anybody else involved in all this that we haven't mentioned by name?'

He shook his head, then looked back at his wife. Her hands were motionless holding the current sock on the darning egg. Her head was tilted a little to one side. Her attitude was of listening, but not to us.

I said: 'The way I got the story, Dr Almore's office nurse put Mrs Almore to bed that night. Would that be the one he was supposed to be playing around with?'

Mrs Grayson said sharply: 'Wait a minute. We never saw the girl. But she had a pretty name. Just give me a minute.'

We gave her a minute. 'Mildred something,' she said, and snapped her teeth.

I took a deep breath. 'Would it be Mildred Haviland, Mrs Grayson?'

She smiled brightly and nodded. 'Of course, Mildred Haviland. Don't you remember, Eustace?'

He didn't remember. He looked at us like a horse that has got into the wrong stable. He opened the door and said: 'What does it matter?'

'And you said Talley was a small man,' I bored on. 'He wouldn't for instance be a big loud bruiser with an overbearing manner?'

'Oh no,' Mrs Grayson said. 'Mr Talley is a man of not more

than medium height, middle-aged, with brownish hair and a very quiet voice. He had a sort of a worried expression. I mean, he looked as if he always had it.'

'Looks as if he needed it,' I said.

Grayson put his bony hand out and I shook it. I felt like shaking hands with a towel-rack.

'If you get him,' he said and clamped his mouth hard on his pipe stem, 'call back with a bill. If you get Almore, I mean, of course.'

I said I knew he meant Almore, but that there wouldn't be any bill.

I went back along the silent hallway. The self-operating elevator was carpeted in red plush. It had an elderly perfume in it, like three widows drinking tea.

24

The house on Westmore Street was a small frame bungalow behind a larger house. There was no number visible on the smaller house, but the one in front showed a stencilled 1618 beside the door, with a dim light behind the stencil. A narrow concrete path led along under windows to the house at the back. It had a tiny porch with a single chair on it. I stepped up on the porch and rang the bell.

It buzzed not very far off. The front door was open behind the screen but there was no light. From the darkness a querulous voice said:

'What is it?'

I spoke into the darkness. 'Mr Talley in?'

The voice became flat and without tone. 'Who wants him?'

'A friend.'

The woman sitting inside in the darkness made a vague sound in her throat which might have been amusement. Or she might just have been clearing her throat.

'All right,' she said. 'How much is this one?'

'It's not a bill, Mrs Talley. I suppose you are Mrs Talley?'

'Oh, go away and let me alone,' the voice said. 'Mr Talley isn't here. He hasn't been here. He won't be here.'

I put my nose against the screen and tried to peer into the room. I could see the vague outlines of its furniture. From where the voice came from also showed the shape of a couch. A woman was lying on it. She seemed to be lying on her back and looking up at the ceiling. She was quite motionless.

'I'm sick,' the voice said. 'I've had enough trouble. Go away and leave me be.'

I said: 'I've just come from talking to the Graysons.'

There was a little silence, but no movement, then a sigh. 'I never heard of them.'

I leaned against the frame of the screen door and looked back along the narrow walk to the street. There was a car across the way with parking lights burning. There were other cars along the block.

I said: 'Yes, you have, Mrs Talley. I'm working for them. They're still in there pitching. How about you? Don't you want something back?'

The voice said: 'I want to be let alone.'

'I want information,' I said. 'I'm going to get it. Quietly if I can. Loud, if it can't be quiet.'

The voice said: 'Another copper, eh?'

'You know I'm not a copper, Mrs Talley. The Graysons wouldn't talk to a copper. Call them up and ask them.'

'I never heard of them,' the voice said. 'I don't have a phone, if I knew them. Go away, copper. I'm sick. I've been sick for a month.'

'My name is Marlowe,' I said. 'Philip Marlowe. I'm a private eye in Los Angeles, I've been talking to the Graysons. I've got something, but I want to talk to your husband.'

The woman on the couch let out a dim laugh which barely reached across the room. 'You've got something,' she said. 'That sounds familiar. My God it does! You've got something. George Talley had something too – once.'

'He can have it again,' I said, 'if he plays his cards right.'

'If that's what it takes,' she said, 'you can scratch him off right now.'

I leaned against the door-frame and scratched my chin instead. Somebody back on the street had clicked a flashlight on. I didn't know why. It went off again. It seemed to be near my car.

The pale blur of face on the couch moved and disappeared. Hair took its place. The woman had turned her face to the wall.

'I'm tired,' she said, her voice now muffled by talking at the wall. 'I'm so damn tired. Beat it, mister. Be nice and go away.'

'Would a little money help any?'

'Can't you smell the cigar smoke?'

I sniffed. I didn't smell any cigar smoke. I said, 'No.'

'They've been here. They were here two hours. God, I'm tired of it all. Go away.'

'Look, Mrs Talley—'

She rolled on the couch and the blur of her face showed again. I could almost see her eyes, not quite.

'Look yourself,' she said. 'I don't know you. I don't want to know you. I have nothing to tell you. I wouldn't tell it, if I had. I live here, mister, if you call it living. Anyway, it's the nearest I can get to living, I want a little peace and quiet. Now you get out and leave me alone.'

'Let me in the house,' I said. 'We can talk this over. I think I can show you—'

She rolled suddenly on the couch again and feet struck the floor. A tight anger came into her voice.

'If you don't get out,' she said, 'I'm going to start yelling my head off. Right now. Now!'

'Okay,' I said quickly. 'I'll stick my card in the door. So you won't forget my name. You might change your mind.'

I got the card out and wedged it into the crack of the screen door. I said: 'Well, good night, Mrs Talley.'

No answer. Her eyes were looking across the room at me, faintly luminous in the dark. I went down off the porch and back along the narrow walk to the street.

Across the way a motor purled gently in the car with the parking lights on it. Motors purl gently in thousands of cars on thousands of streets everywhere.

I got into the Chrysler and started it up.

25

Westmore was a north and south street on the wrong side of town. I drove north. At the next corner I bumped over disused inter-urban tracks and on into a block of junk yards. Behind wooden fences the decomposing carcases of old automobiles lay in grotesque designs, like a modern battlefield. Piles of rusted parts looked lumpy under the moon. Roof-high piles, with alleys between them.

Headlights glowed in my rear view mirror. They got larger. I stepped on the gas and reached keys out of my pocket and unlocked the glove compartment. I took a .38 out and laid it on the car seat close to my leg.

Beyond the junk yards there was a brick field. The tall chimney of the kiln was smokeless, far off over waste land. Piles of dark bricks, a low wooden building with a sign on it, emptiness, no one moving, no light.

The car behind me gained. The low whine of a lightly touched siren growled through the night. The sound loafed over the fringes of a neglected golf course to the east, across the brickyard to the west. I speeded up a bit more, but it wasn't any use. The car behind me came up fast and a huge red spotlight suddenly glared all over the road.

The car came up level and started to cut in. I stood the Chrysler on its nose, swung out behind the police car, and made a U-turn with half an inch to spare. I gunned the motor the other way. Behind me sounded the rough clashing of gears, the howl of an infuriated motor, and the red spotlight swept for what seemed miles over the brickyard.

It wasn't any use. They were behind me and coming fast again. I didn't have any idea of getting away. I wanted to get back where there were houses and people to come out and watch and perhaps to remember.

I didn't make it. The police car heaved up alongside again and a hard voice yelled:

'Pull over, or we'll blast a hole in you!'

I pulled over to the kerb and set the brake. I put the gun back in the glove compartment and snapped it shut. The police car jumped on its springs just in front of my left front fender. A fat man slammed out of it roaring.

'Don't you know a police siren when you hear one? Get out of that car!'

I got out of the car and stood beside it in the moonlight. The fat man had a gun in his hand.

'Gimme your licence!' he barked in a voice as hard as the blade of a shovel.

I took it out and held it out. The other cop in the car slid out from under the wheel and came around beside me and took what I was holding out. He put a flash on it and read.

'Name of Marlowe,' he said. 'Hell, the guy's a shamus. Just think of that, Cooney.'

Cooney said: 'Is that all? Guess I won't need this.' He tucked the gun back in his holster and buttoned the leader flap down over it. 'Guess I can handle this with my little flippers,' he said. 'Guess I can at that.'

The other one said: 'Doing fifty-five. Been drinking, I wouldn't wonder.'

'Smell the bastard's breath,' Cooney said.

The other one leaned forward with a polite leer. 'Could I smell the breath, shamus?'

I let him smell the breath.

'Well,' he said judiciously, 'he ain't staggering. I got to admit that.'

' 'S a cold night for summer. Buy the boy a drink, Officer Dobbs.'

'Now that's a sweet idea,' Dobbs said. He went to the car and got a half-pint bottle out of it. He held it up. It was a third full. 'No really solid drinking here,' he said. He held the bottle out. 'With our compliments, pal.'

'Suppose I don't want a drink,' I said.

'Don't say that,' Cooney whined. 'We might get the idea you wanted feetprints on your stomach.'

I took the bottle and unscrewed the cap and sniffed. The liquor in the bottle smelled just like whisky. Just whisky.

'You can't work the same gag all the time,' I said.

Cooney said: 'Time is eight twenty-seven. Write it down, Officer Dobbs.'

Dobbs went to the car and leaned in to make a note on his report. I held the bottle up and said to Cooney: 'You insist that I drink this?'

'Naw. You could have me jump on your belly instead.'

I tilted the bottle, locked my throat, and filled my mouth

with whisky. Cooney lunged forward and sank a fist in my stomach. I sprayed the whisky and bent over choking. I dropped the bottle.

I bent to get it and saw Cooney's fat knee rising at my face. I stepped to one side and straightened and slammed him on the nose with everything I had. His left hand went to his face and his voice howled and his right hand jumped to his gun holster. Dobbs ran at me from the side and his arm swung low. The blackjack hit me behind the left knee, the leg went dead and I sat down hard on the ground, gritting my teeth and spitting whisky.

Cooney took his hand away from his face full of blood.

'Jesus,' he cracked in a thick horrible voice. 'This is blood, my blood.' He let out a wild roar and swung his foot at my face.

I rolled far enough to catch it on my shoulder. It was bad enough taking it there.

Dobbs pushed between us and said: 'We got enough, Charlie Better not get it all gummed up.'

Cooney stepped backwards three shuffling steps and sat down on the running-board of the police car and held his face. He groped for a handkerchief and used it gently on his nose.

'Just gimme a minute,' he said through the handkerchief. 'Just a minute, pal. Just one little minute.'

Dobbs said: Pipe down. We got enough. That's the way it's going to be.' He swung the blackjack slowly beside his leg. Cooney got up off the running board and staggered forward. Dobbs put a hand against his chest and pushed him gently. Cooney tried to knock the hand out of his way.

'I gotta see blood,' he croaked. 'I gotta see more blood.'

Dobbs said sharply: 'Nothing doing. Pipe down. We got all we wanted.'

Cooney turned and moved heavily away to the other side of the police car. He leaned against it muttering through his handkerchief. Dobbs said to me:

'Up on the feet, boy friend.'

I got up and rubbed behind my knee. The nerve of the leg was jumping like an angry monkey.

'Get in the car,' Dobbs said. 'Our car.'

I went over and climbed into the police car.

Dobbs said: 'You drive the other heap, Charlie.'

'I'll tear every goddamn fender off'n it,' Cooney roared.

Dobbs picked the whisky bottle off the ground, threw it over the fence, and slid into the car beside me. He pressed the starter.

'This is going to cost you,' he said. 'You hadn't oughta to have socked him.'

I said: 'Just why not?'

'He's a good guy,' Dobbs said. 'A little loud.'

'But not funny,' I said. 'Not at all funny.'

'Don't tell him,' Dobbs said. The police car began to move. 'You'd hurt his feelings.'

Cooney slammed into the Chrysler and started it and clashed the gears as if he was trying to strip them. Dobbs tooled the police car smoothly around and started north again along the brickyard.

'You'll like our new jail,' he said.

'What will the charge be?'

He thought for a moment, guiding the car with a gentle hand and watching in the mirror to see that Cooney followed along behind.

'Speeding,' he said. 'Resisting arrest. HBD. HBD is police slang for "had been drinking".'

'How about being slammed in the belly, kicked in the shoulder, forced to drink liquor under threat of bodily harm, threatened with a gun and struck with a blackjack while unarmed? Couldn't you make a little something more out of that?'

'Aw forget it,' he said wearily. 'You think this sort of thing is my idea of a good time?'

'I thought they cleaned this town up,' I said. 'I thought they had it so that a decent man could walk the streets at night without wearing a bullet-proof vest.'

'They cleaned it up some,' he said. 'They wouldn't want it too clean. They might scare away a dirty dollar.'

'Better not talk like that,' I said. 'You'll lose your union card.'

He laughed. 'The hell with them,' he said. 'I'll be in the army in two weeks.'

The incident was over for him. It meant nothing. He took it as a matter of course. He wasn't even bitter about it.

26

The cell block was almost brand-new. The battleship-grey paint on the steel walls and door still had the fresh gloss of newness disfigured in two or three places by squirted tobacco juice. The overhead light was sunk in the ceiling behind a heavy frosted panel. There were two bunks on one side of the cell and a man snored in the top bunk, with a dark-grey blanket wrapped around him. Since he was asleep that early and didn't smell of whisky or gin and had chosen the top berth where he would be out of the way, I judged he was an old lodger.

I sat on the lower bunk. They had tapped me for a gun but they hadn't stripped my pockets. I got out a cigarette and rubbed the hot swelling behind my knee. The pain radiated all the way to the ankle. The whisky I had coughed on my coat front had a rank smell. I held the cloth up and breathed smoke into it. The smoke floated up around the flat square of lighted glass in the ceiling. The jail seemed very quiet. A woman was making a shrill racket somewhere very far off in another part of the jail. My part was as peaceful as a church.

The woman was screaming wherever she was. The screaming had a thin sharp unreal sound, something like the screaming of coyotes in the moonlight, but it didn't have the rising keening note of the coyote. After a while the sound stopped.

I smoked two cigarettes through and dropped the butts into the small toilet in the corner. The man in the upper berth still snored. All I could see of him was damp greasy hair sticking out over the edge of the blanket. He slept on his stomach. He slept well. He was one of the best.

I sat down on the bunk again. It was made of flat steel slats with a thin hard mattress over them. Two dark-grey blankets were folded on it quite neatly. It was a very nice jail. It was on the twelfth floor of the new city hall. It was a very nice city hall. Bay City was a very nice place. People lived there and thought so. If I lived there, I would probably think so. I would see the nice blue bay and the cliffs and the yacht harbour and the quiet streets of houses, old houses brooding under old trees and new houses with sharp green lawns and wire fences and staked saplings set into the parkway in front of them. I knew a girl who lived on Twenty-fifth Street. It was a nice street. She was a nice girl. She liked Bay City.

She wouldn't think about the Mexican and Negro slums stretched out on the dismal flats south of the old inter-urban tracks. Nor of the waterfront dives along the flat shore south of the cliffs, the sweaty little dance halls on the pike, the marijuana joints, the narrow fox faces watching over the tops of newspapers in far too quiet hotel lobbies, nor the pickpockets and grifters of con men and drunk rollers and pimps and queens on the board walk.

I went over to stand by the door. There was nobody stirring across the way. The lights in the cell block were bleak and silent. Business in the jail was rotten.

I looked at my watch. Nine fifty-four. Time to go home and get your slippers on and play over a game of chess. Time for a tall cool drink and a long quiet pipe. Time to sit with your feet up and think of nothing. Time to start yawning over your magazine. Time to be a human being, a householder, a man with nothing to do but rest and suck in the night air and rebuild the brain for tomorrow.

A man in the blue-grey jail uniform came along between the cells reading numbers. He stopped in front of mine and unlocked the door and gave me the hard stare they think they have to wear on their pans for ever and for ever and for ever. I'm a cop, brother, I'm tough, watch your step, brother, or we'll fix you up so you'll crawl on your hands and knees, brother, snap out of it, brother, let's get a load of the truth, brother, let's go, and let's not forget we're tough guys, we're cops, and we do what we like with punks like you.

'Out,' he said.

I stepped out of the cell and he relocked the door and jerked his thumb and we went along to a wide steel gate and he unlocked that and we went through and he relocked it and the keys tinkled pleasantly on the big steel ring and after a while we went through a steel door that was painted like wood on the outside and battleship-grey on the inside.

Degarmo was standing there by the counter talking to the desk sergeant.

He turned his metallic blue eyes on me and said: 'How you doing?'

'Fine.'

'Like our jail?'

'I like your jail fine.'

'Captain Webber wants to talk to you.'

'That's fine,' I said.

'Don't you know any words but fine?'

'Not right now,' I said. 'Not in here.'

'You're limping a little,' he said. 'You trip over something?'

'Yeah,' I said. 'I tripped over a blackjack. It jumped up and bit me behind the left knee.'

'That's too bad,' Degarmo said, blank-eyed. 'Get your stuff from the property clerk.'

'I've got it,' I said. 'It wasn't taken away from me.'

'Well, that's fine,' he said.

'It sure is,' I said. 'It's fine.'

The desk sergeant lifted his shaggy head and gave us both a long stare. 'You ought to see Cooney's little Irish nose,' he said. 'If you want to see something fine. It's spread over his face like syrup on a waffle.'

Degarmo said absently: 'What's the matter? He get in a fight?'

'I wouldn't know,' the desk sergeant said. 'Maybe it was the same blackjack that jumped up and bit him.'

'For a desk sergeant you talk too damn much,' Degarmo said.

'A desk sergeant always talks too goddamn much,' the desk sergeant said. 'Maybe that's why he isn't a lieutenant on homicide.'

'You see how we are here,' Degarmo said. 'Just one great big happy family.'

'With beaming smiles on our faces,' the desk sergeant said, 'and our arms spread wide in welcome, and a rock in each hand.'

Degarmo jerked his head at me and we went out.

27

Captain Webber pushed his sharp bent nose across the desk at me and said: 'Sit down.'

I sat down in a round-backed wooden arm-chair and eased my left leg away from the sharp edge of the seat. It was a large neat corner office. Degarmo sat at the end of the desk and crossed his legs and rubbed his ankle thoughtfully, and looked out of a window.

Webber went on: 'You asked for trouble, and you got it. You were doing fifty-five miles an hour in a residential zone and you attempted to get away from a police car that signalled you to stop with its siren and red spotlight. You were abusive when stopped and you struck an officer in the face.'

I said nothing. Webber picked a match off his desk and broke it in half and threw the pieces over his shoulder.

'Or are they lying – as usual?' he asked.

'I didn't see their report,' I said. 'I was probably doing fifty-five in a residential district, or anyhow within city limits. The police car was parked outside a house I visited. It followed me when I drove away and I didn't at that time know it was a police car. It had no good reason to follow me and I didn't like the look of it. I went a little fast, but all I was trying to do was get to a better-lighted part of town.'

Degarmo moved his eyes to give a bleak meaningless stare. Webber snapped his teeth impatiently.

He said: 'After you knew it was a police car you made a half-turn in the middle of the block and still tried to get away. Is that right?'

I said: 'Yes. It's going to take a little frank talk to explain that.'

'I'm not afraid of a little frank talk,' Webber said. 'I tend to kind of specialize in frank talk.'

I said: 'These cops that picked me up were parked in front of the house where George Talley's wife lives. They were there before I got there. George Talley is the man who used to be a private detective down here. I wanted to see him. Degarmo knows why I wanted to see him.'

Degarmo picked a match out of his pocket and chewed on the soft end of it quietly. He nodded, without expression.

Webber didn't look at him.

I said: 'You are a stupid man, Degarmo. Everything you do is stupid, and done in a stupid way. When you went up against me yesterday in front of Almore's house you had to get tough when there was nothing to get tough about. You had to make me curious when I had nothing to be curious about. You even had to drop hints which showed me how I could satisfy that curiosity, if it became important. All you had to do to protect your friends was to keep your mouth shut until I made a move. I never would have made one, and you would have saved all this.'

Webber said: 'What the devil has all this got to do with your being arrested in the twelve hundred block on Westmore Street?'

'It has to do with the Almore case,' I said. 'George Talley worked on the Almore case – until he was pinched for drunk driving.'

'Well, I never worked on the Almore case,' Webber snapped. 'I don't know who stuck the first knife into Julius Caesar either. Stick to the point, can't you?'

'I am sticking to the point. Degarmo knows about the Almore case and he doesn't like it talked about. Even your prowl-car boys know about it. Cooney and Dobbs had no reason to follow me unless it was because I visited the wife of a man who had worked on the Almore case. I wasn't doing fifty-five miles an hour when they started to follow me. I tried to get away from them because I had a good idea I might get beaten up for going there. Degarmo had given me that idea.'

Webber looked quickly at Degarmo. Degarmo's hard blue eyes looked across the room at the wall in front of him.

I said: 'And I didn't bust Cooney in the nose until after he had forced me to drink whisky and then hit me in the stomach when I drank it, so that I would spill it down my coat front and smell of it. This can't be the first time you have heard of that trick, Captain.'

Webber broke another match. He leaned back and looked at his small tight knuckles. He looked again at Degarmo and said: 'If you got made chief of police today, you might let me in on it.'

Degarmo said. 'Hell, the shamus just got a couple of playful taps. Kind of kidding. If a guy can't take a joke—'

Webber said: 'You put Cooney and Dobbs over there?'

'Well – yes, I did,' Degarmo said. 'I don't see why we have to put up with these snoopers coming into our town and stirring up a lot of dead leaves just to promote themselves a job and work a couple of old suckers for a big fee. Guys like that need a good sharp lesson.'

'Is that how it looks to you?' Webber asked.

'That's exactly how it looks to me,' Degarmo said.

'I wonder what fellows like you need,' Webber said. 'Right now I think you need a little air. Would you please take it, Lieutenant?'

Degarmo opened his mouth slowly. 'You mean you want me to breeze on out?'

Webber leaned forward suddenly and his sharp little chin seemed to cut the air like the forefoot of a cruiser. 'Would you be so kind?'

Degarmo stood up slowly, a dark flush staining his cheekbones. He leaned a hard hand flat on the desk and looked at Webber. There was a little charged silence. He said:

'Okay, Captain. But you're playing this wrong.'

Webber didn't answer him. Degarmo walked to the door and out. Webber waited for the door to close before he spoke.

'Is it your line that you can tie this Almore business a year and a half ago to the shooting in Lavery's place today? Or is it just a smokescreen you're laying down because you know damn well Kingsley's wife shot Lavery?'

I said: 'It was tied to Lavery before he was shot. In a rough sort of way, perhaps only with a granny knot. But enough to make a man think.'

'I've been into this matter a little more thoroughly than you might think,' Webber said coldly. 'Although I never had anything personally to do with the death of Almore's wife and I wasn't chief of detectives at that time. If you didn't even know Almore yesterday morning, you must have heard a lot about him since.'

I told him exactly what I had heard, both from Miss Fromsett and from the Graysons.

'Then it's your theory that Lavery may have blackmailed Dr Almore?' he asked at the end. 'And that may have something to do with the murder?'

'It's not a theory. It's no more than a possibility. I wouldn't be doing a job if I ignored it. The relations, if any, between Lavery and Almore might have been deep and dangerous or just the merest acquaintance, or not even that. For all I positively know they may never even have spoken to each other. But if there was nothing funny about the Almore case, why get so tough with anybody who shows an interest in it? It could be coincidence that George Talley was hooked for drunk driving just when he was working on it. It could be coincidence that Almore called a cop because I stared at his house, and that Lavery was shot before I could talk to him a second time. But it's no coincidence that two of your men were watching Talley's home tonight, ready, willing and able to make trouble for me, if I went there.'

'I grant you that,' Webber said. 'And I'm not done with that incident. Do you want to file charges?'

'Life's too short for me to file charges of assault against police officers,' I said.

He winced a little. 'Then we'll wash all that out and charge it to experience,' he said. 'And as I understand you were not even booked, you're free to go home any time you want to. And if I were you, I'd leave Captain Webber to deal with the Lavery case and with any remote connection it might turn out to have with the Almore case.'

I said: 'And with any remote connection it might have with a woman named Muriel Chess being found drowned in a mountain lake near Puma Point yesterday?'

He raised his little eyebrows. 'You think that?'

'Only you might not know her as Muriel Chess. Supposing that you knew her at all you might have known her as Mildred Haviland, who used to be Dr Almore's office nurse. Who put Mrs Almore to bed the night she was found dead in the garage, and who, if there was any hanky-panky about that, might know who it was, and be bribed or scared into leaving town shortly thereafter.'

Webber picked up two matches and broke them. His small bleak eyes were fixed on my face. He said nothing.

'And at that point,' I said, 'you run into a real basic coincidence, the only one I'm willing to admit in the whole picture. For this Mildred Haviland met a man named Bill Chess in a Riverside beer parlour and for reasons of her own married him and went to live with him at Little Fawn Lake. And Little Fawn Lake was the property of a man whose wife was intimate with Lavery, who had found Mrs Almore's body. That's what I call a real coincidence. It can't be anything else, but it's basic, fundamental. Everything else flows from it.'

Webber got up from his desk and went over to the water-cooler and drank two paper cups of water. He crushed the cups slowly in his hand and twisted them into a ball and dropped the ball into a brown metal basket under the cooler. He walked to the windows and stood looking out over the bay. This was before the dim-out went into effect, and there were many lights in the yacht harbour.

He came slowly back to the desk and sat down. He reached up and pinched his nose. He was making up his mind about something.

He said slowly: 'I can't see what the hell sense there is in trying to mix that up with something that happened a year and a half later.'

'Okay,' I said, 'and thanks for giving me so much of your time.' I got up to go.

'Your leg feel pretty bad?' he asked, as I leaned down to rub it.

'Bad enough, but it's getting better.'

'Police business,' he said almost gently, 'is a hell of a problem. It's a good deal like politics. It asks for the highest type of men, and there's nothing in it to attract the highest type of men. So we have to work with what we get – and we get things like this.'

'I know,' I said. 'I've always known that. I'm not bitter about it. Good night, Captain Webber.'

'Wait a minute,' he said. 'Sit down a minute. If we've got to have the Almore case in this, let's drag it out into the open and look at it.'

'It's about time somebody did that,' I said. I sat down again.

28

Webber said quietly: 'I suppose some people think we're just a bunch of crooks down here. I suppose they think a fellow kills his wife and then calls me up on the phone and says: "Hi, Cap, I got a little murder down here cluttering up the front room.

And I've got five hundred iron men that are not working." And then I say: "Fine. Hold everything and I'll be right down with a blanket." '

'Not quite that bad,' I said.

'What did you want to see Talley about when you went to his house tonight?'

'He had some line on Florence Almore's death. Her parents hired him to follow it up, but he never told them what it was.'

'And you thought he would tell you?' Webber said sarcastically.

'All I could do was try.'

'Or was it just that Degarmo getting tough with you made you feel like getting tough right back at him?'

'There might be a little of that in it too,' I said.

'Talley was a petty blackmailer,' Webber said contemptuously. 'On more than one occasion. Anyway, to get rid of him was good enough. So I'll tell you what it was he had. He had a slipper he had stolen from Florence Almore's foot.'

'A slipper?'

He smiled faintly. 'Just a slipper. It was later found hidden in his house. It was a green velvet dancing-pump with some little stones set into the heel. It was custom-made, by a man in Hollywood who makes theatrical footwear and such. Now ask me what was important about this slipper?'

'What was important about it, Captain?'

'She had two pair of them, exactly alike, made on the same order. It seems that is not unusual. In case one of them gets scuffed or some drunken ox tries to walk up a lady's leg.' He paused and smiled thinly. 'It seems that one pair had never been worn.'

'I think I'm beginning to get it,' I said.

He leaned back and tapped the arms of his chair. He waited.

'The walk from the side door of the house to the garage is rough concrete,' I said. 'Fairly rough. Suppose she didn't walk it, but was carried. And suppose whoever carried her put her slippers on – and got one that had not been worn.'

'Yes?'

'And suppose Talley noticed this while Lavery was telephoning to the doctor, who was out on his rounds. So he took the unworn slipper, regarding it as evidence that Florence Almore had been murdered.'

Webber nodded his head. 'It was evidence if he left it where it was, for the police to find it. After he took it, it was just evidence that he was a rat.'

'Was a monoxide test made of her blood?'

He put his hands on his desk and looked down at them. 'Yes,' he said. 'And there was monoxide all right. Also the investigating officers were satisfied with appearances. There was no sign of violence. They were satisfied that Dr Almore had not murdered his wife. Perhaps they were wrong. I think the investigation was a little superficial.'

'And who was in charge of it?' I asked.

'I think you know the answer to that.'

'When the police came, didn't they notice that a slipper was missing?'

'When the police came there was no slipper missing. You must remember that Dr Almore was back at his home, in response to Lavery's call, before the police were called. All we know about the missing shoe is from Talley himself. He might have taken the unworn shoe from the house. The side door was unlocked. The maids were asleep. The objection to that is that he wouldn't have been likely to know there was an unworn slipper to take. I wouldn't put it past him to think of it. He's a sharp sneaky little devil. But I can't fix the necessary knowledge on him.'

We sat there and looked at each other, thinking about it.

'Unless,' Webber said slowly, 'we can suppose that this nurse of Almore's was involved with Talley in a scheme to put the bite on Almore. It's possible. There are things in favour of it. There are more things against it. What reason have you for claiming that the girl drowned up in the mountains was this nurse?'

'Two reasons, neither one conclusive separately, but pretty powerful taken together. A tough guy who looked and acted like Degarmo was up there a few weeks ago showing a photograph of Mildred Haviland that looked something like Muriel Chess. Different hair and eyebrows and so on, but a fair resemblance. Nobody helped him much. He called himself De Soto and said he was a Los Angeles cop. There isn't any Los Angeles cop named De Soto. When Muriel Chess heard about it, she looked scared. If it was Degarmo, that's easily established. The other reason is that a golden anklet with a heart on it was hidden in a box of powdered sugar in the Chess cabin. It was found after her death, after her husband had been arrested.

On the back of the heart was engraved: *Al to Mildred. June 28 1938. With all my love.'*

'It could have been some other Al and some other Mildred,' Webber said.

'You don't really believe that, Captain.'

He leaned forward and made a hole in the air with his forefinger. 'What do you want to make of all this exactly?'

'I want to make it that Kingsley's wife didn't shoot Lavery. That his death had something to do with the Almore business. And with Mildred Haviland. And possibly with Dr Almore. I want to make it that Kingsley's wife disappeared because something happened that gave her a bad fright, that she may or may not have guilty knowledge, but that she hasn't murdered anybody. There's five hundred dollars in it for me, if I can determine that. It's legitimate to try.'

He nodded. 'Certainly it is. And I'm the man that would help you, if I could see any grounds for it. We haven't found the woman, but the time has been very short. But I can't help you put something on one of my boys.'

I said: 'I heard you call Degarmo Al. But I was thinking of Almore. His name's Albert.'

Webber looked at his thumb. 'But he was never married to the girl,' he said quietly. 'Degarmo was. I can tell you she led him a pretty dance. A lot of what seems bad in him is the result of it.'

I sat very still. After a moment I said: 'I'm beginning to see things I didn't know existed. What kind of girl was she?'

'Smart, smooth and no good. She had a way with men. She could make them crawl over her shoes. The big boob would tear your head off right now, if you said anything against her. She divorced him, but that didn't end it for him.'

'Does he know she is dead?'

Webber sat quiet for a long moment before he said: 'Not from anything he has said. But how could he help it, if it is the same girl?'

'He never found her in the mountains – so far as we know.' I stood up and leaned down on the desk. 'Look, Captain, you're not kidding me, are you?'

'No. Not one damn bit. Some men are like that and some women can make them like it. If you think Degarmo went up there looking for her because he wanted to hurt her, you're as wet as a bar towel.'

'I never quite thought that,' I said. 'It would be possible, provided Degarmo knew the country up there pretty well. Whoever murdered the girl did.'

'This is all between us,' he said. 'I'd like you to keep it that way.'

I nodded, but I didn't promise him. I said good night again and left. He loooked after me as I went down the room. He looked hurt and sad.

The Chrysler was in the police lot at the side of the building with the keys in the ignition and none of the fenders smashed. Cooney hadn't made good on his threat. I drove back to Hollywood and went up to my apartment in the Bristol. It was late, almost midnight.

The green and ivory hallway was empty of all sound except that a telephone bell was ringing in one of the apartments. It rang insistently and got louder as I came near to my door. I unlocked the door. It was my telephone.

I walked across the room in darkness to where the phone stood on the ledge of an oak desk against the side wall. It must have rung at least ten times before I got to it.

I lifted it out of the cradle and answered, and it was Derace Kingsley on the line.

His voice sounded tight and brittle and strained. 'Good Lord, where in hell have you been?' he snapped. 'I've been trying to reach you for hours.'

'All right. I'm here now,' I said. 'What is it?'

'I've heard from her.'

I held the telephone very tight and drew my breath in slowly and let it out slowly. 'Go ahead,' I said.

'I'm not far away. I'll be over there in five or six minutes. Be prepared to move.'

He hung up.

I stood there holding the telephone half-way between my ear and the cradle. Then I put it down very slowly and looked at the hand that had held it. It was half-open and clenched stiff, as if it was still holding the instrument.

29

The discreet midnight tapping sounded on the door and I went over and opened it. Kingsley looked as big as a horse in a creamy Shetland sports coat with a green and yellow scarf around the neck inside the loosely turned-up collar. A dark reddish-brown snapbrim hat was pulled low on his forehead and under its brim his eyes looked like the eyes of a sick animal.

Miss Fromsett was with him. She was wearing slacks and sandals and a dark green coat and no hat and her hair had a wicked lustre. In her ears hung ear-drops made of a pair of tiny artificial gardenia blooms, hanging one above the other, two on each ear. Gillerlain Regal, the Champagne of Perfumes, came in at the door with her.

I shut the door and indicated the furniture and said: 'A drink will probably help.'

Miss Fromsett sat in an arm-chair and crossed her legs and looked around for cigarettes. She found one and lit it with a long casual flourish and smiled bleakly at a corner of the ceiling.

Kingsley stood in the middle of the floor trying to bite his chin. I went out to the dinette and mixed three drinks and brought them in and handed them. I went over to the chair by the chess table with mine.

Kingsley said: 'What have you been doing and what's the matter with the leg?'

I said: 'A cop kicked me. A present from the Bay City police department. It's a regular service they give down there. As to where I've been – in jail for drunk driving. And from the expression on your face, I think I may be right back there soon.'

'I don't know what you're talking about,' he said shortly. 'I haven't the foggiest idea. This is no time to kid around.'

'All right, don't,' I said. 'What did you hear and where is she?'

He sat down with his drink and flexed the fingers of his right hand and put it inside his coat. It came out with an envelope, a long one.

'You have to take this to her,' he said. 'Five hundred dollars. She wanted more, but this is all I could raise. I cashed a cheque at a night-club. It wasn't easy. She has to get out of town.'

I said: 'Out of what town?'

'Bay City somewhere. I don't know where. She'll meet you at a place called the Peacock Lounge, on Arguello Boulevard, at Eighth Street, or near it.'

I looked at Miss Fromsett. She was still looking at the corner of the ceiling as if she had just come along for the ride.

Kingsley tossed the envelope across and it fell on the chess table. I looked inside it. It was money all right. That much of his story made sense. I let it lie on the small polished table with its inlaid squares of brown and pale gold.

I said: 'What's the matter with her drawing her own money? Any hotel would clear a cheque for her. Most of them would cash one. Has her bank account got lockjaw or something?'

'That's no way to talk,' Kingsley said heavily. 'She's in trouble. I don't know how she knows she's in trouble. Unless a pick-up order has been broadcast. Has it?'

I said I didn't know. I hadn't had much time to listen to police calls. I had been too busy listening to live policemen.

Kingsley said: 'Well, she won't risk cashing a cheque now. It was all right before. But not now.' He lifted his eyes slowly and gave me one of the emptiest stares I had ever seen.

'All right, we can't make sense where there isn't any,' I said. 'So she's in Bay City. Did you talk to her?'

'No. Miss Fromsett talked to her. She called the office. It was just after hours but that cop from the beach, Captain Webber, was with me. Miss Fromsett naturally didn't want her to talk at all then. She told her to call back. She wouldn't give any number we could call.'

I looked at Miss Fromsett. She brought her glance down from the ceiling and pointed it at the top of my head. There was nothing in her eyes at all. They were like drawn curtains.

Kingsley went on: 'I didn't want to talk to her. She didn't want to talk to me. I don't want to see her. I guess there's no doubt she shot Lavery. Webber seemed quite sure of it.'

'That doesn't mean anything,' I said. 'What he says and what he thinks don't even have to be on the same map. I don't like her knowing the cops were after her. It's a long time since anybody listened to the police short-wave for amusement. So she called back later. And then?'

'It was almost half-past six,' Kingsley said. 'We had to sit there in the office and wait for her to call. You tell him.' He turned his head to the girl.

Miss Fromsett said: 'I took the call in Mr Kingsley's office.

He was sitting right beside me, but he didn't speak. She said to send the money down to the Peacock place and asked who would bring it.'

'Did she sound scared?'

'Not in the least. Completely calm. I might say, icily calm. She had it all worked out. She realized somebody would have to bring the money she might not know. She seemed to know Derry – Mr Kingsley wouldn't bring it.'

'Call him Derry,' I said. 'I'll be able to guess who you mean.'

She smiled faintly. 'She will go into this Peacock Lounge every hour about fifteen minutes past the hour. I – I guess I assumed you would be the one to go. I described you to her. And you're to wear Derry's scarf. I described that. He keeps some clothes at the office and this was among them. It's distinctive enough.'

It was all of that. It was an affair of fat green kidneys laid down on an egg-yolk background. It would be almost as distinctive as if I was wheeling a red, white and blue wheelbarrow.

'For a blimp brain she's she's doing all right,' I said.

'This is no time to fool around,' Kingsley put in sharply.

'You said that before,' I told him. 'You've got a hell of a crust assuming I'll go down there and take a getaway stake to somebody I know the police are looking for.'

He twisted a hand on his knee and his face twisted into a crooked grin.

'I admit it's a bit thick,' he said. 'Well, how about it?'

'It makes accessories after the fact out of all three of us. That might not be too tough for her husband and his confidential secretary to talk out of, but what they would do to me would be nobody's dream of a vacation.'

'I'm going to make it worth your while,' he said. 'And we wouldn't be accessories, if she hasn't done anything.'

'I'm willing to suppose it.' I said. 'Otherwise I wouldn't be talking to you. And in addition to that, if I decided she did do any murder, I'm going to turn her over to the police.'

'She won't talk to you,' he said.

I reached for the envelope and put it in my pocket. 'She will, if she wants this.' I looked at my strap watch. 'If I start right away, I might make the one-fifteen deadline. They must know her by heart in that bar after all these hours. That makes it nice too.'

'She's dyed her hair dark brown,' Miss Fromsett said. 'That ought to help a little.'

I said: 'It doesn't help me to think she is just an innocent wayfarer.' I finished my drink and stood up. Kingsley swallowed his at a gulp and stood up and got the scarf off his neck and handed it to me.

'What did you do to get the police on your neck down here?' he asked.

'I was using some information Miss Fromsett very kindly got for me. And that led to my looking for a man named Talley who worked on the Almore case. And that led to the clink. They had the house staked. Talley was the dick the Graysons hired,' I added, looking at the tall dark girl. 'You'll probably be able to explain to him what it's all about. It doesn't matter anyway. I haven't time to go into it now. You two want to wait here?'

Kingsley shook his head. 'We'll go to my place and wait for a call from you.'

Miss Fromsett stood up and yawned. 'No, I'm tired, Derry. I'm going home and going to bed.'

'You'll come with me,' he said sharply. 'You've got to keep me from going nuts.'

'Where do you live, Miss Fromsett?' I asked.

'Bryson Tower on Sunset Place. Apartment 716. Why?' She gave me a speculative look.

'I might want to reach you some time.'

Kingsley's face looked bleakly irritated, but his eyes still were the eyes of a sick animal. I wound his scarf around my neck and went out to the dinette to switch off the light. When I came back they were both standing by the door. Kingsley had his arm around her shoulders. She looked very tired and rather bored.

'Well, I certainly hope—' he started to say, then took a quick step and put his hand out. 'You're a pretty level guy, Marlowe.'

'Go on, beat it,' I said. 'Go away. Go far away.'

He gave a queer look and they went out.

I waited until I heard the elevator come up and stop, and the doors open and close again, and the elevator start down. Then I went out myself and took the stairs down to the basement garage and got the Chrysler awake again.

30

The Peacock Lounge was a narrow front next to a gift shop in whose window a tray of small crystal animals shimmered in the street light. The Peacock had a glass brick front and soft light glowed out around the stained-glass peacock that was set into the brick. I went in around a Chinese screen and looked along the bar and then sat at the outer edge of a small booth. The light was amber, the leather was Chinese red and the booths had polished plastic tables. In one booth four soldiers were drinking beer moodily, a little glassy in the eyes and obviously bored even with drinking beer. Across from them a party of two girls and two flashy-looking men were making the only noise in the place. I saw nobody that looked my idea of Crystal Kingsley.

A wizened waiter with evil eyes and a face like a gnawed bone put a napkin with a printed peacock on it down on the table in front of me and gave me a bacardi cocktail. I sipped it and looked at the amber face of the bar clock. It was just past one-fifteen.

One of the men with the two girls got up suddenly and stalked along to the door and went out. The voice of the other man said:

'What did you have to insult the guy for?'

A girl's tinny voice said: 'Insult him? I like that. He pro-positioned me.'

The man's voice said complainingly: 'Well, you didn't have to insult him, did you?'

One of the soldiers suddenly laughed deep in his chest and then wiped the laugh off of his face with a brown hand and drank a little more beer. I rubbed the back of my knee. It was hot and swollen still but the paralysed feeling had gone away.

A tiny, white-faced Mexican boy with enormous black eyes came in with morning papers and scuttled along the booths trying to make a few sales before the barman threw him out. I bought a paper and looked through it to see if there were any interesting murders. There were not.

I folded it and looked up as a slim, brown-haired girl in a

coal-black slacks and a yellow shirt and a long grey coat came out of somewhere and passed the booth without looking at me. I tried to make up my mind whether her face was familiar or just such a standard type of lean, rather hard, prettiness that I must have seen it a thousand times. She went out of the street door around the screen. Two minutes later the little Mexican boy came back in, shot a quick look at the barman, and scuttled over to stand in front of me.

'Mister,' he said, his great big eyes shining with mischief. Then he made a beckoning sign and scuttled out again.

I finished my drink and went after him. The girl in the grey coat and yellow shirt and black slacks was standing in front of the gift shop, looking in at the window. Her eyes moved as I went out. I went and stood beside her.

She looked at me again. Her face was white and tired. Her hair looked darker than dark brown. She looked away and spoke to the window.

'Give me the money, please.' A little mist formed on the plate-glass from her breath.

I said: 'I'd have to know who you are.'

'You know who I am,' she said softly. 'How much did you bring?'

'Five hundred.'

'It's not enough,' she said. 'Not nearly enough. Give it to me quickly. I've been waiting half an eternity for somebody to get here.'

'Where can we talk?'

'We don't have to talk. Just give me the money and go the other way.'

'It's not that simple. I'm doing this at quite a risk. I'm at least going to have the satisfacion of knowing what goes on and where I stand.'

'Damn you,' she said acidly, 'why couldn't he come himself? I don't want to talk. I want to get away as soon as I can.'

'You didn't want him to come himself. He understood that you didn't even want to talk to him on the phone.'

'That's right,' she said quickly and tossed her head.

'But you've got to talk to me,' I said. 'I'm not as easy as he is. Either to me or to the law. There's no way out of it. I'm a private detective and I have to have some protection, too.'

'Well, isn't he charming,' she said. 'Private detective and all.' Her voice held a low sneer.

'He did the best he knew how. It wasn't easy for him to know what to do.'

'What do you want to talk about.'

'You, and what you've been doing and where you've been and what you expect to do. Things like that. Little things, but important.'

She breathed on the glass of the shop window and waited while the mist of her breath disappeared.

'I think it would be much better,' she said in the same cool empty voice, 'for you to give me the money and let me work things out for myself.'

'No.'

She gave me another sharp sideways glance. She shrugged the shoulders of the grey coat impatiently.

'Very well, if it has to be that way. I'm at the Granada, two blocks north on Eighth. Apartment 618. Give me ten minutes. I'd rather go in alone.'

'I have a car.'

'I'd rather go alone.' She turned quickly and walked away.

She walked back to the corner and crossed the boulevard and disappeared along the block under a line of pepper trees. I went and sat in the Chrysler and gave her the ten minutes before I started it.

The Granada was an ugly grey building on a corner. The plate-glass entrance door was level with the street. I drove around the corner and saw a milky globe with 'Garage' painted on it. The entrance to the garage was down a ramp into the hard rubber-smelling silence of parked cars in rows. A lanky negro came out of a glassed-in office and looked the Chrysler over.

'How much to leave this here a short time? I'm going upstairs.'

He gave me a shady leer. 'Kinda late, boss. She needs a good dustin' too. Be a dollar.'

'What goes on here?'

'Be a dollar,' he said woodenly.

I got out. He gave me a ticket. I gave him the dollar. Without my asking him he said the elevator was in back of the office, by the men's room.

I rode up to the sixth floor and looked at numbers on doors and listened to stillness and smelled beach air coming in at the ends of corridors. The place seemed decent enough. There would be a few happy ladies in any apartment house. That would explain the lanky negro's dollar. A great judge of character, that boy.

I came to the door of Apartment 618 and stood outside it a moment and then knocked softly.

31

She still had the grey coat on. She stood back from the door and I went past her into a square room with twin wall beds and a minimum of uninteresting furniture. A small lamp on a window-table made a dim yellowish light. The window behind it was open.

The girl said: 'Sit down and talk then.'

She closed the door and went to sit in a gloomy Boston rocker across the room. I sat down on a thick davenport. There was a dull green curtain hanging across an open door space, at one end of the davenport. That would lead to dressing-room and bathroom. There was a closed door at the other end. That would be the kitchenette. That would be all there was.

The girl crossed her ankles and leaned her head back against the chair and looked at me under long beaded lashes. Her eyebrows were thin and arched and as brown as her hair. It was a quiet, secret face. It didn't look like the face of a woman who would waste a lot of motion.

'I got a rather different idea of you,' I said, 'from Kingsley.'

Her lips twisted a little. She said nothing.

'From Lavery too,' I said. 'It just goes to show that we talk different languages to different people.'

'I haven't time for this sort of talk,' she said. 'What is it you have to know?'

'He hired me to find you. I've been working on it. I supposed you would know that.'

'Yes. His office sweetie told me that over the phone. She

told me you would be a man named Marlowe. She told me about the scarf.'

I took the scarf off my neck and folded it up and slipped it into a pocket. I said:

'So I know a little about your movements. Not very much. I know you left your car at the Prescott Hotel in San Bernardino and that you met Lavery there. I know you sent a wire from El Paso. What did you do then?'

'All I want from you is the money he sent. I don't see that my movements are any of your business.'

'I don't have to argue about that,' I said. 'It's a question of whether you want the money.'

'Well, we went to El Paso,' she said, in a tired voice. 'I thought of marrying him then. So I sent that wire. You saw the wire?'

'Yes.'

'Well, I changed my mind. I asked him to go home and leave me. He made a scene.'

'Did he go home and leave you?'

'Yes. Why not?'

'What did you do then?'

'I went to Santa Barbara and stayed there a few days. Over a week, in fact. Then to Pasadena. Same thing. Then to Hollywood. Then I came down here. That's all.'

'You were alone all this time?'

She hesitated a little and then said: 'Yes.'

'Not with Lavery – any part of it?'

'Not after he went home.'

'What was the idea?'

'Idea of what?' Her voice was a little sharp.

'Idea of going these places and not sending any word. Didn't you know he would be very anxious?'

'Oh, you mean my husband,' she said coolly. 'I don't think I worried much about him. He'd think I was in Mexico, wouldn't he? As for the idea of it all – well, I just had to think things out. My life had got to be a hopeless tangle. I had to be somewhere quite alone and try to straighten myself out.'

'Before that,' I said, 'you spent a month at Little Fawn Lake trying to straighten it out and not getting anywhere. Is that it?'

She looked down at her shoes and then up at me and nodded earnestly. The wavy brown hair surged forward along her cheeks. She put her left hand up and pushed it back and then rubbed her temple with one finger.

'I seemed to need a new place,' she said. 'Not necessarily an interesting place. Just a strange place. Without associations. A place where I would be very much alone. Like an hotel.'

'How are you getting on with it?'

'Not very well. But I'm not going back to Derace Kingsley. Does he want me to?'

'I don't know. Why did you come down here, to the town where Lavery was?'

She bit a knuckle and looked at me over her hand.

'I wanted to see him again. He's all mixed up in my mind. I'm not in love with him, and yet – well, I suppose in a way I am. But I don't think I want to marry him. Does that make sense?'

'That part of it makes sense. But staying away from home in a lot of crummy hotels doesn't. You've lived your own life for years, as I understand it.'

'I had to be alone, to – to think things out,' she said a little desperately and bit the knuckle again, hard. 'Won't you please give me the money and go away?'

'Sure. Right away. But wasn't there any other reason for your going away from Little Fawn Lake just then? Anything connected with Muriel Chess, for instance?'

She looked surprised. But anyone can look surprised. 'Good heavens, what would there be? That frozen-faced little drip – what is she to me?'

'I thought you might have had a fight with her – about Bill.'

'Bill? Bill Chess?' She seemed even more surprised. Almost too surprised.

'Bill claims you made a pass at him.'

She put her head back and let out a tinny and unreal laugh. 'Good heavens, that muddy-faced boozer?' Her face sobered suddenly. 'What's happened? Why all the mystery?'

'He might be a muddy-faced boozer,' I said. 'The police think he's a murderer too. Of his wife. She's been found drowned in the lake. After a month.'

She moistened her lips and held her head on one side, staring at me fixedly. There was a quiet little silence. The damp breath of the Pacific slid into the room around us.

'I'm not too surprised,' she said slowly. 'So it came to that in the end. They fought terribly at times. Did you think that had something to do with my leaving?'

I nodded. 'There was a chance of it,'

'It didn't have anything to do with it at all,' she said seriously, and shook her head back and forth. 'It was just the way I told you. Nothing else.'

'Muriel's dead,' I said. 'Drowned in the lake. You don't get much of a boot out of that, do you?'

'I hardly knew the girl,' she said. 'Really. She kept to herself. After all—'

'I don't suppose you knew she had once worked in Dr Almore's office?'

She looked completely puzzled now. 'I was never in Dr Almore's office,' she said slowly. 'He made a few house calls a long time ago. I – what are you talking about?'

'Muriel Chess was really a girl called Mildred Haviland, who had been Dr Almore's office nurse.'

'That's a queer coincidence,' she said wonderingly. 'I knew Bill met her in Riverside. I didn't know how or under what circumstances or where she came from. Dr Almore's office, eh? It doesn't have to mean anything, does it?'

I said: 'No. I guess it's a genuine coincidence. They do happen. But you see why I had to talk to you. Muriel being found drowned and you having gone away and Muriel being Mildred Haviland who was connected with Dr Almore at one time – as Lavery was also, in a different way. And of course Lavery lives across the street from Dr Almore. Did he, Lavery, seem to know Muriel from somewhere else?'

She thought about it, biting her lower lip gently. 'He saw her up there,' she said finally. 'He didn't act as if he had ever seen her before.'

'And he would have,' I said. 'Being the kind of guy he was.'

'I don't think Chris had anything to do with Dr Almore,' she said. 'He knew Dr Almore's wife. I don't think he knew the doctor at all. So he probably wouldn't know Dr Almore's office nurse.'

'Well, I guess there's nothing in all this to help me,' I said. 'But you can see why I had to talk to you. I guess I can give you the money now.'

I got the envelope out and stood up to drop it on her knee. She let it lie there. I sat down again.

'You do this character very well,' I said. 'This confused innocence with an undertone of hardness and bitterness. People have made a bad mistake about you. They have been thinking of you as a reckless little idiot with no brains and no control. They have been very wrong.'

She stared at me, lifting her eyebrows. She said nothing. Then a small smile lifted the corners of her mouth. She reached for the envelope, tapped it on her knee, and laid it aside on the table. She stared at me all the time.

'You did the Fallbrook character very well too,' I said. 'Looking back on it, I think it was a shade overdone. But at the time it had me going all right. That purple hat that would have been all right on blonde hair but looked like hell on straggly brown, that messed-up make-up that looked as if it had been put on in the dark by somebody with a sprained wrist, the jittery screwball manner. All very good. And when you put the gun in my hand like that – I fell like a brick.'

She snickered and put her hands in the deep pockets of her coat. Her heels tapped on the floor.

'But why did you go back at all?' I asked. 'Why take such a risk in broad daylight, in the middle of the morning?'

'So you think I shot Chris Lavery?' she said quietly.

'I don't think it. I know it.'

'Why did I go back? Is that what you want to know?'

'I don't really care,' I said.

She laughed. A sharp cold laugh. 'He had all my money,' she said. 'He had stripped my purse. He had it all, even silver. That's why I went back. There wasn't any risk at all. I know how he lived. It was really safer to go back. To take in the milk and the newspaper for instance. People lose their heads in these situations. I don't, I didn't see why I should. It's so very much safer not to.'

'I see,' I said. 'Then of course you shot him the night before. I ought to have thought of that, not that it matters. He had been shaving. But guys with dark beards and lady friends sometimes shave the last thing at night, don't they?'

'It has been heard of,' she said almost gaily. 'And just what are you going to do about it?'

'You're a cold-blooded little bitch if ever I saw one,' I said. 'Do about it? Turn you over to the police naturally. It will be a pleasure.'

'I don't think so.' She threw the words out, almost with a lilt. 'You wondered why I gave you the empty gun. Why not? I had another one in my bag. Like this.'

Her right hand came up from her coat pocket and she pointed it at me.

I grinned. It may not have been the heartiest grin in the world, but it was a grin.

'I've never liked this scene,' I said. 'Detective confronts murderer. Murderer produces gun, points same at detective. Murderer tells detective the whole sad story, with the idea of shooting him at the end of it. Thus wasting a lot of valuable time, even if in the end murderer did shoot detective. Only murderer never does. Something always happens to prevent it. The gods don't like this scene either. They always manage to spoil it.'

'But this time,' she said softly and got up and moved towards me softly across the carpet, 'suppose we make it a little different. Suppose I don't tell you anything and nothing happens and I do shoot you?'

'I still wouldn't like the scene,' I said.

'You don't seem to be afraid,' she said, and slowly licked her lips coming towards me very gently without any sound of footfalls on the carpet.

'I'm not afraid,' I lied. 'It's too late at night, too still, and the window is open and the gun would make too much noise. It's too long a journey down to the street and you're not good with guns. You would probably miss me. You missed Lavery three times.'

'Stand up,' she said.

I stood up.

'I'm going to be too close to miss,' she said. She pushed the gun against my chest. 'Like this. I really can't miss now, can I? Now be very still. Hold your hands up by your shoulders and then don't move at all. If you move at all, the gun will go off.'

I put my hands up beside my shoulders. I looked down at the gun. My tongue felt a little thick, but I could still wave it.

Her probing left hand didn't find a gun on me. It dropped and she bit her lip, staring at me. The gun bored into my chest. 'You'll have to turn around now,' she said, polite as a tailor at a fitting.

'There's something a little off key about everything you do,' I said. 'You're definitely not good with guns. You're much too close to me, and I hate to bring this up – but there's that old business of the safety-catch not being off. You've overlooked that too.'

So she started to do two things at once. To take a long step backwards and feel with her thumb for the safety-catch, without taking her eyes off my face. Two very simple things, needing only a second to do. But she didn't like my telling her. She didn't like my thought riding over hers. The minute confusion of it jarred her.

She let out a small choked sound and I dropped my right hand and yanked her face hard against my chest. My left hand smashed down on her right wrist, the heel of my hand against the base of her thumb. The gun jerked out of her hand to the floor. Her face writhed against my chest and I think she was trying to scream.

Then she tried to kick me and lost what little balance she had left. Her hands came up to claw at me. I caught her wrist and began to twist it behind her back. She was very strong, but I was very much stronger. So she decided to go limp and let her whole weight sag against the hand that was holding her head. I couldn't hold her up with one hand. She started to go down and I had to bend down with her.

There were vague sounds of our scuffling on the floor by the davenport, and hard breathing, and if a floorboard creaked I didn't hear it. I thought a curtain-ring checked sharply on a rod. I wasn't sure and I had no time to consider the question. A figure loomed up suddenly on my left, just behind, and out of range of clear vision. I knew there was a man there and that he was a big man.

That was all I knew. The scene exploded into fire and darkness. I didn't even remember being slugged. Fire and darkness and just before the darkness a sharp flash of nausea.

32

I smelled of gin. Not just casually, as if I had taken four or five drinks of a winter morning to get out of bed on, but as if the Pacific Ocean was pure gin and I had nose-dived off the boat deck. The gin was in my hair and eyebrows, on my chin and under my chin. It was on my shirt. I smelled like dead toads.

My coat was off and I was lying flat on my back beside the davenport on somebody's carpet and I was looking at a framed picture. The frame was of cheap soft wood varnished and the picture showed part of an enormously high pale yellow viaduct across which a shiny black locomotive was dragging a Prussian-blue train. Through one lofty arch of the viaduct a wide yellow beach showed and was dotted with sprawled bathers and striped beach umbrellas. Three girls walked close up, with paper parasols, one girl in cerise, one in pale blue, one in green. Beyond the beach a curving bay was bluer than any bay has any right to be. It was drenched with sunshine and flecked and dotted with aching white sails. Beyond the inland curve of the bay three ranges of hills rose in three precisely opposed colours, gold and terra-cotta and lavender.

Across the bottom of the picture was printed in large capitals, SEE THE FRENCH RIVIERA BY THE BLUE TRAIN.

It was a fine time to bring that up.

I reached up wearily and felt the back of my head. It felt pulpy. A shoot of pain from the touch went clear to the soles of my feet. I groaned, and made a grunt out of the groan, from professional pride – what was left of it. I rolled over slowly and carefully and looked at the foot of a pulled-down wall-bed; one twin, the other being still up in the wall. The flourish of design on the painted wood was familiar. The picture had hung over the davenport and I hadn't even looked at it.

When I rolled a square gin bottle rolled off my chest and hit the floor. It was water white, and empty. It didn't seem possible there could be so much gin in just one bottle.

I got my knees under me and stayed on all fours for a while, sniffing like a dog who can't finish his dinner, but hates to leave it. I moved my head around on my neck. It hurt, I moved it around some more and it still hurt, so I climbed up on my feet and discovered I didn't have any shoes on.

The shoes were lying against the baseboard, looking as dissipated as shoes ever looked. I put them on wearily. I was an old man now. I was going down the last long hill. I still had a tooth left though. I felt it with my tongue. It didn't seem to taste of gin.

'It will all come back to you,' I said. 'Some day it will all come back to you. And you won't like it.'

There was the lamp on the table by the open window. There was the fat green davenport. There was the doorway with the green curtain across it. Never sit with your back to a green curtain. It always turns out badly. Something always happens. Who had I said that to? A girl with a gun. A girl with a clear, empty face and dark-brown hair that had been blonde.

I looked around for her. She was still there. She was lying on the pulled-down twin bed.

She was wearing a pair of tan stockings and nothing else. Her hair was tumbled. There were dark bruises on her throat. Her mouth was open and a swollen tongue filled it to over-flowing. Her eyes bulged and the whites of them were not white.

Across her naked belly four angry scratches leered crimson red against the whiteness of flesh. Deep angry scratches, gouged out by four bitter finger-nails.

On the davenport there were tumbled clothes, mostly hers. My coat was there also. I disentangled it and put it on. Something crackled under my hand in the tumbled clothes. I drew out a long envelope with money still in it. I put it in my pocket. Marlowe, five hundred dollars. I hoped it was all there. There didn't seem much else to hope for.

I stepped on the balls of my feet softly, as if walking on very thin ice. I bent down to rub behind my knee and wondered which hurt most, my knee, or my head when I bent down to rub the knee.

Heavy feet came along the hallway and there was a hard mutter of voices. The feet stopped. A hard fist knocked on the door.

I stood there leering at the door, with my lips drawn back tight against my teeth. I waited for somebody to open the door and walk in. The knob was tried, but nobody walked in. The knocking began again, stopped, the voices muttered again. The steps went away. I wondered how long it would take to get the manager with a pass-key. Not very long.

Not nearly long enough for Marlowe to get home from the French Riviera.

I went to the green curtain and brushed it aside and looked down a short dark hallway into a bathroom. I went in there and put the light on. Two wash rugs on the floor, a bath mat folded over the edge of the tub, a pebbled glass window at the corner of the tub. I shut the bathroom door and stood on the edge of the tub and eased the window up. This was the sixth floor. There was no screen. I put my head out and looked into darkness and a narrow glimpse of a street with trees. I looked sideways and saw that the bathroom window of the next apartment was not more than three feet away. A well-nourished mountain goat could make it without any trouble at all.

The question was whether a battered private detective could make it, and if so, what the harvest would be.

Behind me a rather remote and muffled voice seemed to be chanting the policeman's litany: 'Open it up or we'll kick it in.' I sneered back at the voice. They wouldn't kick it in because kicking in a door is hard on the feet. Policemen are kind to their feet. Their feet are about all they are kind to.

I grabbed a towel off the rack and pulled the two halves of the window down and eased out on the sill. I swung half of me over to the next sill, holding on to the frame of the open window. I could just reach to push the next window down, if it was unlocked. It wasn't unlocked. I got my foot over there and kicked the glass over the catch. It made a noise that ought to have been heard in Reno. I wrapped the towel around my left hand and reached in to turn the catch. Down on the street a car went by, but nobody yelled at me.

I pushed the broken window down and climbed across to the other sill. The towel fell out of my hand and fluttered down into the darkness to a strip of grass far below, between the two wings of the building.

I climbed in at the window of the other bathroom.

33

I climbed down into the darkness and groped through darkness to a door and opened it and listened. Filtered moonlight coming through north windows showed a bedroom with twin beds, made up and empty. Not wall beds. This was a larger apartment. I moved past the beds to another door and into a living-room. Both rooms were closed up and smelt musty. I felt my way to a lamp and switched it on. I ran a finger along the wood of a table edge. There was a light film of dust, such as accumulates in the cleanest room when it is left shut up.

The room contained a library dining-table, an arm-chair radio, a book-rack built like a hod, a big bookcase full of novels with their jackets still on them, a dark wood highboy with a siphon and a cut-glass bottle of liquor and four striped glasses upside down on an Indian brass tray. Beside this paired photographs in a double silver frame, a youngish middle-aged man and woman, with round healthy faces and cheerful eyes. They looked out at me as if they didn't mind my being there at all.

I sniffed the liquor, which was Scotch, and used some of it. It made my head feel worse but it made the rest of me feel better. I put the light on in the bedroom and poked into closets. One of them had a man's clothes, tailor-made, plenty of them. The tailor's label inside a coat pocket declared the owner's name to be H. G. Talbot. I went to the bureau and poked around and found a soft blue shirt that looked a little small for me. I carried it into the bathroom and stripped mine off and washed my face and chest and wiped my hair off with a wet towel and put the blue shirt on. I used plenty of Mr Talbot's rather insistent hair tonic on my hair and used his brush and comb to tidy it up. By that time I smelled of gin only remotely, if at all.

The top button of the shirt wouldn't meet its buttonhole so I poked into the bureau again and found a dark-blue crêpe tie and strung it around my neck. I got my coat back on and looked at myself in the mirror. I looked slightly too neat for that hour of the night, even for as careful a man as Mr Talbot's clothes indicated him to be. Too neat and too sober.

I rumpled my hair a little and pulled the tie loose, and went back to the whisky decanter and did what I could about being too sober. I lit one of Mr Talbot's cigarettes and hoped that Mr and Mrs Talbot, wherever they were, were having a much better time than I was. I hoped I would live long enough to come and visit them.

I went to the living-room door, the one giving on the hallway, and opened it and leaned in the opening smoking. I didn't think it was going to work. But I didn't think waiting there for them to follow my trail through the window was going to work any better.

A man coughed a little way down the hall and I poked my

head out farther and he was looking at me. He came towards me briskly, a small sharp man in a neatly pressed police uniform. He had reddish hair and red-gold eyes.

I yawned and said languidly: 'What goes on, officer?'

He stared at me thoughtfully. 'Little trouble next door to you. Hear anything?'

'I thought I heard knocking. I just got home a little while ago.'

'Little late,' he said.

'That's a matter of opinion,' I said. 'Trouble next door, ah?'

'A dame,' he said. 'Know her?'

'I think I've seen her.'

'Yeah,' he said. 'You oughta see her now . . .' He put his hands to his throat and bulged his eyes out and gurgled unpleasantly. 'Like that,' he said. 'You didn't hear nothing, huh?'

'Nothing I noticed – except the knocking.'

'Yeah. What was the name?'

'Talbot.'

'Just a minute, Mr Talbot. Wait there just a minute.'

He went along the hallway and leaned into an open doorway through which light streamed out. 'Oh, Lieutenant,' he said. 'The man next door is on deck.'

A tall man came out of the doorway and stood looking along the hall straight at me. A tall man with rusty hair and very blue blue eyes. Degarmo. That made it perfect.

'Here's the guy who lives next door,' the small neat cop said helpfully. 'His name's Talbot.'

Degarmo looked straight at me, but nothing in his acid blue eyes showed that he had ever seen me before. He came quietly along the hall and put a hard hand against my chest and pushed me back into the room. When he had me half a dozen feet from the door he said over his shoulder:

'Come in here and shut the door, Shorty.'

The small cop came in and shut the door.

'Quite a gag,' Degarmo said lazily. 'Put a gun on him, Shorty.'

Shorty flicked his black belt holster open and had his .38 in his hand like a flash. He licked his lips.

'Oh boy,' he said softly, whistling a little. 'Oh boy. How'd you know, Lieutenant?'

'Know what?' Degarmo asked, keeping his eyes fixed on mine. 'What were you thinking of doing, pal – going down to get a paper – to find out if she was dead?'

'Oh boy,' Shorty said. 'A sex-killer. He pulled the girl's clothes off and choked her with his hands, Lieutenant. How'd you know?'

Degarmo didn't answer him. He just stood there, rocking a little on his heels, his face empty and granite-hard.

'Yah, he's the killer, sure,' Shorty said suddenly. 'Sniff in the air in here, Lieutenant. The place ain't been aired out for days. And look at the dust on those bookshelves. And the clock on the mantel's stopped, Lieutenant. He come in through the — lemme look a minute, can I, Lieutenant?'

He ran out of the room into the bedroom. I heard him fumbling around. Degarmo stood woodenly.

Shorty came back. 'Come in at the bathroom window. There's broken glass in the tub. And something stinks of gin in there something awful. You remember how that apartment smelled of gin when we went in? Here's a shirt, Lieutenant. Smells like it was washed in gin.'

He held the shirt up. It perfumed the air rapidly. Degarmo looked at it vaguely and then stepped forward and yanked my coat open and looked at the shirt I was wearing.

'I know what he done,' Shorty said. 'He stole one of the guy's shirts that lives here. You see what he done, Lieutenant?'

'Yeah.' Degarmo held his hand against my chest and let it fall slowly. They were talking about me is if I was a piece of wood.

'Frisk him, Shorty.'

Shorty ran around me feeling here and there for a gun. 'Nothing on him,' he said.

'Let's get him out the back way,' Degarmo said. 'It's our pinch, if we make it before Webber gets here. That lug Reed couldn't find a moth in a shoe-box.'

'You ain't even been detailed on the case,' Shorty said doubtfully. 'Didn't I hear you was suspended or something?'

'What can I lose?' Degarmo asked, 'if I'm suspended?'

'I can lose this here uniform,' Shorty said.

Degarmo looked at him wearily. The small cop blushed and his bright red-gold eyes were anxious.

'Okay, Shorty. Go and tell Reed.'

The small cop licked his lip. 'You say the word, Lieutenant, and I'm with you. I don't have to know you got suspended.'

'We'll take him down ourselves, just the two of us,' Degarmo said.

'Yeah, sure.'

Degarmo put his finger against my chin. 'A sex-killer,' he said quietly. 'Well, I'll be damned.' He smiled at me thinly, moving only the extreme corners of his wide brutal mouth.

34

We went out of the apartment and along the hall the other way from Apartment 618. Light streamed from the still open door. Two men in plain clothes now stood outside it smoking cigarettes inside their cupped hands, as if a wind was blowing. There was a sound of wrangling voices from the apartment.

We went around the bend of the hall and came to the elevator. Degarmo opened the fire door beyond the elevator shaft and we went down echoing concrete steps, floor after floor. At the lobby floor Degarmo stopped and held his hand on the doorknob and listened. He looked back over his shoulder.

'You got a car?' he asked me.

'In the basement garage.'

'That's an idea.'

We went on down the steps and came out into the shadowy basement. The lanky negro came out of the little office and I gave him my car check. He looked furtively at the police uniform of Shorty. He said nothing. He pointed to the Chrysler.

Degarmo climbed under the wheel of the Chrysler. I got in beside him and Shorty got into the back seat. We went up the ramp and out into the damp cool night air. A big car with twin red spotlights was charging towards us from a couple of blocks away.

Degarmo spat out of the car window and yanked the Chrysler the other way. 'That will be Webber,' he said. 'Late for the funeral again. We sure skinned his nose on that one, Shorty.'

'I don't like it too well, Lieutenant. I don't, honest.'

'Keep the chin up, kid. You might get back on homicide.'

'I'd rather wear buttons and eat,' Shorty said. The courage was oozing out of him fast.

Degarmo drove the car hard for ten blocks and then slowed a little. Shorty said uneasily:

'I guess you know what you're doing, Lieutenant, but this ain't the way to the Hall.'

'That's right,' Degarmo said. 'It never was, was it?'

He let the car slow down to a crawl and then turned into a residential street of small exact houses squatting behind small exact lawns. He braked the car gently and coasted over to the kerb and stopped about the middle of the block. He threw an arm over the back of the seat and turned his head to look back at Shorty.

'You think this guy killed her, Shorty?'

'I'm listening,' Shorty said in a tight voice.

'Got a flash?'

'No.'

I said: 'There's one in the car pocket on the left side.'

Shorty fumbled around and metal clicked and the white beam of the flashlight came on. Degarmo said:

'Take a look at the back of this guy's head.'

The beam moved and settled. I heard the small man's breathing behind me and felt it on my neck. Something felt for and touched the bump on my head. I grunted. The light went off and the darkness of the street rushed in again.

Shorty said: 'I guess maybe he was sapped, Lieutenant. I don't get it.'

'So was the girl,' Degarmo said. 'It didn't show much but it's there. She was sapped so she could have her clothes pulled off and be clawed up before she was killed. So the scratches would bleed. Then she was throttled. And none of this made any noise. Why would it? And there's no telephone in that apartment. Who reported it, Shorty?'

'How the hell would I know? A guy called up and said a woman had been murdered in 618 Granada Apartments on Eighth. Reed was still looking for a cameraman when you come in. The desk said a guy with a thick voice, likely disguised. Didn't give any name at all.'

'All right then,' Degarmo said. 'If you had murdered the girl, how would you get out of there?'

'I'd walk out,' Shorty said. 'Why not? Hey,' he barked at me suddenly, 'why didn't you?'

I didn't answer him. Degarmo said tonelessly: 'You wouldn't climb out of a bathroom window six floors up and then bust in another bathroom window into a strange apartment where people would likely be sleeping, would you? You wouldn't pretend to be the guy that lived there and you wouldn't throw away a lot of your time by calling the police, would you? Hell, that girl could have laid there for a week. You wouldn't throw away the chance of a start like that, would you, Shorty?'

'I don't guess I would,' Shorty said cautiously. 'I don't guess I would call up at all. But you know these sex fiends do funny things, Lieutenant. They ain't normal like us. And this guy could have had help and the other guy could have knocked him out to put him in the middle.'

'Don't tell me you thought that last bit up all by yourself,' Degarmo grunted. 'So here we sit, and the fellow that knows all the answers is sitting here with us and not saying a word.' He turned his big head and stared at me. 'What were you doing there?'

'I can't remember,' I said. 'The crack on the head seems to have blanked me out.'

'We'll help you to remember,' Degarmo said. 'We'll take you up back in the hills a few miles where you can be quiet and look at the stars and remember. You'll remember all right.'

Shorty said: 'That ain't no way to talk, Lieutenant. Why don't we just go back to the Hall and play this the way it says in the rule book?'

'To hell with the rule book,' Degarmo said. 'I like this guy. I want to have one long sweet talk with him. He just needs a little coaxing, Shorty. He's just bashful.'

'I don't want any part of it,' Shorty said.

'What do you want to do, Shorty?'

'I want to go back to the Hall.'

'Nobody's stopping you, kid. You want to walk?'

Shorty was silent for a moment. 'That's right,' he said at last, quietly. 'I want to walk.' He opened the car door and stepped out on to the kerbing. 'And I guess you know I have to report all this, Lieutenant?'

'Right,' Degarmo said. 'Tell Webber I was asking for him. Next time he buys a hamburger, tell him to turn down an empty plate for me.'

'That don't make any sense to me,' the small cop said. He slammed the car door shut. Degarmo let the clutch in and gunned the motor and hit forty in the first block and a half. In the third block he hit fifty. He slowed down at the boulevard and turned east and began to cruise along at a legal speed. A few late cars drifted by both ways, but for the most part the world lay in the cold silence of early morning.

After a little while we passed the city limits and Degarmo spoke. 'Let's hear you talk,' he said quietly. 'Maybe we can work this out.'

The car topped a long rise and dipped down to where the boulevard wound through the park-like grounds of the veterans' hospital. The tall triple electroliers had haloes from the beach fog that had drifted in during the night. I began to talk.

'Kingsley came over to my apartment tonight and said he had heard from his wife over the phone. She wanted some money quick. The idea was I was to take it to her and get her out of whatever trouble she was in. My idea was a little different. She was told how to identify me and I was to be at the Peacock Lounge at Eighth and Arguello at fifteen minutes past the hour. Any hour.'

Degarmo said slowly: 'She had to breeze and that meant she had something to breeze from, such as murder.' He lifted his hands lightly and let them fall on the wheel again.

'I went down there, hours after she had called. I had been told her hair was dyed brown. She passed me going out of the bar, but I didn't know her. I had never seen her in the flesh. All I had seen was what looked like a pretty good snapshot, but could be that and still not a very good likeness. She sent a Mexican kid in to call me out. She wanted the money and no conversation. I wanted her story. Finally she saw she would have to talk a little and told me she was at the Granada. She made me wait ten minutes before I followed her over.'

Degarmo said: 'Time to fix up a plant.'

'There was a plant all right, but I'm not sure she was in on it. She didn't want me to come up there, didn't want to talk. Yet she ought to have known I would insist on some explanation before I gave up the money, so her reluctance could have been just an act, to make me feel that I was controlling the situation. She could act all right. I found that out. Anyhow I went and we talked. Nothing she said made very much sense until we talked about Lavery getting shot. Then she made too much sense too quick. I told her I was going to turn her over to the police.'

Westwood Village, dark except for one all-night service station and a few distant windows in apartment houses, slid away to the north of us.

'So she pulled a gun,' I said. 'I think she meant to use it, but she got too close to me and I got a headlock on her. While we were wrestling around, somebody came out from behind a green curtain and slugged me. When I came out of that the murder was done.'

Degarmo said slowly: 'You get any kind of a look at who slugged you?'

'No. I felt or half-saw he was a man and a big one. And this lying on the davenport, mixed in with clothes.' I reached Kingsley's yellow and green scarf out of my pocket and draped it over his knee. 'I saw Kingsley wearing this earlier this evening,' I said.

Degarmo looked at the scarf. He lifted it under the dashlight. 'You wouldn't forget that too quick,' he said. 'It steps right up and smacks you in the eye. Kingsley, huh? Well, I'm damned. What happened then?'

'Knocking on the door. Me still woozy in the head, not too bright and a bit panicked. I had been flooded with gin and my shoes and coat stripped off and maybe I looked and smelled a little like somebody who would yank a woman's clothes off and strangle her. So I got out through the bathroom window, cleaned myself up as well as I could, and the rest you know.'

Degarmo said: 'Why didn't you lie dormy in the place you climbed into?'

'What was the use? I guess even a Bay City cop would have found the way I had gone in a little while. If I had any chance at all, it was to walk out before that was discovered. If nobody was there who knew me, I had a fair chance of getting out of the building.'

'I don't think so,' Degarmo said. 'But I can see where you didn't lose much trying. What's your idea of the motivation here?'

'Why did Kingsley kill her – if he did? That's not hard. She had been cheating on him, making him a lot of trouble, endangering his job and now she had killed a man. Also, she had money and Kingsley wanted to marry another woman. He might have been afraid that with money to spend she could beat the rap and be left laughing at him. If she didn't beat the rap, and got sent up, her money would be just as thoroughly beyond his reach. He'd also have to divorce her to get rid of her. There's plenty of motive for murder in all that. Also he saw a chance to make me the goat. It wouldn't stick, but it would make confusion and delay. If murderers didn't think they could get away with their murders, very few would be committed.'

Degarmo said: 'All the same it could be somebody else, somebody who isn't in the picture at all. Even if he went down there to see her, it could still be somebody else. Somebody else could have killed Lavery too.'

'If you like it that way.'

He turned his head. 'I don't like it any way at all. But if I crack the case, I'll get by with a reprimand from the police board. If I don't crack it, I'll be thumbing a ride out of town. You said I was dumb. Okay, I'm dumb. Where does Kingsley live? One thing I know is how to make people talk.'

'965 Carson Drive, Beverly Hills. About five blocks on you turn north to the foothills. It's on the left side, just below Sunset. I've never been there, but I know how the block numbers run.'

He handed me the green and yellow scarf. 'Tuck that back into your pocket until we want to spring it on him.'

35

It was a two-storey white house with a dark roof. Bright moonlight lay against its wall like a fresh coat of paint. There were wrought-iron grilles against the lower halves of the front windows. A level lawn swept up to the front door which was set diagonally into the angle of a jutting wall. All the visible windows were dark.

Degarmo got out of the car and walked along the parkway and looked back along the drive to the garage. He moved down the driveway and the corner of the house hid him. I heard the sound of a garage door going up, then the thud as it was lowered again. He reappeared at the corner of the house, shook his head at me, and walked across the grass to the front door. He leaned his thumb on the bell and juggled a cigarette out of his pocket with one hand and put it between his lips.

He turned away from the door to light it and the flare of the match cut deep lines into his face. After a while there was light on the fan over the door. The peephole in the door swung back. I saw Degarmo holding up his shield. Slowly and as if unwillingly the door was opened. He went in.

He was gone four or five minutes. Light went on behind various windows, then off again. Then he came out of the house and while he was walking back to the car the light went off in the fan and the whole house was again as dark as we had found it.

He stood beside the car smoking and looking off down the curve of the street.

'One small car in the garage,' he said. 'The cook says it's hers. No sign of Kingsley. They say they haven't seen him since this morning. I looked in all the rooms. I guess they told the truth. Webber and a print man were there late this afternoon and the dusting powder is still all over the main bedroom. Webber would be getting prints to check against what we found in Lavery's house. He didn't tell me what he got. Where would he be – Kingsley?'

'Anywhere,' I said. 'On the road, in an hotel, in a Turkish bath getting the kinks out of his nerves. But we'll have to try his girl friend first. Her name is Fromsett and she lives at the Bryson Tower on Sunset Place. That's away downtown, near Bullock's Wilshire.'

'She does what?' Degarmo asked, getting in under the wheel.

'She holds the fort in his office and holds his hand out of office hours. She's no office cutie, though. She has brains and style.'

'This situation is going to use all she has,' Degarmo said. He drove down to Wilshire and we turned east again.

Twenty-five minutes brought us to the Bryson Tower, a white stucco palace with fretted lanterns in the forecourt and tall date palms. The entrance was in an L, up marble steps, through a Moorish archway, and over a lobby that was too big and a carpet that was too blue. Blue Ali Baba oil jars were dotted around, big enough to keep tigers. There was a desk and a night clerk with one of those moustaches that get stuck under your fingernail.

Degarmo lunged past the desk towards an open elevator beside which a tired old man sat on a stool waiting for a customer. The clerk snapped at Degarmo's back like a terrier.

'One moment, please. Whom did you wish to see?'

Degarmo spun on his heel and looked at me wonderingly. 'Did he say, "whom"?'

'Yeah, but don't hit him,' I said. 'There is such a word.'

Degarmo licked his lips. 'I knew there was,' he said. 'I often wondered where they kept it. Look, buddy,' he said to the clerk, 'we want up seven-sixteen. Any objection?'

'Certainly I have,' the clerk said coldly. 'We don't announce guests at' – he lifted his arm and turned it neatly to look at the narrow oblong watch on the inside of his wrist – 'at twenty-three minutes past four in the morning.'

'That's what I thought,' Degarmo said. 'So I wasn't going to bother you. You get the idea?' He took his shield out of his pocket and held it so that the light glinted on the gold and the blue enamel. 'I'm a police lieutenant.'

The clerk shrugged. 'Very well. I hope there isn't going to be any trouble. I'd better announce you then. What names?'

'Lieutenant Degarmo and Mr Marlowe.'

'Apartment 716. That will be Miss Fromsett. One moment.'

He went behind a glass screen and we heard him talking on the phone after a longish pause. He came back and nodded.

'Miss Fromsett is in. She will receive you.'

'That's certainly a load off my mind,' Degarmo said. 'And don't bother to call your house-peeper and send him up to the scatter. I'm allergic to house-peepers.'

The clerk gave a small cold smile and we got into the elevator.

The seventh floor was cool and quiet. The corridor seemed a mile long. We came at last to a door with 716 on it in gilt numbers in a circle of gilt leaves. There was an ivory button beside the door. Degarmo pushed it and chimes rang inside the door and it was opened.

Miss Fromsett wore a quilted blue robe over her pyjamas. On her feet were small tufted slippers with high heels. Her dark hair was fluffed out engagingly and the cold cream had been wiped from her face and just enough make-up applied.

We went past her into a rather narrow room with several handsome oval mirrors and grey period furniture upholstered in blue demask. It didn't look like apartment house furniture. She sat down on a slender love seat and leaned back and waited calmly for somebody to say something.

I said: 'This is Lieutenant Degarmo of the Bay City police.

We're looking for Kingsley. He's not at his house. We thought you might be able to give us an idea where to find him.'

She spoke to me without looking at me. 'Is it that urgent?'

'Yes. Something has happened.'

'What has happened?'

Degarmo said bluntly: 'We just want to know where Kingsley is, sister. We don't have time to build up a scene.'

The girl looked at him with a complete absence of expression. She looked back at me and said:

'I think you had better tell me, Mr Marlowe.'

'I went down there with the money,' I said. 'I met her as arranged. I went to her apartment to talk to her. While there I was slugged by a man who was hidden behind a curtain. I didn't see the man. When I came out of it she had been murdered.'

'Murdered?'

I said: 'Murdered.'

She closed her fine eyes and the corners of her lovely mouth drew in. Then she stood up with a quick shrug and went over to a small, marble-topped table with spindly legs. She took a cigarette out of a small embossed silver box and lit it, staring emptily down at the table. The match in her hand was waved more and more slowly until it stopped, still burning, and she dropped it into a tray. She turned and put her back to the table.

'I suppose I ought to scream or something,' she said. 'I don't seem to have any feeling about it at all.'

Degarmo said: 'We don't feel so interested in your feelings right now. What we want to know is where Kingsley is. You can tell us or not tell us. Either way you skip the attitudes. Just make your mind up.'

She said to me quietly: 'The lieutenant here is a Bay City officer?'

I nodded. She turned at him slowly, with a lovely contemptuous dignity. 'In that case,' she said, 'he has no more right in my apartment than any other loud-mouthed bum that might try to toss his weight around.'

Degarmo looked a her bleakly. He grinned and walked across the room and stretched his long legs from a deep downy chair. He waved his hand at me.

'Okay, you work on her. I can get all the co-operation I

need from the LA boys, but by the time I had things explained to them, it would be a week from next Tuesday.'

I said: 'Miss Fromsett, if you know where he is, or where he started to go, please tell us. You can understand that he has to be found.'

She said calmly: 'Why?'

Degarmo put his head back and laughed. 'This babe is good,' he said. 'Maybe she thinks we should keep it a secret from him that his wife has been knocked off.'

'She's better than you think,' I told him. His face sobered and he bit his thumb. He looked her up and down insolently.

She said: 'Is it just because he has to be told?'

I took the yellow and green scarf out of my pocket and shook it out loose and held it in front of her.

'This was found in the apartment where she was murdered. I think you have seen it.'

She looked at the scarf and she looked at me, and in neither of the glances was there any meaning. She said: 'You ask for a great deal of confidence, Mr Marlowe. Considering that you haven't been such a very smart detective after all.'

'I ask for it,' I said, 'and I expect to get it. And how smart I've been is something you don't really know anything about.'

'This is cute,' Degarmo put in. 'You two make a nice team. All you need is acrobats to follow you. But right now—'

She cut through his voice as if he didn't exist. 'How was she murdered?'

'She was strangled and stripped naked and scratched up.'

'Derry wouldn't have done anything like that,' she said quietly.

Degarmo made a noise with his lips. 'Nobody ever knows what anybody else will do, sister. A cop knows that much.'

She still didn't look at him. In the same level tone she asked: 'Do you want to know where we went after we left your apartment and whether he brought me home – things like that?'

'Yes.'

'Because if he did, he wouldn't have had time to go down to the beach and kill her? Is that it?'

I said: 'That's a good part of it.'

'He didn't bring me home,' she said slowly. 'I took a taxi on Hollywood Boulevard, not more than five minutes after we

359

left your place. I didn't see him again. I supposed he went home.'

Degarmo said: 'Usually the bim tries to give her boy friend a bit more alibi than that. But it takes all kinds, don't it?'

Miss Fromsett said to me: 'He wanted to bring me home, but it was a long way out of his way and we were both tired. The reason I was telling you this is because I know it doesn't matter in the least. If I thought it did, I wouldn't tell you.'

'So he did have time,' I said.

She shook her head. 'I don't know. I don't know how much time was needed. I don't know how he could have known where to go. Not from me, not from her through me. She didn't tell me.' Her dark eyes were on mine, searching, probing. 'Is this the kind of confidence you ask for?'

I folded the scarf up and put it back in my pocket. 'We want to know where he is now.'

'I can't tell you because I have no idea.' Her eyes had followed the scarf down to my pocket. They stayed there. 'You say you were slugged. You mean knocked unconscious?'

'Yes. By somebody who was hidden behind a curtain. We still fall for it. She pulled a gun on me and I was busy trying to take it away from her. There's no doubt she shot Lavery.'

Degarmo stood up suddenly. 'You're making yourself a nice smooth scene, fellow,' he growled. 'But you're not getting anywhere. Let's blow.'

I said: 'Wait a minute. I'm not finished. Suppose he had something on his mind, Miss Fromsett, something that was eating pretty deep into him. That was how he looked tonight. Suppose he knew more about all this than we realized – or than I realized – and knew things were coming to a head. He would want to go somewhere quietly and try to figure out what to do. Don't you think he might?'

I stopped and waited, looking sideways at Degarmo's impatience. After a moment the girl said tonelessly: 'He wouldn't run away or hide, because it wasn't anything he could run away and hide from. But he might want a time to himself to think.'

'In a strange place in an hotel,' I said, thinking of the story that had been told me in the Granada. 'Or in a much quieter place than that.'

I looked around for the telephone.

'It's in my bedroom,' Miss Fromsett said, knowing at once what I was looking for.

I went down the room and through the door at the end. Degarmo was right behind me. The bedroom was ivory and ashes of roses. There was a big bed with no footboard and a pillow with the rounded hollow of a head. Toilet articles glistened on a built-in dresser with panelled mirrors on the wall above it. An open door showed mulberry bathroom tiles. The phone was on a night table by the bed.

I sat down on the edge of the bed and patted the place where Miss Fromsett's head had been and lifted the phone and dialled long distance. When the operator answered I asked for Constable Jim Patton at Puma Point, person to person, very urgent. I put the phone back in the cradle and lit a cigarette. Degarmo glowered down at me, standing with his legs apart, tough and tireless and ready to be nasty. 'What now?' he grunted.

'Wait and see.'

'Who's running this show?'

'Your asking me shows that. I am – unless you want the Los Angeles police to run it.'

He scratched a match on his thumbnail and watched it burn and tried to blow it out with a long steady breath that just bent the flame over. He got rid of that much and put another between his teeth and chewed on it. The phone rang in a moment.

'Ready with your Puma Point call.'

Patton's sleepy voice came on the line. 'Yes? This is Patton at Puma Point.'

'This is Marlowe in Los Angeles,' I said. 'Remember me?'

'Sure I remember you, son. I ain't only half awake though.'

'Do me a favour,' I said. 'Although I don't know why you should. Go or send over to Little Fawn Lake and see if Kingsley is there. Don't let him see you. You can spot his car outside the cabin or maybe see lights. And see that he stays put. Call me back as soon as you know. I'm coming up. Can you do that?'

Patton said: 'I got no reason to stop him if he wants to leave.'

'I'll have a Bay City police officer with me who wants to question him about a murder. Not your murder, another one.'

There was a drumming silence along the wire. Patton said: 'You ain't just bein' tricky, are you son?'

'No. Call me back at Tunbridge 2722.'

'Should likely take me half an hour,' he said.

I hung up. Degarmo was grinning now. 'This babe flash you a signal I couldn't read?'

I stood up off the bed. 'No. I'm just trying to read his mind. He's no cold killer. Whatever fire there was is all burned out of him by now. I thought he might go to the quietest and most remote place he knows – just to get a grip of himself. In a few hours he'll probably turn himself in. It would look better for you if you got to him before he did that.'

'Unless he puts a slug in his head,' Degarmo said coldly. 'Guys like him are very apt to do that.'

'You can't stop him until you find him.'

'That's right.'

We went back into the living-room. Miss Fromsett poked her head out of her kitchenette and said she was making coffee, and did we want any. We had some coffee and sat around looking like people seeing friends off at the railroad station.

The call from Patton came through in about twenty-five minutes . There was light in the Kingsley cabin and a car was parked beside it.

36

We ate some breakfast at Alhambra and I had the tank filled. We drove out Highway 70 and started moving past the trucks into the rolling ranch country. I was driving. Degarmo sat moodily in the corner, his hands deep in his pockets.

I watched the fat straight rows of orange trees spin by like the spokes of a wheel. I listened to the whine of the tyres on the road and I felt tired and stale from lack of sleep and too much emotion.

We reached the long slope south of San Dimas that goes up to a ridge and drops down into Pomona. This is the ultimate end of the fog belt, and the beginning of that semi-desert region where the sun is as light and dry as old sherry in the morning, as hot as a blast furnace at noon, and drops like an angry brick at nightfall.

Degarmo stuck a match in the corner of his mouth and said almost sneeringly:

'Webber gave me hell last night. He said he was talking to you and what about.'

I said nothing. He looked at me and looked away again. He waved a hand outwards. 'I wouldn't live in this damn country if they gave it to me. The air's stale before it gets up in the morning.'

'We'll be coming to Ontario in a minute. We'll switch over to Foothill Boulevard and you'll see five miles of the finest grevillea trees in the world.'

'I wouldn't know one from a fireplug,' Degarmo said.

We came to the centre of town and turned north on Euclid, along the splendid parkway. Degarmo sneered at the grevillea trees.

After a while he said: 'That was my girl that drowned in the lake up there. I haven't been right in the head since I heard about it. All I can see is red. If I could get my hands on that guy Chess—'

'You made enough trouble,' I said, 'letting her get away with murdering Almore's wife.'

I stared straight ahead through the windshield. I knew his head moved and his eyes froze on me. I didn't know what his hands were doing. I didn't know what expression was on his face. After a long time his words came. They came through tight teeth and edgeways, and they scraped a little as they came out.

'You a little crazy or something?'

'No,' I said. 'Neither are you. You know as well as anybody could know anything that Florence Almore didn't get up out of bed and walk down to that garage. You know she was carried. You know that was why Talley stole her slipper, the slipper that had never walked on a concrete path. You knew that Almore gave his wife a shot in the arm at Condy's place and that it was just enough and not any too much. He knew his shots in the arm the way you know how to rough up a bum that hasn't any money or any place to sleep. You know that Almore didn't murder his wife with morphine and that if he wanted to murder her, morphine would be the last thing in the world he would use. But you know that somebody else did, and that Almore carried her down to the garage and put her there – technically still alive to breathe in some monoxide, but medically just as dead as though she had stopped breathing. You know all that.'

Degarmo said softly: 'Brother, how did you ever manage to live so long?'

I said: 'By not falling for too many gags and not getting too much afraid of professional hard guys. Only a heel would have done what Almore did, only a heel and a badly scared man who had things on his soul that wouldn't stand daylight. Technically he may even have been guilty of murder. I don't think the point has ever been settled. Certainly he would have a hell of a time proving that she was in such a deep coma that she was beyond any possibility of help. But as a practical matter of who killed her, you know the girl killed her.'

Degarmo laughed. It was a grating unpleasant laugh, not only mirthless, but meaningless.

We reached Foothill Boulevard and turned east again. I thought it was still cool, but Degarmo was sweating. He couldn't take his coat off because of the gun under his arm.

I said: 'The girl, Mildred Haviland, was playing house with Almore and his wife knew it. She had threatened him. I got that from her parents. The girl, Mildred Haviland, knew all about morphine and where to get all of it she needed and how much to use. She was alone in the house with Florence Almore, after she put her to bed. She was in a perfect spot to load a needle with four or five grains and shoot it into an unconscious woman through the same puncture Almore had already made. She would die, perhaps while Almore was still out of the house, and he would come home and find her dead. The problem would be his. He would have to solve it. Nobody would believe anybody else had doped his wife to death. Nobody that didn't know all the circumstances. But you knew. I'd have to think you much more of a damn fool than I think you are to believe you didn't know. You covered the girl up. You were in love with her still. You scared her out of town, out of danger, out of reach, but you covered up for her. You let the murder ride. She had you that way. Why did you go up to the mountains looking for her?'

'And how did I know where to look?' he said harshly. 'It wouldn't bother you to add an explanation of that, would it?'

'Not at all,' I said. 'She got sick of Bill Chess and his boozing and his tempers and his down-at-heels living. But she had to have money to make a break. She thought she was safe now, that she had something on Almore that was safe to use. So she wrote him for money. He sent you up to talk to her. She didn't tell Almore what her present name was or any details or where or how she was living. A letter addressed to Mildred Haviland at Puma Point would reach her. All she had to do was ask for it. But no letter came and nobody connected her with Mildred Haviland. All you had was an old photo and your usual bad manners, and they didn't get you anywhere with those people.'

Degarmo said gratingly: 'Who told you she tried to get money from Almore?'

'Nobody. I had to think of something to fit what happened. If Lavery or Mrs Kingsley had known who Muriel Chess had been, and had tipped it off, you would have known where to find her and what name she was using. You didn't know those things. Therefore the lead had to come from the only person up there who knew who she was, and that was herself. So I assume she wrote to Almore.'

'Okay,' he said at last. 'Let's forget it. It doesn't make any difference any more now. If I'm in a jam, that's my business. I'd do it again, in the same circumstances.'

'That's all right,' I said. 'I'm not planning to put the bite on anybody myself. Not even on you. I'm telling you this mostly so you won't try to hang any murders on Kingsley that don't belong on him. If there is one that does, let it hang.'

'Is that why you're telling me?' he asked.

'Yeah.'

'I thought maybe it was because you hated my guts,' he said.

'I'm all done with hating you,' I said. 'It's all washed out of me. I hate people hard, but I don't hate them very long.'

We are going through the grape country now, the open sandy grape country along the scarred flanks of the foothills. We came in a little while to San Bernardino and I kept on through without stopping.

37

At Crestline, elevation 5,000 feet, it had not yet started to warm up. We stopped for a beer. When we got back into the car, Degarmo took the gun from his under-arm holster and looked it over. It was a .38 Smith and Wesson on a .44 frame, a wicked weapon with a kick like a .45 and a much greater effective range.

'You won't need that,' I said. 'He's big and strong, but he's not that kind of tough.'

He put the gun back under his arm and grunted. We didn't talk any more now. We had no more to talk about. We rolled around the curves along the sharp sheer edges walled with white guard rails and in some places with walls of field stone and heavy iron chains. We climbed through the tall oaks and on to the altitudes where the oaks are not so tall and the pines are taller and taller. We came at last to the dam at the end of Puma Lake.

I stopped the car and the sentry threw his piece across his body and stepped up to the window.

'Close all the windows of your car before proceeding across the dam, please.'

I reached back to wind up the rear window on my side. Degarmo held his shield up. 'Forget it, buddy. I'm a police officer,' he said with his usual tact.

The sentry gave him a solid expressionless stare. 'Close all windows, please,' he said in the same tone he had used before.

'Nuts to you,' Degarmo said. 'Nuts to you, soldier boy.'

'It's an order,' the sentry said. His jaw muscles bulged very slightly. His dull greyish eyes stared at Degarmo. 'And I didn't write the order, Mister. Up with the windows.'

'Suppose I told you to go jump in the lake,' Degarmo sneered.

The sentry said: 'I might do it. I scare easily.' He patted the breech of his rifle with a leathery hand.

Degarmo turned and closed the windows on his side. We drove across the dam. There was a sentry in the middle and one at the far end. The first one must have flashed them some kind of signal. They looked at us with steady watchful eyes, without friendliness.

I drove on through the piled masses of granite and down

through the meadows of coarse grass where cows grazed. The same gaudy slacks and short shorts and peasant handkerchiefs as yesterday, the same light breeze and golden sun and clear blue sky, the same smell of pine needles, the same cool softness of a mountain summer. But yesterday was a hundred years ago, something crystallized in time, like a fly in amber.

I turned off on the road to Little Fawn Lake and wound around the huge rocks and past the little gurgling waterfall. The gate into Kingsley's property was open and Patton's car was standing in the road pointing towards the lake, which was invisible from that point. There was nobody in it. The card sign on the windshield still read, *Keep Jim Patton Constable. He Is Too Old To Go To Work.*

Close to it and pointed the other way was a small battered coupé. Inside the coupé a lion-hunter's hat. I stopped my car behind Patton's and locked it and got out. Andy got out of the coupé and stood staring at us woodenly.

I said: 'This is Lieutenant Degarmo of the Bay City police.

Andy said: 'Jim's just over the ridge. He's waiting for you. He ain't had any breakfast.'

We walked up the road to the ridge as Andy got back into his coupé. Beyond it the road dropped to the tiny blue lake. Kingsley's cabin across the water seemed to be without life.

'That's the lake,' I said.

Degarmo looked down at it silently. His shoulders moved in a heavy shrug. 'Let's go get the bastard,' was all he said.

We went on and Patton stood up from behind a rock. He was wearing the same old Stetson and khaki pants and shirt buttoned to his thick neck. The star on his left breast still had a bent point. His jaws moved slowly, munching.

'Nice to see you again,' he said, not looking at me, but at Degarmo.

He put his hand out and shook Degarmo's hard paw. 'Last time I seen you, Lieutenant, you was wearing another name. Kind of undercover, I guess you'd call it. I guess I didn't treat you right neither. I apologize. Guess I know what that photo of yours was all the time.'

Degarmo nodded and said nothing.

'Likely if I'd been on my toes and played the game right, a lot of trouble would have been saved,' Patton said. 'Maybe a life would have been saved. I feel kind of bad about it, but then again I ain't a fellow that feels too bad about anything very long. Suppose we sit down here and you tell me what it is we're supposed to be doing now.'

Degarmo said: 'Kingsley's wife was murdered in Bay City last night. I have to talk to him about it.'

'You mean you suspect him?' Patton asked.

'And how,' Degarmo grunted.

Patton rubbed his neck and looked across the lake. 'He ain't showed outside the cabin at all. Likely he's still asleep. Early this morning I snuck around the cabin. There was a radio goin' then and I heard sounds like a man would make playing with a bottle and a glass. I stayed away from him. Was that right?'

'We'll go over there now,' Degarmo said.

'You got a gun, Lieutenant?'

Degarmo patted under his left arm. Patton looked at me. I shook my head, no gun.

'Kingsley might have one, too,' Patton said. 'I don't hanker after no fast shooting around here, Lieutenant. It wouldn't do me no good to have a gun-fight. We don't have that kind of community up here. You look to me like a fellow who would jack his gun out kind of fast.'

'I've got plenty of swift, if that's what you mean,' Degarmo said. 'But I want this guy talking.'

Patton looked at Degarmo, looked at me, looked back at Degarmo and spat tobacco juice in a long stream to one side.

'I ain't heard enough to even approach him,' he said stubbornly.

So we sat down on the ground and told him the story. He listened silently, not blinking an eye. At the end he said to me: 'You got a funny way of working for people, seems to me. Personally I think you boys are plumb misinformed. We'll go over and see. I'll go in first – in case you would know what you are talking about and Kingsley would have a gun and would be a little desperate. I got a big belly. Makes a nice target.'

We stood up off the ground and started around the lake the long way. When we came to the little pier. I said:

'Did they autopsy her yet, sheriff?'

Patton nodded. 'She drowned all right. They say they're satisfied that's how she died. She wasn't knifed or shot or had her head cracked in or anything. There's marks on her body, but too many to mean anything. And it ain't a very nice body to work with.'

Degarmo looked white and angry.

'I guess I oughtn't to have said that, Lieutenant,' Patton added mildly. 'Kind of tough to take. Seeing you knew the lady pretty well.'

Degarmo said: 'Let's get it over and do what we have to do.'

We went on along the shore of the lake and came to Kingsley's cabin. We went up the heavy steps. Patton went quietly across the porch to the door. He tried the screen. It was not hooked. He opened it and tried the door. That was unlocked also. He held the door shut, with the knob turned in his hand, and Degarmo took hold of the screen and pulled it wide. Patton opened the door and we walked into the room.

Derace Kingsley lay back in a deep chair by the cold fireplace with his eyes closed. There was an empty glass and an almost empty whisky bottle on the table beside him. The room smelled of whisky. A dish near the bottle was choked with cigarette-stubs. Two crushed empty packs lay on top of the stubs.

All the windows in the room were shut. It was already close and hot in there. Kingsley was wearing a sweater and his face was flushed and heavy. He snored and his hands hung lax outside the arms of the chair, the finger-tips touching the floor.

Patton moved to within a few feet of him and stood looking silently down at him for a long moment before he spoke.

'Mr Kingsley,' he said then, in a calm steady voice, 'we got to talk to you a little.'

38

Kingsley moved with a kind of jerk, and opened his eyes and moved them without moving his head. He looked at Patton, then at Degarmo, lastly at me. His eyes were heavy, but the light sharpened in them. He sat up slowly in the chair and rubbed his hands up and down the sides of his face.

'I was asleep,' he said. 'Fell asleep a couple of hours ago. I was as drunk as a skunk, I guess. Anyway, much drunker than I like to be.' He dropped his hands and let them hang.

Patton said: 'This is Lieutenant Degarmo of the Bay City police. He has to talk to you.'

Kingsley looked briefly at Degarmo and his eyes came around to stare at me. His voice when he spoke again sounded sober and quiet and tired to death.

'So you let them get her?' he said.

I said: 'I would have, but I didn't.'

Kingsley thought about that, looking at Degarmo. Patton had left the front door open. He pulled the brown venetian blinds up at two front windows and pulled the windows up. He sat in a chair near one of them and clasped his hands over his stomach. Degarmo stood glowering down at Kingsley.

'Your wife is dead, Kingsley,' he said brutally. 'If it's any news to you.'

Kingsley stared at him and moistened his lips.

'Takes it easy, don't he?' Degarmo said. 'Show him the scarf.'

I took the green and yellow scarf out and dangled it. Degarmo jerked a thumb. 'Yours?'

Kingsley nodded. He moistened his lips again.

'Careless of you to leave it behind you,' Degarmo said. He was breathing a little too hard. His nose was pinched and deep lines ran from his nostrils to the corners of his mouth.

Kingsley said very quietly: 'Leave it behind me where?' He had barely glanced at the scarf. He hadn't looked at all at me.

'In the Granada Apartments, on Eighth Street, in Bay City. Apartment 618. Am I telling you something?'

Kingsley now very slowly lifted his eyes to meet mine. 'Is that where she was?' he breathed.

I nodded. 'She didn't want me to go there. I wouldn't give her the money until she talked to me. She admitted she killed Lavery. She pulled a gun and planned to give me the same treatment. Somebody came from behind the curtain and knocked me out without letting me see him. When I came to she was dead.' I told him how she was dead and how she looked. I told him what I had done and what had been done to me.

He listened without moving a muscle of his face. When

370

I had done talking he made a vague gesture towards the scarf. 'What has that got to do with it?'

'The lieutenant regards it as evidence that you were the party hidden out in the apartment.'

Kingsley thought that over. He didn't seem to get the implications of it very quickly. He leaned back in the chair and rested his head against the back. 'Go on,' he said at length. 'I suppose you know what you're talking about. I'm quite sure I don't.'

Degarmo said: 'All right, play dumb. See what it gets you. You could begin by accounting for your time last night after you dropped your biddy at her apartment house.'

Kingsley said evenly: 'If you mean Miss Fromsett, I didn't. She went home in a taxi. I was going home myself, but I didn't. I came up here instead. I thought the trip and the night air and the quiet might help me to get straightened out.'

'Just think of that,' Degarmo jeered. 'Straightened out from what, if I might ask?'

'Straightened out from all the worry I had been having.'

'Hell,' Degarmo said, 'a little thing like strangling your wife and clawing her belly wouldn't worry you that much, would it?'

'Son, you hadn't ought to say things like that,' Patton put in from the background. 'That ain't no way to talk. You ain't produced anything yet that sounds like evidence.'

'No?' Degarmo swung his hard head at him. 'What about this scarf, fatty? Isn't that evidence?'

'You didn't fit it in to anything – not that I heard,' Patton said peacefully. 'And I ain't fat, either, just well covered.'

Degarmo swung away from him disgustedly. He jabbed his finger at Kingsley.

'I suppose you didn't go down to Bay City at all,' he said harshly.

'No. Why should I. Marlowe was taking care of that. And I don't see why you are making a point of the scarf. Marlowe was wearing it.'

Degarmo stood rooted and savage. He turned very slowly and gave me his bleak angry stare.

'I don't get this,' he said. 'Honest, I don't. It wouldn't be that somebody is kidding me, would it? Somebody like you?'

I said: 'All I told about the scarf was that it was in the apartment and that I had seen Kingsley wearing it earlier in the evening. That seemed to be all you wanted. I might have added that I had later worn the scarf myself, so the girl I was to meet could identify me that much easier.'

Degarmo backed away from Kingsley and leaned against the wall at the end of the fireplace. He pulled his lower lip out with thumb and forefinger of his left hand. His right hand hung lax at his side, the fingers slightly curved.

I said: 'I told you all I had ever seen of Mrs Kingsley was a snapshot. One of us had to be sure of being able to identify the other. The scarf seemed obvious enough for identification. As a matter of fact I had seen her once before, although I didn't know it when I went to meet her. But I didn't recognize her at once.' I turned to Kingsley. 'Mrs Fallbrook,' I said.

'I thought you said Mrs Fallbrook was the owner of the house,' he answered slowly.

'That's what she said at the time. That's what I believed at the time. Why wouldn't I?'

Degarmo made a sound in his throat. His eyes were a little crazy, I told him about Mrs Fallbrook and her purple hat and her fluttery manner and the empty gun she had been holding and how she gave it to me.

When I stopped, he said very carefully: 'I didn't hear you tell Webber any of that.'

'I didn't tell him. I didn't want to admit I had already been in the house three hours before. That I had gone to talk it over with Kingsley before I reported it to the police.'

'That's something we're going to love you for,' Degarmo said with a cold grin. 'Jesus, what a sucker I've been. How much you paying this shamus to cover up your murders for you, Kingsley?'

'His usual rates,' Kingsley told him emptily. 'And a five hundred dollar bonus if he can prove my wife didn't murder Lavery.'

'Too bad he can't earn that,' Degarmo sneered.

'Don't be silly,' I said. 'I've already earned it.'

There was a silence in the room. One of those charged silences which seem about to split apart with a peal of thunder. It didn't. It remained, hung heavy and solid, like a wall. Kingsley moved a little in his chair, and after a long moment, he nodded his head.

'Nobody could possibly know that better than you know it, Degarmo,' I said.

Patton had as much expression on his face as a chunk of wood. He watched Degarmo quietly. He didn't look at Kingsley at all. Degarmo looked at a point between my eyes, but not as if that was anything in the room with him. Rather as if he was looking at something very far away, like a mountain across a valley.

After what seemed a very long time, Degarmo said quietly: 'I don't see why. I don't know anything about Kingsley's wife. To the best of my knowledge I never laid eyes on her – until last night.'

He lowered his eyelids a little and watched me broodingly. He knew perfectly well what I was going to say. I said it anyway.

'And you never saw her last night. Because she had already been dead for over a month. Because she had been drowned in Little Fawn Lake. Because the woman you saw dead in the Granada Apartments was Mildred Haviland, and Mildred Haviland was Muriel Chess. And since Mrs Kingsley was dead long before Lavery was shot, it follows that Mrs Kingsley did not shoot him.'

Kingsley clenched his fists on the arms of his chair, but he made no sound, no sound at all.

39

There was another heavy silence. Patton broke it by saying in his careful slow voice: 'That's kind of a wild statement, ain't it? Don't you kind of think Bill Chess would know his own wife?'

I said: 'After a month in the water? With his wife's clothes on her and some of his wife's trinkets? With water-soaked blonde hair like his wife's hair and almost no recognizable face? Why would he even have a doubt about it? She left a note that might be a suicide note. She was gone away. They had quarrelled. Her clothes and car had gone away. During the month she was gone, he had heard nothing from her. He had no idea where she had gone. And then this corpse comes up out of the water with Muriel's clothes on it. A blonde woman about his wife's size. Of course there would be differences and if any substitution had been suspected, they would have been found and checked. But there was no reason to suspect any such thing. Crystal Kingsley was still alive. She had gone off with Lavery. She had left her car in San Bernardino. She had sent a wire to her husband from El Paso. She was all taken care of, so far as Bill Chess was concerned. He had no thoughts about her at all. She didn't enter the picture anywhere for him. Why should she?'

Patton said: 'I ought to of thought of it myself. But if I had, it would be one of those ideas a fellow would throw away almost as quick as he thought of it. It would look too kind of far-fetched.'

'Superficially, yes,' I said. 'But only superficially. Suppose the body had not come up out of the lake for a year, or not at all, unless the lake was dragged for it. Muriel Chess was gone and nobody was going to spend much time looking for her. We might never have heard of her again. Mrs Kingsley was a different proposition. She had money and connections and an anxious husband. She would be searched for, as she was, eventually. But not very soon, unless something happened to start suspicion. It might have been a matter of months before anything was found out. The lake might have been dragged, but if a search along her trail seemed to indicate that she had actually left the lake and gone down the hill, even as far as San Bernardino, and the train from there east, then the lake might never have been dragged. And even if it was and the body was found, there was rather better than an even chance that the body would not be correctly identified. Bill Chess was arrested for his wife's murder. For all I know he might even have been convicted of it, and that would have been that, as far as the body in the lake was concerned. Crystal Kingsley would still be missing, and it would be an unsolved mystery. Eventually it would be assumed that something had happened to her and that she was no longer alive. But nobody would know where or when or how it had happened. If it hadn't been for Lavery, we might not be here talking about it now. Lavery is the key to the whole thing. He was in the Prescott Hotel in San Bernardino the night Crystal Kingsley was supposed to have left here. He saw a woman there who had Crystal

Kingsley's car, who was wearing Crystal Kingsley's clothes, and of course he knew who she was. But he didn't have to know there was anything wrong. He didn't have to know they were Crystal Kingsley's clothes or that the woman had put Crysal Kingsley's car in the hotel garage. All he had to know was that he met Muriel Chess. Muriel took care of the rest.'

I stopped and waited for somebody to say anything. Nobody did. Patton sat immovable in his chair, his plump, hairless hands clasped comfortably across his stomach. Kingsley leaned his head back and he had his eyes half-closed and he was not moving. Degarmo leaned against the wall by the fireplace, taut and white-faced and cold, a big hard solemn man whose thoughts were deeply hidden.

I went on talking.

'If Muriel Chess impersonated Crystal Kingsley, she murdered her. That's elementary. All right, let's look at it. We know who she was and what kind of woman she was. She had already murdered before she met and married Bill Chess. She had been Dr Almore's office nurse and his little pal and she had murdered Dr Almore's wife in such a neat way that Almore had to cover up for her. And she had been married to a man in the Bay City police who also was sucker enough to cover up for her. She got the men that way, she could make them jump through hoops. I didn't know her long enough to see why, but her record proves it. What she was able to do with Lavery proves it. Very well, she killed people who got in her way, and Kingsley's wife got in her way too. I hadn't meant to talk about this, but it doesn't matter much now. Crystal Kingsley could make the men do a little jumping through hoops too. She made Bill Chess jump and Bill Chess's wife wasn't the girl to take that and smile. Also, she was sick to death of her life up here – she must have been – and she wanted to get away. But she needed money. She had tried to get it from Almore, and that sent Degarmo up here looking for her. That scared her a little. Degarmo is the sort of fellow you are never quite sure of. She was right not to be sure of him, wasn't she, Degarmo?'

Degarmo moved his foot on the ground. 'The sands are running against you, fellow,' he said grimly. 'Speak your little piece while you can.'

'Mildred didn't positively have to have Crystal Kingsley's car and clothes and credentials and what not, but they helped.

What money she had must have helped a great deal, and Kingsley says she liked to have a good deal of money with her. Also she must have had jewellery which could eventually be turned into money. All this made killing her a rational as well as an agreeable thing to do. This disposes of motive, and we come to means and opportunity.

'The opportunity was made to order for her. She had quarrelled with Bill and he had gone off to get drunk. She knew her Bill and how drunk he could get and how long he would stay away. She needed time. Time was of the essence. She had to assume that there was time. Otherwise the whole thing flopped. She had to pack her own clothes and take them in her car to Coon Lake and hide them there, because they had to be gone. She had to walk back. She had to murder Crystal Kingsley and dress her in Muriel's clothes and get her down in the lake. All that took time. As to the murder itself, I imagine she got her drunk or knocked her on the head and drowned her in the bath-tub in this cabin. That would be logical and simple too. She was a nurse, she knew how to handle things like bodies. She knew how to swim – we have it from Bill that she was a fine swimmer. And a drowned body will sink. All she had to do was guide it down into the deep water where she wanted it. There is nothing in all this beyond the powers of one woman who could swim. She did it, she dressed in Crystal Kingsley's clothes, packed what else of hers she wanted, got into Crystal Kingsley's car and departed. And at San Bernardino she ran into her first snag, Lavery.

'Lavery knew her as Muriel Chess. We have no evidence and no reason whatever to assume that he knew her as anything else. He had seen her up here and he was probably on his way up here again when he met her. She wouldn't want that. All he would find would be a locked-up cabin but he might get talking to Bill and it was part of her plan that Bill should not know positively that she had ever left Little Fawn Lake. So that when, and if, the body was found, he would identify it. So she put her hooks into Lavery at once, and that wouldn't be too hard. If there is one thing we know for certain about Lavery, it is that he couldn't keep his hands off the woman. The more of them the better. He would be easy for a smart girl like Mildred Haviland. So she played him and took him away with her. She took him to El Paso and there sent a wire he knew nothing about. Finally she played him back to Bay City. She probably couldn't help that. He wanted to go home and she couldn't let him get too far from her. Because Lavery was dangerous to her. Lavery alone could destroy all the indications that Crystal Kingsley had actually left Little Fawn Lake. When the search for Crystal Kingsley eventually began, it had to come to Lavery, and at that moment Lavery's life wasn't worth a plugged nickel. His first denials might not be believed, as they were not, but when he opened up with the whole story, that would be believed, because it could be checked. So the search began and immediately Lavery was shot dead in his bathroom, the very night after I went down to talk to him. That's about all there is to it, except why she went back to the house next morning. That's just one of those things that murderers seem to do. She said he had taken her money, but I don't believe it. I think more likely she got to thinking he had some of his own hidden away, or that she had better edit the job with a cool head and make sure it was all in order and pointing the right way; or perhaps it was just what she said, and to take in the paper and the milk. Anything is possible. She went back and I found her there and she put on an act that left me with both feet in my mouth.'

Patton said: 'Who killed her, son? I gather you don't like Kingsley for that little job.'

I looked at Kingsley and said: 'You didn't talk to her on the phone, you said. What about Miss Fromsett? Did she think she was talking to your wife?'

Kingsley shook his head. 'I doubt it. It would be pretty hard to fool her that way. All she said was that she seemed very changed and subdued. I had no suspicion then. I didn't have any until I got up here. When I walked into this cabin last night, I felt there was something wrong. It was too clean and neat and orderly. Crystal didn't leave things that way. There would have been clothes all over the bedroom, cigarette-stubs all over the house, bottles and glasses all over the kitchen. There would have been unwashed dishes and ants and flies. I thought Bill's wife might have cleaned up, and then I remembered that Bill's wife wouldn't have, not on that particular day. She had been too busy quarrelling with Bill and being murdered, or committing suicide, whichever it was. I thought about all this in a confused sort of way, but I don't claim I actually made anything of it.'

Patton got up from his chair and went out on the porch. He

came back wiping his lips with his tan handkerchief. He sat down again, and eased himself over on his left hip, on account of the hip holster on the other side. He looked thoughtfully at Degarmo. Degarmo stood against the wall, hard and rigid, a stone man. His right hand still hung down at his side, with the fingers curled.

Patton said: 'I still ain't heard who killed Muriel. Is that part of the show or is that something that still has to be worked out?'

I said: 'Somebody who thought she needed killing, somebody who had loved her and hated her, somebody who was too much of a cop to let her get away with any more murders, but not enough of a cop to pull her in and let the whole story come out. Somebody like Degarmo.'

40

Degarmo straightened away from the wall and smiled bleakly. His right hand made a hard clean movement and was holding a gun. He held it with a lax wrist, so that it pointed down at the floor in front of him. He spoke to me without looking at me.

'I don't think you have a gun,' he said. 'Patton has a gun but I don't think he can get it out fast enough to do him any good. Maybe you have a little evidence to go with that last guess. Or wouldn't that be important enough for you to bother with?'

'A little evidence,' I said. 'Not very much. But it will grow. Somebody stood behind that green curtain in the Granada for more than half an hour and stood as silently as only a cop on a stake-out knows how to stand. Somebody who had a black-jack. Somebody who knew I had been hit with one without looking at the back of my head. You told Shorty, remember? Somebody who knew the dead girl had been hit with one too, although it wouldn't have showed and he wouldn't have been likely at that time to have handled the body enough to find out. Somebody who stripped her and raked her body with scratches in the kind of sadistic hate a man like you might feel for a woman who had made a small private hell for him.

Somebody who has blood and cuticle under his finger-nails right now, plenty enough for a chemist to work on. I bet you won't let Patton look at the finger-nails of your right hand, Degarmo.'

Degarmo lifted the gun a little and smiled. A wide white smile.

'And just how did I know where to find her?' he asked.

'Almore saw her – coming out of, or going into Lavery's house. That's what made him so nervous, that's why he called you when he saw me hanging around. As to how exactly you trailed her to the apartment, I don't know. I don't see anything difficult about it. You could have hid out in Almore's house and followed her, or followed Lavery. All that would be routine work for a copper.'

Degarmo nodded and stood silent for a moment, thinking. His face was grim, but his metallic blue eyes held a light that was almost amusement. The room was hot and heavy with a disaster that could no longer be mended. He seemed to feel it less than any of us.

'I want to get out of here,' he said at last. 'Not very far, maybe, but no hick cop is going to put the arm on me. Any objections?'

Patton said quietly: 'Can't be done, son. You know I got to take you. None of this ain't proved, but I can't just let you walk out.'

'You have a nice fat belly, Patton. I'm a good shot. How do you figure to take me?'

'I been trying to figure,' Patton said, and rumpled his hair under his pushed-back hat. 'I ain't got very far with it. I don't want no holes in my belly. But I can't let you make a monkey of me in my own territory either.'

'Let him go,' I said. 'He can't get out of these mountains. That's why I brought him up here.'

Patton said soberly: 'Somebody might get hurt taking him. That wouldn't be right. If it's anybody, it's got to be me.'

Degarmo grinned. 'You're a nice boy, Patton,' he said. 'Look, I'll put the gun back under my arm and we'll start from scratch. I'm good enough for that too.'

He tucked the gun under his arm. He stood with his arms hanging, his chin pushed forward a little, watching. Patton chewed softly, with his pale eyes on Degarmo's vivid eyes.

'I'm sitting down,' he complained. 'I ain't as fast as you anyways. I just don't like to look yellow.' He looked at me sadly. 'Why the hell did you have to bring this up here? It ain't any part of my troubles. Now look at the jam I'm in.' He sounded hurt and confused and rather feeble.

Degarmo put his head back a little and laughed. While he was still laughing, his right hand jumped for his gun again.

I didn't see Patton move at all. The room throbbed with the roar of his frontier Colt.

Degarmo's arm shot straight out to one side and the heavy Smith and Wesson was torn out of his hand and thudded against the knotty pine wall behind him. He shook his numbed right hand and looked down at it with wonder in his eyes.

Patton stood up slowly. He walked slowly across the room and kicked the revolver under a chair. He looked at Degarmo, sadly. Degarmo was sucking a little blood off his knuckles.

'You give me a break,' Patton said sadly. 'You hadn't ought ever to give a man like me a break. I been a shooter more years than you been alive, son.'

Degarmo nodded to him and straightened his back and started for the door.

'Don't do that,' Patton told him calmly.

Degarmo kept on going. He reached the door and pushed on the screen. He looked back at Patton and his face was very white now.

'I'm going out of here,' he said. 'There's only one way you can stop me. So long, fatty.'

Patton didn't move a muscle.

Degarmo went out through the door. His feet made heavy sounds on the porch and then on the steps. I went to the front window and looked out. Patton still hadn't moved. Degarmo came down off the steps and started across the top of the little dam.

'He's crossing the dam,' I said. 'Has Andy got a gun?'

'I don't figure he'd use one if he had,' Patton said calmly. 'He don't know any reason why he should.'

'Well, I'll be damned,' I said.

Patton sighed. 'He hadn't ought to have given me a break like that,' he said. 'Had me cold. I got to give it back to him. Kind of puny too. Won't do him a lot of good.'

'He's a killer,' I said.

'He ain't that kind of killer,' Patton said. 'You lock your car?'

I nodded. 'Andy's coming down to the other end of the dam,'

380

I said. 'Degarmo has stopped him. He's speaking to him.'

'He'll take Andy's car, maybe,' Patton said sadly.

'Well, I'll be damned,' I said again. I looked back at Kingsley. He had his head in his hands and he was staring at the floor. I turned back to the window. Degarmo was out of sight beyond the rise. Andy was half-way across the dam, coming slowly, looking back over his shoulder now and then. The sound of a starting car came distantly. Andy looked up at the cabin, then turned back and started to run back along the dam.

The sound of the motor died away. When it was quite gone, Patton said: 'Well, I guess we better go back to the office and do some telephoning.'

Kingsley got up suddenly and went out to the kitchen and came back with a bottle of whisky. He poured himself a stiff drink and drank it standing. He waved a hand at it and walked heavily out of the room. I heard bed-springs creak.

Patton and I went quietly out of the cabin.

41

Patton had just finished putting his calls through to block the highways when a call came through from the sergeant in charge of the guard detail at Puma Lake dam. We went out and got into Patton's car and Andy drove very fast along the lake road through the village and along the lake shore back to the big dam at the end. We were waved across the dam to where the sergeant was waiting in a jeep beside the headquarters hut.

The sergeant waved his arm and started the jeep and we followed him a couple of hundred feet along the highway to where a few soldiers stood on the edge of the canyon looking down. Several cars had stopped there and a cluster of people was grouped near the soldiers. The sergeant got out of the jeep and Patton and Andy and I climbed out of the official car and went over by the sergeant.

'Guy didn't stop for the sentry,' the sergeant said, and there was bitterness in his voice. 'Damn near knocked him off the road. The sentry in the middle of the bridge had to jump fast to get missed. The one at this end had enough. He called the guy to halt. Guy kept going.'

The sergeant chewed his gun and looked down into the canyon.

'Orders are to shoot in a case like that,' he said. 'The sentry shot.' He pointed down to the grooves in the shoulder at the edge of the drop. 'This is where he went off.'

A hundred feet down in the canyon a small coupé was smashed against the side of a huge granite boulder. It was almost upside down, leaning a little. There were three men down there. They had moved the car enough to lift something out.

Something that had been a man.

The Little Sister

1

The pebbled glass door panel is lettered in flaked black paint: *'Philip Marlowe ... Investigations.'* It is a reasonably shabby door at the end of a reasonably shabby corridor in the sort of building that was new about the year the all-tile bathroom became the basis of civilization. The door is locked, but next to it is another door with the same legend which is not locked. Come on in – there's nobody in here but me and a big bluebottle fly. But not if you're from Manhattan, Kansas.

It was one of those clear, bright summer mornings we get in the early spring in California before the high fog sets in. The rains are over. The hills are still green and in the valley across the Hollywood hills you can see snow on the high mountains. The fur stores are advertising their annual sales. The call houses that specialize in sixteen-year-old virgins are doing a land-office business. And in Beverly Hills the jacaranda trees are beginning to bloom.

I had been stalking the bluebottle fly for five minutes, waiting for him to sit down. He didn't want to sit down. He just wanted to do wing-overs and sing the prologue to *Pagliacci*. I had the fly swatter poised in mid-air and I was all set. There was a patch of bright sunlight on the corner of the desk and I knew that sooner or later that was where he was going to light. But when he did I didn't even see him at first. The buzzing stopped and there he was. And then the phone rang.

I reached for it inch by inch with a slow and patient left hand. I lifted the phone slowly and spoke into it softly: 'Hold the line a moment, please.'

I laid the phone down gently on the brown blotter. He was still there, shining and blue green and full of sin. I took a deep breath and swung. What was left of him sailed halfway across the room and dropped to the carpet. I went over and picked him up by his good wing and dropped him into the wastebasket.

'Thanks for waiting,' I said into the phone.

'Is this Mr Marlowe, the detective?' It was a small, rather hurried, little-girlish voice. I said it was Mr Marlowe, the detective. 'How much do you charge for your services, Mr Marlowe?'

'What was it you wanted done?'

The voice sharpened a little. 'I can't very well tell you over the phone. It's – it's very confidential. Before I'd waste time coming to your office I'd have to have some idea—'

'Forty bucks a day and expenses. Unless it's the kind of job that can be done for a flat fee.'

'That's far too much,' the little voice said. 'Why, it might cost hundreds of dollars and I only get a small salary and—'

'Where are you now?'

'Why, I'm in a drug store. It's right next to the building where your office is.'

'You could have saved a nickel. The elevator's free.'

'I – I beg your pardon?'

I said it all over again. 'Come on up and let's have a look at you,' I added. 'If you're my kind of trouble, I can give you a pretty good idea—'

'I have to know something about you,' the small voice said very firmly. 'This is a very delicate matter, very personal. I couldn't talk to just anybody.'

'If it's that delicate,' I said, 'maybe you need a lady detective.'

'Goodness, I didn't know there were any.' Pause. 'But I don't think a lady detective would do at all. You see, Orrin was living in a very tough neighbourhood, Mr Marlowe. At least I thought it was tough. The manager of the rooming house is a most unpleasant person. He smelled of liquor. Do you drink, Mr Marlowe?'

'Well, now that you mention it—'

'I don't think I'd care to employ a detective that uses liquor in any form. I don't even approve of tobacco.'

'Would it be all right if I peeled an orange?'

I caught the sharp intake of breath at the far end of the line. 'You might at least talk like a gentleman,' she said.

'Better try the University Club,' I told her. 'I heard they had a couple left over there, but I'm not sure they'll let you handle them.' I hung up.

It was a step in the right direction, but it didn't go far enough. I ought to have locked the door and hid under the desk.

2

Five minutes later the buzzer sounded on the outer door of the half-office I use for a reception room. I heard the door close again. Then I didn't hear anything more. The door between me and there was half-open. I listened and decided somebody had just looked in at the wrong office and left without entering. Then there was a small knocking on wood. Then the kind of cough you use for the same purpose. I got my feet off the desk, stood up and looked out. There she was. She didn't have to open her mouth for me to know who she was. And nobody ever looked less like Lady Macbeth. She was a small, neat, rather prissy-looking girl with primly smooth brown hair and rimless glasses. She wearing a brown tailormade and from a strap over her shoulder hung one of those awkward-looking square bags that make you think of a Sister of Mercy taking first aid to the wounded. On the smooth brown hair was a hat that had been taken from its mother too young. She had no make-up, no lipstick and no jewellery. The rimless glasses gave her that librarian's look.

'That's no way to talk to people over the telephone,' she said sharply. 'You ought to be ashamed of yourself.'

'I'm just too proud to show it,' I said. 'Come on in.' I held the door for her. Then I held the chair for her.

She sat down on about two inches of the edge. 'If I talked like that to one of Dr Zugsmith's patients,' she said, 'I'd lose my position. He's most particular how I speak to the patients – even the difficult ones.'

'How is the old boy? I haven't seen him since that time I fell off the garage roof.'

She looked surprised and quite serious. 'Why surely you can't know Dr Zugsmith.' The tip of a rather anaemic tongue came out between her lips and searched furtively for nothing.

'I know a Dr George Zugsmith,' I said, 'in Santa Rosa.'

'Oh no. This is Dr Alfred Zugsmith, in Manhattan. Manhattan, Kansas, you know, not Manhattan, New York.'

'Must be a different Dr Zugsmith,' I said. 'And your name?'

'I'm not sure I'd care to tell you.'

'Just window shopping, huh?'

'I suppose you could call it that. If I have to tell my family affairs to a total stranger, I at least have the right to decide whether he's the kind of person I could trust.'

'Anybody ever tell you you're a cute little trick?'

The eyes behind the rimless cheaters flashed. 'I should hope not.'

I reached for a pipe and started to fill it. 'Hope isn't exactly the word,' I said. 'Get rid of that hat and get yourself a pair of those slinky glasses with coloured rims. You know, the ones that are all cockeyed and oriental—'

'Dr Zugsmith wouldn't permit anything like that,' she said quickly. Then, 'Do you really think so?' she asked, and blushed ever so slightly.

I put a match to the pipe and puffed smoke across the desk. She winced back.

'If you hire me,' I said, 'I'm the guy you hire. Me. Just as I am. If you think you're going to find any lay readers in this business, you're crazy. I hung up on you, but you came up here all the same? So you need help. What's your name and trouble?'

She just stared at me.

'Look,' I said. 'You come from Manhattan, Kansas. The last time I memorized the *World Almanac* that was a little town not far from Topeka. Population around twelve thousand. You work for Dr Alfred Zugsmith and you're looking for someone named Orrin. Manhattan is a small town. It has to be. Only half a dozen places in Kansas are anything else. I already have enough information about you to find out your whole family history.'

'But why should you want to?' she asked, troubled.

'Me?' I said. 'I don't want to. I'm fed up with people telling me histories. I'm just sitting here because I don't have any place to go. I don't want to work. I don't want anything.'

'You talk too much.'

'Yes,' I said, 'I talk too much. Lonely men always talk too much. Either that or they don't talk at all. Shall we get down to business? You don't look like the type that goes to see private detectives, and especially private detectives you don't know.'

'I know that,' she said quietly. 'And Orrin would be absolutely livid. Mother would be furious too. I just picked your name out of the phone book—'

'What principle?' I asked. 'And with the eyes closed or open?'

She stared at me for a moment as if I were some kind of freak. 'Seven and thirteen,' she said quietly.

'How?'

'Marlowe has seven letters,' she said, 'and Philip Marlowe has thirteen. Seven together with thirteen—'

'What's *your* name?' I almost snarled.

'Orfamay Quest.' She crinkled her eyes as if she could cry. She spelled the first name out for me, all one word. 'I live with my mother,' she went on, her voice getting rapid now as if my time was costing her. 'My father died four years ago. He was a doctor. My brother Orrin was going to be a surgeon too but he changed into engineering after two years of medical. Then a year ago Orrin came out to work for the Cal-Western Aircraft Company in Bay City. He didn't have to. He had a good job in Wichita. I guess he just sort of wanted to come out here to California. Most everybody does.'

'*Al*most everybody,' I said. 'If you're going to wear those rimless glasses, you might at least try to live up to them.'

She giggled and drew a line along the desk with her fingertip, looking down. 'Did you mean those slanting kind of glasses that make you look kind of oriental?'

'Uh-huh. Now about Orrin. We've got him to California, and we've got him to Bay City. What do we do with him?'

She thought for a moment and frowned. Then she studied my face as if making up her mind. Then her words came with a burst: 'It wasn't like Orrin not to write to us regularly. He only wrote twice to mother and three times to me in the last six months. And the last letter was several months ago. Mother and I got worried. So it was my vacation and I came out to see him. He'd never been away from Kansas before.' She stopped. 'Aren't you going to take any notes?' she asked.

I grunted.

'I thought detectives always wrote things down in little notebooks.'

'I'll make the gags,' I said. 'You tell the story. You came out on your vacation. Then what?'

'I'd written to Orrin that I was coming but I didn't get any answer. Then I sent a wire to him from Salt Lake City but he didn't answer that either. So all I could do was go down where he lived. It's an awful long way. I went in a bus. It's in Bay City. No. 449 Idaho Street.'

She stopped again, then repeated the address, and I still didn't write it down. I just sat there looking at her glasses and her smooth brown hair and the silly little hat and the fingernails with no colour and her mouth with no lipstick and the tip of the little tongue that came and went between the pale lips.

'Maybe you don't know Bay City, Mr Marlowe.'

'Ha,' I said. 'All I know about Bay City is that every time I go there I have to buy a new head. You want me to finish your story for you?'

'Wha-a-at?' Her eyes opened so wide that the glasses made them look like something you see in the deep sea fish tanks.

'He's moved,' I said. 'And you don't know where he's moved to. And you're afraid he's living a life of sin in a penthouse on top of the Regency Towers with something in a long mink coat and an interesting perfume.'

'Well, for goodness' sake!'

'Or am I being coarse?' I asked.

'Please Mr Marlowe,' she said at last, 'I don't think anything of the sort about Orrin. And if Orrin heard you say that you'd be sorry. He can be awfully mean. But I know something has happened. It was just a cheap rooming house, and I didn't like the manager at all. A horrid kind of man. He said Orrin had moved away a couple of weeks before and he didn't know where to and he didn't care, and all he wanted was a good slug of gin. I don't know why Orrin would even live in a place like that.'

'Did you say slug of gin?' I asked.

She blushed. 'That's what the manager said. I'm just telling you.'

'All right,' I said. 'Go on.'

'Well, I called the place where he worked. The Cal-Western Company, you know. And they said he'd been laid off like a lot of others and that was all they knew. So then I went to the post office and asked if Orrin had put in a change of address to anywhere. And they said they couldn't give me any information. It was against the regulations. So I told them how it was and the man said, well if I was his sister he'd go look. So he went and looked and came back and said no. Orrin hadn't put in any change of address. So then I began to get a little frightened. He might have had an accident or something.'

'Did it occur to you to ask the police about that?'

'I wouldn't dare ask the police. Orrin would never forgive me. He's difficult enough at the best of times. Our family—' She hesitated and there was something behind her eyes she tried not to have there. So she went on breathlessly: 'Our family's not the kind of family—'

'Look,' I said wearily. 'I'm not talking about the guy lifting a wallet. I'm talking about him getting knocked down by a car and losing his memory or being too badly hurt to talk.'

She gave me a level look which was not too admiring. 'If it was anything like that, we'd know,' she said. 'Everybody has things in their pockets to tell who they are.'

'Sometimes all they have left is the pockets.'

'Are you trying to scare me, Mr Marlowe?'

'If I am, I'm certainly getting nowhere fast. Just what do you think might have happened?'

She put her slim forefinger to her lips and touched it very carefully with the tip of her tongue. 'I guess if I knew that I wouldn't have to come and see you. How much would you charge to find him?'

I didn't answer for a long moment, then I said: 'You mean alone, without telling anybody?'

'Yes. I mean alone, without telling anybody.'

'Uh-huh. Well, that depends. I told you what my rates were.'

She clasped her hands on the edge of the desk and squeezed them together hard. She had about the most meaningless set of gestures I had ever laid eyes on. 'I thought you being a detective and all you could find him right away,' she said. 'I couldn't possibly afford more than twenty dollars. I've got to buy my meals here and my hotel and the train going back and you know the hotel is so terribly expensive and the food on the train—'

'Which one are you staying at?'

'I – I'd rather not tell you, if you don't mind.'

'Why?'

'I'd just rather not. I'm terribly afraid of Orrin's temper. And, well, I can always call you up, can't I?'

'Uh-huh. Just what is it you're scared of, besides Orrin's temper, Miss Quest?' I had let my pipe go out. I struck a match and held it to the bowl, watching her over it.

'Isn't pipe smoking a very dirty habit?' she asked.

'Probably,' I said. 'But it would take more than twenty bucks to have me drop it. And don't try to sidestep my questions.'

'You can't talk to me like that,' she flared up. 'Pipe smoking *is* a dirty habit. Mother never let father smoke in the house, even the last two years after he had his stroke. He used to sit with that empty pipe in his mouth sometimes. But she didn't like him to do that really. We owed a lot of money too and she said she couldn't afford to give him money for useless things like tobacco. The church needed it much more than he did.'

'I'm beginning to get it,' I said slowly. 'Take a family like yours and somebody in it has to be the dark meat.'

She stood up sharply and clasped the first aid kit to her body. 'I don't like you,' she said. 'I don't think I'm going to employ you. If you're insinuating that Orrin has done something wrong, well, I can assure you that it's not Orrin who's the black sheep of our family.'

I didn't move an eyelash. She swung around and marched to the door and put her hand on the knob and then she swung around again and marched back and suddenly began to cry. I reacted to that just the way a stuffed fish reacts to cut bait. She got out her little handkerchief and tickled the corners of her eyes.

'And now I suppose you'll call the p-police,' she said with a catch in her voice. 'And the Manhattan p-paper will hear all about it and they'll print something n-nasty about us.'

'You don't suppose anything of the sort. Stop chipping at my emotions. Let's see a photo of him.'

She put the handkerchief away in a hurry and dug something else out of her bag. She passed it across the desk. An envelope. Thin, but there could be a couple of snapshots in it. I didn't look inside.

'Describe him the way you see him,' I said.

She concentrated. That gave her a chance to do something with her eyebrows. 'He was twenty-eight years old last March. He has light brown hair, much lighter than mine, and lighter blue eyes, and he brushes his hair straight back. He's very tall, over six feet. But he only weighs a hundred and forty pounds. He's sort of bony. He used to wear a little blond moustache but mother made him cut it off. She said—'

'Don't tell me. The minister needed it to stuff a cushion.'

'You can't talk like that about my mother,' she yelped, getting pale with rage.

'Oh, stop being silly. There's a lot of things about you I don't know. But you can stop pretending to be an Easter lily right now. Does Orrin have any distinguishing marks on him, like moles or scars, or a tattoo of the Twenty-third Psalm on his chest? And don't bother to blush.'

'Well, you don't have to yell at me. Why don't you look at the photograph?'

'He probably has his clothes on. After all, you're his sister. You ought to know.'

'No, he hasn't,' she said tightly. 'He has a little scar on his left hand where he had a wen removed.'

'What about his habits? What does he do for fun – besides not smoking or drinking or going out with girls?'

'Why – how did you know that?'

'Your mother told me.'

She smiled. I was beginning to wonder if she had one in her. She had very even white teeth and she didn't wave her gums. That was something. 'Aren't you silly,' she said. 'He studies a lot and he has a very expensive camera he likes to snap people with when they don't know. Sometimes it makes them mad. But Orrin says people ought to see themselves as they really are.'

'Let's hope it never happens to him,' I said. 'What kind of camera is it?'

'One of those little cameras with a very fine lens. You can take snaps in almost any kind of light. A Leica.'

I opened the envelope and took out a couple of small prints, very clear. 'These weren't taken with anything like that,' I said.

'Oh no. Philip took those, Philip Anderson. A boy I was going with for a while.' She paused and sighed. 'And I guess that's really why I came here, Mr Marlowe. Just because your name's Philip too.'

I just said: 'Uh-huh,' but I felt touched in some vague sort of way. 'What happened to Philip Anderson?'

'But it's about Orrin—'

'I know,' I interrupted. 'But what happened to Philip Anderson?'

'He's still there in Manhattan.' She looked away. 'Mother doesn't like him very much. I guess you know how it is.'

'Yes,' I said, 'I know how it is. You can cry if you want to. I won't hold it against you. I'm just a big soft slob myself.'

I looked at the two prints. One of them was looking down and was no good to me. The other was a fairly good shot of a tall angular bird with narrow-set eyes and a thin straight mouth and a pointed chin. He had the expression I expected to see. If you forgot to wipe the mud off your shoes, he was the boy who would tell you. I laid the photos aside and looked at Orfamay Quest, trying to find something in her face even remotely like his. I couldn't. Not the slightest trace of family resemblance, which of course meant absolutely nothing. It never has.

'All right,' I said. 'I'll go down there and take a look. But you ought to be able to guess what's happened. He's in a strange city. He's making good money for a while. More than he's ever made in his life, perhaps. He's meeting a kind of people he never met before. And it's not the kind of town – believe me it isn't, I know Bay City – that Manhattan, Kansas, is. So he just broke training and he doesn't want his family to know about it. He'll straighten out.'

She just stared at me for a moment in silence, then she shook her head. 'No. Orrin's not the type to do that, Mr Marlowe.'

'Anyone is,' I said. 'Especially a fellow like Orrin. The small-town sanctimonious type of guy who's lived his entire life with his mother on his neck and the minister holding his hand. Out here he's lonely. He's got dough. He'd like to buy a little sweetness and light, and not the kind that comes in the east window of a church. Not that I have anything against that. I mean he already had enough of that, didn't he?'

She nodded her head silently.

'So he starts to play,' I went on, 'and he doesn't know how to play. That takes experience too. He's got himself all jammed up with some floozy and a bottle of hooch and what he's done looks to him as if he'd stolen the bishop's pants. After all, the guy's going on twenty-nine years old and if he wants to roll in the gutter that's his business. He'll find somebody to blame it on after a while.'

'I hate to believe you, Mr Marlowe,' she said slowly. 'I'd hate for mother—'

'Something was said about twenty dollars,' I cut in.

She looked shocked. 'Do I have to pay you now?'

'What would be the custom in Manhattan, Kansas?'

'We don't have any private detectives in Manhattan. Just the regular police. That is, I don't think we do.'

She probed in the inside of her tool kit again and dragged out a red change purse and from that she took a number of bills, all neatly folded and separate. Three fives and five ones. There didn't seem to be much left. She kind of held the purse so I could see how empty it was. Then she straightened the bills out on the desk and put one on top of the other and pushed them across. Very slowly, very sadly, as if she was drowning a favourite kitten.

'I'll give you a receipt,' I said.

'I don't need a receipt, Mr Marlowe.'

'I do. You won't give me your name and address, so I want something with your name on it.'

'What for?'

'To show I'm representing you.' I got the receipt book out and made the receipt and held the book for her to sign the duplicate. She didn't want to. After a moment reluctantly she took the hard pencil and wrote 'Orfamay Quest' in a neat secretary's writing across the face of the duplicate.

'Still no address?' I asked.

'I'd rather not.'

'Call me any time then. My home number is in the phone book, too. Bristol Apartments, Apartment 428.'

'I shan't be very likely to visit you,' she said coldly.

'I haven't asked you yet,' I said. 'Call me around four if you like. I might have something. And then again I might not.'

She stood up. 'I hope mother won't think I've done wrong,' she said, picking at her lip now with the pale fingernail. 'Coming here, I mean.'

'Just don't tell me any more of the things your mother won't like,' I said. 'Just leave that part out.'

'Well, really!'

394

'And stop saying "well, really".'

'I think you're a very offensive person,' she said.

'No, you don't. You think I'm cute. And I think you're a fascinating little liar. You don't think I'm doing this for any twenty bucks, do you?'

She gave me a level, suddenly cool stare. 'Then why?' Then when I didn't answer she added, 'Because spring is in the air?'

I still didn't answer. She blushed a little. Then she giggled.

I didn't have the heart to tell her I was just plain bored with doing nothing. Perhaps it *was* the spring too. And something in her eyes that was much older than Manhattan, Kansas.

'I think you're very nice – really,' she said softly. Then she turned quickly and almost ran out of the office. Her steps along the corridor outside made tiny, sharp pecky sounds, kind of like mother drumming on the edge of the dinner table when father tried to promote himself a second piece of pie. And him with no money any more. No nothing. Just sitting in a rocker on the front porch back there in Manhattan, Kansas, with his empty pipe in his mouth. Rocking on the front porch, slow and easy, because when you've had a stroke you have to take it slow and easy. And wait for the next one. And the empty pipe in his mouth. No tobacco. Nothing to do but wait.

I put Orfamay Quest's twenty hard-earned dollars in an envelope and wrote her name on it and dropped it in the desk drawer. I didn't like the idea of running around loose with that much currency on me.

3

You could know Bay City a long time without knowing Idaho Street. And you could know a lot about Idaho Street without knowing No. 449. The block in front of it had a broken paving that had almost gone back to dirt. The warped fence of a lumberyard bordered the cracked sidewalk on the opposite side of the street. Halfway up the block the rusted rails of a spur track turned in to a pair of high, chained wooden gates that seem not to have been opened for twenty years. Little boys with chalk had been writing and drawing pictures on the gates and all along the fence.

No. 449 had a shallow, paintless front porch on which five

wood and cane rockers loafed dissolutely, held together with wire and the moisture of the beach air. The green shades over the lower windows of the house were two-thirds down and full of cracks. Besides the front door there was a large printed sign: 'No vacancies.' That had been there a long time too. It had got faded and fly-specked. The door opened on a long hall from which stairs went up a third of the way back. To the right there was a narrow shelf with a chained, indelible pencil hanging beside it. There was a push button and a yellow and black sign above which read 'Manager,' and was held up by three thumbtacks no two of which matched. There was a pay phone on the opposite wall.

I pushed the bell. It rang somewhere nearby but nothing happened. I rang it again. The same nothing happened. I prowled along to a door with a black and white metal sign on it: 'Manager.' I knocked on that. Then I kicked it. Nobody seemed to mind my kicking it.

I went back out of the house and down around the side where a narrow concrete walk led to the service entrance. It looked as if it was in the right place to belong to the manager's apartment. The rest of the house would be just rooms. There was a dirty garbage pail on the small porch and a wooden box full of liquor bottles. Behind the screen the back door of the house was open. It was gloomy inside. I put my face against the screen and peered in. Through the open inner door beyond the service porch I could see a straight chair with a man's coat hanging over it and in the chair a man in shirtsleeves with his hat on. He was a small man. I couldn't see what he was doing, but he seemed to be sitting at the end of the built-in breakfast table in the breakfast nook.

I banged on the screen door. The man paid no attention. I banged again, harder. This time he tilted his chair back and showed me a small pale face with a cigarette in it. 'Whatcha want?' he barked.

'Manager.'

'Not in, Bub.'

'Who are you?'

'What's it to you?'

'I want a room.'

'No vacancies, Bub. Can't you read large print?'

'I happen to have different information,' I said.

'Yeah?' He shook ash from his cigarette by flicking it with a nail without removing it from his small sad mouth. 'Go fry your head in it.'

He tilted his chair forward again and went on doing whatever he was doing.

I made noise getting down off the porch and none whatever coming back up on it. I felt the screen door carefully. It was hooked. With the open blade of a penknife I lifted the hook and eased it out of the eye. It made a small tinkle but louder tinkling sounds were being made beyond, in the kitchen.

I stepped into the house, crossed the service porch, went through the door into the kitchen. The little man was too busy to notice me. The kitchen had a three-burner gas stove, a few shelves of greasy dishes, a chipped icebox and the breakfast nook. The table in the breakfast nook was covered with money. Most of it was paper, but there was silver also, in all sizes up to dollars. The little man was counting and stacking it and making entries in a small book. He wetted his pencil without bothering the cigarette that lived in his face.

There must have been several hundred dollars on that table.

'Rent day?' I asked genially.

The small man turned very suddenly. For a moment he smiled and said nothing. It was the smile of a man whose mind is not smiling. He removed the stub of cigarette from his mouth, dropped it on the floor and stepped on it. He reached a fresh one out of his shirt and put it in the same hole in his face, and started fumbling for a match.

'You came in nice,' he said pleasantly.

Finding no match, he turned casually in his chair and reached into a pocket of his coat. Something heavy knocked against the wood of the chair. I got hold of his wrist before the heavy thing came out of the pocket. He threw his weight backwards and the pocket of the coat started to lift towards me. I yanked the chair out from under him.

He sat down hard on the floor and knocked his head against the end of the breakfast table. That didn't keep him from trying to kick me in the groin. I stepped back with his coat and took a .38 out of the pocket he had been playing with.

'Don't sit on the floor just to be chummy,' I said.

He got up slowly, pretending to be groggier than he was. His hand fumbled at the back of his collar and light winked on metal as his arm swept towards me. He was a game little rooster.

I side-swiped his jaw with his own gun and he sat down on the floor again. I stepped on the hand that held the knife. His face twisted with pain but he didn't make a sound. So I kicked the knife into a corner. It was a long thin knife and it looked very sharp.

'You ought to be ashamed of yourself,' I said. 'Pulling guns and knives on people that are just looking for a place to live. Even for these times that's out of line.'

He held his hurt hand between his knees and squeezed it and began to whistle through his teeth. The slap on the jaw didn't seem to have hurt him. 'Okay,' he said, 'Okay. I ain't supposed to be perfect. Take the dough and beat it. But don't ever think we won't catch up with you.'

I looked at the collection of small bills and medium bills and silver on the table. 'You must need a lot of sales resistance, the weapons you carry,' I told him. I walked across to the inner door and tried it. It was not locked. I turned back.

'I'll leave your gun in the mailbox,' I said. 'Next time ask to see the buzzer.'

He was still whistling gently between his teeth and holding his hand. He gave me a narrow, thoughtful eye, then shovelled the money into a shabby briefcase and slipped its catch. He took his hat off, straightened it around, put it back jauntily on the back of his head and gave me a quiet efficient smile.

'Never mind about the heater,' he said. 'The town's full of old iron. But you could leave the skiv with Clausen. I've done quite a bit of work on it to get it in shape.'

'And with it?' I asked.

'Could be.' He flicked a finger at me airily. 'Maybe we'll meet again some day soon. When I got a friend with me.'

'Tell him to wear a clean shirt,' I said. 'And lend you one.'

'My, my,' the little man said chidingly. 'How tough we get, how quick once we get that badge pinned on.'

He went softly past me and down the wooden steps from the back porch. His footsteps tapped to the street and faded. They sounded very much like Orfamay's heels clicking along the corridor in my office building. And for some reason I had that empty feeling of having miscounted the trumps. No reason for it at all. Maybe it was the steely quality about the little man. No whimper, no bluster, just the smile, the whistling between the teeth, the light voice and the unforgetting eyes.

I went over and picked up the knife. The blade was long and round and thin, like a rat-tailed file that has been ground smooth. The handle and guard were light-weight plastic and seemed all one piece. I held the knife by the handle and gave it a quick flip at the table. The blade came loose and quivered in the wood.

I took a deep breath and slid the handle down over the end

398

again and worked the blade loose from the table. A curious knife, with design and purpose in it, and neither of them agreeable.

I opened the door beyond the kitchen and went through it with the gun and knife in one hand.

It was a wall-bed living-room, with the wall-bed down and rumpled. There was an overstuffed chair with a hole burnt in the arm. A high oak desk with tilted doors like old-fashioned cellar doors stood against the wall by the front window. Near this there was a studio couch and on the studio couch lay a man. His feet hung over the end of the couch in knobby grey socks. His head had missed the pillow by two feet. It was nothing much to miss from the colour of the slip on it. The upper part of him was contained in a colourless shirt and a threadbare grey coat-sweater. His mouth was open and his face was shining with sweat and he breathed like an old Ford with a leaky head gasket. On a table beside him was a plate full of cigarette stubs, some of which had a homemade look. On the floor a near-full gin bottle and a cup that seemed to have contained coffee but not at all recently. The room was full mostly of gin and bad air, but there was also a reminiscence of marijuana smoke.

I opened a window and leaned my forehead against the screen to get a little cleaner air into my lungs and looked out into the street. Two kids were wheeling bicycles along the lumberyard fence, stopping from time to time to study the examples of restroom art on the boarding. Nothing else moved in the neighbourhood. Not even a dog. Down at the corner was dust in the air as though a car had passed that way.

I went over to the desk. Inside it was the house register, so I leafed back until I came to the name 'Orrin P. Quest', written in a sharp meticulous handwriting, and the number 214 added in pencil by another hand that was by no means sharp or meticulous. I followed on through to the end of the register but found no new registration for Room 214. A party named G. W. Hicks had Room 215. I shut the register in the desk and crossed to the couch. The man stopped his snoring and bubbling and threw his right arm across his body as if he thought he was making a speech. I leaned down and gripped his nose tight between my first and second fingers and stuffed a handful of his sweater into his mouth. He stopped snoring and jerked his eyes open. They were glazed and bloodshot. He struggled against my hand. When I was sure he was fully awake I let go of him, picked the bottle full of gin off the floor and poured some into a glass that lay

399

on its side near the bottle. I showed the glass to the man.

His hand came out to it with the beautiful anxiety of a mother welcoming a lost child.

I moved it out of his reach and said: 'You the manager?'

He licked his lips stickily and said: 'Gr-r-r-r.'

He made a grab for the glass. I put it on the table in front of him. He grasped it carefully in both hands and poured the gin into his face. The he laughed heartily and threw the glass at me. I managed to catch it and up-end it on the table again. The man looked me over with a studied unsuccessful attempt at sternness.

'What gives?' he croaked in an annoyed tone.

'Manager?'

He nodded and almost fell off the couch. 'Must be I'm drunky,' he said. 'Kind of a little bit drunky.'

'You're not bad,' I said. 'You're still breathing.'

He put his feet on the ground and pushed himself upright. He cackled with sudden amusement, took three uneven steps; went down on his hands and knees and tried to bite the leg of a chair.

I pulled him up on his feet again, set him down in the over-stuffed chair with the burned arm and poured him another slug of his medicine. He drank it, shuddered violently and all at once his eyes seemed to get sane and cunning. Drunks of his type have a certain balanced moment of reality. You never know when it will come or how long it will last.

'Who the hell are you?' he growled.

'I'm looking for a man named Orrin P. Quest.'

'Huh?'

I said it again. He smeared his face with his hands and said tersely: 'Moved away.'

'Moved away when?'

He waved his hand, almost fell out of his chair and waved it again the other way to restore his balance. 'Gimme a drink,' he said.

I poured another slug of the gin and held it out of his reach.

'Gimme,' the man said urgently. 'I'm not happy.'

'All I want is the present address of Orrin P. Quest.'

'Just think of that,' he said wittily and made a loose pass at the glass I was holding.

I put the glass down on the floor and got one of my business cards out for him. 'This might help you to concentrate,' I told him.

He peered at the card closely, sneered, bent it in half and

bent it again. He held it on the flat of his hand, spat on it, and tossed it over his shoulder.

I handed him the glass of gin. He drank it to my health, nodded solemnly, and threw the glass over his shoulder too. It rolled along the floor and thumped the baseboard. The man stood up with surprising ease, jerked a thumb towards the ceiling, doubled the fingers of his hand under it and made a sharp noise with his tongue and teeth.

'Beat it,' he said. 'I got friends.' He looked at the telephone on the wall and back at me with cunning. 'A couple of boys to take care of you,' he sneered. I said nothing. 'Don't believe me, huh?' he snarled, suddenly angry. I shook my head.

He started for the telephone, clawed the receiver off the hook, and dialled the five digits of a number. I watched him. One-three-five-seven-two.

That took all he had for the time being. He let the receiver fall and bang against the wall and he sat down on the floor beside it. He put it to his ear and growled at the wall: 'Lemme talk to the Doc.' I listened silently. 'Vince! The Doc!' he shouted angrily. He shook the receiver and threw it away from him. He put his hands down on the floor and started to crawl in a circle. When he saw me he looked surprised and annoyed. He got shakily to his feet again and held his hand out. 'Gimme a drink.'

I retrieved the fallen glass and milked the gin bottle into it. He accepted it with the dignity of an intoxicated dowager, drank it down with an airy flourish, walked calmly over to the couch and lay down, putting the glass under his head for a pillow. He went to sleep instantly.

I put the telephone receiver back on its hook, glanced out in the kitchen again, felt the man on the couch over and dug some keys out of his pocket. One of them was a pass-key. The door to the hallway had a spring lock and I fixed it so that I could come in again and started up the stairs. I paused on the way to write 'Doc – Vince, 13572' on an envelope. Maybe it was a clue.

The house was quite silent as I went on up.

4

The manager's much filed pass-key turned the lock of Room 214 without noise. I pushed the door open. The room was not empty. A chunky, strongly-built man was bending over a suitcase on the bed, with his back to the door. Shirts and socks and underwear were laid out on the bed cover, and he was packing them leisurely and carefully, whistling between his teeth in a low monotone.

He stiffened as the door hinge creaked. His hand moved fast for the pillow on the bed.

'I beg your pardon,' I said. 'The manager told me this room was vacant.'

He was as bald as a grapefruit. He wore dark grey flannel slacks and transparent plastic suspenders over a blue shirt. His hands came up from the pillow, went to his head, and down again. He turned and he had hair.

It looked as natural as hair ever looked, smooth, brown, not parted. He glared at me from under it.

'You can always try knocking,' he said.

He had a thick voice and a broad careful face that had been around.

'Why would I? If the manager said the room was empty?'

He nodded, satisfied. The glare went out of his eyes.

I came further into the room without invitation. An open love-pulp magazine lay face down on the bed near the suitcase. A cigar smoked in a green glass ashtray. The room was careful and orderly, and, for that house, clean.

'He must have thought you had already moved out,' I said, trying to look like a well-meaning party with some talent for the truth.

'Have it in half an hour,' the man said.

'Okay if I look around?'

He smiled mirthlessly. 'Ain't been in town long, have you?'

'Why?'

'New around here, ain't you?'

'Why?'

'Like the house and the neighbourhood?'

'Not much,' I said. 'The room looks all right.'

He grinned, showing a porcelain jacket crown that was too white for his other teeth. 'How long you been looking?'

'Just started,' I said. 'Why all the questions?'

'You make me laugh,' the man said, not laughing. 'You don't look at rooms in this town. You grab them sight unseen. This burg's so jam-packed even now that I could get ten bucks just for telling there's a vacancy here.'

'That's too bad,' I said. 'A man named Orrin P. Quest told me about the room. So there's one sawbuck you don't get to spend.'

'That so?' Not a flicker of an eye. Not a movement of a muscle. I might as well have been talking to a turtle.

'Don't get tough with me,' the man said. 'I'm a bad man to get tough with.'

He picked his cigar out of the green glass ashtray and blew a little smoke. Through it he gave me the cold grey eye. I got a cigarette out and scratched my chin with it.

'What happens to people that get tough with you?' I asked him. 'You make them hold your toupee?'

'You lay off my toupee,' he said savagely.

'So sorry,' I said.

'There's a "No Vacancy" sign on the house,' the man said. 'So what makes you come here and find one?'

'You didn't catch the name,' I said. 'Orrin P. Quest.' I spelled it for him. Even that didn't make him happy. There was a dead-air pause.

He turned abruptly and put a pile of handkerchiefs into his suitcase. I moved a little closer to him. When he turned back there was what might have been a watchful look on his face. But it had been a watchful face to start with.

'Friend of yours?' he asked casually.

'We grew up together,' I said.

'Quiet sort of guy,' the man said easily. 'I don't pass the time of day with him. Works for Cal-Western, don't he?'

'He did,' I said.

'Oh. He quit?'

'Let out.'

We went on staring at each other. It didn't get either of us anywhere. We both had done too much of it in our lives to expect miracles.

The man put the cigar back in his face and sat down on the side of the bed beside the open suitcase. Glancing into it I saw the square butt of an automatic peeping out from under a pair of badly folded shorts.

'This Quest party's been out of here ten days,' the man said thoughtfully. 'So he still thinks the room is vacant, huh?'

'According to the register it *is* vacant,' I said.

He made a contemptuous noise. 'That rummy downstairs probably ain't looked at the register in a month. Say – wait a minute.' His eyes sharpened and his hand wandered idly over the open suitcase and gave an idle pat to something that was close to the gun. When the hand moved away, the gun was no longer visible.

'I've been kind of dreamy all morning or I'd have wised up,' he said. 'You're a dick.'

'What's the beef?'

'No beef at all. I just wondered why you had the room.'

'I moved from 215 across the hall. This here is a better room. That's all. Simple. Satisfied?'

'Perfectly,' I said, watching the hand that could be near the gun if it wanted to.

'What kind of dick? City? Let's see the buzzer.'

I didn't say anything.

'I don't believe you got no buzzer.'

'If I showed it to you, you're the type of guy who would say it was counterfeit. So you're Hicks.'

He looked surprised.

'George W. Hicks,' I said. 'It's in the register. Room 215. You just got through telling me you moved from 215.' I glanced around the room. 'If you had a blackboard here, I'd write it out for you.'

'Strictly speaking, we don't have to get into no snarling match,' he said. 'Sure I'm Hicks. Pleased to meetcha. What's yours?'

He held his hand out. I shook hands with him, but not as if I had been longing for the moment to arrive.

'My name's Marlowe,' I said. 'Philip Marlowe.'

'You know something,' Hicks said politely, 'you're a goddamn liar.'

I laughed in his face.

'You ain't getting no place with that breezy manner, bub. What's your connection?'

I got my wallet out and handed him one of my business cards. He read it thoughtfully and tapped the edge against his porcelain crown.

'He coulda went somewhere without telling me,' he mused.

'Your grammar,' I said, 'is almost as loose as your toupee.'

'You lay off my toupee, if you know what's good for you,' he shouted.

'I wasn't going to eat it,' I said. 'I'm not that hungry.'

He took a step towards me, and dropped his right shoulder. A scowl of fury dropped his lip almost as far.

'Don't hit me. I'm insured,' I told him.

'Oh hell. Just another screwball.' He shrugged and put his lip back up on his face. 'What's the lay?'

'I have to find this Orrin P. Quest,' I said.

'Why?'

I didn't answer that.

After a moment he said: 'Okay. I'm a careful guy myself. That's why I'm movin' out.'

'Maybe you don't like the reefer smoke.'

'That,' he said emptily, 'and other things. That's why Quest left. Respectable type. Like me. I think a couple of hard boys threw a scare into him.'

'I see,' I said. 'That would be why he left no forwarding address. And why did they throw a scare into him?'

'You just mentioned reefer smoke, didn't you? Wouldn't he be the type to go to headquarters about that?'

'In Bay City?' I asked. 'Why would he bother? Well, thanks a lot, Mr Hicks. Going far?'

'Not far,' he said. 'No. Not very far. Just far enough.'

'What's your racket?' I asked him.

'Racket?' He looked hurt.

'Sure. What do you shake them for? How do you make your dibs?'

'You got me wrong, brother. I'm a retired optometrist.'

'That why you have the .45 in there?' I pointed to the suitcase.

'Nothing to get cute about,' he said sourly. 'It's been in the family for years.' He looked down at the card again. 'Private investigator, huh?' he said thoughtfully. 'What kind of work do you do mostly?'

'Anything that's reasonably honest,' I said.

He nodded. 'Reasonably is a word you could stretch. So is honest.'

I gave him a shady leer. 'You're so right,' I agreed. 'Let's get together some quiet afternoon and stretch them.' I reached out and slipped the card from between his fingers and dropped it into my pocket. 'Thanks for the time,' I said.

I went out and closed the door, then stood against it listening. I don't know what I expected to hear. Whatever it was I didn't hear it. I had a feeling he was standing exactly where I had left him looking at the spot where I had made my exit. I made noise going along the hall and stood at the head of the stairs.

A car drove away from in front of the house. Somewhere a door closed. I went quietly back to Room 215 and used the pass-key to enter. I closed and locked its door silently, and waited just inside.

5

Not more than two minutes passed before Mr George W. Hicks was on his way. He came out so quietly that I wouldn't have heard him if I hadn't been listening for precisely that kind of movement. I heard the slight metallic sound of the door-knob turning. Then slow steps. Then very gently the door was closed. The steps moved off. The faint distant creak of the stairs. Then nothing. I waited for the sound of the front door. It didn't come. I opened the door of 215 and moved along the hall to the stair-head again. Below there was the careful sound of a door being tried. I looked down to see Hicks going into the manager's apartment. The door closed behind him. I waited for the sound of voices. No voices.

I shrugged and went back to 215.

The room showed signs of occupancy. There was a small radio on a night table, an unmade bed with shoes under it, and an old bathrobe hung over the cracked, pull-down green shade to keep the glare out.

I looked at all this as if it meant something, then stepped back into the hall and relocked the door. Then I made another pilgrimage into Room 214. Its door was now unlocked. I searched the room with care and patience and found nothing that connected it in any way with Orrin P. Quest. I didn't expect to. There was no reason why I should. But you always have to look.

I went downstairs, listened outside the manager's door, heard nothing, went in and crossed to put the keys on the desk. Lester B. Clausen lay on his side on the couch with his face to the wall, dead to the world. I went through the desk, found an old account book that seemed to be concerned with rent taken in and expenses paid out and nothing else. I looked at the register again. It wasn't up to date but the party on the couch seemed enough explanation for that. Orrin P. Quest had moved away. Somebody else had taken over his room. Somebody else had the room registered to Hicks. The little man counting money in the kitchen went nicely with the neighbourhood. The fact that he carried a gun and a knife was a social eccentricity that would cause no comment at all on Idaho Street.

I reached the small Bay City telephone book off the hook beside the desk. I didn't think it would be much of a job to sift out the party that went by the name of 'Doc' or 'Vince' and the phone number one-three-five-seven-two. First of all I leafed back through the register. Something which I ought to have done first. The page with Orrin Quest's registration had been torn out. A careful man, Mr George W. Hicks. Very careful.

I closed the register, glanced over at Lester B. Clausen again, wrinkled my nose at the stale air and the sickly sweetish smell of gin and of something else, and started back to the entrance door. As I reached it, something for the first time penetrated my mind. A drunk like Clausen ought to be snoring very loudly. He ought to be snoring his head off with a nice assortment of checks and gurgles and snorts. He wasn't making any sound at all. A brown Army blanket was pulled up around his shoulders and the lower part of his head. He looked very comfortable, very calm. I stood over him and looked down. Something which was not an accidental fold held the Army blanket away from the back of his neck. I moved it. A square yellow wooden handle was attached to the back of Lester B. Clausen's neck. On the side of the yellow handle were printed the words 'Compliments of the Crumsen Hardware Company'. The position of the handle was just below the occipital bulge.

It was the handle of an ice pick ...

I did a nice quiet thirty-five getting away from the neighbourhood. On the edge of the city, a frog's jump from the line, I shut myself in an outdoor telephone booth and called the Police Department.

'Bay City Police. Moot talking,' a furry voice said.

I said: 'Number 449 Idaho Street. In the apartment of the manager. His name's Clausen.'

'Yeah?' the voice said. 'What do we do?'

'I don't know,' I said. 'It's a bit of a puzzle to me. But the man's name is Lester B. Clausen. Got that?'

'What makes it important?' the furry voice said without suspicion.

'The coroner will want to know,' I said, and hung up.

6

I drove back to Hollywood and locked myself in the office with the Bay City telephone book. It took me a quarter-hour to find out that the party who went with the telephone number one-three-five-seven-two in Bay City was a Dr Vincent Lagardie, who called himself a neurologist, had his home and offices on Wyoming Street, which according to my map was not quite in the best residential neighbourhood and not quite out of it. I locked the Bay City telephone book up in my desk and went down to the corner drug store for a sandwich and a cup of coffee and used a pay booth to call Dr Vincent Lagardie. A woman answered and I had some trouble getting through to Dr Lagardie himself. When I did his voice was impatient. He was very busy, in the middle of an examination he said. I never knew a doctor who wasn't. Did he know Lester B. Clausen? He never heard of him. What was the purpose of my inquiry?

'Mr Clausen tried to telephone you this morning,' I said. 'He was too drunk to talk properly.'

'But I don't know Mr Clausen,' the doctor's cool voice answered. He didn't seen to be in quite such a hurry now.

'Well, that's all right then,' I said. 'Just wanted to make sure. Somebody stuck an ice pick into the back of his neck.'

There was a quiet pause. Dr Lagardie's voice was now almost unctuously polite. 'Has this been reported to the police?'

'Naturally,' I said. 'But it shouldn't bother you – unless of course it was your ice pick.'

He passed that one up. 'And who is this speaking?' he inquired suavely.

'The name is Hicks,' I said. 'George W. Hicks, I just moved out of there. I don't want to get mixed up with that sort of thing. I just figured when Clausen tried to call you – this was before he was dead, you understand – that you might be interested.'

'I'm sorry, Mr Hicks,' Dr Lagardie's voice said. 'But I don't *know* Mr Clausen. I have never *heard* of Mr Clausen or had any contact with him whatsoever. And I have an excellent memory for names.'

'Well, that's fine,' I said. 'And you won't meet him now. But somebody *may* want to know why he tried to telephone you – unless I forget to pass the information along.'

There was a dead pause. Dr Lagardie said: 'I can't think of any comment to make on that.'

I said: 'Neither can I. I may call you again. Don't get me wrong, Dr Lagardie. This isn't any kind of a shake. I'm just a mixed-up little man who needs a friend. I kind of felt that a doctor – like a clergyman—'

'I'm at your entire disposal,' Dr Lagardie said. 'Please feel free to consult me.'

'Thank you, Doctor,' I said fervently. 'Thank you very very much.'

I hung up. If Dr Vincent Lagardie was on the level, he would now telephone the Bay City Police Department and tell them the story. If he didn't telephone the police, he wasn't on the level. Which might or might not be useful to know.

7

The phone on my desk rang at four o'clock sharp.

'Did you find Orrin yet, Mr Marlowe?'

'Not yet. Where are you?'

'Why, I'm in the drug store next to—'

'Come on up and stop acting like Mata Hari,' I said.

'Aren't you ever polite to anybody?' she snapped.

I hung up and fed myself a slug of Old Forester to brace my nerves for the interview. As I was inhaling it I heard her steps tripping along the corridor. I moved across and opened the door.

'Come in this way and miss the crowd,' I said.

She seated herself demurely and waited.

'All I could find out,' I told her, 'is that the dump on Idaho Street is peddling reefers. That's marijuana cigarettes.'

'Why, how disgusting,' she said.

'We have to take the bad with the good in this life,' I said. 'Orrin must have got wise and threatened to report it to the police.'

'You mean,' she said in her little-girl manner, 'that they might hurt him for doing that?'

'Well, most likely they'd throw a scare into him first.'

'Oh, they couldn't scare Orrin, Mr Marlowe,' she said decisively. 'He just gets mean when people try to run him.'

'Yeah,' I said. 'But we're not talking about the same things. You can scare anybody – with the right technique.'

She set her mouth stubbornly. 'No, Mr Marlowe. They couldn't scare Orrin.'

'Okay,' I said. 'So they didn't scare him. Say they just cut off one of his legs and beat him over the head with it. What would he do then – write to the Better Business Bureau?'

'You're making fun of me,' she said politely. Her voice was as cool as boarding-house soup. 'Is that all you did all day? Just find Orrin had moved and it was a bad neighbourhood? Why, I found that out for myself, Mr Marlowe. I thought you being a detective and all—' She trailed off, leaving the rest of it in the air.

'I did a little more than that,' I said. 'I gave the landlord a little gin and went through the register and talked to a man named Hicks. George W. Hicks. He wears a toupee. I guess maybe you didn't meet him. He has, or had, Orrin's room. So I thought maybe—' It was my turn to do a little trailing in the air.

She fixed me with her pale blue eyes enlarged by the glasses. Her mouth was small and firm and tight, her hands clasped on the desk in front of her over her large square bag, her whole body stiff and erect and formal and disapproving.

'I paid you twenty dollars, Mr Marlowe,' she said coldly. 'I understood that was in payment of a day's work. It doesn't seem to me that you've done a day's work.'

'No,' I said. 'That's true. But the day isn't over yet. And don't bother about the twenty bucks. You can have it back if you like. I didn't even bruise it.'

I opened the desk drawer and got out her money. I pushed it across the desk. She looked at it but didn't touch it. Her eyes came up slowly to meet mine.

'I didn't mean it like that. I know you're doing the best you can, Mr Marlowe.'

'With the facts I have.'

'But I've told you all I know.'

'I don't think so,' I said.

'Well, I'm sure I can't help what you think,' she said tartly. 'After all, if I knew what I wanted to know already, I wouldn't have come here and asked you to find it out, would I?'

'I'm not saying you know all you want to know,' I answered. 'The point is I don't know all I want to know in order to do a job for you. And what you tell me doesn't add up.'

'What doesn't add up? I've told you the truth. I'm Orrin's sister. I guess I know what kind of person he is.'

'How long did he work for Cal-Western?'

'I've told you that. He came out to California just about a year ago. He got work right away because he practically had the job before he left.'

'He wrote home how often? Before he stopped writing.'

'Every week. Sometimes oftener. He'd take turns writing to mother and me. Of course the letters were for both of us.'

'About what?'

'You mean what did he write about?'

'What did you think I meant?'

'Well, you don't have to snap at me. He wrote about his work and the plant and the people there, and sometimes about a show he'd been to. Or it was about California. He'd write about church too.'

'Nothing about girls?'

'I don't think Orrin cared much for girls.'

'And lived at the same address all this time?'

She nodded, looking puzzled.

'And he stopped writing how long ago?'

That took thought. She pressed her lips and pushed a finger-tip around the middle of the lower one. 'About three or four months,' she said at last.

'What was the date of his last letter?'

'I – I'm afraid I can't tell you exactly the date. But it was like I said, three or four—'

I waved a hand at her. 'Anything out of the ordinary in it? Anything unusual said or anything unusual unsaid?'

'Why no. It seemed just like all the rest.'

'Don't you have any friends or relatives in this part of the country?'

She gave me a funny stare, started to say something, then shook her head sharply. 'No.'

'Okay. Now I'll tell you what's wrong. I'll skip over your not telling me where you're staying, because it might be just that you're afraid I'll show up with a quart of hooch under my arm and make a pass at you.'

'That's not a very nice way to talk,' she said.

'Nothing I say is nice. I'm not nice. By your standards no-body with less than three prayer-books could be nice. But I *am* inquisitive. What's wrong with this picture is that you're not scared. Neither you personally nor your mother. And you ought to be scared as hell.'

She clutched her bag to her bosom with tight little fingers. 'You mean something has happened to him?' Her voice faded off into a sort of sad whisper, like a mortician asking for a down payment.

'I don't know that anything has. But in your position, know-ing the kind of guy Orrin was, the way his letters came through and then didn't, I can't see myself waiting for my summer vacation to come around before I start asking questions. I can't see myself by-passing the police who have an organization for finding people. And going to a lone-wolf operator you never heard of, asking him to root around for you in the rubble. And I can't see your dear old mother just sitting there in Manhattan, Kansas, week after week darning the minister's winter underwear. No letter from Orrin. No news. And all she does about it is take a long breath and mend up another pair of pants.'

She came to her feet with a lunge. 'You're a horrid, disgusting person,' she said angrily. 'I think you're vile. Don't you dare say mother and I weren't worried. Just don't you dare.'

I pushed the twenty dollars' worth of currency a little closer to the other side of the desk. 'You were worried twenty dollars' worth, honey,' I said. 'But about what I wouldn't know. I guess I don't really want to know. Just put this hunk of the folding back in your saddle-bag and forget you ever met me. You might want to lend it to another detective tomorrow.'

She snapped her bag shut viciously on the money. 'I'm not very likely to forget your rudeness,' she said between her teeth. 'Nobody in the world's ever talked to me the way you have.'

I stood up and wandered around the end of the desk. 'Don't think about it too much. You might get to like it.'

I reached up and twitched her glasses off. She took half a step back, almost stumbled, and I reached an arm around her by pure instinct. Her eyes widened and she put her hands against my chest and pushed. I've been pushed harder by a kitten.

'Without the cheaters those eyes are really something,' I said in an awed voice.

She relaxed and let her head go back and her lips open a little. 'I suppose you do that to all the clients,' she said softly. Her hands now had dropped to her sides. The bag whacked against my leg. She leaned her weight on my arm. If she wanted me to let go of her, she had her signals mixed.

'I just didn't want you to lose your balance,' I said.

'I knew you were the thoughtful type.' She relaxed still more. Her head went back now. Her upper lids drooped, fluttered a bit, and her lips came open a little farther. On them appeared the faint provocative smile that nobody ever has to teach them. 'I suppose you thought I did it on purpose,' she said.

'Did what on purpose?'

'Stumbled, sort of.'

'Wel-l-l-l.'

She reached a quick arm around my neck and started to

pull. So I kissed her. It was either that or slug her. She pushed her mouth hard at me for a long moment then quietly and very comfortably wriggled around in my arms and nestled. She let out a long easy sigh.

'In Manhattan, Kansas, you could be arrested for this,' she said.

'If there was any justice, I could be arrested just for being there,' I said.

She giggled and poked the end of my nose with a fingertip. 'I suppose you really prefer fast girls,' she said, looking up at me sideways. 'At least you won't have to wipe off any lip rouge. Maybe I'll wear some next time.'

'Maybe we'd better sit down on the floor,' I said. 'My arm's getting tired.

She giggled again and disengaged herself gracefully. 'I guess you think I've been kissed lots of times,' she said.

'What girl hasn't?'

She nodded, gave me the up-from-under look that made her eyelashes cut across the iris. 'Even at the church socials they play kissing games,' she said.

'Or there wouldn't be any church socials,' I said.

We looked at each other with no particular expression.

'Well-l-l—' she began at last. I handed her back her glasses. She pulled them on. She opened her bag, looked at herself in a small mirror, rooted around in her bag and came out with her hand clenched.

'I'm sorry I was mean,' she said, and pushed something under the blotter of my desk. She gave me another frail little smile and marched to the door and opened it.

'I'll call you,' she said intimately. And out she went, tap, tap, tap down the hall.

I went over and lifted the blotter and smoothed out the crumpled currency that lay under it. It hadn't been much of a kiss, but it looked like I had another chance at the twenty dollars.

The phone rang before I had quite started to worry about Mr Lester B. Clausen. I reached for it absently. The voice I heard was an abrupt voice, but thick and clogged, as if it was being strained through a curtain or somebody's long white beard.

'You Marlowe?' it said.

'Speaking.'

'You got a safe-deposit box, Marlowe?'

I had enough of being polite for one afternoon. 'Stop asking and start telling,' I said.

'I asked you a question, Marlowe.'

'I didn't answer it,' I said. 'Like this.' I reached over and pressed down the riser on the phone. Held it that way while I fumbled around for a cigarette. I knew he would call right back. They always do when they think they're tough. They haven't used their exit line. When it rang again I started right in.

'If you have a proposition, state it. And I get called "mister" until you give me some money.'

'Don't let that temper ride you so hard, friend. I'm in a jam. I need help. I need something kept in a safe place. For a few days. Not longer. And for that you make a little quick money.'

'How little?' I asked. 'And how quick?'

'A C note. Right here and waiting. I'm warming it for you.'

'I can hear it purr,' I said. 'Right where and waiting?' I was listening to the voice twice, once when I heard it and once when it echoed in my mind.

'Room 332, Van Nuys Hotel. Knock two quick ones and two slow ones. Not too loud. I got to have live action. How fast can you—'

'What is it you want me to keep?'

'That'll wait till you get here. I said I was in a hurry.'

'What's your name?'

'Just Room 332.'

'Thanks for the time,' I said. 'Goodbye.'

'Hey. Wait a minute, dope. It's nothing hot like you think. No ice. No emerald pendants. It just happens to be worth a lot of money to me – and nothing at all to anybody else.'

'The hotel has a safe.'

'Do you want to die poor, Marlowe?'

'Why not? Rockefeller did. Goodbye again.'

The voice changed. The furriness went out of it. It said sharply and swiftly: 'How's every little thing in Bay City?'

I didn't speak. Just waited. There was a dim chuckle over the wire. 'Thought that might interest you, Marlowe. Room 332 it is. Tramp on it, friend. Make speed.'

The phone clicked in my ear. I hung up. For no reason a pencil rolled off the desk and broke its point on the glass doohickey under one of the desk legs. I picked it up slowly and carefully sharpened it in the Boston sharpener screwed to the edge of the window frame, turning the pencil around to get it nice and even. I laid it down in the tray on the desk and dusted off my hands. I had all the time in the world. I looked out of the window. I didn't see anything. I didn't hear anything.

And then, for even less reason, I saw Orfamay Quest's face

with the glasses, and polished and painted and with blonde hair piled up high on the forehead with a braid around the middle of it. And bedroom eyes. They all have to have bedroom eyes. I tried to imagine this face in a vast close-up being gnawed by some virile character from the wide-open spaces of Romanoff's bar.

It took me twenty-nine minutes to get to the Van Nuys Hotel.

8

Once, long ago, it must have had a certain elegance. But no more. The memories of old cigars clung to its lobby like the dirty gilt on its ceiling and the sagging springs of its leather lounging chairs. The marble of the desk had turned a yellowish-brown with age. But the floor carpet was new and had a hard look, like the room clerk. I passed him up and strolled over to the cigar counter in the corner and put down a quarter for a package of Camels. The girl behind the counter was a straw blonde with a long neck and tired eyes. She put the cigarettes in front of me, added a packet of matches, dropped my change into a slotted box marked 'The Community Chest Thanks You'.

'You'd want me to do that, wouldn't you?' she said, smiling patiently. 'You'd want to give your change to the poor little underprivileged kids with bent legs and stuff, wouldn't you?'

'Suppose I didn't,' I said.

'I dig up seven cents,' the girl said, 'and it would be very painful.' She had a low lingering voice with a sort of moist caress in it like a damp bath towel. I put a quarter after the seven cents. She gave her big smile then. It showed more of her tonsils.

'You're nice,' she said. 'I can see you're nice. A lot of fellows would have come in here and made a pass at a girl. Just think. Over seven cents. A pass.'

'Who's the house peeper here now?' I asked her, without taking up the option.

'There's two of them.' She did something slow and elegant to the back of her head, exhibiting what seemed like more than one handful of blood-red fingernails in the process. 'Mr Hady is on nights and Mr Flack is on days. It's day now, so it would be Mr Flack would be on.'

'Where could I find him?'

She leaned over the counter and let me smell her hair, pointing with a half-inch fingernail towards the elevator bank. 'It's down along that corridor there, next to the porter's room. You can't miss the porter's room on account of it has a half-door and says PORTER on the upper part in gold letters. Only that half is folded back like, so I guess maybe you can't see it.'

'I'll see it,' I said. 'Even if I have to get a hinge screwed to my neck. What does this Flack look like?'

'Well,' she said, 'he's a little squatty number, with a bit of a moustache. A sort of chunky type. Thick-set like, only not tall.' Her fingers moved languidly along the counter to where I could have touched them without jumping. 'He's not interesting,' she said. 'Why bother?'

'Business,' I said, and made off before she threw a half-nelson on me.

I looked back at her from the elevators. She was staring after me with an expression she probably would have said was thoughtful.

The porter's room was halfway down the corridor to the Spring Street entrance. The door beyond it was half-open. I looked around its edge, then went in and closed it behind me.

A man was sitting at a small desk which had dust on it, a very large ashtray and very little else. He was short and thick-set. He had something dark and bristly under his nose about an inch long. I sat down across from him and put a card on the desk.

He reached for the card without excitement, read it, turned it over and read the back with as much care as the front. There was nothing on the back to read. He picked up half of a cigar out of his ashtray and burned his nose lighting it.

'What's the gripe?' he growled at me.

'No gripe. You Flack?'

He didn't bother to answer. He gave me a steady look which may or may not have concealed his thoughts, depending on whether he had any to conceal.

'Like to get a line on one of the customers,' I said.

'What name?' Flack asked, with no enthusiasm.

'I don't know what name he's using here. He's in Room 332.'

'What name was he using before he came here?' Flack asked. 'I don't know that either.'

'Well, what did he look like?' Flack was suspicious now. He re-read my card but it added nothing to his knowledge.

'I never saw him as far as I know.'

Flack said: 'I must be overworked. I don't get it.'

'I had a call from him,' I said. 'He wanted to see me.'

'Am I stopping you?'

'Look, Flack. A man in my business makes enemies at times. You ought to know that. This party wants something done. Tells me to come on over, forgets to give his name, and hangs up. I figured I'd do a little checking before I went up there.'

Flack took the cigar out of his mouth and said patiently: 'I'm in terrible shape. I still don't get it. Nothing makes sense to me any more.'

I leaned over the desk and spoke to him slowly and distinctly: 'The whole thing could be a nice way to get me into a hotel room and knock me off and then quietly check out. You wouldn't want anything like that to happen in your hotel, would you, Flack?'

'Supposing I cared,' he said. 'You figure you're that important?'

'Do you smoke that piece of rope because you like it or because you think it makes you look tough?'

'For forty-five bucks a week,' Flack said, 'would I smoke anything better?' He eyed me steadily.

'No expense account yet,' I told him. 'No deal yet.'

He made a sad sound and got up wearily and went out of the room. I lit one of my cigarettes and waited. He came back in a short time and dropped a registration card on the desk. *Dr G. W. Hambleton, El Centro, California* was written on it in a firm round hand in ink. The clerk had written other things on it, including the room number and daily rate. Flack pointed a finger that needed a manicure or, failing that, a nail brush.

'Came in at 2.47 p.m.,' he said. 'Just today, that is. Nothing on his bill. One day's rent. No phone calls. No nothing. That what you want?'

'What does he look like?' I asked.

'I didn't see him. You think I stand out there by the desk and take pictures of them while they register?'

'Thanks,' I said. 'Dr G. W. Hambleton, El Centro. Much obliged.' I handed him back the registration card.

'Anything I ought to know,' Flack said as I went out. 'Don't forget where I live. That is, if you call it living.'

I nodded and went out. There are days like that. Everybody you meet is a dope. You begin to look at yourself in the glass and wonder.

9

Room 332 was at the back of the building near the door to the fire escape. The corridor which led to it had a smell of old carpet and furniture oil and the drab anonymity of a thousand shabby lives. The sand bucket under the racked fire hose was full of cigarette and cigar stubs, an accumulation of several days. A radio pounded brassy music through an open transom. Through another transom people were laughing fit to kill themselves. Down at the end by Room 332 it was quieter.

I knocked the two longs and two shorts as instructed. Nothing happened. I felt jaded and old. I felt as if I had spent my life knocking at doors in cheap hotels that nobody bothered to open. I tried again. Then turned the knob and walked in. A key with a red fibre tab hung in the inside keyhole.

There was a short hall with a bathroom on the right. Beyond the hall the upper half of a bed was in view, and a man lay on it in shirt and pants.

I said: 'Dr Hambleton?'

The man didn't answer. I went past the bathroom door towards him. A whiff of perfume reached me and I started to turn, but not quickly enough. A woman who had been in the bathroom was standing there holding a towel in front of the lower part of her face. Dark glasses showed above the towel. And then the brim of a wide-brimmed straw hat in a sort of dusty delphinium blue. Under that was fluffed-out pale blonde hair. Blue earbuttons lurked somewhere back in the shadows. The sunglasses were in white frames with broad flat sidebows. Her dress matched her hat. An embroidered silk or rayon coat was open over the dress. She wore gauntleted gloves and there was an automatic in her right hand. White bone grip. Looked like a .32.

'Turn around and put your hands behind you,' she said through the towel. The voice muffled by the towel meant as little to me as the dark glasses. It was not the voice which had talked to me on the telephone. I didn't move.

'Don't ever think I'm fooling,' she said. 'I'll give you exactly three seconds to do what I say.'

'Couldn't you make it a minute? I like looking at you.'

She made a threatening gesture with the little gun. 'Turn around,' she snapped. 'But fast.'

'I like the sound of your voice too.'

'All right,' she said, in a tight dangerous tone. 'If that's the way you want it, that's the way you want it.'

'Don't forget you're a lady,' I said, and turned around and put my hands up to my shoulders. A gun muzzle poked into the back of my neck. Breath almost tickled my skin. The perfume was an elegant something or other, not strong, not decisive. The gun against my neck went away and a white flame burned for an instant behind my eyes. I grunted and fell forward on my hands and knees and reached back quickly. My hand touched a leg in a nylon stocking, but slipped off, which seemed a pity. It felt like a nice leg. The jar of another blow on my head took the pleasure out of this and I made the hoarse sound of a man in desperate shape. I collapsed on the floor. The door opened. A key rattled. The door closed. The key turned. Silence.

I climbed to my feet and went into the bathroom. I bathed my head with a towel from the rack soaked with cold water. It felt as if the heel of a shoe had hit me. Certainly it was not a gun butt. There was a little blood, not much. I rinsed the towel out and stood there patting the bruise and wondering why I didn't run after her screaming. But what I was doing was staring into the open medicine cabinet over the basin. The upper part of a can of talcum had been prised off the shoulder. There was talcum all over the shelf. A toothpaste tube had been cut open. Someone had been looking for something.

I went back to the little hallway and tried the room door. Locked from the outside. I bent down and looked through the keyhole. But it was an up-and-down lock, with the outer and inner keyholes on different levels. The girl in the dark glasses with the white rims didn't know much about hotels. I twisted the night latch, which opened the outside lock, opened the door, looked along the empty corridor, and closed the door again.

Then I went towards the man on the bed. He had not moved during all this time, for a somewhat obvious reason.

Beyond the little hallway the room widened towards a pair of windows through which the evening sun slanted in a shaft that reached almost across the bed and came to a stop under the neck of the man that lay there. What it stopped on was blue and white and shining and round. He lay quite comfortably half on his face with his hands down at his sides and his shoes off. The side of his face was on the pillow and he seemed relaxed. He was wearing a toupee. The last time I had talked to him his name had been George W. Hicks. Now it was Dr G. W. Hambleton. Same initials. Not that it mattered any more. I wasn't going to be talking to him again. There was no blood.

None at all, which is one of the few nice things about an expert ice-pick job.

I touched his neck. It was still warm. While I was doing it the shaft of sunlight moved away from the knob of the ice-pick towards his left ear. I turned away and looked the room over. The telephone bell box had been opened and left open. The Gideon Bible was thrown in the corner. The desk had been searched. I went to a closet and looked into that. There were clothes in it and a suitcase I had seen before. I found nothing that seemed important. I picked a snap-brim hat off the floor and put it on the desk and went back to the bathroom. The point of interest now was whether the people who had ice-picked Dr Hambleton had found what they came for. They had had very little time.

I searched the bathroom carefully. I moved the top of the toilet and drained it. There was nothing in it. I peered down the overflow pipe. No thread hung there with a small object at the end of it. I searched the bureau. It was empty except for an old envelope. I unhooked the window screens and felt under the sills outside. I picked up the Gideon Bible off the floor and leafed through it again. I examined the backs of three pictures and studied the edge of the carpet. It was tacked close to the wall and there were little pockets of dust in the depressions made by the tacks. I got down on the floor and examined the part under the bed. Just the same. I stood on a chair, looked into the bowl of the light fixture. In contained dust and dead moths. I looked the bed over. It had been made up by a professional and not touched since. I felt the pillow under the dead man's head, than got the extra pillow out of the closet and examined its edges. Nothing.

Dr Hambleton's coat hung over a chair back. I went through that, knowing it was the least likely place to find anything. Somebody with a knife had worked on the lining and the shoulder padding. There were matches, a couple of cigars, a pair of dark glasses, a cheap handkerchief not used, a Bay City movie theatre ticket stub, a small comb, an unopened package of cigarettes. I looked at it in the light. It showed no sign of having been disturbed. I disturbed it. I tore off the cover, went through it, found nothing but cigarettes.

That left Dr Hambleton himself. I eased him over and got into his trousers pockets. Loose change, another handkerchief, a small tube of dental floss, more matches, a bunch of keys, a folder of bus shedules. In a pigskin wallet was a book of stamps, a second comb (here was a man who really took care of his toupee), three flat packages of white powder, seven printed cards reading *Dr G. W. Hambleton, O.D. Tustin Building, El Centro, California, Hours 9–12 and 2–4, and by Appointment. Telephone El Centro 50406.* There was no driver's licence, no social security card, no insurance cards, no real identification at all. There was $164.00 in currency in the wallet. I put the wallet back where I found it.

I lifted Dr Hambleton's hat off the desk and examined the sweatband and the ribbon. The ribbon bow had been picked loose with a knife point, leaving hanging threads. There was nothing hidden inside the bow. No evidence of any previous ripping and restitching.

This was the take. If the killers knew what they were looking for, it was something that could be hidden in a book, a telephone box, a tube of toothpaste, or a hat band. I went back into the bathroom and looked at my head again. It was still oozing a tiny trickle of blood. I gave it more cold water and dried the cut with toilet paper and flushed that down the bowl. I went back and stood a moment looking down on Dr Hambleton, wondering what his mistake had been. He had seemed a fairly wise bird. The sunlight had moved over to the far edge of the room now, off the bed and down into a sad dusty corner.

I grinned suddenly, bent over and quickly and with the grin still on my face, out of place as it was, pulled off Dr Hambleton's toupee and turned it inside out. As simple as all that. To the lining of the toupee a piece of orange-coloured paper was fastened by Scotch tape, protected by a square of cellophane. I pulled it loose, turned it over, and saw that it was a numbered claim check belonging to the Bay City Camera Shop. I put it in my wallet and put the toupee carefully back on the dead egg-bald head.

I left the room unlocked because I had no way to lock it.

Down the hall the radio still blared through the transom and the exaggerated alcoholic laughter accompanied it from across the corridor.

10

Over the telephone the Bay City Camera Shop man said: 'Yes, Mr Hicks. We have them for you. Six enlarged prints on glossy from your negative.'

'What time do you close?' I asked.

'Oh, in about five minutes. We open at nine in the morning.'

'I'll pick them up in the morning. Thanks.'

I hung up, reached mechanically into the slot and found somebody else's nickel. I walked over to the lunch counter and bought myself a cup of coffee with it, and sat there sipping and listening to the auto horns complaining on the street outside. It was time to go home. Whistles blew. Motors raced. Old brake linings squeaked. There was a dull steady mutter of feet on the sidewalk outside. It was just after five-thirty. I finished the coffee, stuffed a pipe, and strolled a half-block back to the Van Nuys Hotel. In the writing-room I folded the orange camera shop check into a sheet of hotel stationery and addressed an envelope to myself. I put a special delivery stamp on it and dropped it in the mail chute by the elevator bank. Then I went along to Flack's office again.

Again I closed his door and sat down across from him. Flack didn't seem to have moved an inch. He was chewing morosely on the same cigar butt and his eyes were still full of nothing. I relit my pipe by striking a match on the side of his desk. He frowned.

'Dr Hambleton doesn't answer his door,' I said.

'Huh?' Flack looked at me vacantly.

'Party in 332. Remember? He doesn't answer his door.'

'What should I do – bust my girdle?' Flack asked.

'I knocked several times,' I said. 'No answer. Thought he might be taking a bath or something, although I couldn't hear anything. Went away for a while, then tried again. Same no answer again.'

Flack looked at a turnip watch he got from his vest. 'I'm off at seven,' he said. 'Christ. A whole hour to go, and more. Boy, am I hungry.'

'Working the way you do,' I said, 'you must be. You have to keep your strength up. Do I interest you at all in Room 332?'

'You said he wasn't in,' Flack said irritably. 'So what? He wasn't in.'

'I didn't say he wasn't in. I said he didn't answer his door.'

Flack leaned forward. Very slowly he removed the debris of the cigar from his mouth and put in in the glass tray. 'Go on. Make me like it,' he said, carefully.

'Maybe you'd like to run up and look,' I said. 'Maybe you didn't see a first-class ice-pick job lately.'

Flack put his hands on the arms of his chair and squeezed the wood hard. 'Aw,' he said painfully. 'Aw.' He got to his feet and opened the desk drawer. He took out a large black gun, flicked the gate open, studied the cartridges, squinted down the barrel, snapped the cylinder back into place. He unbuttoned his vest and tucked the gun down inside the waistband. In an emergency he could probably have got to it in less than a minute. He put his hat on firmly and jerked a thumb at the door.

We went up to the third floor in silence. We went down the corridor. Nothing had changed. No sound had increased or diminished. Flack hurried along to 332 and knocked from force of habit. Then tried the door. He looked back at me with a twisted mouth.

'You said the door wasn't locked,' he complained.

'I didn't exactly say that. It *was* unlocked, though.'

'It ain't now,' Flack said, and unshipped a key on a long chain. He unlocked the door and glanced up and down the hall. He twisted the knob slowly without sound and eased the door a couple of inches. He listened. No sound came from within. Flack stepped back, took the black gun out of his waistband. He removed the key from the the door, kicked it wide open, and brought the gun up hard and straight, like the wicked foreman of the Lazy Q. 'Let's go,' he said out of the corner of his mouth.

Over his shoulder I could see Dr Hambleton lay exactly as before, but the ice-pick handle didn't show from the entrance. Flack leaned forward and edged cautiously into the room. He reached the bathroom door and put his eye to the crack, then pushed the door open until it bounced against the tub. He went in and came out, stepped down into the room, a tense and wary man who was taking no chances.

He tried the closet door, levelled his gun and jerked it wide open. No suspects in the closet.

'Look under the bed,' I said.

Flack bent swiftly and looked under the bed.

'Look under the carpet,' I said.

'You kidding me?' Flack added nastily.

'I just like to watch you work.'

He bent over the dead man and studied the ice pick.

'Somebody locked that door,' he sneered. 'Unless you're lying about its being unlocked.'

I said nothing.

'Well, I guess it's the cops,' he said slowly. 'No chance to cover up on this one.'

'It's not your fault,' I told him. 'It happens even in good hotels.'

The red-headed intern filled out a DOA form and clipped his stylus to the outside pocket of his white jacket. He snapped the book shut with a faint grin on his face.

'Punctured spinal cord just below the occipital bulge, I'd say,' he said carelessly. 'A very vulnerable spot. If you know how to find it. And I suppose you do.'

Detective Lieutenant Christy French growled. 'Think it's the first time I've seen one?'

'No, I guess not,' the intern said. He gave a last quick look at the dead man, turned and walked out of the room. 'I'll call the coroner,' he said over his shoulder. The door closed behind him.

'What a stiff means to those birds is what a plate of warmed-up cabbage means to me,' Christy French said sourly to the closed door. His partner, a cop named Fred Beifus, was down on one knee by the telephone box. He had dusted it for fingerprints and blown off the loose powder. He was looking at the smudge through a small magnifying glass. He shook his head, then picked something off the screw with which the box had been fastened shut.

'Grey cotton undertaker's gloves,' he said disgustedly. 'Cost about four cents a pair wholesale. Fat lot of good printing this joint. They were looking for something in the telephone box, huh?'

'Evidently something that could be there,' French said. 'I didn't expect prints. These ice-pick jobs are a speciality. We'll get the experts after a while. This is just a quickover.'

He was stripping the dead man's pockets and laying what had been in them out on the bed beside the quiet and already waxy corpse. Flack was sitting in a chair by the window, looking out morosely. The assistant manager had been up, said nothing with a worried expression, and gone away. I was leaning against the bathroom wall and sorting out my fingers.

Flack said suddenly: 'I figure an ice-pick job's a dame's work. You can buy them anywhere. Ten cents. If you want one fast, you can slip it down inside a garter and let it hang there.'

Christy French gave him a grief glance which had a kind of wonder in it. Beifus said: 'What kind of dames you been running around with, honey? The way stockings cost nowadays a dame would as soon stick a saw down her sock.'

'I never thought of that,' Flack said.

Beifus said: 'Leave us do the thinking, sweetheart. It takes equipment.'

'No need to get tough,' Flack said.

Beifus took his hat off and bowed. 'You mustn't deny us our little pleasures, Mr Flack.'

Christy French said: 'Besides, a woman would keep on jabbing. She wouldn't even know how much was enough. Lots of punks don't. Whoever did this one was a performer. He got the spinal cord the first try. And another thing – you have to have the guy quiet to do it. That means more than one guy, unless he was doped, or the killer was a friend of his.'

I said: 'I don't see how he could have been doped, if he's the party that called me on the phone.'

French and Beifus both looked at me with the same expression of patient boredom. 'If,' French said, 'and since you don't know the guy – according to you – there's always the faint possibility that you wouldn't know his voice. Or am I being too subtle?'

'I don't know,' I said. 'I haven't read your fan mail.'

French grinned.

'Don't waste it on him,' Beifus told French. 'Save it for when you talk to the Friday Morning Club. Some of them old ladies in the shiny-nose league go big for the nicer angles of murder.'

French rolled himself a cigarette and lit it with a kitchen match he struck on the back of a chair. He sighed.

'They worked the technique out in Brooklyn,' he explained. 'Sunny Moe Stein's boys specialized in it, but they run it into the ground. It got so you couldn't walk across a vacant lot without finding some of their work. Then they came out here, what was left of them. I wonder why did they do that?'

'Maybe we just got more vacant lots,' Beifus said.

'Funny thing, though,' French said, almost dreamily. 'When Weepy Moyer had the chill put on Sunny Moe Stein over on Franklin Avenue last February, the killer used a gun. Moe wouldn't have liked that at all.'

'I betcha that was why his face had that disappointed look, after they washed the blood off,' Beifus remarked.

'Who's Weepy Moyer?' Flack asked.

'He was next to Moe in the organization,' French told him. 'This could easily be his work. Not that he'd have done it personal.'

'Why not?' Flack asked sourly.

'Don't you guys ever read a paper? Moyer's a gentleman now. He knows the nicest people. Even has another name. And as for the Sunny Moe Stein job, it just happened we had him in jail on a gambling rap. We didn't get anywhere. But we did make him a very sweet alibi. Anyhow he's a gentleman like I said, and gentlemen don't go around sticking ice-picks into people. They hire it done.'

'Did you ever have anything on Moyer?' I asked.

French looked at me sharply. 'Why?'

'I just had an idea. But it's very fragile,' I said.

French eyed me slowly. 'Just between us girls in the powder room,' he said, 'we never even proved the guy we had *was* Moyer. But don't broadcast it. Nobody's supposed to know but him and his lawyer and the DA and the police beat and the city hall and maybe two or three hundred other people.'

He slapped the dead man's empty wallet against his thigh and sat down on the bed. He leaned casually against the corpse's leg, lit a cigarette and pointed with it.

'That's enough time on the vaudeville circuit. Here's what we got, Fred. First off, the customer here was not too bright. He was going by the name of Dr G. W. Hambleton and had the cards printed with an El Centro address and a phone number. It took just two minutes to find out there ain't any such address or any such phone number. A bright boy doesn't lay open that easy. Next, the guy is definitely not in the chips. He has fourteen smackeroos folding in here and about two bucks loose change. On his key ring he don't have any car key or any safe-deposit key or any house key. All he's got is a suitcase key and seven filed Yale master keys. Filed fairly recently at that. I figure he was planning to sneak the hotel a little. Do you think these keys would work in your dump, Flack?'

Flack went over and stared at the keys. 'Two of them are the right size,' he said. 'I couldn't tell if they'd work by just looking. If I want a master key I have to get it from the office. All I carry is a pass-key. I can only use that if the guest is out.' He took a key out of his pocket, a key on a long chain, and compared it. He shook his head. 'They're no good without more work,' he said. 'Far too much metal on them.'

French flicked ash into the palm of his hand and blew it off as dust. Flack went back to his chair by the window.

'Next point,' Christie French announced. 'He don't have a driver's licence or any identification. None of his outside clothes were bought in El Centro. He had some kind of a grift, but he don't have the looks or personality to bounce cheques.'

'You really didn't see him at his best,' Beifus put in.

'And this hotel is the wrong dump for that anyway,' French went on. 'It's got a crummy reputation.'

'Now wait a minute!' Flack began.

French cut him short with a gesture. 'I know every hotel in the metropolitan district, Flack. It's my business to know. For fifty bucks I could organize a double-strip act with French trimmings inside of an hour in any room in this hotel. Don't kid me. You earn your living and I'll earn mine. Just don't kid me. All right. The customer had something he was afraid to keep around. That means he knew somebody was after him and getting close. So he offers Marlowe a hundred bucks to keep it for him. But he doesn't have that much money on him. So what he must have been planning on was getting Marlowe here to gamble with him. It couldn't have been hot jewellery then. It had to be something semi-legitimate. That right, Marlowe?'

'You could leave out the semi,' I said.

French grinned faintly. 'So what he had was something that could be kept flat or rolled up – in a phone box, a hatband, a Bible, a can of talcum. We don't know whether it was found or not. But we do know there was very little time. Not much more than half an hour.'

'If Dr Hambleton did the phoning,' I said. 'You opened that can of beans yourself.'

'It's kind of pointless any other way. The killers wouldn't be in a hurry to have him found. Why should they ask anybody to come over to his room?' He turned to Flack. 'Any chance to check his visitors?'

Flack shook his head gloomily. 'You don't even have to pass the desk to get to the elevators.'

Beifus said: 'Maybe that was one reason he came here. That, and the homey atmosphere.'

'All right,' French said. 'Whoever knocked him off could come and go without any questions asked. All he had to know was his room number. And that's about all we know. Okay, Fred?'

Beifus nodded.

I said: 'Not quite all. It's a nice toupee, but it's still a toupee.'

French and Beifus both swung around quickly. French reached, carefully removed the dead man's hair, and whistled. 'I wondered what that damn intern was grinning at,' he said. 'The bastard didn't even mention it. See what I see, Fred?'

'All I see is a guy without no hair,' Beifus answered.

'Maybe you never knew him at that. Mileaway Marston. Used to be a runner for Ace Devore.'

'Why, sure enough,' Beifus chuckled. He leaned over and patted the dead bald head gently. 'How you been all this time, Mileaway? I didn't see you in so long I forgot. But you know me, pal. Once a softy always a softy.'

The man on the bed looked old and hard and shrunken without his toupee. The yellow mask of death was beginning to set his face into rigid lines.

French said calmly: 'Well, that takes a load off my mind. This punk ain't going to be no twenty-four-hour-a-day job. The hell with him.' He replaced the toupee over one eye and stood up off the bed. 'That's all for you two,' he said to Flack and me.

Flack stood up.

'Thanks for the murder, honey,' Beifus told him. 'You get any more in your nice hotel, don't forget our services. Even when it ain't good, it's quick.'

Flack went down the short hall and yanked the door open. I followed him out. On the way to the elevator we didn't speak. Nor on the way down. I walked with him along to his little office, followed him in and shut the door. He seemed surprised.

He sat down at his desk and reached for his telephone. 'I got to make a report to the Assistant Manager,' he said. 'Something you want?'

I rolled a cigarette around on my fingers, put a match to it and blew smoke softly across the desk. 'One hundred and fifty dollars,' I said.

Flack's small, intent eyes became round holes in a face washed clean of expression. 'Don't get funny in the wrong place,' he said.

'After those two comedians upstairs, you could hardly blame me if I did. But I'm not being funny.' I beat a tattoo on the edge of the desk and waited.

Tiny beads of sweat showed on Flack's lip above his little moustache. 'I got business to attend to,' he said, more throatily this time. 'Beat it and keep going.'

'Such a tough little man,' I said. 'Dr Hambleton had $164.00 currency in his wallet when I searched him. He promised me a hundred as retainer, remember? Now, in the same wallet he has fourteen dollars. And I *did* leave the door of his room unlocked. And somebody else locked it. You locked it, Flack.'

Flack took hold of the arms of his chair and squeezed. His voice came from the bottom of a well, saying: 'You can't prove a damn thing.'

'Do I have to try?'

He took the gun out of his waistband and laid it on the desk in front of him. He stared down at it. It didn't have any message for him. He looked up at me again. 'Fifty-fifty, huh?' he said brokenly.

There was a moment of silence between us. He got his old shabby wallet out and rooted in it. He came up with a handful of currency and spread bills out on the desk, sorted them into two piles and pushed one pile my way.

I said: 'I want the whole hundred and fifty.'

He hunched down in his chair and stared at a corner of the desk. After a long time, he sighed. He put the two piles together and pushed them over – to my side of the desk.

'It wasn't doing him any good,' Flack said. 'Take the dough and breeze. I'll remember you, buddy. All you guys make me sick to my stomach. How do I know you didn't take half a grand off him?'

'I'd take it all. So would the killer. Why leave fourteen dollars?'

'So why did I leave fourteen dollars?' Flack asked, in a tired voice, making vague movements along the desk edge with his fingers. I picked up the money, counted it and threw it back at him.

'Because you're in the business and could size him up. You knew he'd at least have room rent, and a few dollars for loose change. The cops would expect the same thing. Here, I don't want the money. I want something else.'

He stared at me with his mouth open.

'Put that dough out of sight,' I said.

He reached for it and crammed it back in his wallet. 'What something else?' His eyes were small and thoughtful. His tongue pushed out his lower lip. 'It don't seem to me *you're* in a very hot trading position either.'

'You could be a little wrong about that. If I have to go back up there and tell Christy French and Beifus I was up there before and searched the body, I'd get a tongue lashing all right. But he'd understand that I haven't been holding out just to be smart. He'd know that somewhere in the background I had a client I was trying to protect. I'd get tough talk and bluster. But that's not what *you'd* get.' I stopped and watched the faint glisten of moisture forming on his forehead now. He swallowed hard. His eyes were sick.

'Cut out the wise talk and lay your deal on the desk,' he said. He grinned suddenly, rather wolfishly. 'Got here a little late to protect her, didn't you?' The fat sneer he lived with was coming home again, slowly, but gladly.

I killed my cigarette and got another one out and went through all the slow futile face-saving motions of lighting it, getting rid of the match, blowing smoke off to one side, inhaling deeply as though that scrubby little office was a hilltop overlooking the bouncing ocean – all the tired clichéd mannerisms of my trade.

'All right,' I said. 'I'll admit it was a woman. I'll admit she must have been up there while he was dead, if that makes you happy. I guess it was just shock that made her run away.'

'Oh, sure,' Flack said nastily. The fat sneer was all the way home now. 'Or maybe she hadn't ice-picked a guy in a month. Kind of lost touch.'

'But why would she take his key?' I said, talking to myself. 'And why leave it at the desk? Why not just walk away and leave the whole thing? What if she did think she had to lock the door? Why not drop the key in a sand jar and cover it up? Or take it away with her and lose it? Why do something with that key that would connect her with that room?' I brought my eyes down and gave Flack a thick leaden stare. 'Unless of course she was seen to leave the room – with the key already in her hand – and followed out of the hotel.'

'What for would anybody do that?' Flack asked.

'Because whoever saw her could have got into that room at once. He had a pass-key.'

Flack's eyes flicked up at me and dropped all in one motion.

'So he must have followed her,' I said. 'He must have seen her dump the key at the desk and stroll out of the hotel and he must have followed her a little farther than that.'

Flack said derisively: 'What makes you so wonderful?'

I leaned down and pulled the telephone towards me. 'I'd better call Christy and get this over with,' I said. 'The more I think about it the scareder I get. Maybe she did kill him. I can't cover up for a murderer.'

I took the receiver off the hook. Flack slammed his moist paw down hard on top of my hand. The phone jumped on the desk. 'Lay off.' His voice was almost a sob. 'I followed her to a car parked down the street. Got the number. Christ sake, pal, give me some kind of a break.' He was fumbling wildly in his pockets. 'Know what I make on this job? Cigarette and cigar money and hardly a dime more. Wait a minute now. I think—' He looked down and played solitaire with some dirty envelopes, finally selected one and tossed it over to me. 'Licence number,' he said wearily, 'and if it's any satisfaction to you, I can't even remember what it was.'

I looked down at the envelope. There was a scrawled licence number on it all right. Ill-written and faint and oblique, the way it would be written hastily on a paper held in a man's hand on the street. 6 N 333. California 1947.

'Satisfied?' That was Flack's voice. Or it came out of his mouth. I tore the number off and tossed the envelope back to him.

'4P 327,' I said watching his eyes. Nothing flicked in them. No trace of derision or concealment. 'But how do I know this isn't some licence number you had already?'

'You just got to take my word for it.'

'Describe the car,' I said.

'Caddy convertible, not new, top up. About 1942 model. Sort of dusty blue colour.'

'Describe the woman.'

'Want a lot for your dough, don't you, peeper?'

'Dr Hambleton's dough.'

He winced. 'All right. Blonde. White coat with some coloured stitching on it. Wide blue straw hat. Dark glasses. Height about five two. Built like a Conover model.'

'Would you know her again – without the glasses?' I asked carefully.

He pretended to think. Then shook his head, no.

'What was that licence number again, Flackie?' I caught him off guard.

'Which one?' he said.

I leaned across the desk and dropped some cigarette ash on his gun. I did some more staring into his eyes. But I knew he was licked now. He seemed to know too. He reached for his gun, blew off the ash and put it back in the drawer of his desk.

'Go on. Beat it,' he said between his teeth. 'Tell the cops I frisked the stiff. So what? Maybe I lose a job. Maybe I get tossed in the fish-bowl. So what? When I come out I'm solid. Little Flackie don't have to worry about coffee and crullers. Don't think for a minute those dark cheaters fool little Flackie. I've seen too many movies to miss that lovely puss. And if you ask me that babe'll be around for a long time. She's a comer – and who knows' – he leered at me triumphantly – 'she'll need a body-guard one of these days. A guy to have around, watch things, keep her out of jams. Somebody that knows the ropes and ain't unreasonable about dough ... What's the matter?'

I had put my head on one side and was leaning forward. I was listening. 'I thought I heard a church bell,' I said.

'There ain't any church around here,' he said contemptuously.

431

'It's that platinum brain of yours getting cracks in it.'

'Just one bell,' I said. 'Very slow. Tolling is the word, I believe.'

Flack listened with me. 'I don't hear anything,' he said sharply.

'Oh, you wouldn't hear it,' I said. 'You'd be the one guy in the whole world who wouldn't hear it.'

He just sat there and stared at me with his nasty little eyes half-closed and his nasty little moustache shining. One of his hands twitched on the desk, an aimless movement.

I left him to his thoughts, which were probably as small, ugly and frightened as the man himself.

12

The apartment house was over on Doheny Drive, just down the hill from the Strip. It was really two buildings, one behind the other, loosely connected by a floored patio with a fountain and a room built over the arch. There were mail boxes and bells in the imitation marble foyer. Three out of the sixteen had no names over them. The names that I read meant nothing to me. The job needed a little more work. I tried the front door, found it unlocked, and the job still needed more work.

Outside stood two Cadillacs, a Lincoln Continental and a Packard Clipper. Neither of the Cadillacs had the right colour or licence. Across the way a guy in riding breeches was sprawled with his legs over the door of a low-cut Lancia. He was smoking and looking up at the pale stars which know enough to keep their distance from Hollywood. I walked up the steep hill to the boulevard and a block east and smothered myself in an outdoor sweat-box phone booth. I dialled a man named Peoria Smith, who was so-called because he stuttered – another little mystery I hadn't had time to work out.

'Mavis Weld,' I said. 'Phone number. This is Marlowe.'

'S-s-s-ure,' he said. 'M-M-Mavis Weld huh? You want h-h-her ph-ph-phone number?'

'How much?'

'Be-b-b-be ten b-b-b-bucks,' he said.

'Just forget I called,' I said.

'W-W-Wait a minute! I ain't supposed to give out with them

b-b-babes' phone numbers. An assistant prop man is taking a hell of a chance.'

I waited and breathed back my own breath.

'The address goes with it naturally,' Peoria whined, forgetting to stutter.

'Five bucks,' I said. 'I've got the address already. And don't haggle. If you think you're the only studio grifter in the business of selling unlisted telephone numbers—'.

'Hold it,' he said wearily, and went to get his little red book. A left-handed stutterer. He only stuttered when he wasn't excited. He came back and gave it to me. A Crestview number, of course. If you don't have a Crestview number in Hollywood you're a bum.

I opened up the steel-and-glass cell to let in some air while I dialled again. After two rings a drawling sexy voice answered. I pulled the door shut.

'Ye-e-e-s,' the voice cooed.

'Miss Weld, please.'

'And who is calling Miss Weld, if you please?'

'I have some stills Whitey wants me to deliver tonight.'

'Whitey? And who is Whitey, amigo?'

'The head still-photographer at the studio,' I said. 'Don't you know that much? I'll come up if you'll tell me which apartment. I'm only a couple of blocks away.'

'Miss Weld is taking a bath.' She laughed. I guess it was a silvery tinkle where she was. It sounded like somebody putting away saucepans where I was. 'But of course bring up the photographs. I am sure she is dying to see them. The apartment number is fourteen.'

'Will you be there too?'

'But of course. But naturally. Why do you ask that?'

I hung up and staggered out into the fresh air. I went down the hill. The guy in the riding breeches was still hanging out of the Lancia but one of the Cadillacs was gone and two Buick convertibles had joined the cars in front. I pushed the bell to Number 14, went on through the patio where scarlet Chinese honeysuckle was lit by a peanut spotlight. Another light glowed down on the big ornamental pool full of fat goldfish and silent lily pads, the lilies folded tight for the night. There were a couple of stone seats and a lawn swing. The place didn't look very expensive except that every place was expensive that year. The apartment was on the second floor, one of the two doors facing across a wide landing.

The bell chimed and a tall dark girl in jodhpurs opened the

door. Sexy was very faint praise for her. The jodphurs, like her hair, were coal black. She wore a white silk shirt with a scarlet scarf loose around her throat. It was not as vivid as her mouth. She held a long brown cigarette in a pair of tiny golden tweezers. The fingers holding it were more than adequately jewelled. Her black hair was parted in the middle and a line of scalp as white as snow went over the top of her head and dropped out of sight behind. Two thick braids of her shining black hair lay one on each side of her slim brown neck. Each was tied with a small scarlet bow. But it was a long time since she was a little girl.

She looked sharply down at my empty hands. Studio stills are usually a little too big to put in your pocket.

I said: 'Miss Weld, please.'

'You can give me the stills.' The voice was cool, drawling and insolent, but the eyes were something else. She looked almost as hard to get as a haircut.

'For Miss Weld personally. Sorry.'

'I told you she was taking a bath.'

'I'll wait.'

'Are you quite sure you have the stills, amigo?'

'As sure as I'll ever be. Why?'

'Your name?' Her voice froze on the second word, like a feather taking off in a sudden draft. Then it cooed and hovered and soared and eddied and the silent invitation of a smile picked delicately at the corners of her lips, very slowly like a child trying to pick up a snowflake.

'Your last picture was wonderful, Miss Gonzales.'

The smile flashed like lightning and changed her whole face. The body became erect and vibrant with delight. 'But it was stinking,' she glowed. 'Positively goddamned stinking, you sweet lovely man. You know but positively goddamn well it was stinking.'

'Nothing with you in it stinks for me, Miss Gonzales.'

She stood away from the door and waved me in. 'We will have a drink,' she said. 'The goddamnedest drink we will have. I adore flattery, however dishonest.'

I went in. A gun in the kidney wouldn't have surprised me a bit. She stood so that I had to practically push her mammaries out of the way to get through the door. She smelled the way the Taj Mahal looked by moonlight. She closed the door and danced over to a small portable bar.

'Scotch? Or would you prefer a mixed drink? I mix a perfectly loathsome Martini,' she said.

'Scotch is fine, thanks.'

She made a couple of drinks in a couple of glasses you could almost have stood umbrellas in. I sat down in a chintz chair and looked around. The place was old-fashioned. It had a false fireplace with gas logs and a marble mantel, cracks in the plaster, a couple of vigorously coloured daubs on the walls that looked lousy enough to have cost money, an old black chipped Steinway and for once no Spanish shawl on it. There were a lot of new-looking books in bright jackets scattered around and a double-barrelled shotgun with a handsomely carved stock stood in the corner with a white satin bow tied around the barrels. Hollywood wit.

The dark lady in the jodhpurs handed me a glass and perched on the arm of my chair. 'You may call me Dolores if you wish,' she said, taking a hearty swig out of her own tumbler.

'Thanks.'

'And what may I call you?'

I grinned.

'Of course,' she said, 'I am most fully aware that you are a goddamn liar and that you have no stills in your pockets. Not that I wish to inquire into your no doubt very private business.'

'Yeah?' I inhaled a couple of inches of my liquor. 'Just what kind of bath is Miss Weld taking? And old-fashioned soap or something with Arabian spices in it?'

She waved the remains of the brown cigarette in the small gold clasp. 'Perhaps you would like to help her. The bathroom is over there – through the arch and to the right. Most probably the door is not locked.'

'Not if it's that easy,' I said.

'Oh,' she gave me the brilliant smile again. 'You like to do the difficult things in life. I must remember to be less approachable, must I not?' She removed herself elegantly from the arm of the chair and ditched her cigarette, bending over enough so that I could trace the outline of her hips.

'Don't bother, Miss Gonzales. I'm just a guy who came here on business. I don't have any idea of raping anybody.'

'No?' The smile became soft, lazy and, if you can't think of a better word, provocative.

'But I'm sure as hell working up to it,' I said.

'You are an amusing son-of-a-bitch,' she said with a shrug and went off through the arch, carrying her half-quart of Scotch and water with her. I heard a gentle tapping on a door and her voice: 'Darling, there's a man here who says he has some stills from the studio. He says. *Muy simpàtico. Muy guapo tambièn. Con cojones.*'

A voice I had heard before said sharply: 'Shut up, you little bitch. I'll be out in a second.'

The Gonzales came back through the archway humming. Her glass was empty. She went to the bar again. 'But you are not drinking,' she cried, looking at my glass.

'I ate dinner. I only have a two-quart stomach anyway. I understand a little Spanish.'

She tossed her head. 'You are shocked?' Her eyes rolled. Her shoulders did a fan dance.

'I'm pretty hard to shock.'

'But you heard what I said? *Madre de Dios.* I'm so terribly sorry.

'I'll bet,' I said.

She finished making herself another highball.

'Yes. I am so sorry,' she sighed. 'That is, I think I am. Sometimes I am not sure. Sometimes I do not give a good goddamn. It is so confusing. All my friends tell me I am far too outspoken. I do shock you, don't I?' She was on the arm of my chair again.

'No. But if I wanted to be shocked I'd know right where to come.' She reached her glass behind her indolently and leaned towards me.

'But I do not live here,' she said. 'I live at the Château Bercy.'

'Alone?'

She slapped me delicately across the tip of my nose. The next thing I knew I had her in my lap and she was trying to bite a piece off my tongue. 'You are a very sweet son-of-a-bitch,' she said. Her mouth was as hot as ever a mouth was. Her lips burned like dry ice. Her tongue was driving hard against my teeth. Her eyes looked enormous and black and the whites showed under them.

'I am so tired,' she whispered into my mouth. 'I am so worn, so incredibly tired.'

I felt her hand in my breast pocket. I shoved her off hard, but she had my wallet. She danced away with it laughing, flicked it open and went through it with fingers that darted like little snakes.

'So glad you two got acquainted,' a voice off to one side said coolly. Mavis Weld stood in the archway.

Her hair was fluffed out carelessly and she hadn't bothered with make-up. She wore a hostess gown and very little else. Her legs ended in little green and silver slippers. Her eyes were empty, her lips contemptuous. But she was the same girl all right, dark glasses on or off.

The Gonzales gave her a quick darting glance, closed my wallet and tossed it. I caught it and put it away. She strolled to a table and picked up a black bag with a long strap, hooked it over her shoulder and moved towards the door.

Mavis Weld didn't move, didn't look at her. She looked at me. But there was no emotion of any kind in her face. The Gonzales opened the door and glanced outside and almost closed it and turned.

'The name is Philip Marlowe,' she said to Mavis Weld. 'Nice, don't you think?'

'I didn't know you bothered to ask them their names,' Mavis Weld said. 'You so seldom know them long enough.'

'I see,' the Gonzales answered gently. She turned and smiled at me faintly. 'Such a charming way to call a girl a whore, don't you think?'

Mavis Weld said nothing. Her face had no expression.

'At least,' the Gonzales said smoothly as she pulled the door open again, 'I haven't been sleeping with any gunmen lately.'

'Are you sure you can remember?' Mavis Weld asked her in exactly the same tone. 'Open the door, honey. This is the day we put the garbage out.'

The Gonzales looked back at her slowly, levelly, and with a knife in her eyes. Then she made a faint sound with her lips and teeth and yanked the door wide. It closed behind her with a jarring smash. The noise didn't even flicker the steady dark blue glare in Mavis Weld's eyes.

'Now suppose you do the same – but more quietly,' she said.

I got out a handkerchief and scrubbed the lipstick off my face. It looked exactly the colour of blood, fresh blood. 'That could happen to anybody,' I said. 'I wasn't petting her. She was petting me.'

She marched to the door and heaved it open. 'On your way, dreamboat. Make with the feet.'

'I came here on business, Miss Weld.'

'Yes. I can imagine. Out. I don't know you. I don't want to know you. And if I did, this wouldn't be either the day or the hour.'

'Never the time and place and the loved one all together,' I said.

'What's that?' She tried to throw me out with the point of her chin, but even she wasn't that good.

'Browning. The poet, not the automatic. I feel sure you'd prefer the automatic.'

'Look, little man, do I have to call the manager to bounce you downstairs like a basketball?'

I went over and pushed the door shut. She held on to the last moment. She didn't quite kick me, but it cost her an effort not to. I tried to ease her away from the door without appearing to. She didn't ease worth a darn. She stood her ground, one hand reaching for the door-knob, her eyes full of dark-blue rage.

'If you're going to stand that close to me,' I said, 'maybe you'd better put some clothes on.'

She took her hand back and swung it hard. The slap sounded like Miss Gonzales slamming the door, but it stung. And it reminded me of the sore place on the back of my head.

'Did I hurt you?' she asked softly.

I nodded.

'That's fine.' She hauled off and slapped me again, harder if anything. 'I think you'd better kiss me,' she breathed. Her eyes were clear and limpid and melting. I glanced down casually. Her right hand was balled into a very business-like fist. It wasn't too small to work with, either.

'Believe me,' I said. 'There's only one reason I don't. Even if you had your little black gun with you. Or the brass knuckles you probably keep on your night table.

She smiled politely.

'I might just happen to be working for you,' I said. 'And I don't go whoring around after every pair of legs I see.' I looked down at hers. I could see them all right and the flag that marked the goal line was no larger than it had to be. She pulled the hostess gown together and turned and walked over to the little bar shaking her head.

'I'm free, white and twenty-one,' she said. 'I've seen all the approaches there are. I think I have. If I can't scare you, lick you, or seduce you, what the hell can I buy you with?'

'Well—'

'Don't tell me,' she interrupted sharply and turned with a glass in her hand. She drank and tossed the loose hair around and smiled a thin little smile. 'Money, of course. How damned stupid of me to overlook that.'

'Money would help,' I said.

Her mouth twisted in wry disgust but the voice was almost affectionate. 'How much money?'

'Oh, a hundred bucks would do to start with.'

'You're cheap. It's a cheap little bastard, isn't it? A hundred

438

bucks it says. Is a hundred bucks money in your circle, darling?'

'Make it two hundred then. I could retire on that.'

'Still cheap. Every week of course. In a nice clean envelope?'

'You could skip the envelope. I'd only get it dirty.'

'And just what would I get for this money, my charming little gumshoe? I'm quite sure of what you are, of course.'

'You'd get a receipt. Who told you I was a gumshoe?'

She stared out of her own eyes for a brief instant before the act dropped over her again. 'It must have been the smell.' She sipped her drink and stared at me over it with a faint smile of contempt.

'I'm beginning to think you write your own dialogue,' I said. 'I've been wondering just what was the matter with it.'

I ducked. A few drops splattered me. The glass splintered on the wall behind me. The broken pieces fell soundlessly.

'And with that,' she said, completely calm, 'I must have used up my entire stock of girlish charm.'

I went over and picked up my hat. 'I never thought *you* killed him,' I said. 'But it would help to have some sort of reason for not telling you were there. It's a help to have money enough for a retainer just to establish myself. And enough information to justify my accepting the retainer.'

She picked a cigarette out of a box, tossed it in the air, caught it between her lips effortlessly and lit it with a match that came from nowhere.

'My goodness. Am I supposed to have killed somebody?' she asked. I was still holding the hat. It made me feel foolish. I don't know why. I put it on and started for the door.

'I trust you have the carfare home,' the contemptuous voice said behind me.

I didn't answer. I just kept going. When I had the door ready to open she said: 'I also trust Miss Gonzales gave you her address and phone number. You should be able to get almost anything out of her – including, I am told, money.'

I let go of the door-knob and went back across the room fast. She stood her ground and the smile on her lips didn't slip a millimetre.

'Look,' I said. 'You're going to find this hard to believe. But I came over here with the quaint idea that you might be a girl who needed some help – and would find it rather hard to get anyone you could bank on. I figured you went to that hotel room to make some kind of a pay-off. And the fact that you went by yourself and took chances of being recognized – and *were* recognized by a house dick whose standards of ethics would take about as much strain as a very tired old cobweb – all this made me think you might be in one of those Hollywood jams that really mean curtains. But you're not in any jam. You're right up front under the baby spot pulling every tired ham gesture you ever used in the most tired B-picture you ever acted in – if acting is the word—'

'Shut up,' she said, between teeth so tight they grated. 'Shut up, you slimy, blackmailing keyhole peeper.'

'You don't need me,' I said. 'You don't need anybody. You're so goddamn smart you could talk your way out of a safe-deposit box. Okay. Go ahead and talk your way out. I won't stop you. Just don't make me listen to it. I'd burst out crying to think a mere slip of an innocent little girl like you should be so clever. You do things to me, honey. Just like Margaret O'Brien.'

She didn't move or breathe when I reached the door, nor when I opened it. I don't know why. The stuff wasn't *that* good.

I went down the stairs and across the court and out of the front door, almost bumping into a slim dark-eyed man who was standing there lighting a cigarette.

'Excuse me,' he said quietly, 'I'm afraid I'm in your way.'

I started to go around him, then I noticed that his lifted right hand held a key. I reached out and snapped it out of his hand for no reason at all. I looked at the number stamped on it. No. 14. Mavis Weld's apartment. I threw it off behind some bushes.

'You don't need that,' I said. 'The door isn't locked.'

'Of course,' he said. There was a peculiar smile on his face. 'How stupid of me.'

'Yeah,' I said. 'We're both stupid. Anybody's stupid that bothers with that tramp.'

'I wouldn't quite say that,' he answered quietly, his small sad eyes watching me without any particular expression.

'You don't have to,' I said. 'I just said it for you. I beg your pardon. I'll get your key.' I went over behind the bushes, picked it up and handed it to him.

'Thank you very much,' he said. 'And by the way—' He stopped. I stopped. 'I hope I don't interrupt an interesting quarrel,' he said. 'I should hate to do that. No?' He smiled. 'Well, since Miss Weld is a friend in common, may I introduce myself. My name is Steelgrave. Haven't I seen you somewhere?'

'No, you haven't seen me anywhere, Mr Steelgrave,' I said.

'My name's Marlowe, Philip Marlowe. It's extremely unlikely that we've met. And, strange to relate, I never heard of you, Mr Steelgrave. And I wouldn't give a damn, even if your name was Weepy Moyer.' I never knew quite why I said that. There was nothing to make me say it, except that the name had been mentioned. A peculiar stillness came over his face. A peculiar fixed look in his silent black eyes. He took the cigarette out of his mouth, looked at the tip, flicked a little ash off it, although there was no ash to flick off, looking down as he said: 'Weepy Moyer. Peculiar name. I don't think I ever heard that. Is he somebody I should know?'

'Not unless you're unusually fond of ice picks,' I said, and left him. I went on down the steps, crossed to my car, looked back before I got in. He was standing there looking down at me, the cigarette between his lips. From that distance I couldn't see whether there was any expression on his face. He didn't move or make any kind of gesture when I looked back at him. He didn't even turn away. He just stood there. I got in and drove off.

13

I drove east on Sunset but I didn't go home. At La Brea I turned north and swung over to Highland, out over Cahuenga Pass and down on to Ventura Boulevard, past Studio City and Sherman Oaks and Encino. There was nothing lonely about the trip. There never is on that road. Fast boys in stripped-down Fords shot in and out of the traffic streams, missing fenders by a sixteenth of an inch, but somehow always missing them. Tired men in dusty coupés and sedans winced and tightened their grip on the wheel and ploughed on north and west towards home and dinner, an evening with the sports page, the blatting of the radio, the whining of their spoiled children and the gabble of their silly wives. I drove on past the gaudy neons and the false fronts behind them, the sleazy hamburger joints that look like palaces under the colours, the circular drive-ins as gay as circuses with the chipper hard-eyed car-hops, the brilliant counters, and the sweaty greasy kitchens that would have poisoned a toad. Great double trucks rumbled down over Sepulveda from Wilmington and San Pedro and crossed towards the Ridge Route, starting up in low low from the traffic lights with a growl of lions in the zoo.

Behind Encino an occasional light winked from the hills

through thick trees. The homes of screen stars. Screen stars, phooey. The veterans of a thousand beds. Hold it, Marlowe, you're not human tonight.

The air got cooler. The highway narrowed. The cars were so few now that the headlights hurt. The grade rose against chalk walls and at the top a breeze, unbroken from the ocean, danced casually across the night.

I ate dinner at a place near Thousand Oaks. Bad but quick. Feed 'em and throw 'em out. Lots of business. We can't bother with you sitting over your second cup of coffee, mister. You're using money space. See those people over there behind the rope? They want to eat. Anyway they think they have to. God knows why they want to eat here. They could do better home out of a can. They're just restless. Like you. They have to get the car out and go somewhere. Sucker-bait for the racketeers that have taken over the restaurants. Here we go again. You're not human tonight, Marlowe.

I paid off and stopped in a bar to drop a brandy on top of the New York cut. Why New York, I thought. It was Detroit where they made machine tools. I stepped out into the night air that nobody had yet found out how to option. But a lot of people were probably trying. They'd get around to it.

I drove on to the Oxnard cut-off and turned back along the ocean. The big eight-wheelers and sixteen-wheelers were streaming north, all hung over with orange lights. On the right a great fat solid Pacific trudging into shore like a scrubwoman going home. No moon, no fuss, hardly a sound of the surf. No smell. None of the harsh wild smell of the sea. A Californian ocean. California, the department-store state. The most of everything and the best of nothing. Here we go again. You're not human tonight, Marlowe.

All right. Why should I be? I'm sitting in that office, playing with a dead fly and in pops this dowdy little item from Manhattan, Kansas, and chisels me down to a shop-worn twenty to find her brother. He sounds like a creep but she wants to find him. So with this fortune clasped to my chest, I trundle down to Bay City and the routine I go through is so tired I'm half-asleep on my feet. I meet nice people, with and without ice picks in their necks. I leave, and I leave myself wide-open too. Then she comes in and takes the twenty away from me and gives me a kiss and gives it back to me because I didn't do a full day's work.

So I go see Dr Hambleton, retired (and how) optometrist from El Centro, and meet again the new style in neckwear. And I don't tell the cops. I just frisk the customer's toupee and put on an act. Why? Who am I cutting my throat for this time? A blonde with sexy eyes and too many door keys? A girl from Manhattan, Kansas? I don't know. All I know is that something isn't what it seems and the old tired but always reliable hunch tells me that if the hand is played the way it is dealt the wrong person is going to lose the pot. Is that my business? Well, what is my business? Do I know? Did I ever know? Let's not go into that. You're not human tonight, Marlowe. Maybe I never was or ever will be. Maybe I'm an ectoplasm with a private licence. Maybe we all get like this in the cold half-lit world where always the wrong thing happens and never the right.

Malibu. More movie stars. More pink and blue bathtubs. More tufted beds. More Chanel No. 5. More Lincoln Continentals and Cadillacs. More wind-blown hair and sunglasses and attitudes and pseudo-refined voices and water-front morals. Now, wait a minute. Lots of nice people work in pictures. You've got the wrong attitude, Marlowe. You're not human tonight.

I smelled Los Angeles before I got to it. It smelled stale and old like a living-room that had been closed too long. But the coloured lights fooled you. The lights were wonderful. There ought to be a monument to the man who invented neon lights. Fifteen storeys high, solid marble. There's a boy who really made something out of nothing.

So I went to a picture show and it had to have Mavis Weld in it. One of those glass-and-chromium deals where everybody smiled too much and talked too much and knew it. The women were always going up a long curving staircase to change their clothes. The men were always taking monogrammed cigarettes out of expensive cases and snapping expensive lighters at each other. And the help was round-shouldered from carrying trays with drinks across the terrace to a swimming pool about the size of Lake Huron but a lot neater.

The leading man was an amiable ham with a lot of charm. some of it turning a little yellow at the edges. The star was a bad-tempered brunette with contemptuous eyes and a couple of bad close-ups that showed her pushing forty-five backwards almost hard enough to break a wrist. Mavis Weld played second lead and she played it with wraps on. She was good, but she could have been ten times better. But if she had been ten times better half her scenes would have been yanked out to protect the star. It was as neat a bit of tightrope walking as I ever saw. Well, it wouldn't be a tightrope she'd be walking from now on. It would be a piano wire. It would be very high. And there wouldn't be any net under it.

14

I had a reason for going back to the office. A special delivery letter with an orange claim check ought to have arrived there by now. Most of the windows were dark in the building, but not all. People work nights in other businesses than mine. The elevator man said 'Howdy' from the depths of his throat and trundled me up. The corridor had lighted open doors where the scrubwomen were still cleaning up the debris of the wasted hours. I turned a corner past the slobbery hum of a vacuum cleaner, let myself into my dark office and opened the windows. I sat there at the desk doing nothing, not even thinking. No special delivery letter. All the noise of the building, except the vacuum cleaner, seemed to have flowed out into the street and lost itself among the turning wheels of innumerable cars. Then, somewhere along the hall outside, a man started whistling 'Lili Marlene' with elegance and virtuosity. I knew who that was. The night man checking office doors. I switched the desk lamp on and he passed without trying mine. His steps went away, then came back with a different sound, more of a shuffle. The buzzer sounded in the other office which was still unlocked. That would be special delivery. I went out to get it, only it wasn't.

A fat man in sky-blue pants was closing the door with that beautiful leisure only fat men can achieve. He wasn't alone, but I looked at him first. He was a large man and wide. Not young nor handsome, but he looked durable. Above the sky-blue gaberdine slacks he wore a two-tone leisure jacket which would have been revolting on a zebra. The neck of his canary-yellow shirt was open wide, which it had to be if his neck was going to get out. He was hatless and his large head was decorated with a reasonable amount of salmon-coloured hair. His nose had been broken but well set, and it hadn't been a collector's item in the first place.

The creature with him was a weedy number with red eyes and sniffles. Age about twenty, five feet nine, thin as a broom straw. His nose twitched and his mouth twitched and his hands twitched and he looked very unhappy.

The big man smiled genially. 'Mr Marlowe, no doubt?'

I said: 'Who else?'

'It's a little late for a business call,' the big man said and hid half the office by spreading out his hands. 'I hope you don't mind. Or do you already have all the business you can handle?'

'Don't kid me. My nerves are frayed,' I said. 'Who's the junky?'

'Come along, Alfred,' the big man said to his companion. 'And stop acting girlish.'

'In a pig's valise,' Alfred told him.

The big man turned to me placidly. 'Why do all these punks keep saying that? It isn't funny. It isn't witty. It doesn't mean anything. Quite a problem, this Alfred. I got him off the stuff, you know, temporarily at least. Say "How do you do" to Mr Marlowe, Alfred.'

'Screw him,' Alfred said.

The big man sighed. 'My name's Toad,' he said. 'Joseph P. Toad.'

I didn't say anything.

'Go ahead and laugh,' the big man said. 'I'm used to it. Had the name all my life.' He came towards me with his hand out. I took it. The big man smiled pleasantly into my eyes. 'Okay, Alfred,' he said without looking back.

Alfred made what seemed to be a very slight and unimportant movement at the end of which a heavy automatic was pointing at me.

'Careful, Alfred,' the big man said, holding my hand with a grip that would have bent a girder. 'Not yet.'

'In a pig's valise,' Alfred said. The gun pointed at my chest. His finger tightened around the trigger. I watched it tighten. I knew at precisely what moment that tightening would release the hammer. It didn't seem to make any difference. This was happening somewhere else in a cheesy programme picture. It wasn't happening to me.

The hammer of the automatic clicked dryly on nothing. Alfred lowered the gun with a grunt of annoyance and it disappeared whence it had come. He started to twitch again. There was nothing nervous about his movements with the gun. I wondered just what junk he was off of.

The big man let go of my hand, the genial smile still over his large healthy face.

He patted a pocket. 'I got the magazine,' he said. 'Alfred ain't reliable lately. The little bastard might have shot you.'

Alfred sat down in a chair and tilted it against the wall and breathed through his mouth.

I let my heels down on the floor again.

'I bet he scared you,' Joseph P. Toad said.

I tasted salt on my tongue.

'You ain't so tough,' Toad said, poking me in the stomach with a fat finger.

I stepped away from the finger and watched his eyes.

'What does it cost?' he asked almost gently.

'Let's go into my parlour,' I said.

I turned my back on him and walked through the door into the other office. It was hard work but I made it. I sweated all the way. I went around behind the desk and stood there waiting. Mr Toad followed me in placidly. The junky came twitching in behind him.

'You don't have a comic book around, do you?' Toad asked. 'Keeps him quiet.'

'Sit down,' I said. 'I'll look.'

He reached for the chair arms. I jerked a drawer open and got my hand around the butt of a Luger. I brought it up slowly, looking at Alfred. Alfred didn't even look at me. He was studying the corner of the ceiling and trying to keep his mouth out of his eye.

'This is as comic as I get,' I said.

'You won't need that,' the big man said, genially.

'That's fine,' I said, like somebody else talking, far away behind a wall. I could just barely hear the words. 'But if I do, here it is. And this one's loaded. Want me to prove it to you?'

The big man looked as near worried as he would ever look. 'I'm sorry you take it like that,' he said. 'I'm so used to Alfred I hardly notice him. Maybe you're right. Maybe I ought to do something about him.'

'Yeah,' I said. 'Do it this afternoon before you come up here. It's too late now.'

'Now wait a minute, Mr Marlowe.' He put his hand out. I slashed at it with the Luger. He was fast, but not fast enough. I cut the back of his hand open with the sight of the gun. He grabbed at it and sucked at the cut. 'Hey, please! Alfred's my nephew. My sister's kid. I kind of look after him. He wouldn't hurt a fly, really.'

'Next time you come up I'll have one for him not to hurt,' I said.

'Now don't be like that, mister. Please don't be like that. I've got quite a nice little proposition—'

'Shut up,' I said. I sat down very slowly. My face burned. I had difficulty speaking clearly at all. I felt a little drunk. I said, slowly and thickly: 'A friend of mine told me about a fellow that had something like this pulled on him. He was at a desk the way I am. He had a gun, just the way I have. There were two men on the other side of the desk, like you and Alfred. The man on my side began to get mad. He couldn't help himself. He began to shake. He couldn't speak a word. He just had this gun in his hand. So without a word he shot twice under the desk, right where your belly is.'

The big man turned a sallow green colour and started to get up. But he changed his mind. He got a violent-looking handkerchief out of his pocket and mopped his face. 'You seen that in a picture,' he said.

'That's right,' I said. 'But the man who made the picture told me where he got the idea. *That* wasn't in any picture.' I put the Luger down on the desk in front of me and said in a more natural voice: 'You've got to be careful about firearms, Mr Toad. You never know but what it may upset a man to have an Army .45 snapped in his face – especially when he doesn't know it's not loaded. It made me kind of nervous for a minute. I haven't had a shot of morphine since lunchtime.'

Toad studied me carefully with narrow eyes. The junky got up and went to another chair and kicked it around and sat down and tilted his greasy head against the wall. But his nose and hands kept on twitching.

'I heard you were kind of hardboiled,' Toad said slowly, his eyes cool and watchful.

'You heard wrong. I'm a very sensitive guy. I go all to pieces over nothing.'

'Yeah, I understand.' He stared at me a long time without speaking. 'Maybe we played this wrong. Mind if I put my hand in my pocket? I don't wear a gun.'

'Go ahead,' I said. 'It would give me the greatest possible pleasure to see you try to pull a gun.'

He frowned, then very slowly got out a flat pigskin wallet and drew out a crisp new one-hundred-dollar bill. He laid it on the edge of the glass top, drew out another just like it, then one by one, three more. He laid them carefully in a row along the desk, end to end. Alfred let his chair settle to the floor and stared at the money with his mouth quivering.

'Five Cs,' the big man said. He folded his wallet and put it away. I watched every movement he made. 'For nothing at all but keeping the nose clean. Check?'

I just looked at him.

'You ain't looking for nobody,' the big man said. 'You

couldn't find nobody. You don't have time to work for nobody. You didn't hear a thing or see a thing. You're clean. Five Cs clean. Okay?'

There was no sound in the office but Alfred's sniffling. The big man half turned his head. 'Quiet, Alfred. I'll give you a shot when we leave,' the big man told him. 'Try to act nice.' He sucked again at the cut on the back of his hand.

'With you for a model that ought to be easy,' I said.

'Screw you,' Alfred said.

'Limited vocabulary,' the big man told me. 'Very limited. Get the idea, chum? He indicated the money. I fingered the butt of the Luger. He leaned forward a little. 'Relax, can't you. It's simple. This is a retainer. You don't do a thing for it. Nothing is what you do. If you keep on doing nothing for a reasonable length of time you get the same amount later on. That's simple, isn't it?'

'And who am I doing this nothing for?' I asked.

'Me. Joseph P. Toad.'

'What's your racket?'

'Business representative, you might call me.'

'What else could I call you? Besides what I could think up myself?'

'You could call me a guy that wants to help out a guy that don't want to make trouble for a guy.'

'And what could I call that lovable character?' I asked.

Joseph P. Toad gathered the five hundred-dollar bills together, lined up the edges neatly and pushed the packet across the desk. 'You can call him a guy that would rather spill money than blood,' he said. 'But he don't mind spilling blood if it looks like that's what he's got to do.'

'How is he with an ice pick?' I asked. 'I can see how lousy he is with a .45.'

The big man chewed his lower lip, then pulled it out with a blunt forefinger and thumb and nibbled on the inside of it softly, like a milch cow chewing her cud. 'We're not talking about ice picks,' he said at length. 'All we're talking about is how you might get off on the wrong foot and do yourself a lot of harm. Whereas if you don't get off on no foot at all, you're sitting pretty and money coming in.'

'Who is the blonde?' I asked.

He thought about that and nodded. 'Maybe you're into this too far already,' he sighed. 'Maybe it's too late to do business.'

After a moment he leaned forward and said gently: 'Okay.

I'll check back with my principal and see how far out he wants to come. Maybe we can still do business. Everything stands as it is until you hear from me. Check?'

I let him have that one. He put his hands on the desk and very slowly stood up, watching the gun I was pushing around on the blotter.

'You can keep the dough,' he said. 'Come on, Alfred.' He turned and walked solidly out of the office.

Alfred's eyes crawled sideways watching him, then jerked to the money on the desk. The big automatic appeared with the same magic in his thin right hand. Dartingly as an eel he moved over to the desk. He kept the gun on me and reached for the money with his left hand. It disappeared into his pocket. He gave me a smooth cool empty grin, nodded and moved away, apparently not realizing for a moment that I was holding a gun too.

'Come on, Alfred,' the big man called sharply from outside the door. Alfred slipped through the door and was gone.

The outer door opened and closed. Steps went along the hall. Then silence. I sat there thinking back over it, trying to make up my mind whether it was pure idiocy or just a new way to toss a scare.

Five minutes later the telephone rang.

A thick pleasant voice said: 'Oh, by the way, Mr Marlowe, I guess you know Sherry Ballou, don't you?'

'Nope.'

'Sheridan Ballou, Incorporated. The big agent? You ought to look him up sometime.'

I held the phone silently for a moment. Then I said: 'Is he her agent?'

'He might be,' Joseph P. Toad said, and paused a moment. 'I suppose you realize we're just a couple of bit players, Mr Marlowe. That's all. Just a couple of bit players. Somebody wanted to find out a little something about you. It seemed the simplest way to do it. Now, I'm not so sure.'

I didn't answer. He hung up. Almost at once the phone rang again.

A seductive voice said: 'You do not like me so well, do you, amigo?'

'Sure I do. Just don't keep biting me.'

'I am at home at the Château Bercy. I am lonely.'

'Call an escort bureau.'

'But please. That is no way to talk. This is business of a great importance.'

'I bet. But not the business I'm in.'

'That slut— What does she say about me?' she hissed.

'Nothing. Oh, she might have called you a Tijuana hooker in riding pants. Would you mind?'

That amused her. The silvery giggle went on for a little while. 'Always the wisecrack with you. Is it not so? But you see I did not then know you were a detective. That makes a very big difference.'

I could have told her how wrong she was. I just said: 'Miss Gonzales, you said something about business. What kind of business, if you're not kidding me?'

'Would you like to make a great deal of money? A very great deal of money?'

'You mean without getting shot?' I asked.

Her incaught breath came over the wire. '*Sí*,' she said thoughtfully. 'There is also that to consider. But you are so brave, so big, so—'

'I'll be at my office at nine in the morning, Miss Gonzales. I'll be a lot braver then. Now if you'll excuse me—'

'You have a date? Is she beautiful? More beautiful than I am?'

'For Christ's sake,' I said. 'Don't you ever think of anything but one thing?'

'The hell with you, darling,' she said, and hung up in my face.

I turned out the light and left. Halfway down the hall I met a man looking at numbers. He had a special delivery in his hand. So I had to go back to the office and put it in the safe. And the phone rang again while I was doing this.

I let it ring. I had had enough for one day. I just didn't care. It could have been the Queen of Sheba with her cellophane pyjamas on – or off – I was too tired to bother. My brain felt like a bucket of wet sand.

It was still ringing as I reached the door. No use. I had to go back. Instinct was stronger than weariness. I lifted the receiver.

Orfamay Quest's twittery little voice said: 'Oh, Mr Marlowe, I've been trying to get you for just the longest time. I'm so upset. I'm—'

'In the morning,' I said. 'The office is closed.'

'Please, Mr Marlowe – just because I lost my temper for a moment—'

'In the morning.'

'But I tell you I have to see you.' The voice didn't quite rise to a yell. 'It's terribly important.'

'Uh-huh.'

She sniffed. 'You – you kissed me.'

'I've kissed better since,' I said. To hell with her. To hell with all women.

'I've heard from Orrin,' she said.

That stopped me for a moment, then I laughed. 'You're a nice little liar,' I said. 'Goodbye.'

'But really I have. He called me. On the telephone. Right here where I'm staying.'

'Fine,' I said. 'Then you don't need a detective at all. And if you did, you've got a better one than I am right in the family. I couldn't even find out where you were staying.'

There was a little pause. She still had me talking to her anyway. She'd kept me from hanging up. I had to give her that much.

'I wrote to him where I'd be staying,' she said at last.

'Uh-huh. Only he didn't get the letter because he had moved and he didn't leave any forwarding address. Remember? Try again some time when I'm not so tired. Good night, Miss Quest. And you don't have to tell me where you are staying now. I'm not working for you.'

'Very well, Mr Marlowe. I'm ready to call the police now. But I don't think you'll like it. I don't think you'll like it at all.'

'Why?'

'Because there's murder in it, Mr Marlowe, and murder is a very nasty word – don't you think?'

'Come on up,' I said. 'I'll wait.'

I hung up. I got the bottle of Old Forester out. There was nothing slow about the way I poured myself a drink and dropped it down my throat.

15

She came in briskly enough this time. Her motions were small and quick and determined. There was one of those thin little, bright little smiles on her face. She put her bag down firmly, settled herself in the customer's chair and went on smiling.

'It's nice of you to wait for me,' she said. 'I bet you haven't had your dinner yet, either.'

'Wrong,' I said. 'I have had my dinner. I am now drinking whisky. You don't approve of whisky drinking, do you?'

'I certainly do not.'

'That's just dandy,' I said. 'I hoped you hadn't changed your mind.' I put the bottle up on the desk and poured myself another slug. I drank a little of it and gave her a leer above the glass.

'If you keep on with that you won't be in any condition to listen to what I have to say,' she snapped.

'About this murder,' I said. 'Anybody I know? I can see you're not murdered – yet.'

'Please don't be unnecessarily horrid. It's not my fault. You doubted me over the telephone so I had to convince you. Orrin did call me up. But he wouldn't tell me where he was or what he was doing. I don't know why.'

'He wanted you to find out for yourself,' I said. 'He's building your character.'

'That's not funny. It's not even smart.'

'But you've got to admit it's nasty,' I said. 'Who was murdered? Or is that a secret too?'

She fiddled a little with her bag, not enough to overcome her embarrassment, because she wasn't embarrassed. But enough to needle me into taking another drink.

'That horrid man in the rooming house was murdered. Mr – Mr – I forget his name.'

'Let's both forget it,' I said. 'Let's do something together for once. I dropped the whisky bottle into the desk drawer and stood up. 'Look, Orfamay, I'm not asking how you know all this. Or rather how Orrin knows it all. Or if he *does* know it. You've found him. That's what you wanted me to do. Or he's found you, which comes to much the same thing.'

'It's not the same thing,' she cried. 'I haven't really found him. He wouldn't tell me where he was living.'

'Well, if it is anything like the last place, I don't blame him.'

She set her lips in a firm line of distaste. 'He wouldn't tell me anything really.'

'Just about murders,' I said. 'Trifles like that.'

She laughed bubblingly. 'I just said that to scare you. I don't really mean anybody was murdered, Mr Marlowe. You sounded so cold and distant. I thought you wouldn't help me any more. And – well, I just made it up.'

I took a couple of deep breaths and looked down at my hands. I straightened out the fingers slowly. Then I stood up. I didn't say anything.

'Are you mad at me?' she asked timidly, making a little circle on the desk with the point of a finger.

'I ought to slap your face off,' I said. 'And quit acting innocent. Or it mightn't be your face I'd slap.'

Her breath caught with a jerk. 'Why, how dare you!'

'You used that line,' I said. 'You used it too often. Shut up and get the hell out of here. Do you think I enjoy being scared to death? Oh – there's this.' I yanked a drawer open, got out her twenty dollars and threw them down in front of her. 'Take this money away. Endow a hospital or a research laboratory with it. It makes me nervous having it around.'

Her hand reached automatically for the money. Her eyes behind the cheaters were round and wondering. 'Goodness,' she said, assembling her handbag with a nice dignity. 'I'm sure I didn't know you scared that easy. I thought you were tough.'

'That's just an act,' I growled, moving the desk. She leaned back in her chair away from me. 'I'm only tough with little girls like you that don't let their fingernails grow too long. I'm all mush inside.' I took hold of her arm and yanked her to her feet. Her head went back. Her lips parted. I was hell with the women that day.

'But you will find Orrin for me, won't you?' she whispered. 'It was all a lie. Everything I've told you was a lie. He didn't call me up. I – don't know anything.'

'Perfume,' I said, sniffing. 'Why, you little darling. You put perfume behind your ears – and all for me!'

She nodded her little chin half an inch. Her eyes were melting. 'Take my glasses off,' she whispered. 'Philip. I don't mind if you take a little whisky once in a while. Really I don't.'

Our faces were about six inches apart. I was afraid to take her glasses off. I might have socked her on the nose.

'Yes,' I said in a voice that sounded like Orson Welles with his mouth full of crackers. 'I'll find him for you, honey, if he's still alive. And for free. Not a dime of expense involved. I only ask one thing.'

'What, Philip?' she asked softly and opened her lips a little wider.

'Who was the black sheep in your family?'

She jerked away from me like a startled fawn might, if I had a startled fawn and it jerked away from me. She stared at me stony-faced.

'You said Orrin wasn't the black sheep in your family. Remember? With a very peculiar emphasis. And when you mentioned your sister Leila, you sort of passed on quickly as if the subject was distasteful.'

'I – I don't remember saying anything like that,' she said very slowly.

'So I was wondering,' I said. 'What name does your sister Leila use in pictures?'

'Pictures?' she sounded vague. 'Oh, you mean motion pictures? Why, I never said she was in pictures. I never said anything about her like that.'

I gave her my big homely lop-sided grin. She suddenly flew into a rage.

'Mind your business about my sister Leila,' she spat at me. 'You leave my sister Leila out of your dirty remarks.'

'What dirty remarks?' I asked. 'Or should I try to guess?'

'All you think about is liquor and women,' she screamed. 'I hate you!' She rushed to the door and yanked it open and went out. She practically ran down the hall.

I went back around my desk and slumped into the chair. A very strange little girl. Very strange indeed. After a while the phone started ringing again, as it would. On the fourth ring I leaned my head on my hand and groped for it, fumbled it to my face.

'Utter McKinley Funeral Parlours,' I said.

A female voice said: 'Wha-a-t?' and went off into a shriek of laughter. That one was a riot at the police smoker in 1921. What a wit. Like a humming-bird's beak. I put the lights out and went home.

16

Eight-forty-five the next morning found me parked a couple of doors from the Bay City Camera Shop, breakfasted and peaceful and reading the local paper through a pair of sunglasses. I had already chewed my way through the Los Angeles paper, which contained no item about ice picks in the Van Nuys or any other hotel. Not even MYSTERIOUS DEATH IN DOWNTOWN HOTEL, with no names or weapons specified. The Bay City News wasn't too busy to write up a murder. They put it on the first page, right next to the price of meat.

LOCAL MAN FOUND STABBED IN
IDAHO STREET ROOMING HOUSE

'An anonymous telephone call late yesterday sent police speeding to an address on Idaho Street opposite the Seamans and Jansing Company's lumberyard. Entering the unlocked door of his apartment, officers found Lester B. Clausen, 45, manager of the rooming house, dead on the couch in his apartment. Clausen had been stabbed in the neck with an ice pick which was still in his body. After a preliminary examination, Coroner Frank L. Crowdy announced that Clausen had been drinking heavily and may have been unconscious at the time of his death. No signs of a struggle were observed by the police.

'Detective Lieutenant Moses Maglashan immediately took charge and questioned tenants of the rooming house on their return from work, but no light has so far been thrown on the circumstances of the crime. Interviewed by this reporter, Coroner Crowdy stated that Clausen's death might have been suicide but that the position of the wound made this unlikely. Examination of the rooming house register disclosed that a page had recently been torn out. Lieutenant Maglashan, after questioning the tenants at length, stated that a thick-set middle-aged man with brown hair and heavy features had been noticed in the hallway of the rooming house on several occasions, but that none of the tenants knew his name or occupation. After carefully checking all rooms, Maglashan further gave it as his opinion that one of the roomers had left recently and in some haste. The mutilation of the register, however, the character of the neighbourhood, the lack of an accurate description of the missing man, made the job of tracing him extremely difficult.

' "I have no idea at present why Clausen was murdered," Maglashan announced at a late hour last night. "But I have had my eye on this man for some time. Many of his associates are known to me. It's a tough case, but we'll crack it." '

It was a nice piece and only mentioned Maglashan's name twelve times in the text and twice more in picture captions. There was a photo of him on page three holding an ice pick and looking at it with profound thought wrinkling his brows. There was a photo of 449 Idaho Street which did it more than justice, and a photo of something with a sheet over it on a couch and Lieutenant Maglashan pointing at it sternly. There was also a close-up of the mayor looking as executive as hell behind his official desk and an interview with him on the subject of post-war crime. He said just what you would expect a mayor to say – a watered-down shot of J. Edgar Hoover with some extra bad grammar thrown in.

At three minutes to nine the door of the Bay City Camera Shop opened and an elderly negro began to sweep dirt across the sidewalk into the gutter. At nine a.m. a neat-appearing young guy in glasses fixed the lock on the door and I went in there with the black and orange check Dr G. W. Hambleton had pasted to the inside of his toupee.

The neat-appearing young man gave me a searching glance as I exchanged the check and some money for an envelope containing a tiny negative and half a dozen shiny prints blown up eight times the size of the negative. He didn't say anything, but the way he looked at me gave me the impression that he remembered I was not the man who had left the negative.

I went out and sat in my car and looked over the catch. The prints showed a man and a blonde girl sitting in a crowded booth in a restaurant with food in front of them. They were looking up as though their attention had suddenly been attracted and they had only just had time to react before the camera had clicked. It was clear from the lighting that no flashbulb had been used.

The girl was Mavis Weld. The man was rather small, rather dark, rather expressionless. I didn't recognize him. There was no reason why I should. The padded leather seat was covered with tiny figures of dancing couples. That made the restaurant The Dancers. This added to the confusion. Any amateur camera hound that tried to flash a lens in there without getting an okay from the management would have been thrown out so hard that he would have bounced all the way down to Hollywood and Vine. I figured it must have been the hidden camera trick, the way they took Ruth Snyder in the electric chair. He would have the little camera up hanging by a strap under his coat collar, the lens just peeping out from his open jacket, and he would have rigged a bulb release that he could hold in his pocket. It wasn't too hard for me to guess who had taken the picture. Mr Orrin P. Quest must have moved fast and smooth to get out of there with his face still in front of his head.

I put the pictures in my vest pocket and my fingers touched a crumpled piece of paper. I got it out and read: 'Doctor Vincent Lagardie, 965 Wyoming Street, Bay City.' That was the Vince I had talked to on the phone, the one Lester B. Clausen might have been trying to call.

An elderly flat-foot was strolling down the line of parked cars, marking tyres with yellow chalk. He told me where Wyoming Street was. I drove out there. It was a cross-town street well out beyond the business district, parallel with two numbered streets. Number 965, a grey-white frame house, was on a corner.

On its door a brass plate said *Vincent Lagardie, MD, Hours* 10.00 *to* 12.00 *and* 2.30 *to* 4.00.

The house looked quiet and decent. A woman with an unwilling small boy was going up the steps. She read the plate, looked at a watch pinned to her lapel and chewed irresolutely on her lip. The small boy looked around carefully, then kicked her on the ankle. She winced but her voice was patient. 'Now, Johnny, you mustn't do that to Aunty Fern,' she said mildly.

She opened the door and dragged the little ape in with her. Diagonally across the intersection was a big white colonial mansion with a portico which was roofed and much too small for the house. Floodlight reflectors were set into the front lawn. The walk was bordered by tree roses in bloom. A large black and silver sign over the portico said: 'The Garland Home of Peace.' I wondered how Dr Lagardie liked looking out of his front windows at a funeral parlour. Maybe it made him careful.

I turned around at the intersection and drove back to Los Angeles, and went up to the office to look at my mail and lock my catch from the Bay City Camera Shop up in the battered green safe – all but one print. I sat down at the desk and studied this through a magnifying glass. Even with that and the camera shop blow-up the detail was still clear. There was an evening paper, a *News-Chronicle*, lying on the table in front of the dark thin expressionless man who sat beside Mavis Weld. I could just read the headline. LIGHT HEAVYWEIGHT CONTENDER SUCCUMBS TO RING INJURIES. Only a noon or late sports edition would use a headline like that. I pulled the phone towards me. It rang just as I got my hand on it.

'Marlowe? This is Christy French downtown. Any ideas this morning?'

'Not if your teletype's working. I've seen a Bay City paper.'

'Yeah, we got that,' he said casually. 'Sounds like the same guy, don't it? Same initials, same description, same method of murder, and the time element seems to check. I hope to Christ this doesn't mean Sunny Moe Stein's mob have started in business again.'

'If they have, they've changed their technique,' I said. 'I was reading up on it last night. The Stein mob used to jab their victims full of holes. One of them had over a hundred stab wounds in him.'

'They could learn better,' French said a little evasively, as if he didn't want to talk about it. 'What I called you about was Flack. Seen anything of him since yesterday afternoon?'

'No.'

'He skipped out. Didn't come to work. Hotel called his landlady. Packed up and left last night. Destination unknown.'

'I haven't seen him or heard from him,' I said.

'Didn't it strike you as kind of funny our stiff only had fourteen bucks in his kick?'

'It did a little. You answered that yourself.'

'I was just talking. I don't buy that any more. Flack's either scared out or come into money. Either he saw something he didn't tell and got paid to breeze, or else he lifted the customer's case dough, leaving the fourteen bucks to make it look better.'

I said: 'I'll buy either one. Or both at the same time. Whoever searched that room so thoroughly wasn't looking for money.'

'Why not?'

'Because when this Dr Hambleton called me up I suggested the hotel safe to him. He wasn't interested.'

'A type like that wouldn't have hired you to hold his dough anyway,' French said. 'He wouldn't have hired you to keep anything for him. He wanted protection or he wanted a sidekick – or maybe just a messenger.'

'Sorry,' I said. 'He told me just what I told you.'

'And seeing he was dead when you got over there,' French said with a too casual drawl, 'you could hardly have given him one of your business cards.'

I held the phone too tight and thought back rapidly over my talk with Hicks in the Idaho Street rooming house. I saw him holding my card between his fingers, looking down at it. And then I saw myself taking it out of his hand quickly, before he froze to it. I took a deep breath and let it out slowly.

'Hardly,' I said. 'And stop trying to scare me to death.'

'He had one, chum. Folded twice across in his pants watch pocket. We missed it the first time.'

'I gave Flack a card,' I said, stiff-lipped.

There was a silence. I could hear voices in the background and the clack of a typewriter. Finally French said dryly: 'Fair enough. See you later.' He hung up abruptly.

I put the phone down very slowly in its cradle and flexed my cramped fingers. I stared down at the photo lying on the desk in front of me. All it told me was that two people, one of whom I knew, were having lunch at The Dancers. The papers on the table told me the date, or would.

I dialled the *News-Chronicle* and asked for the sports section. Four minutes later I wrote on a pad: 'Ritchy Belleau, popular young light heavyweight contender, died in the Sisters Hospital just before midnight February 19th as a result of ring injuries sustained the previous evening in the main event at the Hollywood Legion Stadium. The *News-Chronicle* Noon Sports Edition for February 20th carried the headline.'

I dialled the same number again and asked for Kenny Haste in the City Room. He was an ex-crime reporter I had known for years. We chatted around for a minute and then I said:

'Who covered the Sunny Moe Stein killing for you?'

'Tod Barrow. He's on the *Post-Despatch* now. Why?'

'I'd like the details, if any.'

He said he would send to the morgue for the the file and call me, which he did ten minutes later. 'He was shot twice in the head, in his car, about two blocks from the Château Bercy on Franklin. Time, about 11.15 p.m.'

'Date, February 20th,' I said, 'or was it?'

'Check, it was. No witnesses, no arrests except the usual police stock company of book-handlers, out-of-work fight managers and other professional suspects. What's in it?'

'Wasn't a pal of his supposed to be in town about that time?'

'Nothing here says so. What name?'

'Weepy Moyer. A cop friend of mine said something about a Hollywood money man being held on suspicion and then released for lack of evidence.'

Kenny said: 'Wait a minute. Something's coming back to me – yeah. Fellow named Steelgrave, owns The Dancers, supposed to be a gambler and so on. Nice guy. I've met him. That was a bust.'

'How do you mean, a bust?'

'Some smart monkey tipped the cops he was Weepy Moyer and they held him for ten days on an open charge for Cleveland. Cleveland brushed it off. That didn't have anything to do with the Stein killing. Steelgrave was under glass all that week. No connection at all. Your cop friend has been reading pulp magazines.'

'They all do,' I said. 'That's why they talk so tough. Thanks, Kenny.'

We said goodbye and hung up and I sat leaning back in my chair and looking at my photograph. After a while I took scissors and cut out the piece that contained the folded newspaper with the headline. I put two pieces in separate envelopes and put them in my pocket with the sheet from the pad.

I dialled Miss Mavis Weld's Crestview number. A woman's voice answered after several rings. It was a remote and formal voice that I might or might not have heard before. All it said was, 'Hello?'

'This is Philip Marlowe. Is Miss Weld in?'

'Miss Weld will not be in until late this evening. Do you care to leave a message?'

'Very important. Where could I reach her?'

'I'm sorry. I have no information.'

'Would her agent know?'

'Possibly.'

'You're quite sure *you're* not Miss Weld?'

'Miss Weld is not in.' She hung up.

I sat there and listened to the voice. At first I thought yes, then I thought no. The longer I thought the less I knew. I went down to the parking lot and got my car out.

17

On the terrace at The Dancers a few early birds were getting ready to drink their lunch. The glass-fronted upstairs room had the awning let down in front of it. I drove on past the curve that goes down into the Strip and stopped across the street from a square building of two storeys of rose-red brick with small white leaded bay windows and a Greek porch over the front door and what looked, from across the street, like an antique pewter door-knob. Over the door was a fanlight and the name Sheridan Ballou, Inc in black wooden letters severely stylized. I locked my car and crossed to the front door. It was white and tall and wide and had a keyhole big enough for a mouse to crawl through. Inside this keyhole was the real lock. I went for the knocker, but they had thought of that too. It was all in one piece and didn't knock.

So I patted one of the slim fluted white pillars and opened the door and walked directly into the reception room which filled the entire front of the building. It was furnished in dark antique-looking furniture and many chairs and settees of quilted chintz-like material. There were lace curtains at the windows and chintz boxes around them that matched the chintz of the furniture. There was a flowered carpet and a lot of people waiting to see Mr Sheridan Ballou.

Some of them were bright and cheerful and full of hope. Some looked as if they had been there for days. One small dark girl was sniffling into her handkerchief in the corner. Nobody paid any attention to her. I got a couple of profiles at nice angles before the company decided I wasn't buying anything and didn't work there.

A dangerous-looking redhead sat languidly at an Adam desk talking into a pure-white telephone. I went over there and she put a couple of cold blue pellets into me with her eyes and then stared at the cornice that ran around the room.

'No,' she said into the phone. 'No. So sorry. I'm afraid it's no use. Far, far too busy.' She hung up and ticked off something on a list and gave me some more of her steely glance.

'Good morning. I'd like to see Mr Ballou,' I said. I put my plain card on her desk. She lifted it by one corner, smiled at it amusedly.

'Today?' she inquired amiably. 'This week?'

'How long does it usually take?'

'It *has* taken six months,' she said cheerfully. 'Can't somebody else help you?'

'No.'

'So sorry. Not a chance. Drop in again, won't you? Somewhere about Thanksgiving.' She was wearing a white wool skirt, a burgundy silk blouse and a black velvet over-jacket with short sleeves. Her hair was a hot sunset. She wore a golden topaz bracelet and topaz earrings and a topaz dinner ring in the shape of a shield. Her fingernails matched her blouse exactly. She looked as if it would take a couple of weeks to get her dressed.

'I've got to see him,' I said.

She read my card again. She smiled beautifully. 'Everyone has,' she said. 'Why – er – Mr Marlowe. Look at all these lovely people. Every one of them has been here since the office opened two hours ago.'

'This is important.'

'No doubt. In what way if I may ask?'

'I want to peddle a little dirt.'

She picked a cigarette out of a crystal box and lit it with a crystal lighter. 'Peddle? You mean for money – in Hollywood?'

'Could be.'

'What kind of dirt? Don't be afraid to shock me.'

'It's a bit obscene, Miss – Miss—' I screwed my head around to read the plaque on her desk.

'Helen Grady,' she said. 'Well, a little well-bred obscenity never did any harm, did it?'

'I didn't say it was well-bred.'

She leaned back carefully and puffed smoke in my face.

'Blackmail, in short.' She sighed. 'Why the hell don't you lam out of here, bud? Before I throw a handful of fat coppers in your lap?'

I sat on the corner of her desk, grabbed a double handful of her cigarette smoke and blew it into her hair. She dodged angrily. 'Beat it, lug,' she said in a voice that could have been used for paint remover.

'Oh oh. What happened to the Bryn Mawr accent?'

Without turning her head she said sharply: 'Miss Vane.'

A tall slim elegant dark girl with supercilious eyebrows looked up. She had just come through an inner door camouflaged as a stained-glass window. The dark girl came over. Miss Grady handed her my card: 'Spink.'

Miss Vane went back through the stained-glass window with the card.

'Sit down and rest your ankles, big stuff,' Miss Grady informed me. 'You may be here all week.'

I sat down in a chintz winged chair, the back of which came eight inches above my head. It made me feel shrunken. Miss Grady gave me her smile again, the one with the hand-honed edge, and bent to the telephone once more.

I looked around. The little girl in the corner had stopped crying and was making up her face with calm unconcern. A very tall distinguished-looking party swung up a graceful arm to stare at his elegant wrist watch and oozed gently to his feet. He set a pearl-grey homburg at a rakish angle on the side of his head, checked his yellow chamois gloves and his silver-knobbed cane, and strolled languidly over to the red-headed receptionist.

'I have been waiting two hours to see Mr Ballou,' he said icily in a rich sweet voice that had been modulated by a lot of training. 'I'm not accustomed to waiting two hours to see anybody.'

'So sorry, Mr Fortescue. Mr Ballou is just too busy for words this a.m.'

'I'm sorry I cannot leave him a cheque,' the elegant tall party remarked with a weary contempt. 'Probably the only thing that would interest him. But in default of that—'

'Just a minute, kid.' The redhead picked up a phone and said into it: 'Yes? ... Who says so besides Goldwyn? Can't you reach somebody that's not crazy? ... Well, try again.' She slammed the telephone down. The tall party had not moved.

'In default of that,' he resumed as if he had never stopped speaking, 'I should like to leave a short personal message.'

'Please do,' Miss Grady told him. 'I'll get it to him somehow.'

'Tell him with my love that he is a dirty polecat.'

'Make it skunk, darling,' she said. 'He doesn't know any English words.'

'Make it skunk and double skunk,' Fortescue told her. 'With a slight added nuance of sulphuretted hydrogen and a very cheap grade of whore-house perfume.' He adjusted his hat and gave his profile the once-over in a mirror. 'I now bid you good morning and to hell with Sheridan Ballou, Incorporated.'

The tall actor stalked out elegantly, using his cane to open the door.

'What's the matter with him?' I asked.

She looked at me pityingly. 'Billy Fortescue? Nothing's the matter with him. He isn't getting any parts so he comes in every day and goes through that routine. He figures somebody might see him and like it.'

I shut my mouth slowly. You can live a long time in Hollywood and never see the part they use in pictures.

Miss Vane appeared through the inner door and made a chin-jerk at me. I went in past her. 'This way. Second on the right.' She watched me while I went down the corridor to the second door, which was open. I went in and closed the door.

A plump white-haired Jew sat at the desk smiling at me tenderly. 'Greetings,' he said. 'I'm Moss Spink. What's on the thinker, pal? Park the body. Cigarette?' He opened a thing that looked like a trunk and presented me with a cigarette which was not more than a foot long. It was an individual glass tube.

'No thanks,' I said. 'I smoke tobacco.'

He sighed. 'All right. Give. Let's see. Your name's Marlowe. Huh? Marlowe. Marlowe. Have I ever heard of anybody named Marlowe?'

'Probably not,' I said. 'I never heard of anybody named Spink. I asked to see a man named Ballou. Does that sound like Spink? I'm not looking for anybody named Spink. And just between you and me, the hell with people named Spink.'

'Anti-Semitic, huh?' Spink said. He waved a generous hand on which a canary-yellow diamond looked like an amber traffic light. 'Don't be like that,' he said. 'Sit down and dust off the brains. You don't know me. You don't want to know me. Okay. I ain't offended. In a business like this you got to have somebody around that don't get offended.'

'Ballou,' I said.

'Now be reasonable, pal. Sherry Ballou's a very busy guy. He works twenty hours a day and even then he's way behind schedule. Sit down and talk it out with little Spinky.'

'You're what around here?' I asked him.

'I'm his protection, pal. I gotta protect him. A guy like Sherry can't see everybody. I see people for him. I'm the same as him – up to a point you understand.'

'Could be I'm past the point you're up to,' I said

'Could be,' Spink agreed pleasantly. He peeled a thick tape off an aluminium individual cigar container, reached the cigar out tenderly and looked it over for birthmarks. 'I don't say not. Why not demonstrate a little? Then we'll know. Up to now all you're doing is throwing a line. We get so much of that in here it don't mean a thing to us.'

I watched him clip and light the expensive-looking cigar. 'How do I know you wouldn't double-cross him?' I asked cunningly.

Spink's small tight eyes blinked and I wasn't sure but that there were tears in them. 'Me cross Sherry Ballou?' he asked brokenly in a hushed voice, like a six-hundred-dollar funeral. 'Me? I'd sooner double-cross my own mother.'

'That doesn't mean anything to me either,' I said. 'I never met your mother.'

Spink laid his cigar aside in an ashtray the size of a bird bath. He waved both his arms. Sorrow was eating into him. 'Oh, pal. What a way to talk,' he wailed. 'I love Sherry Ballou like he was my own father. Better. My father – well, skip it. Come on, pal. Be human. Give with a little of the old trust and friendliness. Spill the dirt to little Spinky, huh?'

I drew an envelope from my pocket and tossed it across the desk to him. He pulled the single photograph from it and stared at it solemnly. He laid it down on the desk. He looked up at me, down at the photo, up at me. 'Well,' he said woodenly, in a voice suddenly empty of the old trust and friendliness he had been talking about. 'What's it got that's so wonderful?'

'Do I have to tell you who the girl is?'

'Who's the guy?' Spink snapped.

I said nothing.

'I said who's the guy?' Spink almost yelled at me. 'Cough up, mug. Cough up.'

I still didn't say anything. Spink reached slowly for his telephone, keeping his hard bright eyes on my face.

'Go on. Call them,' I said. 'Call downtown and ask for Lieutenant Christy French in the homicide bureau. There's another boy that's hard to convince.'

Spink took his hand off the phone. He got up slowly and went out with the photograph. I waited. Outside on Sunset Boulevard traffic went by distantly, monotonously. The minutes dropped silently down a well. The smoke of Spink's freshly lit cigar played in the air for a moment, then was sucked through the vent of the air-conditioning apparatus. I looked at the innumerable inscribed photos on the walls, all inscribed to Sherry Ballou with somebody's eternal love. I figured they were back numbers if they were in Spink's office.

18

After a while Spink came back and gestured to me. I followed him along the corridor through double doors into an ante-room with two secretaries. Past them towards more double doors of heavy black glass with silver peacocks etched into the panels. As we neared the doors they opened of themselves.

We went down three carpeted steps into an office that had everything in it but a swimming pool. It was two storeys high, surrounded by a balcony loaded with bookshelves. There was a concert grand Steinway in the corner and a lot of glass and bleached wood furniture and a desk about the size of a badminton court and chairs and couches and tables and a man lying on one of the couches with his coat off and his shirt open over a Charvet scarf you could have found in the dark by listening to it purr. A white cloth was over his eyes and forehead, and a lissom blonde girl was wringing out another in a silver bowl of ice water at a table beside him.

The man was a big shapely guy with wavy dark hair and a strong brown face below the white cloth. An arm dropped to the carpet and a cigarette hung between fingers, wisping a tiny thread of smoke.

The blonde girl changed the cloth deftly. The man on the couch groaned. Spink said: 'This is the boy, Sherry. Name of Marlowe.'

The man on the couch groaned. 'What does he want?'

Spink said: 'Won't spill.'

The man on the couch said: 'What did you bring him in for then? I'm tired.'

Spink said: 'Well, you know how it is, Sherry. Sometimes you kind of got to.'

The man on the couch said: 'What did you say his beautiful name was?'

Spink turned to me. 'You can tell us what you want now. And make it snappy, Marlowe.'

465

I said nothing.

After a moment the man on the couch slowly raised the arm with the cigarette at the end of it. He got the cigarette wearily into his mouth and drew on it with the infinite languor of a decadent aristocrat mouldering in a ruined château.

'I'm talking to you, pal,' Spink said harshly. The blonde changed the cloth again, looking at nobody. The silence hung in the room as acrid as the smoke of the cigarette. 'Come on, lug. Snap it up.'

I got one of my Camels out and lit it and picked out a chair and sat down. I stretched my hand out and looked at it. The thumb twitched up and down slowly every few seconds.

Spink's voice cut into this furiously: 'Sherry don't have all day, you.'

'What would he do with the rest of the day?' I heard myself asking. 'Sit on a white satin couch and have his toenails gilded?'

The blonde turned suddenly and stared at me. Spink's mouth fell open. He blinked. The man on the couch lifted a slow hand to the corner of the towel over his eyes. He removed enough so that one seal-brown eye looked at me. The towel fell softly back into place.

'You can't talk like that in here,' Spink said in a tough voice.

I stood up. I said: 'I forgot to bring my prayer-book. This is the first time I knew God worked on commission.'

Nobody said anything for a minute. The blonde changed the towel again.

From under it the man on the couch said calmly: 'Get the hell out of here, darlings. All but the new chum.'

Spink gave me a narrow glare of hate. The blonde left silently.

Spink said: 'Why don't I just toss him out on his can?'

The tired voice under the towel said: 'I've been wondering about that so long I've lost interest in the problem. Beat it.'

'Okay, boss,' Spink said. He withdrew reluctantly. He paused at the door, gave me one more silent snarl and disappeared.

The man on the couch listened to the door close and then said: 'How much?'

'You don't want to buy anything.'

He pushed the towel off his head, tossed it to one side and sat up slowly. He put his bench-made pebble grain brogues on the carpet and passed a hand across his forehead. He looked tired but not dissipated. He fumbled another cigarette from somewhere, lit it and stared morosely through the smoke at the floor.

'Go on,' he said.

'I don't know why you wasted all the build-up on me,' I said.

'But I credit you with enough brains to know you couldn't buy anything, and know it would stay bought.'

Ballou picked up the photo that Spink had put down near him on a long low table. He reached out a languid hand. 'The piece that's cut out would be the punch line, no doubt,' he said.

I got the envelope out of my pocket and gave him the cut-out corner, watched him fit the two pieces together.

'With a glass you can read the headline,' I said.

'There's one on my desk. Please.'

I went over and got the magnifying glass off his desk. 'You're used to a lot of service, aren't you, Mr Ballou?'

'I pay for it.' He studied the photograph through the glass and sighed. 'Seems to me I saw that fight. They ought to take more care of these boys.'

'Like you do of your clients,' I said.

He laid down the magnifying glass and leaned back to stare at me with cool untroubled eyes.

'That's the chap that owns The Dancers. Name's Steelgrave. The girl is a client of mine, of course.' He made a vague gesture towards a chair. I sat down on it. 'What were you thinking of asking, Mr Marlowe?'

'For what?'

'All the prints and the negative. The works.'

'Ten grand,' I said, and watched his mouth. The mouth smiled, rather pleasantly.

'It needs a little more explanation, doesn't it? All I see is two people having lunch in a public place. Hardly disastrous to the reputation of my client. I assume that was what you had in mind.'

I grinned. 'You can't buy anything, Mr Ballou. I could have had a positive made from the negative and another negative from the positive. If that snap is evidence of something, you could never know you had suppressed it.'

'Not much of a sales talk for a blackmailer,' he said, still smiling.

'I always wonder why people pay blackmailers. They can't buy anything. Yet they do pay them, sometimes over and over and over again. And in the end are just where they started.'

'The fear of today,' he said, 'always overrides the fear of tomorrow. It's a basic fact of the dramatic emotions that the part is greater than the whole. If you see a glamour star on the screen in a position of great danger, you fear for her with one part of your mind, the emotional part. Notwithstanding that, your reasoning mind knows that she is the star of the picture and nothing very bad is going to happen to her. If suspense and menace didn't defeat reason, there would be very little drama.'

I said: 'Very true, I guess,' and puffed some of my Camel smoke around.

His eyes narrowed a little. 'As to really being able to buy anything, if I paid you a substantial price and didn't get what I bought, I'd have you taken care of. Beaten to a pulp. And when you got out of the hospital, if you felt aggressive enough, you could try to get me arrested.'

'It's happened to me,' I said. 'I'm a private eye. I know what you mean. Why are you talking to me?'

He laughed. He had a deep pleasant effortless laugh. 'I'm an agent, sonny. I always tend to think traders have a little something in reserve. But we won't talk about any ten grand. She hasn't got it. She only makes a grand a week so far. I admit she's very close to the big money, though.'

'That would stop her cold,' I said, pointing to the photo. 'No big money, no swimming pool with underwater lights, no platinum mink, no name in neons, no nothing. All blown away like dust.'

He laughed contemptuously.

'Okay if I show this to the johns down town, then?' I said.

He stopped laughing. His eyes narrowed. Very quietly he asked:

'Why would they be interested?'

I stood up. 'I don't think we're going to do any business, Mr Ballou. And you're a busy man. I'll take myself off.'

He got off the couch and stretched, all six feet two of him. He was a very fine hunk of man. He came over and stood close to me. His seal-brown eyes had little gold flecks in them. 'Let's see who you are, sonny.'

He put his hand out. I dropped my open wallet into it. He read the photostat of my licence, poked a few more things out of the wallet and glanced at them. He handed it back.

'What would happen, if you did show your little picture to the cops?'

'I'd first of all have to connect it up with something they're working on – something that happened in the Van Nuys Hotel yesterday afternoon. I'd connect it up through the girl – who won't talk to me – that's why I'm talking to you.'

'She told me about it last night,' he sighed.

'Told you how much?' I asked.

'That a private dectective named Marlowe had tried to force

her to hire him, on the ground that she was seen in a downtown hotel inconveniently close to where a murder was committed.'

'How close?' I asked.

'She didn't say.'

'Nuts she didn't.'

He walked away from me to a tall cylindrical jar in the corner. From this he took one of a number of short thin malacca canes. He began to walk up and down the carpet, swinging the cane deftly past his right shoe.

I sat down again and killed my cigarette and took a deep breath. 'It could only happen in Hollywood,' I grunted.

He made a neat about turn and glanced at me. 'I beg your pardon.'

'That an apparently sane man could walk up and down inside the house with a Piccadilly stroll and a monkey stick in his hand.'

He nodded. 'I caught the disease from a producer at MGM. Charming fellow. Or so I've been told.' He stopped and pointed the cane at me. 'You amuse the hell out of me, Marlowe. Really you do. You're so transparent. You're trying to use me for a shovel to dig yourself out of a jam.'

'There's some truth in that. But the jam I'm in is nothing to the jam your client would be in if I hadn't done the thing that put me in the jam.'

He stood quite still for a moment. Then he threw the cane away from him and walked over to a liquor cabinet and swung the two halves of it open. He poured something into a couple of pot-bellied glasses. He carried one of them over to me. Then he went back and got his own. He sat down with it on the couch.

'Armagnac,' he said. 'If you knew me, you'd appreciate the compliment. This stuff is pretty scarce. The Krauts cleaned most of it out. Our brass got the rest. Here's to you.'

He lifted the glass, sniffed and sipped a tiny sip. I put mine down in a lump. It tasted like good French brandy.

Ballou looked shocked. 'My God, you sip that stuff, you don't swallow it whole.'

'I swallow it whole,' I said. 'Sorry. She also told you that if somebody didn't shut my mouth, she would be in a lot of trouble.'

He nodded.

'Did she suggest how to go about shutting my mouth?'

'I got the impression she was in favour of doing it with some kind of heavy blunt instrument. So I tried out a mixture of

469

threat and bribery. We have an outfit down the street that specializes in protecting picture people. Apparent they didn't scare you and the bribe wasn't big enough.'

'They scared me plenty,' I said. 'I damn near fanned a Luger at them. That junky with the .45 puts on a terrific act. And as for the money not being big enough, it's all a question of how it's offered to me.'

He sipped a little more of his Armagnac. He pointed at the photograph lying in front of him with the two pieces fitted together.

'We got to where you were taking that to the cops. What then?'

'I don't think we got that far. We got to why she took this up with you instead of with her boyfriend. He arrived just as I left. He has his own key.'

'Apparently she just didn't.' He frowned and looked down into his Armagnac.

'I like that fine,' I said. 'I'd like it still better if the guy didn't have her door-key.'

He looked up rather sadly. 'So would I. So would we all. But show business has always been like that – any kind of show business. If these people didn't live intense and rather disordered lives, if their emotions didn't ride them too hard – well, they wouldn't be able to catch those emotions in flight and imprint them on a few feet of celluloid or project them across the footlights.'

'I'm not talking about her love life,' I said. 'She doesn't have to shack up with a red-hot.'

'There's no proof of that, Marlowe.'

I pointed to the photograph. 'The man that took that is missing and can't be found. He's probably dead. Two other men who lived at the same address are dead. One of them was trying to peddle those pictures just before he got dead. She went to his hotel in person to take delivery. So did whoever killed him. She didn't get delivery and neither did the killer. They didn't know where to look.'

'And you did?'

'I was lucky. I'd seen him without his toupee. None of this is what I call proof, maybe. You could build an argument against it. Why bother? Two men have been killed, perhaps three. She took an awful chance. Why? She wanted that picture. Getting it was worth an awful chance. Why, again? It's just two people having lunch on a certain day. The day Moe Stein was shot to death on Franklin Avenue. The day a character named Steelgrave was in jail because the cops got a tip he was a Cleveland red-hot named Weepy Moyer. That's what the record shows. But the photo says he was out of jail. And by saying that about him on that particular day it says who he is. And she knows it. And he still has her door-key.'

I paused and we eyed each other solidly for a while. I said: 'You don't really want the cops to have that picture, do you? Win, lose or draw, they'd crucify her. And when it was all over it wouldn't make a damn bit of difference whether Steelgrave was Moyer or whether Moyer killed Stein or had him killed or just happened to be out on a jail pass the day he was killed. If he got away with it, there'd always be enough people to think it was a fix. She wouldn't get away with anything. She's a gangster's girl in the public mind. And as far as your business is concerned, she's definitely and completely through.'

Ballou was silent for a moment, staring at me without expression. 'And where are you all this time?' he asked softly.

'That depends a good deal on you, Mr Ballou.'

'What do you really want?' His voice was thin and bitter now.

'What I wanted from her and couldn't get. Something that gives me a colourable right to act in her interests up to the point where I decided I can't go any farther.'

'By suppressing evidence?' he asked tightly.

'If it *is* evidence. The cops couldn't find out without smearing Miss Weld. Maybe I can. They wouldn't be bothered to try; they don't care enough. I do.'

'Why?'

'Let's say it's the way I earn my living. I might have other motives, but that one's enough.'

'What's your price?'

'You sent it to me last night. I wouldn't take it then. I'll take it now. With a signed letter employing my services to investigate an attempt to blackmail one of your clients.'

I got up with my empty glass and went over and put it down on the desk. As I bent down I heard a soft whirring noise. I went around behind the desk and yanked open a drawer. A wire recorder slid out on a hinged shelf. The motor was running and the fine steel wire was moving steadily from one spool to the other. I looked across at Ballou.

'You can shut it off and take the record with you,' he said. 'You can't blame me for using it.'

I moved the switch over to rewind and the wire reversed direction and picked up speed until the wire was winding so fast I couldn't see it. It made a sort of high keening noise, like a couple of pansies fighting for a piece of silk. The wire came loose and the machine stopped. I took the spool off and dropped it into my pocket.

'You might have another one,' I said. 'I'll have to chance that.'

'Pretty sure of yourself, aren't you, Marlowe?'

'I only wish I was.'

'Press that button on the end of the desk, will you?'

I pressed it. The black glass doors opened and a dark girl came in with a stenographer's notebook.

Without looking at her, Ballou began to dictate. 'Letter to Mr Philip Marlowe, with his address. Dear Mr Marlowe: This agency herewith employs you to investigate an attempt to blackmail one of its clients, particulars of which have been given to you verbally. Your fee is to be one hundred dollars a day with a retainer of five hundred dollars, receipt of which you acknowledge on the copy of this letter. Blah, blah, blah. That's all, Eileen. Right away, please.'

I gave the girl my address and she went out.

I took the wire spool out of my pocket and put it back in the drawer.

Ballou crossed his knees and danced the shiny tip of his shoe up and down, staring at it. He ran his hand through crisp dark hair.

'One of these days,' he said, 'I'm going to make the mistake which a man in my business dreads above all other mistakes. I'm going to find myself doing business with a man I can trust and I'm going to be just too goddamn smart to trust him. Here, you'd better keep this.' He held out the two pieces of the photograph.

Five minutes later I left. The glass doors opened when I was three feet from them. I went past the two secretaries and down the corridor past the open door of Spink's office. There was no sound in there, but I could smell his cigar smoke. In the reception room exactly the same people seemed to be sitting around in the chintzy chairs. Miss Helen Grady gave me her Saturday night smile. Miss Vane beamed at me.

I had been forty minutes with the boss. That made me as gaudy as a chiropractor's chart.

19

The studio cop at the semi-circular glassed-in desk put down his telephone and scribbled on a pad. He tore off the sheet and pushed it through the narrow slit not more than three-quarters of an inch wide where the glass did not quite meet the top of his desk. His voice coming through the speaking device set into the glass panel had a metallic ring.

'Straight through to the end of the corridor,' he said, 'you'll find a drinking fountain in the middle of the patio. George Wilson will pick up there.'

I said: 'Thanks. Is this bullet-proof glass?'

'Sure. Why?'

'I just wondered,' I said. 'I never heard of anybody shooting his way into the picture business.'

Behind me somebody snickered. I turned to look at a girl in slacks with a red carnation behind her ear. She was grinning.

'Oh, brother, if a gun was all it took.'

I went over to an olive-green door that didn't have any handle. It made a buzzing sound and let me push it open. Beyond was an olive green corridor with bare walls and a door at the far end. A rat trap. If you got into that and something was wrong, they could still stop you. The far door made the same buzz and click. I wondered how the cop knew I was at it. So I looked up and found his eyes staring at me in a tilted mirror. As I touched the door the mirror went blank. They thought of everything.

Outside in the hot midday sun, flowers rioted in a small patio with tiled walks and a pool in the middle and a marble seat. The drinking fountain was beside the marble seat. An elderly and beautifully dressed man was lounging on the marble seat watching three tan-coloured boxer dogs root up some tea-rose begonias. There was an expression of intense but quiet satisfaction on his face. He didn't glance at me as I came up. One of the boxers, the biggest one, came over and made a wet on the marble seat beside his pants leg. He leaned down and patted the dog's hard short-haired head.

'You Mr Wilson?' I asked.

He looked up at me vaguely. The middle-sized boxer trotted up and sniffed and wet after the first one.

'Wilson?' He had a lazy voice with a touch of drawl to it. 'Oh no. My name's not Wilson. Should it be?'

'Sorry.' I went over to the drinking fountain and hit myself in the face with a stream of water. While I was wiping it off with a handkerchief the smallest boxer did his duty on the marble bench.

The man whose name was not Wilson said lovingly: 'Always do it in the exact same order. Fascinates me.'

'Do what?' I asked.

'Pee,' he said. 'Question of seniority it seems. Very orderly. First Maisie. She's the mother. Then Mac. Year older than Jock, the baby. Always the same. Even in my office.'

'In your office?' I said, and nobody ever looked stupider saying anything.

He lifted his whitish eyebrows at me, took a plain brown cigar out of his mouth, bit the end off and spat it into the pool.

'That won't do the fish any good,' I said.

He gave me an up-from-under look. 'I raise boxers. The hell with fish.'

I figured it was just Hollywood. I lit a cigarette and sat down on the bench. 'In your office,' I said. 'Well, every day has its new idea, hasn't it.'

'Up against the corner of the desk. Do it all the time. Drives my secretaries crazy. Gets into the carpet, they say. What's the matter with women nowadays? Never bothers me. Rather like it. You get fond of dogs, you even like to watch them pee.'

One of the dogs heaved a full-blown begonia plant into the middle of the tiled walk at his feet. He picked it up and threw it into the pool.

'Bothers the gardeners, I suppose,' he remarked as he sat down again. 'Oh well, if they're not satisfied, they can always—' he stopped dead and watched a slim mail girl in yellow slacks deliberately detour in order to pass through the patio. She gave him a quick side glance and went off making music with her hips.

'You know what's the matter with this business?' he asked me.

'Nobody does,' I said.

'Too much sex,' he said. 'All right in its proper time and place. But we get it in carload lots. Wade through it. Stand up to our necks in it. Gets to be like fly paper.' He stood up. 'We have too many flies too. Nice to have met you, Mister—'

'Marlowe,' I said. 'I'm afraid you don't know me.'

'Don't know anybody,' he said. 'Memory's going. Meet too many people. Name's Oppenheimer.'

'Jules Oppenheimer?'

He nodded. 'Right. Have a cigar.' He held one out to me. I

showed my cigarette. He threw the cigar into the pool, then frowned. 'Memory's going,' he said sadly. 'Wasted fifty cents. Oughtn't to do that.'

'You run this studio,' I said.

He nodded absently. 'Ought to have saved that cigar. Save fifty cents and what have you got?'

'Fifty cents,' I said, wondering what the hell he was talking about.

'Not in this business. Save fifty cents in this business and all you have is five dollars' worth of book-keeping.' He paused and made a motion to the three boxers. They stopped whatever they were rooting at and watched him. 'Just run the financial end,' he said. 'That's easy. Come on, children, back to the brothel.' He sighed. 'Fifteen hundred theatres,' he added.

I must have been wearing my stupid expression again. He waved a hand around the patio. 'Fifteen hundred theatres is all you need. A damn sight easier than raising pure-bred boxers. The motion picture business is the only business in the world in which you can make all the mistakes there are and still make money.'

'Must be the only business in the world where you can have three dogs pee up against your office desk,' I said.

'You have to have the fifteen hundred theatres.'

'That makes it a little harder to get a start,' I said.

He looked pleased. 'Yes. That *is* the hard part.' He looked across the green clipped lawn at a four-storey building which made one side of the open square. 'All offices over there,' he said. 'I never go there. Always redecorating. Makes me sick to look at the stuff some of these people put in their suites. Most expensive talent in the world. Give them anything they like, all the money they want. Why? No reason at all. Just habit. Doesn't matter a damn what they do or how they do it. Just give me fifteen hundred theatres.'

'You wouldn't want to be quoted on that, Mr Oppenheimer?'

'You a newspaper man?'

'No.'

'Too bad. Just for the hell of it I'd like to see somebody try to get that simple elementary fact of life into the papers.' He paused and snorted. 'Nobody'd print it. Afraid to. Come on, children!'

The big one, Maisie, came over and stood beside him. The middle-sized one paused to ruin another begonia and then trotted up beside Maisie. The little one, Jock, lined up in order, then, with a sudden inspiration, lifted a hind leg at the cuff of

Oppenheimer's pants. Maisie blocked him off casually.

'See that?' Oppenheimer beamed. 'Jock tried to get out of turn. Maisie wouldn't stand for it.' He leaned down and patted Maisie's head. She looked up at him adoringly.

'The eyes of your dog,' Oppenheimer mused. 'The most unforgettable thing in the world.'

He strolled off down the tiled path towards the executive building, the three boxers trotting sedately beside him.

'Mr Marlowe?'

I turned to find that a tall sandy-haired man with a nose like a straphanger's elbow had sneaked up on me.

'I'm George Wilson. Glad to know you. I see you know Mr Oppenheimer.'

'Been talking to him. He told me how to run the picture business. Seems all it takes is fifteen hundred theatres.'

'I've been working here five years. I've never even spoken to him.'

'You just don't get pee'd on by the right dogs.'

'You could be right. Just what can I do for you, Mr Marlowe?'

'I want to see Mavis Weld.'

'She's on the set. She's in a picture that's shooting.'

'Could I see her on the set for a minute?'

He looked doubtful. 'What kind of pass did they give you?'

'Just a pass, I guess.' I held it out to him. He looked it over.

'Ballou sent you. He's her agent. I guess we can manage. Stage 12. Want to go over there now?'

'If you have time.'

'I'm the unit publicity man. That's what my time is for.'

We walked along the tiled path towards the corners of two buildings. A concrete roadway went between them towards the back lot and the stages.

'You in Ballou's office?' Wilson asked.

'Just came from there.'

'Quite an organization, I hear. I've thought of trying that business myself. There's nothing in this but a lot of grief.'

We passed a couple of uniformed cops, then turned into a narrow alley between two stages. A red wig-wag was swinging in the middle of the alley, a red light was on over a door marked 12, and a bell was ringing steadily above the red light. Wilson stopped beside the door. Another cop in a tilted-back chair nodded to him, and looked me over with that dead grey expression that grows on them like scum on a water tank.

The bell and the wig-wag stopped and the red light went off.

Wilson pulled a heavy door open and I went in past him. Inside was another door. Inside that what seemed after the sunlight to be pitch darkness. Then I saw a concentration of lights in the far corner. The rest of the enormous sound stage seemed to be empty.

We went towards the lights. As we drew near the floor seemed to be covered with thick black cables. There were rows of folding chairs, a cluster of portable dressing-rooms with names on the doors. We were wrong way on to the set and all I could see was the wooden backing and on either side a big screen. A couple of back-projection machines sizzled off to the side.

A voice shouted: 'Roll 'em.' A bell rang loudly. The two screens came alive with tossing waves. Another calmer voice said: 'Watch your positions, please, we may have to end up matching this little vignette. All right, action.'

Wilson stopped dead and touched my arm. The voices of the actors came out of nowhere, neither loud nor distinct, an unimportant murmur with no meaning.

One of the screens suddenly went blank. The smooth voice, without change of tone, said: 'Cut.'

The bell rang again and there was a general sound of movement. Wilson and I went on. He whispered in my ear: 'If Ned Gammon doesn't get this take before lunch, he'll bust Torrance on the nose.'

'Oh. Torrance in this?' Dick Torrance at the time was a ranking star of the second grade, a not uncommon type of Hollywood actor that nobody really wants but a lot of people in the end have to take for lack of better.

'Care to run over the scene again, Dick?' the calm voice asked, as we came around the corner of the set and saw what it was – the deck of a pleasure yacht near the stern. There were two girls and three men in the scene. One of them was middle-aged, in sports clothes, lounging in a deck chair. One wore whites and had red hair and looked like the yacht's captain. The third was the amateur yachtsman, with the handsome cap, the blue jacket with gold buttons, the white shoes and slacks and the supercilious charm. This was Torrance. One of the girls was a dark beauty who had been younger; Susan Crawley. The other was Mavis Weld. She wore a wet white sharkskin swimsuit, and had evidently just come aboard. A make-up man was spraying water on her face and arms and the edges of her blonde hair.

Torrance hadn't answered. He turned suddenly and stared at the camera. 'You think I don't know my lines?'

A grey-haired man in grey clothes came forward into the light from the shadowy background. He had hot black eyes, but there was no heat in his voice.

'Unless you changed them intentionally,' he said, his eyes steady on Torrance.

'It's just possible that I'm not used to playing in front of a back projection screen that has a habit of running out of film only in the middle of a take.'

'That's a fair complaint,' Ned Gammon said. 'Trouble is he only has two hundred and twelve feet of film, and that's my fault. If you could take the scene just a little faster—'

'Huh.' Torrance snorted. 'If *I* could take it a little faster. Perhaps Miss Weld could be prevailed upon to climb aboard this yacht in rather less time than it would take to build the damn boat.'

Mavis Weld gave him a quick, contemptuous look.

'Weld's timing is just right,' Gammon said. 'Her performance is just right too.'

Susan Crawley shrugged elegantly. 'I had the impression she could speed it up a trifle, Ned. It's good, but it *could* be better.'

'If it was any better, darling,' Mavis Weld told her smoothly, 'somebody might call it acting. You wouldn't want anything like that to happen in *your* picture, would you?'

Torrance laughed. Susan Crawley turned and glared at him. 'What's funny, Mister Thirteen?'

Torrance's face settled into an icy mask. 'The name again?' he almost hissed.

'Good heavens, you mean you didn't know,' Susan Crawley said wonderingly. 'They call you Mister Thirteen because any time you play a part it means twelve other guys have turned it down.'

'I see,' Torrance said coolly, then burst out laughing again. He turned to Ned Gammon. 'Okay, Ned. Now everybody's got the rat poison out of their system, maybe we can give it to you the way you want it.'

Ned Gammon nodded. 'Nothing like a little hamming to clear the air. All right, here we go.'

He went back beside the camera. The assistant shouted 'roll 'em' and the scene went through without a hitch.

'Cut,' Gammon said. 'Print that one. Break for lunch everybody.'

The actors came down a flight of rough wooden steps and nodded to Wilson. Mavis Weld came last, having stopped to put on a terrycloth robe and a pair of beach sandals. She stopped dead when she saw me. Wilson stepped forward.

'Hello, George,' Mavis Weld said, staring at me. 'Want something from me?'

'Mr Marlowe would like a few words with you. Okay?'

'Mr Marlowe?'

Wilson gave me a quick sharp look. 'From Ballou's office. I supposed you knew him.'

'I may have seen him.' She was still staring at me. 'What is it?'

I didn't speak.

After a moment she said: 'Thanks, George. Better come along to my dressing-room, Mr Marlowe.'

She turned and walked off around the far side of the set. A green and white dressing-room stood against the wall. The name on the door was Miss Weld. At the door she turned and looked around carefully. Then she fixed her lovely blue eyes on my face.

'And now, Mr Marlowe?'

'You *do* remember me?'

'I believe so.'

'Do we take up where we left off – or have a new deal with a clean deck?'

'Somebody let you in here. Who? Why? That takes explaining.'

'I'm working for you. I've been paid a retainer and Ballou has the receipt.'

'How very thoughtful. And suppose I don't want you to work for me? Whatever your work is.'

'All right, be fancy,' I said. I took the Dancers photo out of my pocket and held it out. She looked at me a long and steady moment before she dropped her eyes. Then she looked at the snapshot of herself and Steelgrave in the booth. She looked at it gravely without movement. Then very slowly she reached up and touched the tendrils of damp hair at the side of her face. Ever so slightly she shivered. Her hand came out and she took the photograph. She stared at it. Her eyes came up again slowly, slowly.

'Well?' she asked.

'I have the negative and some other prints. You would have had them, if you had had more time and known where to look. Or if he had stayed alive to sell them to you.'

'I'm a little chilly,' she said. 'And I have to eat some lunch.' She held the photo out to me.

'You're a little chilly and you have to eat some lunch,' I said.

I thought a pulse beat in her throat. But the light was not too good. She smiled very faintly. The bored aristocrat touch.

'The significance of all this escapes me,' she said.

'You're spending too much time on yachts. What you mean is I know you and I know Steelgrave, so what has this photo got that makes anybody give me a diamond dog collar?'

'All right,' she said. 'What?'

'I don't know,' I said. 'But if finding out is what it takes to shake you out of this duchess routine, I'll find out. And in the meantime you're still chilly and you still have to eat some lunch.'

'And you've waited too long,' she said quietly. 'You haven't anything to sell. Except perhaps your life.'

'I'd sell that cheap. For love of a pair of dark glasses and a delphinium blue hat and a crack on the head from a high-heeled slipper.'

Her mouth twitched as if she was going to laugh. But there was no laughter in her eyes.

'Not to mention three slaps in the face,' she said. 'Goodbye, Mr Marlowe. You came too late. Much, much too late.'

'For me – or for you?' She reached back and opened the door of the dressing-room.

'I think for both of us.' She went in quickly, leaving the door open.

'Come in and shut the door,' her voice said from the dressing-room.

I went in and shut the door. It was no fancy custom-built star's dressing-room. Strictly utility only. There was a shabby couch, one easy chair, a small dressing-table with mirror and two lights, a straight chair in front of it, a tray that had held coffee.

Mavis Weld reached down and plugged in a round electric heater. Then she grabbed up a towel and rubbed the damp edges of her hair. I sat down on the couch and waited.

'Give me a cigarette.' She tossed the towel to one side. Her eyes came close to my face as I lit the cigarette for her. 'How did you like that little scene we adlibbed on the yacht?'

'Bitchy.'

'We're all bitches. Some smile more than others, that's all. Show business. There's something cheap about it. There always has been. There was a time when actors went in at the back door. Most of them still should. Great strain, great urgency, great hatred, and it comes out in nasty little scenes. They don't mean a thing.'

'Cat talk,' I said.

She reached up and pulled a fingertip down the side of my cheek. It burned like a hot iron. 'How much money do you make, Marlowe?'

'Forty bucks a day and expenses. That's the asking price. I take twenty-five. I've taken less.' I thought about Orfamay's worn twenty.

She did that with her finger again and I just didn't grab hold of her. She moved away from me and sat in the chair, drawing the robe close. The electric heater was making the little room warm.

'Twenty-five dollars a day,' she said wonderingly.

'Little lonely dollars.'

'Are they very lonely?'

'Lonely as lighthouses.'

She crossed her legs and the pale glow of her skin in the light seemed to fill the room.

'So ask me the questions,' she said, making no attempt to cover her thighs.

'Who's Steelgrave?'

'A man I've known for years. And liked. He owns things. A restaurant or two. Where he comes from – that I don't know.'

'But you know him very well.'

'Why don't you ask me if I sleep with him?'

'I don't ask that kind of questions.'

She laughed and snapped ash from her cigarette. 'Miss Gonzales would be glad to tell you.'

'The hell with Miss Gonzales.'

'She's dark and lovely and passionate. And very, very kind.'

'And exclusive as a mailbox,' I said. 'The hell with her. About Steelgrave – has he ever been in trouble?'

'Who hasn't?'

'With the police.'

Her eyes widened a little too innocently. Her laugh was a little too silvery. 'Don't be ridiculous. The man is worth a couple of million dollars.'

'How did he get it?'

'How would I know?'

'All right. You wouldn't. That cigarette's going to burn your fingers.' I leaned across and took the stub out of her hand. Her hand lay open on her bare leg. I touched the palm with a fingertip. She drew away from me and tightened the hand into a fist.

'Don't do that,' she said sharply.

'Why? I used to do that to girls when I was a kid.'

'I know.' She was breathing a little fast. 'It makes me feel very young and innocent and kind of naughty. And I'm far from being young and innocent any more.'

'Then you don't really know anything about Steelgrave.'

'I wish you'd make up your mind whether you are giving me a third degree or making love to me.'

'My mind has nothing to do with it,' I said.

After a silence she said: 'I really do have to eat something, Marlowe. I'm working this afternoon. You wouldn't want me to collapse on the set, would you?'

'Only stars do that.' I stood up. 'Okay, I'll leave. Don't forget I'm working for you. I wouldn't be if I thought you'd killed anybody. But you were there. You took a big chance. There was something you wanted very badly.'

She reached the photo out from somewhere and stared at it, biting her lip. Her eyes came up without her head moving.

'It could hardly have been this.'

'That was the one thing he had so well hidden that it was not found. But what good is it? You and a man called Steelgrave in a booth at The Dancers. Nothing in that.'

'Nothing at all,' she said.

'So it has to be something about Steelgrave – or something about the date.'

Her eyes snapped down to the picture again. 'There's nothing to tell the date,' she said quickly. 'Even if it meant something. Unless the cut-out piece—'

'Here.' I gave her the cut-out piece. 'But you'll need a magnifier. Show it to Steelgrave. Ask *him* if it means anything. Or ask Ballou.'

I started towards the exit of the dressing-room. 'Don't kid yourself the date can't be fixed,' I said over my shoulder. 'Steelgrave won't.'

'You're just building a sandcastle, Marlowe.'

'Really?' I looked back at her, not grinning. 'You really think that? Oh no you don't. You went there. The man was murdered. You had a gun. He was a known crook. And I found something the police would love to have me hide from them. Because it must be as full of motive as the ocean is full of salt. As long as the cops don't find it I have a licence. And as long as somebody else doesn't find it I don't have an ice pick in the back of my neck. Would you say I was in an overpaid profession?'

She just sat there and looked at me, one hand on her kneecap, squeezing it. The other moving restlessly, finger by finger, on the arm of the chair.

All I had to do was turn the knob and go out. I don't know why it had to be so hard to do.

20

There was the usual coming and going in the corridor outside my office, and when I opened the door and walked into the musty silence of the little waiting-room there was the usual feeling of having been dropped down a well dried up twenty years ago to which no one would come back ever. The smell of old dust hung in the air as flat and stale as a football interview.

I opened the inner door and inside there it was the same dead air, the same dust along the veneer, the same broken promise of a life of ease. I opened the windows and turned on the radio. It came up too loud and when I had it turned down to normal the phone sounded as if it had been ringing for some time. I took my hat off it and lifted the receiver.

It was high time I heard from her again. Her cool compact voice said: 'This time I really mean it.'

'Go on.'

'I lied before. I'm not lying now. I really have heard from Orrin.'

'Go on.'

'You're not believing me. I can tell by your voice.'

'You can't tell anything by my voice. I'm a detective. Heard from him how?'

'By phone from Bay City.'

'Wait a minute.' I put the receiver down on the stained brown blotter and lit my pipe. No hurry. Lies are always patient. I took it up again.

'We've been through that routine,' I said. 'You're pretty forgetful for your age. I don't think Dr Zugsmith would like it.'

'Please don't tease me. This is very serious. He got my letter. He went to the post office and asked for his mail. He knew where I'd be staying. And about when I'd be here. So he called up. He's staying with a doctor he got to know down there. Doing some kind of work for him. I told you he had two years' medical.'

'Doctor have a name?'

'Yes. A funny name. Dr Vincent Lagardie.'

'Just a minute. There's somebody at the door.'

I laid the phone down very carefully. It might be brittle. It might be made of spun glass. I got a handkerchief out and wiped the palm of my hand, the one that had been holding it. I got up and went to the built-in wardrobe and looked at my face in the flawed mirror. It was me all right. I had a strained look. I'd been living too fast.

Dr Vincent Lagardie, 965 Wyoming Street. Catty-corners from The Garland Home of Peace. Frame house on the corner. Quiet. Nice neighbourhood. Friend of the extinct Clausen. Maybe. Not according to him. But still maybe.

I went back to the telephone and squeezed the jerks out of my voice. 'How would you spell that?' I asked.

She spelled it – with ease and precision. 'Nothing to do then, is there?' I said. 'All jake to the angels – or whatever they say in Manhattan, Kansas.'

'Stop sneering at me. Orrin's in a lot of trouble. Some—' her voice quivered a little and her breath came quickly. 'Some gangsters are after him.'

'Don't be silly, Orfamay. They don't have gangsters in Bay City. They're all working in pictures. What's Dr Lagardie's phone number?'

She gave it to me. It was right. I won't say the pieces were beginning to fall into place, but at least they were getting to look like parts of the same puzzle. Which is all I ever get or ask.

'Please go down there and see him and help him. He's afraid to leave the house. After all, I did pay you.'

'I gave it back.'

'Well, I offered it to you again.'

'You more or less offered me other things that are more than I'd care to take.'

There was silence.

'All right,' I said. 'All right. If I can stay free that long. I'm in a lot of trouble myself.'

'Why?'

'Telling lies and not telling the truth. It always catches up with me. I'm not as lucky as some people.'

'But I'm not lying, Philip. I'm not lying. I'm frantic.'

'Take a deep breath and get frantic so I can hear it.'

'They might kill him,' she said quietly.

'And what is Dr Vincent Lagardie doing all this time?'

'He doesn't know, of course. Please, please go at once. I have the address here. Just a moment.'

And the little bell rang, the one that rings far back at the end of the corridor, and is not loud, but you'd better hear it. No matter what other noises there are you'd better hear it.

'He'll be in the phone book,' I said. 'And by an odd coincidence I have a Bay City phone book. Call me around four. Or five. Better make it five.'

I hung up quickly. I stood up and turned the radio off, not having heard a thing it said. I closed the windows again. I opened the drawer of my desk and took out the Luger and strapped it on. I fitted my hat on my head. On the way out I had another look at the face in the mirror.

I looked as if I had made up my mind to drive off a cliff.

21

They were just finishing a funeral service at The Garland Home of Peace. A big grey hearse was waiting at the side entrance. Cars were clotted along both sides of the street, three black sedans in a row at the side of Dr Vincent Lagardie's establishment. People were coming sedately down the walk from the funeral chapel to the corner and getting into their cars. I stopped a third of a block away and waited. The cars didn't move. Then three people came out with a woman heavily veiled and all in black. They half carried her down to a big limousine. The boss mortician fluttered around making elegant little gestures and body movements as graceful as a Chopin ending. His composed grey face was long enough to wrap twice around his neck.

The amateur pallbearers carried the coffin out the side door and professionals eased the weight from them and slid it into the back of the hearse as smoothly as if it had no more weight than a pan of butter rolls. Flowers began to grow into a mound over it. The glass doors were closed and motors started all over the block.

A few moments later nothing was left but one sedan across the way and the boss mortician sniffing a tree-rose on his way back to count the take. With a beaming smile he faded into his neat colonial doorway and the world was still and empty again. The sedan that was left hadn't moved. I drove along and made a U-turn and came up behind it. The driver wore blue serge and a soft cap with a shiny peak. He was doing a crossword puzzle from the morning paper. I stuck a pair of those diaphanous mirror sunglasses on my nose and strolled past him towards Dr Lagardie's place. He didn't look up. When I was a few yards ahead I took the glasses off and pretended to polish them on my handkerchief. I caught him in one of the mirror lenses. He still didn't look up. He was just a guy doing a cross-word puzzle. I put the mirror glasses back on my nose, and went around to Dr Lagardie's front door.

The sign over the door said: Ring and Enter. I rang, but the door wouldn't let me enter. I waited. I rang again. I waited again. There was silence inside. Then the door opened a crack very slowly, and a thin expressionless face over a white uniform looked out at me.

'I'm sorry. Doctor is not seeing any patients today.' She blinked at the mirror glasses. She didn't like them. Her tongue moved restlessly inside her lips.

'I'm looking for a Mr Quest. Orrin P. Quest.'

'Who?' There was a dim reflection of shock behind her eyes.

'Quest. Q as in quintessential, U as in uninhibited, E as in Extrasensory, S as in Subliminal, T as in Toots. Put them all together and they spell Brother.'

She looked at me as if I had just come up from the floor of the ocean with a drowned mermaid under my arm.

'I beg your pardon. Dr Lagardie is not—'

She was pushed out of the way by invisible hands and a thin dark haunted man stood in the half-open doorway.

'I am Dr Lagardie. What is it, please?'

I gave him a card. He read it. He looked at me. He had the white pinched look of a man who is waiting for a disaster to happen.

'We talked over the phone,' I said. 'About a man named Clausen.'

'Please come in,' he said quickly. 'I don't remember, but come in.'

I went in. The room was dark, the blinds drawn, the windows closed. It was dark, and it was cold.

The nurse backed away and sat down behind a small desk. It was an ordinary living-room with light painted woodwork which had once been dark, judging by the probable age of the house. A square arch divided the living-room from the dining-room. There were easy-chairs and a centre table with magazines. It looked like what it was – the reception room of a doctor practising in what had been a private home.

The telephone rang on the desk in front of the nurse. She started and her hand went out and then stopped. She stared at the telephone. After a while it stopped ringing.

'What was the name you mentioned?' Dr Lagardie asked me softly.

'Orrin Quest. His sister told me he was doing some kind of work for you, Doctor. I've been looking for him for days. Last night he called her up. From here, she said.'

'There is no one of that name here,' Dr Lagardie said politely. 'There hasn't been.'

'You don't know him at all?'

'I have never heard of him.'

'I can't figure why he would say that to his sister.'

The nurse dabbed at her eyes furtively. The telephone on her desk burred and made her jump again. 'Don't answer it,' Dr Lagardie said without turning his head.

We waited while it rang. Everybody waits while a telephone rings. After a while it stopped.

'Why don't you go home, Miss Watson? There's nothing for you to do here.'

'Thank you, Doctor.' She sat without moving, looking down at the desk. She squeezed her eyes shut and blinked them open. She shook her head hopelessly.

Dr Lagardie turned back to me. 'Shall we go into my office?'

We went across through another door leading to a hallway. I walked on eggs. The atmosphere of the house was charged with foreboding. He opened a door and ushered me into what must have once been a bedroom, but nothing suggested a bedroom. It was a small compact doctor's office. An open door showed a part of an examination room. A sterilizer was working in the corner. There were a lot of needles cooking in it.

'That's a lot of needles,' I said, always quick with an idea.

'Sit down, Mr Marlowe.'

He went behind the desk and sat down and picked up a long thin letter-opening knife.

He looked at me levelly from his sorrowful eyes. 'No, I don't know anyone named Orrin Quest, Mr Marlowe. I can't imagine any reason in the world why a person of that name should say he was in my house.'

'Hiding out,' I said.

His eyebrows went up. 'From what?'

'From some guys that might want to stick an ice pick in the back of his neck. On account of he is a little too quick with his little Leica. Taking people's photographs when they want to be private. Or it could be something else, like peddling reefers and he got wise. Am I talking in riddles?'

'It was you who sent the police here,' he said coldly.

I didn't say anything.

'It was you who called up and reported Clausen's death.'

I said the same as before.

'It was you who called me up and asked me if I knew Clausen. I said I did not.'

'But it wasn't true.'

'I was under no obligation to give you information, Mr Marlowe.'

I nodded and got a cigarette out and lit it. Dr Lagardie glanced at his watch. He turned in his chair and switched off the sterilizer. I looked at the needles. A lot of needles. Once before I had had trouble in Bay City with a guy who cooked a lot of needles.

'What makes it?' I asked him. 'The yacht harbour?'

He picked up the wicked-looking paper knife with a silver handle in the shape of a nude woman. He pricked the ball of his thumb. A pearl of dark blood showed on it. He put it to his mouth and licked it. 'I like the taste of blood,' he said softly.

There was a distant sound as of the front door opening and closing. We both listened to it carefully. We listened to retreating steps on the front steps of the house. We listened hard.

'Miss Watson has gone home,' Dr Lagardie said. 'We are all alone in the house.' He mulled that over and licked his thumb again. He laid the knife down carefully on the desk blotter. 'Ah, the question of the yacht harbour,' he added. 'The proximity of Mexico you are thinking of, no doubt. The ease with which marijuana—'

'I wasn't thinking so much of marijuana any more.' I stared again at the needles. He followed my stare. He shrugged.

I said: 'Why so many of them?'

'Is it any of your business?'

'Nothing's any of my business.'

'But you seem to expect your questions to be answered.'

'I'm just talking,' I said. 'Waiting for something to happen. Something's going to happen in this house. It's leering at me from corners.'

Dr Lagardie licked another pearl of blood off his thumb.

I looked hard at him. It didn't buy me a way into his soul. He was quiet, dark and shattered and all the misery of life was in his eyes. But he was still gentle.

'Let me tell you about the needles,' I said.

'By all means.' He picked the long thin knife up again.

'Don't do that,' I said sharply. 'It gives me the creeps. Like petting snakes.'

He put the knife down again gently and smiled. 'We do seem to talk in circles,' he suggested.

'We'll get there. About the needles. A couple of years back I had a case that brought me down here and mixed me up with a doctor named Almore. Lived over on Altair Street. He had a funny practice. Went out nights with a big case of hypodermic needles – all ready to go. Loaded with the stuff. He had a peculiar practice. Drunks, rich junkies, of whom there are far more than people think, overstimulated people who had driven themselves beyond the possibility of relaxing. Insomniacs – all the neurotic types that can't take it cold. Have to have their little pills and little shots in the arm. Have to help them over the humps. It gets to be all humps after a while. Good business for the doctor. Almore was the doctor for them. It's all right to say it now. He died a year or so back. Of his own medicine.'

'And you think I may have inherited his practice?'

'Somebody would. As long as there are the patients, there will be the doctor.'

He looked even more exhausted than before. 'I think you are an ass, my friend. I did not know Dr Almore. And I do not have the sort of practice you attribute to him. As for the needles – just to get that trifle out of the way – they are in somewhat constant use in the medical profession today, often for such innocent medicaments as vitamin injections. And needles get dull. And when they are dull they are painful. Therefore in the course of the day one may use a dozen or more. Without narcotics in a single one.'

He raised his head slowly and stared at me with a fixed contempt.

'I can be wrong,' I said. 'Smelling that reefer smoke over at Clausen's place yesterday, and having him call your number on the telephone – and call you by your first name – all this probably made me jump to wrong conclusions.'

'I have dealt with addicts,' he said. 'What doctor has not? It is a complete waste of time.'

'They get cured sometimes.'

'They can be deprived of their drug. Eventually after great suffering they can do without it. That is not curing them, my friend. That is not removing the nervous or emotional flaw which made them become addicts. It is making them dull negative people who sit in the sun and twirl their thumbs and die of sheer boredom and inanition.'

'That's a pretty raw theory, Doctor.'

'You raised the subject. I have disposed of it. I will raise another subject. You may have noticed a certain atmosphere and strain about this house. Even with those silly mirror glasses on. Which you may now remove. They don't make you look in the least like Cary Grant.'

I took them off. I'd forgotten all about them.

'The police have been here, Mr Marlowe. A certain Lieutenant Maglashan, who is investigating Clausen's death. He would be pleased to meet you. Shall I call him? I'm sure he would come back.'

'Go ahead, call him,' I said. 'I just stopped off here on my way to commit suicide.'

His hand went towards the telephone but was pulled to one side by the magnetism of the paper knife. He picked it up again. Couldn't leave it alone, it seemed.

'You could kill a man with that,' I said.

'Very easily,' and he smiled a little.

'An inch and a half in the back of the neck, square in the centre, just under the occipital bulge.'

'An ice pick would be better,' he said. 'Especially a short one, filed down very sharp. It would not bend. If you miss the spinal cord, you do no great damage.'

'Takes a bit of medical knowledge then?' I got out a poor old package of Camels and untangled one from the cellophane.

He just kept on smiling. Very faintly, rather sadly. It was not the smile of a man in fear. 'That would help,' he said softly. 'But any reasonably dexterous person could acquire the technique in ten minutes.'

'Orrin Quest had a couple of years' medical,' I said.

'I told you I did not know anybody of that name.'

'Yeah, I know you did. I didn't quite believe you.'

He shrugged his shoulders. But his eyes as always went to the knife in the end.

'We're a couple of sweethearts,' I said. 'We just sit here making with the old over-the-desk dialogue. As though we hadn't a care in the world. Because both of us are going to be in the clink by nightfall.'

He raised his eyebrows again. I went on:

'You, because Clausen knew you by your first name. And you may have been the last man he talked to. Me, because I've been doing all the things a PI never gets away with. Hiding evidence, hiding information, finding bodies and not coming in with my hat in my hand to these lovely incorruptible Bay City cops. Oh, I'm through. Very much through. But there's a wild perfume in the air this afternoon. I don't seem to care. Or I'm in love. I just don't seem to care.'

'... have been drinking,' he said slowly.

'Only Chanel No. 5, and kisses, and the pale glow of lovely legs, and the mocking invitation in deep blue eyes. Innocent things like that.'

He just looked sadder than ever. 'Women can weaken a man terribly, can they not?' he said.

'Clausen.'

'A hopeless alcoholic. You probably know how they are. They drink and drink and don't eat. And little by little the vitamin deficiency brings on the symptoms of delirium. There is only one thing to do for them.' He turned and looked at the sterilizer. 'Needles, and more needles. It makes me feel dirty. I am a graduate of the Sorbonne. But I practise among dirty little people in a dirty little town.'

'Why?'

'Because of something that happened years ago – in another city. Don't ask me too much, Mr Marlowe.'

'He used your first name.'

'It is a habit with people of a certain class. One-time actors especially. And one-time crooks.'

'Oh,' I said. 'That all there is to it?'

'All.'

'Then the cops coming here doesn't bother you on account of Clausen. You're just afraid of this other thing that happened somewhere else long gone. Or it could even be love.'

'Love?' He dropped the word slowly off the end of his tongue, tasting it to the last. A bitter little smile stayed after the word, like powder smell in the air after a gun is fired. He shrugged and pushed a desk cigarette box from behind a filing tray and over to my side of the desk.

'Not love then,' I said. 'I'm trying to read your mind. Here you are, a guy with a Sorbonne degree and a cheap little practice in a cheap and nasty little town. I know it well. So what are you doing here? What are you doing with people like Clausen? What was the rap, Doctor? Narcotics, abortions, or were you by any chance a medic for the gang boys in some hot Eastern city?'

'As for instance?' he smiled thinly.

'As for instance Cleveland.'

'A very wild suggestion, my friend.' His voice was like ice now.

'Wild as all hell,' I said. 'But a fellow like me with very limited brains tends to try to fit the things he knows into a pattern. It's often wrong, but it's an occupational disease with me. It goes like this, if you want to listen.'

'I am listening.' He picked the knife up again and pricked lightly at the blotter on his desk.

'You knew Clausen. Clausen was killed very skilfully with an ice pick, killed while I was in the house, upstairs talking to a grifter named Hicks. Hicks moved out fast, taking a page of the register with him, the page that had Orrin Quest's name on it. Later that afternoon Hicks was killed with an ice pick in LA. His room had been searched. There was a woman there who had come to buy something from him. She didn't get it. I had more time to search. I did get it. Presumption A. Clausen and Hicks killed by same man, not necessarily for same reason. Hicks killed because he muscled in on another guy's racket and muscled the other guy out. Clausen killed because he was a babbling drunk and might know who would be likely to kill Hicks. Any good so far?'

'Not the slightest interest to me,' Dr Lagardie said.

'But you *are* listening. Sheer good manners, I suppose. Okay. Now what did I find? A photo of a movie queen and an ex-Cleveland gangster, maybe, now a Hollywood restaurant owner, etc. having lunch on a particular day. Day when this ex-Cleveland gangster was supposed to be in hock at the County Jail, also day when ex-Cleveland gangster's one-time sidekick was shot dead on Franklin Avenue in Los Angeles. Why was he in hock? Tip-off that he was who he was, and say what you like against the LA cops, they do try to run back-East hot shots out of town. Who gave them the tip? The guy they pinched gave it to them himself, because his ex-partner was being troublesome and had to be rubbed out, and being in jail was a first-class alibi when it happened.'

'All fantastic,' Dr Lagardie smiled wearily. 'Utterly fantastic.'

'Sure. It gets worse. Cops couldn't prove anything on ex-gangster. Cleveland police not interested. The LA cops turn him loose. But they wouldn't have turned him loose if they'd seen that photo. Photo therefore strong blackmail material, first against ex-Cleveland character, if he really is the guy; secondly against movie queen for being seen around with him in public. A good man could make a fortune out of that photo. Hicks not good enough. Paragraph. Presumption B: Orrin Quest, the boy I'm trying to find, took that photo. Taken with Contax or Leica, without flashbulb, without subjects knowing they were being photographed. Quest had a Leica and liked to do things like that. In this case of course he had a more commercial motive. Question, how did he get a chance to take photo? Answer, the movie queen was his sister. She would let him come up and speak to her. He was out of work, needed money. Likely enough she gave him some and made it a condition he stay away from her. She wants no part of her family. Is it still utterly fantastic, Doctor?'

He stared at me moodily. 'I don't know,' he said slowly. 'It begins to have possibilities. But why are you telling this rather dangerous story to me?'

He reached a cigarette out of the box and tossed me one casually. I caught it and looked it over. Egyptian, oval and fat, a little rich for my blood. I didn't light it, just sat holding it between my fingers, watching his dark unhappy eyes. He lit his own cigarette and puffed nervously.

'I'll tie you in on it now,' I said. 'You knew Clausen. Professionally, you said. I showed him I was a dick. He tried at once to call you up. He was too drunk to talk to you. I caught the number and later told you he was dead. Why? If you were on the level, you would call the cops. You didn't. Why? You knew Clausen, you could have known some of his roomers. No proof either way. Paragraph. Presumption C: you knew Hicks or Orrin Quest or both. The LA cops couldn't or didn't establish identity of ex-Cleveland character – let's give him his new name, call him Steelgrave. But *somebody* had to be able to – if that photo was worth killing people over. Did you ever practise medicine in Cleveland, Doctor?'

'Certainly not.' His voice seemed to come from far off. His eyes were remote too. His lips opened barely enough to admit his cigarette. He was very still.

I said: 'They have a whole roomful of directories over at the telephone office. From all over the country. I checked you up.'

'A suite in a downtown office building,' I said. 'And now this – an almost furtive practice in a little beach town. You'd have liked to change your name – but you couldn't and keep your licence. Somebody had to mastermind this deal, Doctor. Clausen was a bum, Hicks a stupid lout, Orrin Quest a nasty-minded creep. But they could be used. You couldn't go up against Steelgrave directly. You wouldn't have stayed alive long enough to brush your teeth. You had to work through pawns – expendable pawns. Well – are we getting anywhere?'

He smiled faintly and leaned back in his chair with a sigh. 'Presumption D, Mr Marlowe,' he almost whispered. 'You are an unmitigated idiot.'

I grinned and reached for a match to light his fat Egyptian cigarette.

'Added to all the rest,' I said. 'Orrin's sister calls me up and tells me he is in your house. There are a lot of weak arguments taken one at a time, I admit. But they do seem to sort of focus on you.' I puffed peacefully on the cigarette.

He watched me. His face seemed to fluctuate and become vague, to move far off and come back. I felt a tightness in my chest. My mind had slowed to a turtle's gallop.

'What's going on here?' I heard myself mumble.

I put my hands on the arms of the chair and pushed myself up. 'Been dumb, haven't I?' I said, with the cigarette still in my mouth and me still smoking it. Dumb was hardly the word. Have to coin a new word.

I was out of the chair and my feet were stuck in two barrels of cement. When I spoke my voice seemed to come through cottonwool.

I let go of the arms of the chair and reached for the cigarette. I missed it clean a couple of times, then got my hand around it. It didn't feel like a cigarette. It felt like the hind leg of an elephant. With sharp toenails. They stuck into my hand. I shook my hand and the elephant took his leg away.

A vague but enormously tall figure swung around in front of me and a mule kicked me in the chest. I sat down on the floor.

'A little potassium hydrocyanide,' a voice said, over the transatlantic telephone. 'Not fatal, not even dangerous. Merely relaxing ...'

I started to get up off the floor. You ought to try it some time. But have somebody nail the floor down first. This one looped the loop. After a while it steadied a little. I settled for an angle of forty-five degrees. I took hold of myself and started to go somewhere. There was a thing that might have been Napoleon's tomb on the horizon. That was a good enough objective. I started that way. My heart beat fast and thick and I was having trouble opening my lungs. Like after being winded at football. You think your breath will never come back. Never, never, never.

Then it wasn't Napoleon's tomb any more. It was a raft on a swell. There was a man on it. I'd seen him somewhere. Nice fellow, we'd got on fine. I started towards him and hit a wall with my shoulder. That spun me around. I started clawing for something to hold on to. There was nothing but the carpet. How did I get down there? No use asking. It's a secret. Every time you ask a question they just push the floor in your face. Okay, I started to crawl along the carpet. I was on what formerly had been my hands and knees. No sensation proved it. I crawled towards a dark wooden wall. Or it could have been black marble. Napoleon's tomb again. What did I ever do to Napoleon? What for should he keep shoving his tomb at me?

'Need a drink of water,' I said.

I listened for the echo. No echo. Nobody said anything. Maybe I didn't say it. Maybe it was just an idea I thought better of. Potassium cyanide. That's a couple of long words to be worrying about when you're crawling through tunnels. Nothing fatal, he said. Okay, this is just fun. What you might call semi-fatal. Philip Marlowe, 38, a private licence operator of shady reputation, was apprehended by police last night while crawling through the Ballona Storm Drain with a grand piano on his back. Questioned at the University Heights Police Station, Marlowe declared he was taking the piano to the Maharajah of Coot-Berar. Asked why he was wearing spurs, Marlowe declared that a client's confidence was sacred. Marlowe is being held for investigation. Chief Hornside said police were not yet ready to say more. Asked if the piano was in tune, Chief Hornside declared that he had played the Minute Waltz on it in thirty-five seconds and so far as he could tell there were no strings in the piano. He intimated that something else was. A complete statement to the press will be made within twelve hours, Chief Hornside said abruptly. Speculation is rife that Marlowe was attempting to dispose of a body.

A face swam towards me out of the darkness. I changed direction and started for the face. But it was too late in the afternoon. The sun was setting. It was getting dark rapidly. There was no face. There was no wall, no desk. Then there was no floor. There was nothing at all.

I wasn't even there.

22

A big black gorilla with a big black paw had his big black paw over my face and was trying to push it through the back of my neck. I pushed back. Taking the weak side of an argument is my speciality. Then I realized that he was trying to keep me from opening my eyes.

I decided to open my eyes just the same. Others have done it, why not me? I gathered my strength and very slowly, keeping the back straight, flexing the thighs and knees, using the arms as ropes, I lifted the enormous weight of my eyelids.

I was looking at the ceiling, lying on my back on the floor, a position in which my calling has occasionally placed me. I rolled my head. My lungs felt stiff and my mouth felt dry. The room was just Dr Lagardie's consulting room. Same chair, same desk, same walls and window. There was a shuttered silence hanging around.

I got up on my haunches and braced myself on the floor and shook my head. It went into a flat spin. It spun down about five thousand feet and then I dragged it out and levelled off. I blinked. Same floor, same desk, same walls. But no Dr Lagardie.

I wet my lips and made some kind of a vague noise to which nobody paid any attention. I got up on my feet. I was as dizzy as a dervish, as weak as a worn-out washer, as low as a badger's belly, as timid as a titmouse, and as unlikely to succeed as a ballet dancer with a wooden leg.

I groped my way over behind the desk and slumped into Lagardie's chair and began to paw fitfully through his equipment for a likely looking bottle of liquid fertilizer. Nothing doing. I got up again. I was as hard to lift as a dead elephant. I staggered around looking into cabinets of shining white enamel which contained everything somebody else was in a hurry for. Finally, after what seemed like four years on the road gang, my little hand closed around six ounces of ethyl alcohol. Just what the label said. All I needed now was a glass and some water. A good man ought to be able to get that far. I started through the door to the examination room. The air still had the aromatic perfume of overripe peaches. I hit both sides of the doorway going through and paused to take a fresh sighting.

At that moment I was aware that steps were coming down the hall. I leaned against the wall wearily and listened.

Slow, dragging steps, with a long pause between each. At first they seemed furtive. Then they just seemed very, very tired. An old man trying to make it to his last armchair. That made two of us. And then I thought, for no reason at all, of Orfamay's father back there on the porch in Manhattan, Kansas, moving quietly along to his rocking chair with his cold pipe in his hand, to sit down and look out over the front lawn and have himself a nice economical smoke that required no matches and no tobacco and didn't mess up the living-room carpet. I arranged his chair for him. In the shade at the end of the porch where the bougainvillaea was thick I helped him sit down. He looked up and thanked me with the good side of his face. His fingernails scratched on the arms of the chair as he leaned back.

The fingernails scratched, but it wasn't on the arm of any chair. It was a real sound. It was close by, on the outside of a closed door that led from the examination room to the hallway. A thin, feeble scratch, possibly a young kitten wanting to be let in. Okay, Marlowe, you're an old animal lover. Go over and let the kitten in. I started. I made it with the help of the nice examination couch with the rings on the end and the nice clean towels. The scratching had stopped. Poor little kitten, outside and wanting to come in. A tear formed itself in my eye and trickled down my furrowed cheek. I let go of the examination table and made a smooth four yards to the door. The heart was bumping inside me. And the lungs still had that feeling of having been in storage for a couple of years. I took a deep breath and got hold of the door-knob and opened it. Just at the last moment it occurred to me to reach for a gun. It occurred to me but that's as far as I got. I'm a fellow that likes to take an idea over by the light and have a good look at it. I'd have had to let go of the door-knob. It seemed like too big an operation. I just twisted the knob and opened the door instead.

He was braced to the door-frame by four hooked fingers made of white wax. He had eyes an eighth of an inch deep, pale grey-blue, wide open. They looked at me but they didn't see me. Our faces were inches apart. Our breathing met in mid-air. Mine was quick and harsh, his was the far-off whisper which has not yet begun to rattle. Blood bubbled from his mouth and ran down his chin. Something made me look down. Blood drained slowly down the inside of his trouser leg and out on his shoe and from his shoe it flowed without haste to the floor. It was already a small pool.

I couldn't see where he had been shot. His teeth clicked and I thought he was going to speak, or try to speak. But that was the only sound from him. He had stopped breathing. His jaw fell slack. Then the rattle started. It isn't a rattle at all, of course. It isn't anything like a rattle.

Rubber heels squeaked on the linoleum between the rug and the door sill. The white fingers slid away from the door-frame. The man's body started to wind up on the legs. The legs refused to hold it. They scissored. His torso turned in mid-air, like a swimmer in a wave, and jumped at me.

In the same moment his other arm, the one that had been out of sight, came up and over in a galvanic sweep that seemed not to have any possible living impetus behind it. It fell across my left shoulder as I reached for him. A bee stung me between the shoulder-blades. Something besides the bottle of alcohol I had been holding thumped to the floor and rattled against the bottom of the wall.

I clamped my teeth hard and spread my feet and caught him under the arms. He weighed like five men. I took a step back and tried to hold him up. It was like trying to lift one end of a fallen tree. I went down with him. His head bumped the floor. I couldn't help it. There wasn't enough of me working to stop it. I straightened him out a bit and got away from him. I climbed up on my knees, and bent down and listened. The rattle stopped. There was a long silence. Then there was a muted sigh, very quiet and indolent and without urgency. Another silence. Another still slower sigh, languid and peaceful as a summer breeze drifting past the nodding roses.

Something happened to his face and behind his face, the indefinable thing that happens in that always baffling and inscrutable moment, the smoothing out, the going back over the years to the age of innocence. The face now had a vague inner amusement, an almost roguish lift at the corners of the mouth. All of which was very silly, because I knew damn well, if I ever knew anything at all, that Orrin P. Quest had not been that kind of boy.

In the distance a siren wailed. I stayed kneeling and listened. It wailed and went away. I got to my feet and went over and looked out of the side window. In front of The Garland Home of Peace another funeral was forming up. The street was thick with cars again. People walked slowly up the path past the tree-roses. Very slowly, the men with their hats in their hands long before they reached the little colonial porch.

I dropped the curtain and went over and picked up the bottle of ethyl alcohol and wiped it off with my handkerchief and laid it aside. I was no longer interested in alcohol. I bent down again and the bee-sting between my shoulder-blades reminded me that there was something else to pick up. A thing with a round white wooden handle that lay against the baseboard. An ice pick with a filed-down blade not more than three inches long. I held it against the light and looked at the needle-sharp tip. There might or might not have been a faint stain of my blood on it. I pulled a finger gently beside the point. No blood. The point was very sharp.

I did some more work with my handkerchief and then bent down and put the ice pick on the palm of his right hand, white and waxy against the dull nap of the carpet. It looked too arranged. I shook his arm enough to make it roll off his hand to the floor. I thought about going through his pockets, but a more ruthless hand than mine would have done that already.

In a flash of sudden panic I went through mine instead.

Nothing had been taken. Even the Luger under my arm had been left. I dragged it out and sniffed at it. It had not been fired, something I should have known without looking. You don't walk around much after being shot with a Luger.

I stepped over the dark red pool in the doorway and looked along the hall. The house was still silent and waiting. The blood trail led me back and across to a room furnished like a den. There was a studio couch and a desk, some books and medical journals, an ashtray with five fat oval stubs in it. A metallic glitter near the leg of the studio couch turned out to be a used shell from an automatic, .32 calibre. I found another under the desk. I put them in my pocket.

I went back out and up the stairs. There were two bedrooms, both in use, one pretty thoroughly stripped of clothes. In an ashtray more of Dr Lagardie's oval stubs. The other contained Orrin Quest's meagre wardrobe, his spare suit and overcoat neatly hung in the closet, his shirts and socks and underwear equally neat in the drawers of a chest. Under the shirts at the back I found a Leica with an F.2 lens.

I left all these things as they were and went back downstairs into the room where the dead man lay indifferent to these trifles. I wiped off a few more door-knobs out of sheer perverseness, hesitated over the phone in the front room, and left without touching it. The fact that I was still walking around was a pretty good indication that the good Dr Lagardie hadn't killed anybody.

People were still crawling up the walk to the oddly undersized colonial porch of the funeral parlour across the street. An organ was moaning inside.

I went around the corner of the house and got into my car and left. I drove slowly and breathed deeply from the bottom of my lungs, but I still couldn't seem to get enough oxygen.

Bay City ends about four miles from the ocean. I stopped in front of the last drug store. It was time for me to make one more of my anonymous phone calls. Come and pick up the body, fellows. Who am I? Just a lucky boy who keeps finding them for you. Modest too. Don't even want my name mentioned.

I looked at the drug store and in through the plate-glass front. A girl with slanted cheaters was reading a magazine. She looked something like Orfamay Quest. Something tightened up my throat.

I let the clutch in and drove on. She had a right to know first, law or no law. And I was far outside the law already.

23

I stopped at the office door with the key in my hand. Then I went noiselessly along to the other door, the one that was always unlocked, and stood there and listened. She might be in there already, waiting, with her eyes shining behind the slanted cheaters and the small moist mouth willing to be kissed. I would have to tell her a harder thing than she dreamed of, and then after a while she would go and I would never see her again.

I didn't hear anything. I went back and unlocked the other door and picked the mail up and carried it over and dumped it on the desk. Nothing in it made me feel any taller. I left it and crossed to turn the latch in the other door and after a long slow moment I opened it and looked out. Silence and emptiness. A folded piece of paper lay at my feet. It had been pushed under the door. I picked it up and unfolded it.

'Please call me at the apartment house. Most urgent. I must see you.' It was signed D.

I dialled the number of the Château Bercy and asked for Miss Gonzales. Who was calling, please? One moment please, Mr Marlowe. Buzz, buzz. Buzz, buzz.

''Allow?'

'The accent's a bit thick this afternoon.'

'Ah, it is you, amigo. I waited so long in your funny little office. Can you come over here and talk to me?'

'Impossible. I'm waiting for a call.'

'Well, may I come there?'

'What's it all about?'

'Nothing I could discuss on the telephone, amigo.'

'Come ahead.'

I sat there and waited for the telephone to ring. It didn't ring. I looked out of the window. The crowd was seething on the boulevard, the kitchen of the coffee shop next door was pouring the smell of Blue Plate Specials out of its ventilator shaft. Time passed and I sat there hunched over the desk, my chin in a hand, staring at the mustard-yellow plaster of the end wall, seeing on it the vague figure of a dying man with a short ice pick in his hand, and feeling the sting of its point between my shoulder-blades. Wonderful what Hollywood will do to a nobody. It will make a radiant glamour queen out of a drab little wench who ought to be ironing a truck driver's shirts, a he-man hero with shining eyes and brilliant smile reeking of sexual charm out of some overgrown kid who was meant to go to work with a lunchbox. Out of a Texas car hop with the literacy of a character in a comic strip it will make an international courtesan, married six times to six millionaires and so blase and decadent at the end of it that her idea of a thrill is to seduce a furniture-mover in a sweaty under-shirt.

And by remote control it might even take a small-town prig like Orrin Quest and make an ice-pick murderer out of him in a matter of months, elevating his simple meanness into the classic sadism of the multiple killer.

It took her a little over ten minutes to get there. I heard the door open and close and I went through to the waiting-room and there she was, the All-American Gardenia. She hit me right between the eyes. Her own were deep and dark and unsmiling.

She was all in black, like the night before, but a tailormade outfit this time, a wide black straw hat set at a rakish angle, the collar of a white silk shirt folded out over the collar of her jacket, and her throat brown and supple and her mouth as red as a new fire engine.

'I waited a long time,' she said. 'I have not had any lunch.'

'I had mine,' I said. 'Cyanide. Very satisfying. I've only just stopped looking blue.'

'I am not in an amusing mood this morning, amigo.'

'You don't have to amuse me,' I said. 'I amuse myself. I do a brother act that has me rolling in the aisle. Let's go inside.'

We went into my private thinking parlour and sat down.

'You always wear black?' I asked.

'But yes. It is more exciting when I take my clothes off.'

'Do you have to talk like a whore?'

'You do not know much about whores, amigo. They are always most respectable. Except, of course, the very cheap ones.'

'Yeah,' I said. 'Thanks for telling me. What is the urgent matter we have to talk about? Going to bed with you is not urgent. It can be done any day.'

'You are in a nasty mood.'

'Okay, I'm in a nasty mood.'

She got one of her long brown cigarettes out of her bag and fitted it carefully into the golden tweezers. She waited for me to light it for her. I didn't, so she lit it herself with a golden lighter.

She held this doohickey in a black gauntleted glove and stared at me out of depthless black eyes that had no laughter in them now.

'Would you like to go to bed with me?'

'Most anyone would. But let's leave sex out of it for now.'

'I do not draw a very sharp line between business and sex,' she said evenly. 'And you cannot humiliate me. Sex is a net with which I catch fools. Some of these fools are useful and generous. Occasionally one is dangerous.'

She paused thoughtfully.

I said: 'If you're waiting for me to say something that lets on I know who a certain party is – Okay, I know who he is.'

'Can you prove it?'

'Probably not. The cops couldn't.'

'The cops,' she said contemptuously, 'do not always tell all they know. They do not always prove everything they could prove. I suppose you know he was in jail for ten days last February.'

'Yes.'

'Did it not occur to you as strange that he did not get bail?'

'I don't know what charge they had him on. If it was as a material witness—'

'Do you not think he could get the charge changed to something bailable – if he really wanted to?'

'I haven't thought much about it,' I lied. 'I don't know the man.'

'You have never spoken to him?' she asked idly, a little too idly.

I didn't answer.

She laughed shortly. 'Last night, amigo. Outside Mavis Weld's apartment. I was sitting in a car across the street.'

'I may have bumped into him accidentally. Was that the guy?'

'You do not fool me at all.'

'Okay. Miss Weld was pretty rough with me. I went away sore. Then I met this ginzo with her door-key in his hand. I yank it out of his hand and toss it behind some bushes. Then I apologize and go get it for him. He seemed like a nice little guy too.'

'Ver-ry nice,' she drawled. 'He was *my* boyfriend also.'

I grunted.

'Strange as it may seem I'm not a hell of a lot interested in your love life, Miss Gonzales. I assume it covers a wide field – all the way from Stein to Steelgrave.'

'Stein?' she asked softly. 'Who is Stein?'

'A Cleveland hot shot that got himself gunned in front of your apartment house last February. He had an apartment there.

I thought perhaps you might have met him.'

She let out a silvery little laugh. 'Amigo, there are men I do not know. Even at the Château Bercy.'

'Reports say he was gunned two blocks away,' I said. 'I like it better that it happened right in front. And you were looking out of the window and saw it happen. And saw the killer run away and just under a street light he turned back and the light caught his face and darned if it wasn't old man Steelgrave. You recognized him by his rubber nose and the fact that he was wearing his tall hat with the pigeons on it.'

She didn't laugh.

'You like it better that way,' she purred.

'We could make more money that way.'

'But Steelgrave was in jail,' she smiled. 'And even if he was not in jail – even if, for example, I happened to be friendly with a certain Dr Chalmers who was county jail physician at the time and he told me, in an intimate moment, that he had given Steelgrave a pass to go to the dentist – with a guard, of course, but the guard was a reasonable man – on the very day Stein was shot – even if this happened to be true, would it not be a very poor way to use the information by blackmailing Steelgrave?'

'I hate to talk big,' I said, 'but I'm not afraid of Steelgrave – or a dozen like him in one package.'

'But I am, amigo. A witness to a gang murder is not in a very safe position in this country. No, we will not blackmail Steelgrave. And we will not say anything about Mr Stein, whom I may not have known. It is enough that Mavis Weld is a close friend of a known gangster and is seen in public with him.'

'We'd have to prove he was a known gangster,' I said.

'Can we not do that?'

'How?'

She made a disappointed mouth. 'But I felt sure that was what you had been doing these last couple of days.'

'Why?'

'I have private reasons.'

'They mean nothing to me while you keep them private.'

She got rid of the brown cigarette stub in my ashtray. I leaned over and squashed it out with the stub of a pencil. She touched my hand lightly with a gauntleted finger. Her smile was the reverse of anaesthetic. She leaned back and crossed her legs. The little lights began to dance in her eyes. It was a long time between passes – for her.

'Love is such a dull word,' she mused. 'It amazes me that the

English language, so rich in the poetry of love, can accept such a feeble word for it. It has no life, no resonance. It suggests to me little girls in ruffled summer dresses, with little pink smiles, and little shy voices, and probably the most unbecoming underwear.'

I said nothing. With an effortless change of pace she became businesslike again.

'Mavis will get seventy-five thousand dollars a picture from now on, and eventually one hundred and fifty thousand dollars. She has started to climb and nothing will stop her. Except possibly a bad scandal.'

'Then somebody ought to tell her who Steelgrave is,' I said. 'Why don't you? And incidentally, suppose we did have all this proof, what's Steelgrave doing all the time we're putting the bite on Weld?'

'Does he have to know? I hardly think she would tell him. In fact, I hardly think she would go on having anything to do with him. But that would not matter to us – if we had our proof. And if she knew we had it.'

Her black gauntleted hand moved towards her black bag, stopped, drummed lightly on the edge of the desk, and so got back to where she could drop it in her lap. She hadn't looked at the bag. I hadn't either.

I stood up. 'I might happen to be under some obligation to Miss Weld. Ever think of that?'

She just smiled.

'And if that was so,' I said, 'don't you think it's about time you got the hell out of my office?'

She put her hands on the arms of her chair and started to get up, still smiling. I scooped up the bag before she could change direction. Her eyes filled with glare. She made a spitting sound.

I opened the bag and went through and found a white envelope that looked a little familiar. Out of it I shook the photo at The Dancers, the two pieces fitted together and pasted on another piece of paper.

I closed the bag and tossed it to her.

She was on her feet now, her lips drawn back over her teeth. She was very silent.

'Interesting,' I said, and snapped a digit at the glazed surface of the print. 'If it's not a fake. Is that Steelgrave?'

The silvery laugh bubbled up again. 'You are a ridiculous character, amigo. You really are. I did not know they made such people any more.'

'Pre-war stock,' I said. 'We're getting scarcer every day. Where did you get this?'

'From Mavis Weld's purse in Mavis Weld's dressing-room. While she was on the set.'

'She knows?'

'I wonder where she got it.'

'From you.'

'Nonsense.' I raised my eyebrows a few inches. 'Where would *I* get it?'

She reached the gauntleted hand across the desk. Her voice was cold. 'Give it back to me, please.'

'I'll give it back to Mavis Weld. And I hate to tell you this, Miss Gonzales, but I'd never get anywhere as a blackmailer. I just don't have the engaging personality.'

'Give it back to me!' she said sharply. 'If you do not—'

She cut herself off. I waited for her to finish. A look of contempt showed on her smooth features.

'Very well,' she said. 'It is my mistake. I thought you were smart. I can see that you are just another dumb private eye. This shabby little office,' she waved a black gloved hand at it, 'and the shabby little life that goes on here – they ought to tell me what sort of idiot you are.'

'They do,' I said.

She turned slowly and walked to the door. I got around the desk and she let me open it for her.

She went out slowly. The way she did it hadn't been learned at business college.

She went on down the hall without looking back. She had a beautiful walk.

The door bumped against the pneumatic door-closer and very softly clicked shut. It seemed to take a long time to do that. I stood there watching it as if I had never seen it happen before. Then I turned and started back towards my desk and the phone rang.

I picked it up and answered it. It was Christy French. 'Marlowe? We'd like to see you down at headquarters.'

'Right away?'

'If not sooner,' he said and hung up.

I slipped the pasted-together print from under the blotter and went over to put it in the safe with the others. I put my hat on and closed the window. There was nothing to wait for. I looked at the green tip on the sweep hand of my watch. It was a long time until five o'clock. The sweep hand went around and around the dial like a door to door salesman. The hands stood at four-ten. You'd think she'd have called up by now. I peeled my coat off and unstrapped the shoulder harness and locked it with the Luger in the desk drawer. The cops don't like you to be wearing a gun in their territory. Even if you have the right to wear one. They like you to come in properly humble, with your hat in your hand, and your voice low and polite, and your eyes full of nothing.

I looked at the watch again. I listened. The building seemed quiet this afternoon. After a while it would be silent and then the madonna of the dark grey mop would come shuffling along the hall, trying door-knobs.

I put my coat back on and locked the communicating door and switched off the buzzer and let myself out into the hallway. And then the phone rang. I nearly took the door off its hinges getting back to it. It was her voice all right, but it had a tone I had never heard before. A cool, balanced tone, not flat or empty or dead, or even childish. Just the voice of a girl I didn't know and yet did know. What was in that voice I knew before she said more than three words.

'I called you up because you told me to,' she said. 'But you don't have to tell me anything. I went down there.'

I was holding the phone with both hands.

'You went down there,' I said. 'Yes. I heard that. So?'

'I – borrowed a car,' she said. 'I parked across the street. There were so many cars you would never have noticed me. There's a funeral home there. I wasn't following you. I tried to go after you when you came out but I don't know the streets down there at all. I lost you. So I went back.'

'What did you go back for?'

'I don't really know. I thought you looked kind of funny when you came out of the house. Or maybe I just had a feeling. He being my brother and all. So I went back and rang the bell. And nobody answered the door. I thought that was funny too. Maybe I'm psychic or something. All of a sudden I seemed to have to get into that house. And I didn't know how to do it, but I had to.'

'That's happened to me,' I said, and it was my voice, but somebody had been using my tongue for sandpaper.

'I called the police and told them I had heard shots,' she said. 'They came and one of them got into the house through a window. And then he let the other one in. And after a while they let me in. And they wouldn't let me go. I had to tell them all about it, who he was, and that I had lied about the shots, but I was afraid something had happened to Orrin. And I had to tell them about you too.'

'That's all right,' I said. 'I'd have told them myself as soon as I could get a chance to tell *you*.'

'It's kind of awkward for you, isn't it?'

'Yes.'

'Will they arrest you or something?'

'They could.'

'You left him lying there on the floor. Dead. You had to, I guess.'

'I had my reasons,' I said. 'They won't sound too good, but I had them. It made no difference to him.'

'Oh, you'd have your reasons all right,' she said. 'You're very smart. You'd always have reasons for things. Well, I guess you'll have to tell the police your reasons too.'

'Not necessarily.'

'Oh yes, you will,' the voice said, and there was a ring of pleasure in it I couldn't account for. 'You certainly will. They'll make you.'

'We won't argue about that,' I said. 'In my business a fellow does what he can to protect a client. Sometimes he goes a little too far. That's what I did. I've put myself where they can hurt me. But not entirely for you.'

'You left him lying on the floor, dead,' she said. 'And I don't care what they do to you. If they put you in prison, I think I would like that. I bet you'll be awfully brave about it.'

'Sure,' I said. 'Always a gay smile. Do you see what he had in his hand?'

'He didn't have anything in his hand.'

'Well, lying near his hand.'

'There wasn't anything. There wasn't anything at all. What sort of thing?'

'That's fine,' I said. 'I'm glad of that. Well, goodbye. I'm going down to headquarters now. They want to see me. Good luck, if I don't see you again.'

'You'd better keep your good luck,' she said. 'You might need it. And I wouldn't want it.'

'I did my best for you,' I said. 'Perhaps if you'd given me a little more information in the beginning—'

She hung up while I was saying it.

I put the phone down in its cradle as gently as if it was a baby. I got out a handkerchief and wiped the palms of my hands. I went over to the wash-basin and washed my hands and face. I sloshed cold water on my face and dried it off hard with the towel and looked at it in the mirror.

'You drove off a cliff all right,' I said to the face.

24

In the centre of the room was a long yellow oak table. Its edges were unevenly grooved with cigarette burns. Behind it was a window with wire over the stippled glass. Also behind it with a mess of papers spread out untidily in front of him was Detective-Lieutenant Fred Beifus. At the end of the table leaning back on two legs of an armchair was a big burly man whose face had for me the vague familiarity of a face previously seen in a half-tone on newsprint. He had a jaw like a park bench. He had the butt end of a carpenter's pencil between his teeth. He seemed to be awake and breathing, but apart from that he just sat.

There were two roll-top desks at the other side of the table and there was another window. One of the roll-top desks was backed to the window. A woman with orange-coloured hair was typing out a report on a typewriter stand beside the desk. At the other desk, which was endways to the window, Christy French sat in a tilted back swivel chair with his feet on the corner of the desk. He was looking out of the window, which was open and afforded a magnificent view of the police parking lot and the back of a billboard.

'Sit down there,' Beifus said, pointing.

I sat down across from him in a straight oak chair without arms. It was far from new and when new had not been beautiful.

'This is Lieutenant Moses Maglashan of the Bay City police,' Beifus said. 'He don't like you any better than we do.'

Lieutenant Moses Maglashan took the carpenter's pencil out of his mouth and looked at the teeth marks in the fat octagonal pencil butt. Then he looked at me. His eyes went over me slowly, exploring me, noting me, cataloguing me. He said nothing. He put the pencil back in his mouth.

Beifus said: 'Maybe I'm queer, but for me you don't have no more sex appeal than a turtle.' He half turned to the typing woman in the corner. 'Millie.'

She swung around from the typewriter to a shorthand notebook. 'Name's Philip Marlowe,' Beifus said. 'With an "e" on the end, if you're fussy. Licence number?'

He looked back at me. I told him. The orange queen wrote

without looking up. To say she had a face that would have stopped a clock would have been to insult her. It would have stopped a runaway horse.

'Now if you're in the mood,' Beifus told me, 'you could start in at the beginning and give us all the stuff you left out yesterday. Don't try to sort it out. Just let it flow natural. We got enough stuff to check you as you go along.'

'You want me to make a statement?'

'A very full statement,' Beifus said. 'Fun, huh?'

'This statement is to be voluntary and without coercion?'

'Yeah. They all are.' Beifus grinned.

Maglashan looked at me steadily for a moment. The orange queen turned back to her typing. Nothing for her yet. Thirty years of it had perfected her timing.

Maglashan took a heavy worn pigskin glove out of his pocket and put it on his right hand and flexed his fingers.

'What's that for?' Beifus asked him.

'I bite my nails times,' Maglashan said. 'Funny. Only bite 'em on my right hand.' He raised his slow eyes to stare at me. 'Some guys are more voluntary than others,' he said idly. 'Something to do with the kidneys, they tell me. I've known guys of the not-so-voluntary type that had to go to the can every fifteen minutes for weeks after they got voluntary. Couldn't seem to hold water.'

'Just think of that,' Beifus said wonderingly.

'Then there's the guys can't talk above a husky whisper,' Maglashan went on. 'Like punch-drunk fighters that have stopped too many with their necks.'

Maglashan looked at me. It seemed to be my turn.

'Then there's the type that won't go to the can at all,' I said. 'They try too hard. Sit in a chair like this for thirty hours straight. Then they fall down and rupture a spleen or burst a bladder. They over-cooperate. And after sunrise court, when the tank is empty, you find them dead in a dark corner. Maybe they ought to have seen a doctor, but you can't figure everything, can you, Lieutenant?'

'We figure pretty close down in Bay City,' he said. 'When we got anything to figure with.'

There were hard lumps of muscle at the corners of his jaws. His eyes had a reddish glare behind them.

'I could do lovely business with you,' he said, staring at me. 'Just lovely.'

'I'm sure you could, Lieutenant. I've always had a swell time in Bay City – while I stayed conscious.'

'I'd keep you conscious a long long time, baby. I'd make a point of it. I'd give it my personal attention.'

Christy French turned his head slowly and yawned. 'What makes you Bay City cops so tough?' he asked. 'You pickle your nuts in salt-water or something?'

Beifus put his tongue out so that the tip showed and ran it along his lips.

'We've always been tough,' Maglashan said, not looking at him. 'We like to be tough. Jokers like this character here keep us tuned up.' He turned back to me. 'So you're the sweetheart that phoned in about Clausen. You're right handy with a pay phone, ain't you, sweetheart?'

I didn't say anything.

'I'm talking to you, sweetheart,' Maglashan said. 'I asked you a question, sweetheart. When I ask a question I get answered. Get that, sweetheart?'

'Keep on talking and you'll answer yourself,' Christy French said. 'And maybe you won't like the answer, and maybe you'll be so damn tough you'll have to knock yourself out with that glove. Just to prove it.'

Maglashan straightened up. Red spots the size of half-dollars glowed dully on his cheeks.

'I come up here to get cooperation,' he told French slowly. 'The big razzoo I can get to home. From my wife. Here I don't expect the wise numbers to work out on me.'

'You'll get cooperation,' French said. 'Just don't try to steal the picture with that nineteen-thirty dialogue.' He swung his chair around and looked at me. 'Let's take out a clean sheet of paper and play like we're just starting this investigation. I know all your arguments. I'm no judge of them. The point is, do you want to talk or get booked as a material witness?'

'Ask the questions,' I said. 'If you don't like the answers, you can book me. If you book me, I get to make a phone call.'

'Correct,' French said, '*if* we book you. But we don't have to. We can ride the circuit with you. It might take days.'

'And canned cornbeef hash to eat,' Beifus put in cheerfully.

'Strictly speaking, it wouldn't be legal,' French said. 'But we do it all the time. Like you do a few things which you hadn't ought to do maybe. Would you say you were legal in this picture?'

'No.'

Maglashan let out a deep-throated 'Ha!'

I looked across at the orange queen who was back to her notebook, silent and indifferent.

'You got a client to protect,' French said.

'Maybe.'

'You mean you did have a client. She ratted on you.'

I said nothing.

'Name's Orfamay Quest,' French said, watching me.

'Ask your questions,' I said.

'What happened down there on Idaho Street?'

'I went there looking for her brother. He'd moved away, she said, and she'd come out here to see him. She was worried. The manager, Clausen, was too drunk to talk sense. I looked at the register and saw another man had moved into Quest's room. I talked to this man. He told me nothing that helped.'

French reached around and picked a pencil off the desk and tapped it against his teeth. 'Ever see this man again?'

'Yes. I told him who I was. When I went back downstairs Clausen was dead. And somebody had torn a page out of the register. The page with Quest's name on it. I called the police.'

'But you didn't stick around?'

'I had no information about Clausen's death.'

'But you didn't stick around,' French repeated. Maglashan made a savage noise in his throat and threw the carpenter's pencil clear across the room. I watched it bounce against the wall and floor and come to a stop.

'That's correct,' I said.

'In Bay City,' Maglashan said, 'we could murder you for that.'

'In Bay City you could murder me for wearing a blue tie,' I said.

He started to get up. Beifus looked sideways at him and said: 'Leave Christy to handle it. There's always a second show.'

'We could break you for that,' French said to me without inflexion.

'Consider me broke,' I said. 'I never liked the business anyway.'

'So you came back to your office. What then?'

'I reported to the client. Then a guy called me up and asked me over to the Van Nuys Hotel. He was the same guy I had talked to down on Idaho Street, but with a different name.'

'You could have told us that, couldn't you?'

'If I had, I'd have had to tell you everything. That would have violated the conditions of my employment.'

French nodded and tapped his pencil. He said slowly: 'A murder wipes out agreements like that. Two murders ought to do it double. And two murders by the same method, treble. You don't look good, Marlowe. You don't look good at all.'

'I don't even look good to the client,' I said, 'after today.'

'What happened today?'

'She told me her brother had called her up from this doctor's house. Dr Lagardie. The brother was in danger. I was to hurry on down and take care of him. I hurried on down. Dr Lagardie and his nurse had the office closed. They acted scared. The police had been there.' I looked at Maglashan.

'Another of his phone calls,' Maglashan snarled.

'Not me this time,' I said.

'All right. Go on,' French said, after a pause.

'Largardie denied knowing anything about Orrin Quest. He sent his nurse home. Then he slipped me a doped cigarette and I went away from there for a while. When I came to I was alone in the house. Then I wasn't. Orrin Quest, or what was left of him, was scratching at the door. He fell through it and died as I opened it. With his last ounce of strength he tried to stick me with an ice pick.' I moved my shoulders. The place between them was a little stiff and sore, nothing more.

French looked hard at Maglashan. Maglashan shook his head, but French kept on looking at him. Beifus began to whistle under his breath. I couldn't make out the tune at first, and then I could. It was Old Man Mose is Dead.

French turned his head and said slowly: 'No ice pick was found by the body.'

'I left it where it fell,' I said.

Maglashan said: 'Looks like I ought to be putting on my glove again.' He stretched it between his fingers. 'Somebody's a goddamn liar and it ain't me.'

'All right,' French said. 'All right. Let's not be theatrical. Suppose the kid did have an ice pick in his hand, that doesn't prove he was born holding one.'

'Filed down,' I said. 'Short. Three inches from the handle to the tip of the point. That's not the way they come from the hardware store.'

'Why would he want to stick you?' Beifus asked with his derisive grin. 'You were his pal. You were down there to keep him safe for his sister.'

'I was just something between him and the light,' I said. 'Something that moved and could have been a man and could have been the man that hurt him. He was dying on his feet. I'd never seen him before. If he ever saw me, I didn't know it.'

'It could have been a beautiful friendship,' Beifus said with a sigh. 'Except for the ice pick, of course.'

'And the fact that he had it in his hand and tried to stick me with it could mean something.'

'For instance what?'

'A man in his condition acts from instinct. He doesn't invent new techniques. He got me between the shoulder-blades, a sting, the feeble last effort of a dying man. Maybe it would have been a different place and a much deeper penetration if he had had his health.'

Maglashan said: 'How much longer we have to barber round with this monkey? You talk to him like he was human. Leave me talk to him my way.'

'The captain doesn't like it,' French said casually.

'Hell with the captain.'

'The captain doesn't like small town cops saying the hell with him,' French said.

Maglashan clamped his teeth tight and the line of his jaw showed white. His eyes narrowed and glistened. He took a deep breath through his nose.

'Thanks for the cooperation,' he said, and stood up. 'I'll be on my way.' He rounded the corner of the table and stopped beside me. He put his left hand out and tilted my chin up again.

'See you again, sweetheart. In *my* town.'

He lashed me across the face twice with the wrist end of the glove. The buttons stung sharply. I put my hand up and rubbed my lower lip.

French said: 'For Chrissake, Maglashan, sit down and let the guy speak his piece. And keep your hands off him.'

Maglashan looked back at him and said: 'Think you can make me?'

French just shrugged. After a moment Maglashan rubbed his big hand across his mouth and strolled back to his chair. French said:

'Let's have your ideas about all this, Marlowe.'

'Among other things Clausen was probably pushing reefers,' I said. 'I sniffed marijuana smoke in his apartment. A tough little guy was counting money in the kitchen when I got there. He had a gun and a sharpened rat-tail file, both of which he tried to use on me. I took them away from him and he left. He would be the runner. But Clausen was liquored to a point where you wouldn't want to trust him any more. They don't go for that in the organizations. The runner thought I was a dick. Those people wouldn't want Clausen picked up. He would be too easy to milk. The minute they smelled dick around the house Clausen would be missing.'

French looked at Maglashan. 'That make any sense to you?'

'It could happen,' Maglashan said grudgingly.

French said: 'Suppose it was so, what's it got to do with this Orrin Quest?'

'Anybody can smoke reefers,' I said. 'If you're dull and lonely and depressed and out of a job, they might be very attractive. But when you smoke them you get warped and calloused emotions. And marijuana affects different people different ways. Some it makes very tough and some it just makes never-no-mind. Suppose Quest tried to put the bite on somebody and threatened to go to the police. Quite possibly all three murders are connected with the reefer gang.'

'That don't jibe with Quest having a filed-down ice pick,' Beifus said.

I said: 'According to the lieutenant here he didn't have one. So I must have imagined that. Anyhow, he might just have picked it up. They might be standard equipment around Dr Lagardie's house. Get anything on him?'

He shook his head. 'Not so far.'

'He didn't kill me, probably he didn't kill anybody,' I said. 'Quest told his sister – according to her – that he was working for Dr Lagardie, but that some gangsters were after him.'

'This Lagardie,' French said, prodding at his blotter with a pen point, 'what do you make of him?'

'He used to practise in Cleveland. Downtown in a large way. He must have had his reasons for hiding out in Bay City.'

'Cleveland, huh?' French drawled and looked at a corner of the ceiling. Beifus looked down at his papers. Maglashan said:

'Probably an abortionist. I've had my eye on him for some time.'

'Which eye?' Beifus asked him mildly.

Maglashan flushed.

French said: 'Probably the one he didn't have on Idaho Street.'

Maglashan stood up violently. 'You boys think you're so goddamn smart it might interest you to know that we're just a small town police force. We got to double in brass once in a while. Just the same, I like that reefer angle. It might cut down my work considerable. I'm looking into it right now.'

He marched solidly to the door and left. French looked after him. Beifus did the same. When the door closed they looked at each other.

'I betcha they pull that raid again tonight,' Beifus said.

French nodded.

Beifus said: 'In a flat over a laundry. They'll go down on the beach and pull in three or four vagrants and stash them in the flat and then they'll line them up for the camera boys after they pull the raid.'

French said: 'You're talking too much, Fred.'

Beifus grinned and was silent. French said to me: 'If you were guessing, what would you guess they were looking for in that room at the Van Nuys?'

'A claim check for a suitcase full of weed.'

'Not bad,' French said. 'And still guessing where would it have been?'

'I thought about that. When I talked to Hicks down at Bay City he wasn't wearing his muff. A man doesn't around the house. But he was wearing it on the bed at the Van Nuys. Maybe he didn't put it on himself.'

French said: 'So?'

I said: 'Wouldn't be a bad place to stash a claim check.'

French said: 'You could pin it down with a piece of scotch tape. Quite an idea.'

There was a silence. The orange queen went back to her typing. I looked at my nails. They weren't as clean as they might be. After the pause French said slowly:

'Don't think for a minute you're in the clear, Marlowe. Still guessing, how come Dr Lagardie to mention Cleveland to you?'

'I took the trouble to look him up. A doctor can't change his name if he wants to go on practising. The ice pick made you think of Weepy Moyer. Weepy Moyer operated in Cleveland. Sunny Moe Stein operated in Cleveland. It's true the ice-pick technique was different, but it was an ice pick. You said yourself the boys might have learned. And always with these gangs there's a doctor somewhere in the background.'

'Pretty wild,' French said. 'Pretty loose connection.'

'Would I do myself any good if I tightened it up?'

'Can you?'

'I can try.'

French sighed. 'The little Quest girl is okay,' he said. 'I talked to her mother back in Kansas. She really did come out here to look for her brother. And she really did hire you to do it. She gives you a good write-up. Up to a point. She really did suspect her brother was mixed up in something wrong. You make any money on the deal?'

'Not much,' I said. 'I gave her back the fee. She didn't have much.'

'That way you don't have to pay income tax on it,' Beifus said.

French said: 'Let's break this off. The next move is up to the DA. And if I know Endicott, it will be a week from Tuesday before he decides how to play it.' He made a gesture towards the door.

I stood up. 'Will it be all right if I don't leave town?' I asked. They didn't bother to answer that one.

I just stood there and looked at them. The ice-pick wound between my shoulders had a dry sting, and the flesh around the place was stiff. The side of my face and mouth smarted where Maglashan had sideswiped me with his well-used pigskin glove. I was in the deep water. It was dark and unclear and the taste of the salt was in my mouth.

They just sat there and looked back at me. The orange queen was clacking her typewriter. Cop talk was no more treat to her than legs to a dance director. They had the calm weathered faces of healthy men in hard condition. They had the eyes they always have, cloudy and grey like freezing water. The firm set mouth, the hard little wrinkles at the corners of the eyes, the hard hollow meaningless stare, not quite cruel and a thousand miles from kind. The dull ready-made clothes, worn without style, with a sort of contempt; the look of men who are poor and yet proud of their power, watching always for ways to make it felt, to shove it into you and twist it and grin and watch you squirm, ruthless without malice, cruel and yet not always unkind. What would you expect them to be? Civilization had no meaning for them. All they saw of it was the failures, the dirt, the dregs, the aberrations and the disgust.

'What you standing there for?' Beifus asked sharply. 'You want us to give you a great big spitty kiss? No snappy comeback, huh? Too bad.' His voice fell away into a dull drone. He frowned and reached a pencil off the desk. With a quick motion of his fingers he snapped it in half and held the two halves out on his palm.

'We're giving you that much break,' he said thinly, the smile all gone. 'Go on out and square things up. What the hell you think we're turning you loose for? Maglashan bought you a rain check. Use it.'

I put my hand up and rubbed my lip. My mouth had too many teeth in it.

Beifus lowered his eyes to the table, picked up a paper and began to read it. Christy French swung around in his chair and put his feet on the desk and stared out of the open window at the parking lot. The orange queen stopped typing. The room was suddenly full of heavy silence, like a fallen cake.

I went on out, parting the silence as if I was pushing my way through water.

25

The office was empty again. No leggy brunettes, no little girls with slanted glasses, no neat dark men with gangsters' eyes.

I sat down at the desk and watched the light fade. The going home sounds had died away. Outside the neon signs began to glare at one another across the boulevard. There was something to be done, but I didn't know what. Whatever it was it would be useless. I tidied up my desk, listening to the scrape of a bucket on the tiling of the corridor. I put my papers away in the drawer, straightened the pen stand, got out a duster and wiped off the glass and then the telephone. It was dark and sleek in the fading light. It wouldn't ring tonight. Nobody would call me again. Not now, not this time. Perhaps not ever.

I put the duster away folded with the dust in it, leaned back and just sat, not smoking, not even thinking. I was a blank man. I had no face, no meaning, no personality, hardly a name. I didn't want to eat. I didn't even want a drink. I was the page from yesterday's calendar crumpled at the bottom of the wastebasket.

So I pulled the phone towards me and dialled Mavis Weld's number. It rang and rang and rang. Nine times. That's a lot of ringing, Marlowe. I guess there's nobody home. Nobody home to you. I hung up. Who would you like to call now? You got a friend somewhere that might like to hear your voice? No. Nobody.

Let the telephone ring, please. Let there be somebody to call up and plug me into the human race again. Even a cop. Even a Maglashan. Nobody has to like me. I just want to get off this frozen star.

The telephone rang.

'Amigo,' her voice said. 'There is trouble. Bad trouble. She wants to see you. She likes you. She thinks you are an honest man.'

'Where?' I asked. It wasn't really a question, just a sound I made. I sucked on a cold pipe and leaned my head on my hand, brooding at the telephone. It was a voice to talk to anyway.

'You will come?'

'I'd sit up with a sick parrot tonight. Where do I go?'

'I will come for you. I will be before your building in fifteen minutes. It is not easy to get where we go.'

'How is it coming back,' I asked, 'or don't we care?'

But she had already hung up.

Down at the drug-store lunch counter I had time to inhale two cups of coffee and a melted cheese sandwich with two slivers of ersatz bacon embedded in it, like dead fish in the silt at the bottom of a drained pool.

I was crazy. I liked it.

26

It was a black Mercury convertible with a light top. The top was up. When I leaned in at the door Dolores Gonzales slid over towards me along the leather seat.

'You drive please, amigo. I do not really ever like to drive.'

The light from the drug-store caught her face. She had changed her clothes again, but it was still all black, save for a flame-coloured shirt. Slacks and a kind of loose coat like a man's leisure jacket.

I leaned on the door of the car. 'Why didn't she call me?'

'She couldn't. She did not have the number and she had very little time.'

'Why?'

'It seemed to be while someone was out of the room for just a moment.'

'And where is this place she called from?'

'I do not know the name of the street. But I can find the house. That is why I come. Please get into the car and let us hurry.'

'Maybe,' I said. 'And again maybe I am not getting into the car. Old age and arthritis have made me cautious.'

'Always the wisecrack,' she said. 'It is a very strange man.'

'Always the wisecrack where possible,' I said, 'and it is a very ordinary guy with only one head — which has been rather harshly used at times. The times usually started out like this.'

'Will you make love to me tonight?' she asked softly.

'That is an open question. Probably not.'

'You would not waste your time. I am not one of those synthetic blondes with a skin you could strike matches on. These ex-laundresses with large bony hands and sharp knees and unsuccessful breasts.'

'Just for half an hour,' I said, 'let's leave the sex to one side. It's great stuff, like chocolate sundaes. But there comes a time you would rather cut your throat. I guess maybe I'd better cut mine.'

I went around the car and slid under the wheel and started the motor.

'We go west,' she said, 'through the Beverly Hills and then farther on.'

I let the clutch in and drifted around the corner to go south to Sunset. Dolores got one of her long brown cigarettes out.

'Did you bring a gun?' she asked.

'No. What would I want a gun for?' The inside of my left arm pressed against the Luger in the shoulder harness.

'It is better not perhaps.' She fitted the cigarette into the little golden tweezer thing and lit it with the golden lighter. The light flaring in her face seemed to be swallowed up by her depthless black eyes.

I turned west on Sunset and swallowed myself up in three lanes of race track drivers who were pushing their mounts hard to get nowhere and do nothing.

'What kind of trouble is Miss Weld in?'

'I do not know. She just said that it was trouble and she was much afraid and she needed you.'

'You ought to be able to think up a better story than that.'

She didn't answer. I stopped for a traffic signal and turned to look at her. She was crying softly in the dark.

'I would not hurt a hair of Mavis Weld's head,' she said. 'I do not quite expect that you would believe me.'

'On the other hand,' I said, 'maybe the fact that you don't have a story helps.'

She started to slide along the seat towards me.

'Keep to your own side of the car,' I said. 'I've got to drive this heap.'

'You do not want my head on your shoulder?'

'Not in this traffic.'

I stopped at Fairfax with the green light to let a man make a left turn. Horns blew violently behind. When I started again the car that had been right behind swung out and pulled level and a fat guy in a sweatshirt yelled:

'Aw go get yourself a hammock!'

He went on, cutting in so hard that I had to brake.

'I used to like this town,' I said, just to be saying something and not to be thinking too hard. 'A long time ago. There were trees along Wilshire Boulevard. Beverly Hills was a country town. Westwood was bare hills and lots offering at eleven hundred dollars and no takers. Hollywood was a bunch of frame houses on the inter-urban line. Los Angeles was just a big dry sunny place with ugly homes and no style, but good-hearted and peaceful. It had the climate they just yap about now. People used to sleep out on porches. Little groups who thought they were intellectual used to call it the Athens of America. It wasn't that, but it wasn't a neon-lighted slum either.'

We crossed La Cienega and went into the curve of the Strip. The Dancers was a blaze of light. The terrace was packed. The parking lot was like ants on a piece of overripe fruit.

'Now we get characters like this Steelgrave owning restaurants. We get guys like that fat boy that bawled me out back there. We've got the big money, the sharpshooters, the percentage workers, the fast dollar boys, the hoodlums out of New York and Chicago and Detroit – and Cleveland. We've got the flash restaurants and night clubs they run, and the hotels and apartment houses they own, and the grifters and con men and female bandits that live in them. The luxury trades, the pansy decorators, the Lesbian dress designers, the riff-raff of a big hardboiled city with no more personality than a paper cup. Out in the fancy suburbs dear old Dad is reading the sports page in front of a picture window, with his shoes off, thinking he is high class because he has a three-car garage. Mom is in front of her princess dresser trying to paint the suitcases out from under her eyes. And Junior is clamped on to the telephone calling up a succession of high school girls that talk pidgin English and carry contraceptives in their make-up kit.'

'It is the same in all big cities, amigo.'

'Real cities have something else, some individual bony structure under the muck. Los Angeles has Hollywood – and hates it. It ought to consider itself damn lucky. Without Hollywood it would be a mail order city. Everything in the catalogue you could get better somewhere else.'

'You are bitter tonight, amigo.'

'I've got a few troubles. The only reason I'm driving this car with you beside me is that I've got so much trouble a little more will seem like icing.'

'You have done something wrong?' she asked, and came close to me along the seat.

'Well, just collecting a few bodies,' I said. 'Depends on the point of view. The cops don't like the work done by us amateurs. They have their own service.'

'What will they do to you?'

'They might run me out of town and I couldn't care less. Don't push me so hard. I need this arm to shift gears with.'

She pulled away in a huff. 'I think you are very nasty to get along with,' she said. 'Turn right at the Lost Canyon Road.'

After a while we passed the University. All the lights of the city were on now, a vast carpet of them stretching down the slope to the south and on into the almost infinite distance. A plane droned overhead, losing altitude, its two signal lights winking on and off alternately. At Lost Canyon I swung right, skirting the big gates that led into Bel-Air. The road began to twist and climb. There were too many cars; the headlights glared angrily down the twisting white concrete. A little breeze blew down over the pass. There was the odour of wild sage, the acrid tang of eucalyptus, and the quiet smell of dust. Windows glowed on the hill-side. We passed a big white two-storeyed Monterey house that must have cost $70,000 and had a cut-out illuminated sign in front: 'Cairn Terriers.'

'The next to the right,' Dolores said.

I made the turn. The road got steeper and narrower. There were houses behind walls and masses of shrubbery but you couldn't see anything. Then we came to the fork and there was a police car with a red spotlight parked at it and across the right side of the fork two cars parked at right angles. A torch waved up and down. I slowed the car and stopped level with the police car. Two cops sat in it smoking. They didn't move.

'What goes on?'

'Amigo, I have no idea at all.' Her voice had a hushed withdrawn sound. She might have been a little scared. I didn't know what of.

A tall man, the one with the torch, came around the side of the car and poked the flash at me, then lowered it.

'We're not using this road tonight,' he said. 'Going anywhere in particular?'

I set the brake, reached for a flash which Dolores got out of the glove compartment. I snapped the light on to the tall man. He wore expensive-looking slacks, a sports shirt with initials on the pocket and a polka dot scarf knotted around his neck. He had horn-rimmed glasses and glossy wavy black hair. He looked as Hollywood as all hell.

I said: 'Any explanation – or are you just making law?'

'The law is over there, if you want to talk to them.' His voice held a tone of contempt. 'We are merely private citizens. We live around here. This is a residential neighbourhood. We mean to keep it that way.'

A man with a sporting gun came out of the shadows and stood beside the tall man. He held the gun in the crook of his left arm, pointed muzzle down. But he didn't look as if he just had it for ballast.

'That's jake with me,' I said. 'I didn't have any other plans. We just want to go to a place.'

'What place?' the tall man asked coolly.

I turned to Dolores. 'What place?'

'It is a white house on the hill, high up,' she said.

'And what did you plan to do up there?' the tall man asked.

'The man who lives there is my friend,' she said tartly.

He shone the flash in her face for a moment. 'You look swell,' he said. 'But we don't like your friend. We don't like characters that try to run gambling joints in this kind of neighbourhood.'

'I know nothing about a gambling joint,' Dolores told him sharply.

'Neither do the cops,' the tall man said. 'They don't even want to find out. What's your friend's name, darling?'

'That is not of your business,' Dolores spat at him.

'Go on home and knit socks, darling,' the tall man said. He turned to me.

'The road's not in use tonight,' he said. 'Now you know why.'

'Think you can make it stick?' I asked him.

'It will take more than you to change our plans. You ought to see our tax assessments. And those monkeys in the prowl car – and a lot more like them down at the City Hall – just sit on their hands when we ask for the law to be enforced.'

I unlatched the car door and swung it open. He stepped back and let me get out. I walked over to the prowl car. The two cops in it were leaning back lazily. Their loudspeaker was turned low, just audibly muttering. One of them was chewing gum rhythmically.

'How's to break up this road block and let the citizens through?' I asked him.

'No orders, buddy. We're just here to keep the peace. Anybody starts anything, we finish it.'

'They say there's a gambling house up the line.'

'They say,' the cop said.

'You don't believe them?'

'I don't even try, buddy,' he said, and spat past my shoulder.

'Suppose I have urgent business up there.'

He looked at me without expression and yawned.

'Thanks a lot, buddy,' I said.

I went back to the Mercury, got my wallet out and handed the tall man a card. He put his flash on it, and said: 'Well?'

He snapped the flash off and stood silent. His face began to take form palely in the darkness.

'I'm on business. To me it's important business. Let me through and perhaps you won't need this block tomorrow.'

'You talk large, friend.'

'Would I have the kind of money it takes to patronize a private gambling club?'

'*She* might,' he flicked an eye at Dolores. 'She might have brought you along for protection.'

He turned to the shotgun man. 'What do you think?'

'Chance it. Just two of them and both sober.'

The tall one snapped his flash on again and made a sidesweep with it back and forth. A car motor started. One of the block cars backed around on to the shoulder. I got in and started the Mercury, went on through the gap and watched the block car in the mirror as it took up position again, then cut its high beam lights.

'Is this the only way in and out of here?'

'They think it is, amigo. There is another way, but it is a private road through an estate. We would have had to go around by the valley side.'

'We nearly didn't get through,' I told her. 'This can't be very bad trouble anybody is in.'

'I knew you would find a way, amigo.'

'Something stinks,' I said nastily. 'And it isn't wild lilac.'

'Such a suspicious man. Do you not even want to kiss me?'

'You ought to have used a little of that back at the road block. That tall guy looked lonely. You could have taken him off in the bushes.'

She hit me across the mouth with the back of her hand. 'You son of a bitch,' she said casually. 'The next driveway on the left, if you please.'

We topped a rise and the road ended suddenly in a wide black circle edged with whitewashed stones. Directly ahead was a wire fence with a wide gate in it, and a sign on the gate: Private Road. No Trespassing. The gate was open and a padlock hung from one end of a loose chain on the posts. I turned the car around a white oleander bush and was in the motoryard of a long low white house with a tile roof and a four-car garage in the corner, under a walled balcony. Both the wide garage doors were closed. There was no light in the house. A high moon made a bluish radiance on the white stucco walls. Some of the lower windows were shuttered. Four packing cases full of trash stood in a row at the foot of the steps. There was a big garbage can upended and empty. There were two steel drums with papers in them.

There was no sound from the house, no sign of life. I stopped the Mercury, cut the lights and the motor, and just sat. Dolores moved in the corner. The seat seemed to be shaking. I reached across and touched her. She was shivering.

'What's the matter?'

'Get – get out, please,' she said as if her teeth chattered.

'How about you?'

She opened the door on her side and jumped out. I got out my side and left the door hanging open, the keys in the lock. She came around the back of the car and as she got close to me I could almost feel her shaking before she touched me. Then she leaned up against me hard, thigh to thigh and breast to breast. Her arms went around my neck.

'I am being very foolish,' she said softly. 'He will kill me for this – just as he killed Stein. Kiss me.'

I kissed her. Her lips were hot and dry. 'Is he in there?'

'Yes.'

'Who else?'

'Nobody else – except Mavis. He will kill her too.'

'Listen—'

'Kiss me again. I have not very long to live, amigo. When you are the finger for a man like that – you die young.'

I pushed her away from me, but gently.

She stepped back and lifted her right hand quickly. There was a gun in it now.

I looked at the gun. There was a dull shine on it from the high moon. She held it level and her hand wasn't shaking now.

'What a friend I would make if I pulled this trigger,' she said.

'They'd hear the shot down the road.'

She shook her head. 'No, there is a little hill between. I do not think they would hear, amigo.'

I thought the gun would jump when she pulled the trigger. If I dropped just at the right moment—

I wasn't that good. I didn't say anything. My tongue felt large in my mouth.

She went on slowly, in a soft, tired voice: 'With Stein it did not matter. I would have killed him myself, gladly. That filth. To die is not much, to kill is not much. But to entice people to

524

their deaths—' She broke off with what might have been a sob. 'Amigo, I liked you for some strange reason. I should be far beyond such nonsense. Mavis took him away from me, but I did not want him to kill her. The world is full of men who have enough money.'

'He seems like a nice little guy,' I said, still watching the hand that held the gun. Not a quiver in it now.

She laughed contemptuously. 'Of course he does. That is why he is what he is. You think you are tough, amigo. You are a very soft peach compared with Steelgrave.' She lowered the gun and now it was my time to jump. I still wasn't good enough.

'He has killed a dozen men,' she said. 'With a smile for each one. I have known him for a long time. I knew him in Cleveland.'

'With ice picks?' I asked.

'If I give you the gun, will you kill him for me?'

'Would you believe me if I promised?'

'Yes.' Somewhere down the hill there was the sound of a car. But it seemed as remote as Mars, as meaningless as the chattering of monkeys in the Brazilian jungle. It had nothing to do with me.

'I'd kill him if I had to,' I said, licking along my lips.

I was leaning a little, knees bent, all set for a jump again.

'Good night, amigo. I wear black because I am beautiful and wicked – and lost.'

She held the gun out to me. I took it. I just stood there holding it. For another silent moment neither of us moved. Then she smiled and tossed her head and jumped into the car. She started the motor and slammed the door shut. She idled the motor down and sat looking out at me. There was a smile on her face now.

'I was pretty good in there, no?' she said softly.

Then the car backed violently with a harsh tearing of the tyres on the asphalt paving. The lights jumped on. The car curved away and was gone past the oleander bush. The lights turned left, into the private road. The lights drifted off among trees and the sound faded into the long-drawn whee of tree frogs. Then that stopped and for a moment there was no sound at all. And no light except the tired old moon.

I broke the magazine from the gun. It had seven shells in it. There was another in the breach. Two less than a full load. I sniffed at the muzzle. It had been fired since it was cleaned. Fired twice, perhaps.

I pushed the magazine into place again and held the gun on

the flat of my hand. It had a white bone grip. .32 calibre.

Orrin Quest had been shot twice. The two exploded shells I picked up on the floor of the room were .32 calibre.

And yesterday afternoon, in Room 332 of the Hotel Van Nuys, a blonde girl with a towel in front of her face had pointed a .32 calibre automatic with a white bone grip at me.

You can get too fancy about these things. You can also not get fancy enough.

27

I walked on rubber heels across to the garage and tried to open one of the two wide doors. There were no handles, so it must have been operated by a switch. I played a tiny pencil flash on the frame, but no switch looked at me.

I left that and prowled over to the trash barrels. Wooden steps went up to a service entrance. I didn't think the door would unlock for my convenience. Under the porch was another door. This was unlocked and gave on darkness and the smell of corded eucalyptus wood. I closed the door behind me and put the little flash on again. In the corner there was another staircase, with a thing like a dumb waiter beside it. It wasn't dumb enough to let me work it. I started up the steps.

Somewhere remotely something buzzed. I stopped. The buzzing stopped. I started again. The buzzing didn't. I went on up to a door with no knob, set flush. Another gadget.

But I found the switch to this one. It was an oblong movable plate set into the door-frame. Too many dusty hands had touched it. I pressed it and the door clicked and fell back off the latch. I pushed it open, with the tenderness of a young intern delivering his first baby.

Inside was a hallway. Through shuttered windows moonlight caught the white corner of a stove and the chromed griddle on top of it. The kitchen was big enough for a dancing class. An open arch led to a butler's pantry tiled to the ceiling. A sink, a huge ice box set into the wall, a lot of electrical stuff for making drinks without trying. You pick your poison, press a button, and four days later you wake up on the rubbing table in a re-conditioning parlour.

Beyond the butler's pantry a swing door. Beyond the swing door a dark dining-room with an open end to a glassed-in lounge into which the moonlight poured like water through the flood-gates of a dam.

A carpeted hall led off somewhere. From another flat arch a flying buttress of a staircase went up into more darkness, but shimmered as it went in what might have been glass brick and stainless steel.

At last I came to what should be the living-room. It was curtained and quite dark, but it had the feel of great size. The darkness was heavy in it and my nose twitched at a lingering odour that said somebody had been there not too long ago. I stopped breathing and listened. Tigers could be in the darkness watching me. Or guys with large guns, standing flatfooted, breathing softly with their mouths open. Or nothing and nobody and too much imagination in the wrong place.

I edged back to the wall and felt around for a light switch. There's always a light switch. Everybody has light switches. Usually on the right side as you go in. You go into a dark room and you want light. Okay, you have a light switch in a natural place at a natural height. This room hadn't. This was a different kind of house. They had odd ways of handling doors and lights. The gadget this time might be something fancy like having to sing A above high C, or stepping on a flat button under the carpet, or maybe you just spoke and said: 'Let there be light,' and a mike picked it up and turned the voice vibration into a low-power electrical impulse and a transformer built that up to enough voltage to throw a silent mercury switch.

I was psychic that night. I was a fellow who wanted company in a dark place and was willing to pay a high price for it. The Luger under my arm and the .32 in my hand made me tough. Two-gun Marlowe, the kid from Cyanide Gulch.

I took the wrinkles out of my lip and said aloud: 'Hello again. Anybody here needing a detective?'

Nothing answered me, not even a stand-in for an echo. The sound of my voice fell on silence like a tired head on a swansdown pillow.

And then amber light began to grow high up behind the cornice that circumnavigated the huge room. It brightened very slowly, as if controlled by the rheostat panel in a theatre. Heavy apricot-coloured curtains covered the windows.

The walls were apricot too. At the far end was a bar off to one side, a little catty-corner, reaching back into the space by the butler's pantry. There was an alcove with small tables and padded seats. There were floor lamps and soft chairs and love seats and the usual paraphernalia of a living-room, and there were long shrouded tables in the middle of the floor space.

The boys back at the road block had something after all. But the joint was dead. The room was empty of life. It was almost empty. Not quite empty.

A blonde in a pale cocoa fur coat stood leaning against the side of a grandfather's chair. Her hands were in the pockets of the coat. Her hair was fluffed out carelessly and her face was not chalk white because the light was not white.

'Hello again yourself,' she said in a dead voice. 'I still think you came too late.'

'Too late for what?'

I walked towards her, a movement which was always a pleasure. Even then, even in that too silent house.

'You're kind of cute,' she said. 'I didn't think you were cute. You found a way in. You—' her voice clicked off and strangled itself in her throat.

'I need a drink,' she said after a thick pause. 'Or maybe I'll fall down.'

'That's a lovely coat,' I said. I was up to her now. I reached out and touched it. She didn't move. Her mouth moved in and out, trembling.

'Stone marten,' she whispered. 'Forty thousand dollars. Rented. For the picture.'

'Is this part of the picture?' I gestured around the room.

'This is the picture to end all pictures – for me. I – I do need that drink. If I try to walk—' the clear voice whispered away into nothing. Her eyelids fluttered up and down.

'Go ahead and faint,' I said. 'I'll catch you on the first bounce.'

A smile struggled to arrange her face for smiling. She pressed her lips together, fighting hard to stay on her feet.

'Why did I come too late?' I asked. 'Too late for what?'

'Too late to be shot.'

'Shucks, I've been looking forward to it all evening. Miss Gonzales brought me.'

'I know.'

I reached out and touched the fur again. Forty thousand dollars is nice to touch, even rented.

'Dolores will be disappointed as hell,' she said, her mouth edged with white.

'No.'

'She put you on the spot – just as she did Stein.'

'She may have started out to. But she changed her mind.'

She laughed. It was a silly pooped out little laugh like a child trying to be supercilious at a playroom tea party.

528

'What a way you have with the girls,' she whispered. 'How the hell do you do it, wonderful? With doped cigarettes? It can't be your clothes or your money or your personality. You don't have any. You're not too young, nor too beautiful. You've seen your best days and—'

Her voice had been coming faster and faster, like a motor with a broken governor. At the end she was chattering. When she stopped, a spent sigh drifted along the silence and she caved at the knees and fell straight forward into my arms.

If it was an act it worked perfectly. I might have had guns in all nine pockets and they would have been as much use to me as nine little pink candles on a birthday cake.

But nothing happened. No hard characters peeked at me with automatics in their hands. No Steelgrave smiled at me with the faint dry remote killer's smile. No stealthy footstep crept up behind me.

She hung in my arms as limp as a wet tea towel and not as heavy as Orrin Quest, being less dead, but heavy enough to make the tendons in my knee joints ache. Her eyes were closed when I pushed her head away from my chest. Her breath was inaudible and she had that bluish look on the parted lips.

I got my right hand under her knees and carried her over to a gold couch and spread her out on it. I straightened up and went along to the bar. There was a telephone on the corner of it but I couldn't find the way through to the bottles. So I had to swing over the top. I got a likely-looking bottle with a blue and silver label and five stars on it. The cork had been loosened. I poured dark and pungent brandy into the wrong kind of glass and went back over the bar top, taking the bottle with me.

She was lying as I had left her, but her eyes were open.

'Can you hold a glass?'

She could, with a little help. She drank the brandy and pressed the edge of the glass hard against her lips as if she wanted to hold them still. I watched her breathe into the glass and cloud it. A slow smile formed itself on her mouth.

'It's cold tonight,' she said.

She swung her legs over the edge of the couch and put her feet on the floor.

'More,' she said, holding the glass out. I poured into it. 'Where's yours?'

'Not drinking. My emotions are being worked on enough without that.'

The second drink made her shudder. But the blue look had gone away from her mouth and her lips didn't glare like stoplights and the little etched lines at the corners of her eyes were not in relief any more.

'Who's working on your emotions?'

'Oh, a lot of women that keep throwing their arms around my neck and fainting on me and getting kissed and so forth. Quite a full couple of days for a beat-up gumshoe with no yacht.'

'No yacht,' she said. 'I'd hate that. I was brought up rich.'

'Yeah,' I said. 'You were born with a Cadillac in your mouth. And I could guess where.'

Her eyes narrowed. 'Could you?'

'Didn't think it was a very tight secret, did you?'

'I – I—' she broke off and made a helpless gesture. 'I can't think of any lines tonight.'

'It's the technicolor dialogue,' I said. 'It freezes up on you.'

'Aren't we talking like a couple of nuts?'

'We could be sensible. Where's Steelgrave?'

She just looked at me. She held the empty glass out and I took it, and put it somewhere or other without taking my eyes off her. Nor she hers off me. It seemed as if a long minute went by.

'He was here,' she said at last, as slowly as if she had to invent the words one at a time. 'May I have a cigarette?'

'The old cigarette stall,' I said. I got a couple out and put them in my mouth and lit them. I leaned across and tucked one between her ruby lips.

'Nothing's cornier that that,' she said. 'Except maybe butterfly kisses.'

'Sex is a wonderful thing,' I said. 'When you don't want to answer questions.'

She puffed loosely and blinked, then put her hand up to adjust the cigarette. After all these years I can never put a cigarette in a girl's mouth where she wants it.

She gave her head a toss and swung the soft loose hair around her cheeks and watched me to see how hard that hit me. All the whiteness had gone now. Her cheeks were a little flushed. But behind her eyes things watched and waited.

'You're rather nice,' she said, when I didn't do anything sensational. 'For the kind of guy you are.'

I stood that well too.

'But I don't really know what kind of guy you are, do I?' She laughed suddenly and a tear came from nowhere and slid down her cheek. 'For all I know you might be nice for any kind of guy.' She snatched the cigarette loose and put her hand to her mouth and bit on it. 'What's the matter with me? Am I drunk?'

'You're stalling for time,' I said. 'But I can't make up my mind whether it's to give someone time to get here – or to give some-body time to get far away from here. And again it could just be brandy on top of shock. You're a little girl and you want to cry into your mother's apron.'

'Not my mother,' she said. 'I could get as far crying into a rain barrel.'

'Dealt and passed. So where is Steelgrave?'

'You ought to be glad wherever he is. He had to kill you. Or thought he had.'

'You wanted me here, didn't you? Were you that fond of him?'

She blew cigarette ash off the back of her hand. A flake of it went into my eye and made me blink.

'I must have been,' she said, 'once.' She put a hand down on her knee and spread the fingers out, studying the nails. She brought her eyes up slowly without moving her head. 'It seems like about a thousand years ago I met a nice quiet little guy who knew how to behave in public and didn't shoot his charm around every bistro in town. Yes, I liked him. I liked him a lot.'

She put her hand up to her mouth and bit a knuckle. Then she put the same hand into the pocket of the fur coat and brought out a white-handled automatic, the brother of the one I had myself.

'And in the end I liked him with this,' she said.

I went over and took it out of her hand. I sniffed the muzzle. Yes. That made two of them fired around.

'Aren't you going to wrap it up in a handkerchief, the way they do in the movies?'

I just dropped it into my other pocket, where it could pick up a few interesting crumbs of tobacco and some seeds that grow only on the south-east slope of the Beverly Hills City Hall. It might amuse a police chemist for a while.

28

I watched her for a minute, biting at the end of my lip. She watched me. I saw no change of expression. Then I started prowling the room with my eyes. I lifted up the dust cover on one of the long tables. Under it was a roulette layout but no wheel. Under the table was nothing.

'Try that chair with the magnolias on it,' she said.

She didn't look towards it so I had to find it myself. Surprising how long it took me. It was a highbacked wing chair, covered in flowered chintz, the kind of chair that a long time ago was intended to keep the draught off while you sat crouched over a fire of cannel coal.

It was turned away from me. I went over there, walking softly, in low gear. It almost faced the wall. Even at that it seemed ridiculous that I hadn't spotted him on my way back from the bar. He leaned in the corner of the chair with his head tilted back. His carnation was red and white and looked as fresh as though the flower girl had just pinned it into his lapel. His eyes were half-open as such eyes usually are. They stared at a point in the corner of the ceiling. The bullet had gone through the outside pocket of his double-breasted jacket. It had been fired by someone who knew where the heart was.

I touched his cheek and it was still warm. I lifted his hand and let it fall. It was quite limp. It felt like the back of somebody's hand. I reached for the big artery in his neck. No blood moved in him and very little had stained his jacket. I wiped my hands off on my handkerchief and stood for a little longer looking down at his quiet little face. Everything I had done or not done, everything wrong and everything right – all wasted.

I went back and sat down near her and squeezed my knee-caps.

'What did you expect me to do?' she asked. 'He killed my brother.'

'Your brother was no angel.'

'He didn't have to kill him.'

'Somebody had to – and quick.'

Her eyes widened suddenly.

I said: 'Didn't you ever wonder why Steelgrave never went after me and why he let you go to the Van Nuys yesterday instead of going himself? Didn't you ever wonder why a fellow with his resources and experience never tried to get hold of those photographs, no matter what he had to do to get them?'

She didn't answer.

'How long have you known the photographs existed?' I asked.

'Weeks, nearly two months. I got one in the mail a couple of days after – after that time we had lunch together.'

'After Stein was killed.'

'Yes, of course.'

'Did you think Steelgrave had killed Stein?'

'No. Why should I? Until tonight, that is.'

'What happend after you got the photo?'

'My brother Orrin called me up and said he had lost his job and was broke. He wanted money. He didn't say anything about the photo. He didn't have to. There was only one time it could have been taken.'

'How did he get your number?'

'Telephone? How did you?'

'Bought it.'

'Well—' she made a vague movement with her hand. 'Why not call the police and get it over with.'

'Wait a minute. Then what? More prints of the photo?'

'One every week. I showed them to *him*.' She gestured towards the chintzy chair. 'He didn't like it. I didn't tell him about Orrin.'

'He must have known. His kind find things out.'

'I suppose so.'

'But not where Orrin was hiding out,' I said. 'Or he wouldn't have waited this long. *When* did you tell Steelgrave?'

She looked away from me. Her fingers kneaded her arm. 'Today,' she said in a distant voice.

'Why today?'

Her breath caught in her throat. 'Please,' she said. 'Don't ask me a lot of useless questions. Don't torment me. There's nothing you can do. I thought there was – when I called Dolores. There isn't now.'

I said: 'All right. There's something you don't seem to understand. Steelgrave knew that whoever was behind that photograph wanted money – a lot of money. He knew that sooner or later the blackmailer would have to show himself. That was what Steelgrave was waiting for. He didn't care anything about the photo itself, except for your sake.'

'He certainly proved that,' she said wearily.

'In his own way,' I said.

Her voice came to me with glacial calm. 'He killed my brother. He told me so himself. The gangster showed through then all right. Funny people you meet in Hollywood, don't you – including me.'

'You were fond of him once,' I said brutally.

Red spots flared on her cheeks.

'I'm not fond of anybody,' she said. 'I'm all through being fond of people.' She glanced briefly towards the highbacked chair. 'I stopped being fond of him last night. He asked me about you, who you were and so on. I told him. I told him that I would have to admit that I was at the Van Nuys Hotel when that man was lying there dead.'

'You were going to tell the police that?'

'I was going to tell Julius Oppenheimer. He would know how to handle it.'

'If he didn't, one of his dogs would,' I said.

She didn't smile. I didn't either.

'If Oppenheimer couldn't handle it, I'd be through in pictures,' she added without interest. 'Now I'm through everywhere else as well.'

I got a cigarette out and lit it. I offered her one. She didn't want one. I wasn't in any hurry. Time seemed to have lost its grip on me. And almost everything else. I was flat out.

'You're going too fast for me,' I said, after a moment. 'You didn't know when you went to the Van Nuys that Steelgrave was Weepy Moyer.'

'No.'

'Then what did you go there for?'

'To buy back those photographs.'

'That doesn't check. The photographs didn't mean anything to you then. They were just you and him having lunch.'

She stared at me and winked her eyes tight, then opened them wide. 'I'm not going to cry,' she said. 'I said I didn't *know*. But when he was in jail that time, I had to know there was something about him that he didn't care to have known. I knew he had been in some kind of racket, I guess. But not killing people.'

I said: 'Uh-huh.' I got up and walked around the high-backed chair again. Her eyes travelled slowly to watch me. I leaned over the dead Steelgrave and felt under his arm on the left side. There was a gun there in the holster. I didn't touch it. I went back and sat down opposite her again.

'It's going to cost a lot of money to fix this,' I said.

For the first time she smiled. It was a very small smile, but it was a smile. 'I don't have a lot of money,' she said. 'So that's out.'

'Oppenheimer has. You're worth millions to him by now.'

'He wouldn't chance it. Too many people have their knives into the picture business these days. He'll take his loss and forget it in six months.'

'You said you'd go to him.'

'I said if I got into a jam and hadn't really done anything, I'd go to him. But I have done something now.'

'How about Ballou? You're worth a lot to him too.'

'I'm not worth a plugged nickel to anybody. Forget it, Marlowe. You mean well, but I know these people.'

'That puts it up to me,' I said. 'That would be why you sent for me.'

'Wonderful,' she said. 'You fix it, darling. For free.' Her voice was brittle and shallow again.

I went and sat beside her on the davenport. I took hold of her arm and pulled her hand out of the fur pocket and took hold of that. It was almost ice-cold, in spite of the fur.

She turned her head and looked at me squarely. She shook her head a little. 'Believe me, darling, I'm not worth it – even to sleep with.'

I turned the hand over and opened the fingers out. They were stiff and resisted. I opened them out one by one. I smoothed the palm of her hand.

'Tell me why you had the gun with you.'

'The gun?'

'Don't take time to think. Just tell me. Did you mean to kill him?'

'Why not, darling? I thought I meant something to him. I guess I'm a little vain. He fooled me. Nobody means anything to the Steelgraves of this world. And nobody means anything to the Mavis Welds of this world any more.'

She pulled away from me and smiled thinly. 'I oughtn't to have given you that gun. If I killed you I might get clear yet.'

I took it out and held it towards her. She took it and stood up quickly. The gun pointed at me. The small tired smile moved her lips again. Her finger was very firm on the trigger.

'Shoot high,' I said. 'I'm wearing my bullet-proof underwear.'

She dropped the gun to her side and for a moment she just stood staring at me. Then she tossed the gun down on the davenport.

'I guess I don't like the script,' she said. 'I don't like the lines. It just isn't me, if you know what I mean.'

She laughed and looked down at the floor. The point of her shoe moved back and forth on the carpeting. 'We've had a nice chat, darling. The phone's over there at the end of the bar.'

'Thanks, do you remember Dolores' number?'

'Why Dolores?'

When I didn't answer she told me. I went along the room to the corner of the bar and dialled. The same routine as before. Good evening, the Château Bercy, who is calling Miss Gonzales please. One moment, please, buzz, buzz, and then a sultry voice saying: 'Hello?'

'This is Marlowe. Did you really mean to put me in a spot?'

I could almost hear her breath catch. Not quite. You can't

really hear it over the phone. Sometimes you think you can.

'Amigo, but I am glad to hear your voice,' she said. 'I am so very glad.'

'Did you or didn't you?'

'I – I don't know. I am very sad to think that I might have. I like you very much.'

'I'm in a little trouble here.'

'Is he—' long pause. Apartment house phone. Careful. 'Is he there?'

'Well – in a way. He is and yet he isn't.'

I really did hear her breath this time. A long indrawn sigh that was almost a whistle.

'Who else is there?'

'Nobody. Just me and my homework. I want to ask you something. It is deadly important. Tell me the truth. Where did you get that thing you gave me tonight?'

'Why, from him. He gave it to me.'

'When?'

'Early this evening. Why?'

'How early?'

'About six o'clock, I think.'

'*Why* did he give it to you?'

'He asked me to keep it. He always carried one.'

'Asked you to keep it, why?'

'He did not say, amigo. He was a man that did things like that. He did not often explain himself.'

'Notice anything unusual about it? About what he gave you?'

'Why – no, I did not.'

'Yes, you did. You noticed that it had been fired and that it smelled of burned powder.'

'But I did not—'

'Yes, you did. Just like that. You wondered about it. You didn't like to keep it. You didn't keep it. You gave it back to him. You don't like them around anyhow.'

There was a long silence. She said at last: 'But of course. But why did he want me to have it? I mean, if that was what happened.'

'He didn't tell you why. He just tried to ditch a gun on you and you weren't having any. Remember?'

'That is something I have to tell?'

'*Si.*'

'Will it be safe for me to do that?'

'When did you ever try to be safe?'

She laughed softly. 'Amigo, you understand me very well.'

536

'Good night,' I said.

'One moment, you have not told me what happened.'

'I haven't even telephoned you.'

I hung up and turned.

Mavis Weld was standing in the middle of the floor watching me.

'You have your car here?' I asked.

'Yes.'

'Get going.'

'And do what?'

'Just go home. That's all.'

'You can't get away with it,' she said softly.

'You're my client.'

'I can't let you. I killed him. Why should you be dragged into it?'

'Don't stall. And when you leave go the back way. Not the way Dolores brought me.'

She stared me straight in the eyes and repeated in a tense voice: 'But I killed him.'

'I can't hear a word you say.'

Her teeth took hold of her lower lip and held it cruelly. She seemed hardly to breathe. She stood rigid. I went over close to her and touched her cheek with a fingertip. I pressed it hard and watched the white spot turn red.

'If you want to know my motive,' I said, 'it has nothing to do with you. I owe it to the johns. I haven't played clean cards in this game. They know. I know. I'm just giving them a chance to use the loud pedal.'

'As if anyone ever had to give them that,' she said, and turned abruptly and walked away. I watched her to the arch and waited for her to look back. She went on through without turning. After a long time I heard a whirring noise. Then the bump of something heavy – the garage door going up. A car started a long way off. It idled down and after another pause the whirring noise started again.

When that stopped, the motor faded off into the distance. I heard nothing now. The silence of the house hung around me in thick loose folds like that fur coat around the shoulders of Mavis Weld.

I carried the glass and bottle of brandy over to the bar and climbed over it. I rinsed the glass in a little sink and set the bottle back on the shelf. I found the trick catch this time and swung the door open at the end opposite the telephone. I went back to Steelgrave.

I took the gun Dolores had given me out and wiped it off and put his small limp hand around the butt, held it there and let go. The gun thudded to the carpet. The position looked natural. I wasn't thinking about fingerprints. He would have learned long ago not to leave them on any gun.

That left me with three guns. The weapon in his holster I took out and went and put it on the bar shelf under the counter, wrapped in a towel. The Luger I didn't touch. The other white-handled automatic was left. I tried to decide about how far away from him it had been fired. Beyond scorching distance, but probably very close beyond. I stood about three feet from him and fired two shots past him. They nicked peacefully into the wall. I dragged the chair around until it faced into the room. I laid the small automatic down on the dust cover of one of the roulette tables. I touched the big muscle in the side of his neck, usually the first to harden. I couldn't tell whether it had begun to set or not. But his skin was colder than it had been.

There was not a hell of a lot of time to play around with.

I went to the telephone and dialled the number of the Los Angeles Police Department. I asked the police operator for Christy French. A voice from homicide came on, said he had gone home and what was it. I said it was a personal call he was expecting. They gave me his phone number at home, reluctantly, not because they cared, but because they hate to give anybody anything any time.

I dialled and a woman answered and screamed his name. He sounded rested and calm.

'This is Marlowe. What were you doing?'

'Reading the funnies to my kid. He ought to be in bed. What's doing?'

'Remember over at the Van Nuys yesterday you said a man could make a friend if he got you something on Weepy Moyer?'

'Yeah.'

'I need a friend.'

He didn't sound very interested. 'What you got on him?'

'I'm assuming it's the same guy. Steelgrave.'

'Too much assuming, kid. We had him in the fish-bowl because we thought the same. It didn't pan any gold.'

'You got a tip. He set that tip up himself. So the night Stein was squibbed off he would be where you knew.'

'You just making this up – or got evidence?' He sounded a little less relaxed.

'If a man got out of jail on a pass from the jail doctor, could you prove that?'

There was a silence. I heard a child's voice complaining and a woman's voice speaking to the child.

'It's happened,' French said heavily. 'I dunno. That's a tough order to fill. They'd send him under guard. Did he get to the guard?'

'That's my theory.'

'Better sleep on it. Anything else?'

'I'm out at Stillwood Heights. In a big house where they were setting up for gambling and the local residents didn't like it.'

'Read about it. Steelgrave there?'

'He's here. I'm here alone with him.'

Another silence. The kid yelled and I thought I heard a slap. The kid yelled louder. French yelled at somebody.

'Put him on the phone,' French said at last.

'You're not bright tonight, Christy. Why would I call *you*?'

'Yeah,' he said. 'Stupid of me. What's the address there?'

'I don't know. But it's up at the end of Tower Road in Stillwood Heights, and the phone number is Halldale 9-5033. I'll be waiting for you.'

He repeated the number and said slowly: 'This time you wait, huh?'

'It had to come sometime.'

The phone clicked and I hung up.

I went back through the house putting on lights as I found them, and came out at the back door at the top of the stairs. There was a floodlight for the motoryard. I put that on. I went down the steps and walked along to the oleander bush. The private gate stood open as before. I swung it shut, hooked up the chain and clicked the padlock. I went back, walking slowly, looking up at the moon, sniffing the night air, listening to the tree frogs and the crickets. I went into the house and found the front door and put the light on over that. There was a big parking space in front and a circular lawn with roses. But you had to slide back around the house to the rear to get away.

The place was a dead end except for the driveway through the neighbouring grounds. I wondered who lived there. A long way off through trees I could see the lights of a big house. Some Hollywood big shot, probably, some wizard of the slobbery kiss, and the pornographic dissolve.

I went back in and felt the gun I had just fired. It was cold enough. And Mr Steelgrave was beginning to look as if he meant to stay dead.

No siren. But the sound of a car coming up the hill at last. I went out to meet it, me and my beautiful dream.

29

They came in as they should, big, tough and quiet, their eyes flickering with watchfulness and cautious with disbelief.

'Nice place,' French said. 'Where's the customer?'

'In there,' Beifus said, without waiting for me to answer.

They went along the room without haste and stood in front of him looking down solemnly.

'Dead, wouldn't you say?' Beifus remarked, opening up the act.

French leaned down and took the gun that lay on the floor with thumb and finger on the trigger guard. His eyes flicked sideways and he jerked his chin. Beifus took the other white-handled gun by sliding a pencil into the end of the barrel.

'Fingerprints all in the right places, I hope,' Beifus said. He sniffed. 'Oh yeah, this baby's been working. How's yours, Christy?'

'Fired,' French said. He sniffed again. 'But not recently.' He took a clip flash from his pocket and shone it into the barrel of the black gun. 'Hours ago.'

'Down at Bay City, in a house on Wyoming Street,' I said.

Their heads swung around to me in unison.

'Guessing?' French asked slowly.

'Yes.'

He walked over to the covered table and laid the gun down some distance from the other. 'Better tag them right away, Fred. They're twins. We'll both sign the tags.'

Beifus nodded and rooted around in his pockets. He came up with a couple of tie-on tags. The things cops carry around with them.

French moved back to me. 'Let's stop guessing and get to the part you know.'

'A girl I know called me this evening and said a client of mine was in danger up here – from him.' I pointed with my chin at the dead man in the chair. 'This girl rode me up here. We passed the road block. A number of people saw us both. She left me in back of the house and went home.'

'Somebody with a name?' French asked.

'Dolores Gonzales, Château Bercy Apartments. On Franklin. She's in pictures.'

'Oh ho,' Beifus said and rolled his eyes.

'Who's your client? Same one?' French asked.

'No. This is another party altogether.'

'She have a name?'

'Not yet.'

They stared at me with hard bright faces. French's jaw moved almost with a jerk. Knots of muscles showed at the sides of his jawbone.

'New rules, huh?' he said softly.

I said: 'There has to be some agreement about publicity. The DA ought to be willing.'

Beifus said: 'You don't know the DA good, Marlowe. He eats publicity like I eat tender young garden peas.'

French said: 'We don't give you any undertaking whatsoever.'

'She hasn't any name,' I said.

'There's a dozen ways we can find out, kid,' Beifus said. 'Why go into this routine that makes it tough for all of us?'

'No publicity,' I said, 'unless charges are actually filed.'

'You can't get away with it, Marlowe.'

'Goddamn it,' I said, 'this man killed Orrin Quest. You take that gun down town and check it against the bullets in Quest. Give me that much at least, before you force me into an impossible position.'

'I wouldn't give you the dirty end of a burnt match,' French said.

I didn't say anything. He stared at me with cold hate in his eyes. His lips moved slowly and his voice was thick saying: 'You here when he got it?'

'No.'

'Who was?'

'He was,' I said, looking across at the dead Steelgrave.

'Who else?'

'I won't lie to you,' I said. 'And I won't tell you anything I don't want to tell – except on the terms I stated. I don't know who was here when he got it.'

'Who was here when you got here?'

I didn't answer. He turned his head slowly and said to Beifus: 'Put the cuffs on him. Behind.'

Beifus hesitated. Then he took a pair of steel handcuffs out of his left hip pocket and came over to me. 'Put your hands behind you,' he said in an uncomfortable voice.

I did. He clicked the cuffs on. French walked over slowly and stood in front of me. His eyes were half-closed. The skin around them was greyish with fatigue.

'I'm going to make a little speech,' he said. 'You're not going to like it.'

I didn't say anything.

French said: 'It's like this with us, baby. We're coppers and everybody hates our guts. And as if we didn't have enough trouble, we have to have you. As if we didn't get pushed around enough by the guys in the corner offices, the City Hall gang, the day chief, the night chief, the chamber of commerce, His Honour the Mayor in his panelled office four times as big as the three lousy rooms the whole homicide staff has to work out of. As if we didn't have to handle one hundred and fourteen homicides last year out of three rooms that don't have enough chairs for the whole duty squad to sit down in at once. We spend our lives turning over dirty underwear and sniffing rotten teeth. We go up dark stairways to get a gun punk with a skinful of hop and sometimes we don't get all the way up, and our wives wait dinner that night and all the other nights. We don't come home any more. And nights we do come home, we come home so goddamn tired we can't eat or sleep or even read the lies the papers print about us. So we lie awake in the dark in a cheap house on a cheap street and listen to the drunks down the block having fun. And just about the time we drop off the phone rings and we get up and start all over again. Nothing we do is right, not ever. Not once. If we get a confession, we beat it out of the guy, they say, and some shyster calls us Gestapo in court and sneers at us when we muddle our grammar. If we make a mistake they put us back in uniform on Skid Row and we spend the nice cool summer evenings picking drunks out of the gutter and being yelled at by whores and taking knives away from greaseballs in zoot suits. But all that ain't enough to make us entirely happy. We got to have you.'

He stopped and drew in his breath. His face glistened a little as if with sweat. He leaned forward from his hips.

'We got to have you,' he repeated. 'We got to have sharpers with private licences hiding information and dodging around corners and stirring up dust for us to breathe in. We got to have you suppressing evidence and framing set-ups that wouldn't fool a sick baby. You wouldn't mind me calling you a goddamn cheap double-crossing keyhole peeper, would you, baby?'

'You want me to mind?' I asked him.

He straightened up. 'I'd love it,' he said. 'In spades redoubled.'

'Some of what you say is true,' I said. 'Not all. Any private eye wants to play ball with the police. Sometimes it's a little hard to find out who's making the rules of the ball game. Sometimes he doesn't trust the police, and with cause. Sometimes he just gets in a jam without meaning to and has to play his hand out the way it's dealt. He'd usually rather have a new deal. He'd like to keep on earning a living.'

'Your licence is dead,' French said. 'As of now. That problem won't bother you any more.'

'It's dead when the commission that gave it to me says so. Not before.'

Beifus said quietly: 'Let's get on with it, Christy. This could wait.'

'I'm getting on with it,' French said. 'My way. This bird hasn't cracked wise yet. I'm waiting for him to crack wise. The bright repartee. Don't tell me you're all out of the quick stuff, Marlowe.'

'Just what is it you want me to say?' I asked him.

'Guess,' he said.

'You're a man-eater tonight,' I said. 'You want to break me in half. But you want an excuse. And you want me to give it to you?'

'That might help,' he said between his teeth.

'What would you have done in my place?' I asked him.

'I couldn't imagine myself getting that low.'

He licked at the point of his upper lip. His right hand was hanging loose at his side. He was clenching and unclenching the fingers without knowing it.

'Take it easy, Christy,' Beifus said. 'Lay off.'

French didn't move. Beifus came over and stepped between us. French said: 'Get out of there, Fred.'

'No.'

French doubled his fist and slugged him hard on the point of the jaw. Beifus stumbled back and knocked me out of the way. His knees wobbled. He bent forward and coughed. He shook his head slowly in a bent-over position. After a while he straightened up with a grunt. He turned and looked at me. He grinned.

'It's a new kind of third degree,' he said. 'The cops beat hell out of each other and the suspect cracks up from the agony of watching.'

His hand went up and felt the angle of his jaw. It already showed swelling. His mouth grinned but his eyes were still a little vague. French stood rooted and silent.

Beifus got out a pack of cigarettes and shook one loose and held the pack out to French. French looked at the cigarette, looked at Beifus.

'Seventeen years of it,' he said. 'Even my wife hates me.'

He lifted his open hand and slapped Beifus across the cheek with it lightly. Beifus kept on grinning.

French said: 'Was it you I hit, Fred?'

Beifus said: 'Nobody hit me, Christy. Nobody that I can remember.'

French said: 'Take the cuffs off him and take him out to the car. He's under arrest. Cuff him to the rail if you think it's necessary.'

'Okay.' Beifus went around behind me. The cuffs came loose. 'Come along, baby,' Beifus said.

I stared hard at French. He looked at me as if I was the wallpaper. His eyes didn't seem to see me at all.

I went out under the archway and out of the house.

30

I never knew his name, but he was rather short and thin for a cop, which was what he must have been, partly because he was there, and partly because when he leaned across the table to reach a card I could see the leather under-arm holster and the butt end of a police .38.

He didn't speak much, but when he did he had a nice voice, a soft-water voice. And he had a smile that warmed the whole room.

'Wonderful casting,' I said, looking at him across the cards.

We were playing double Canfield. Or he was. I was just there, watching him, watching his small and very neat and very clean hands go out across the table and touch a card and lift it delicately and put it somewhere else. When he did this he pursed his lips a little and whistled without tune, a low soft whistle, like a very young engine that is not yet sure of itself.

He smiled and put a red nine on a black ten.

'What do you do in your spare time?' I asked him.

'I play the piano a good deal,' he said. 'I have a seven-foot Steinway. Mozart and Bach mostly. I'm a bit old-fashioned. Most people find it dull stuff. I don't.'

'Perfect casting,' I said, and put a card somewhere.

'You'd be surprised how difficult some of that Mozart is,' he said. 'It sounds so simple when you hear it played well.'

'Who can play it well?' I asked.

'Schnabel.'

'Rubenstein?'

He shook his head. 'Too heavy. Too emotional. Mozart is just music. No comment needed from the performer.'

'I bet you get a lot of them in the confession mood,' I said. 'Like the job?'

He moved another card and flexed his fingers lightly. His nails were bright but short. You could see he was a man who loved to move his hands, to make little neat inconspicuous motions with them, motions without any special meaning, but smooth and flowing and light as swansdown. They gave him a feel of delicate things delicately done, but not weak. Mozart, all right. I could see that.

It was about five-thirty, and the sky behind the screened window was getting light. The roll-top desk in the corner was rolled shut. The room was the same room I had been in the afternoon before. Down at the end of the table the square carpenter's pencil was lying where somebody had picked it up and put it back after Lieutenant Maglashan of Bay City threw it against the wall. The flat desk at which Christy French had sat was littered with ash. An old cigar butt clung to the extreme edge of a glass ashtray. A moth circled around the overhead light on a drop cord that had one of those green and white glass shades they still have in country hotels.

'Tired?' he asked.

'Pooped.'

'You oughtn't to get yourself involved in these elaborate messes. No point in it that I can see.'

'No point in shooting a man?'

He smiled the warm smile. 'You never shot anybody.'

'What makes you say that?'

'Common sense – and a lot of experience sitting here with people.'

'I guess you do like the job,' I said.

'It's night work. Gives me the days to practise. I've had it for twelve years now. Seen a lot of funny ones come and go.'

He got another ace out, just in time. We were almost blocked.

'Get many confessions?'

'I don't take confessions,' he said. 'I just establish a mood.'

'Why give it all away?'

He leaned back and tapped lightly with the edge of a card on the edge of the table. The smile came again. 'I'm not giving anything away. We got you figured long ago.'

'Then what are they holding me for?'

He wouldn't answer that. He looked around at the clock on

the wall. 'I think we could get some food now.' He got up and went to the door. He half opened it and spoke softly to someone outside. Then he came back and sat down again and looked at what we had in the way of cards.

'No use,' he said. 'Three more up and we're blocked. Okay with you to start over?'

'Okay with me if we never started at all. I don't play cards. Chess.'

He looked up at me quickly. 'Why didn't you say so? I'd rather have played chess too.'

'I'd rather drink some hot black coffee as bitter as sin.'

'Any minute now. But I won't promise the coffee's what you're used to.'

'Hell, I eat anywhere ... Well, if I didn't shoot him, who did?'

'Guess that's what is annoying them.'

'They ought to be glad to have him shot.'

'They probably are,' he said. 'But they don't like the way it was done.'

'Personally I thought it was as neat a job as you could find.'

He looked at me in silence. He had the cards between his hands, all in a lump. He smoothed them out and flicked them over on their faces and dealt them rapidly into the two decks. The cards seemed to pour from his hands in a stream, in a blur.

'If you were that fast with a gun,' I began.

The stream of cards stopped. Without apparent motion a gun took their place. He held it lightly in his right hand pointed at a distant corner of the room. It went away and the cards started flowing again.

'You're wasted in here,' I said. 'You ought to be in Las Vegas.'

He picked up one of the packs and shuffled it slightly and quickly cut it, and dealt me a king high flush in spades.

'I'm safer with Steinway,' he said.

The door opened and a uniformed man came in with a tray.

We ate canned cornbeef hash and drank hot but weak coffee. By that time it was full morning.

At eight-fifteen Christy French came in and stood with his hat on the back of his head and dark smudges under his eyes.

I looked from him to the little man across the table. But he wasn't there any more. The cards weren't there either. Nothing was there but a chair pushed in neatly to the table and the dishes we had eaten off gathered on a tray. For a moment I had that creepy feeling.

Then Christy French walked around the table and jerked the chair out and sat down and leaned his chin on his hand. He took his hat off and rumpled his hair. He stared at me with hard morose eyes. I was back in cop-town again.

31

'The DA wants to see you at nine o'clock,' he said. 'After that I guess you can go on home. That is, if he doesn't hang a pinch on you. I'm sorry you had to sit up in that chair all night.'

'It's all right,' I said. 'I needed the exercise.'

'Yeah, back in the groove again,' he said. He stared moodily at the dishes on the tray.

'Got Lagardie?' I asked him.

'No. He's a doctor all right, though.' His eyes moved to mine. 'He practised in Cleveland.'

I said: 'I hate it to be that tidy.'

'How do you mean?'

'Young Quest wants to put the bite on Steelgrave. So he just by pure accident runs into the one guy in Bay City that could prove who Steelgrave was. *That*'s too tidy.'

'Aren't you forgetting something?'

'I'm tired enough to forget my name. What?'

'Me too,' French said. '*Somebody* had to tell him who Steelgrave was. When that photo was taken Moe Stein hadn't been squibbed off. So what good was the photo unless somebody knew who Steelgrave was?'

'I guess Miss Weld knew,' I said. 'And Quest was her brother.'

'You're not making much sense, chum.' He grinned a tired grin. 'Would she help her brother put the bite on her boyfriend and on her too?'

'I give up. Maybe the photo was just a fluke. His other sister – my client that was – said he liked to take candid camera shots. The candider the better. If he'd lived long enough you'd have had him for mopery.'

'For murder,' French said indifferently.

'Oh?'

'Maglashan found that ice pick all right. He just wouldn't give out to you.'

'There'd have to be more than that.'

'There is, but it's a dead issue. Clausen and Mileaway Marston both had records. The kid's dead. His family's respectable. He had an off-streak in him and he got in with the wrong people. No point in smearing his family just to prove the police can solve a case.'

'That's white of you. How about Steelgrave?'

'That's out of my hands.' He started to get up. 'When a gangster gets his, how long does the investigation last?'

'Just as long as it's front page stuff,' I said. 'But there's a question of identity involved here.'

'No.'

I stared at him. 'How do you mean, no?'

'Just no. We're sure.' He was on his feet now. He combed his hair with his fingers and rearranged his tie and hat. Out of the corner of his mouth he said in a low voice: 'Off the record – we were always sure. We just didn't have a thing on him.'

'Thanks,' I said, 'I'll keep it to myself. How about the guns?'

He stopped and stared down at the table. His eyes came up to mine rather slowly. 'They both belonged to Steelgrave. What's more, he had a permit to carry a gun. From the sheriff's office in another county. Don't ask me why. One of them' – he paused and looked up at the wall over my head – 'one of them killed Quest ... The same gun killed Stein.'

'Which one?'

He smiled faintly. 'It would be hell if the ballistics man got them mixed up and we didn't know,' he said.

He waited for me to say something. I didn't have anything to say. He made a gesture with his hand.

'Well, so long. Nothing personal you know, but I hope the DA takes your hide off – in long, thin strips.'

He turned and went out.

I could have done the same, but I just sat there and stared across the table at the wall, as if I had forgotten how to get up. After a while the door opened and the orange queen came in. She unlocked her roll-top desk and took her hat off her impossible hair and hung her jacket on a bare hook in the bare wall. She opened the window near her and uncovered her typewriter and put paper in it. Then she looked across at me.

'Waiting for somebody?'

'I room here,' I said. 'Been here all night.'

She looked at me steadily for a moment. 'You were here yesterday afternoon. I remember.'

She turned to her typewriter and her fingers began to fly. From the open window behind her came the growl of cars filling up the parking lot. The sky had a white glare and there was not much smog. It was going to be a hot day.

The telephone rang on the orange queen's desk. She talked into it inaudibly, and hung up. She looked across at me again.

'Mr Endicott's in his office,' she said. 'Know the way?'

'I worked there once. Not for him, though. I got fired.'

She looked at me with that City Hall look they have. A voice that seemed to come from anywhere but her mouth said:

'Hit him in the face with a wet glove.'

I went over near her and stood looking down at the orange hair. There was plenty of grey at the roots.

'Who said that?'

'It's the wall,' she said. 'It talks. The voices of the dead men who have passed through on the way to hell.'

I went out of the room walking softly and shut the door against the closer so that it wouldn't make any noise.

32

You go in through double swing doors. Inside the double doors there is a combination PBX and Information desk at which sits one of those ageless women you see around municipal offices everywhere in the world. They were never young and will never be old. They have no beauty, no charm, no style. They don't have to please anybody. They are safe. They are civil without ever quite being polite, and intelligent and knowledgeable without any real interest in anything. They are what human beings turn into when they trade life for existence and ambition for security.

Beyond this desk there is a row of glassed-in cubicles stretching along one side of a very long room. On the other side is the waiting-room, a row of hard chairs all facing one way, towards the cubicles.

About half the chairs were filled with people waiting who had the look of long waiting on their faces and the expectation of still longer waiting to come. Most of them were shabby. One was from the jail, in denim, with a guard. A white-faced kid built like a tackle, with sick, empty eyes.

At the back of the line of cubicles a door was lettered SEWELL ENDICOTT DISTRICT ATTORNEY. I knocked and went on into a big airy corner room. A nice enough room, old-fashioned with padded black leather chairs and pictures of former DAs and Governors on the walls. Breeze fluttered the net curtain at four windows. A fan on a high shelf purred and swung slowly in a languid arc.

Sewell Endicott sat behind a flat dark desk and watched me come. He pointed to a chair across from him. I sat down. He was tall, thin and dark with loose black hair and long delicate fingers.

'You're Marlowe?' he said in a voice that had a touch of the soft South.

I didn't think he really needed an answer to that. I just waited.

'You're in a bad spot, Marlowe. You don't look good at all. You've been caught suppressing evidence helpful to the solution of a murder. That is obstructing justice. You could go up for it.'

'Suppressing what evidence?' I asked.

He picked a photo off his desk and frowned at it. I looked across at the other two people in the room. They sat in chairs side by side. One of them was Mavis Weld. She wore the dark glasses with the wide white bows. I couldn't see her eyes, but I thought she was looking at me. She didn't smile. She sat very still.

By her side sat a man in an angelic pale grey flannel suit with a carnation the size of a dahlia in his lapel. He was smoking a monogrammed cigarette and flicking the ashes on the floor, ignoring the smoking stand at his elbow. I knew him by pictures I had seen in the papers. Lee Farrell, one of the hottest trouble-shooting lawyers in the country. His hair was white but his eyes were bright and young. He had a deep outdoor tan. He looked as if it would cost a thousand dollars to shake hands with him.

Endicott leaned back and tapped the arm of his chair with his long fingers. He turned with polite deference to Mavis Weld.

'And how well did you know Steelgrave, Miss Weld?'

'Intimately. He was very charming in some ways. I can hardly believe—' she broke off and shrugged.

'And you are prepared to take the stand and swear as to the time and place when this photograph was taken?' He turned the photograph over and showed it to her.

Farrell said indifferently: 'Just a moment. Is that the evidence Mr Marlowe is supposed to have suppressed?'

'I ask the questions,' Endicott said sharply.

Farrell smiled. 'Well, in case the answer is yes, that photo isn't evidence of anything.'

Endicott said softly: 'Will you answer my question, Miss Weld?'

She said quietly and easily: 'No, Mr Endicott, I couldn't swear when that picture was taken or where. I didn't know it was being taken.'

'All you have to do is look at it,' Endicott suggested.

'And all I know is what I get from looking at it,' she told him.

I grinned. Farrell looked at me with a twinkle. Endicott caught the grin out of the corner of his eye. 'Something you find amusing?' he snapped at me.

'I've been up all night. My face keeps slipping,' I said.

He gave me a stern look and turned to Mavis Weld again. 'Will you amplify that, Miss Weld?'

'I've had a lot of photos taken of me, Mr Endicott. In a lot of different places and with a lot of different people. I have had lunch and dinner at The Dancers with Mr Steelgrave and with various other men. I don't know what you want me to say.'

Farrell put in smoothly: 'If I understand your point, you would like Miss Weld to be your witness to connect this photo up. In what kind of proceeding?'

'That's my business,' Endicott said shortly. 'Somebody shot Steelgrave to death last night. It could have been a woman. It could even have been Miss Weld. I'm sorry to say that, but it seems to be on the cards.'

Mavis Weld looked down at her hands. She twisted a white glove between her fingers.

'Well, let's assume a proceeding,' Farrell said. 'One in which that photo is part of your evidence – if you can get it in. But you can't get it in. Miss Weld won't get it in for you. All she knows about the photo is what she sees by looking at it. What anybody can see. You'd have to connect it up with a witness who could swear as to when how and where it was taken. Otherwise I'd object – if I happened to be on the other side. I could even introduce experts to swear the photo was faked.'

'I'm sure you could,' Endicott said dryly.

'The only man who could connect it up for you is the man who took it,' Farrell went on without haste or heat. 'I understand he's dead. I suspect that was why he was killed.'

Endicott said: 'This photo is clear evidence of itself that at a certain time and place Steelgrave was not in jail and therefore had no alibi for the killing of Stein.'

Farrell said: 'It's evidence when and if you get it introduced in evidence, Endicott. For Pete's sake, I'm not trying to tell you the law. You know it. Forget that picture. It proves nothing whatsoever. No paper would dare print it. No judge would admit it in evidence, because no competent witness can connect it up. And if that's the evidence Marlowe suppressed, then he didn't in a legal sense suppress evidence at all.'

'I wasn't thinking of trying Steelgrave for murder,' Endicott said, dryly. 'But I *am* a little interested in who killed him. The police department, fantastically enough, also has an interest in that. I hope our interest doesn't offend you.'

Farrell said: 'Nothing offends me. That's why I'm where I am. Are you sure Steelgrave was murdered?'

Endicott just stared at him. Farrell said easily: 'I understand two guns were found, both the property of Steelgrave.'

'Who told you?' Endicott asked sharply. He leaned forward, frowning.

Farrell dropped his cigarette into the smoking stand and shrugged. 'Hell, these things come out. One of these guns had killed Quest and also Stein. The other had killed Steelgrave. Fired at close quarters too. I admit those boys don't as a rule take that way out. But it could happen.'

Endicott said gravely: 'No doubt. Thanks for the suggestion. It happens to be wrong.'

Farrell smiled a little and was silent. Endicott turned slowly to Mavis Weld.

'Miss Weld, this office – or the present incumbent of it at least – doesn't believe in seeking publicity at the expense of people to whom a certain kind of publicity might be fatal. It is my duty to determine whether anyone should be brought to trial for any of these murders, and to prosecute them, if the evidence warrants it. It is not my duty to ruin your career by exploiting the fact that you had the bad luck or bad judgement to be the friend of a man who, although never convicted or even indicted for any crime, was undoubtedly a member of a criminal mob at one time. I don't think you have been quite candid with me about this photograph, but I won't press the matter now. There is not much point in my asking you whether you shot Steelgrave. But I do ask you whether you have any knowledge that would point to who may have or might have killed him.'

Farrell said quickly: 'Knowledge, Miss Weld – not mere suspicion.'

She faced Endicott squarely. 'No.'

He stood up and bowed. 'That will be all for now then. Thanks for coming in.'

Farrell and Mavis Weld stood up. I didn't move. Farrell said: 'Are you calling a press conference?'

'I think I'll leave that to you, Mr Farrell. You have always been very skilful in handling the press.'

Farrell nodded and went to open the door. They went out. She didn't seem to look at me when she went out, but something touched the back of my neck lightly. Probably accidental. Her sleeve.

Endicott watched the door close. He looked across the desk at me. 'Is Farrell representing you? I forgot to ask him.'

'I can't afford him. So I'm vulnerable.'

He smiled thinly. 'I let them take all the tricks and then salve my dignity by working out on you, eh?'

'I couldn't stop you.'

'You're not exactly proud of the way you have handled things, are you, Marlowe?'

'I got off on the wrong foot. After that I just had to take my lumps.'

'Don't you think you owe a certain obligation to the law?'

'I would – if the law was like you.'

He ran his long pale fingers through his tousled black hair. 'I could make a lot of answers to that,' he said. 'They'd all sound about the same. The citizen is the law. In this country we haven't got around to understanding that. We think of the law as an enemy. We're a nation of cop-haters.'

'It'll take a lot to change that,' I said. 'On both sides.'

He leaned forward and pressed a buzzer. 'Yes,' he said quietly. 'It will. But somebody has to make a beginning. Thanks for coming in.'

As I went out a secretary came in another door with a fat file in her hand.

33

A shave and a second breakfast made me feel a little less like the box of shavings the cat had had kittens in. I went up to the office and unlocked the door and sniffed in the twice-breathed air and the smell of dust. I opened a window and inhaled the fry cook smell from the coffee shop next door. I sat down at my desk and felt the grit on it with my fingertips. I filled a pipe and lit it and leaned back and looked around.

'Hello,' I said.

I was just talking to the office equipment, the three green filing cases, the threadbare piece of carpet, the customers' chair across from me, and the light fixture in the celing with three dead moths in it that had been there for at least six months. I was talking to the pebbled glass panel and the grimy woodwork and the pen set on the desk and the tired, tired telephone. I was talking to the scales on an alligator, the name of the alligator being Marlowe, a private detective in our thriving little community. Not the brainiest guy in the world, but cheap. He started out cheap and he ended cheaper still.

I reached down and put the bottle of Old Forester up on the desk. It was about a third full. Old Forester. Now who gave you that, pal? That's green label stuff. Out of your class entirely. Must have been a client. I had a client once.

And that got me thinking about her, and maybe I have stronger thoughts than I know. The telephone rang, and the funny little precise voice sounded just as it had the first time she called me up.

'I'm in that telephone booth,' she said. 'If you're alone, I'm coming up.'

'Uh-huh.'

'I suppose you're mad at me,' she said.

'I'm not mad at anybody. Just tired.'

'Oh yes you are,' her tight little voice said. 'But I'm coming up anyway. I don't care if you *are* mad at me.'

She hung up. I took the cork out of the bottle of Old Forester and gave a sniff at it. I shuddered. That settled it. Any time I couldn't smell whisky without shuddering I was through.

I put the bottle away and got up to unlock the communicating door. Then I heard her tripping along the hall. I'd know those tight little footsteps anywhere. I opened the door and she came up to me and looked at me shyly.

It was all gone. The slanted cheaters, and the new hair-do and the smart little hat and the perfume and the prettied-up touch. The costume jewellery, the rouge, the everything. All gone. She was right back where she started that first morning. Same brown tailormade, same square bag, same rimless glasses, same prim little narrow-minded smile.

'It's me,' she said. 'I'm going home.'

She followed me into my private thinking parlour and sat down primly, and I sat down just any old way and stared at her.

'Back to Manhattan,' I said. 'I'm surprised they let you.'

'I may have to come back.'

'Can you afford it?'

554

She gave a quick little half-embarrassed laugh. 'It won't cost me anything,' she said. She reached up and touched the rimless glasses. 'These feel all wrong now,' she said. 'I liked the others. But Dr Zugsmith wouldn't like them at all.' She put her bag on the desk and drew a line along the desk with her fingertip. That was just like the first time too.

'I can't remember whether I gave you back your twenty dollars or not,' I said. 'We kept passing it back and forth until I lost count.'

'Oh, you gave it to me,' she said. 'Thank you.'

'Sure?'

'I never make mistakes about money. Are you all right? Did they hurt you?'

'The police? No. And it was as tough a job as they ever didn't do.'

She looked innocently surprised. Then her eyes glowed. 'You must be awfully brave,' she said.

'Just luck,' I said. I picked up a pencil and felt the point. It was a good sharp point, if anybody wanted to write anything. I didn't. I reached across and slipped the pencil through the strap of her bag and pulled it towards me.

'Don't touch my bag,' she said quickly and reached for it.

I grinned and drew it out of her reach. 'All right. But it's such a cute little bag. It's so like you.'

She leaned back. There was a vague worry behind her eyes, but she smiled. 'You think I'm cute – Philip? I'm so ordinary.'

'I wouldn't say so.'

'You wouldn't?'

'Hell no, I think you're one of the most unusual girls I ever met.' I swung the bag by its strap and set it down on the corner of the desk. Her eyes fastened on it quickly, but she licked her lip and kept on smiling at me.

'And I bet you've known an awful lot of girls,' she said. 'Why' – she looked down and did that with her fingertip on the desk again – 'why didn't you ever get married?'

I thought of all the ways you could answer that. I thought of all the women I had liked that much. No, not all. But some of them.

'I suppose I know the answer,' I said. 'But it would just sound corny. The ones I'd maybe like to marry – well, I haven't what they need. The others you don't have to marry. You just seduce them – if they don't beat you to it.'

She flushed to the roots of her mousy hair.

'You're horrid when you talk like that.'

'That goes for some of the nice ones too,' I said. 'Not what you said. What I said. You wouldn't have been so hard to take yourself.'

'Don't talk like that, please!'

'Well, would you?'

She looked down at the desk. 'I wish you'd tell me,' she said slowly, 'what happened to Orrin. I'm all confused.'

'I told you he probably went off the rails. The first time you came in. Remember?'

She nodded slowly, still blushing.

'Abnormal sort of home life,' I said. 'Very inhibited sort of guy with a very highly developed sense of his own importance. It looked at you out of the picture you gave me. I don't want to go psychological on you, but I figure he was just the type to go very completely haywire, if he went haywire at all. Then there's that awful money hunger that runs in your family – all except one.'

She smiled at me now. If she thought I meant her, that was jake with me.

'There's one question I want to ask you,' I said. 'Was your father married before?'

She nodded, yes.

'That helps. Leila had another mother. That suits me fine. Tell me some more. After all, I did a lot of work for you, for a very low fee of no dollars net.'

'You got paid,' she said sharply. 'Well paid. By Leila. And don't expect me to call her Mavis Weld. I won't do it.'

'You didn't know I was going to get paid.'

'Well' – there was a long pause, during which her eyes went to her bag again – 'you did get paid.'

'Okay, pass that. Why wouldn't you tell me who she was?'

'I was ashamed. Mother and I were both ashamed.'

'Orrin wasn't. He loved it.'

'Orrin?' There was a tidy little silence while she looked at her bag again. I was beginning to get curious about that bag. 'But he had been out here and I suppose he'd got used to it.'

'Being in pictures isn't that bad, surely.'

'It wasn't just that,' she said swiftly, and her tooth came down on the outer edge of her lower lip and something flared in her eyes and very slowly died away. I just put another match to my pipe. I was too tired to show emotions, even if I felt any.

'I know. Or anyway I kind of guessed. How did Orrin find out about Steelgrave that the cops didn't know?'

'I – I don't know,' she said slowly, picking her way among her words like a cat on a fence. 'Could it have been that doctor?'

'Oh sure,' I said, with a big, warm smile. 'He and Orrin got

'Oh sure,' I said, with a big, warm smile. 'He and Orrin got to be friends somehow. A common interest in sharp tools maybe.'

She leaned back in her chair. Her little face was thin and angular now. Her eyes had a watchful look.

'Now you're just being nasty,' she said. 'Every so often you have to be that way.'

'Such a pity,' I said. 'I'd be a lovable character if I'd let myself alone. Nice bag.' I reached for it and pulled it in front of me and snapped it open.

She came out of her chair and lunged.

'You let my bag alone!'

I looked her straight in the rimless glasses. 'You want to go home to Manhattan, Kansas, don't you? Today? You got your ticket and everything?'

She worked her lips and slowly sat down again.

'Okay,' I said. 'I'm not stopping you. I just wondered how much dough you squeezed out of the deal.

She began to cry. I opened the bag and went through. Nothing until I came to the zipper pocket at the back. I unzipped and reached in. There was a flat packet of new bills in there. I took them out and riffled them. Ten centuries. All new. All nice. An even thousand dollars. Nice travelling money.

I leaned back and tapped the edge of the packet on my desk. She sat silent now, staring at me with wet eyes. I got a handkerchief out of her bag and tossed it across to her. She dabbed at her eyes. She watched me around the handkerchief. Once in a while she made a nice little appealing sob in her throat.

'Leila gave the money to me,' she said softly.

'What size chisel did you use?'

She just opened her mouth and a tear ran down her cheek into it.

'Skip it,' I said. I dropped the pack of money back into the bag, snapped the bag shut and pushed it across the desk to her. 'I guess you and Orrin belong to that class of people that can convince themselves that everything they do is right. He can blackmail his sister and then when a couple of small-time crooks get wise to his racket and take it away from him, he can sneak up on them and knock them off with an ice pick in the back of the neck. Probably didn't even keep him awake that night. You can do much the same. Leila didn't give you that money. Steelgrave gave it to you. For what?'

'You're filthy,' she said. 'You're vile. How dare you say such things to me?'

'Who tipped off the law that Dr Lagardie knew Clausen? Lagardie thought I did. I didn't. So you did. Why? To smoke out your brother who was not cutting you in – because right then he had lost his deck of cards and was hiding out. I'd like to see some of those letters he wrote home. I bet they're meaty. I can see him working at it, watching his sister, trying to get her lined up for his Leica, with the good Dr Lagardie waiting quietly in the background for his share of the take. What did you hire me for?'

'I didn't know,' she said evenly. She wiped her eyes again and put the handkerchief away in the bag and got herself all collected and ready to leave. 'Orrin never mentioned any names. I didn't even know Orrin had lost his pictures. But I knew he had taken them and that they were very valuable. I came out to make sure.'

'Sure of what?'

'That Orrin had treated me right. He could be awfully mean sometimes. He might have kept all the money himself.'

'Why did he call you up night before last?'

'He was scared. Dr Lagardie wasn't pleased with him any more. He didn't have the pictures. Somebody else had them. Orrin didn't know who. But he was scared.'

'I had them. I still have,' I said. 'They're in that safe.'

She turned her head very slowly to look at the safe. She ran a fingertip questioningly along her lip. She turned back.

'I don't believe you,' she said, and her eyes watched me like a cat watching a mousehole.

'How's to split that grand with me. You get the pictures.'

She thought about it. 'I could hardly give you all that money for something that doesn't belong to you,' she said, and smiled. 'Please give them to me. Please, Philip. Leila ought to have them back.'

'For how much dough?'

She frowned and looked hurt.

'She's my client now,' I said. 'But double-crossing her wouldn't be bad business – at the right price.'

'I don't believe you have them.'

'Okay.' I got up and went to the safe. In a moment I was back with the envelope. I poured the prints and the negative out on the desk – my side of the desk. She looked down at them and started to reach.

I picked them up and shuffled them together and held one so that she could look at it. When she reached for it I moved it back.

'But I can't see it so far away,' she complained.

'It costs money to get closer.'

'I never thought you were a crook,' she said with dignity.

'I didn't say anything. I relit my pipe.'

'I could make you give them to the police,' she said.

'You could try.'

Suddenly she spoke rapidly. 'I couldn't give you this money I have, really I couldn't. We – well, mother and I owe money still on account of father and the house isn't clear and—'

'What did you sell Steelgrave for the grand?'

Her mouth fell open and she looked ugly. She closed her lips and pressed them together. It was a tight hard little face that I was looking at.

'You had one thing to sell,' I said. 'You knew where Orrin was. To Steelgrave that information was worth a grand. Easy. It's a question of connecting up evidence. You wouldn't understand. Steelgrave went down there and killed him. He paid you the money for the address.'

'Leila told him,' she said in a far-away voice.

'Leila told me she told him,' I said. 'If necessary Leila would tell the world she told him. Just as she would tell the world she killed Steelgrave – if that was the only way out. Leila is a sort of free and easy Hollywood babe that doesn't have very good morals. But when it comes to bedrock guts – she has what it takes. She's not the ice-pick type. And she's not the blood-money type.'

The colour flowed away from her face and left her as pale as ice. Her mouth quivered, then tightened up hard into a little knot. She pushed her chair back and leaned forward to get up.

'Blood-money,' I said quietly. 'Your own brother. And you set him up so they could kill him. A thousand dollars blood-money. I hope you'll be happy with it.'

She stood away from the chair and took a couple of steps backward. Then suddenly she giggled.

'Who could prove it?' she half squealed. 'Who's alive to prove it? You? Who are you? A cheap shyster, a nobody.' She went off into a shrill peal of laughter. 'Why, even twenty dollars buys you.'

I was still holding the packet of photos. I struck a match and dropped the negative into the ashtray and watched it flare up.

She stopped dead, frozen in a kind of horror. I started to tear the pictures into strips. I grinned at her.

'A cheap shyster,' I said. 'Well, what would you expect. I don't have any brothers or sisters to sell out. So I sell out my clients.'

She stood rigid and glaring. I finished my tearing-up job and lit the scraps of paper in the tray.

'One thing I regret,' I said. 'Not seeing your meeting back in Manhattan, Kansas, with dear old Mom. Not seeing the fight over how to split that grand. I bet that would be something to watch.'

I poked at the paper with a pencil to keep it burning. She came slowly, step by step, to the desk, and her eyes were fixed on the little smouldering heap of torn prints.

'I could tell the police,' she whispered. 'I could tell them a lot of things. They'd believe me.'

'I could tell them who shot Steelgrave,' I said. 'Because I know who didn't. They might believe *me*.'

The small head jerked up. The light glinted on the glasses. There were no eyes behind them.

'Don't worry,' I said. 'I'm not going to. It wouldn't cost me enough. And it would cost somebody else too much.'

The telephone rang and she jumped a foot. I turned and reached for it and said: 'Hello.'

'Amigo, are you all right?'

There was a sound in the background. I swung around and saw the door click shut. I was alone in the room.

'Are you all right, amigo?'

'I'm tired. I've been up all night. Apart from—'

'Has the little one called you up?'

'The little sister? She was just in here. She's on her way back to Manhattan with the swag.'

'The swag?'

'The pocket money she got from Steelgrave for fingering her brother.'

There was a silence, then she said gravely: 'You cannot know that, amigo.'

'Like I know I'm sitting leaning on this desk holding on to this telephone. Like I know I hear your voice. And not quite so certainly, but certainly enough like I know who shot Steelgrave.'

'You are somewhat foolish to say that to me, amigo. I am not above reproach. You should not trust me too much.'

'I make mistakes, but this won't be one. I've burned all the photographs. I tried to sell them to Orfamay. She wouldn't bid high enough.'

'Surely you are making fun, amigo.'

'Am I? Who of?'

She tinkled her laugh over the wire. 'Would you like to take me to lunch?'

'I might. Are you home?'

'*Sí.*'

'I'll come over in a little while.'

'But I shall be delighted.'

I hung up.

The play was over. I was sitting in the empty theatre. The curtain was down and projected on it dimly I could see the action. But already some of the actors were getting vague and unreal. The little sister above all. In a couple of days I would forget what she looked like. Because in a way she *was* so unreal. I thought of her tripping back to Manhattan, Kansas, and dear old Mom, with that fat little new little thousand dollars in her purse. A few people had been killed so she could get it, but I didn't think that would bother her for long. I thought of her getting down to the office in the morning – what was the man's name? Oh yes. Dr Zugsmith – and dusting off his desk before he arrived and arranging the magazines in the waiting-room. She'd have her rimless cheaters on and a plain dress and her face would be without make-up and her manners to the patients would be most correct.

'Dr Zugsmith will see you now, Mrs Whoosis.'

She would hold the door open with a little smile and Mrs Whoosis would go past her and Dr Zugsmith would be sitting behind his desk as professional as hell with a white coat and his stethoscope hanging around his neck. A case file would be in front of him and his note pad and prescription pad would be neatly squared off. Nothing that Dr Zugsmith didn't know. You couldn't fool him. He had it all at his fingertips. When he looked at a patient he knew the answers to all the questions he was going to ask just as a matter of form.

When he looked at his receptionist, Miss Orfamay Quest, he saw a nice quiet young lady, properly dressed for a doctor's office, no red nails, no loud make-up, nothing to offend the old-fashioned type of customer. An ideal receptionist, Miss Quest.

Dr Zugsmith, when he thought about her at all, thought of her with self-satisfaction. He had made her what she was. She was just what the doctor ordered.

Most probably he hadn't made a pass at her yet. Maybe they don't in those small towns. Ha, ha! I grew up in one.

I changed position and looked at my watch and got that bottle of Old Forester up out of the drawer after all. I sniffed it. It smelled good. I poured myself a good stiff jolt and held it up against the light.

'Well, Dr Zugsmith,' I said out loud, just as if he was sitting there on the other side of the desk with a drink in his hand, 'I don't know you very well and you don't know me at all. Ordinarily I don't believe in giving advice to strangers, but I've had a short intensive course of Miss Orfamay Quest and I'm breaking my rule. If ever that little girl wants anything from you, give it to her quick. Don't stall around or gobble about your income tax and your overheads. Just wrap yourself in a smile and shell out. Don't get involved in any discussions about what belongs to who. Keep the little girl happy, that's the main thing. Good luck to you, Doctor, and don't leave any harpoons lying around the office.'

I drank off half my drink and waited for it to warm me up. When it did that I drank the rest and put the bottle away.

I knocked the cold ashes out of my pipe and refilled it from the leather humidor an admirer had given me for Christmas, the admirer by an odd coincidence having the same name as mine.

When I had the pipe filled I lit it carefully, without haste, and went on out and down the hall, as breezy as a Britisher coming in from a tiger hunt.

34

The Château Bercy was old but made over. It had the sort of lobby that asks for plush and india rubber plants, but gets glass brick, cornice lighting, three-cornered glass tables, and a general air of having been redecorated by a parolee from a nut hatch. Its colour scheme was bile green, linseed poultice brown, sidewalk grey and monkey-bottom blue. It was as restful as a split lip.

The small desk was empty but the mirror behind it could be diaphanous, so I didn't try to sneak up the stairs. I rang a bell and a large soft man oozed out from behind a wall and smiled at me with moist soft lips and bluish-white teeth and unnaturally bright eyes.

'Miss Gonzales,' I said. 'Name's Marlowe. She's expecting me.'

'Why, yes, of course,' he said, fluttering his hands. 'Yes, of course. I'll telephone up at once.' He had a voice that fluttered too.

He picked up the telephone and gurgled into it and put it down.

'Yes, Mr Marlowe. Miss Gonzales says to come right up. Apartment 412.' He giggled. 'But I suppose you know.'

'I know now,' I said. 'By the way, were you here last February?'

'Last February? Last February? Oh yes, I was here last February.' He pronounced it exactly as spelled.

'Remember the night Stein got chilled out front?'

The smile went from his fat face in a hurry. 'Are you a police officer?' His voice was now thin and reedy.

'No. But your pants are unzipped, if you care.'

He looked down with horror and zipped them up with hands that almost trembled.

'Why, thank you,' he said. 'Thank you.' He leaned across the low desk. 'It was not exactly out front,' he said. 'That is not exactly. It was almost to the next corner.'

'Living here, wasn't he?'

'I'd rather not talk about it. Really I'd rather not talk about it.' He paused and ran his pinkie along his lower lip. 'Why do you ask?'

'Just to keep you talking. You want to be more careful, bud. I can smell it on your breath.'

The pink flowed all over him right down to his neck. 'If you suggest I have been drinking—'

'Only tea,' I said. 'And not from a cup.'

I turned away. He was silent. As I reached the elevator I looked back. He stood with his hands flat on the desk and his head strained around to watch me. Even from a distance he seemed to be trembling.

The elevator was self-service. The fourth floor was cool grey, the carpet thick. There was a small bell-push beside Apartment 412. It chimed softly inside. The door was swung open instantly. The beautiful deep dark eyes looked at me and the red red mouth smiled at me. Black slacks and the flame-coloured shirt, just like last night.

'Amigo,' she said softly. She put her arms out. I took hold of her wrists and brought them together and made her palms touch. I played patacake with her for a moment. The expression in her eyes was languorous and fiery at the same time.

I let go of her wrists, closed the door with my elbow and slid past her. It was like the first time.

'You ought to carry insurance on those,' I said, touching one. It was real enough. The nipple was as hard as a ruby.

She went into her joyous laugh. I went on and looked the place over. It was French grey and dusty blue. Not her colours, but very nice. There was a false fireplace with gas logs, and enough chairs and tables and lamps, but not too many. There was a neat little cellarette in the corner.

'You like my little apartment, amigo?'

'Don't say little apartment. That sounds like a whore too.'

I didn't look at her. I didn't want to look at her. I sat down on a davenport and rubbed a hand across my forehead.

'Four hours' sleep and a couple of drinks,' I said. 'And I'd be able to talk nonsense to you again. Right now I've barely strength to talk sense. But I've got to.'

She came to sit close to me. I shook my head. 'Over there. I really do have to talk sense.'

She sat down opposite and looked at me with grave dark eyes. 'But yes, amigo, whatever you wish. I am your girl – at least I would gladly be your girl.'

'Where did you live in Cleveland?'

'In Cleveland?' Her voice was very soft, almost cooing. 'Did I say I had lived in Cleveland?'

'You said you knew him there.'

She thought back and then nodded. 'I was married then, amigo. What is the matter?'

'You did live in Cleveland then?'

'Yes,' she said softly.

'You got to know Steelgrave how?'

'It was just that in those days it was fun to know a gangster. A form of inverted snobbery, I suppose. One went to the places where they were said to go, and if one was lucky, perhaps some evening—'

'You let him pick you up.'

She nodded brightly. 'Let us say I picked him up. He was a very nice little man. Really, he was.'

'What about the husband? Your husband. Or don't you remember?'

She smiled. 'The streets of the world are paved with discarded husbands,' she said.

'Isn't it the truth? You find them everywhere. Even in Bay City.'

That bought me nothing. She shrugged politely. 'I would not doubt it.'

'Might even be a graduate of the Sorbonne. Might even be mooning away in a measly small town practice. Waiting and hoping. That's one coincidence I'd like to eat. It has a touch of poetry.'

The polite smile stayed in place on her lovely face.

'We've slipped far apart,' I said. 'Ever so far. And we got to be pretty clubby there for a while.'

I looked down at my fingers. My head ached. I wasn't even forty per cent of what I ought to be. She reached me a crystal cigarette box and I took one. She fitted one for herself into the golden tweezers. She took it from a different box.

'I'd like to try one of yours,' I said.

'But Mexican tobacco is so harsh to most people.'

'As long as it's tobacco,' I said, watching her. I made up my mind. 'No, you're right. I wouldn't like it.'

'What,' she asked carefully, 'is the meaning of this by-play?'

'Desk clerk's a muggle-smoker.'

She nodded slowly. 'I have warned him,' she said. 'Several times.'

'Amigo,' I said.

'What?'

'You don't use much Spanish, do you? Perhaps you don't know much Spanish. Amigo gets worn to shreds.'

'We are not going to be like yesterday afternoon, I hope,' she said slowly.

'We're not. The only thing Mexican about you is a few words and a careful way of talking that's supposed to give the impression of a person speaking a language they had to learn. Like saying "do not" instead of "don't". That sort of thing.'

She didn't answer. She puffed gently on her cigarette and smiled.

'I'm in bad trouble down town,' I went on. 'Apparently Miss Weld had the good sense to tell it to her boss – Julius Oppenheimer – and he came through. Got Lee Farrell for her. I don't think they think she shot Steelgrave. But they think I know who did, and they don't love me any more.'

'And do you know, amigo?'

'Told you over the phone I did.'

She looked at me steadily for a longish moment. 'I was there.' Her voice had a dry serious sound for once.

'It was very curious, really. The little girl wanted to see the gambling house. She had never seen anything like that and there had been in the papers—'

'She was staying here – with you?'

'Not in my apartment, amigo. In a room I got for her here.'

'No wonder she wouldn't tell me,' I said. 'But I guess you didn't have time to teach her the business.'

She frowned very slightly and made a motion in the air with the brown cigarette. I watched its smoke write something unreadable in the still air.

'Please. As I was saying, she wanted to go to that house. So I called him up and he said to come along. When we got there he was drunk. I have never seen him drunk before. He laughed and put his arm around little Orfamay and told her she had earned her money well. He said he had something for her, then he took from his pocket a bill-fold wrapped in a cloth of some kind and gave it to her. When she unwrapped it there was a hole in the middle of it and the hole was stained with blood.'

'That wasn't nice,' I said. 'I wouldn't even call it characteristic.'

'You did not know him very well.'

'True. Go on.'

'Little Orfamay took the billfold and stared at it and then stared at him, and her white little face was very still. Then she thanked him and opened her bag to put the bill-fold in it, as I thought – it was all very curious—'

'A scream,' I said. 'It would have had me gasping on the floor.'

'—but instead she took a gun out of her bag. It was a gun he had given Mavis, I think. It was like the one—'

'I know exactly what it was like,' I said. 'I played with it some.'

'She turned around and shot him dead with one shot. It was very dramatic.'

She put the brown cigarette back in her mouth and smiled at me. A curious, rather distant smile, as if she was thinking of something far away.

'You made her confess to Mavis Weld,' I said.

She nodded.

'Mavis wouldn't have believed *you*, I guess.'

'I did not care to risk it.'

'It wasn't you gave Orfamay the thousand bucks, was it, darling? To make her tell? She's a little girl who would go a long way for a thousand bucks.'

'I do not care to answer that,' she said with dignity.

'No. So last night when you rushed me out there, you already knew Steelgrave was dead and there wasn't anything to be afraid of and that act with the gun was just an act.'

'I do not like to play God,' she said softly. 'There was a

566

situation and I knew that somehow or other you would get Mavis out of it. There was no one else who would. Mavis was determined to take the blame.'

'I better have a drink,' I said. 'I'm sunk.'

She jumped up and went to the little cellarette. She came back with a couple of huge glasses of Scotch and water. She handed me one and watched me over her glass as I tried it out. It was wonderful. I drank some more. She sank down into her chair again, and reached for the golden tweezers.

'I chased her out,' I said, finally. 'Mavis, I'm talking about. She told me she had shot him. She had the gun. The twin of the one you gave me. You didn't probably notice that yours had been fired.'

'I know very little about guns,' she said softly.

'Sure. I counted the shells in it, and assuming it had been full to start with, two had been fired. Quest was killed with two shots from a .32 automatic. Same calibre. I picked up the empty shells in the den down there.'

'Down where, amigo?'

It was beginning to grate. Too much amigo, far too much.

'Of course I couldn't know it was the same gun, but it seemed worth trying out. Only confuse things up a little anyhow, and give Mavis that much break. So I switched guns on him, and put his behind the bar. His was a black .38. More like what he would carry, if he carried one at all. Even with a checked grip you can leave prints, but with an ivory grip you're apt to leave a fair set of finger marks on the left side. Steelgrave wouldn't carry that kind of gun.'

Her eyes were round and empty and puzzled. 'I am afraid I am not following you too well.'

'And if he killed a man he would kill him dead, and be sure about it. This guy got up and walked a bit.'

A flash of something showed in her eyes and was gone.

'I'd like to say he talked a bit,' I went on. 'But he didn't. His lungs were full of blood. He died at my feet. Down there.'

'But down where? You have not told me where it was that this—'

'Do I have to?'

She sipped from her glass. She smiled. She put the glass down. I said:

'You were present when little Orfamay told him where to go.'

'Oh yes, of course.' Nice recovery. Fast and clean. But her smile looked a little more tired.

'Only he didn't go,' I said.

Her cigarette stopped in mid-air. That was all. Nothing else. It went on slowly to her lips. She puffed elegantly.

'That's what's been the matter all along,' I said. 'I just wouldn't buy what was staring me in the face. Steelgrave is Weepy Moyer. That's solid, isn't it?'

'Most certainly. And it can be proved.'

'Steelgrave is a reformed character and doing fine. Then this Stein comes out bothering him, wanting to cut in. I'm guessing, but that's about how it would happen. Okay, Stein has to go. Steelgrave doesn't want to kill anybody – and he has never been accused of killing anybody. The Cleveland cops won't come out and get him. No charges pending. No mystery – except that he had been connected with a mob in some capacity. But he has to get rid of Stein. So he gets himself pinched. And then he gets out of jail by bribing the jail doctor, and he kills Stein and goes back into jail at once. When the killing shows up, whoever let him out of jail is going to run like hell and destroy any records there might be of his going out. Because the cops will come over and ask questions.'

'Very naturally, amigo.'

I looked her over for cracks, but there weren't any yet.

'So far so good. But we've got to give this lad credit for a few brains. Why did he let them hold him in jail for ten days? Answer One, to make himself an alibi. Answer Two, because he knew that sooner or later this question of him being Moyer was going to get aired, so why not give them the time and get it over with? That way any time a racket boy gets blown down around here they're not going to keep pulling Steelgrave in and trying to hang the rap on him.'

'You like the idea, amigo?'

'Yes. Look at it this way. Why would he have lunch in a public place the very day he was out of the cooler to knock Stein off? And if he did, why would young Quest happen around to snap that picture? Stein hadn't been killed, so the picture wasn't evidence of anything. I like people to be lucky, but that's *too* lucky. Again, even if Steelgrave didn't know his picture had been taken, he knew who Quest was. Must have. Quest had been tapping his sister for eating money since he lost his job, maybe before. Steelgrave had a key to her apartment. He must have known something about this brother of hers. Which simply adds up to the result, that *that* night of all nights Steelgrave would *not* have shot Stein – even if he had planned to.'

'It is now for me to ask you who did,' she said politely.

'Somebody who knew Stein and could get close to him.

Somebody who already knew that photo had been taken, knew who Stein was, knew that Mavis Weld was on the edge of becoming a big star, knew that her association with Steelgrave was dangerous, but would be a thousand times more dangerous if Steelgrave could be framed for the murder of Stein. Knew Quest, because he had been to Mavis Weld's apartment, and had met him there and given him the works, and he was a boy that could be knocked clean out of his mind by that sort of treatment. Knew that those bone-handled .32s were registered to Steelgrave, although he had only bought them to give to a couple of girls, and if he carried a gun himself, it would be one that was not registered and could not be traced to him. Knew—'

'Stop!' Her voice was a sharp stab of sound, but neither frightened nor even angry. 'You will stop at once, please! I will not tolerate this another minute. You will now go!'

I stood up. She leaned back and a pulse beat in her throat. She was exquisite, she was dark, she was deadly. And nothing would ever touch her, not even the law ...

'Why did you kill Quest?' I asked her.

She stood up and came close to me, smiling again. 'For two reasons, amigo. He was more than a little crazy and in the end he would have killed me. And the other reason is that none of this – absolutely none of it – was for money. It was for love.'

I started to laugh in her face. I didn't. She was dead serious. It was out of this world.

'No matter how many lovers a woman may have,' she said softly, 'there is always one she cannot bear to lose to another woman. He was the one.'

I just stared into her lovely dark eyes. 'I believe you,' I said at last.

'Kiss me, amigo.'

'Good God!'

'I must have men, amigo. But the man I loved is dead. I killed him. That man I would not share.'

'You waited a long time.'

'I can be patient – as long as there is hope.'

'Oh, nuts.'

She smiled a free, beautiful and perfectly natural smile. 'And you cannot do a damn thing about all this, darling, unless you destroy Mavis Weld utterly and finally.'

'Last night she proved she was willing to destroy herself.'

'If she was not acting.' She looked at me sharply and laughed. 'That hurt, did it not? You are in love with her.'

I said slowly: 'That would be kind of silly. I could sit in

the dark with her and hold hands, but for how long? In a little while she will drift off into a haze of glamour and expensive clothes and froth and unreality and muted sex. She won't be a real person any more. Just a voice from a sound track, a face on a screen. I'd want more than that.'

I moved towards the door without putting my back to her. I didn't really expect a slug. I thought she liked better having me the way I was – and not being able to do a damn thing about any of it.

I looked back as I opened the door. Slim, dark and lovely and smiling. Reeking with sex. Utterly beyond the moral laws of this or any world I could imagine.

She was one for the book all right. I went out quietly. Very softly her voice came to me as I closed the door.

'*Querido* – I have liked you very much. It is too bad.'

I shut the door.

As the elevator opened at the lobby a man stood there waiting for it. He was tall and thin and his hat was pulled low over his eyes. It was a warm day but he wore a thin topcoat with the collar up. He kept his chin low.

'Dr Lagardie,' I said softly.

He glanced at me with no trace of recognition. He moved into the elevator. It started up.

I went across to the desk and banged the bell. The large fat soft man came out and stood with a pained smile on his loose mouth. His eyes were not quite so bright.

'Give me the phone.'

He reached down and put it on the desk. I dialled Madison 7911. The voice said: 'Police.' This was the Emergency Board.

'Château Bercy Apartments, Franklin and Girard in Hollywood. A man named Dr Vincent Lagardie wanted for questioning by homicide Lieutenants French and Beifus, has just gone up to Apartment 412. This is Philip Marlowe, a private detective.'

'Franklin and Girard. Wait there please. Are you armed?'

'Yes.'

'Hold him if he tries to leave.'

I hung up and wiped my mouth off. The fat softy was leaning against the counter, white around the eyes.

They came fast – but not fast enough. Perhaps I ought to have stopped him. Perhaps I had a hunch what he would do, and deliberately let him do it. Sometimes when I'm low I try to reason it out. But it gets too complicated. The whole damn case was that way. There was never a point where I could do the natural obvious thing without stopping to rack my head dizzy with figuring how it would affect somebody I owed something to.

When they cracked the door he was sitting on the couch holding her pressed against his heart. His eyes were blind and there was bloody foam on his lips. He had bitten through his tongue.

Under her left breast and tight against the flame-coloured shirt lay the silver handle of a knife I had seen before. The handle was in the shape of a naked woman. The eyes of Miss Dolores Gonzales were half-open and on her lips there was the dim ghost of a provocative smile.

'The Hippocrates smile,' the ambulance intern said, and sighed. 'On her it looks good.'

He glanced across at Dr Lagardie who saw nothing and heard nothing, if you could judge by his face.

'I guess somebody lost a dream,' the intern said. He bent over and closed her eyes.

Raymond Chandler
The Chandler Collection Volume 2 £5.95

The High Window, The Long Good-bye, Playback

'In everything that can be called art there is a quality of redemption. It may be pure tragedy if it is high tragedy, and it may be pity and irony, and it may be the raucous laughter of the strong man. But down these mean streets a man must go who is not himself mean, who is neither tarnished nor afraid. The detective in this kind of story must be such a man. He is the hero, he is everything . . . He is a relatively poor man or he would not be a detective at all. He is a common man or he could not go among common people. He has a sense of character or he would not know his job. He is a lonely man and his pride is that you will treat him as a proud man or be very sorry you ever saw him. He talks as the man of his age talks, that is with rude wit, a lively sense of the grotesque, a disgust for sham and a contempt for pettiness . . . If there were enough like him, I think the world would be a very safe place to live in, and yet not too dull to be worth living in'
RAYMOND CHANDLER, THE SIMPLE ART OF MURDER

Dashiell Hammett
The Four Great Novels £5.95

The Dain Curse, The Glass Key, The Maltese Falcon, Red Harvest

'Hammett had seen the rotten underbelly of his country and wanted others to see it . . . Not just the first of the tough school of crime-writing but the best' THE TIMES

'Hammett . . . took murder out of the Venetian vase and dropped it into the alley. He was spare, frugal, hard-boiled, but he did over and over again what only the best writers can ever do at all' RAYMOND CHANDLER

'The genius of the American detective story' TIME OUT

'The America of Prohibition days, and over all is the stink of corruption and cordite and hard liquor' OXFORD TIMES

Italo Calvino
Marcovaldo £2.50

'*Marcovaldo* is an enchanting collection of stories both melancholy and funny about an Italian peasant's struggle to reconcile country habits with urban life. Oblivious to the garish attractions of the town, Marcovaldo is the attentive recorder of natural phenomena. Marcovaldo's problem is that he is a dreamer and not very bright. At every turn, the city is there to thwart his inclinations. The reader's heart bleeds for Marcovaldo in his tenacious pursuit of lost domains, but the stories are full of mirth and fun.' BOOKS AND BOOKMEN

'Marcovaldo lives through the stories as the double of the writer, observing, reflecting and comparing in a perfectly detached way. *Marcovaldo* conveys the sensuous, tangible qualities of life.' NEW YORK TIMES BOOK REVIEW

'One of the best works of fiction to be published this year' SAN FRANCISCO CHRONICLE

Adam, One Afternoon £2.95

'Confirms the part he has played in revitalizing the fiction of our time . . . Calvino's special gift is to link the physical and immediate with an allegorical timelessness . . . All the characters and creatures in these stories conspire to convey a feeling of wonder, mystery and terror of life' GUARDIAN

'Back in the 1940s, Calvino was writing fables and stories of comparative simplicity and considerable gaiety. These have at last been published here . . . a collection of animals and men, their sombre implications faintly visible below the surface of laughter' BOOKS AND BOOKMEN

'The best of his allegorical fantasies have the power of the Brothers Grimm, rollicking stories on the surface, with an underlying savagery' LISTENER

James M. Cain
The Five Great Novels of James M. Cain £4.95

'Cain's work is the poetry of small, failing businesses. Swindlers and sharks, drifters and cheats – these are his subjects, rather than the muscle-and-fur mob more often associated with those contemporaries of his who concentrated on crime . . . His characters are a combustible mixture of poverty and greed, people who have lost the ability to draw distinctions between the claims of love and money' THE FICTION MAGAZINE

'They (the novels) represent a kind of native American expressionism, in which livid elements familiar from pulp fiction are recast by a transcendent starkness, and in which literary embellishment is eschewed, with the result that they seem all the more metaphoric' NEW YORK REVIEW OF BOOKS

'Cain has established a formidable reputation of furious pace, harsh and masterful realism, tough, raw speech right out of the mouths of the people' SATURDAY REVIEWS

Edward Limonov
It's Me, Eddie £2.95

'Who was I over there? I was a poet, an unofficial underground poet. That's over forever, and now I am one of yours. I am scum. I'm the one to whom you feed rotten cheap Californian wine . . .' Eddie is an exile from Soviet Russia, a pawn in a cultural cold war, an unlikely passenger aboard the free world's flagship USA. He is Russian dissident and samizdat poet, bisexual omnivore with a taste for the good life and at least a sliver of American pie, scraping by on welfare on the seedy underside of Fun City, New York. Subtitled 'a fictional memoir', *It's Me, Eddie* is a blend of picaresque novel and personal testament.

M. Ageyev
Novel with Cocaine £2.95

One of the century's most unusual books: a rediscovered Russian
masterpiece about seduction, drug addiction, adolescence, and the 1917
Revolution, by a mysterious, pseudonymous author.

'This novel reminds me above all of Proust. Mr Ageyev is a genius; his *Novel
with Cocaine* belongs to that rare class of moving and complex books which
confirm line by line the lessons of your own life' LE POINT

'A masterpiece preserved for all time' VENDREDI-SAMEDI-DIMANCHE